The Country Set

FIONA WALKER is the bestselling author of seventeen novels. She lives in Warwickshire with her partner and two children plus an assortment of horses and dogs. Visit Fiona's website at www.fionawalker.com.

By Fiona Walker

The Country Set

FIONA WALKER

HEAD
ZEUS

First published in the UK in 2017 by Head of Zeus Ltd
This paperback edition first published in 2018 by Head of Zeus Ltd

9 7 5 3 1 2 4 6 8

A catalogue record for this book is available from
the British Library.

ISBN (XTPB): 9781784977245

Typeset by Adrian McLaughlin

Printed and bound in Germany by
CPI Books GmbH

Head of Zeus Ltd
First Floor East
5–8 Hardwick Street
London EC1R 4RG

WWW.HEADOFZEUS.COM

The Country Set

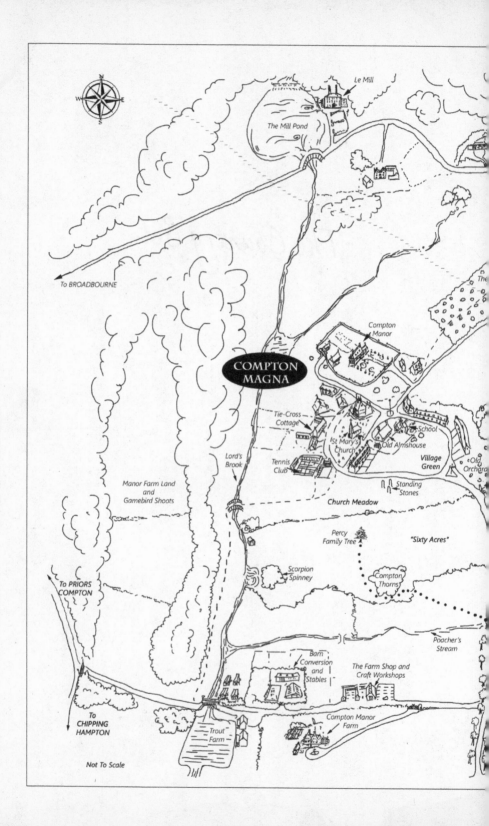

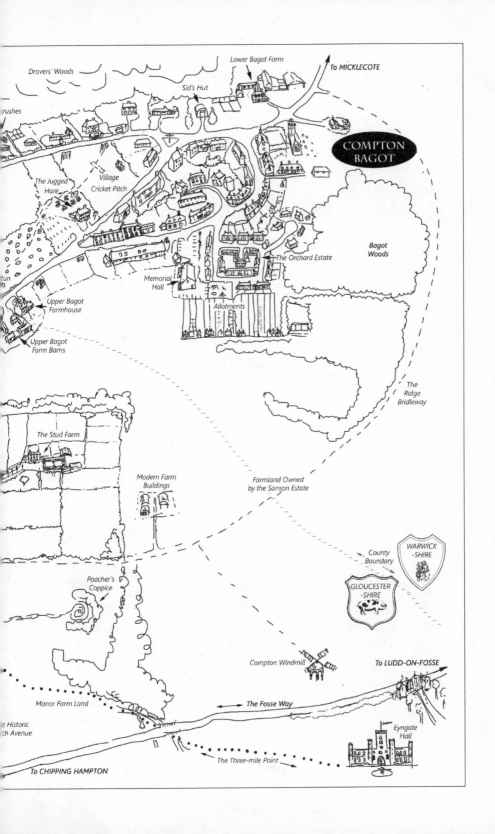

THE PERCY FAMILY

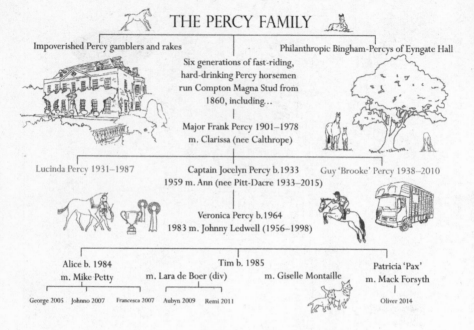

Impoverished Percy gamblers and rakes

Philanthropic Bingham-Percys of Eyngate Hall

Six generations of fast-riding,
hard-drinking Percy horsemen
run Compton Magna Stud from
1860, including...

Major Frank Percy 1901–1978
m. Clarissa (nee Calthrope)

Lucinda Percy 1931–1987

Captain Jocelyn Percy b.1933
1959 m. Ann (nee Pitt-Dacre 1933–2015)

Guy 'Brooke' Percy 1938–2010

Veronica Percy b.1964
1983 m. Johnny Ledwell (1956–1998)

Alice b. 1984
m. Mike Petty

Tim b. 1985
m. Lara de Boer (div)
m. Giselle Montaille

Patricia 'Pax'
m. Mack Forsyth

George 2005   Johnno 2007   Francesca 2007   Aubyn 2009   Remi 2011

Oliver 2014

THE GUNN FAMILY

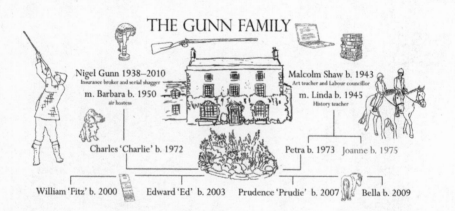

Nigel Gunn 1938–2010
Insurance broker and serial shagger
m. Barbara b. 1950
air hostess

Malcolm Shaw b. 1943
Art teacher and Labour councillor
m. Linda b. 1945
History teacher

Charles 'Charlie' b. 1972

Petra b. 1973   Joanne b. 1975

William 'Fitz' b. 2000   Edward 'Ed' b. 2003   Prudence 'Prudie' b. 2007   Bella b. 2009

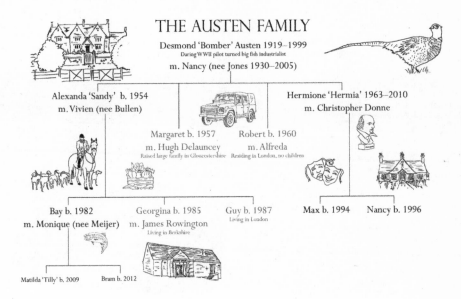

THE AUSTEN FAMILY

Desmond 'Bomber' Austen 1919–1999
Daring WWII pilot turned big fish industrialist
m. Nancy (nee Jones 1930–2005)

Alexanda 'Sandy' b. 1954
m. Vivien (nee Bullen)

Margaret b. 1957
m. Hugh Delauncey
Raised large family in Gloucestershire

Robert b. 1960
m. Alfreda
Residing in London, no children

Hermione 'Hermia' 1963–2010
m. Christopher Donne

Bay b. 1982
m. Monique (nee Meijer)

Georgina b. 1985
m. James Rowington
Living in Berkshire

Guy b. 1987
Living in London

Max b. 1994   **Nancy b. 1996**

Matilda 'Tilly' b. 2009   Bram b. 2012

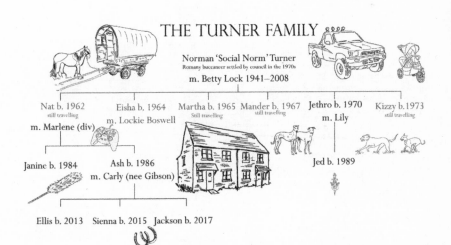

THE TURNER FAMILY

Norman 'Social Norm' Turner
Romany buccaneer settled by council in the 1970s
m. Betty Lock 1941–2008

Nat b. 1962
still travelling
m. Marlene (div)

Eisha b. 1964
m. Lockie Boswell

Martha b. 1965
Still travelling

Mander b. 1967
still travelling

Jethro b. 1970
m. Lily

Kizzy b.1973
still travelling

Janine b. 1984

Ash b. 1986
m. Carly (nee Gibson)

Jed b. 1989

Ellis b. 2013   Sienna b. 2015   Jackson b. 2017

Dramatis Personae

Captain Jocelyn Percy: the sixth generation of small, fierce Percys to run Compton Magna Stud. Stubbornly anti-social and bibulous since the death of his formidable wife Ann.

Veronica 'Ronnie Percy' Ledwell: the Captain's only child, a fast-riding blonde whose ill-fated marriage to handsome Johnny Ledwell ended with a swift exit in a lover's sports car.

Alice Petty: her estranged daughter, a bossy Pony Club stalwart.

Tim Ledwell: Ronnie's son, a debonair wine merchant with a complicated love life in South Africa.

Giselle: his French second wife, adding to the complication.

Patricia 'Pax' Forsyth: their younger sister, the family peacemaker whose marriage to tough Scot **Mack** is a battlefield.

Lester: the stud's tight-lipped stallion man, dedicated to his horses, his routine and a quiet life.

Blair Robertson: craggy Australian three-day-event rider known as Mr Sit-Tight.

Verity Verney: his wife, a reclusive Wiltshire landowner.

Roo Verney: a defiant aristo anti-hunt protestor.

Pauline 'Pip' Edwards: baking addict and village busybody who runs a homecare service for the elderly.

Kit Donne: acclaimed theatre director and weekender, over-fond of leading ladies and Scotch.

Hermia Austen: his late wife, a talented actress born in the village.

Orla Gomez: one-time Hollywood A-lister working her way back up the alphabet via Broadway.

Ferdie and Donald: theatrical agent and his actor husband, both fine-dining RSC devotees.

Petra Gunn: historical novelist and neglected wife, founder of the village Saddle Bags whose gossipy hacks keep her sane.

Charlie Gunn: Petra's elusive barrister husband.

William 'Fitz' Gunn: the Gunns' oldest son, a quick-thinking centennial.

Ed: his affably lazy younger brother.

Prudie: their sister, a sparkly daddy's girl.

Bella: the pony-mad youngest Gunn.

Barbara 'Gunny' Gunn: their grandmother, a Machiavellian merry widow and silver surfer.

Kenneth: the Gunns' veggie-growing neighbour.

Gill Walcote: straight-talking member of the Saddle Bags who runs a local veterinary practice with Kiwi husband **Paul Wish**.

Dixie: one of the Walcote-Wishes' three clever daughters.

Mo Dawkins: the jolliest of the Saddle Bags, a tirelessly hard-working farmer's daughter.

Barry Dawkins: Mo's rotund and rubicund tractor driver husband.

Grace Dawkins: another pony-mad eight-year-old.

Sid and Joan Stokes and daughter **Pam:** Mo's parents and sister, old-time village smallholders.

Bridge Mazur: hipster Saddle Bag on a prolonged baby break, married to volatile **Aleš**.

Bay Austen: dashing agricultural entrepreneur, hunt thruster and serial flirt.

Monique Austen: his steely Dutch wife.

Tilly: their daughter, pony-mad friend of Bella Gunn and Grace Dawkins.

Sandy and Viv Austen: Bay's parents, well-connected incumbents of Compton Manor Farm.

Leonie the caterer: waspish whirler of canapes with very sharp elbows.

Peter Sanson: tax exile billionaire who owns huge tracts of Compton farmland.

Carly Turner: animal-loving young mum, adjusting to village life and job juggling.

Ash Turner: her ex-soldier husband whose family rule the Orchard Estate.

Ellis, Sienna and baby **Jackson,** their three children.

Janine Turner: Ash's older sister, queen of cleaning and nail art empires.

Jed Turner: their lurcher-loving cousin, a guileful thug.

'Social' Norm: the emphysemic Turner family patriarch, a settled Romany.

Ink, Hardcase, Skully: Ash's old school friends and drinking buddies.

Flynn the farrier: another childhood friend, the Bon Jovi of the anvil.

Mrs Hedges: one of Pip's elderly clients.

Brian and Chris Hicks: officious chairman of the Parish Council and his timid wife.

Paranoid Landlord: the crooked proprietor and chef of the Jugged Hare.

Animals

Top Gun/Spirit: a wall-eyed colt with a big man attitude and a bright future.

Cruisoe: the stud's foundation stallion whose winning progeny inherit his lion heart.

The stud's broodmares: an opinionated bunch of matriarchs.

Beck: spoiled warmblood stallion, as stunning as he is screwed up.

The Redhead: Petra's rabble-rousing mare and her three pony sidekicks.

Olive and Enid: Ronnie's sprightly little Lancashire Heelers, a squabbling mother and daughter.

Stubbs: Lester's unswervingly loyal fox terrier.

Wilf: the Gunns' wayward springer spaniel.

Pricey: a bull lurcher bred for coursing.

Part One

HIGH SUMMER,
HAY-MAKING
AND HACKING

'Go past it, you daft bat.' Petra urged her horse on with her legs, but the mare had planted herself firmly on the verge, backed up against a Cotswold stone wall, rigid with indignation at the sight of a scarecrow in the garden on the opposite side of the lane, its lumpy body swathed in a psychedelic Boden kaftan, head styled with a woolly hat and a Donald Trump party mask.

'I donated that dress to the fête's nearly-new stall!' Petra recognised it.

'Not really your colour,' observed Gill, whose super-obedient dressage horse strode past without a sideways glance.

'Not his either!' said Bridge, her young Irish pony dancing sideways and ramming Petra.

The mare stood firm, chestnut ears shooting llama high as she spotted another scarecrow in the garden next door, this one in an old pinstriped suit, its head a pink balloon in a multi-coloured Afro wig.

Behind Petra, her two other hacking buddies were experiencing similar difficulties, hoofs clattering on tarmac, snorts rising.

'You've got to admire the village committee,' said Petra, calves nudging frantically. 'It's very bold to give this year's scarecrow competition a non-binary transgender theme. Come *on*, Redhead.'

'Gerronwithit!' Further back still, Mo gave the familiar cry, issued to stubborn cobs, cows, sheep and children. 'No offence, but he don't like the look of that dress, Petra.'

The Saddle Bags, as they'd dubbed themselves, were out in the early morning. Gathered together by Petra, they were mothers, wives, villagers and horse-owners, sharing a close bond of sisterly secrets and a love of peering over their neighbours' hedges. Together, they took to the lanes and bridle-paths around Compton Magna and Compton Bagot at least once a week to let off steam about husbands, hormones, horses and – very occasionally – horticulture.

'Don't you just love Open Gardens Week?' Petra glanced over her shoulder.

'Are the scarecrows always this disturbing?' asked Bridge. A Belfast-born, shoot-from-the-lip hipster chick, she was their most recent recruit, a maverick incomer with black-rimmed specs and a constellation of star tattoos on her wrists and ankles (she called them 'ermine marks'). Fearless and speed-loving, she'd only recently broken in her sharp little Connemara pony, who was, she liked to boast, a lot less paranoid than her volatile Polish husband.

'Our straw man is very dapper.' Tall, thin and gimlet-eyed, local vet Gill Walcote was in her early fifties but seemed to belong to a different era, when men tipped the brims of their hats. 'We chose a golfing theme this year. We've nicknamed him SergioGar-seagrass.' She was also a fan of extremely bad puns.

'The goat always eats ours.' Broad-berthed farmer's daughter Mo Dawkins let out her trademark laugh. She joked that the only time she got to sit down was on her armchair of a piebald cob.

'When I suggested to my lot that we make Worzel Gummidge, they had to get their phones out to google him. If he's not the very embodiment of Jon Pertwee, I'm docking their screen time.' Petra was constantly on the lookout for distractions from, and inspiration for, the racy historical romances she churned out in a shed in her garden, much of it coming from her opinionated chestnut mare, known simply as the Redhead, still stubbornly refusing to go past Donald Trump.

'Open Gardens Week used to be a lot better,' said Mo, 'but the townies who've moved in don't take village events seriously.'

The Comptons were idyllic outposts on the tip of the Cotswolds' northernmost Fosse Hills, jewels in the crown of an area affectionately known as the 'Bardswolds' for its proximity to Stratford-upon-Avon. Although small, it boasted an abundance of steeply wooded river valleys skirted with orchards and dotted with golden villages into which families ripe for change dropped sweetly each year. The area's grandest houses – stately Elizabethan and Jacobean piles hidden amid deer parks – had long attracted the super-rich in search of privacy a short helicopter flight from London and Birmingham, and actors settled in villages close to the RSC. In recent years, though, the Bardswolds' manors and rectories had been traded between media types like Top Trumps, while its cottages attracted theatre-junkie retirees and thirty-something professionals, all leading a procession out of London to find more bang for their buck. Of the Fosse Hill villages, the small and much-photographed Compton Magna was the star, regularly outshining nearby 'ugly sister' Bagot, despite the latter's far longer history.

Although it looked centuries old, Compton Magna had been largely created at the whim of a local family to house their estate workers. With its golden houses grouped in a figure of eight around the Green, its two-room school, the duck-pond and the tiny Gothic Revival church tucked between tall yew trunks and ancient meadows with standing stones, it was a stage set in which squires, smallholders and cottagers had played no part. Beloved of film and television crews, Compton Magna had appeared in everything from costume dramas to tampon adverts, pop videos and a grisly crime series.

Heavily diluted by an influx of settlers aspiring to a gingham-bunting-Farrow-&-Ball English country life, the intense rivalry between the villages had lost its earthy edge. Open Gardens Week – dreaded by villagers and horse-riders alike – had become far more focused on the scarecrow competition and lavish cake-baking than on showing off one's sweet peas.

'It should be about the standard of the cornflowers, not corn men,' lamented Gill.

'We're not all green-fingered,' said Petra, knowing she was still classified as a 'townie' even after a decade living in the Cotswolds, more than half of it in this village. 'And it gets seriously expensive when you're shamed into spending a fortune at the garden centre at the last minute to make your beds look half decent.'

'One can't just click a ready-made herbaceous border on Amazon Prime, Petra,' chided Gill, her glossy bay now strutting past a straw man in a scream mask brandishing a scythe. 'I'm very proud of my achilleas this year, although last night's storm finished off the delphies.'

'Dad's been having terrible trouble with his osteospermum,' admitted Mo.

'Has he tried holistic medicine?' asked Bridge, whose little Connemara had now spotted the scream mask. Moments later, they shot off at speed across the Green.

'I thought you and Charlie had a gardener?' Mo asked Petra, as she gave her a lead past the offending scarecrows, the chestnut mare taking exaggerated antelope leaps.

'We had to let him go.' Petra hung on gamely as they pogoed from verge to verge. 'Kenneth next door accused him of sabotaging his floral hedge and it all got very tawdry. A Forsythia Saga,' she added, for Gill's benefit, and was rewarded with an appreciative hoot.

'Like gladioli, an absolute crime in a country garden,' tutted the vet, glaring at the garish front beds of one of the holiday cottages as they waited for Bridge to rejoin them, her trendy grey hair extensions matching the pony's white tail as both streamed behind them. 'And those hanging baskets are offensive. Nothing lets down a village like a desiccated begonia at eye-level.'

'Don't be such a snob!' Petra had just bought several ready-planted, overpriced wildflower wicker ones from the farm shop to liven up Upper Bagot Farmhouse's austere façade. She thickened her Yorkshire accent to *Last of the Summer Wine* creaminess in their defence. 'I bloody love mine.'

'They add a nice splash of colour,' agreed Mo, who had jolly pink fuchsias at the rundown DIY livery yard she ran at her parents' farm in the hope they would attract wealthy clients.

'What's your opinion on hanging baskets, Bridge?' Gill asked, as she came up alongside them again, the dappled grey rocking horse now blowing hard and still boggling at everything.

Bridge's eyes boggled too. 'My opinion is that if you keep talking to me about fecking gardening I'm digging out my body protector and joining the Life Hackers.' They were a rival riding posse, a bunch of daredevil pros and hunt members, none of whom idled along bridleways coffee-shopping about lobelias.

'Trust me, they're incredibly dull,' insisted Petra, who had ridden out with them. 'They might jump big ditches, but all they talk about is farming yields and racing form.'

'Well, I think they're ghastly,' said Gill.

'Not hunky Bay Austen and his merry men, surely?' Mo chuckled, looking pointedly at Petra.

'I was talking about hanging baskets,' Gill said archly.

'Petra's admirer is pretty offensive too.' Bridge scowled. 'All that bloodthirsty old-school-tie privilege.'

'He's not my admirer,' Petra grumbled, although she felt a frisson of delight at the mention of the handsome landowner. 'Our daughters are summer-holiday BFFs. Mo's in the same boat. Those three girls are the unholy trinity of the Pony Club under tens.' Bella Gunn, Tilly Austen and their friend Grace Dawkins were currently inseparable.

'Bay doesn't text me personally to invite Gracie for play dates, funnily enough,' sighed Mo.

'Must have lost your number,' Petra deflected. 'Really, there's no flirtation between us.'

With regrettable timing, a Land Rover appeared through a gate further along the lane, an arm dangling from the driver's side, checked shirt rolled up to reveal Riviera-tanned skin, heavy Tag watch and glinting signet ring. It lifted in greeting as the driver spotted the riders in his wing mirror.

Heart racing, blush rising, Petra waved back as he roared away.

'Admit it, he's your hot new SMC,' teased Bridge, the Safe Married Crush being a Saddle Bags rite of passage.

'Please let's not bang on about it.'

'Beats fecking gardening.' The Connemara, catching sight of a whole family of lop-sided scarecrows in one garden, started to go backwards. 'Oh, heck.'

'Ride on my inside,' Gill ordered briskly.

As the foursome moved into a brisk trot, Petra quashed a suspicion that Gill might be shadowing the grey to hide Bridge's pink flowery wellies. They made an incongruous pair, school prefect with a naughty pupil, but that was true of all the Bags – one reason she was so absurdly fond of her lovely horse collective.

The Bags' conversations had got a bit prosaic lately, mind you. Petra wished something exciting would happen in the village to give them something new to talk about. A few scarecrows hardly measured up to the Bardswolds' big-cat sightings last year, or the transgender vicar, hot-headed Bridge almost leaving husband Aleš on a weekly basis, or Mo's dilemma when she thought her elderly parents were no longer coping as crisis followed crisis. Even dry-humoured Gill was usually guaranteed to keep them agog with tales from the equine clinic she ran with her cycling-fanatic husband Paul, a hub of local horse gossip and marital discord, but it had been a very dull summer.

The Bags had a rule: what's said in the saddle stays in the saddle. It was why they could all speak about their marriages so openly, sharing secrets with unswerving support, understanding, and gales of laughter. Petra owed it to them to liven things up a bit, especially as she'd been the one to introduce the idea of the Safe Married Crush, their way of cheerfully deflecting from those neglectful husbands. Emotional infidelity didn't count, she'd told the Saddle Bags cheerily. Feeling attracted to someone other than one's spouse was as healthy as reading an escapist novel – or, in her case, writing one; you were secure in the knowledge that it was all in the mind. Now that her marriage was nearing the end of its second decade and lovemaking had waned to high days and holidays, Petra always tried to keep at least one SMC on the go. She justified these innocent infatuations by thinking of them as research. Inspiration for histori-cal erotica was hard to come by when one's entire life sometimes felt like a never-ending rota of drop-offs and pick-ups, co-ordinating the complicated demands of her teenage and tweeny children, commuter husband Charlie, and their menagerie of animals, often at the expense of her own fading career. The Safe Married Crush unleashed something wild in buxom, smoky-eyed Petra, which helped her write steamy fiction, as well as immunising her against her husband's indifference.

None of the Bags took the crushes seriously – Bridge's on sleazy farrier Flynn was a cause of much hilarity, Mo's on devilish lurcher-enthusiast and lamper Jed Turner more so, Gill's on the oleaginous local MP an obvious smokescreen – but they were comforters that helped them through the long weeks between *Poldark* series or anything starring James Norton, especially if one's husband was only home at weekends, as Petra's was.

Bridge was right: she did have quite a big crush on Bay, Compton's dishiest farmer, but it was at a very delicate stage. The whole point of a Safe Married Crush was that it was innocent, and this one felt unnervingly reciprocal. The texts had been bouncing back and forth all summer, *all the best Petra* and *regards Bay* quickly becoming '*Pxx*' and '*Bx*'. They'd be carving their names in tree trunks next.

Lusting after Bay Austen was hardly an exclusive gig. The sexy, roguish agricultural entrepreneur had long been the local pin-up, a good-looking charmer, whose cool *Dragon's Den* business head had turned his parents' large arable holding, with its fishery and shoot, into a huge money-earner. Compton Manor Farm was now a Mecca for craftsmen, holidaymakers, yummy-mummies and foodies, with its business units, farm shop, micro-brewery, yurts and Wagyu cattle, while its small, exclusive shoot was legendary. Taking a gun at one of the Austens' cliquey invitation-only days had long been an ambition of shooting-mad Charlie; celebrities and royals were reported to be regulars, along with enough City hedge-funders to enclose the Square Mile in privet and – most importantly to Charlie, whose occasionally ragged career at the Bar relied heavily upon old-school ties in the Legal 500 – a great many high-flying, crack-shot solicitors. His enthusiasm for an alliance between Bay and the Gunn family made her crush even more awkward: Charlie had even encouraged the dashing farmer to buy Petra's books for his very beautiful, very bored wife.

Bay had bought Petra's entire backlist – *Got one for all the family! B* – then teased her when he found out how racy the plots were: *Kept them all to myself. Up all night reading, I am officially your biggest fan. Bx.* A handsome, bouncy Labrador of a man, he was hard to put on a discreet pedestal. It had been so much easier to harbour her longing for London theatre director Kit Donne, who visited his cottage so rarely that it was like fancying a distant celebrity. He'd once owned the Gunns' farmhouse yet had no idea who Petra was. Bay, by contrast, had her number on speed-dial, a terrible reputation as a flirt and a way of looking at her that made her feel sexier than she had in years.

'You got an idea for your new book yet?' Mo huffed beside her.

'No, but I've a feeling it's going to have lots of bedroom scenes.' She grinned.

*

'So have you gone to bed yet, mate?' Ed Gunn hung upside down off his bunk ladder talking into his phone camera.

'No, mate. How cool was that game? I cracked open a Monster. Still buzzin'.'

'Same here! It's, like, da boss—' The phone was plucked out of his hand, the Skype call to a school friend abruptly ended. 'What the fuh?'

'Did you ask permission to use my phone?'

Ed glared up at his older brother, a thin-lipped mask behind an overlong fringe, sixteen-year-old disciplinarian to thirteen-year-old upstart.

'It's not your phone, bro. It's Dad's old one.'

'Which he gave to *me* when he upgraded.'

'Yeah but you're still using Mum's old iPhone, so the BlackBerry is up for grabs.' Ed turned the right way up and clambered down from the ladder. 'Mine's jank, you know that, and the webcam's broken on my laptop.'

'Not the point. Dad gave this to *me*. And you went into my room, went through *my* stuff, and took it without asking.'

'Chill.' Ed held up his hands, then slouched out of his room to go downstairs and FaceTime on his mother's tablet instead. 'I saw in your bedside drawer by the way. *Kinky*.'

Fitz lobbed a pillow after him, knowing his brother had seen nothing more incriminating than a few flash sticks and old trading cards. The most perverted thing in there by far was the phone, but he'd made sure its darkest secret was protected with a password that even geeky genius Ed would never crack. Their father was a dolt with technology, which was why Fitz had seen what he had on there. He was still working out what to do with it.

He went up to the attic floor and put the phone back in his bedside drawer. Last night Fitz had lain awake trying to work out what to do for the best. He was still no closer to an answer.

Named William, after a grandfather he'd disliked intensely, he had somewhat pretentiously adopted the name of his mother's old college, Fitzwilliam, to differentiate him from the three other Williams in his year at boarding school. Good-looking, charming and manipulative, he'd entered his GCSE year in every first team and top set, his parents' golden boy, predicted to wipe the board with straight A stars come the summer. He'd worked blisteringly hard all year to maintain his momentum. Last term that had been turned upside down. Now Fitz was on borrowed time.

Grabbing the phone back out of the drawer, he swiped to the app, typing *You bastard!* and sending it. Then he went to wake his sisters.

Carly had eight-week-old Jackson asleep on her shoulder, like a hot, damp gym towel, as she spilled out breakfast cereal for Sienna and Ellis, both squabbling furiously over who got which bowl.

'Want Toe Nauts!' toddler Sienna yelled, gripping tightly onto Captain Barnacle with both hands.

'Peppa Pig is for *girls!*' insisted Ellis, a diehard Octonauts fan who at four already had a bias against all things pink. Carly blamed Great-granddad Norm, the Turner family's very own Vito Corleone, who greeted the little boy from the confines of his wheelchair with shadow-boxing grimaces and said things like 'Who's my big tough man, then?'

The Turner family's real big tough man – three feet taller and sixty kilos heavier than his scowling son – was still in bed.

Leaving the children as they shovelled up sweet, milky treats, she took Ash a mug of tea. When he had been in the army, he'd always been the first up. Now day-to-day life reminded Carly of the weeks he'd been away on exercise in a different time zone, Skyping sleepily at two a.m. to find him squinting in broad daylight.

Curtains still drawn, their bedroom was a sultry, shadowed hangover den.

He stretched back, muscles moving beneath tattoos, a smile flashing through the stubble. Then he spotted Jackson and frowned. 'Put him in his cot and get back into bed, bae.'

'I can't. I'm taking the kids out.'

'It's half seven.'

'They've been up since six. I've been up all night. They want to see the foals.'

'You want to see them, you mean. Ellis just wants to go to the playground with his cousins. I was the same growing up.'

Carly smiled vaguely, already aware that the Turners were far from the welcoming new regiment she'd hoped for – she didn't share their bond of Traveller's blood, which Ash claimed that decades of settling in one place and marrying out could never dilute. The horde of Turner kids, almost all much bigger than hers, currently ruled the village playground through the long school holidays, teens by night, tweens by day. She worried Ash was undergoing a similar Jekyll and Hyde transformation, his clan reabsorbing him as he shook off army discipline and embraced a more nebulous timetable. Unlike Carly, whose days revolved rigidly around the kids and her two part-time jobs, Ash had no fixed routine until his college course started in September. They'd moved into the Orchard Estate three months ago, and Carly was still struggling to learn the names of his nocturnal gang of drinking friends and the many family members who were now neighbours, none of whom had shown much interest in her.

'Where did you get to last night?' She kept her voice deliberately light.

'Out with the lads. You knew that.'

'Until after four?'

'Didn't fancy walking back in that storm.'

Thunder and lightning had ripped back and forth along their Cotswold ridge most of the night. It had made it impossible to settle Jackson, whose colicky screams had doubled under the onslaught, his brother and sister waking too.

'Ended up at Flynn's,' he said now. 'Lost sight of time, you know.'

'Yeah, I know.' She stooped to kiss him, feeling his tongue against her teeth, which she kept clamped together in a placating smile. Carly didn't trust Flynn, the village's double-denimed rock-god throwback, an old school friend of Ash, recently divorced and out to prove he could do whatever he liked – mostly watching box sets and drinking home brew at antisocial hours. Married to the army for eight years, Ash was out to prove much the same thing.

Jackson let out a bleat of protest.

'Have some more kip,' Carly told Ash. 'I'm working lunchtime, remember? I'll leave them with your mum. We'll all get out of your hair.' It had grown wild since he'd quit the army. Carly's Facebook friends oohed and aahed about how handsome he was whenever she shared a family selfie, but she missed her clean-cut soldier.

He'd left the army four months ago, having served Queen and country long enough to receive his eight-year bonus. Despite a reputation for rebellion and a few close shaves with the military police, he'd done his regiment proud, received campaign and service medals, and was, his commander told him upon discharge, the very body of a soldier.

Ash insisted it had always been his dream to settle with his family in the village where he'd grown up. 'This will be our for-ever-after,' he'd promised Carly, when they'd first walked around number three, almost asphyxiated by bleach and Febreze, compensated by every upstairs window looking out to fields and woods and allotments.

Carly was good at moving house. An army daughter then wife, she'd done it countless times, and she was still only in her twenties. But this time they'd moved all alone without the regiment around them. And she wasn't sure she'd wanted for-ever-after just yet.

Ash's elder sister had organised a council house for them. Carly was wary of Janine, whose possessive, controlling hold over the family was an unwelcome part of life. It was Janine's three-bed semi in which she and Ash now lived, number three Quince Drive. The Turner family rented at least nine of the Orchard Estate houses from the local authority, but the names on the tenancy agreements bore no relation to their occupants. Janine lived in Granddad Norm's four-bedroomed link-detached on Damson Road, with three teenage children, only one of whom was hers. She had never married. After Robbie Williams and nail art, the biggest love of her life was little brother Ash.

Propping Jackson in the crook of her arm, Carly clenched her fists, trying to discharge the static electricity in her fingertips. She'd felt a sense of foreboding since the storm had passed, chest tight, hands tingling. She'd suffered from it all her life, sometimes so bad that she could barely pick up a cup for the scalding heat in her fingers, the fire in her lungs making her mute. Her mum had called it a 'healing gift' and said it came from her grandmother. She'd been tested, but her palpitations and hot hands were medical oddities, dismissed vaguely as psychosomatic stress.

It must be because she was worried about Ash. He pretended all was well, but his temper was quicker, his tall tales longer, their conversations briefer. Her fusilier was in danger of turning into a short-fused liar.

Downstairs, Captain Barnacles' and Peppa's faces had reappeared at the bottom of two bowls.

'Are you ready to go and see Spirit?' They'd nick-named their favourite foal after the Disney horse because he was the same unusual colour that they called 'buckskin' in the movie but was labelled 'dun' in the old encyclopaedia of horses Carly had bought at the village fête.

Ellis and Sienna dropped down to pull their wellies onto the wrong feet. As they did so, Carly caught the glint of gold jewellery and a flash of tanned thigh as Janine paused at the side gate, pink talons scrabbling at the bolt to let herself into the garden. A stranger to doorbells, Janine preferred the proprietorial stealth of bursting in through the back door on dawn raids.

She ran her cleaning business, Feather Dusters, like an East End protection racket, with mops and Henry Hoovers in place of fire-arms. She had the monopoly on domestic and commercial contracts in the village and guaranteed cheap labour from family members. Carly's work-rate was twice that of most of Janine's team, meaning she was always in demand for the rota. While she appreciated the extra money, and the kids were coping fine with their nan looking after them on the days she worked, today she had a waitressing shift at a local hotel and didn't want Janine to strong-arm her into calling in sick so she could help her bring up a weekend cottage's wet-room grout like new.

Never had two children been inserted into a double buggy faster. Carly jumped into her trainers as she unlatched the door and – ignoring a muffled voice calling, 'Only *meee*!' – made her getaway through the front door, Jackson still asleep on her shoulder.

As the Saddle Bags trotted along the main lane leading out of Compton Magna, a car engine approaching behind them made the horses' ears prick back. It was travelling far too fast, Abba booming out from within.

'Brace yourselves, it's Pip Edwards!' Gill thrust up her crop hand to ask the driver to slow down as they regrouped to a single-file walk, swinging around in their saddles to see a small blue hatchback career into view.

The riders hurriedly flattened their horses tight against the steeply banked verge below a row of thatched cottages, setting off a barking dog. Bridge's grey pony barged forwards in horror, springing up the bank and cowering under the mossy eaves.

As the car roared past, 'Knowing Me, Knowing You' at full blast, the horn gave a cheerful beep that sent Petra's chestnut mare up the bank too, dislodging a hanging basket. It landed neatly in her arms, like a trophy bowl at a horse show. It contained a set of door keys.

'What is it with that woman?' she complained, hanging it back up while the Redhead snacked on a window box. 'You'd think she'd drive more carefully past horses, given she works at the stud.'

'Pip Edwards has no horse sense whatsoever,' said Gill.

'Isn't she a groom there?' asked Petra, as they rode on. Pip Edwards had appeared on her radar around a year ago as part of a short-lived local writing circle she'd agreed to help. Petra often saw her little blue car race past her driveway as it flew along the lane between Compton Bagot, where Pip lived in a bungalow that had belonged to her parents, and Compton Magna, where she worked at the august old stud. Its big-barrelled mares and bounding foals were as much a village landmark as the standing stones in the church meadows they were riding past now.

'Goodness, no. Officially Pip's the Captain's part-time housekeeper. Unofficially she's a private carer who co-ordinates his healthcare visits, cooks him nice soft food and monitors his gout.'

'She runs a service locally for old folks,' Mo elaborated. 'Shopping and baking cakes for them. Home Comforts, it's called.'

'That's a kind thing to do,' said Bridge, as the grey barged ahead.

'She's a menace around horses,' said Gill, catching up to block out the wellies from a passing commuter. 'She "helps" old Lester, the stallion man, on the yard in her spare time, but she just holds him up – and the stud's hopelessly understaffed as it is. All the vets dread her being there on a visit, fussing around and getting in the way. We call her the Understudy.'

As they rode on, they looked across the hedged fields to Compton Magna's famous stud, a vision of honey-coloured, horse-filled loveliness – apart from the car now speeding along its distant furlong of poplar-lined driveway.

The Percy family had run the stud for more than a century, breeding quality hunters and hacks. Small, blond and fierce, far more interested in four legs than four walls, the beauty of their home was largely wasted on its occupants. The splendour of their horses, however, was legendary.

'I'd work there.' Bridge sighed. 'Sod HR.'

'Not an easy man to work for, the Captain,' said Mo. 'How Lester's stuck it out all these years is a mystery. Must have the hide of a Hereford bull.'

With its Queen Anne symmetry, as perfect as a tapestry sampler, the Captain's house was considered by many to be the loveliest in the Compton villages. To its left was a high-walled Victorian kitchen garden filled with beet and carrots. To its right, two Cotswold-stone stableyards, gleaming from cobbles to clock-towers, led out through wide arches to a hundred acres of curving pasture, with a hidden valley, bluebell woods and bubbling brooks, the very embodiment of green and pleasant. Jocelyn Percy, its paterfamilias, known to all as the Captain, was a widower in failing health who rarely ventured out.

'The place is surviving on a shoestring,' Gill told them. 'Ann Percy was the only one who could ever balance the books and that was mostly to rest her gin glass on, God rest her soul. He's quite lost without her.'

'How long ago did she die?' asked Petra.

'Must be coming up for two years,' Mo recalled. 'There was a fire, wasn't there, Gill?'

'That's right. Not long after Pip started.'

'Maybe she bumped her off,' whispered Bridge in mock-horror.

Petra adopted a movie trailer voiceover tone: 'Her ambitions to become the next Mrs P knew no bounds. Her path ruthless, her victims stood little chance – especially if she was at the wheel of a Nissan Micra.'

'It's like *Kind Hearts and Coronets*,' chuckled Mo.

'Maybe she and old Lester are in cahoots,' Bridge suggested excitedly. 'The Fred and Rose West of the Comptons.'

'You lot are *awful*!' Gill gasped, her eyes glowing.

Petra grinned, relaxing at last as the Bags refocused from Safe Married Crushes and hanging baskets to village scandal again.

2

From the feed room, Lester heard the shriek of a clutch and the groan of gears, obliterating the Handel Violin Concerto playing on his old stereo. It was a familiar prelude to morning stables.

He called his fox terrier, Stubbs, ensuring the little bearded sentry was well away from the arrivals yard as a small blue car careered in, like a detective appearing at the scene of a crime, tyres hissing through storm puddles.

'Sorry I'm late!' Pip leaped out, a blurry vision in a bright pink fleece. Lester's vision – which had been gradually worsening this year – no longer picked out the little moles on her neat, snub nose and chin, but there was no mistaking the huge downturned eyes and picket fence of small teeth being bared at him.

'Had to get Mr Thorne out of bed and drop off some shortbread. All his hollyhocks were flattened in last night's storm. Wasn't it a corker? He says another's on its way and then we're in for a heat-wave. I baked extra biccies for us and brought you a cake. I'll do nets, shall I?'

'If you like.' He returned to the feed room and Handel, his mouth watering at the prospect of Pip's biscuits, the lightest and most buttery imaginable. As the Captain was fond of saying, 'It doesn't matter how bloody awful the woman, the cook is the last one you shoot in the jungle, Lester.' Pip had been housekeeping at Compton Magna Stud for almost two years, during which the Captain had retreated between the leather blinkers of his wing-chair in his study, drinking too much, watching the racing and grieving his late wife. He was increasingly reliant upon Pip and her Teflon coating was as tough as her bakeware when it came to tolerating his foul temper.

Lester was more tolerant of pug-like Pip and her voluntary extra hours than the Captain was, although, like his boss, he seldom showed much gratitude, aware that to give Pip any encouragement would be to have her under your feet for ever. She was self-obsessed, overbearing and occasionally very foolish, and she never stopped to think or ask, but she had batteries that never went flat, which made her useful. She just worked and talked. Non-stop.

She was talking now, despite being three stone-walled bays from him. He cranked up the stereo slightly, scooping the boiled linseed out of the big cauldron in the corner, enjoying the steam rising to his face. It was far too cold for a heatwave, the rain and wind growing increasingly tempestuous as August drew closer. The hay still hadn't been cut, the yearlings going feral as they waited to move across the lane from their hilly spring pasture onto freshly shorn flat fields as soon as the bales were stacked and taken away. Lester always loved that moment: it spoke of harvest, hunters getting fit and pheasants being released, the count-down to autumn sport. The Captain's mood would surely pick up at the prospect, even if summer had stubbornly refused to show its face.

The Saddle Bags turned up the bridleway that ran alongside paddocks of glossy stud mares, some of which trotted over to snort at them, making Bridge's pony spook away.

'Where have the foals gone?' Petra scanned the pasture dotted with fat-girthed oaks.

'Weaned this week,' Gill said matter-of-factly. 'They all get shut in a barn and the mums taken away.'

'That's awful!' Petra thought of the tears she'd shed when Charlie had had his way and their boys were sent one by one to his old boarding school. She had flatly refused to consider boarding for their daughters, who were younger.

'They soon get used to it,' said Gill, sounding just like Charlie. 'It's not my preferred method, but the Captain's always been old-fashioned.'

'And a tightwad,' Mo muttered behind them.

'Ssh,' Gill said, as though the mares might be offended if they overheard.

'You're the one who said he's cash-strapped,' Bridge pointed out.

'It's a tough time for British breeding. Fortunes change and studs adapt. Jocelyn and Ann Percy had bred three Badminton contenders by the time I qualified as a vet. His father, Major Percy, produced hunters for royalty, his father before him cavalry horses and point-to-pointers. They've run Compton Magna Stud for donkey's years.'

'Thoroughbred years,' Petra corrected.

'Brilliant!' Gill beamed. 'Although technically these are now sports horses. Having a Percy horse was once a byword for class, but now that the moneyed owners are all buying direct from the Continent, their stock has fallen. It's tragic.'

Looking at the beautiful mares floating alongside them, Petra found it hard to believe nobody was buying. They crowded together to watch as the riders waited for Mo to unhitch a gate leading to a wide track, on the far side of which a shimmering sea of corn stretched as far as the horizon. 'When I was a nipper, all this land belonged to the stud,' Mo said. 'Right the way down to the Fosse it went, fields full of horses and cross-country jumps and hunt coverts. When the Percys sold it, Sanson Holdings ripped out the hedges and ploughed it all up.'

'That was Bay's fault,' Gill remembered, as they filed through. 'The Austens wanted it, but Jocelyn and Ann refused to sell to them because Bay had offended them.'

'Nothing new there.' Mo chuckled, swinging the gate closed with a clang. 'Those families have been feuding for years. Taking offence at the Austens is sport to the Percys. They've always looked down on them. Old money to new.'

'Like monarchs looking down on oligarchs, you mean?' suggested Bridge. The little grey danced beneath her in anticipation, knowing they were about to go faster.

Beside her, Petra sat out a flurry of bucks from the Redhead as they all broke into a canter. She let the mare have her head, imagination sparked by the village's feuding families. 'So the Percys and the Austens were once the Montagues and Capulets of the Comptons?'

'Nothing so romantic.' Gill accelerated to keep up until the bouncy canter levelled to racing pace. 'It's all about land gain not love lost!' she called. 'The Sixty Acres, between the church meadows and Poacher's Stream, has changed hands more often than Berwick-upon-Tweed, won and lost in Austen wagers and Percy gambles. It used to be part of Manor Farm but the stud has it now. Sandy Austen is desperate to buy it back. They should have joined forces by marriage generations ago to redraw their field maps, but the Percys have always put horses first.'

'The horse before the cartography?' Petra suggested breathlessly, her mare trying to steam ahead, the other two Bags dropping far behind as the cob idled and the pony spooked.

'I wish I'd thought of that one! It can make for very unstable relationships. Just look at what happened to Ronnie.'

'Who's he?'

'*She!* You *must* know the story. The Bardswold Bolter! Veronica Ledwell was her married name, but everybody round here still thinks of her as Ronnie Percy.'

'I've never heard of her.'

'Good God, this village is fractured.' Gill gathered the bay into a more leisurely hunting canter. 'I always forget you haven't been here long.'

'Seven years!' Petra was breathless from galloping. 'I'm on the fête committee and the parish council.'

'By local standards you've hardly unpacked.' Gill dropped back to a trot. 'And you never go to meetings. Where were you when that awful eco developer was threatening to annex the old cricket field for hobbit houses with a reed-bed loo each?'

'Working hundred-hour weeks to pay for fossil fuel and oats.' She'd only got a seat on the parish council because Charlie had resigned from his at about the same time he'd decided to take advantage of their Pimlico tenants giving notice and stay in the London flat on week nights. Having been co-opted into her husband's seat, Petra had intended to step down as soon as the elections came round. Three years later, she was still searching for a replacement, her truancy rate increasing. 'Why did Ronnie Percy bolt?'

'*Adultery*,' Gill breathed, with a shudder of revulsion. 'The village was jolly shaken. The stud's Percys usually make very dull marriages, unlike their cousins at Eyngate Hall, who all murdered each other in crimes of passion – it was like a game of Cluedo over there.'

Petra had trawled the children around the local stately pile many times in search of writing inspiration in its grand ballroom and Gothic follies. Notoriously well connected and oversexed, the Percys had once boasted enough highly strung women, love-rat cads, infidelity and scandal to fill a shelf of romantic historical fiction. The big Regency wedding cake of architectural excess was now a favourite landing spot for coachloads of pensioners in search of tea and a wee. When media tycoon tax exile Peter Sanson had bought the Eyngate Estate in the eighties, he'd wasted no time in separating the house from its valuable agricultural and sporting assets and placing it in a charitable trust to turn it into a tourist attraction. Sanson Holdings' tenanted properties and arable agricultural land – farmed by contractors like Mo's husband, Barry – dominated the Comptons, like a new era of feudal landlords.

They pulled to a halt, waiting for the others to catch up. They were high on the ridge, almost able to see across to the huge hall cupped in its own valley of Capability Brown parkland with tree-lined rides, a five-acre lake and a scimitar-shaped ha-ha. 'The Eyngate Hall lot were the Bingham-Percys,' Gill told Petra, 'totally obsessed with pretty architecture. They built the stud for the Captain's great-great-grandfather. His mob are just plain Percys and distinctly poor rellies.'

Petra turned to look down to the stud again, far less grand in proportion than Eyngate Hall, but no less fuel for creative imagination, gleaming in its fold of the ridge, like a golden hare. She was ashamed that she rode past its fields of mares and foals almost every day, and even coveted the beautiful house, yet knew so little of its occupants. 'I always think of it as Birtwick Park,' she said fondly.

'Is that National Trust?'

'Beauty, Ginger and Merrylegs live there. It's Squire Gordon's house.'

'Now why is that familiar? Do the Gordons hunt with the Fosse and Wolds?'

Petra didn't answer, transported back to her childhood obsession with *Black Beauty*, both the book and the seventies television series. For many years, it was her single-minded ambition to live in Squire

Gordon's beautiful country house, with a black gelding, a small white pony and a chestnut mare. When not writing – nobody had ever taken Petra Shaw's childhood dreams of literary fame very seriously, least of all Petra – she had spent a lot of time belting around the Dales on the loan pony she shared with her younger sister, fantasising that she was galloping side-saddle to Squire Gordon's aid. Even her eleven-plus essay had been crammed with ostlers and nosebags.

The much-loved middle daughter of two jovial Yorkshire teachers whose love of history and animals she'd inherited – they'd named her after the *Blue Peter* dog – Petra had barely shrugged off her Cambridge gown, sights set on a masters' degree in eighteenth-century romanticism, when she'd had her first novel published and been hailed as a precocious new talent. That novel, written for fun on a six-month placement archiving records in an isolated stately home, had propelled her from junior researcher to bestselling author. In a twenty-year career that had taken her from early critical and commercial success to the less audacious times she was enduring now, Petra had never let go of her dream. It remained her greatest inspiration, that Birtwick Park fantasy of racing to the rescue, ringlets bobbing beneath her bowler.

Looking down at Compton Magna Stud, she fought a desperate urge to jump the golden-stone wall and gallop across the field towards it, whispering, 'Come on, Beauty!'

'The Percy family's notoriously tricky.' Gill pulled a packet of mints out of her pocket to offer across. 'I've been treating the Captain's horses for over twenty years and I can count the number of times he's said, "Thank you," on one hand, which is five more than his late wife ever gave me. Selling this land to a big-scale agri-magnate like Sanson was just Ann's style. Whatever Bay did to offend her, he was a marked man.'

'You really don't know what happened?' Petra handed her mint down to the Redhead, whiskery lips lifting it from her palm with the delicacy of a jewel thief.

'No idea.' Gill turned as the others caught up at last. 'I was away in Newmarket learning colic surgery. He can't have been much more than a teenager. Bay's at least ten years younger than me.' She gave Petra a penetrating look.

'You have a toy-boy admirer!' Bridge grinned at Petra, trying to pull up but the grey shot straight past them, ears flat back.

'*I'm* at least ten years younger than Gill!'

'Seven years and three months.' Gill was a stickler for detail. 'D'you know what Bay did that put the Percys' backs up, Mo?' she asked, as their friend and her cob lumbered up, both blowing hard.

'He had a fling with the Captain's granddaughter, didn't he?'

'Definitely not.' Gill shook her head. 'Alice married a Petty. They met at Young Farmers when they were fourteen.'

'The other one. The redhead, Patricia. What was it everyone called her? Pash?'

'Pax. And you're right. Summer romance. Didn't last long because she buggered off to work in London. Shame, really. We all thought she'd run the stud one day. She was a blisteringly good rider.' She gave Petra a crushing look as she lolled on the Redhead with her stirrups kicked out. 'He could never resist a Lucy Glitters.'

'Wasn't she an *X Factor* finalist?' asked Bridge, now turning wild circles around them, still hauling on the brakes.

'It's a character in a book, a foxhunting glamour girl,' Petra explained, illogically jealous of the youngest Percy granddaughter and her riding prowess.

'Bay likes a woman who can take on big Cotswold timber.' Mo's chuckles were breathlessly *Carry On*.

'Pax was the Captain's favourite,' Gill remembered. 'Tipped to take over the stud, but sodded off to join an uncle's architecture firm. Some sort of structural engineer now.'

'The nuts and bolter!' Bridge offered Gill, gratified with an explosion of laughter.

'Not as notorious as her mother,' Mo conceded. 'They say Ronnie ran off with her lover in a sports car wearing just her bikini.'

'Wasn't it her dressing-gown?'

Before speculation could be satisfied, Bridge's pony took exception to something in the cornfield opposite them, this time unstoppable in her panic.

'Oh, shit, she's bolting.' Gill set off in pursuit.

'That's exactly what they said about Veronica Percy.' Mo kicked the fat cob into action and he broke into a steady trot.

Knowing the Redhead was faster than any of them and would catch the pony first, Petra let the brake off and they streaked into action.

When Ellis was born, Carly had taken up running to get fit. With Sienna it had been boxercise. With Jackson, off-roading with the double buggy. The three-wheeled colossus was nicknamed 'Mum's Truck' because the first thing Ash had spent a chunk of his service bonus on had been a snarling twin-cab pickup that Ellis called 'Dad's Big Truck'. They'd bought the double buggy on Gumtree. It took a toddler in front, and the baby car seat clicked in over the back seat so a newborn could smile as his sweaty mother lugged her weighty child-barrow over the ruts and potholes of the Cotswold Hills, Ellis racing alongside.

After its first few outings, it was clear Ellis couldn't manage the long walks on foot, so today Carly had left the car seat behind and strapped the baby to her chest. Now the buggy was even heavier to push, the ground wet and slippery from the storm, which made it tough going along the track that emerged at the highest point of the Compton ridge, the most breath-taking place to admire the view from the Fosse Hills. Here, she could see for miles, her panorama across the Vale of Fosse celestial, a Philadelphia moment in a hard cheese world.

Carly had been fifteen when she'd met Ash in a nightclub, sneaking in with a mate and false ID. She'd been a wisecracker with nerves of steel, hard-knock schooled through her parents' divorce, which had taken her from army family to awkward baggage for a single mum with a new boyfriend.

She'd known straight away that she wanted to marry the tall, olive-skinned stranger, who looked like a *Vampire Diaries* heart-throb, his eyes as pale as a husky's. They'd danced without blinking, bodies getting closer and closer, an hour of hard-core drum 'n' bass foreplay, until he'd bought her a drink and told her he was in the Fusiliers. She'd told him she was doing her GCSEs.

He'd put a hand on her arm. 'I'm afraid, as you're under age, it's my duty to accompany you outside.' On a dark, litter-strewn pavement, he'd kissed her thoroughly, taken her number and put her into a cab home. 'You'll thank me for this.'

Gobby daredevil Carly Gibson was lost for words and totally in love.

The text arrived before the taxi even got to the end of the street. *When can I take you out for your sixteenth birthday?*

Ash was fun-loving, horny, a little wild and definitely one of the lads. He'd said almost nothing about his background at first, accustomed to being marked out for it in a uniform world, and by the time Carly learned his father was a Traveller, she saw the army as his family. The life-and-soul, Ash was always on the edge of trouble in his regiment for poor discipline and rule bending. But he was a brave soldier, who would have laid down his life for his country and his brothers in arms, and thrived on institutional life – like a hound, he needed to run with a pack.

'I'm a lifer,' he told Carly early on. 'They fused my boots to my feet when they put them on.'

They'd got engaged after two years of largely long-distance love, for much of which he was on tour in Iraq at the end of Operation Telic. She wrote him emails almost every day, full of misspelt, horny fantasies and her alien abduction plans for her stepdad, Gary, which made him laugh.

She loved all the uniforms at their wedding, the rowdy speeches, the camaraderie. That day, his two families – now hers – had briefly come together: soldiers and Travellers. His heritage was an old Romany one. Although their customs had long since been dulled by settling down and marrying out, Carly was still aware that she was entering into another world, which she found as strange as the army was comforting.

Carly had adored married life in a garrison town, embracing army-wife friendships, and the brigade of bumps she'd joined when she fell pregnant. She was back where she belonged. Ash doted on their new son. Ellis was so like his father, with those big silver eyes and his graze of black hair; Sienna followed eighteen months later while Ash was still serving in Afghanistan.

Carly was a loving wife, a plain speaker and close collaborator, yet she'd suffered from post-natal depression after both births, terrifying disconnects from her new-born babies which she'd battled to overcome with the help of her mother, friends and her GP. She'd kept it from Ash, the battle in her head tiny by comparison to that of a world in conflict.

When Ash came back from Afghanistan, that sense of unfamiliarity had returned, disconcerting and disorienting. Only it was Ash who was the stranger. Something had changed him from her laughing, daredevil, sexy-as-hell husband to a man who could barely look her in the eye, who woke up every night drenched in sweat, whose hands shook so much sometimes that he couldn't pick things up or type a text.

He was fine, he snapped. He was just tired. He had a week's leave and they went away to their favourite holiday park. He stared out to a grey sea for hours on end.

'How would you feel if I left the army?'

'Like crying,' she said honestly.

He didn't mention it again. They made sandcastles with Ellis, gave Sienna her first ice-cream. Ash talked properly for the first time about his childhood, part of a big extended family growing up in the beautiful Cotswold village he'd taken her to not long before they'd married. He made his early years there sound idyllic – all apple-scrumping, hay-making and gypsy fairs, although she knew from previous conversations that he'd been bored rigid and had got into a lot of trouble.

Back at barracks, Ash seemed to relax into the familiar routine. He still woke up trembling sometimes, but he and Carly found sex a great cure for that. Jackson had been conceived when Sienna was barely a year old. When his unit went away on a training exercise to Brunei, they'd Skyped with silly conversations and laughter like the old days.

When he got back, they visited his family in Compton Bagot in the Cotswolds. The Turners' long-standing hold over the Orchard Estate made them unofficial village clan leaders. They had spread through the estate since the early seventies when Ash's Traveller grandparents, Norm and Betty Turner, and their four children had been rehoused by the council. 'Social' Norm was now great-grandfather to eleven, respected elder to those who had remained settled, while others, like Ash's father, Nat, were back on the road, in clink or just off radar.

Ash and his sister had been brought up largely by their grandparents. Their mother, an apologetic little woman who lived with the television permanently on at her maisonette, had become a severe agoraphobic after her husband's departure.

'She's a Gorgio,' Ash had explained. 'Not born a Traveller.'

'So I'm a Gorgio too?'

'I'm not like my dad. We travel together. And you're tougher.'

It was the first time Carly had encountered most of the Turners since the wedding. She had trouble working out who was who: they all shared the same dark hair and silver eyes, which seemed to slide sideways to watch her while Ash was welcomed like a hero.

Domineering Janine was the family princess – now caring for widowed Norm, who was almost housebound with emphysema – and unofficial landlady to the Turner property portfolio.

'To my family regiment!' Ash had toasted them all, to table-thumping cheers.

It had been a horrible wet day in March, with grey clouds lower than a sagging tent roof. Ash insisted on taking them for a walk around the villages, Ellis on his shoulders shouting that he wanted to go home, rain drumming on the plastic buggy hood over a sleeping Sienna. They had paused by a pretty Cotswold-stone school, with a clock-tower and two big gables, like a spiky M.

'This is where I learned my three Rs – reading, rioting and rutting. Beautiful, isn't it?'

Sienna had started to cry, so they had moved on to walk past a pretty church, then on to a meadow, its curving contours dented by a stream and pond, rising to a group of three weathered standing stones. Once they had been as tall as men, but were now reduced to little more than bollards, having endured four thousand years of the same driving, hilltop rain.

The only thing Carly had enjoyed about the wet walk was stopping at a field gate to watch some foals, only a few days old. They'd turned away from the rain and were pressed to their mothers' sides, fragile and ribby, with their coats flattened wet. One was watching her, a wide white mark running down his face, one eye blue and the other darkest chocolate brown. Bigger than the others, golden coat rain-streaked, like tiger bread, he made his way across to the gate, uneven white stockings splattered with mud. As he stood snorting and watching them, Ellis pointed, said, 'Hoss!' repeatedly, and Sienna, awake now, chuckled from beneath the buggy hood.

'Isn't he a beauty?' Carly had breathed, her love instant and unconditional.

But Ash's pale eyes had narrowed. 'This place belongs to a right bastard. Horse-whipped me once.'

'Did he really *whip* you?'

'Yeah, called me a pikey, then clouted me round the head for joy-riding on the hunt's quad bike.'

'I'm glad they banned foxhunting.'

'Try telling that to people round here. Knowing you, you will. Beautiful village, isn't it?' He'd turned around, arms wide. 'Welcome to your new home.'

Carly hadn't felt at home at all.

Now she pushed the double buggy through an open gateway to walk on the wide grassy headland alongside a crop, her hands numb and sweaty on the handles as the familiar heat coursed through them. Her 'healing gift' was getting on her nerves. Today it was like a tic in her fingertips and a throb at her temples, and she felt continuous spasms of worry for her family. Her marriage was being absorbed by the Turners, Ash to ashes, dust to duster.

Jackson was grizzling in his sleep, his little back arching, colicky discomfort. Carly sang lullabies as she pushed the cumbersome buggy, throwing in Beyoncé's 'Running' for good measure – she'd been the army wife karaoke star in their garrison with that track – but while Sienna and Ellis's heads lolled in front of her, the baby squirmed. A cry burst out of him now, and there was a loud squelching noise. The smell made her hold her breath.

'What's that pong?' Ellis woke up with a start.

'Your brother's filled his nappy.' In fact, it was an explosion so epic it was leaking out of the sides, staining his Babygro. 'Ewww!' Ellis leaned away, almost toppling the buggy over because he was far too big for it. 'Make it go away!'

'Get out and walk if you don't like it,' snapped Carly.

Ellis clambered out of the buggy and ran ahead, charging into the wheat crop they were walking beside with a war cry that sent up a deer. It bounded away.

Her phone buzzed in her pocket. A photo-text from Ash. *Where are you, bae? Come back to bed. This needs you.* Still hung-over, he'd photographed a lot of duvet, some muscular thigh and a corner of hairy ball, but she could guess the rest. She texted *Laters xx* as she pushed on.

The smell really was very bad. Putting the brake on the buggy, she looked around. She'd just have to change the nappy here – it was sunny now, at least, and the grass was dry enough to lay out the mat. As she did so, pulling back the nappy's tabs and leaning away from the sight inside, she heard the thud of hoofs and Sienna let out a shriek of excitement. 'Horsie!'

Looking up, Carly saw a small grey horse thundering towards them, its rider's eyes wide as she tugged frantically at the reins. 'I can't stop! Get out of the way!'

Carly's reactions were lightning fast. Gathering up Jackson, she kicked off the buggy brake and reversed it into the crop, screaming at Ellis to stay back.

The pony spotted the changing mat with the full nappy on it and applied the brakes, almost shooting his rider over his neck, her stick flying through the air and landing in the buggy. She and the pony swerved away from Carly and the kids, came up against the hedge, reared back until they were almost sitting down, then set off at full speed back the way they had come.

'Horsie gone!' Sienna started to cry.

'Shit, that was close!' Carly breathed, kissing her daughter's head while jiggling a bawling, smelly Jackson at her chest, some of the contents of his nappy now plastered over her hands and T-shirt.

'Mum said "shit"!'

She felt a light smack on her bottom and irritably retrieved the crop from Ellis's grip, surprised at its weight, its sparkly purple end shaped like a star. Poor horse.

'Horsie!' Sienna shrieked happily, as more thundering hoofbeats approached, this time out of sight behind the hedge, accompanied by the bleating of sheep. A moment later another rider flew over four feet of birch, almost landing on top of the changing mat. As her chestnut touched down, the rider looked at Carly in shock. 'Sorry! Christ.'

'They went that way.' Carly pointed the magic-wand crop at the retreating white shape.

'Goodness, you've a baby there. Are you all right?'

'We're fine.'

With great effort, the woman turned the horse in a tight circle.

Carly recognised them from the big farmhouse by the barn conversions – she stopped at its paddock gate to talk to the chestnut mare and her pony friends most days if they were out, and sometimes saw the woman in the stableyard at the far end. She had wondered what it would be like to be married to a rich husband and live in a beautiful big house.

Now she backed further into the corn as they plunged around on the track, feeling uncomfortably like a serf looking up at a royal. 'You're not far behind.' She held out the crop like a race steward, indicating the departing grey. 'You'll catch them if you're quick.'

'Damn! I thought I'd cut them off. Thanks!' They set off in pursuit.

'… and there's a John le Carré film on BBC One we can all watch one night next week – or is it Jim Carrey? The one you both like,' Pip was saying loudly to an out-of-sight Lester as she filled nets, planning a few evenings of company for him and the Captain. Both men claimed to prefer to be alone, but she didn't believe it, and they loved their television. It must be terribly lonely here nowadays. The Captain was deeply antisocial, rarely stepping across his threshold, too proud to use the walking frame Pip had acquired for him from the NHS, along with a shower seat and grab-rails.

The Captain's fierce raptor of a wife, Ann, had employed Pip, reluctantly taking on her only applicant for the role of part-time housekeeper. A thirty-something former job-centre manager, Pip had recently started up her Home Comforts carer service after taking voluntary redundancy to look after her ageing parents: 'You obviously didn't do a very good job as they're both now dead, but at least English is your first language and you live in the village, so you'll have to do.' There had been impatience in Ann Percy's manner, which Pip took to be typical of her breed, but it turned out her need to find someone to look after her gout-ridden husband was urgent:

she'd underplayed her on-off battle with cancer for almost a decade and the disease was spreading into her lungs and liver. Just three months later Ann Percy's funeral had brought so many mourners to the village they'd opened the church meadows for extra parking.

Pip was honoured that Ann Percy had entrusted her house and husband to her care, the former's beauty more than capable of making up for the latter's beastliness. She gazed lovingly out from the hay store now at the tiny top dormers and tall chimneys visible over the golden stone stableyard roofs.

In the village, the stud was a star attraction architecturally, its clock-tower and pretty house a landmark that visitors saw first as they approached Compton Magna along the die-straight narrow lane up from the Fosse Way. The oh-so-handsome face, with its symmetrical sash windows, flirty dormers and limestone quoins, was like a perfect dolls' house.

Although known affectionately in the village as Percy Place, the main house at Compton Magna Stud had never been given a name. Unlike its Stables Cottage and Groom's Flat, it wasn't separately listed in the records of the Eyngate Estate to which it had once belonged. Pip rather liked its anonymity, like the mares in its oldest stud books with only stable names written in. Lester had explained that their bloodline was more important than their individual merits. That was how she felt as its part-time châtelaine. Just Pip. A tiny part of its history, and a seed that might find a place to root there.

Whenever she introduced herself to somebody new, Pip would tell them, 'My dad nicknamed me Pipsqueak. Everyone calls me Pip.' It wasn't strictly true. Both parents had always addressed her as Pauline but she had chosen to bury Pauline Edwards with them and Pip, the village's happiest helper and bounciest baker, had been born.

There weren't many hay nets to make up at this time of year – just those of the stallion, the box-resting point-to-pointer, and a few of the visiting mares, given private quarters well away from the broad-span barn where their foals had just been weaned. The rest of the broodmares were all out at grass, far from earshot of their offspring's plaintive cries. The stud always separated mother and foal in high summer so that the mare, pregnant again, wouldn't have more taken out of her by her big, milk-guzzling foal at foot.

'There's no room for sentimentality in horse breeding,' Lester had told Pip, the first day she'd come in to help on the yard.

Pip wasn't sentimental, so that suited her. When she'd started as housekeeper, there had been two stallions standing at Compton Magna: 'Old but serviceable,' the Captain would bark, on each occasion they were led ceremonially past him. Not long after his wife's death, they'd lost the legendary old thoroughbred, father of the first Magna Badminton winner.

Only roman-nosed Cruisoe was left, by far the tougher horse for his 'quarter of Irish bog-trotter', according to Lester, who wouldn't let Pip handle him. His dedicated care guaranteed that the horse's gold coat and black points gleamed like a *concours d'élégance* Ferrari badge.

She popped her head around the feed-room door. Lester was listening to his classical music, feed buckets lined up in military order in wheelbarrows ready to throw over stable doors and decant into long foal troughs. 'I'll take these round.' She'd seen how perilously the old boy moved over wet cobbles with a full barrow.

'Don't forget to check the—'

'Water buckets. I'm on it.' She barrowed away, wheel squeaking, proud of how expert she was these days. There had been a time when Lester wouldn't let her pick up a yard brush. The sun was already illuminating gingerbread stone walls and gleaming cobbles, like toffees.

It was on the Compton Magna stableyards that its historic architects had lavished their most extravagant flourishes – two grand courtyards of twenty stables apiece, interlinked with three Gothic stone arches, the first topped with a dovecote and weathervane, the central arch crowned by the clock-tower and the one at the rear boasting a copper-domed lookout of such structural ingenuity it still drew engineering students. The views from the little tower across to Eyngate Park were spectacular and entirely wasted on the colony of pipistrelles it had housed for more than seventy years. Having rescued many babies from grilles and gutters, and thinking of them as her little namesakes, Pip was determined that their home wouldn't be disturbed on her watch. Developers prowled regularly, and she knew from filing the Captain's post that there had been several unsolicited approaches since Ann's death, but he hadn't dignified them with a reply.

She wheeled beneath the tower now and out towards the modern barns, where the little foal group in the first enclosure started to shift, snort and whinny in anticipation, shuffling, barging, nipping and cow-kicking their way into rank order. There were six this year. A quartet of strapping juveniles vied for supremacy; the two younger ones, still in individual weaning pens, craned over to watch, squealing and whickering plaintively.

In the past decade, the breeding programme had been scaled down, visiting mares a priority. The majority of Compton Magna's homebred stock had traditionally been sold on as yearlings to keep costs down, staff numbers kept lean as the Percys aged and money thinned, only the cream of the crop retained to produce. When Pip had first become housekeeper, a work rider had come in from a neighbouring village and helped to break them in, but she hadn't been around for more than a year, and there seemed to be a lot of horses. Bossy Gill Walcote, the vet who came to check foals and scan mares, said there were far too many. None had been sold or broken in since Ann Percy's death, so the four-year-olds that should have started their careers were now great lanky adolescents with nothing to do but battle over their herd position like gang members.

Pip couldn't tell most of them apart. She liked the foals when they were tiny, and rideable horses like Horace, the point-to-pointer, and Lester's hunting cob, which were so well mannered they stood aside and waited for you to go through doors first, like old gents. But she found the broodmares boring and the youngsters intimidating – even at five months old they could nip and kick so hard it bruised bone. She chucked the food into the barns now, missing most of the troughs, already thinking about her tea and shortbread.

She did a quick check over the gates at the herds out in the fields – not that she could see where any of them were in the far distance. A bobbing line of brightly coloured helmet silks beyond the furthest boundary hedge meant riders on the bridleway, which always drew the stud horses across to watch. Forgetting the water troughs and the buckets in the foal barn, Pip hurried back to Lester to share a quick tea break, eager to talk to him again about her summer pensioner outings until it was time to wake the Captain.

'I can't stay long,' she said, leading the way into his little cottage and putting the kettle on. 'He'll give me hell if he misses the racing news again. Now, Lester, what's your opinion of a day at an outlet village, and do you think the Captain could be persuaded to come along? I have lots of mature single ladies on my books.'

'She was definitely right here.' Petra pulled up, looking at a patch of flattened straw. 'A blonde woman with three children.'

'Well, they're not here now,' said Gill.

'I can't see my stick,' complained Bridge.

'What if she was traumatised?' Petra fretted. 'We almost galloped over her new-born, Bridge.'

'She'll be fine,' Bridge said breezily. 'But what about my bloody stick? Aleš gave me it.'

'There's an earring here.' Gill jumped off to retrieve it, holding it up.

'It's a phone charm.' Petra examined the glittery little crescent. 'A letter C.'

'I thought I recognised her.' Bridge studied it too. 'She came to my mummy-yoga class in the village hall when the baby was still a bump – she was with that lot from the estate. She has Cs tattooed bloody everywhere. Third trimester and still lean as a marathon runner, lucky thing.'

'That'll be young Ash Turner's wife,' said Mo, whose bungalow was in the cul-de-sac that led directly off the Orchard Estate. 'Carla. Carrie? Pretty blonde, am I right?'

'Blondie didn't fetch a mat or take out her earphones, just watched us warm up and walked out, saying she preferred fresh air.'

'Ash Turner used to be a right tearaway,' Mo remembered, with a smile. 'War hero now. Probably sent wifey on a recce, Bridge. He's retraining to be a fitness instructor, I heard.'

'He's welcome to run my class. The sooner I get back into HR the better.'

'We really should push off,' Gill urged. 'Sanson's estate managers

are very quick to come down on riders threatening their steward-
ship scheme by trampling the field margins – not to mention his
valuable crops.'

Petra conceded defeat. She was still worried about the young
mum with the haunted eyes, but her own children would soon be
up and wanting breakfast. She didn't entirely trust Fitz to oversee
them. Last time she'd left him in charge, his younger brother, Ed, had
consumed an entire loaf of bread, toasted with Nutella, ten-year-old
wannabe Junior MasterChef Prudie had tried flambéing pineapple
on the Aga, smoke alarms shrieking, and baby-of-the-family Bella
had brought their Shetland pony into the kitchen to sample her
apple and marshmallow smoothie. 'Let's cut back through the sheep
fields. It's quicker.'

'That's Austen land.' Mo shook her head.

'Bay's even tougher on trespassers than Sanson,' warned Gill,
'especially when he's just released all the poults.' Compton Manor
Farm's drives were far from prying eyes, its fat, high-flying pheasant
and partridge closely guarded.

'Hates anyone going near his birds, does Bay.' Mo glanced up
at the woodland on the far brow where a Land Rover was parked.
'That might be his car.'

'Maybe that's what Petra's hoping,' scoffed Bridge.

'It takes a game bird to cross his land uninvited.' Gill's puns never
got better.

'Ha-bloody-ha.' Petra headed for a hunt jump. 'Is everyone up to
this? Shall I give you a lead?'

'You go ahead, Lucy Glitters!' Mo called.

Realising too late that an extra rail had been added behind the
tiger trap to allow for the summer sheep wire, Petra got left behind
as the Redhead put in a huge leap, losing both stirrups quickly followed by her dignity as the mare landed and bucked, propelling her
up her neck where she dangled as long as she could before sliding
gently into a patch of boggy, sedge-tufted ground. Standing over
her, the chestnut mare prodded her for signs of life with her nose,
long accustomed to her mistress falling off. Petra made a lot of
unscheduled dismounts, which Gill insisted was because she had an
insecure seat, like a marginal MP.

'I'm fine!' she said, springing up to take a bow. 'My fault!'

Leading a round of applause from the track, Mo rode to the nearby gate and put the combination in the padlock so that she could let the others through to the field without the need to jump. 'Barry does a lot of tractor work for the Austens,' she explained. 'He knows all the codes. Took him ages to remember. Nineteen... eighty-two... There we go! The year Bay was born.'

'Falklands War,' Gill remembered solemnly.

'Under-ten gymkhana race champion, Arthrington Show, Petra Shaw riding her evil loan pony Cecil to glory.' Petra sighed fondly. 'We shared an ice-cream, then Dad took me and my sister to see *E.T.*'

He *is* a toy-boy, she realised, as she led the mare back to the fence to use it as a mounting block. That was a first for the Safe Married Crush. Knowing Bay was younger made it feel safer. He was late thirties to her mid-forties.

They cantered along the edge of the sheep field, crossing through to adjoining pasture and riding single file along a wide, elder-flanked dry ditch, then scrambling up to the narrow gate that led back onto the track.

'Nineteen seventy-seven.' Mo put in the code. 'Year Sandy and Viv Austen got married.'

'The Queen's Silver Jubilee,' Gill remembered nostalgically, holding the gate open for the others. 'I was four.' Petra rode out onto the track, pulling her vibrating phone from her pocket. 'In fairy wings at an Ilkley street party.'

'I was minus ten.' Bridge burst through the gate last, making them all feel old. Unlocking her screen with fat riding-glove fingers on the third attempt, Petra saw the text was from Bay with a familiar spike of adrenalin.

'You all right, pet?' Mo was watching her. 'You've gone very blotchy.'

'Show!' Gill beckoned for the phone.

'We've been spotted trespassing.' She showed them the picture text that had just arrived, a blurred close-up of her balancing on his hunt jump, remounting the Redhead. *Get off my bloody land, gorgeous. Bx*

'How did he get a bum shot like that?' Bridge said, leaning across to look at it.

'Drones,' Gill said darkly. 'Sanson Holdings has dozens of them, and Bay's always wanted what they have. They're probably watching our every move.' Her eyes rolled from the woods to the hills to emphasise the point.

'Phone camera.' Mo quashed the notion. 'Bay, or his dad, always drives around the farm before breakfast. I thought that was his Defender parked up by Ten Ash Thicket. Best say sorry and keep my name out if he asks about the gate codes.'

Torn between embarrassment at being caught falling off and jubilation at being called 'gorgeous', Petra texted back an unapologetic *Off! x*

Don't do it again. Bay had a lightning thumb. *See anything odd? W@?*

Had visitors last night. After the storm. Lamping deer.

Petra would have liked to think that an instinctive bond of sisterhood stopped her grassing up the nappy-changing blonde from the estate, but the rest of the Bags were riding off and it was too complicated to type with one thumb on horseback. Carly, with her C tattoos, hadn't looked like a poacher.

Soz! she texted, aware that her witty repartee needed honing. The Redhead danced and spun impatiently, triggering a long row of accidental exclamation marks. At least they weren't kisses.

The others had set off at a fast trot. Taking a heavenly gulp of early-morning air, warm horse and refreshed crush, Petra set off in pursuit at full tilt, whooping loudly.

3

L ester managed to deflect all talk of picnics, pensioner days out and blind dates for at least twenty minutes, largely by keeping his mouth crammed with shortbread so that all he could do was look thoughtful and shrug.

'Look at you bending my ear!' Pip said brightly, taking their teacups to wash at the cottage sink. 'Can't keep the Captain waiting!'

Lester glanced at the carriage clock on the mantelpiece. Jocelyn Percy loathed unpunctuality, but the chances were he'd be too discombobulated to notice when he was woken up with a tray breakfast and the papers. The old boy slept much longer these days, and took more time to gather his wits.

Lester felt a pang of regret that he would almost certainly be the last of the three of them left. It should have been Johnny. Huntsman to his whip to the Captain's master. Every autumn, the trio would charge at dawn through the local landscape after Fosse foxhounds, like the Three Musketeers in rat-catcher, then hunting pink against a lowering sun as winter stole through the hills. When Jocelyn had resigned his mastership and his son-in-law had accepted the role, the heir had never been more apparent. Johnny Ledwell had been an extraordinary horseman, his knowledge and eye for breeding unrivalled.

For the first time in many months, Lester found himself reliving the awful day that the police had arrived to tell them Johnny was dead. The Captain, who had taken the news of human and horse tragedies many times in his life, had seemed broken by it.

Following Pip outside, Lester watched her trot off through the arch towards the main house. He could guess why she put off going inside until the last possible moment: the guv'nor had always been insufferably bad-tempered before midday. In the five decades that he'd checked the yard every morning at eight thirty sharp, a stickler for detail, his roars of fury had regularly been heard across the valley. Lester would give anything to hear that sound echoing around the stone walls again.

He wiped shortbread crumbs from his lips, buttoned up his coat and went back into the feed room to collect an extra bucketful for the ones he knew Pip would have missed. Heading out through the yards, grateful to have his beloved silence back, he set off to check the foals properly and fill their water buckets.

The scream from the house stopped him in his tracks.

Carly heard a distant shriek, but the horse-riders were far from view.

They had reached the point where Manor Farm's land met that of the Compton Magna Stud. Ahead, across a park-rail fence, familiar horses were grazing. Where were the foals?

'Horsie!' Sienna clamoured to be let out of the buggy. Carly stooped to unclip her.

Thwack, thwack, thwack!

Trailing behind, Ellis was smacking a hedge with a familiar purple stick.

'I told you to leave that where we found it!' Carly scolded.

The sense of foreboding she'd felt all morning was stronger here, her chest corseted. She took a deep breath and blew out hard to try to dislodge it. It could never again be as bad as when her mum was ill, Carly reminded herself. She'd known straight away, before even the official diagnosis, that she would lose her before Jackson was born. This was distant fire by comparison.

She could smell the poo stain and longed to rip off the T-shirt and wash it in the stream that trickled beneath the hedge boundary.

A yelp made her swing around again, exasperated. 'What you doing *now*, Ellis?'

'It wasn't me, it was the dog!'

'What dog?'

'In the grass. I din' mean to hit it.'

She hurried across to see. Lying behind a high bank of reeds, half submerged in red-stained stream water, was a huge dog, its brindle coat covered with blood. It looked close to death. 'Ellis, go and help your sister give the horses their carrots, yeah?'

'Did I kill it?'

'No, you didn't, baby.' She tried to keep her voice calm as she took in the dog's stillness, the skeletal ribs and open wounds. Eyes white with terror, it cowered away but couldn't move far. 'You found it. That's a very good thing. Now go to Sienna.' He pottered away.

The little boy's hedge-whacking whip had caught the injured dog across its side – Carly could see the stripe on its muddy coat and touched it gently and apologetically, surprised by the soft warmth – but the injuries were far worse than anything a small child could inflict. Its throat and sides had been gouged multiple times, the blood clotted now, proud flesh showing, one white-pawed brindle leg twisted completely the wrong way. Yet its eyes pleaded with her, bright copper dulled by pain, its will to live fierce.

'Oh, what happened to you?' She crouched closer, reaching out to comfort it, the dome of its head velvet against her palm. Her hands were burning now, her heart hammering, blood rushing too loudly in her ears for her to hear an approaching engine.

Ash would know what to do. He'd been raised around dogs – his family had packs of them. She fumbled for her phone, but there was no signal.

Somehow the big dog managed to drag itself fractionally closer, head pressed harder against her fingers, refusing to be let go.

'This field is private property,' drawled an angry voice. 'Just what in hell are you doing?'

Spinning round, Carly wanted to weep with relief at the sight of a toff in a flat cap towering over her, even if he was looking furious and filming her on his mobile.

'Me and my kids found an injured dog. It needs to go to a vet.'

The man stepped forward and took no more than a cursory look at the animal before glancing across at the buggy and the two small figures feeding the last carrot to the stud horses. 'Better get your children out of the way.' Then he turned back to retrace his steps.

'What are you going to do?'

'Put the wretched thing out of its misery,' he explained, striding along the field edge.

'You can't do that!' She hurried after him. 'We need to fetch a vet.'

'Don't be ridiculous,' he snapped. 'That animal was brought here by a bunch of city psychos who wanted to film it shredding a hare or fox, or in this case fighting to the death with a stag. I found him all bled out in a game copse earlier. Nobody "won" this time but it'll already be on a private video share channel, I can guarantee you.'

'The dog still deserves a chance!' she shouted at his broad-shouldered back. 'Please don't kill him.'

'It's the kindest thing,' he barked over his shoulder. 'It'll be dead inside an hour whatever we do.'

'You've got a car here?' She spotted the roof of a Land Rover on the other side of the hedge.

'And a gun.' He disappeared out of sight to open the tailgate, telling the dogs inside to stay there.

'You wouldn't use that in front of little kids.' She stood her ground as he reappeared.

'Which is why I'm now going to take your name and address so you can remove your children and we can talk about the trespassing later.' Gun resting on his shoulder, he flicked his phone on again and waited for her to dictate them, blue eyes unexpectedly attractive. They homed in now on the poo patch on her T-shirt.

'No!' Carly's hands felt as though she'd plunged them into scalding hot water. '*You*, mate, will help me pick up the dog, put it in the back of your car and take it to a vet to try to save its life.'

'Or what?'

'We'll all stand and watch it die together and you can explain to my kids why you won't help save it. And then *I'll* share that on bloody YouTube.' She got out her phone and started videoing him.

His mouth pursed, but he clearly knew she had far more powerful weapons than he did: a deep respect for all animals, a fierce mother love, three children under five and a 64GB memory card.

Pip had screamed more from protocol than fear. Wasn't it what you were supposed to do when you found a corpse? It was all too exciting and unexpected to think straight. And upsetting, of course. Pip's second death since her parents. She was becoming an old hand now, although on reflection the length of the bloodcurdling scream had been amateurish.

Had she found the Captain dead in his bed, as she had her own father, she might have contained herself, but her octogenarian boss was wedged nose-down between the clarets and Malbecs at the bottom of the cellar steps, the eighty-fourth birthday-present slippers she'd given him last week still bearing their price-tags on the soles. She'd bought them in the summer sales, a size too big but, in his favourite Black Watch tartan at a bargain price, they had been too good an opportunity to miss.

She and Lester waited for the ambulance in the big farmhouse kitchen, with warm sweet tea on tap. The drawing room could come later when they rounded up the suspects and revealed the murderer.

'Must've tripped,' Lester muttered, his face still bone white, which, given his ruddy complexion, was like seeing Ayers Rock covered with snow.

'Or been pushed?'

He didn't appear to be listening. 'Fetching more wine.'

'I left a bottle of claret out as usual. Maybe he had company.'

'He didn't.'

'I always said I should come back later to see him into bed. Maybe he saw a ghost.' She imagined that bulldog face lifting in brief, frozen valediction at the sight of Ann in full hunting gear.

'Heart attack's my guess. That's how his dad, the Major, went. Watching the Derby, he was, saw his horse win by ten lengths. Good way to go.'

'Tell that to Emily Davison!' She let loose a brittle sob, thinking it the right moment. But the obstinate tears wouldn't come: she was too pumped. 'At least there wasn't blood. I can't abide blood.'

Lester was familiar with shock. He'd seen a great many lives end, most of them four-legged ones that he'd shared from joyful, slithering birth to all manner of deaths, waved off in the kennelman's trailer. The Captain had been saying his adieu for a long time. When a man lost interest in his horses, he lost interest in living. Johnny had been the same by the end.

He could see Pip was struggling to take it in, now cooking the Captain's kippers – she always ate in a crisis – but instead of dropping them into the pan boiling on the Aga, she put them into the toaster and sat down again.

The secret was to be practical and keep busy.

'We must let the family know,' he said matter-of-factly.

'He hasn't been declared dead yet!'

'Nothing a paramedic can do.'

They'd already tried to dislodge him and lay him down, but rigor mortis had started to set in. It was going to be a hell of a job to move him: he wasn't a small man.

Under Lester's beady gaze, Pip picked up the phone handset that lived by the Aga and ran her eye along the list of numbers written on the noticeboard in big black figures so that the Captain could read them. He made a lot of calls, shouting at his bookie, his solicitor, his family – his deafness made him bellow at everyone.

She called Alice first, adopting her best breaking-bad-news manner. A voicemail message greeted her.

None of the grandchildren were answering their phones. As each outgoing message told her they were unavailable, she pieced together what she could remember from recent family visits – wasn't it this week Alice was overseeing Pony Club Camp on a windswept Warwickshire hill? Tim was *loco vinum* all month, visiting vineyards in South Africa; Pax was on holiday with her husband and kids in Italy.

Pip started to relax. It was still her drama. Having left messages to ask each in turn to ring her urgently, she set the phone down. 'Shall I call Ronnie?'

'Absolutely not.'

'In that case, I'll make more tea.'

It had been a task to squeeze two adults, two kids, a baby, a double buggy and three dogs – one on its last gasps – inside a Land Rover already rammed with gun racks and gamebird feeders. The posh landowner, who Carly now knew was called Bay, made no bones about his opinion of their emergency dash, but at last they were on their way. The big dog was now wrapped in a tartan rug on the floor between the bench seats, on one of which Carly perched, trying to cuddle a wailing Jackson while reaching down to staunch fresh bleeding. Mother and child were covered with blood as well as poo, the ultimate unsavoury hijackers.

'Still hanging on in there?' Bay called back.

'Yes, but hurry!'

Bay's dogs swayed on the passenger seat beside him at the front; Ellis and Sienna were strapped into the row behind them, rattling from side to side, thoroughly overexcited by the mission.

'Doggie! Save doggie!' Sienna chanted.

'Is it much further?' Carly reached down to reassure the injured dog.

'Five minutes max.' Their reluctant ambulance driver forded a stream. 'I've forgotten your name, sorry.'

'Carly.'

In front, her son introduced himself too. 'I am Ellis Peter Turner and I'm four.'

'Turner, you say?'

'That's right.' Carly was getting used to local reaction to the surname. He let out a cynical laugh.

'I might have guessed.' He had an amused, drawly voice, like a posh Simon Cowell. 'Something tells me I've just been had here.'

'How so?'

'It's your lot behind all this lamping business in the first place.'

'What are you talking about?'

'We caught Jed Turner twice last year. Your boys promise the urban coursers a night's entertainment, spring the gates, act as guides. What do you charge to find them a good spot?'

'I have no idea what you're banging on about, lover, but you'd better bloody step on it.' The dog was starting to fit, eyes rolling back, legs jerking and twitching. 'Faster!'

They turned into a wide driveway with Compton Equine Clinic signs to either side, then bounced over speed bumps to a modern Cotswold-stone state-of-the-art surgery surrounded by stableyards and turn-out paddocks.

'It's a horse hospital.' She panicked they wouldn't agree to see the dog.

'A vet's a vet, especially when they're an old friend.' Bay leaped out and ran inside. Moments later he reappeared with a small, bearded man, whom he was briefing on the run: 'I'm bloody sorry to land this on you, Paul, but you're closest, and I don't want the Turners putting some gypsy curse on this shooting season because their best bull-lurcher pegged it in my car.'

'We're not really set up for small-animal surgery, Bay.'

'You've not seen the size of this dog.' They wrenched the tailgate open and levered out the big lurcher.

The vet, Paul Wish, was a New Zealander with a gentle, no-nonsense manner, calling on a team of veterinary nurses, who prepared the animal, clinging to its last thread of life, to be rushed into an operating theatre.

'This is going to take a while,' Paul told Bay and Carly, as he prepared to leave them in the waiting room, a mobile phone pressed to his ear. 'I'll do what I can, but I don't think—' He broke off to leave a message: 'Gill, call me the moment you get this. I could use your suturing skills right now.' The phone was lowered. 'I don't think there's a lot of hope.'

'Do what you can,' pleaded Carly.

'And do it quickly.' Bay glanced at his watch. 'We've got a pony booked in for a scan later. Do you want a lift home?' he asked Carly.

'I'll stay here to see how the dog does, thanks.'

No way she was leaving the dog with the pleading eyes.

Eight metal shoes clattered along the Plum Run between the Comptons at trot.

'Time for a quick coffee?' asked Petra.

'Why not?' Gill replied.

It was their much-repeated catchphrase, delivered with French and Saunders aplomb.

Petra counted Gill among her closest village friends. Kind, practical and immensely likeable – as long as you didn't mind old-school bluntness, drinks mixed so strong they were dangerous near naked flames and four-by-four road rage along narrow local lanes. She was a lot more fun than the starchy front implied, with a ticklish sense of humour for all its bad puns. She also knew a lot more about Petra's marriage than most villagers.

To outsiders, the Gunns' was a materially enviable life. The family owned a Cotswold farmhouse and a London pied-à-terre and their children were privately educated. They drove around in gas-guzzling off-roaders, had plenty of gadgets to play with and took two holidays a year. They owned three ponies and one horse, as well as a delinquent dog and several chickens. Petra had achieved the have-it-all generation's dream of family and career, even if it had come at a price: their marriage was uncommunicative, seldom sexual, still less affectionate, and a financial minefield. Their social lives were largely conducted separately, and Petra was fond of saying that putting Charlie first meant she had the last laugh, but she struggled to find much her husband said amusing now. So it was funny that she still cared about him so much. In between wanting to kill him. But, after eighteen years of marriage, they loved their children and their house and, grudgingly, each other.

Friendships like that with Gill helped enormously, although they had none of the deep heart-to-hearts she had once or twice a year with old college friends; it was the day-to-day rhythm of life they shared, its reasons to be cheerful or irritated, the underlying unhappiness with their marriages implicitly understood, a silent pact broken only in a crisis. Married to small, cycling-mad beta Paul for more than twenty years, Gill treated him like a fourth child and craved adult company. Her delaying going into the clinic – 'It's only paperwork and drug reps on Thursday mornings' – was a regular occurrence.

The two women consequently squeezed in a coffee between early-morning hacking and work, a secret indulgence stolen after they'd waved off Mo and Bridge in Compton Bagot. They always seemed to have a lot still to talk about, happy to put off work for another half-hour, and Petra's welcoming kitchen was on Gill's way home.

Georgian-fronted Upper Bagot Farmhouse was on the lane between Comptons Bagot and Magna. Seven years earlier, the Gunns had traded up from a chocolate-box thatch in Chipping Hampton. It had ticked every one of Charlie's extensive wish-list requirements, including the game larder, walled garden and railed paddocks, apart from affordability, especially since his daily commute had proved so punishing. That he now used the London flat during the week meant its rental income no longer helped to pay off the Cotswold mortgage. Seven years ago, Petra's wish list had been simpler: somewhere peaceful to write, and somewhere to keep horses. That she would spend so long working in one to pay for the other was trade off she hadn't fully appreciated then, but she was proud of the neat little stableyard where she kept the Redhead and her daughters' ponies.

The old ironstone stables that had been part of the original farm-yard had been converted when Upper Bagot Farm was developed, and the farmhouse had its own modern courtyard of four wooden loose boxes, tack room and store. Here was where Bella's spoilt Welsh pony was lavished with kisses, watched jealously by Prudie's largely neglected New Forest. The outgrown family Shetland mowed the lawn and gave rides at the fête every year, and the stroppy Redhead ruled the roost, with a lot of door-kicking.

The original milking parlour and timbered barns had all been converted into luxury homes, creating a pocket-sized community that locals had nicknamed 'WI' because its inhabitants had all come from London. Among their neighbours were a glamorous former dentist in the Old Byre, rarely at home for more than a week at a time between cruises; a pair of elderly tennis enthusiasts in the Barn; two jolly foodies in the Stables; and lonely retired airline pilot Kenneth in the Granary, a keen gardener who had left Petra his usual canvas bag of goodies hanging on a fence post this morning – lettuces, radishes and freshly cut flowers.

'I wish I had a Kenneth next door,' sighed Gill, whose sprawling, historic cottage on the far edge of Compton Magna was flanked by holiday lets.

'He can talk for an hour and a half about aphids without pausing for breath,' Petra reminded her.

'So can my husband.'

The coffee pod machine grumbled out two Guatemalan lungos, milk-frothed clouds poured on top. The two women took their caffeine fix at the breakfast bar.

A Hansel and Gretel trail of breakfast cereal, dressing-gowns and slippers led off to the snug, from which the television boomed and voices shrieked.

'They keep lining up like the Brady Bunch offering to do the washing-up; I've told them they need to relax.' Petra pulled a what-can-I-say face. 'I love having them all home, but I classify summer holidays as a manic episode. One minute.'

She stuck her head around the door to find three figures silhouetted against the television screen, eyes inches from *Scooby Doo*: Ed, soft, round tummy showing in outgrown *Hobbit* pyjamas, Prudie standing in ballet third position in a Coolest Kid Ever nightie, Bella with her Joules pony pyjamas on inside out, dark hair on end as usual. Wilf, the delinquent spaniel, was helpfully washing up the cereal bowls abandoned by sag bags on the floor. No sign of Fitz.

'I'm home!' she told them brightly. 'Everything okay?'

They murmured vague assents.

'How long until you all go to Italy?' Gill asked, when she came back.

'A fortnight. We've got Gunny's summer visit first.' Charlie's mother was travelling up from Kent the next day for a week's stay, a tri-annual ritual Petra anticipated with the same foreboding and need for gin as getting a manuscript back from a pedantic copy-editor. 'I've a packed schedule planned. Thank heaven for Tesco vouchers.'

'And Open Garden Week. Bring her to admire the Walcote Wishes – we'll sedate her with Paul's elderberry wine and his guided tour of his veg patch.'

'She'll critique it all on her blog. *The flat delphiniums at Tie Cross Cottage were an utter disgrace.* You'll find your herbaceous borders named, shamed and face-tagged.'

Barbara 'Gunny' Gunn, an early adopter of silver surfing, was a keen blogger, unsparing in her opinions on social class, marriage, books, gardening and food, which she now shared with her legion of subscribers. Her son's family and their lives in the Cotswolds were favourite subjects for Gunn Points posts.

'Is Charlie taking time off while she's here?'

'What do you think?'

'Sudden heavy caseload?'

'You guessed it.'

'We're all still placing bets as to how you killed him,' Gill said now. Regularly away shooting in winter and playing cricket in summer,

Charlie was an elusive Compton weekender, especially when his mother was visiting. On the rare occasions he did appear, he was so gregariously sociable and charming that everyone was left wanting more.

Petra had come to realise that her husband looked magnificent in a wig, an adversarial pin-up, and was well-liked, immensely sociable and superb at networking, but he wasn't very good at winning for his clients. Like his hair, his cases were thinner on the ground each year. He and Petra earned roughly the same, yet his routine was never compromised by sick children, broken dishwashers or visiting grandparents.

'This is delicious coffee.' Gill sucked off the white moustache from her first sip. 'You're one mother of a barista, Gunn.'

'No, Gunny's the mother of a barrister. I'm his wife.' Petra boom-boomed.

'Don't you forget that.' Gill adopted her mock-schoolmarm air, but her eyes were serious. 'You have a good marriage. Bay really does have a terrible reputation as a flirt.'

'Tell that to Charlie! My husband's been trying to befriend Bay for years, remember? He'd quite happily pimp me and the kids if it gets him an invitation to the Well-hung supper.'

'Not a chance,' Gill said. The Austen family threw a notoriously cliquey party to gather the county's movers and shakers as soon as the season's first pheasants were deemed gamey enough to stew in a vat of Calvados and cream. 'And especially not if you keep flirting with Bay.'

'I told you, we're just trapped in a *manège à trois* of Pony Clubbers. Charlie's delighted.'

As an old-fashioned networker, her husband had made it his mission to infiltrate the village hierarchy over several seasons, with dedicated church-going and bonhomie at local events. Being a top-class delegator, he'd thrust that mantle to Petra as court cases in London took up more of his time. Over the moon that a social connection between the Gunn and Austen families had at last been forged – albeit by eight-year-olds bonding between gymkhana potato races – Charlie had encouraged his wife to chat up the party-throwing, landowning, moneyed Austens while supporting their daughters at

Pony Club rallies and other competitions all summer. Sociable and ever-grateful to be away from her desk, it was an easy enough task for Petra to get talking to other parents. Tellingly, Charlie had no interest in befriending Gracie's less glamorous family, another of the village's oldest farming clan, but her warm-hearted, perennially broke mother Mo had become a firm friend and hacking buddy, while Tilly's cool, stand-offish mother would never be a Saddle Bag. Petra had disliked Bay's wife on instinct.

'I have no idea why men are attracted to ice queens like Monique,' she said now.

'Sex,' Gill said crushingly. 'I meet Moni Austen a lot on the dressage circuit, and she's a very tough cookie – she's known as the Assassin in the warm-up arena because she'd ride over anyone.'

An ultra-slim Dutch dressage fanatic, Monique Austen had taken Petra's mobile number months ago, saying she'd text to arrange a play-date for the girls but never had. Text addict Bay, by contrast, had been hitting send such a lot recently that, had his wife not been quite so beautiful, she might have mistrusted his intentions.

'Are you warning me off him?' She took in Gill's stern expression.

'I hardly think I need to do that, do I? I'm just saying you should try to focus on what's important.' Those brown eyes looked pointedly to the door that led to the snug and her children. 'And you really don't want to cross Monique Austen.'

'Especially not in working trot M to K,' Petra muttered.

Gill's phone chirruped in her pocket. She plucked it out impatiently. Moments later, she was throwing back her coffee dregs and sprinting around the kitchen island as though the lungo had been shot straight into a vein.

'I need to borrow your car. Emergency at the clinic. Can you hang onto my big chap until I get back?'

'Of course. What's happened?' Petra felt guiltily relieved that a veterinary emergency had put an end to the morality lecture.

'No idea, but Paul's patching something up in theatre and he stitches like a saddler.' Gill was already out of the door, Petra grabbing the key fob to follow.

'It's a push-button ignition,' she explained, as Gill jumped into the Gunns' SUV. 'Put your foot on the brake. *Voilà!*'

It was only while waving her off that Petra realised she still had the fob in her hand.

'Whatever you do, don't stall the engine!' she shouted, but the car was already accelerating along Plum Run.

At the stud, the paramedics, police officers and undertakers all knew each other of old: it was a death-scene reunion. Boiling the kettle so often that her pores were opening, Pip kept her ears trained for hints of suspicious circumstances, but they mostly spoke in low, respectful tones that were a far cry from *Luther*.

'Been busy lately?' Pip overheard one say to another as she crossed the courtyard while they vaped outside the back door.

'They're piling up, bro. Same every year. Summer holidays and Christmas, we always get a rush on.'

'Nice place, this. Better than most shouts. No family to tiptoe round yet either.'

'Tell me about it. I had one last week where the wife was hand-bagging the son over the body.'

'The worst is where they announce the death on Facebook while you're still there and you can hear notifications coming in, pop, pop, pop. "Sorry for your loss." They fall apart as soon as that starts.'

'Don't think this old boy can have much of a family.'

'Got a lot of horses, though.'

'Not big on grief, horses.'

'You kidding me? My wife's got one. No end of grief she gives me.'

Pip felt an urgent need for grief, yet hers still refused to come. Lester was even more buttoned-up and pragmatic, currently helping the police take apart the wine racks – there was a bit of difficulty getting the body out.

There *should* be family here. They would refuse to let this death pass without wanting to know why now, why today, why so sudden.

Pip hurried up the old observation tower where her network signal was strong enough for 3G. She could see the horses from here, black, grey, brown and gold shapes beyond the mould-laced glass windows.

Her breath caught in her throat. The Captain would have wanted his daughter here. She googled Ronnie Percy, knowing exactly which stepping stones of clicks would lead to her phone number.

Pip liked to keep online tabs on all the Percy family and Ronnie in particular. She was a single-minded surfer, using search engines like a government agent closing in on suspects, but Ronnie Percy moved mostly beneath the radar, with no social media account or up-to-date professional profile.

She'd known better than to ask the elderly Percys about their only daughter, the mere mention of her name enough to bring on an angina attack, and Lester was equally tight-lipped, but the long-term village residents whom Pip cared for were far more forthcoming about the infamous Bardswold Bolter.

In the post-war era Major Frank Percy, the Captain's father, had brought fame to Compton Magna by breeding high-class hacks and hunters for the gentry, including the Queen, whose visits had caused much verge-scything, hedge-trimming and hat-buying excitement in the village. Son Jocelyn, a dashing blond blade, had done a stint in the Household Cavalry before he'd taken over at the stud in the late fifties. The young Captain and his hunting-mad wife, Ann, had introduced the very best thoroughbred blood to add the stamina that would take Percy horses out of the show ring and across all country, hailing a new era for the stud.

Less enthusiastic about parenthood, they had just one daughter, Veronica.

Raised in the saddle, Ronnie was pretty, vivacious, fearless, competing at the top level in three-day-eventing's heyday, chasing Princess Anne and Lucinda Prior-Palmer across private parkland, and going on to be selected for the British team at just eighteen. Not long afterwards she'd married the handsome, brooding Johnny Ledwell, the couple barely checking between coverts as they produced three children in swift succession, Alice, Tim and Pax, destined to follow in the family hoofprints.

Then in the early eighties, still just twenty-five, Ronnie had deserted her marriage, children, horses and the stud in a dramatic bolt, still talked about by the likes of the Misses Evans in the thatched cottage by the tennis club. Ran off with a handsome fancy man in his sports car, she did. Those poor little kiddies. Nobody had seen it coming. Such a pretty, friendly young mum she'd been, always full of beans.

As far as Pip could tell, she'd fled to the wilds of Cumbria and seemed to have stayed in the north for almost two decades. More recently she'd been based in Germany, dealing horses for a few years, although information was scant.

Pip had pieced together enough to know that she now lived in Wiltshire where she helped organise a big horse trials. The event website had her listed on its contacts page with an office address on a country estate, along with landline.

A male voice message told callers that the phone was only manned on Mondays and Tuesdays and gave an email address for horse-trials enquiries.

Undeterred, Pip searched on.

From her research, she also knew that Ronnie owned two competition horses ridden by a brooding Aussie veteran, the fortunes of which she'd been following all year on the British Eventing website and, more revealingly, on his head girl's busy Twitter feed.

Pip went there now, rewarded straight away with a photo tweeted the previous evening of people relaxing with champagne flutes in folding picnic chairs by a horsebox, the most glamorous of whom was laughing as the two small dogs on her lap gave her kisses on both cheeks.

Pip didn't need to check the schedules to know Ronnie Percy was watching her horses compete in a big international trials near Milton Keynes. The Aussie event rider's number was listed on several sites selling horses. She rang it.

A voice as deep, rough and Australian as a dried bush creek answered. 'Yeah?'

'Is Veronica Percy there, please?'

There was a long, muffled pause, then Pip heard an echoing Tannoy, a whistle blow and a horse's hoofs approaching.

The crackly Australian voice came back. 'Who is this?'

'It's personal.'

Another pause, during which the hoof beats got louder, stopped for a moment, then thundered on amid a smattering of applause and whoops.

'Tell them to fuck off.' A husky voice laughed in the background. The line went dead.

Pip gritted her teeth and texted. *Captain Jocelyn Percy died last night.*

The phone rang less than a minute afterwards. 'Who is this?'

4

'Taking root here, I see?'

Carly looked up in shock. Bay was back. The toff cared! 'They're still in surgery. The dog's died on the table twice.'

'That's over two hours.'

'Is it?' Carly was shocked, glancing guiltily at her children, but they were more settled here than at home, Ellis playing Crossy Roads on her phone, Sienna entranced by the bead maze in the corner and Jackson asleep.

'Every dog has his day. Some have groundhog days. I'm a repeat customer,' Bay told the receptionist. 'Brought a pony for a bone-cyst scan. Austen.'

'Might not be quite ready for you. Can you fill in the consent forms while you wait?'

A small girl with lop-sided bunches burst in through the entrance. 'Daddy, I've unloaded Toffee, but he's not happy without a hay net. It's *really* unfair to make him wait.' She eyed Carly and her brood warily.

'Tilly darling, this is Carly, whose dog's life-saving surgery is causing the delay. He's already stopped breathing twice, so if it's third time lucky, Toffee will be straight in.'

'Wow.' The child's eyes stretched wide. 'That's, like, *really* serious.'

Carly thought it was a terrible thing to say to a child, but Tilly seemed remarkably robust, delighted, even. 'I *really* wish I could be in there watching, don't you? I'm going to be an equine vet one day, along with my friends Grace and Bella. We plan to open our own clinic and call it Horse-pital. Is this your baby?'

'Yes.'

'I don't like babies much. You have lots of tattoos, don't you? Is that poo on your shirt?'

'She takes after her mother,' Bay apologised over his shoulder, putting a hand on his daughter's head and turning it ninety degrees until Tilly's eyes alighted on a pile of *Pony* magazines.

Carly paced fretfully around the waiting room while Bay took calls, voice languid and privileged, apologising to someone he was supposed to be meeting: 'Bloody bizarre morning – I'll tell you when I see you. Yes, next week's good.' Then taking another: 'Thanks for calling back, Lockie. You had any illegal lamping going on in your neck of the woods? Bloody nasty bastards left a bull-lurcher dying in one of my sheep fields. I'm going to chat to the rural crime guy at Broadbourne nick later...'

Jackson had woken up, nappy heavier than concrete shoes in the Thames, but seemed too hypnotised by the sparkly mood lights in the ceiling to notice. Ellis had gravitated towards Tilly, both entranced by a flat screen showing colic operations and terrifying dental footage.

'Uuuuuugh!' He pointed, thrilled by the goo and gore.

'Diastemas are oral fissures usually due to jaw misalignment and prone to painful infection,' she explained to him, in an eight-year-old-talking-to-a-simpleton voice, then returned to a word search in *Pony*.

'Shudda brushed his teef prop'ly.' He chuckled.

Bay was now lounging on a leather sofa with a macchiato, making calls and texting as though he had all the time in the world.

He had a handsome face in a posh sort of way, Carly noted, the sort you saw in aftershave ads aimed at older men, all straight nose and strong jaw staring out of power boardrooms across the City, not usually hauling battered dogs out of hedgerows.

As she observed him, his eyes developed a frozen look. 'Are you quite sure he's dead?'

Carly felt a sharp bolt of dread as she imagined the vet calling through from the operating theatre, not wanting to break the news in front of such small children.

'An ambulance means nothing,' Bay was saying. 'Oh, the police too?'

Carly relaxed, guiltily relieved that the death wasn't their hunting dog's, and the wide smile breaking across Bay's face suggested it was no close friend.

'Are you sure it's not Lester?... Oh, right. Bloody hell. Poor sod.' He clenched his fist in a discreet air punch.

He rang off, scrolled to a number in his Contacts and dialled straight out. 'Kelvin! Bay Austen. I might have some land acquisitions coming up for you to handle and I need you to be straight on it if so.'

Guessing the two calls weren't unconnected, Carly was shocked by his gall.

Standing by the front desk now, she noticed the pretty young receptionist was discreetly checking her Instagram feed on her phone. 'You got any vacancies coming up here?'

'Oh, yah, I think there's an application form for volunteers somewhere.'

'Paid jobs.' Carly crossed her arms in front of her filthy T-shirt.

'You'd have to talk to someone more senior than me. I'm only here on work experience.'

'What I've learned from experience,' Carly whispered kindly, 'is to demand the minimum wage.'

'Totes! Ha-ha.' The girl pretended to be busy with the photocopier.

'You have jobs, don't you, Daddy?' Tilly had been listening in.

Writing another text now, Bay Austen didn't look up. 'You're after a job?'

'Yeah. Part time.'

'Give me your number. I'll put my farm-shop manager in touch.'

'Thanks.' Astonished, Carly dictated it, catching Tilly's eye, and decided perhaps the little girl wasn't quite so brattish as she'd thought.

'It's always busy around harvest.' Bay saved her number. 'The pay's good and you get free veg if you don't mind bent courgettes and ugly peppers.'

'I believe in equal-opportunities ratatouille.'

'Then it's your lucky day.' He looked up at her, the blue eyes sparkling. 'I can see past the fact you're a Turner.'

Carly's gaze shifted instinctively and proudly to her children with their father's coal-black hair and wolf-pale eyes. If she hadn't wanted a job away from Janine and Feather Dusters so badly, she'd have told Bay to look at her middle finger.

A harassed female vet came out of a side door, surgical greens creased and splattered, peppery hair sprouting from the sides of an inadequate paper cap, bear-like eyes focused on him. 'You know that dog's been bred to kill?'

'Aren't we all, Gill?'

'Lost half its blood, femur split like kindling and a bashed head that's clotted to hell. It should be dead. No idea how you kept it alive long enough to get it here.'

'Here's your miracle worker.' Bay indicated Carly.

'Are you veterinary-trained?' demanded Gill.

'No.' She glanced down at her fingers wringing together, cold and sweaty now. 'Women in my family have healing hands, Mum always said. Please tell me he'll pull through.'

'*She*'ll pull through if I have anything to do with it. So you practised Reiki on her?' The corner of her mouth curled, not unkindly.

'Dunno. Mum swore I picked up a bird with a broken wing when I was a toddler and it flew clean away.'

'Quite impossible,' the vet said, 'but there's great potency in adrenalin, belief and kindness.'

'And cranks who rub their hands together at the prospect of laying them on wads of cash.' Bay chortled. 'There's your job opportunity, sweetheart. Chap my wife's friends are fond of charges fifty quid to wave his pinkies over their horses' chakras and pep their piaffes.'

'Not all dressage riders are that naïve, Bay,' the vet hissed. 'Whatever you did,' she turned to Carly, 'it's practical magic. I've not seen such a fierce will to live in a long time.' Recognising that Carly was distressed, she smiled stiffly. 'The worst bit's over. She's already coming around from the anaesthetic. Wouldn't surprise me if she bounces straight up, like Katie Jordan, ready for a *Hi There* shoot after a boob job!' She forced a jolly laugh.

Carly looked at her blankly.

'Katie Price? OK?' suggested young Tilly.

'Don't be so impertinent, Matilda Austen. I know who I mean.' The vet had turned to Bay again. 'I gather she's a rescue case. The RSPCA are usually pretty good at stepping in with veterinary funding, and we'll call today pro bono. Paul's ringing around sanctuaries now to try to find her a place.'

Carly thought of the animal's desperate trust in her, a lifetime's bond.

'How much will it cost to keep her?' She had a small cash legacy from her mum, still on deposit for a rainy day. Waitressing was already bringing in a bit of cash, and if she added more cleaning shifts for Janine and maybe some farm-shop work she'd have a regular wage coming in again. She was sure she could cover the extra expense.

'She'll need referral to the orthopaedic specialist for a wire frame on that leg,' the wild-haired vet explained. 'Then physio, probably hydrotherapy, plus repeat visits to adjust and finally remove the wires. Spaying is mandatory in cases like this, and she's riddled with worms. There will undoubtedly be a high degree of training, sociali-sation and rehabilitation involved, for which I can recommend a canine behaviour therapist locally.' The figure she came up with was more than Ash's flashy truck, the wall-mounted TV, games console and gym sub combined.

'I can't cover that,' Carly said in a small voice.

'Daddy, we can pay, can't we?' said the sing-song one.

Carly was seriously liking Tilly now.

'No.' Bay was adamant.

'Let's look at what's best for this dog, shall we?' The vet pulled off her green paper hat, revealing more untamed iron-grey curls. 'There's a super charity locally that rehabilitates lurchers, and I really think they're the champions for your girl right now. If Paul can get her a place there, it's her best chance of a future.'

Carly nodded, too choked to speak. Living with Ash was already like tiptoeing around a hound that had lost his pack. He had no head-space for a sick dog. She couldn't hope to offer her the happy, loving home she deserved.

She looked to Bay for reassurance, but he was on the phone again, his back turned to them. 'We all knew he was on his way out... Absolutely. Place has been going downhill for years, doubt they'll keep it going as a stud.'

'Can I at least give her a name?' she asked the vet.

'What?' The vet was listening to Bay's conversation now.

'The dog. Can I name her?'

The vet's eyes focused on Carly again. 'Please do. Anything would be better than "stray bitch admitted at eight twenty-five".'

'Pricey,' she said decisively.

'That's so cool!' Tilly sealed their unlikely friendship.

Lester had always appreciated the rituals surrounding death, not least tea-drinking. Pip was an enthusiastic tea-maker. The paramedics had swigged English Breakfast while they waited for the police; the police had waited for the funeral directors while drinking Assam; the funeral directors had waited for the GP nursing Ceylon; the GP had been given Earl Grey. The coroners' office would have to be involved, they were told, a post-mortem held. The GP concurred with the medics that it was likely to have been a heart attack, the circumstances of death unusual and unfortunate but not suspicious.

Lester was keeping his emotions in check and carrying on with his yard duties when time allowed. Pip grew more agitated as the morning wore on, a far from silent witness clutching a tea tray. 'Such a terrible scene to find! It's just like a Sunday-night whodunit on TV. Do you need to take photographs? Are SOCO coming?'

She refused to believe the excitement was evaporating so fast, that no grizzled, squabbling CID duo were going to arrive in a vintage car to examine the evidence.

'He would never willingly die like this,' she'd told the police emphatically. 'He was far too proud. When Mrs Percy passed on with all that fuss, he was furious. She was in the bath, you know – huge aneurysm, instant, still had a ciggie on the go. Tufted mat went up like stubble. The family Labrador was locked in there with her. Terrible scene. The Captain never got another dog after that.' She added breathlessly, 'He drank a lot more after Mrs Percy died. Always sneaking down to the cellar for another bottle. But he knew those steps better than anyone.'

Once the Captain's body had been removed and all the unfamiliar cars had gone, Pip went into uncharacteristic overdrive, waving a cloth around the house in a token gesture to its fur coats of dust – Lester had noticed that cleaning wasn't Pip's strong point

– organising the post, going through the fridge and freezer to throw out perishables, stripping the bed, any intention to help him on the yard thankfully forgotten. 'Why not go home and have some rest?' he suggested.

'I have to go and prepare old Mrs Bentley's lunch in a minute.' She looked at her watch. 'I'll come straight back afterwards. I thought we'd watch the racing from Goodwood in the Captain's honour. I'll make your lunch too.'

'Sussex Stakes today.' And suddenly he could hardly stand up for sadness. It hit him like a big wave against a seafront. Tears seemed to be coming from everywhere – his fingers, his jaw, his chest, his back, flooding in. He watched her plucking rows of keys out of the press, although she was becoming too blurred to see. *Focus, man!* He heard the Captain's voice in his head, barking at him as it had for sixty years, since his first day of national service with the Household Cavalry, the handsome young Captain Percy telling him there was no room for sentiment with horses, soldiers or women. *The only living creature on God's earth that should see a man's fear, his suffering or his pain is his dog.*

Stubbs was looking up at him worriedly. The tears were rising higher. Lester stood up tall, lifting his nose and chin, as though trapped in an upturned boat in an ever-shrinking air pocket, face twisted with the effort of not drowning.

'Let's put a bet on!' Pip suggested brightly. She turned to Lester, relieved to find he had a curious half-smile on his face, gazing mistily up at the ceiling.

'The Captain fancied the Coolmore colt,' he told Pip, and she distinctly heard an amused catch in his throat, a curious sort of choking noise. He was taking strangely deep breaths, she noticed, hoping he'd remembered to use his asthma inhaler today. The last thing she wanted on top of everything else was a trip to A and E.

Pip pressed her eyes tight shut against a much-anticipated deluge of tears, but still they remained obstinately dry. 'I'll place an online bet from Mrs B's. Now I'm going to lock this place up in case the police need the scene preserved. They haven't done the autopsy yet.'

His breathing really was very odd. 'Any word from the children?'

Pip noticed he skipped a generation when he spoke of them, just as the Captain had: 'the children', not 'grandchildren'. 'I've tried them all again twice.' The hiatus no longer felt reassuringly normal, but like a gathering storm, and they already had one of those, with distant thunder rumbling on the far horizon.

Pip felt indignant on the Captain's behalf. She knew they all had busy lives – they'd visited less often lately, familial tolerance waning. He'd become so intractable, less interested in them than his television screen. Most recently, Alice had complained about the smell and the state of the house. Pip knew that wasn't her fault: the Captain didn't see dirt and he always insisted that watching her mop was torture. But to cover herself, she'd already texted Janine Turner, saying she needed her team for an urgent deep-clean; the housekeeping float could easily cover it, and she'd get a receipt.

Outside the day was unfittingly perfect, the sky now Lego-block blue. Pip triple-locked the back door, secure in the knowledge that the house was impenetrable. 'I'll be back before you know it,' she promised Lester, heaving her clanking bag onto the passenger seat.

His head was bowed, but at least his breathing seemed normal again.

With dam-bursting relief, Lester waved her off, Stubbs at his side as she hurtled out along the driveway, exhaust bobbing smokily.

From his high-hedged field, Cruisoe the stallion charged alongside, letting out angry bellows as he saw the car off.

'Now that's a lot of horse, Lester.' Laugh as loud as a fevered sneeze. Gorsebridge Sales, 1993. A rare dun sports horse bred in the purple ('Never breed for colour, Lester, but if you happen to throw a rainbow there's a crock at the end'). The Captain nodding almost imperceptibly in time to the auctioneer's rising price, fast climbing higher than Lester's annual salary and higher again. 'Tell me when to stop.'

Lester had said nothing.

Cruisoe had earned his hammer price back many times over.

Lester turned back to the yard, remembering it full of visiting mares, the lorries and trailers coming and going every day, Ann's fierce welcomes, the three-hour three-bottle lunches, the Captain's loud laughter, the yard phone ringing non-stop.

The yard Tannoy *was* ringing, the phone-line wired to loud-speakers.

There was an extension in Stables Cottage, attached to the wall with a long, curled flex that had tangled itself so tightly over many years that it was now impossible to move more than a foot away from the base set. Lester was seldom called upon to answer it. He used it to ring through feed orders or summon the vet.

He disliked it so intensely that sometimes he chose to ignore it, as he did now, marching into the cottage to feed Stubbs, then selecting a Fray Bentos pie to heat up for his lunch. He had eaten meat pies on rotation for longer than there had been a telephone in Stables Cottage. His horses always ate the same food and Lester saw no reason to do otherwise. Sweet treats were a different matter.

The small fruit cake Pip had left him smelt like a Turkish spice market, jewelled with dates, cherries and sultanas. The Captain had been particularly fond of rich fruit cake with a glass of port.

His eyes watered again.

The infernal phone was still ringing.

When answering a call, which he was increasingly reluctant to do, Lester addressed the mouthpiece with the same gruff greeting: 'Stud.' This had caused such amusement to some local teenage girls in the seventies that they'd rung repeatedly from the red box on the Green, so that they could shriek, 'Your place or mine?'

He was reminded of those girls now as he marched across to answer it.

'Stud.'

Within a breath of the reply, he knew whom he was speaking to.

'Lester, I need you to make up two stables. Shavings, not straw.'

No preamble. So like the Captain.

He turned automatically to look up at the faded festoons of rosettes along the beams, heart hammering, appetite vanished. 'Right you are, Mrs Ledwell.'

Then she ruined it with a warm laugh. 'For God's sake, don't do the Parker thing on me, Lester, today of all days. Call me Ronnie.'

*

Kit Donne was stuck behind a horsebox on the twisting climb between Chipping Hampton and the Fosse ridge.

Trying to ring his son to apologise that he would be late for lunch, he repeatedly redialled his last outgoing call by mistake, theatrical agent and old friend Ferdie.

'How hung-over are you, dear boy?'

'Mildly,' he said, through gritted teeth.

'Stay on the line and I'll patch a call through on my other line. Are you meeting up at the house?'

'No, the Mill – *Le* Mill, now it's been shleb-cheffed and Michelin-starred.'

'*Quelle surprise*,' came the sing-song sarcasm. 'No corner of the Cotswolds is spared a little *jus*, these days, which is why this little Jew prefers life up here in the Brum-burbs of Stratford or down in the ghetto of London. I'm dialling your firstborn from the other line now.'

The Fosse Hills was the current Cotswold-property hotspot for celebrities in the know stepping away from London.

Cooler and more cultural than the Castle Combe chocolate boxes in the south, less media-tarnished than the east's seedy Chipping Norton set, not as snobbishly inbred as the Badminton and Highgrove west wing, it had become almost impossible to open a property section without finding the Bardswolds namechecked. This high spur of Jurassic limestone escarpment, which scythed its way around the lush folds of the Fosse Valley, was no longer the Cotswolds' best-kept secret.

Those who had discovered it years ago remained tight-lipped, fearful that it would soon become another franchise outlet for Soho House and Daylesford Organics, narrow lanes overrun with Range Rover Evoques. Others, like Kit, who had loved it in another lifetime, now avoided it as much as possible. He based himself in London all year and soon in New York.

'Tell me, dear boy, have you cast your Broadway lead?' Ferdie was asking.

'I have,' Kit said, head throbbing. His Broadway lead could drink a lot of vodka.

'Have you couched your Broadway lead?'

'I resent that.'

Kit's recent National Theatre production, based on a little-known Jacobean comedy, had been a huge commercial success, going on to sell out the regional tour circuit, then three months in the West End. Transferring it to Broadway was always going to be challenging, an American audience unlikely to catch the zeitgeist of a modern-day reworking of a Thomas Middleton satire set among high-end London property developers playing off oligarchs against Chinese investors. They'd needed a big name attached.

American A-lister Orla Gomez's reputation was notorious. She'd been in rehab more than she'd been on a set in recent years, but the only needles she put in her arm now were insulin pens for her diabetes. However, her sugar-rush mind, sharp tongue and bitter regrets made her volatile. To risk that on stage six nights a week in a comedy was certifiable, yet when she'd read for the part in New York, she'd outclassed all the other actresses by a league. Kit's mind was made up from his first gale of laughter. She'd flown into London this week to watch the original cast, telling Kit she'd wanted to work with him since seeing his production of *Medea* as an exchange student: 'Five goddam pissing times! You changed my life, Kit Donne.'

Orla was beautiful, unbelievably talented and probably still in bed in his London flat, sleeping off a moonlit performance of Medea's speech to Jason on his rooftop garden, decrying women's subjugation to their husbands, followed by a demonstration of what turned her on in his wet room and an all-out seduction in his kitchen. He'd cleared an empty bottle of Chase vodka from his work surface that morning while dunking out his teabag, his head feeling insanely cheerful, possibly because he was still drunk. Then he'd looked up at the calendar and noticed the date, and it was as though someone had picked up that vodka bottle and hit him over the skull with it.

'Your son, my godson and theatre's future is finally on line one.' Ferdie had adopted an Essex dental receptionist's lilt.

'It's Mum's birthday.' The familiar voice was as clear as a radio play through his car speakers. 'You'd forgotten, hadn't you? We've been waiting over an hour. We're leaving now.'

'Hello? Sorry! Stuck in traffic!' Kit shouted. 'Going to be late! Order for me!'

In twenty-seven years, Kit had never once forgotten his wife's birthday until today. It was like forgetting Christmas.

Ferdie reappeared on the line, his voice wrapped in a self-satisfied smile. 'You are beneath contempt, dear boy. I am beyond agent. And given you're practically next door to our mutually beloved Stratford, you can bloody well come here to talk to Donald about playing Lear. He's got frightful collywobbles. We're here until the weekend.'

Ferdie's husband Donald was one of the country's best-loved actors and a notorious drama queen. Having gladly accepted the invitation to direct his long-anticipated Lear at the RSC the following summer, Kit might have guessed his leading man would be gripped by stage fright with a year to curtain up.

'Sorry, Ferd.' He tried to swing past the horsebox again, almost going head-on into a white van. 'It's a flying visit.'

'The sort that involves the seat of your pants, I don't doubt. I'm not sure I like you very much right now, and that is spoken as your oldest friend.'

Kit had studiously avoided kindness for a long time, seeing few old acquaintances outside the safe professional confines of rehearsal room or theatre bar. Work was a way of channelling his grief, but he was drinking too much and a series of well-publicised affairs with his leading ladies – his 'caught in the actress', as Ferdie called it – had left him hollow with loneliness.

'I will make this up to you, Ferdie, I promise.'

'Make it up to yourself first. The rest of us have lower expectations. I know it's in the theatre-director job description to seduce actresses, but must they always be so much younger than you? If acting your age is too much to ask, dear boy, at least cast it.'

Kit laughed. 'It's on the bucket list.'

'Trouble with bloody bucket lists is that one generally kicks it before one ticks it.'

'I'm coming up for Donald's *Uncle Vanya* preview in a couple of weeks, bringing some of the old Royal Court crowd. I'll take you all out to lunch beforehand.'

'He'll appreciate that.' Mollified, Ferdie's voice lost a little of its scalpel edge. There was a long pause. 'Put a pebble on her grave from me.' He rang off.

The lorry in front of him now slowed to a crawl on the steep hill.

Kit glared at the ramp in front of him. 'CAUTION HORSES', said the letters across it. 'Too bloody right.' Swinging out, seeing clear carriageway, he floored it, flicking his finger out of the sunroof in celebration, spotting the speed camera too late, the oncoming car later still. Cresting the hill, he swerved back into his own lane in the nick of time, then blasted past the Gatso, with the horsebox's furious beep in his ears. He already had nine points on his licence. Had it flashed?

The dun colt had escaped from the foal barn, sailing over sheep hurdles, gates, posts and rails to rejoin his mother in the top field. Lester trudged after it, cursing under his breath. There were always one or two that tried, but he'd never known one get this far. Lester had picked the foal out as special straight away. The Captain had known it too, his waning interest briefly revived at the sight of it at a day old, charging around the nursery paddock. 'That's our Olympic horse, Lester.'

The Captain had let Pip christen it, which meant the poor chap owed his registered name, Top Gun, to a movie she liked about fighter pilots – 'He's by Cruisoe and it stars Tom Cruise, get it?' To Lester he was simply Tom, and he was breathtaking.

He watched him move now, that ground-covering, fetlock-flicking action eager to play catch, knowing he had Lester beat from the off, trotting away with hocks and head high.

'I'm not even going to try,' Lester told him, going up to his mother instead and buckling on a head-collar. 'I know you're still a mummy's boy.'

The foal watched as he led the mare down to the gate. He let out an indignant high-pitched whinny, but he didn't follow.

Lester took the mare out of the field and waited. Leaning back against the gate patiently, he pulled an aniseed ball from his pocket to suck, looking down at the stableyard. Although his eyes blurred things now, his mind and memory were crystal clear, filling in the soft spots.

From here, he could see across the stud's rooftops to the stallion paddock where the foal's father was scratching his golden, dorsal-striped rump on the metal tree guard around the oak trunk. Beyond that, the front paddocks flanked the drive to the lane, park rails meeting stone walls, hunt jump and hedge, Austen land to the left, the village to the right, and directly ahead the hayfield still waiting to be cut, silver as wolf fur.

Stubbs came and sat beside him, leaning hard against his leg and looking up, old-man eyebrows serious.

'It's all right, I'm not going to cry,' he told him. 'We saw that one off.'

He could vividly remember standing up here with the Captain and Mrs Percy the year they'd planted all the whips for the new field hedging, watching Ronnie and her friend, riding bareback, pony-tails bobbing, charging off across the fields to the church meadows, climbing the hill to slalom through the standing stones, then plunging down into the churchyard to scatter tables, chairs and nervous village ladies as they bought cakes from the stall to cram into saddle bags before setting off on some day-long adventure.

The Captain had roared with laughter, sending his wife to apologise to the vicar and bring back a Victoria sponge.

Church volunteers had run the cake stall every Saturday throughout the sixties and seventies, serving cream teas all summer to a roaring trade. The church had been at the heart of village life then. Those two little girls had been christened and married there; one was now buried there. Soon the Captain would be lowered beneath its earth too, joining his wife and forefathers.

Lester could see the unicorn horn of the spire peeking above the yews, a glint from the tall glass dome on the vicarage roof in the foreground, and the barley-sugar twists of the Old Almshouses' chimneys closer still, its garden backing onto the Green. To the right was the little school – the 'terrors' hadn't attended that, one educated by nuns, the other by a boater-throwing local preparatory then boarding school, where she'd denied her bright mind by staring out of the window through lessons, dreaming of eventing glory.

An unfamiliar horsebox was turning into the arrivals yard. Lester's heart jumped from trot to gallop. A hiss of air brakes, the thump of impatient hoofs kicking partitions, the whinnies from stables as they registered newcomers. Then the engine rattled to a stop and he could hear the skylarks again, their shrill, lyrical trills rising and falling.

Behind him, the colt let out another indignant whinny.

Ignoring him, Lester watched the cab door open, then two small dogs spilling out followed by a diminutive figure.

His eyesight might not be so good these days, but he knew without question it was Ronnie, still slim as a teenager and athletic enough to jump down in one. She raked back the blonde bob and marched to the back of the horsebox, pulling down the ramp to check her horses. Then she emerged and stood looking up at the house, its golden face and hers basking in lunchtime sun, Percy family tragedy stealing none of their beauty.

He could feel his arthritic fingers aching worse than ever and realised his hands had formed into swollen-knuckled fists.

For all the prolonged schism, she was an only daughter who had just lost her father, Lester reminded himself. Let her have a moment. She wouldn't thank him for interfering – they'd hardly parted on good terms.

'Mnee-he-he-he-he.' Behind him, the colt came a few steps closer.

Not looking round, Lester slotted the aniseed ball from one cheek to the other and let the mare keep slowly edging out of sight of her foal behind the hedge as she grazed the track.

Ronnie was on her mobile now. Lester, who disliked speaking on the phone at the best of times, was baffled by the modern plague of impatience that turned people into walking telephone booths.

The day she'd left Johnny, she'd spent half the morning in the old red phone box by the Green.

The foal nickered, closer still now.

Beyond the stableyard, there was a screech of brake and the roar of burned clutch that told Lester Pip was returning. A moment later he spotted the little blue car racing along the drive between the poplars. She can deal with Ronnie, he decided with relief. Women were better at tea and sympathy. Or, in Pip's case, tea.

Then he spotted a glint of red at the stud gates. A hundred yards behind Pip, turning off the village lane, came the battered Shogun of the Captain's eldest grandchild, Alice. It pulled up at the bottom of the drive and she got out, also on the phone, gesticulating furiously. For a moment, he wondered if she could be speaking with Ronnie, then dismissed the notion. To Lester's knowledge, mother and daughter hadn't spoken since Ann Percy's funeral, when Alice had wished Ronnie in Hell in front of three hundred witnesses, including the editor of *Horse & Hound* and the Duchess of Cornwall.

'Oh, bloody hell!' he cursed under his breath.

With a squeal, the colt reeled away.

Inserting another aniseed ball, Lester let the mare graze on.

5

The vast lavender-fringed and much-raked gravel rectangle beside the old watermill was playing host to more glossy marques than a Knightsbridge underground car park.

Kit posted his filthy ten-year-old Saab between two Aston Martins, wishing he'd booked somewhere less pretentious. Hermia would have loved it, but their twenty-three-year-old son had donated his last acting fee to Médicins Sans Frontières and their daughter was a Marxist vegan. The dishes here cost more than their local food bank's annual budget.

His phone had buzzed with messages throughout his drive from London. Pulling his reading glasses from brow to nose to find *Orla (10)* banded across his screen, he scrolled through them, jpeg attachments loading with the laboured pace of a reluctant roller blind coming down. Orla belonged to the generation for whom the selfie had replaced a thousand words, all of them tightening his groin without challenging his mind.

Kit sent a smiley emoticon, ironically minimalist. His children were waiting, his own smiley face irrepressible at the prospect. He switched the phone off, a parallel life that was no longer an active window.

The maître d', who was an RSC member and had discreetly prepared his staff for a big-talent VIP lunching with them today, was profoundly disappointed to find that Christopher 'Kit' Donne looked more like a country auctioneer than a theatre director, a newsboy flat cap shielding his mane of oaky hair and clever grey eyes. Anybody expecting luvvie flamboyance didn't know the sharp intellect behind

Kit's award-winning productions, or appreciate that his children remained quite his favourite power couple to lunch with.

They were sitting at an outside table along the small balcony over-looking the millwheel: an angry idealist in a tweed waistcoat and pork-pie hat, with a countrified hippie chick in a flowered dress and gumboots, blonde hair piled up with pins that couldn't hope to take its weight, sharing a bottle of red wine and the sort of ribald sibling laughter that's as comfortable as old shoes. He felt his chest hollow with love and pride.

'Sorry! Sorry so late. Have you ordered?'

'We're disordered.' His daughter rose for a kiss.

'You're *fucking* late.' His son tipped his chair back. 'I take it you're in a hurry as usual. Shall we skip lunch and go straight to Mum's grave?'

'We're here to celebrate her birthday.' Kit dragged up a chair. 'We don't need to stand on top of her. Let's eat.' His hangover needed ballast. 'God, but it's good to see you both!'

The food, when it arrived, lacked the carbohydrates he craved, sculptured little taste-bud-teasing cameos on huge white plates that the waitress turned to ensure the Le Mill logo was at twelve o'clock.

'When did "The" become "Le"?' Kit asked her, with jaded irony, but she didn't know the answer, and offering to find out. 'Really, don't bother.'

'Enjoy your meal.' She smiled and backed away, tugging her white cuffs down over tattooed wrists. Lots of tiny Cs interlinked, he noticed. Orla had a tattoo of a bird of paradise on her hip. Hermia had hated tattoos. It was one of the few things she'd been as snobbish about as her family. As far as he was aware, their children still had none – at least none visible.

He regarded them both now, his lifeblood with some of his DNA, and relaxed into listening mode as his daughter launched into a convoluted story about losing her bag at a party the previous night.

People often mistook Kit's quietness for disapproval, but thought was a conversation in his head too fast to voice out loud. When he'd been young, he'd been plagued by a bad stutter. It was why he'd always kept notes, his pockets bulging with hardback pads crammed with tight lines of largely illegible text. When he spoke with his cast and crew, he referred to the books constantly, slowing himself down with pre-written lines, slower still because it took him so long to read his own tiny writing, his many pairs of reading glasses never to hand. He no longer stuttered, but his mind in freeform worked so quickly and constantly it was beyond language. The little leather pad and pen sat on the table beside him as habitually as a mobile phone.

His son was now describing researching the role he was about to play, glaring at the pad as he spoke, as though daring Kit to take notes.

They all picked unenthusiastically at desiccated edamame and beetroot soil on chia and pea-shoot salad, see-through slivers of three varieties of organic radish fanned artfully around it, and he remembered bringing Hermia here years earlier. They had served T-bones on cast-iron griddles that took half an hour to cool down enough to eat, mountains of garlic bread weeping butter. His stomach rumbled at the memory.

'So the heart attack is scheduled when?' His son set down his fork. 'I'll diarise it.'

'"Diarise" is not a word.'

'Unlike "mid-life crisis".'

'That's technically a hypothesis legitimised as a turn of phrase.'

The fork lifted accusingly. 'That's technically bullshit.'

'*That's* technically CH_4,' he snapped, then forced a smile, hangover pounding afresh. 'Although, like any good farmer's daughter, your mother would have been quick to point out that's just methane.'

'Hot air.' His daughter gave him a wise look. 'From a windbag having a mid-life crisis.'

'Bullshit.' His son grinned. 'From a slimy moldwarp.'

'Puttock.'

'Loon.'

'Ratsbane.' Kit laughed, leaning back as the waitress brought more wine.

Years ago, somebody had given the family fridge magnets of Shakespearian insults, which Hermia had adored. Even when her speech had been so laboured that it was almost impossible to understand her, they could all identify her glorying in 'cream-faced loon' and 'bunch-back'd toad'.

'Your mother would have been fifty-three today.' He raised his refilled glass. 'To Hermia!'

His children followed suit. 'To Mum!'

For a moment, the lump in Kit's throat was too cumbersome to work round, but he held the smile. A natural pessimist, he had none the less always striven to ensure his children saw their mother's life in a positive light to counter the tragedy of her early death.

Three glasses stayed raised. His son stretched back, six foot four of lean, bearded muscle and lack of drive. His daughter's big French grey eyes looked straight across at him, dark-rimmed and tangle-lashed; her mother's eyes, demanding and compelling.

Both children had followed their parents into the theatre. Both had talent – his son emotional and explosive on stage, his daughter a cool-headed pedant of prop table and lighting cue. Neither had the fanatical drive he'd possessed at their age, a chippy small-town northern lad sharing a cramped Vauxhall basement with a bunch of impoverished fellow Cambridge graduates, insomniac actors and writers whose lives all revolved around the stage. His kids, brought up confident and metropolitan, drifted between loftier landscapes as jobs and lovers changed; they used the family cottage in Compton Magna as a party pad, their father's London flat as an administrative address and dumping ground; they were bright and breezy and savvy enough not to live to work, and on days like this, Kit had to remind himself repeatedly that he loved them precisely because they weren't like him. When they had been tiny, Hermia had spent bedtime hours with her lips pressed to their little pink ears, telling them to aim high and fear nothing. Kit had ribbed her fondly for giving them unrealistic expectations. To be proven right twice over with no voice to say 'told you so' remained devastating.

Kit Donne and Hermia Austen had met through mutual friends in London in the late eighties, ambitious young director and bright, brave actress, one as antagonistically academic and working class as the other was broad-mindedly liberal and well-born, an alchemy of opposites that had forged a golden young Theatreland couple. When Hermia had been expecting their first child, they'd bought a rundown Cotswolds farm as an escape from London and to be closer to her family. Between directing and acting commitments, Kit had set about restoring the house and raising rare-breed sheep as a hobby, while Hermia bred and competed her beloved Welsh cobs. In the decade that had followed they'd spent as many weekends and long holidays there as possible. They were the village golden couple by then too, generous and sociable, with their outgoing children and an infectious passion for theatre, particularly the Royal Shakespeare Company. With a stint as artistic director of the Royal Court and a string of award-winning productions under his belt, Kit had been hotly tipped as a future artistic director there.

Then, just days after her fortieth birthday, Hermia had suffered a serious head injury falling from a young horse onto the road. She'd been in hospital for months, multiple operations bringing no hope of her returning to the life she'd once led. Despite years of chasing medical science, she never recovered her co-ordination enough to walk unaided or her speech enough to be clearly understood, her mental health blighted by long-term cognitive problems and bouts of deep depression. At times, her desire to end her half-life had been overwhelming. Seven years after the accident, a huge stroke granted that wish, and Kit had finally lost his greatest love and companion, relief and grief too tightly twisted together to reconcile, his mourning raw and conflicted. Six summers on, it could still consume him on days like this.

The children now found it hard to remember Mum without her 'thinking gaps', the tics, slurs and frustration that had held their vibrant, clever mother hostage until her death. Kit told them one of the anecdotes he'd scribbled down in his notepad, remembering a family camping weekend knee-deep in festival mud when they'd been babes in arms, their mother determined that they'd all see Bob Dylan, Tori Amos and 'a panoply of nineties bands singing like Betjeman on Ecstasy'.

'Is that why you hate their music, because not long afterwards Mum's frontal lobe turned into Pulp and life became a Primal Scream Blur?' His son turned, hat tipped back like James Dean now. He was an artful poser of questions as well as stances.

Kit held his gaze, not trusting the beat in his carotid artery. They inevitably saw through his rose-tinted memories to the thorns. He wished he'd been a better husband when she was happy and healthy. He'd been furiously bad-tempered throughout that trip.

He was grateful that the waitress chose that moment to clear their plates. A phone number was written in biro on the back of her hand beneath *Lurcher Rescue*. Hermia had been absurdly fond of lurchers, calling them the Iagos of the dog world, all eyes aside and guile.

'I go to New York in a couple of weeks,' he told them. 'I've got the new lead actors over here right now to workshop the script with the London cast.' He didn't mention Orla by name, uncomfortably aware that his son's puberty had coincided with her starring role as a glossy television vampire. Posters of the woman he'd shared a bed with last night had featured on bedroom walls and almost certainly in fantasies. 'You must come out and visit. Bring girlfriends, boyfriends, whatever.' Like tattoos, it was safest not to ask.

His daughter was tipping down her brother's pork-pie hat brim playfully as they launched into a spat about his Tinder-dependent love life and her 'non-binary' taste.

'One, one, oh, one, oh, one, two,' Kit muttered.

'Is that the code to your safe?' Two grey eyes turned to him. Hermia's amused gaze.

'No, Dad's more left-field than that. Don't tell me.' The hat was lifted; Hermia's smile. '*To be or not to be* reloaded?'

'Binary for fifty-three.' He picked up his glass, finding it empty.

'Mum always said you were too clever by half.' Her blonde hair was escaping its pins, just like her mother's used to, as she splashed out the last of the bottle of red. 'What's that in binary?'

'Zero point one.'

His son raised his glass. 'Lady and gentleman, I give you the only Cambridge mathematician to win two Oliviers and a Tony.'

His daughter clinked it. 'Mum won an Olivier.'

'Medea.' Kit nodded, swallowing uncomfortably. 'At the Royal Court.'

Afterwards she'd taken a break from acting, wanting to spend more time with the children. She wanted them to base the family in Compton Magna year-round and aim for secondary education at the good Warwickshire grammars. She couldn't wait to focus more on her pony breeding and catch up with childhood friends, like the one in the Lake District with whom she exchanged ridiculously long, old-fashioned letters that she re-read endlessly ('You'll love her!' she'd always promised, their plans to meet up ill-fated). Hermia's family farmed just half a mile along the lane; parties and visits were planned, the future a limitless horizon.

They'd come here, to *the* Mill for her fortieth birthday that year. She was wearing a poppy-red dress and a necklace shaped from a row of snaffles, sent to her by the Lake District friend. 'These will be my unbridled forties!'

After her death Kit had boxed up that necklace, along with every personal item he could find relating to horses, and sent it to storage. They were still there. He couldn't dispose of them – they had been a part of her – but he couldn't bear them in his sight. He felt much the same way about horses.

Careering into the stud's arrivals yard at her usual breakneck speed, Pip was so overexcited at the sight of Ronnie Percy – perched on a horsebox ramp talking on the phone and looking thrillingly aris-tocratic – that she didn't notice the two little black and tan dogs bounding forward until the last minute, one disappearing beneath her car.

She screamed, swerved and closed her eyes, driving blindly into the hay barn and coming to a soft halt against a wall of bales. When she looked around, Ronnie had both waggy-tailed dogs at foot and was hurrying across to her.

'My goodness, are you all right?'

Pip rolled down the window. 'Yes! I often park here. Nice and shady.' She gathered up the Tupperware container that had just fallen off the front seat, her egg salad now transformed into a beet-root massacre. 'My deepest sympathies at your father's passing.' She leaped out breathlessly, not realising that Ronnie was still talking on the phone. 'I was the one who found him. Such a sorry tragedy.'

Ronnie held up her hand apologetically as she said a hasty fare-well to her caller: 'I have to go. I don't know when I'll be back in Wiltshire, but not tonight... Okay, well, if you can, then let me know. I'd like that.' She rang off, holding out her hand to squeeze

Pip's. 'Horribly rude of me. You must be Pauline. I'm Veronica Percy. Are you really okay?'

Clutching her Tupperware box, Pip nodded eagerly and arranged her face into one of pity. 'They've taken your dad to the morgue for the…' she cleared her throat and mouthed '…autopsy. I'm keeping the house locked to preserve the scene, but I'll put on the tack-room kettle so we can have a nice cup of tea. I've made an egg salad, and there's fruit cake.'

'How wonderfully organised you are.' Close to, Ronnie's face was quite lined, but she was exquisitely pretty, with those big blue upper-class British eyes, high cheekbones and a generous smile. 'I need to unload my horses first.' Her husky voice was forthright, like the Captain's. 'Are there a couple of stables made up?'

'I'll go and see!' she offered, thrilled at the chance to play head girl, putting the egg salad on the roof of her car and wondering where Lester was. 'Any special requirements?'

Ronnie's face froze as a big red off-roader turned into the yard, its driver's face equally stricken. Alice was out in a flash, still wearing her Wolds Pony Club polo-shirt, arms sunburned, a lanyard around her neck from which a whistle and a roll of gold stickers dangled. 'Mummy, how *dare* you?'

'Darling, Grandpa has just died. Let's not fight.'

'So you thought you'd load up your horses and move straight back in?'

'Don't be ridiculous. We were at a competition when I heard the news.'

'Did you win anything?' Pip asked brightly, eager to cover up who had been the one to break the news to Ronnie. She'd always been wary of the Captain's eldest granddaughter, not her biggest fan.

'Couldn't you have just stayed there?' Alice was obviously trying very hard not to cry. 'Let us handle this, Mummy.'

'I want to be here. Today is just awful. I know how important he was to you three.'

Alice took after her late father, a handsomely broken-nosed Worcestershire huntsman, who appeared in photos all over the house, glowering with the low-browed, broad-shouldered misanthropy of a Brontë hero, in a scarlet jacket. Ronnie was all fine-boned femininity.

'We don't need you here!' Alice fumed.

'Daddy would have wanted it.'

'He bloody didn't!'

'I disagree.'

'He *so* didn't.'

'You're wrong.'

Ronnie's mobile, abandoned on a hay bale, was ringing, its tone a soothing classical air. Pip picked it up to offer it to her, but she waved it away. The picture flashing up on screen of a man in a bush hat – seriously sexy eyes, Pip noted – disappeared as the call timed out, along with the word *Blair*.

'Just go, Mummy! Throw up your ramp and go!' Alice was barking, a mashup of 'I Will Survive' and evicting a recalcitrant pony clubber from camp. 'Pax can't take it.'

'Pax is in Italy,' Pip pointed out helpfully, admiring Ronnie's phone, which was a version up from hers.

'Let's go into the house and talk, Alice.' Ronnie's voice was consoling, etched with a heavy hint of mounting irritation. 'Pippa here's offered to look after my horses, and I'm dying for a pee.'

'Best use the yard loo.' Pip stood to attention, determined the house would stay locked down to spare the grieving family its less savoury corners until Janine Turner's cleaning team had been in. 'I'll make tea. Milk and sugar? It's Pip, by the way.'

But Alice was already talking across her: 'Mummy, I really think this is all best conducted through lawyers. There's the stud to consider.'

'I don't give a fig about that right now.' The big blue eyes sought out Pip. 'Was it quick, his death?'

'I wasn't there.' She saw again the slipper soles at the bottom of the cellar steps, the lifeless veined ankles. 'I found him this morning. He'd passed over some time before. Around midnight, they think.'

'Oh, God, he was all alone.'

'What do you care?' Alice was raging now. 'You roll up here the moment he dies, like you have a right to be a part of this family, of this place. You're a stranger here now. You're not needed. You never saw him.'

Pip felt cross. She could hear a voice in her head respectfully pointing out that neither of them had seen much of the Captain towards the end. But she said nothing, heartbeat suddenly revving to max.

Pip had always struggled with her emotions, her parents responding to tears and tantrums with the same mistrust prompted by pop music, spicy food and television channels not prefixed by 'BBC'. 'Happy' and 'cross' seemed to cover most bases, Pip had found. Lying awake in the dark brought out other feelings so she kept two bedside lights permanently switched on and an emergency torch in her bedside drawer. Being faced with other people's emotions was as bad as a power cut.

'Alice, he was my father!' Ronnie raked back her hair, which sprang back to cloud glossily around her face, like an advert for conditioner.

'Which is why we all loved and protected him from what you did to him!' Alice squared up to her mother. 'He looked after us after you pissed off and then after Daddy died. Grumps brought us up. I have a *right* to be upset. You don't!' As she stepped back with a Donald Trump finger jab, she inadvertently trod hard on Pip's foot.

'Ow!'

'Oh, dry up, Pip.'

Pip wanted to shout, *I* was the one who saw him every day! *I* washed for him, cooked for him, cared for him! *I* saw his breath get shallower. *I* saw him struggle to walk. He was the toughest, nastiest man I cared for but I *did* care for him. Me! And *I* saw his dead body.

At last, this was feeling real. Yet still the tears didn't come.

'Just leave!' Alice was snarling at her mother.

Ronnie rolled her eyes in defiant exasperation. 'Why don't we let Pip make us that cup of tea?'

'Pip should leave too!' Alice growled. 'You had *no* right to call Mummy.'

Pip's anger was incendiary now. 'None of the rest of you picked up.'

'We do have lives!'

'Unlike *Grumps*!' Pip flashed. Oh. Shit.

Alice turned to her mother, saying in a throat-burning undertone: '*I requiem meam doleat!*'

Now they were talking in tongues! Pip's chest was a fire-pit, her grief a forest blaze roaring through her.

'Oh, God.' Ronnie was doing the hair thing with her hands again, husky laughter trapped in a sob. 'Daddy insisted every Percy should be able to ride well enough to race under rules, add up well enough to wager, write well enough to apologise, and speak Latin well enough to—'

'Garden!' Alice interrupted, leaving Pip with the distinct impression that the Captain had used a less wholesome example.

'*Omnia mors aequat.* I must pee.' Ronnie hurried to the yard loo.

Alice marched after her and Pip went to the tack room to put the kettle on, only realising she was still carrying Ronnie's phone when it vibrated in her hand. The photo of handsome Blair was back on screen.

'Phone call!' She hurried out.

Alice was now addressing the closed door of the yard's ancient privy, listing her mother's many failings.

Pip stood on the tack-room step, a threshold that had felt like a portal to the Holy Grail two years ago.

The man's face on the screen was looking straight at her, his dark eyes ninety per cent cocoa. Guessing it had to be important for him to call twice, she swiped the green Accept.

'You okay?' His voice was pure gravel. 'Don't even bother answering that. Brian Sedgewick's lending me his car. I'll drive down as soon as I've ridden my last round. I booked somewhere called Le Mill. Usual name. See you there. Be strong, kid.' He rang off before Pip could explain.

There was something heroic in that voice: Crocodile Dundee was on his way, Indiana Jones was galloping in, Wolverine had transport!

Be strong, kid. Pip felt better just for hearing it. Ronnie *was* strong, standing up for herself against Alice's barrage.

'For goodness' sake, let's pull together!' The loo door slammed now as she emerged, ancient cistern refilling loudly, setting the old pipes rattling through the feed and tack rooms, like plate-banging prisoners. 'Daddy would expect us all to jump to it, not mud-sling. There's a lot to get on with.' That husky voice was splitting. 'Alice, we're all in shock.'

The yard pipes, rattling and humming their final refrain, shuddered to silence. As they did so, Pip sensed the anger between the two women finally ebb.

Alice's face contorted with the effort of not crying. She turned away, hand pressed to her mouth, the other held out to stop her mother touching her arm in comfort.

Ronnie and Alice stood together for a long time, not reconciled and yet too closely bonded by grief to move apart.

Pip hovered, wondering whether it would be a good moment to mention the recent mobile call.

Alice was the first to pull herself together with a determined sniff. 'Where the bloody hell's Lester?'

'Up in the top fields, I should think,' Pip volunteered, grateful to be back in the conversation. 'It's where he always goes when he needs to mull things over.' Or hide. The stallion man was as brave as a lion with Percy horses, less so with Percy women. 'Poor old Lester.' Ronnie sighed. 'This will be incredibly hard on him. They knew each other more than sixty years.'

Pip watched her make her way back to her lorry ramp, slight and determined. But instead of walking up it to fetch out a horse, she started heaving it closed. 'I'll take these two straight home and leave you in charge, Alice,' she called. 'Let's please speak tomorrow.'

'No!' Pip leaped towards her. 'You have to stay!' Pip had personally brought Ronnie Percy back to Compton Magna. She was vibrant and she belonged here. It was the Elgin Marbles coming home to Greece, the Rosetta Stone to Egypt, Michelle Fowler to Albert Square. 'I need you to stay!'

'This isn't about you, Pip!' Alice snapped.

'Blair's on his way!'

The ramp hovered, the big blue eyes startled. 'What?'

'I took the call,' Pip told Ronnie breathlessly, holding up the phone. 'He says he's booked a room at Le Mill in the usual name.' As she spoke the words, she realised that perhaps she should have kept that bit quiet.

'Oh, Christ, Mummy,' Alice flared. 'You haven't got your claws into Blair Robertson?'

'He's one of my oldest allies,' Ronnie said, eyes flashing at Pip. 'If Blair's father died, I'd be there for him too. We make friends for life in this sport.'

'It's just your family you walk out on.'

She rested her forehead against the lorry ramp for a moment. 'I asked for that.'

The bolts clicked in.

Pip felt her heartbeat fly to three figures again. 'The Captain has left you the stud!' she told Ronnie shrilly.

Ronnie looked at her, not comprehending,

Alice was far quicker to work it out. 'How do you know?'

'I witnessed his will. He changed it a few months after Mrs Percy passed on. This whole place is now in trust to Ronnie for the rest of her life, then it passes to you, Tim and Pax.'

'I don't believe you.' Alice's cheeks were turning an odd aubergine colour.

'This conversation is for another day.' Ronnie moved towards her lorry cab.

'You *knew*!' Alice exploded.

'Alice, let's just leave it.'

Alice chased after her. 'After everything you did to Dad, to Pax, after everything, *you* get the stud! How could he do that? What bloody manipulation tactics did you use on him?' She barred her mother's way. 'You're going nowhere, Mummy. Don't you *dare* run away from this one! Unload the horses, Pip.'

Pip hurried to lower the ramp. No need to mention that Lester hadn't let her unload a horse since one of the visiting mares had ended up in the walled garden. Everyone deserved a second chance. She did. So did Ronnie.

'*Don't* unload my horses, Pip.' Ronnie's voice was a ghostly echo of the Captain's. 'I'll do it.'

'Good!' Alice looked astonished to have her bluff called. 'Time to do the right thing, Mummy. I'm going to find Lester. He must be in bits.' She dashed off, already dialling out on her mobile phone.

Pip gazed at Ronnie in awe. 'Are you really staying?'

The bluest eyes in Gloucestershire crinkled, the deep, throaty voice making laughter of sadness. 'Percys all stay the distance, Pip. Some of us just don't stick to the course.'

6

Kit sensed his edgy, point-scoring family trinity pulling together as they walked from the restaurant along the mill chase to the river, its fast-flowing path snaking away, sinewy and reed-banked, towards Ludd-on-Fosse. Their footprints trailed behind them, deeply embossed on the storm-muddied footpath, companionably close. Arms cuffed, jokes ribbed , memories surfaced, voices overlapping. At their best, the Donnes were an indistinguishable stream of bright, laughing voices.

'What was that Crafty Craft Race they used to run here on the river?'

'The Compton Raftgatta. Villagers riding the rapids on planks roped to barrels that usually sank without trace.'

'Remember the outdoor village Shakespeare? Manor Farm, late nineties, Mum directing. We were waves. Cousin Bay was back from boarding school and insisted on playing Ariel like a Tarantino character. Then the man playing Prospero—'

'Henry Walcote, the old vet.'

'—fell ill and you read in the part on the last night. Remember that big electrical storm blew in during Act Five up by the standing stones and you kept throwing yourself on the ground during the "revels are ended" speech?'

'I think you'll find Kevin Spacey experimented with much the same concept at the Old Vic.' Kit was accustomed to being ribbed about his hatred of storms.

'Storm's coming in again now, Dad.' His son's smile challenged him, Hermia incarnate. The irony of Kit directing *Lear* next year was not lost on either of them.

Kit looked at his gym-pumped child, still trying to lock horns. He'd been doing it ever since his mother's death, an instinctive urge to be alpha. But Kit knew the alphabet all the way to omega: the last word and last laugh should be shared.

'*Stormy weather...*' He started to sing.

They all broke into harmony. Hermia had loved Ella Fitzgerald.

Dragonflies hummed past, midge clouds floated in and out, their ankles were caught by nettles, brambles and bracken in swift rotation. Thrips were gathering, sweat rising.

They marched Indian file along a narrow section of path, singing at the tops of their voices, flattening against a hedge for a gaggle of heads-down dog-walkers, who nodded politely and steered a wide path around the noisy arty farties in inappropriate footwear, whom they took to be typical Le Mill lunchers.

They stopped at the small waterfall known locally as the Hare's Ladder, one of Hermia's favourite spots, a gushing glass staircase to the river curtained with reeds and weeping willows.

Kit felt her memory standing by his side as he read the customary birthday sonnet, accompanied by a distant rumble of returning thunder, uncomfortably aware that his children were indulging him rather than engaging.

This year it was Sonnet VII, the seventh anniversary of a birthday now in remembrance not active service. Its metaphor took the sunrise of youth to the sunset of old age, claiming it pointless without children. Kit read it from his phone, its pertinence lifting his stumbled recital: '*Resembling strong youth in his middle age, Yet mortal looks adore his beauty still, Attending on his...* blasted screen lock... *golden pilgrimage.*' The low-battery warning bleated, its screen banded with *Orla (6)*. He switched it off hastily, the parallel door closed once more.

'Shall we go to Mum's grave now?'

'This is enough.'

'Come to the house, Dad.'

'We're having a barbecue later. And Pimm's jelly. Stay the night, Dad. Dance in the rain and all that crap.'

Thunder rumbled.

He shook his head. 'I'll go to the grave before I leave for New York. I always visit for Lughnasa.'

The four Celtic fire festivals: Samhain as winter closed in, Imbolc as spring burst, Beltane as summer budded and Lughnasa in harvest, his and Hermia's private joke to remind them that they had been wild young pagan travellers once, had lost three days at Burning Man in Nevada, danced all night at the Puck Fair in Ireland and slept under the stars woaded in Glastonbury mud long before their children claimed it for their generation.

Kit heard Hermia's voice in his head, defiant and amused: *You and your big bunch of lilies four times a year, like quarterly dividends and VAT returns. You really don't need to. I'm not there. It's the last place you'd find me.*

As they started to walk back, he told his children: 'I've been thinking about selling the Old Almshouses.'

'No!' They spoke in horrified unison. 'It's our house, Mum's house.'

Kit looked from one to the other, knowing that for them the Old Almshouses had far fewer of the negative connotations than it held for him. It had been bought in such a time of strain, the pressing need to relocate Hermia in adaptable living space when she came back from hospital, properties limited in the village, the sale of their beloved farm a huge wrench. His relationship with it had always been ambivalent. For at least a decade it had been his lime-tree bower and hermitage, now crammed with so many possessions that the notion of selling it was fanciful. Ferdie joked that the reason Kit no longer went there was because there was nowhere to sit, every piece of furniture piled with books. His kids just sat on the floor, happy amid the childhood never meant for them.

'The place is wasted on us,' he insisted.

'On you, maybe. You're afraid to set bloody foot in it.'

'I am bloody well not!'

'When did you last go there?'

'Not long ago.' Almost three months. Beltane. The children in the village school had been dancing around their maypole. He'd visited the church to lay flowers on Hermia's grave, crossed the lane to let himself into the house to pick up some books and notes, then driven away so fast he'd taken out three verge-staked fête posters.

'Come back with us now!'

'There's loads of wine in.'

They were walking in their own footsteps in reverse, brambles lashing them afresh.

'It's Open Gardens week – we've made a Donald Trump scarecrow.'

'Yes, Dad, the garden needs serious attention. You're that age. Maybe that could be your project.'

'I bloody hate gardening!'

'The village has lots of social activities for the over-sixties.'

'I'm still in my fifties!' He knew they were winding him up, but today pride came before being the fall guy.

'The big six-oh isn't far off.'

'You'll be needing single-storey living yourself soon. Mad to sell it.'

'I'm not even fifty-nine till September, you maggot.' He heard himself sounding like an enraged Keswick sheep farmer. 'And I have a single-storey flat in Stoke Newington. Three floors up.' With a new lover waiting. 'The steps of which I take two at a bleeding time.'

'Try living here for a month, Dad, and see if you feel the same.' His daughter turned to stand in his path, tossing her head back, grey eyes wide and direct, Hermia inviting him home. 'You keep on telling us you're going to take a sabbatical to finish the Siegfried Sassoon script. It's the perfect retreat.'

'I'm in New York until Christmas.'

They were back in the grounds of Le Mill, skirting the banks of the wide expanse of tarnished silver water, the clouds overhead as dark as the tree canopy from which they'd just emerged, a sharp new wind throwing up hair and collars.

'So are you coming back with us now?'

He stooped to pick up a pebble, turning it in his fingers, remembering Ferdie asking him to place one on her grave. With a silent apology to his dear friend, he turned to spin it across the mill pool. It ducked and draked. Seven jumps. 'No.'

★

The horsebox parked in front of the stud rocked lightly on its axles.

'This is just for the night, sunshine,' Ronnie told the whinnying ball of cooped-up energy as she clipped on the lead rope.

Standing well back, Pip watched as a dark bay exploded down the ramp, its mane curly from being plaited, its delicate, steely limbs wrapped in brightly coloured leg-warmer travelling boots, high-stepping, like a majorette. Lapping the yard at speed, Ronnie peered over stable doors, located a suitable one and started removing Velcro tapes with deft rips.

Pip hurried to help her, gathering up the boots and holding open the door to a stable, relieved that Lester had already made it up. He'd even put new binder twine loops on the tie-rings, she noticed. The more OCD attention the stallion man paid to the fine details, the more he rated his charges. Only the best visiting mares got this level of cobweb-stripped, mat-scrubbed accommodation. Ronnie's horses were certainly classy, even to Pip's untrained eye.

The second to come out of the lorry was the colour of Caramac, also sporting a curly clown mane and the longest, floppiest ears she'd seen. 'Won her section this morning, so she's very pleased with herself,' Ronnie told Pip, pulling off the travel boots and handing them straight over this time.

We're already a team, Pip realised happily. 'First intermediate outing?' She'd mugged up on Ronnie's horses just days ago, never imagining it would come in so useful.

'Goodness, you know your stuff. Not that I'd expect my father to have anybody less horse savvy onside. I'd like to turn both these horses out later, if I can.' Glancing up at the sky through the half-door, she grimaced. 'We'll see what the storm does.'

'You don't have to worry about a thing,' Pip assured her. 'I'll make sure they're looked after.'

'You're an angel.'

Pip hoped that meant she wasn't out of a job. A small pay rise and title like stud administrator would go a long way to cushioning the shock of losing the Captain.

It was only when the mare was inside her stable rolling enthusiastically in the straw that Pip remembered to hand Ronnie her phone. 'Blair said "stay strong".' She inadvertently did an Australian accent, sounding like a dodgy *Prisoner Cell Block H* lifer. 'He's borrowed a car from someone called Brian.'

'Which means he'll have the bonnet up in a Buckinghamshire layby soon.' Ronnie's face grew watchful. 'You two had quite a chat.'

'Oh, I didn't say anything,' Pip assured her, trusty stud administrator to boss. 'He thought I was you.'

There was a long pause. Then the smile came back, dazzling, all too brief. 'You're probably better at being me than I am right now.'

Pip's heart was won. 'I hope I didn't get you in trouble with Alice?'

'I've been in trouble with Alice for a lot longer than this. She really needs you at the moment, Pip. They all do. You're very strong. The fact you were with their grandfather in his last days means a lot. Please keep talking to them. It'll help you all. Grief's the loneliest boat to find oneself in. The less you talk, the further out to sea you drift.'

Feeling valued and trusted once more, Pip puffed with pride. 'I think we could both use a cup of tea, don't you? I bet you haven't eaten all day. I know *exactly* what will make you feel better. Follow me!' She hurried to the hay barn to fetch it, lifting the Tupperware container off her car roof in triumph. 'Egg salad!' She spun round, not anticipating that Ronnie would have followed so close behind. The salad container banged hard against the side of her head, the contents spilling out in a strong-smelling purple explosion. 'Oh, shit! Sorry!'

Knocked sideways, Ronnie staggered back a few steps.

'It was an accident!' Mortified, Pip's hopes died in flashes before her eyes: no stud administrator job, no go-between messages to convey from sexy Blair, no foals and no Lester, exiled from the place she loved most.

To her surprise, Ronnie laughed, the loveliest throatiest sound. She'd ducked away fast enough to avoid an all-over dousing, but one side of her bob was transformed from gold to beetroot crimson, her arm was coated and she had a radicchio epaulette on one shoulder. 'Ugh! There are anchovies in here.'

'Good for the bones,' Pip pointed out. 'Lots of Omega 3 and iron.'

There was a curious snorting sound, and she looked at Ronnie in alarm. For the briefest moment, giggles gripped the older woman. Pip understood grief did this sometimes, but it was hard to know how to react. Joining in felt a bit odd, although she threw in a few good-natured ha-has to show willing.

Pulling herself together, Ronnie straightened up, shaking lumps of egg from her hair. 'God, I'm sorry.' Underfoot, her dogs were already crowding in to clean up the spillage. 'I must wash this off.'

'Go straight to the hotel!' Pip suggested, all too aware of the state of the house bathrooms. 'There's a lovely spa there. Treat yourself to a seaweed wrap.'

'That's the last thing I bloody want. Although I suppose poor Lester's going to get caught in a storm one way or another if I stay.'

'He's very frail, these days.'

'Oh, God, is he?'

'He just needs time to let it all sink in. Come back tomorrow. I'll keep an eye on everything here, get hold of Tim and Pax one way or another, and call you later with an update. The storm's coming in, so there's no point in us all standing about here getting wet.' Pip knew she'd almost turned this around. 'And I'll have a quiet word with Alice about the grief-boat thing. Make sure she knows how much you care and that she'll never drift out to sea while I'm here to help.'

Ronnie's blue eyes were unusually bright. 'You are unbelievably kind, Pip.'

'I'm a good egg!' Pip watched for another giggling fit, half hopeful.

The smile flashed on and off lightning fast, coinciding with a distant rumble of thunder. The silliness had gone, the mood blackening, like the sky. 'Call me later.'

Lester knew the colt could feel the storm closing in. He was near to the gate now, pretending to graze but really just looking to his mother for reassurance, every distant rumble making him throw up his head. Letting him steal closer, Lester watched the horsebox making its way back down the drive, the low branches flailing against its shiny alloy Luton. Years ago, Ronnie had nicknamed the stud's old wooden lorry 'the Drum' because she said the sound of the poplars hitting its roof was like sitting inside Keith Moon's floor tom.

Through the early eighties, Ronnie Percy became the face of the stud, a fearless and popular young competitor, who held many trophies over her blonde head, the bluest eyes in Gloucestershire always full of laughter. The press loved the tiny blonde sylph who took on the biggest fences, talking to her horses all the way, her husky giggle infectious. Soon finding herself a pin-up in the horse world as well as in the loyal Comptons, Ronnie flirted her way into more than one close scrape on the notoriously naughty eventing circuit, although the Captain kept her on a very tight leash.

When the Fosse and Wolds had acquired a dashing new huntsman, Johnny Ledwell, it had been easy to predict that he'd fall in love with Ronnie, just as every red-blooded man did. What had been more of a surprise was the Captain's active encouragement of the union, taking Lester by shock as it did many others, who saw Ronnie as a girl who had her pick from Mick Jagger to Prince Charles. Johnny was the youngest son of a Worcestershire farming family, with modest prospects on a hunt servant's income. Yet he rode more beautifully than any man ever had across Fosse country, and hounds sang for him like an operatic choir. Johnny was cool-headed and emotionally aloof, which made him utterly intoxicating to Ronnie and his ability to school up a rough, newly broken youngster in no time had astonished her. Unlike the leering event riders who normally pursued her, he was punctual, courteous, honourable and maddeningly sexy.

Talk of marriage came almost indecently soon, ameliorated when a favourite uncle unexpectedly bequeathed him a large chunk of Worcestershire farmland, guaranteeing Ann Percy was onside as eagerly as Mrs Bennet peddling Bingley to Jane. Madly in love and lust, Ronnie had been too caught up in the moment to stop and think before saying, 'Yes, please!' to his old-fashioned proposal.

On a flawless June day, dressed in a huge silk meringue, nineteen-year-old Ronnie had married handsome Johnny Ledwell in her family's pretty village church, cheered on by two hundred family, friends and villagers.

The horsebox was turning onto the lane. Lester's chest burned as though he'd swallowed a Roman candle.

He could see Alice coming towards him up the field track, immediately identifiable despite his cataracts. He pressed a checked-cotton shoulder deftly into each eye to mop up any sweat and tears, pulling down his cuffs and standing to attention.

Out of breath by the time she reached him, able only to nod in greeting, she turned to admire the view and wheeze discreetly, reeking of Silk Cut. Alice smoked as heavily as her parents and grandparents had, a rarity now.

He bowed his head. 'It's a sad day. Your grandfather was a great man. I'm very sorry for you and the family.'

'Thank you. He was.' She offered no sympathy in return and he was grateful for it. Plenty of others would soon gush about his long service, loyalty and uncertain future. He had lost his oldest friend. He could cope with that just as long as nobody dared pity him.

'What are you doing up here?' she asked, when she'd got her breath back.

'Foal doesn't want his mum, just his freedom.' He pointed out the dun colt showboating gaily around the field now that he had a new audience. 'Never known one like it. Can't catch the bugger.'

'Why bother?'

'Most valuable youngster on the yard. Captain bought this mare straight off the racetrack.' He patted her chestnut rump fondly. 'He swore this chap will bring eventing glory back to Compton. Your grandfather's been waiting thirty years for that.'

'Too late now,' she said brusquely. 'You know he's left Mummy the stud?'

'Not my business to ask.' It never ceased to amaze Lester how quickly the bereaved focused upon the bequeathed.

'She'll get rid of you in a heartbeat.'

'If you say so.' He put the mare back in the field and saluted the uncatchable colt, a rare defeat, but he couldn't help admiring the perpetrator.

'If it's true Grumps left her everything, we'll have to contest it,' she said, as they started back down the track, Stubbs racing ahead. 'I've just had a long phone chat with the solicitor who is totally onside.'

Lester's voice had sharpened steel through it. 'Bury him first, Alice.'

To his discomfort, she burst into noisy, desperate tears, a grief-stricken child once more. 'I j-just can't believe he's g-gone!'

Alice was one of the few women Lester was taller than. He gathered her into an awkward Heimlich manoeuvre hug, their bodies rigid with inhibition. Of all the grandchildren, Alice had loved the Captain with the most blinkered, unquestioning loyalty, receiving the least gratitude in return. Tim was his high-flying indulgence, Pax his talented golden girl. Alice had no such charm but, like her father, she'd stayed as close and fierce as a terrier, and she knew how to drive the fastest, fleetest fox to earth.

'I will *not* let her do this!' she sobbed. 'I know I can count on your loyalty, Lester. She let us all down. She mustn't be allowed to do it again.'

Lester maintained the awkward hug for far longer than felt comfortable, looking back up the track where, beyond the gate, the dun colt had trotted straight to his mother's teats for a sly feed, receiving a sharp cow-kick reminder that the milk bar was closed. Moments later they were charging across the field side by side, both racing for fun.

Six decades of stud work had taught him to be wary of mothers who seemed not to care. They were usually the kindest of the lot.

7

When Kit dashed back to the car park, rain was already coming down like a power shower, machine-gunning the smooth surface of the millpond. A large horsebox was parked alongside the Saab.

'CAUTION HORSES' warned the familiar lettering on its ramp. Letting out a sardonic huff, he felt for his keys, head bowed against the downpour. His fingers plunged straight through the loose seam. This was the jacket with the ripped lining. He'd been losing keys out of the bloody thing all year.

He looked around, finally spotting a glint of fob under the horse-box.

His head cracked against its dripping metal skirting. 'Shit! Ow!' He hit out at it angrily and a locker opened, cracking down on his skull with a splash of trapped water.

'Fuck!' He tried to stand up, hitting his head again. A saddle landed on him like an attacking stingray. 'Argh!' 'Mate, what are you doing?' asked a deep voice behind him, as Australian as eucalyptus creaking in the storm.

'Trying to get my bloody keys. Ouch!' Another saddle crashed down.

Both saddles were deftly lifted. 'Stop head-butting the bloody tack, mate.'

He tugged at the keyring, a ridiculously OTT thing his daughter had bought him with tragedy and comedy masks dangling from it. 'They're stuck under the tyre.'

A large, muscular back in a wet T-shirt blocked his view. 'Move aside.'

The man – younger and more sinewy than his voice had suggested – dropped athletically beneath the lorry and dragged the keyring out to hand up to him, its masks bent. There was no ignition key attached.

'Thanks, but—'

'No worries.' Jumping up, he slammed the locker shut and sauntered off as though the downpour wasn't happening. Kit kicked the lorry tyre.

His phone was buzzing madly with an incoming call.

'Why do you Brits always keep your awards in the john?' Her voice was languid. 'I'm lying in your bath playing with your gongs. You've got some real big ones, baby. In the interests of fairness, I'm going to show you my Oscar. Coming atcha. Look.'

An MSM buzzed through: a selfie of a small scar on her forehead. *Knocked out by a Kansas twister.*

Water splashed on the screen. Kit held the phone to his ear again. 'I love your Oz scar.' He laughed. 'And I can't wait to see your Tony.'

'Toe knee! I get it. Hang on, I'll take a shot.'

It hadn't been meant as a joke, but her *joie de vivre* was infectious.

'What I really want is a Kit in my pussy,' her voice growled. 'Come back, baby. I'm doing things with three Oliviers that should never be allowed. I'll send you a Snapchat.'

'Three, you say?' He closed his eyes, his parallel lives colliding.

'Man, you are *so* talented. You even won a Best Actress!' The line went quiet. 'Holy shit.' There was a splashing sound as she got out of the bath. 'Ohmygod, I'm so, so sorry! Medea. My heroine. She was your wife! The one that died!'

'That one, yes.' As if there had ever been another

'I feel so bad.' She started sobbing, sounding terribly young.

'Please don't,' he urged, suspecting she didn't feel as bad as he did right now, the door between his parallel lives swinging on its hinges as the heavens opened. 'I'll be back as soon as I can,' he promised, his phone triple-bleeping to warn that its battery was a screen swipe away from dying. His charger was in the car. His way back to Orla was in his car. Rain was lashing down.

*

The Le Mill receptionist cast his eye down the register on his screen. 'Nothing obvious, sir.'

'How many clients do you have who arrive in a horsebox?'

'You'd be surprised.'

'May I see?'

He turned the screen a fraction.

'Mr and Mrs Blenheim-Badminton in the Hopsack Suite?'

'I can make a discreet enquiry.'

A small, disgruntled blonde was summoned, braless in a T-shirt and jeans, Medusa snakes of wet hair, half red half blonde.

'You'll need a coat,' he told her.

'No point if I'm getting straight back into the shower you just interrupted.'

Outside the rain had let up, but the sky was blacker than ever.

He followed her to the car park, noticing that she was still wearing the hotel's free white slippers.

She clambered into the cab, starting the engine. Then, to his surprise, she jumped back out, screwdriver in hand.

'Aren't you going to move it?'

'The air brakes need to come up to pressure.'

Thunder ripped through the sky, chased by a shard of lightning. Kit flattened himself against the side of the box. She didn't flinch, marching round to the tack locker that had fallen open on his head earlier and fiddling with its locking mechanism.

Kit, who took an academic approach to changing a lightbulb, had grudgingly to admire her resourcefulness. She was typical of older, well-bred horsy women, whom he encountered mercifully rarely: tough and wiry, the ludicrous punky half-red hair probably a second-wind rebellion.

'Are you local?' he asked, to pass the time.

'That's up for debate.' She gave a gruff little laugh. 'You?'

'Nebulous.'

'Aren't we all? You can dream in England but your digital memory's in a cloud in South America.' She turned to look at him properly, eyes extraordinarily blue. 'To think we used to pull back the tracing paper on each page of a photograph album as if it was a sacred veil.'

Not so horse-mad and narrow-minded, maybe.

The locker fell open behind her. 'Blast!'

'My parents had a mountain of albums.' He watched her jabbing the screwdriver into the lock, now less convinced she was a master engineer. 'After they died, we went through them to share out the memories. In over three thousand photographs Dad featured in less than fifty. The rest were all bloody landscapes.'

That gruff laugh again. 'My darling dad photographed horses. The people on them were incidental. He died today.' She attached the last three words so casually he almost missed it.

'I'm sorry.'

'Forget I said it.' She tested the locker, this time tightly closed. 'Trying not to think about it. Easier to talk about the weather.' Another lightning strike forked out uncomfortably close. Kit ducked low as thunder bellowed.

'Are you okay? You're shaking.'

'Not fond of storms.'

'Shelter in the cab while I move this if you like.' She hauled open the passenger door, releasing a Pandora's box of old familiar smells – wet dogs, cigarettes, coffee and, above all, horse.

'Thanks, I'm fine.'

She shrugged. 'Not fond of horseboxes either?'

'You got it. You made me late for lunch earlier.'

She looked at his car. 'You're the prat who overtook me on Fosse Hill.'

'I was late for lunch with my kids. It was their mother's birthday.'

'That's no excuse. I'm sure your wife doesn't want to be made a widow on her birthday.'

'Her husband's already her widower.'

'Then don't make your kids orphans.' She didn't miss a beat for compassion. 'Drive better next time. You almost killed us both.'

'I wouldn't have dreamed of overtaking if you hadn't been going so slowly. Surely the point of these things is that they should travel marginally faster than the horses they're transporting.'

To his surprise, she let out a brief, husky laugh. 'If my box offends you, I suggest you need to think outside it.' The red dye in her hair was coming out, he realised, pink water streaming down her T-shirt, like blood.

'Have we met?'

She shook her head. 'I'd remember. One of us would. *'Tis in my memory lock'd and you yourself shall keep the key of it.* Poor Ophelia and Laertes never made it to senior moments.' She headed back to the driver's door.

How did a horsebox-driving harridan know *Hamlet*?

But before he could work it out, she'd reversed neatly, liberating his key, still miraculously intact when he plucked it up from its gravel casing.

'Thank you!' he shouted up at the cab. 'Sorry to have been so much trouble!'

Nodding, she drove forwards again, almost mowing him down.

He waited in the rain to apologise and bid her farewell, but she stayed in the cab, digging through the glovebox. More thunder rumbled. Holding up his hand in farewell, he got into his car, plugged his phone onto its charger, cranked up Ella Fitzgerald and drove away at speed.

In the cab of the lorry, Ronnie pulled out a heavy coin from her glovebox. She'd just realised who he was. She turned it round in her hand. It went everywhere with her to competitions and had done for half a century. A commemorative crown handed out to school children to celebrate the silver wedding anniversary of Queen Elizabeth II and Prince Philip in 1972, later swapped between two small girls who'd painted them with nail varnish initials as friendship tokens. The varnish had long since chipped off, but Ronnie could still remember the V daubed with her mother's conservative coral pink, while on the other side, in far bolder scarlet, a curly H.

'Happy birthday, Hermia,' she breathed, pressing it to her lips. 'By God, he misses you, that difficult man of yours. That makes two of us.'

'Has Key Man gone?' Blair came out of the bathroom towelling his wet hair. He had a dark red bruise across his ribs.

'Key Man has gone.' She lifted his arm to examine it closer, but he waved the gesture away. 'Funny thing, he was married to a friend of mine.'

'Small world. You get talking?'

'Not really. He's no idea who I am – we never met. They got together after I'd left Johnny. She and I wrote to each other on and off, but then we lost touch.' Ronnie had a trick she'd adopted long ago to share facts about her past without their allied pain, a throwaway lightness of tone and amused crease of the eye.

After she'd left Johnny she'd counted the friends who remained in touch on one hand. For years, Hermia's name would have been the first finger she'd have lifted when asked who had remained loyal, but that had changed abruptly.

She leaned against him, head under his chin.

'Tough day.' He wrapped his arms round her.

'Tough day.' She sighed, grateful for the tightness of the hug. 'Thank you for driving over here.'

'I'd only be sitting in the lorry park worrying about you if I hadn't. My first ride tomorrow isn't until late morning.' While no longer arriving at events with the small cavalry of horses he'd once had – all for sale at the right price, his six-horse transporter known as the Dealing Ring – Blair was still competing in classes every day this week. His was the travelling circus life typical of eventers, one he found hard to give up. They both did.

'How are the family bearing up?'

'Still gathering.' She didn't mention the animosity of her encounter with Alice. Blair would listen if she needed to get it all off her chest but he knew none of the characters involved. She had never asked him to invest in that part of her life, and having him here was enough. Ultra-competitive, diamond-tough and known for taking things that mattered very seriously, Blair was the *yin* to her *yang*.

Stealing his towel for her own hair, she sat down on the bed.

'How long will you need to stay on to sort things out?' Blair asked.

'Not long,' she said, lying back on the bed, the crook of one elbow over her eyes, the flight urge lighting up her nerve endings. 'Alice needs to be in complete control of this. Tim's the entertainer so he'll make the funeral a big production. Pax will ensure nobody feels left out and everything is fair. I just stir things up.'

'Maybe they need stirring.' She felt his weight shift onto the mattress beside her.

'The silver spoon in this mouth got melted down a long time ago to keep horses in shoes.' She rolled over, propping her chin on his chest to look at him.

'Doesn't stop it speaking its mind.'

'A family trait all Percys inherit.' She smiled. 'Pip's the stirrer, I suspect. I bet she's counted the spoons.'

'Who's Pip?'

'Daddy's carer, who's running around like an adrenalin collie. Strange woman. Clever, though. I quite like her.'

'Not as clever as you. You're fierce.' Blair reached up a hand to cup her face and she pressed her cheek tightly to it. He had wonderful hands, sensitive to a horse's mouth and a woman's body.

'Rub my back.' She sat up to drag off her T-shirt and flopped back down on her front.

His thumbs hard in the knots of tension bunched there brought out a sigh so deep she felt her soul might sneak out with it. The tears rolled for a while, a huge relief to be able to let them out, and to be with a man who understood not to try to baby-talk her into feeling better. They weren't straightforward feelings: raw grief for the father she had lost today, frustration at being rejected again as a mother, the yearning for a long-lost friend, but there was no need to separate them out. Like tangled laundry, they all got washed together.

At last the sad blindness passed, the seizures shuddering away. She rolled over and smiled up at him, a moment of supreme calm. 'Shall we have sex?'

'Isn't that kind of disrespectful?'

'Only if the coffin's in the room.'

Graveside humour made them crease together with laughter, Blair hand clamped on his bruised chest.

She reached up to move it aside and touch the red skin. He wince as her fingertips tested it. 'You fell off?'

'Three from bloody home. Rider error. Going too fast.'

His mind had been off the game because he was thinking a getting here for me, she realised. That was never part of the either. The flight nerves hummed.

She slid off her jeans and climbed on top of him.

Blair and Ronnie enjoyed having sex together immensely. Such were the stop-start timetable and prying eyes of competition lorry-park life that they'd been known to start making love before breakfast, take it a stage further mid-morning, pick up where they'd left off at teatime and finish the job at bedtime. Conversely, Blair sometimes came to her cottage with just minutes to spare. They'd barely have closed the door before they were joined at the hip, no words exchanged between entry, finale and the door slamming again. Although she'd never admit it to anybody but herself, Ronnie occasionally struggled to keep up with the super-fit Australian – he could be very controlling as well as athletic, flipping between passion and detachment with bewildering unpredictability – but he also accused her of tuning out, so they were perfectly matched to give pleasure while not always paying it their full attention.

But now, when she was kneeling on those steel-hard riding thighs, with his even harder shaft revving deliciously inside her, his thumb soft drumming just the right spot to give her a body-melt climax, she found herself so stuffed with sadness she could barely breathe. The hot fix melted shamefully away.

'Let's stop.' Blair drew her close, pulses slamming against hers. 'Poor baby. Ssh. It's okay.'

They lay together for a long time, heartbeats slowing in tandem, empathy coupling them tightly together, intimacy knotted from forehead to toes. Eventually, Ronnie got up to make a cup of tea. If sex and death were the forces by which humans erred, boiling the kettle was the first line of British defence.

'What will happen to your father's stud?' he asked.

'Not my decision ultimately. The sooner I can sign away any interest the better.'

'That's what he wanted?'

She thought back to the awful lunches in recent memory at which her father had shouted a lot, knowing his health was failing. 'He wanted the last thirty-five years back.'

'And you?'

'I want today back.' She closed her eyes. But instead of reliving the news of her father's death, she saw Hermia's widower cowering against the storm, his eyes as lost as hers. *Everyone can master a grief but he that has it.*

Small, felt-like ears flicking back and forth at the sound of thunder, Stubbs looked up from his bed in the corner of the tack room at an unlikely human pack drawn together in adversity: Alice and Lester were sheltering from the storm with the last of the cake and yet more tea brewed by Pip.

Retreating behind the rug racks, Alice made a series of urgent phone calls, not as hush-hush as she'd clearly have liked because she had to shout to be heard over the storm, was continually cut off, then had to repeat herself loudly.

'... solicitors are emailing me the will now... The WILL, yes. We're executors, as are they. It's vitally important we— What? I told you, he fell down the stairs. Heart attack, they think. Let's not worry about that now, Pax. We can talk about this when you're— Pax? Pax? Bugger!'

'You get the best mobile reception up in the observation tower,' Pip said helpfully, as lightning discharged through a distant telegraph pole with a loud bang.

Red-eyed, Alice peered out at the wild weather. 'I'll use the phone in the house. I need to call my brother's family again. Can I have the keys, Pip?'

'*Very* crackly line in bad weather,' Pip said quickly. 'There's an extension in Lester's cottage.'

To her relief, a power cut put paid to Alice's notion and they were plunged into gloomy monochrome.

'Happens a lot,' Pip told Alice.

'I *did* grow up here,' she snapped. 'Now, it's essential the stud functions as normally as possible.' She took command, a small, busty silhouette marching between saddle racks, whistle swinging on its lanyard as though she was about to run a keep-fit class. 'I need you both up to speed with what's going on.'

Pip stood to attention, perked up to be counted still as part of the team given Alice's customary disregard for her position. She owed it to Ronnie to report all this verbatim to her later. She reminded herself to visualise Alice as a small boat drifting on a sea of grief, the string that could pull her back in her own hand.

'Pax,' Alice told them, helping herself to cake, 'is going to try to get a flight back from Italy tonight and should be here mid-morning tomorrow. Tim's ex-wife knows where he is – halfway up some mountain apparently – and is driving out there now from Cape Town to… break… the… news.' She was suddenly too choked to speak, and Pip rushed to comfort her, only to find herself batted away. 'Too many raisins in this fruitcake.'

'Just how your grandfather liked it.' Pip stood up even taller. Think boat.

'Shilling a slice.' Lester struck a match to light a hurricane lamp, his leathery face as sunken as Pip had ever seen it. 'They sold it at the church for a shilling a slice.'

'I think Pip should stay here with you tonight, Lester,' Alice said firmly.

Pip and the old stallion man looked at each other in horror. Mute in complicity, they listened as Alice forged on with her staff briefing, a tiny Queen Victoria addressing her trusty retainers: 'Now that all the immediate family know – we'll take Tim as read – the news can be broken more widely. Friends, locals, professional associates. Of course, there's this delay waiting for the coroner, but I've called the lawyer and have a meeting with him first thing tomorrow. There's the funeral to arrange. That's Tim's mandate when he flies in but I want you both to start thinking of any names his family might not be aware of, especially you, Lester, mare owners, suppliers, trades and so forth. Grumps knew an awful lot of people.' She rubbed her forehead fretfully. 'He was admired by so many.'

'Most of them are dead now,' Pip pointed out helpfully, 'and he refused to talk to quite a lot of the rest, didn't he, Lester?'

'He was a one for picking fights and holding grudges.' Lester nodded fondly.

'He was certainly a strong-minded man.' Alice cleared her throat. 'I'll need his diary and address book, Pip. And it goes without saying we'll want you to make lots of your delicious cakes for the wake.' She managed a stiff, condescending smile. 'Using fewer raisins.'

Pip made a mental note to tell Ronnie about the meeting with the solicitor, which seemed indecently hasty.

'Any questions so far?'

'Farrier's coming,' Lester said.

'What?'

'The farrier's coming to trim them all tomorrow. Do I put him off?'

'No. Horses' hoofs don't stop growing out of respect, Lester. This is why we need to get ourselves organised. The sooner I can go through Grumps's paperwork the better. Is it all kept together, Pip?'

'Your grandfather had an eccentric filing system' – "Just shove it in a bloody drawer or bin it, Pip!" – 'but as soon as the lawyers tell you what you need, I can find it for you in a trice. No point looking now.' The lights flickered. She willed the power to stay off.

'Agreed. I'm better off at home where I can make calls and muck in.' Alice opened the door, a blast of wind making the rosettes on the wall flutter like bunting. 'Hopefully Mummy will push off pretty pronto tomorrow so we don't have her under our feet. I'm still furious with you for calling her, Pip,' she snarled over her shoulder. 'This is a family matter.' The door was caught in a gust, banging against the outside wall, rosettes dropping like shot birds. 'The rain's almost stopped. I might make a dash for it.'

Thinking she'd gone, Pip harrumphed under her breath and turned back to Lester. 'Can you *believe* that? Ronnie *is* family. I'm calling her later. She knows who to trust.'

He made a growling sound in the base of his throat as the lights flickered back on, revealing Alice still framed in the door.

'*I* will call Mummy, Pip.' She marched back in. 'She's staying at the Mill, I believe.'

'Le Mill, yes, but I don't know what name it's booked under. I've got her mobile number, if you need it?'

Alice lifted her square little chin, reluctant to admit that she didn't have her own mother's number. 'Best jot it down to save me time.'

Pip did so, reading from her little screen. 'I've added Blair Robertson's too in case he has better reception.'

'Thank you.' Alice coloured.

Lester hissed through his teeth, catching Pip's eye with a rheumy warning. She ignored it, thinking about the little grief boat floating out to sea. 'Mrs Petty – Alice – we're always here for you. *I'm* always here for you. Bereavement is such a lonely place. I have some knowledge of grief therapy.'

Tucking into a second piece of cake, Lester coughed a piece of date across the room. Thunder bellowed closer again. The lights plunged off once more.

Ignoring Lester and divine signs, Pip ploughed on: 'I've lost my beloved parents in recent years, and I know how important it is to be able to lean on those you trust. I won't let you down. My door is open day or night.'

'Then I suggest you invest in better security measures,' Alice said briskly, handing her an empty cup and heading outside.

Carly cadged a lift home from Le Mill with a workmate, rain hammering down on the car roof from a black sky as she called the vet's surgery on the way to check how Pricey was doing.

'Barking the place down!' the flaky young work-for-free receptionist told her. 'They're just waiting for her bloods back, yah, but it all looks super-good. The lurcher sanctuary's going to take her. She'll probably go there tomorrow.'

'Can I have the address? I'd like to visit.' She let out a whoop when, eventually, she rang off.

'You're way too soft,' her workmate told her, having heard the story of the rescued bull-lurcher between serving tables. 'Those coursing dogs are psychos.' Having collected the kids from Ash's mother's dingy, toy-crammed little maisonette, she and Ellis pushed the double buggy across the estate as fast as they could beneath a too-small umbrella, shouting back at thunderclaps to show them they weren't scared. Carly expected the house to be empty, but a familiar sound of gunfire was coming from the lounge.

The curtains were drawn, a trio of lager cans on the side table as the console twisted this way and that.

'I thought you were going to the gym?'

'Storm broke again.'

It was still circling the ridge, rumbling round to terrorise Eyngate Park once more.

'Look, Dad! Look what I got!' Ellis thundered in with the purple riding crop. Carly hadn't realised he'd kept hold of it – it must have been left in the buggy.

'That's not yours.' She made a grab for it, but he'd already thwacked it down on the leather arm of the settee, inches from Ash.

'Jesus, fuck!' Ash exploded from the seat, beer cans and console controller flying. He looked deranged.

Face crumpling, Ellis ran out.

Shooting Ash an accusing look, Carly rushed after their son, hugging him tightly on the stairs as he wept and shook. 'Ssh, ssh, baby. Your dad didn't mean it – you took him by surprise, that's all. He gets jumpy like that from being a soldier.' Her hands were hot again. She cupped his face with them. 'Ssh. Why don't you both say sorry and make up, eh?'

Ellis nodded, blinking the tears away, his brave little face so like his father's.

But when they went back into the front room, Ash was back on his game, eyes still wide and fixed, his reaction to Ellis's stuttered apology a distracted fist-bump.

Carly picked up the crop and they retreated. 'This has to go back to the lady who dropped it,' she told Ellis, putting it on top of the hall cupboard.

'It's my 'Splorer Stick.'

'*Explorer.*' She smiled. 'I'll find you something else.'

Carly glanced round the hall. Her Feather Dusters cleaning kit and tabard were tucked beneath the stairs, a new multi-coloured fluffy duster poking up still in its plastic sleeve. She plucked it out. 'Magic Explorer Stick. Keeps you safe.' She pulled off the cellophane sleeve and it puffed out.

Grinning, he took it.

Posting Ellis and his duster in front of CBeebies in her and Ash's bedroom, she put Sienna down for her afternoon nap, gave Jackson his bottle and set him down too, then changed into joggers and threw her waitressing uniform into the washing-machine with that morning's clothes.

When she took Ash a mug of tea, he'd lost the manic look, turning to thank her with a familiar cheeky wink.

'The day I've had!' She sagged on the sofa, still so new it squeaked and puffed out its showroom leather smell.

'Tell me about it. Janine's been giving me earache since first thing. Says she needs you all day tomorrow. Couldn't get hold of you on your phone.'

Carly had ignored the calls. 'I've got an interview at the farm shop, then going to visit the lurcher sanctuary. It's important. You can look after the kids, can't you?'

'I've got your back.' Still stalking KGB operatives around dark alleys on screen with a Kalashnikov, he half listened as she told him about finding the injured dog and rushing it to the vet, about the out-of-control horse-riders, arrogant flat-capped Bay Austen and the mystery stiff, then the customer at Le Mill who had traded weird insults with his children and tipped her more than her day-shift rate.

'Bet he wanted to get in your knickers.'

'I think he was more of a head man.'

'Filthy fucker.'

'He knew French and binary and stuff.'

'Kinky with it.' The controller was laid down and he turned to face her, grinning. 'Nobody gets to be kinky with my wife.' He slipped his hand inside her waistband.

'Apart from you.' She nudged her hips closer.

Ash was looking at her mouth, a sure sign that he wanted sex.

Lightning flashed outside. They could hear animated vegetables singing upstairs.

'Ellis is wide awake up there,' she whispered, glancing up at the ceiling. 'If *Something Special* comes on, we stop. He can't stand Mr Tumble.'

'You are something special down here,' he breathed against her lips, slipping two fingers inside her to test the territory, his cock already springing from his fly.

'Hung like a porn star,' he'd boasted, when they were first together, handsome Fusilier Ash Turner with his big wolf eyes, bigger ego and quick tongue. At that point she'd never witnessed a porn star in action so she couldn't judge, but it had felt plenty big enough. It always did.

Today it lacked its usual straight rhythm, its partner in pleasure still out of shape from her third long labour. They hit and missed as it slipped out repeatedly through hasty, sofa-squeaking changes of position and waistband adjustments, finally keeping connected and catching enough friction to bring him off, his head rammed against a cushion, hers banging painfully against his shoulder.

'Love you, bae. You're the best.' He slapped her buttock affectionately.

'You too.'

Carly drew his sweating forehead to her lips, grateful to feel this close, heartbeats crashing skin to skin, even if it hadn't been great sex.

The back door banging made them both sit up.

'*Only me!*' came a familiar call from the kitchen, the perfume already snaking beneath the sitting-room door like tear gas.

Waistbands were snapped up just in time for Janine to bustle in, peeling off a RainMate.

'Carly, Feather Dusters needs you tomorrow. Has Ash said? Can you do a double shift?'

'I've got plans.' She looked to him for support.

But Ash was already back on the console, eyes locked on target. The last five minutes might not have happened. 'Ash?'

'Do what you like.' It didn't matter that his semen was still dribbling out of her, his tooth-marks on her areolas; his mind was utterly focused on the screen.

'This sofa's like the inside of a new Jag, isn't it?' Janine sniffed appreciatively.

Boom-boom-boom went his Kalashnikov. Upstairs, Ellis was jumping up and down on their bed.

'I thought that was you two when I came in!' Janine snorted with laughter, elbowing Carly. 'Now, tell me you can do it. I'll pay extra.'

'I'm busy.'

'I'll do your nails.' Janine planned to set up a mobile nail bar once she'd saved enough for the van.

'Not good with nappies.'

'So just do it for the money. What about that motorbike you're saving up for that Ash says is unladylike?'

'Triumph Bonneville.' She sighed. Her dream of becoming a biker was a big Turner family joke. In their world, only men were allowed throbbing engines between their legs. 'I'm saving for something else now.'

'Not a bloody horse? Ash told me about that.'

Carly shook her head, wondering how Janine got so much information out of him when she could hardly get him to say yes or no to a cup of tea. Or look at her during sex. She thought about the dog, war-torn and tough, like him. 'How much extra?'

'Twenty.'

'Make it fifty.'

'Are you kidding? Thirty-five.'

'Okay, I'll do it,' Carly said, adding a last-minute 'if you can tell me about lamping.'

The bright pink lips pursed. 'Is that like a light-therapy thing?'

'You know what it is. Lurchers. And coursing too.'

'If you're really interested, I can do better than that. I'll get someone to take you.'

'Who?'

'Wise up, Carl. There's men in this family could light up the eyes of the cow jumping over the moon on a good night, hey, Ash?'

He wasn't listening, the pixilation glittering as the gun-barrel on the screen swung from side to side. Carly remembered Bay Austen saying a Turner cousin had been caught poaching red-handed not long ago. 'So who was out last night? Was it Jed?'

The pink lips disappeared as they were rolled between Janine's teeth, reappearing with a small kissing sound. 'Not likely in that storm. Be townies. Nasty sorts. Leave it, Carl. Best not to ask too much.'

8

Blair had a tremendous capacity to catch up on sleep in short doses. Ronnie left him napping and went out onto the balcony to smoke three puffs of a roll-up.

'Haven't you quit those bloody things yet?' her father had barked at her, when they'd first met for lunch a few weeks after her mother had died, lighting up his own.

They'd been sitting in a sunny restaurant courtyard at a country-house hotel near Bath. His invitation, as furtively arranged as a tryst with a mistress, had been full of warm entreaties about making peace. Within a minute of meeting, he'd picked up her cigarette packet with liver-spotted fingers, pocketing it in his blazer as though she was still fourteen. 'Smoking killed your mother.'

She looked at her lighter now, flicking the flame on and off. *Out, out, brief candle.*

Tears threatened. She couldn't bear to think of him lying alone in the cellar last night.

She gazed fixedly across the millpond instead, remembering the year the Young Farmers had hired swan-shaped boats for the summer ball here, leading to a lot of skinny-dipping and a huge cumulative dry-cleaning bill. Not yet fourteen, Ronnie had borrowed her mother's best taffeta, hurriedly taken in to fit her with great tacking stitches, and had floated about like Millais's *Ophelia*. Hermia, resembling one of Waterhouse's nymphs in a training bra and immaculately white knickers, had dipped and dived around her reciting Gertrude's *There is a willow grows aslant a brook* speech. They'd both been high as kites on Jeremy Perriman's spliff, thinking themselves wildly sophisticated.

Goodness, but her father had been angry after that, grounding her for the rest of the summer. Ronnie had exchanged long letters with Hermia – also grounded – handed to the postman amid much secrecy to deliver three hundred yards along the lane, just as they corresponded during term-time from schools three hundred miles apart.

With their precocious blonde charm and boundless energy, Percy daughters – rarities in any given generation – made friends easily and were fiercely loyal allies. For Ronnie that ally was fellow Pony Clubber and near neighbour Hermione 'Hermia' Austen, the youngest and most overlooked of a large pack of farming offspring. Both girls had been taught to ride by Lester, whose terrifying challenges imbued them with such high-speed stickability that they were unbeatable in pairs hunter-trials classes, fearless daredevils in the saddle.

From the ages of six to eleven, the two girls had been inseparable. Both blonde, bubbly and generous, often mistaken for twins, the duo had been at the heart of village life, a youthful bridge between their stand-offish families and the villagers in an era when the old order was being shaken by social revolution.

They were forcibly separated when they were sent to different senior schools, cosseted far from IRA terrors, the first European Referendum and *The Good Life*, but they remained as close as sisters, writing those long letters every week and joined at the hip during holidays, even when grounded.

Lighting another cigarette, Ronnie watched a heron glide low over the millpond, landing on a protruding tree root at its edge, instantly still as a statue, its long beak angled to bayonet the surface for a fish. In her head, she could still hear the laughter and music of that ball – Abba's 'Mamma Mia', Donna Summer's 'I Feel Love', Rod Stewart's 'Maggie May', 'In the Summertime' by Mungo Jerry, 'Spirit in the Sky'…Who the devil sang that? Hermia would know.

She looked up at the sky, a deep-cleaned blue, the heat of the sun finally throwing its full blowtorch strength into the afternoon. Why was she thinking about Hermia on the day of her father's death?

I hate him, I hate him, I hate him, I HATE HIM! she'd confessed in those long summer letters.

'I hate him for dying,' she breathed now.

And it was Hermia she sensed close by.

Ronnie took out the anniversary crown from her jeans pocket and flipped it. Queen Elizabeth II, unfamiliar in swan-necked, braided-hair youth: no trace of a coral V remained across that Greek-bust stern face.

She looked across the millpond once more. The heron hadn't moved. *Patience on a monument...* How did the quote go? Hermia would know that too. She'd been a brilliant Viola.

By the time thirteen-year-old Hermia Austen had bobbed about in her undies to T. Rex quoting Hamlet, she'd already learned Shakespeare's juiciest female speeches, her passion for theatre fuelled by trips to the nearby RSC and a starring role in the village panto. She was soon directing ambitious productions staged in the church meadows between summer horse shows, most often with a cast of just two. Liberated from weeks shivering in a cold Scottish dorm fantasising that Harvey Smith would gallop in to rescue her in full *Ivanhoe* armour, Ronnie had been very taken with dressing up and high drama, but it was Hermia whose talent and passion dazzled, and Ronnie had challenged her friend to follow her dream profes-sionally. 'You just *have* to act on the main stage at Stratford.'

'Only if you ride round Badminton.'

'Of course I will,' she'd said matter-of-factly, amazed it was ever in doubt. 'I'll get that Whitbread Trophy. And the *Evening Standard* Best Actress Award goes to... Hermia Austen!'

They'd neither of them liked the names they were christened with, one taking the boyish abbreviation for Veronica, the other trying out many different variations of her own, none suiting her so well as the character in Shakespeare's great fantasy romantic comedy, hers to play on through her professional life.

Highly flirtatious and endlessly inquisitive, Ronnie was the touch-paper who all too often got them into trouble, Hermia the fast-talking, quick-thinking diplomat who got them out. They'd shared the same taste in clothes and boys, sometimes swapping both when they grew bored. In their last summer before leaving school, they pursued a rock star who had bought a neighbouring manor, escaping through his bathroom window when things had got out of hand.

From the hotel room, she heard 'Wild Horses' playing as Blair's phone rang and was answered.

While Hermia had gone on to win a place at a London drama school, Ronnie remained in the Cotswolds where her competitive horse-trials career had quickly taken off from Pony Club to professional, a career path as meticulously planned by her parents as the breeding of the horses she rode. By contrast, her impulsive love life had lacked forethought. If she'd walked the course beforehand, she might have taken a different route.

'Your mother could never see her way to forgiving you,' her father had explained irritably, at that first lunch together. 'Not for what you did, but for what you didn't do. You had so much potential.'

A splash made her turn to look across the lake. The heron had a silver fish wriggling in its beak.

Patience on a monument smiling at grief, she remembered, looking up at the unbroken hot blue canopy. 'So tell me, Hermia, who sang "Spirit in the Sky"?'

'Norman Greenbaum.' Blair wandered outside, yawning and raking up his silver-streaked pelt of hair. He stooped in front of her. 'You okay?'

She nodded, already knowing what he was going to say: it had stolen all the joy from his eyes. 'You have to go home.'

Ronnie didn't need to ask why, but today had been so upside down it spilled out without thinking. 'Is Vee okay?'

He flinched almost imperceptibly. They never spoke about his wife. Of course Vee wasn't okay. How could she be?

He kissed her again, dropping onto his haunches. 'I'll call you later. The room's paid for. Order what you like from room service.'

'Company?'

'You know I hate to do this to you.'

'Hey.' She cupped his face, aware how hard it was for him. 'I'm grateful you came, in every sense. I have my girls.' Her dogs were spread out on the baking deck in the afternoon sun, like two seal pups. 'We'll go for a walk where the willow grows aslant the brook.'

'Wear a hat.' He fetched his battered baseball cap out of a back pocket and slotted it on her head. 'The heatwave's arrived.'

★

'Will you really, *really* be all right?' Pip asked Lester, watching him finish off afternoon stables, noticing his increasing pallor and shaking hands, despite the sudden rise in temperature. The yard thermometer was already pushing thirty. 'Why not come back with me to the Bulrushes? I've got the new *Game of Thrones* box set and seafood lasagne. I can drop you back here later.'

'*Go*,' was all he said. She took the cue gratefully.

As she parked on the neat tarmac rectangle in front of the Bulrushes' yellow garage door, a predictably illiterate text came through from Janine Turner: *Jst conferming tomz. Myself and my best girl C @10. Cash plz. xx*

Pip smiled with relief.

There was a PS. *Is it true the old man there's snuffed it?*

Out of respect for the family, Pip didn't reply. But meeting Ronnie Percy had been the sunrise that eclipsed tragedy. Pip had a mission in cyberspace to examine the corona more closely.

Convinced that Ronnie and gravel-voiced Blair were more than just owner and rider, she hurried straight into the bungalow to research the Australian horseman in more detail.

Her other clients would just have to wait. She was supposed to be taking a cake to one and picking up fresh groceries for another, but she was too engrossed in her task, calling them both with a hurried apology. 'There's been a terrible tragedy at the yard. I can't go into details, but the family have been informed.'

Cat curled up like a purring ammonite on her lap and digital mouse in hand, she whizzed past all the search engine results she was familiar with from playing detective on Ronnie in the past – the Australian rider's Wikipedia entry, his long competition track-record and Olympic team golds – and went deeper. Although Blair rarely gave interviews, there was plenty of information about eventing's senior tough-man on equestrian news sites, his legendary three-decade career guaranteeing acres of Google Image photographs. Stories of rivalries and ride-offs abounded, along with loyal friendships he'd held close for three decades, and the devoted aristocratic owners he'd ridden for. One in particular had caused a scandal back in the nineties.

Still in his early thirties then, three-times world champion, notorious serial-shagger Blair had outraged both the Establishment and the equestrian world when he'd set up home with one of the most prolific owners in eventing, Lady Verney, a blue-blooded former show-jumper fifteen years his senior. At the time, she'd been the wife of outspoken Tory peer and Prince Charles's hunting crony Earl Verney, their pack of chisel-chinned children freshly fledged and cavorting across *Tatler*'s social pages.

'That's twenty-first-century *Downton*!' Pip told the cat excitedly. 'Blair stole Cora!'

She scrolled the few photographs of them together, craggy sexpot alongside a high-cheekboned ageing Audrey Hepburn. The chemistry sizzled like rock star and cougar.

'She must be coming up for seventy now,' Pip calculated, digging around for up-to-date photographs. There were none. After the late-noughties, Verity had vanished from view, like the first Mrs Rochester.

9

Like the rainfall from that week's storms still running off the hills into the Fosse valley, news and rumours of Jocelyn Percy's death spread through the Comptons. Alice's phone calls to friends and family from her farmhouse kitchen couldn't hope to keep pace with the quickening tide of news.

At Manor Farm, the Austen family were quietly celebratory beneath decorously unsmiling faces. At the equine clinic, soul of discretion Gill Walcote was furious when husband Paul carelessly mentioned it to the most gossipy equine dentist in Gloucestershire. Twenty minutes later it was on all social feeds. 'Talk about straight from the horse's mouth.'

She felt that justified her calling Petra to relay the news. 'I wonder if Ronnie will come back and run the stud now. That'll liven things up. There was *such* a scandal when she ran off with the jump jockey in the eighties. My father was the stud vet at the time. He said half the mares foaled early with the shock.'

'How horribly Mitford.' Standing in her kitchen, whisk in hand, envisaging tight breeches, shoulder pads and big hair, Petra thought it sounded excitingly like something from *Dynasty*. 'Did she ever return?'

'Only for funerals. Her husband Johnny died in a smash-up on the Fosse Way a few years later, pickled with Scotch, so it was pretty clear he drove straight at the tree. They'd never divorced so Ronnie probably thought she'd cash in, but Johnny died beanless. She pushed off PDQ when she realised there was no fatted calf on offer. The same when her mother died. I was there – huge turnout, standing room only – and she kept the engine revving, lover at the wheel. He's probably putting his driving gloves on as we speak.'

'The woman sounds like a monster.' Petra imagined a Cruella de Vil character sliding into town in a Rolls, swathed in furs, cigarette holder at a jaunty angle, pound signs in her eyes.

Meanwhile Pip's pensioner network had hit the telephones as soon as they heard the word 'tragedy', cause of death still a mystery. Suspicious circumstances, they'd heard. One had discovered that cutting equipment had been involved. Had the Captain died in his car, like his son-in-law? As talk of a fatal kick spread one way along the landline and suicide the other, Janine and her cleaning Mafia picked up the thread from their on-the-job radar and spread the jungle drums, tapping it through their texting thumbs with an alto-gether cooler-headed rap. *Old boy from the stud snuffed it. Must have been worth a packet.*

The dog-walkers crossing paths on Plum Run were soon whisper-ing in grave undertones, fearful for the future of the village. What if the stud was sold? Developers would be straight in there. What if the hobbit house man came back and built eco-shacks all over the paddocks?

The farm shop was abuzz by closing time, a cloud of midges outside, gossip within. Petra, who had walked across the fields with her daughters and Wilf to buy ice-cream, found a small gaggle discussing the Captain's death at the till. 'Did you hear? The old boy from the stud got trapped under his quad bike. Lay there all night and died of his injuries. His horses formed a circle around him and literally wept.'

'We rode right past the stud just this morning.' She handed a tenner across, ice-cream blissfully cool in its bag against her side. 'Poor old chap.'

'He was a paardenlul.' Petra's other side felt even colder as Monique Austen slid in beside her, super-thin in grey Pikeur breeches, white-blonde hair scraped back in a rider's bun so tight she almost looked shaven-headed. 'That's Dutch for horse dick. Hello, Petra.'

'Monique!' Petra charitably assumed Bay's wife was referring to the Captain's field of expertise, the phrase somewhat lost in translation.

Having pushed to the front of the queue, Monique was waving a bottle of designer water and a packet of kale crisps at the manageress. 'I'm taking these, okay?'

'Can I just scan them for stock-keeping, Mrs A?' She held up her barcode reader.

Monique had the sing-song voice of a Eurovision act, with Stasi manners, ending each sentence with a determined exclamation: 'I've no time for that, okay. You can sort it out.' She turned on her heel and gave Petra a frosty look. 'I know you.'

'Monique, hi! Petra Gunn. Tilly and Bella are friends,' Petra greeted her, overenthusiasm masking dislike. 'She's just outside with her sister.' She gestured through the glass doors.

'Tilly's at a sleepover, okay.'

Oh, no! Had she sounded as if she was angling for an invitation? 'Mine hardly seem to be home this summer. Such bliss on days like this when I have them all to myself.'

Outside, Bella and Prudie were giving each other Chinese burns.

'No kidding.' The cool Botoxed face regarded Petra's red one, still sweaty from walking at hard-pulling-spaniel speed.

Mindful of Gill's stern warning not to cross the woman, Petra said: 'Isn't it awful news about the Captain? We were only talking about him today.'

'Don't be a hypocrite. Nobody round here liked him, okay. They only care about his house.' She strode off, her bottom small and pert.

She turned back to take her change, grateful for the look of amused empathy from the manageress who lowered her voice: 'The stud's going to be auctioned, I heard. An Arab sheikh offered the family a blank cheque for it once.'

'What about the daughter?' asked Petra. 'The Bolter?'

'Oh, she won't want to come back,' said a husky little voice behind her, a local she didn't recognise with a packet of chicken fillets. She moved forwards to the counter now, tiny and tough in a baseball cap and vest-top, her slim tanned arms landscaped with freckled muscles. 'Are these priced right?'

'Yes, madam. The meat is from a one hundred per cent organic pasture-fed Ixworth bird, raised here on the farm.'

'Did it have a name? For this price I'd expect a full obit. How did it die? Is its coop on the open market yet?' Her voice had a deep, teasing quality, but there was steel too. The manageress smiled nervously, then offered ten per cent off.

Petra walked out alongside her, and the woman gathered up the leads of two little dogs tied there. 'I bought your supper, girls!' She strode away in the direction of the footpath along Lord's Brook.

The dogs bounded eagerly in their mistress's wake, one darting the wrong side of Petra so that the lead caught her ankles. High-stepping over it, Petra dropped her canvas bag, tubs tumbling out. One cracked, spilling a gory splat of raspberry sorbet onto the tarmac.

'Oh, hell, I'm sorry.' The woman turned. 'I'll buy you another.'

'Really, don't worry.' Petra stooped to clear it up as best she could. 'It was my fault.'

'Stay there.' She marched inside while Petra reclaimed Wilf, tugging him away from the sorbet splash.

The late-afternoon sun was blisteringly hot. Prudie and Bella were grumbling. One of the woman's small dogs whined.

The shop door opened, but it was a pair of elderly ladies in checked shirtdresses, baskets of new-season rhubarb hooked on one arm, talking in excited undertones. 'I tell you, Cynthia, she *is* Ronnie Percy.'

'She'd be *far* older.'

Petra gazed into the shop again, seeing a flash of blonde hair. It was perfectly possible she'd be in the village if her father had just died.

A minute later the little dogs were wagging all over and a cold replacement tub was pressed into Petra's hand. It was gazpacho soup, but she appreciated the gesture, her thanks waved away with a freckled hand as the woman strode again towards the path along the bank of Lord's Brook.

Finding herself on the same track, Petra hung back awkwardly, not wanting to impinge on her grief. The blonde was far faster, with the jaunty, swinging gait bred to cross moors, walk hunter-trials courses and nail a gay Gordon in an ancestral ballroom. Before she could stop them, though, the girls raced shrieking ahead, soon leading them all, tossing twigs into the stream and chasing them along like white-water rafting Pooh sticks. Wilf was pulling her arm out to catch them up, doubly so when the blonde's small dogs were let off their leads to trot obediently beside her. A well-practised mutineer, the spaniel threw himself down and wriggled until he was free of his collar.

A fraction too late, Petra made a grab for his ruff. Bounce, bounce, splash. 'Woof!' He was in the fast-moving water, alluring as a dolphin on the Riviera Maya as he plunged along its course. Come swim with me! He writhed around in the cool, stone-contoured shallows.

The small dogs needed no more invitation, plunging in after him with beach-babe eagerness.

The diminutive blonde strode on, seeming not to notice.

'Sorry!' Petra hurried after her.

'What?' She stopped. Her eyes were astonishingly blue.

'He's the Tom Daley of this parish.' Petra made a big look-over-there gesture at Wilf and the little dogs in the water.

'Who?' The gruff voice was last-century upper class.

'He of the budgie-smugglers. As opposed to pheasant, grouse or one hundred per cent organic pasture-raised Ixworth.'

'I'm hopeless with names.' She shook her head apologetically, those blue eyes moreish.

'Tom Daley, the Olympic diver.' Petra beamed at her, realising she must sound like a dog-walking loon. 'White teeth, spray tan, washboard stomach. Not that Wilf has that. Or a tan.'

'Does he live in the village?'

This was getting awkward. The dogs were charging up and down the stream, showing no sign of coming out. 'Sorry. Forget I mentioned him. I have no idea why I did. I just wanted to apologise for my dog. Not that I'm implying the need to apologise for Tom Daley, who I'm sure is very sportsmanlike. Oh, God, there I go again. He's not someone I ever think about, unless the television's live-streaming sports and he is literally bouncing on a board, but now I can't shut up about him.'

Then, like birdsong, the most deliciously husky giggle bubbled up, the blue eyes creasing with fleeting, all-too-infectious amusement.

'Sorry,' Petra said again.

'I'm afraid I know nothing about divers, but I do know my gun-dogs. That's a fine-looking springer. Do you shoot?'

'Only my mouth off.' Petra whistled for Wilf, who ignored her.

'Good for you.' The blue gaze stayed on her face. 'Not enough people prepared to speak their mind.'

'Even if it's full of gibberish.'

'Oh, mine always is. Earworms, unidentifiable quotes, half-forgotten to-do lists, petty grudges, quiet passions, racing form. Like an old handbag.' Her smile was enchanting.

The dogs were plunging their noses into water-vole holes, snorting furiously.

Petra had started to doubt this was the Bardswolds Bolter – Gill had described her as evil incarnate. 'Are you from the village?'

'Once upon a time. You?'

'Not originally. Happy-ever-aftering.' If she said it often enough, Petra hoped it would come true. Guiltily remembering her daughters, she turned to find they'd both climbed the fence into the hayfield that stretched from the stream to the lane and were racing towards the tumbledown wooden barn that always fascinated them. 'Girls, you're trespassing!'

'The landowner won't mind,' the woman assured her, setting off at her brisk walk. 'I always cut across it. Come on.'

'What about the dogs?' Petra had been known to lose half a day trying to coax Wilf out of Lord's Brook.

'Oh, they'll follow.' She was already climbing deftly over a park rail.

They cut across the hayfield. All three wet dogs were hard on their heels, as she had predicted, snaking through the tall grass to dry off, Wilf besottedly following the little double act, not caring that the older one snapped and snarled at him.

'*I am your spaniel...*' Petra laughed, watching him. '*The more you beat me, I will fawn on you.*'

She almost walked into the blonde, who had swung round to gaze at her, deathly pale.

'It's *A Midsummer Night's Dream*,' Petra explained. 'Hermia speaking to Demetrius.'

'I know.'

'*Use me but as your spaniel – spurn me, strike me,*
Neglect me, lose me. Only give me leave,
Unworthy as I am, to follow you.'

Off she strode through the grass, diminutive in stature but long in shadow. Petra hurried after her, the remainder of the ice-cream melting in the bag. At the big field's midpoint there was a huge cedar, incongruously tall, which she had often admired from a distance. Her girls had already scaled its lower branches and were sitting astride them. 'Mummy! Look!'

'Wow!' She gazed up at it in awe. Rows of iron horseshoes had been hammered onto its fat trunk, spiralling upwards. There had to be close to a hundred, as though a herd had defied gravity and stampeded up to the top.

Beside her, the blonde's jaw had that fixed tetanus look of the well-bred when outraged, distraught, in severe pain or all three. 'The family tree,' she muttered, as she gazed up too, blue eyes squinting against the hot afternoon sun lasering through its branches. 'Every Bingham-Percy born at Eyngate Hall got a horseshoe nailed up there by the estate workers.'

'That's so cool,' said Prudie. 'Can we plant one, Mummy?'

'Why don't you both go and pick some wildflowers for Gunny?' Petra suggested, sensing that climbing it must be deeply disrespectful. As they slithered down, she looked from one shoe to the next, each a little bit of romantic history that fired her imagination.

'That threesome is Great-great-granny Mary, who couldn't make up her mind.' The blonde was pointing up at a high row of rusty crescents. 'A ribbon-tied shoe was added whenever a Percy married, and only real philanderers had a full set. Above Mary, Howard outlived three wives. The shoes were painted black when one died, although it wears off in a year. When I was little I thought that was the point at which their souls went up to Heaven. Now I know it's just oxidisation.' She reached up and patted one, large and robust with studs still screwed in it. 'Second-cousin Philip sold the entire village after the war to pay for repairs to the Hall once the garrisoned soldiers left.'

Petra knew exactly who she was. How could she have doubted it? 'Are you up here?'

'We're on the other side.' She marched round the trunk where a far more modest track of shoes made its way up. 'Guess which I am.'

Petra spotted an upside-down loner overhead, hanging by just one loose nail. Righting it and pressing the nail back into its hole, she turned back questioningly.

A husky, infectious laugh sounded out. 'Dear queer Uncle Brooke never stays the right way up. I'm the racing plate over there. Fast, lightweight and never rusts. Your girls are beautiful.' She nodded at Prudie and Bella, one as tall and willowy as the other was small and solid, already clutching enough meadow flowers to have Gunny reaching for the Piriton.

'I think so too. Thank you.'

Ronnie traced three horseshoes on the trunk and turned away with a sad half-smile.

They parted company at the standing stones without ceremony. 'Who was that lady?' Bella asked, as they made their way through the apple orchards.

'She never said, but I think she's called Ronnie.'

'Does she live in this village?'

'I'm hoping she might.' She could hear the *Black Beauty* theme tune in her head.

Ronnie's mobile rang at exactly seven fifteen – even bereavement didn't stop Alice listening to *The Archers* – the incoming number assigned to a favourite old photograph of a small, determined child on a pony. It was the first time it had ever lit up as an incoming call on her screen. The milestone was a blunt one.

As deliberately emotionless as a fifties housewife dictating a shopping list to her butcher, Alice offered an abrupt summary of those she'd spoken with and possible funeral dates. 'Pax flies into Birmingham tomorrow morning at ten and will come straight to the farm. Tim can't make it until after the weekend.' Ronnie sensed a pencil ticking off points. 'The vicar will call in at the farm tomorrow, as will the Austens and the funeral director. Please don't come to pick up your horses before eleven. I think we're all agreed it's probably best you don't hang around, yes?'

Johnny had done the same, retreating behind bullet points shouted like hounds' names and hunt commands – that need for sharp consonants: Palmer, Petrel, Pontiff, Ware Riot! Hopkins, Horace, Hornet, Forrard! You. Will. Not. Forsake. This. Marriage.

'I'll come at eleven,' she said wearily, hurrying out to her balcony to light a cigarette.

At the other end of the line, she heard a matching spark striking and a deep inhale. Her heart cracked a little more. She stubbed hers straight out. 'Alice, we have to make peace.'

'Mummy, please don't fuck this up.' The call ended.

Horses, hunting and cigarettes were probably the only enduring things that Ronnie had ever had in common with aloof, taciturn Johnny Ledwell.

Ronnie and Johnny, a rhyming couplet for a domestic tragedy that was never going to work. One was gregarious, impulsive and determined to make a better fist of family life than her starchy, detached parents. The other, brought up ducking a father's fist, was monosyllabic socially and held an idealised, archaic view of a wife; his flame-haired Irish mother had died when he was young; he greatly admired his in-laws for their solid fortitude.

The marriage had started to go downhill almost as soon as the honeymoon car snaked into the Fosse valley and Ronnie had stroked her handsome new husband's thigh, fingers creeping towards his crotch.

A hand had clamped over hers, wedding ring shining. '*I'm driving.*'

Johnny was an alpha in bed, as uncommunicative between the sheets as between guests at a dinner party. The aggressive, stolen moments of enthusiasm that Ronnie had mistaken for passion before their marriage turned out to be her husband's only gear. Obsessed with breeding – cattle, then hounds, horses and now his own lineage – he wanted to start a family straight away.

'I've got a dozen horses to compete and I'm long-listed for the Olympics!' Ronnie had laughed disbelievingly. But she'd never been destined to go to Los Angeles, her career course already walked, the maternity suite the next fence ahead: Johnny had sired his first child with the same determination as the Captain's latest acquisition, a wiry little flat-racing stallion newly put to work in the covering barn. He'd been bought to strengthen the stud's famous line, much as his son-in-law had been. Clamping onto the mare's back, teeth deep in her withers, half a dozen thrusts and it was over, the first of a new generation on its way.

An unheated hunt cottage was by then deemed too damp for babies and the career of huntsman too unsociable. At Jocelyn's insistence, Johnny had moved with his pregnant wife the short distance from the Ludd-on-Fosse kennels to Compton Magna to manage the stud. He worked closely alongside his father-in-law and Lester, with whom he developed a strong bond, both men taciturn and fanatical about pedigree. All three regularly sat in the Jugged Hare in Compton Bagot until the early hours, planning bloodlines. It was where the trio received the news, phoned in to the landlord by Ann, that Ronnie had given birth to a daughter.

'Better luck next time.' The Captain had famously patted his son-in-law on the back and bought a round for everybody.

The village loved the Ledwells, babies apparently coming easily to Ronnie, first dark, then blonde, then Titian, her bumps riding out proudly to the fore until weeks before the births, then strapped into basket saddles as soon as they could sit up to follow the Fosse hounds on Shetlands, towed by a stern grandmother shouting, 'Up! Down!' and a jolly nanny hired to enable Ronnie to keep competing the stud horses.

Very few onlookers had ever guessed all was not well in the Ledwell marriage. Ronnie was too good a performer, adept at welcoming, placating, charming and distracting, and far too grateful for company to frighten it off.

By the time Pax had arrived, the Ledwells' marriage had become lonely and loveless, thereafter sexless too. Brought up to stay the distance, Ronnie had buttoned up her show jacket and got on with the job. She'd grown up in a household of hard-drinking, hard-riding misogyny; her mother insisted that men always went a bit off the boil when their wives were milky new mothers. Friends like Hermia, free-wheeling her way around London in an orgy of boom, bust and marching-dust eighties parties, had no experience of marriage, and Ronnie wouldn't have dreamed of troubling them for advice, striking on positively, her children and horses her focus.

She had gathered her growing family to heel as naturally as the terriers that had always travelled with her, horsebox gypsies rattling between one-day events, catching happiness where she could, infectiously passing it through to the children, who always got the best of both their parents. They were too young to pick up the toxicity that consumed the Ledwells out of hours. Although no longer campaigning at the highest level, Ronnie had remained something of a local celebrity, welcomed at village events, a child on each hip and one at foot, all wearing smiles as wide as a Cotswold horizon.

Compton Magna had been prouder than ever of their stud, its beautiful progeny and its long history of brave, blond Percys. 'Such a lovely family!'

Until the day the Bardswolds Bolter had run.

Her phone rang again, a teenage photograph, gawky and doe-eyed, hair as red as a fallow deer. The blast of guilt was always instant.

'Pax.' She wanted to sympathise, ask how she was bearing up, but her throat had constricted as though swallowing a poison draught.

'Where are you, Mum?' Her daughter's voice was a soft cello D string.

'The Mill.' Ronnie looked up at the stars – how had it got so dark? They blurred and disappeared, like sugar stirred into black coffee.

'You'll be at the farm tomorrow?'

'Briefly.'

'Wait for me. You have to wait for me.'

'Please don't worry. I told Alice I don't want any of it.' The poison was working through her chest now, a silent thief that took her breath away. She sank down on the deck as grief mugged her, jaws clamped with the effort of sparing her daughter its messiness.

'We'll see about that.' The D string drew a long sigh. 'I'll see you tomorrow.'

As soon as the call ended, Ronnie let loose the sobs, cut through with grateful laughter when the small, elderly alpha dog of her two-pack marched out and deposited a neat pile of chopped one hundred per cent organic pasture-raised Ixworth fillet beside her, swiftly and disapprovingly regurgitated, then sat down to peer at it with distaste.

Her phone lit up with Blair's face, that bloody cello D string again, deep within the four chords opening Elgar's Concerto. She'd change it to something more cheerful.

'How are you bearing up?' he asked, road noise rumbling.

Big ploppy tears. Bloody grief. 'Great! You?'

'Vee tried to go riding again.' It was a day for breaking rules.

'Oh, fuck.'

'It's fine. She didn't even get the tack on. But I've got to get rid of the horse.'

'I'll take him back.'

'No.'

'I sold him to you.' Ronnie sat back on the deck and looked up at the stars, clearly focused now, Venus flying like a kite above the moon. That stallion could jump the moon with Venus between his knees. She should have guessed he'd turn out to be as unruly as Sleipnir, Norse god Odin's legendary eight-legged warhorse who could out-leap, out-gallop and outwit all others.

An owl shrieked overhead. It repeated in stereo on her phone. 'Where are you?'

'I just pulled into the hotel. I can see your silhouette.'

'Keep the engine ticking.'

'You can't run away from this, Ronnie.'

10

'Feather Dusters calling!'

'Who?'

'Your cleaner. I'm Carly. I've been ringing this thing ten minutes.'

Opening the electric gates and peering around her front door, Petra blinked sleep from her eyes. 'You know it's twenty to eight?'

'I'll make sure you're not charged for the late start.' A whip of energy bustled in with a cleaning tray and a Henry Hoover, blonde hair scraped back to reveal two inches of far prettier dark root. 'Janine texted you, yeah? I'll start down here, shall I?'

Petra's phone had been left in her handbag overnight, a regular accidental sleepover that placed her off radar. She fished it out now. Finding a signal, the device gave its usual neglected fandango, battery striking off with below-ten-per-cent chirrup. Then a fast-bullet ricochet of chimes told her she had tens of messages queuing for an answer. No doubt the majority were from her mother-in-law, who would arrive in a cloud of brimstone and sulphur later that morning, expecting boutique-hotel standards and all her food cooked to recipes devised by a Michelin-starred chef ('Nigella is for slatterns, Jamie for slobs and the Hairy Bikers for northerners').

'Lovely house.' The cleaner was already wiping years of grime from the light fitting.

Petra reeled sleepily around her kitchen island, picking up the wrappings from several of Fitz's midnight feasts – at sixteen, he didn't so much eat as inhale food from its packaging – and apologising while the kettle boiled. 'I hadn't expected you quite so early.'

She looked short-sightedly for some glasses, pausing to squint at a message from Gill sent late last night. *Gossip! Call me. G.*

'We've got a lot of work on today.' The girl was spraying everything in sight with Cif. 'Janine said starting here eightish would be fine.'

'That's a no-ish.' Petra yawned, having lain awake far too late reading a thriller in which everyone seemed to have dunit. 'I need you to blitz the annexe after this – my mother-in-law's staying there from tonight. She packs white gloves specifically to trail across picture frames and cornicing. Downstairs in this side of the house will need the full monty, too, upstairs just a flick. I'll try to get the children to tidy before you venture in to vacuum.'

'I've only been booked two hours.'

Petra gritted her teeth. She'd had a weekly half-day Friday-morning slot for at least two years, usually with a team of two. Janine was always doing this. 'In that case forget upstairs this week. Also the playroom. And ignore my study. It's beyond hope and I'm not going back in there until September.'

'Janine says you're a famous writer.' The girl carried a mop bucket to the sink at speed.

'Half-truths are the foundation of all fiction.' Petra watched her stoop to cuddle Wilf as she passed. He gave an appreciative body-wag, claws skittering on the flagstones. 'He's called Wilf.'

'I love dogs.'

'Wilf's a Gunn-dog, ha-ha. He's on gardening leave until October which means he's a total delinquent. Typical seasonal worker.'

'I think it's cruel using dogs for hunting.'

'Wilf flushes and picks up rather than hunts – he's like a meno-pausal mother of teenagers – but I agree. Dogs should spend their entire lives looking at us adoringly, which is what Wilf does best.'

The girl started mopping. 'They're pack creatures, though, aren't they?'

'Wilf unpacks.'

'You don't think he gets lonely on his own?'

'Possibly. I'm here most of the time.' *New girl Carly wil be with you furst thing, fully loaded. Gud at grout. Janine T xx*, she read now. Why was the name Carly familiar? She squinted at her again, battling another yawn, wishing she'd worked out whodunit in her bedside reading before falling asleep with it pressed to her face at three o'clock.

'You could maybe give her a home?' the girl was saying now. 'I've got pictures on my phone I can show you.' She fished a sparkly smartphone out of her pocket.

Gratefully locating a pair of glasses in a fruit bowl, Petra put them on and found herself looking at something that resembled roadkill.

'Like I say, she's a rescue dog. She'll be coming up for adoption soon, when she's healed. You could rehome her here. You've got loads of space and you're obviously animal lovers.'

Petra could see the girl's face in focus now. 'OhmyGod, you're the girl whose children my horse almost jumped on yesterday!'

'Sorry about that.'

'No, I should be the one to apologise. We came back to look for you. I hope we didn't totally ruin your walk. Were the children terrified?'

'It's fine. We love horses. All animals.' She was mopping energetically, throwing chairs onto the kitchen table as she went, like a publican after last orders. There was nothing to her, but she was Herculean.

Petra moved aside as Carly powered towards her once more. 'By all means give me the details of the rescue dog. We'd love another, as long as it's not a pit-bull or anything terrifying.' Seeing the mop moving towards her, like a swishing jellyfish, Petra hurried to pull on her boots. 'Just popping out to check over the horses.'

'My baby boy loves your little ponies. We say hello through the hedge on the lane.'

'That's sweet. Bring him round to meet them properly.'

Carly loved the house. It was her dream home, although it needed a much better cleaning team than Janine's: there were corners hammocked in spiders' webs, the kitchen kick-boards were a disgrace, and the white goods hadn't been wiped over in many a month. Yet it was the friendliest and huggiest house Carly could ever remember entering. She wouldn't have been surprised if the Muppets came bursting out of the hand-made kitchen cupboard to get the party started. She danced a couple of steps.

'Are you the new cleaner?' A languid blond youth was watching her from the door through to the kitchen, probably no older than sixteen despite nifty sideburns.

'No, I'm burgling the place. Stop walking on my wet floor.'

'I can walk on water.' He padded towards her in artfully mismatched socks, holding up a phone in a pink glitter case. 'This yours?'

She reached to take it, but he snatched it away out of reach and took a selfie. 'Is this model any good? Dad gave me his old BlackBerry when his contract was renewed, but I can't get my head round it. It looks like a calculator and is full of shit. This one is way neater.'

'It's okay.' Carly had got it cheap off one of Ash's cousins.

'You ever use the instant-messaging app?'

'Some.'

'There, I've added my number to your contacts.' He handed over the phone. 'Fitz.'

'Carly.'

'Nice inks. My kid sister's pony has dapples like that.'

Carly tilted her head to look at him irritably. She didn't have time for some precocious teenager practising his pick-up lines on her. 'My husband's got Roman armour tattooed across one shoulder. Spartacus has steelwork like that.'

'Fitz, you're up!' cried Petra from the patio doors. 'Gunny's coming today. I need you to hide the entire top floor of this house. I'm sure you have the technology to cloak it under a force shield or something. Or just pick up all your clothes. Now stop distracting Carla.'

'Lee. Car*lee*,' he corrected fiercely. Then, with a wink at Carly, he melted away.

Janine picked Carly up in her little van just before ten.

'How d'you like the farmhouse? Lovely, yeah? Petra's a doll.'

'It's okay.' She glanced over her shoulder as they drove away, longing to hold onto the heart-lift its messy cheerfulness had given her. Petra had made her two cups of tea, fed her lots of double-choc cookies and told her she was Janine's secret weapon, which she already knew but it was good to hear, especially from someone as smart as Petra Gunn.

'*Such* a nice lady. I bet you thought Catherine Zeta-Jones, yeah? Hubby looks like Jude Law. Hot. Bit bald, mind you.' She turned into the driveway of the stud. 'I usually clean their house personally, but I had business to attend to this morning.'

Cooking the books and drinking one too many cans of Monster, Carly suspected, her eyes stretching wide as they drove up to a house as big as a barrack block. 'Is this place for real?'

'There used to be a back drive for trade, Granddad Norm says, but the old man here sold the land and got denied access so we get the full frontal,' Janine said, as they swung into a big cobbled parking area, already rammed with cars. 'He dropped dead yesterday. Be a bit sensitive. This lot make the Mitchell family look loved up.'

Carly recognised Bay's Land Rover and Flynn the farrier's truck, alongside half a dozen shiny saloons and muddy pickups, and a few rusting farm vehicles.

A chunky little woman, who looked like a pug in a fright wig, hurried up. 'Thank God! There's not a moment to lose. I've made a start in the drawing room where we're receiving well-wishers and officials. I've made the rest of the house off limits, even the toilet, so you'd best start there. The vicar's looking a bit desperate. Do your magic, Janine.' She ushered them in through a side door. Carly had never seen a house so old-fashioned, decaying and unloved. Compared to the bright, fragrant shabby chic of the farmhouse, it was a dark, filthy museum.

Janine assigned herself polishing, maxing her way through the big boxes of pound-shop anti-bacterial wipes and microfibre cloths as she shone up pottery, porcelain, silverware and bronze, discreetly check-ing out the bases for manufacturers' marks, taking a few snaps on her phone of her favourites – 'In case they accuse us of damage,' she told Carly unconvincingly – and then getting out her portable steam cleaner for tricky crevices. Carly, tasked with floors, dusting, de-cobwebbing, airing drapes and washing down white goods, was equipped with an extendable duster, a bucket of bleachy water and a sponge.

Janine's laziness maddened Carly, but the house made her race along in her fastest gear, mopping and waxing and dusting and disinfecting, desperate to bring it back to life.

'It's weird,' Janine whispered. 'All sorts of suits are here, but none of the family have turned up yet. The bigwigs probably just want a good snoop. Bet they never came here when he was alive. Scary old bastard, may God rest his soul.'

Carly recalled Ash telling her that he'd been horse-whipped by the owner. She imagined him as Grinch-like, unloved by anyone except his horses.

But when Alice, the eldest grandchild, arrived, she was a proper swollen-eyed, pale-faced mourner in a black trouser suit.

'Been to the lawyer's,' Janine hissed to Carly, as they cleaned the big hallway. 'Not good news by the look of it.'

The voices rose and fell in the drawing room.

Carly took a cigarette break outside, gravitating towards farrier Flynn, who was sitting on his tailgate in his leather apron with a mug of tea, shaking his bleached highlights to his iPod, like a head-banger at a silent disco.

Flynn was one of Ash's pre-army band of brothers, this one without leadership or discipline. The kids he'd grown up with, now hulking men, were regulars in Carly's sitting room where they gathered to play shoot-'em-up games on the high-tech television, a case of beer within easy reach. Carly liked them more than she'd expected to – gentle, silent Ink, a close relative and Traveller, with his wetsuit of tattoos right up to his chin, was surprisingly courteous and polite; Hardcase, the roadie-turned-plumber, played soulful guitar. Of them all, she found Flynn the most accessible, with his ready smile and cheeky banter. For all his ripped denim rock-star posturing and Tinder love life, he was brilliant with her kids, and beneath the painted leather and carousing, there was a hard-working dad.

'D'you know what's going on round here?' Carly asked him as he pulled the speaker buds from his ears. 'It's well weird in there.'

'Not a clue, sweetlips.' He raked back the Kurt Cobain hair, offering a light for her dying rollie. 'Lester's trap's tighter than a snare on a rabbit leg.'

'Who's Lester?'

He pointed out a tiny wizened figure in a three-piece tweed suit with a black armband herding horses into the stableyard. In their midst was a small, familiar gold rebel, with a blond-streaked Mohican mane, black tail high.

'Spirit!' Carly laughed, running to the gate. With a high-pitched nicker, the colt high-stepped to greet her, thrusting his nose through the wooden cross bars.

'Get a rope on him!' yelled the wizened man.

Flynn was straight over the gate in a move that briefly put Carly in uncomfortably close proximity with his armpit and crotch. The foal charged off across the cobbles.

'Blast and bother!' the tweedy old man cursed, as Flynn laughed, arms lifted in defeat.

Proud of the foal for his anarchic streak, Carly turned to watch a fresh convoy of cars arriving in the yard, including a brace of identikit funeral-director saloons.

'Never known it as busy as this.' Flynn let himself back through the gate. 'Just shows it takes a death to breathe life into a place.'

They were all arriving now. Another Percy-family granddaughter – a jaw-dropping beauty with chestnut hair and a deeply freckled tan – followed by a man in a suit, then a locksmith.

Carly gazed into Flynn's van, transfixed by the furnace and tools, the shelves of freshly forged metal crescents, the pile of old ones below, twisted nails sprouting from them. 'Does it hurt the horses having shoes nailed on?'

'No more than Janine's acrylic jobs hurt you.'

'I don't let her do mine.' She showed him her short-nailed fingertips. The heat was coursing through them again, telling her something. 'Hard-working hands, these.'

'Long nails feel good on your back, sweetlips,' he chuckled.

'Not so great in your balls,' she muttered. 'What's it like as a job then, farriery?'

'Pays well. Good for booty calls. Shit for your marriage. Ash has already turned me down so no point asking, sweetlips.'

'Come again?'

'I've been looking for an apprentice a while now,' Flynn explained. 'Most of the lads are flakes. Ash always was a good grafter and has the Turner knack with neds. I suggested he could learn the trade and we'd make it a partnership eventually. Says he's not interested.'

'He's going to be a personal trainer.'

'More fool him.'

'He reckons the Cotswolds are full of fat bankers who want to look ripped.'

'And their bored pretty wives.'

Dismissing him with an irritated wave, Carly headed back into the house where she found Janine listening in at the closed sitting-room door, leggings straining over a bottom that was twerking with excitement. 'I think they're reading out the will,' she breathed.

A moment later, the door burst open and she leaped away, waving her hand-held steamer at a large wooden sculpture of a bear, sporting a lot of hats, as Pip dashed out with the flame-haired daughter and the red-eyed one in the power suit, who cannoned into the other two when she spotted Janine's cloudy blasts.

'Christ, what *is* that?'

'The cleaner, Mrs Petty. Very professional,' Pip assured her.

'The bear in the hats.'

'Mummy gave it to Grumps for his seventy-fifth,' said the redhead. 'It came from Germany. It's been there ages.'

'She can have it back,' Alice said, with satisfaction. 'Now let's find somewhere quiet to telephone a few more names on this list and break the news. The library.' She opened a door, then backed out as a small, disc-shaped robot shot between her legs.

'It's an electronic floor cleaner,' Janine told her proudly. 'You'll find it's all ready for you.' She beckoned them in, spotting too late that the robot had left more puddles than a new puppy and massacred the Persian rug.

Not that anyone noticed. They all missed a beat as air brakes hissed outside and a horsebox rolled into the yard.

'That'll be Mummy.' Alice clicked her low heels together. 'Better break the news.'

'Let me go,' insisted her sister, who was a head taller and looked at least a decade younger, with remarkable blue eyes that flashed warily as one of the men in suits appeared in the doorway.

'I'm afraid I need someone to sign forms.'

'I'll do that,' snapped Alice. 'You talk to Mummy, Pax. Have we got anything stronger to offer people than tea, Pip? Whatever it is, pour me a large one.' She stomped back in without waiting for an answer.

When the red-haired sister had gone outside, Pip muttered to Janine: 'Have you done the cellar yet?'

'It's next on the list,' the cleaner assured her. 'Carly will go down there while I give the late Captain's bedroom a thorough clean.' As Carly opened her mouth to protest, she lifted a long talon, hissing, 'You're being paid extra for this, remember.'

Carly glared at her, thinking how much more fun it would be to shoe beautiful horses belonging to pretty Cotswold wives, like Petra Gunn.

Ronnie, appalled to find that her horses appeared to have been stuck in their stables for almost twenty-four hours, bit back her anger when she saw how contented and well rested they looked, their beds spotless, coats gleaming from being brushed to best velvet nap. It was a blisteringly hot day, yet inside their boxes it was cool, the back windows all tilted open to let what little breeze was available circulate. The horseflies would be maddening out in the little paddocks at this time of day. She couldn't wait to get them home to the rolling twenty-acre field they shared with her old campaigner Dickon. His was the neck her unwept tears needed to find.

She stooped to feel along the sorrel mare's tendons, which were prone to blowing up like frankfurters after competing. But they were cool and slim as bow strings. Fitting that at that moment a voice as sweet as a cello said: 'Hello, Mum.'

Ronnie looked up to see a silhouette over the half-door, all wild hair and slim shoulders. 'Pax!'

Even grief-stricken, sleep-deprived and sent out on a solo bomb-disposal mission, Pax had a smile that soothed souls.

Ronnie's heart climbed into her throat so that she had no breath. Her voice was a one-note tin whistle when she said: 'Before you say anything, I'm devastated. I love you and I want nothing, *nothing*, from this place.' She hurried out of the stable.

Stepping back, Pax nodded, eyes mistrustful, like a hare's. 'Grumps made that quite difficult. Will you come inside the house?' she entreated.

Ronnie shook her head. 'I'd only wind up Alice.'

'You're probably right. And Pip Edwards now appears to be having the place fumigated.'

'She's very efficient.'

'Grumps insisted he only kept her on because saying, "Tootle pip, Pip" amused him so much, but he depended on her totally by the end.'

They fell silent, riding out a brief swell of grief that gripped them both.

They could hear the farrier's rasp working rhythmically. Ronnie's little dogs raced back from the Big Yard with hoof trims clenched in their teeth.

Pax broke the silence: 'The funeral will be held a fortnight today.' She added quickly, 'If that suits you too.'

'Of course.'

'Alice thinks a small family ceremony best. She's being a bit spiky about you getting involved, but I can calm her down.'

'I'll keep a low profile.'

'I know you probably don't want to talk about the stud and Grumps's will, but—'

'You're right, I don't. It's far too soon.' She snatched up a pair of travelling boots and let herself back into the stable, the voice in her head hissing, *Run, run, run.* Her father was taking control, as she'd known he would, the consequences all-consuming. 'I'm loading my horses.'

'We have to talk about it, Mum. There's no money to pay the running costs here. If we don't sort things out quickly, it spells disaster.'

'Fine.' She strapped boots onto the mare with deft tugs. 'What do you need me to do?'

'Alice saw the solicitor this morning. Grumps has left his entire estate in trust. You benefit from a life interest, which means that you're the only one entitled to profit from the stud and its assets, but you can't sell any of it.'

Ronnie reached for another boot, leaning back as the horse waggled a padded leg. 'How do I give that back?'

'You resign as a trustee, but you have to name a successor or, if not, the other trustees must agree one.'

'Will you do it?' She stepped back outside for the other two boots.

'I already am one – we all are. You're the only one of us with the *life* legacy. That gives you special privileges.'

'Can't I renounce them?' She crouched beneath a shower of hay, attaching front boots.

'It's not that simple. When I say you're the only one with a life legacy, I mean you're the only family member, but there are others to whom Grumps left an irrevocable trust. It confers on them less power, but they're safe for their lifetimes basically, and effectively in our care. Lester's one.'

Ronnie straightened up. 'Of course. Daddy would want him looked after.' Letting herself out, she could hear him buzzing around on the quad bike, herding young-stock back up a field track, making good his escape. They were both frightful cowards. *Run, run, run* urged the voice.

Pax cleared her throat awkwardly. 'It's not *just* Lester.'

'Not the funny little housekeeper, surely.' She moved along to the next stable, stooping for another set of boots.

'No, not Pip, much to her pique – Alice is convinced she wanted to be the next Mrs Percy. There are almost twenty additional life trusts in total individually named in the will. I had no idea he called his broodmares after female politicians.'

'Shirley Williams was his favourite.' Ronnie half sobbed, half laughed as she realised what the Captain had done. 'The silly old fool. Oh, God, Daddy, you had to keep calling the shots, didn't you, even the knacker man's?' She let her gaze run around the empty stables, once filled with a face at every door and a brass name-plate below it, now safeguarded for the care of Maggie, Nancy, Barbara and a host of others. 'Nothing sentimental about breeding, he always said.'

'He's been pretty unsentimental about which bloodlines he wants saved. I've got a copy of his letter of wishes for you to take back with you, along with the will. Not all the mares are listed by any means. The letter's very specific. We all thought he'd lost interest in the horses after Granny died, but he'd been plotting this all along.'

Ronnie pressed her forehead against a warm chestnut knee, breathing. She'd only known his wishes in the broadest terms, never realising just how meticulously he had planned it. *Run, run, run,* the voice in her head screamed.

Pax rubbed tired eyes. 'This place has been losing money for years, so even if the assets weren't frozen we'd be selling off the Wemyss-ware to pay the feed-merchant's bills. It's all complicated by inheritance tax, in theory minimal because as a farm we get agricultural-property relief, but Granny and Grumps split the title a few years ago to release equity from the house and bail out the stud. They only discovered later that doing so might reclassify the house outside the farm, which means it now gets taxed at top rate, as well as there being a mortgage to pay off. Grumps agreed a land deal with the Austens to cover that, the pasture over the lane. They're on the case already. Sandy never lets the grass grow.'

'Hay needs cutting in there anyway.' Ronnie had stopped listening properly, blood drumming in her ears as she led out her little bay gelding to load in the lorry. 'What do I sign to make all this go away?'

Pax followed her. 'Alice wants the trustees to agree to release the house and garden from the trust so that it can be sold as soon as probate is granted. Tim's been on an open line all morning, saying much the same. The family retains the stables, some paddock land, Lester's cottage and the stud business, as Grumps wanted.'

Spitting, spuming magma coursed through Ronnie's veins. Her father's voice roared in her ears: *The house belongs to the stud! You can't rip them apart! It's been in the Percy family since it was built!*

Not trusting herself to speak, she felt those kind hare eyes on her as she crossed the yard with the horse on a loose lead, bounded up into her horsebox with him, clipped on his bungie, pulled the partition across and stalked back out to find Pax waiting at the foot of the ramp.

'Is that what you want, too?' she asked, carefully modulating her anger.

'It doesn't matter what I want, Mum.'

'It bloody does. Don't let them bully you.'

Ronnie watched her closely as she turned to look up at the house, its walls so brightly gold in the sun that they reflected against her beautiful freckled skin.

'I'll go with the majority decision,' Pax said in that reassuringly deep monotone. 'If you support the idea, the solicitor seems to think it's practicable under the terms of the will. Stopping this place going under means thinking fast.'

Ronnie crossed the yard again and fetched out the mare, a high-stepping astronaut in her moon boots, then swiftly loaded her beside her stablemate.

Pax scaled the ramp to help close the side gates, admiring the chestnut over them. 'I like this one.' She'd always had the Percy good eye for a horse.

'You'd suit her,' Ronnie told her. 'No brakes, never falls.' Pax had also been a speed freak across country.

Ronnie knew her daughter was being far too calm. The more panic-stricken Pax became, the less of herself she revealed, internalising everything, that perfect balance always maintained, balletic in mind and stature. It had made her an exquisite rider. Like a great stage actress, the terrible nerves that caused her to throw up for hours before big competitions were entirely subjugated in the saddle, her horses never sensing anything but calm confidence.

'It would help to have your feedback before you go, Mum.'

'This isn't a bloody market-research survey.' Ronnie rubbed her aching temples. 'Sorry. It's too soon, Pax, too awful. He died yesterday.' She scrunched her face up against the pain of acknowledging it all over again. 'It's obscene to be talking about this at all. His body's in some anonymous hospital fridge. This is *his* home. Right now, I don't give a stuff about whatever this bloody trust is all about. And I *don't* want a small funeral. We have to bury him with honours. He threw the biggest parties here once. Loud jazz. Punch so strong you could light it with a match.'

'Granny horse-trading furiously, the more sherries she had.'

From their standpoint on top of the ramp they could see down into the walled garden, hopelessly overgrown now.

'She sold three yearlings to the members of the swing band once.'

'At least one horse was always brought out to jump over the net on the tennis lawn for a bet and one drunk ended up in the carp pond.'

'And one gunshot could be guaranteed before midnight, usually Daddy telling everyone to bugger off home.'

They caught each other's eye, a shared smile snatched from despair and striped with regret: parties attended in different lifetimes.

'I don't care much about the details of any of it either,' Pax admitted. 'I just want him still here. He fought and fought to keep this place going, and after Granny died he needed us really badly, but we were all so bloody busy and found him so hard to like. You weren't even allowed to *see* him.'

Ronnie turned to stroke the white face of her mare, who was prodding her shoulder over the ramp gates. 'I saw him, Pax.'

'When?'

'Three or four times a year. The last time was about six months ago. Awful lunches when he told me what I was expected to do after he died.'

'Which was what?'

Turning to look out across the yard once more, Ronnie watched a swallow swoop into a dove hole in the stone wall to its nest in the eaves. The second clutch of eggs of the summer would be hatching. It always amazed her the way they waved off their first fledglings and laid the next eggs while the nest was still warm, like busy hoteliers turning around rooms.

'He told me it was my job to make this place a commercial success again.'

Aware that his grandchildren would be left with little choice but to sell the stud if it was passed straight to them in its present state, his task was straightforward: *Give them something too profitable to sell, girl. It's your chance to make amends at last. You're the reason it got like this.*

'Could you do that?'

Ronnie couldn't deny the truth of it, however reluctantly voiced. 'Pax, I don't want to come back to live here, and I know you don't want to ask me to. But, theoretically, yes. I could probably turn it round.'

'How quickly?'

'It could take a very long time. And even then there'd be no guarantees.'

Pax sucked her teeth. 'Even supposing we could afford to take that risk, the others aren't prepared to wait.'

'Of course not.' She started down the ramp. 'Daddy was always the gambler. He studied pedigree and form. He was relying on the fact that you're too much of a sentimentalist to want this place broken up, and that contesting a will costs a fortune, which Tim would rule out. That only leaves Alice, and while she would rather sell the house than see me living in it, she's always ultimately done as her grandfather told her.'

'And you?' Pax followed her down.

'I've always done the opposite.' *Run, run, run.*

'And if we all ask you to come back?'

'I'll come back.'

'You have to hang around for just a bit longer,' Pax said, in a strangled voice. 'I need to renegotiate.' She was already running towards the house.

Ronnie sighed, whistling for her dogs. She walked them up into the top pasture fields, hoping she might bump into Lester and bury the hatchet for better or worse, but he'd gone firmly to earth. The broodmares drifted around her with polite, tail-flicking interest, each curved belly containing next year's foal, currently no bigger than a kitten. They were a glossy Munnings oil-painting of perfect sloping shoulders and long necks, her father's keepers by far the cream of the crop. Looking them over, she felt another wash of grief so strong it threatened to take her legs away.

She lit a roll-up, saying a silent apology to her father. If I come back, I will give up. But we both know the chances of that.

Three riders were trotting along the bridleway in the distance, helmet silks bright and bobbled, a woman and two children. Squinting against the sun, Ronnie recognised the kind-eyed brunette from the farm shop and her two little daughters. Such a perfect Cotswolds tableau, which she'd never shared with her own children, their early excursions on lead reins more often overseen by her mother and the nanny while she was out competing. She'd made the big profits then, but that was a long time ago when she'd been young and fearless with no regrets. She was none of those now.

11

When Ronnie walked back onto the yard, dogs bounding ahead, Pax was prowling around the lorry with a mug in her hand.

'I have a proposal. The others have agreed to it because they don't think you'll do it. The door stays open until Christmas.'

'To do what?'

Pax's hare eyes screamed into hers. 'Come back. It took a *lot* of persuading.'

'Pax, I have a life away from this place,' she said carefully.

'And we have a death here, remember? There are conditions attached.'

'I thought there might be.'

'You put up the money. You write a business plan. You don't make any decisions about breeding, selling or anything else without the trust's approval.'

'I can't agree to that.'

Pax looked away, fingernails working against her tea mug like chalk on blackboard, jaw clenched.

'Have it your own way.' She nodded tightly. 'Funeral in a fortnight. No jazz, guns or punch. But it will be big and you will behave.' She found her calm bass note at last, struggling to hold it. 'I'll see you there. I love you too by the way.' Distractedly handing over the mug, she hugged herself tightly, ducking behind the lorry, footsteps retreating.

Smelling Scotch, Ronnie looked down at the innocuous brown tea and almost gagged. Her father had enjoyed two fingers of rare malt every night at precisely yardarm; Johnny, by contrast, had

144

laced everything he drank with it, from his wakeup mug of Tetley's to his cocoa nightcap, with a bottle of Famous Grouse in between.

'My poisoned chalice raises a toast to Captain Jocelyn Percy,' she muttered, tossing its contents away.

Ronnie hurried around the lorry in pursuit of Pax, but she'd already disappeared. In her place, Pip Edwards was parading across the cobbles with a stack of Tupperware containers and an excited smile. 'A little bird tells me you'll be moving back soon!' She thrust her plastic tower at Ronnie. 'I've baked these for you – and Blair – to enjoy. Just a few cupcakes, fondant fancies, tarts and pastries. Call me day or night.' She dropped her voice. 'I had that word with Alice about the grief boat. I think it went down well— Oh, not that one!' She plucked the top box off the pile. 'Where's Lester gone? He was here a minute ago.' She turned to look at a lone wheelbarrow piled with shavings.

'Give me to the end of the drive and you can tell him it's safe to come out.' Ronnie sighed, climbing into her lorry cab with the cake boxes and her two dogs.

'Just call the moment you want a bed made up!' Pip shouted over the engine starting.

As she pulled the lorry round, avoiding Lester's abandoned barrow, Ronnie distinctly remembered her father ranting: 'You've made your bed, and now you must damned well lie in it!'

She glanced across at the house. 'Sleep well, Daddy.'

'Sorry, sorry, sorry I'm late!'

Petra's perfect mother-in-law welcome was blown from the moment she dashed onto the platform at Broadbourne station still wearing her breeches and hairnet to find Gunny sitting irritably on a bench, posting insults about bad timekeeping on Instagram.

Charlie's parents had been separated for at least a decade when his philandering father had suffered an untimely heart attack, but Barbara had adopted the role of widow with such conviction that nobody dared question it, least of all Charlie, who had accepted her claim on his father's estate without a fight. An old-fashioned battle-axe, softened with just the slightest hint of camp and a lot of facial filler, she was now enjoying a high life of holidays, self-improvement, spa treatments and leisure sports, all documented in her blog and on her Twitter feed @GunnPoint. She had carved out an enjoyable life for herself in her beloved Kent. She claimed in her blog to be devoted to her son and grandchildren but, to Petra's relief, that didn't involve seeing them very often. Summer was an exception, and she always set aside at least a week to take up occupancy in the farmhouse annexe and criticise the way Petra ran her home, her marriage and her children. Having been on several expensive writing courses in Mediterranean spa hotels, to which she attributed the quality and popularity of her blog, Gunny was particularly fond of needling her daughter-in-law on literary technique.

Always immaculately coiffured, pearled and suited, Barbara Gunn's Botox and ill humour had conspired to prevent her smiling since the noughties. Dark glasses propped in her expensively streaked bob, make-up immaculate, she regarded her daughter-in-law's appearance with dismay, taking a photograph of Petra to add to her feed. 'Did you fall off?'

'Several times. Dragged by the stirrup across three fields. Had to pop my dislocated shoulder back in. Sorry again.' She offered a kiss on both cheeks, which Gunny took with a chin-back nose-crinkle at the smell of horse.

'I can never tell whether you're joking or not, Petra.'

'I was joking.'

'Sarcasm rarely suffices with a sophisticated audience, I find, and I'm speaking as someone voted wittiest over-sixties blogger three times in a row by *Good Housekeeping* online. They've stopped reviewing your books, I noticed.'

'Everyone's stopped reviewing my books online, Barbara, but that's no bad thing, given social media's largely populated by trolls, egoists and bullies. Thankfully, by some miracle, people are still reading them. Good journey?'

After that, the visit grew even less picture-perfect on the @GunnPoint streams. Having complained non-stop about the sudden heatwave, the strange smell in Petra's car – later identified as an abandoned riding hat – and the state of the house ('Is this what they call shabby chic?'), Gunny settled down in the sun-drenched walled garden to eat a simple lunch of fluffiest home-made smoked-mackerel mousse, pea-shoot salad from Kenneth's veggie plot next door, and the farm shop's poshest artisan horseradish soda bread.

Petra had been confident the food, at least, would pass muster. But the martyred smile said it all.

'What a coincidence! I had the loveliest smoked-mackerel mousse in Seasalter last night. It's Michelin-starred – you can't beat Kent for fish.'

By a cruel (surely not deliberate) twist of Fate, she found a small bone in her first mouthful and staged a Queen Mother choking fit, washed away by Prosecco that she identified in her near-death throes as a sub-fiver Aldi bargain – 'Two stars in the *Daily Mail*.'

'Eat marshmallows, Gunny!' insisted practical Bella. 'Mummy always makes us do that when we get her fish bones stuck. Wait there! I have some in my room.'

'*Once*,' Petra breathed. 'You got a bone stuck *once*, Bella Gunn. A supermarket fishcake. They gave us cinema vouchers when I complained and you asked for those fishcakes every day for a month afterwards.'

Gunny said sweetly, 'Is the marshmallow trick a Yorkshire thing, Petra?'

Why did her mother-in-law always make her feel so inadequate and uncouth and northern? she fumed. And why, as soon as Gunny arrived, did her children become co-conspirators in an all-out campaign to discredit her catering?

Prudie now claimed to have bitten into a minuscule slug on her home-grown salad leaf, pea-shooting it across the table at her sister, who retaliated with a blade of the artisan bread crust as sharp as an arrow tip. Looking up wearily from his phone screen, Fitz – whom Petra had bribed to charm his grandmother with compliments – muttered, 'Gunny, we deserve better than this,' and retreated to his attic room once more.

'Is he worried about his GCSE results?' Gunny asked, taking a close-up shot of the smoked-mackerel mousse, by now a sun-melted slagheap of bony peril subsiding into its cucumber garnish.

Ed coughed into his hand. To a finely tuned mother's ear, the word 'wanking' was just about audible. 'He fancies the new cleaner,' Ed was telling his grandmother. 'She has tattoos and huge—'

'Strawberries!' Petra leaped up to fetch pudding and found a text from Charlie on her phone. *Busy day. Tied up until late. ETA 22.47 train. Cx*

Not for the first time, she closed her eyes to a split-second's collision of literal and imaginative interpretation: her husband in a Chelsea basement in studded-collar bondage, looking up Chiltern Railways train times.

'When's Charlie due back?' Gunny asked, as strawberries were dumped in front of her.

'When he's untied. Madagascan vanilla soft scoop, lime sorbet or fresh cream?'

'Is it whipped?'

'Lightly flagellated.'

At that point, Wilf gambolled winningly across the lawn to Gunny, charm assassin to the rescue with his handsome spaniel smile – 'Charlie's dog really is *such* a sweet chap, isn't he? Just like his master' – and disgraced himself by cocking his leg on her handbag.

Which at least gave Petra the excuse to take him out.

The children had started to play croquet on a striped baize green lawn, their grandmother prowling eagerly around the Pollock-colourful herbaceous borders, snapping photographs of Upper Bagot Farmhouse's contribution to Open Garden Week, lupins fat as loofahs, aliums like lollipop ladies and rambling roses dancing with butterflies.

Chasing Wilf's waggy, stumpy liver and white tail through the orchards, Petra walked to Lord's Brook in his wake, breathing deeply, and ringing Gill.

'Where have you *been* all day?'

'Gunny.'

'Oh, yes. Going well?'

'Probably slightly better than usual. I've only tried three different ways of murdering her so far. None worked, although I got close with cheap fizz.'

'Give it time. You wait until you hear the latest from the stud. This'll take your mind off it. Flynn's just popped into the clinic and apparently the Bolter's been back. Nobody's seen her, but I have it on very good authority she was here *in the village*.'

Petra watched Wilf snaking back and forth in the stream, smiling and bouncing with a tail-wagging invitation to join him. 'Really?'

Ronnie Percy had something quite magical about her, the sort of charm one wanted to keep all to oneself.

'She's bound to be sniffing round the pot,' Gill was saying.

'Or paying her respects to a father she's just lost.'

Gill let out a sceptical harrumph. 'Bay's already let slip the Austens are buying the Sixty Acres by the church meadows. It has the best coverts in Fosse and Wolds' country.'

'That's the field with the cedar?'

'That's right. Bay came to pick up a pony this morning and was full of talk about hunting there before Christmas, but I think this thing has a long legal tail. Oh, he also said he's getting a drone, so make sure you keep your bathroom curtains closed. He was telling Paul it's an MoD-issue super-surveillance one with night vision that can practically take your fingerprints without being heard. Your neighbour Kenneth has a contact apparently. All very hush-hush.'

'Who knew? By day a mild-mannered gardening enthusiast, by night a spy in the sky.'

'Code name Rhododendrone from the Royal Air Squadrone.'

'Ha-ha-ha. His Open Garden's like Waterloo station today. Ours is a ghost town.'

'That's because you've got two of the most off-putting things growing in it.'

'What?'

'Teenage boys.'

At the farmhouse, Fitz had just checked his dad's old phone. Things had hotted up since Fitz's *You bastard* message, which was hardly surprising given the BlackBerry, passed from father to son months ago, still logged onto all its accounts. It meant the sender was displayed as Charles G, and whilst Charlie secretly knew full well what a bastard he was, he didn't like admitting it, even to himself.

Since discovering the app, Fitz had been so filled with hostility that he preferred to imagine he wasn't Charlie Gunn's biological son. The fact that his parents had married several months after his conception had never been a secret. They'd always insisted it would have happened regardless of Petra's pregnancy, but Fitz had his doubts based on years of evidence gleaned at close quarters. He'd also done the maths. He was a Millennium-night creation, conceived the final time his mother partied like it was nineteen ninety-nine. And his current, comforting fantasy was that it had been a party which Charlie Gunn hadn't attended.

Petra Shaw had partied hard through the late nineties among the glittering young publishing set, according to Fitz's funky godmother Pearl. Fitz had read the inscriptions in the books on the landing shelves, many signed by male authors she'd met on the road – rebels of chemical fiction and high-brow concept, edgy music journalists and lad-lit chancers – and decided he was the result of a passionate affair with a secret literary lover, who'd abandoned her pregnant and in need of a father elect. Why else marry a 404 like Charlie, whose favourite authors were Jeremy Clarkson and Dan Brown? She hadn't so much settled down as dumbed down.

Fitz now saw right through his father, picking apart the very fabric of the man and finding not a thread of himself in him: there was no moral fibre. His grandmother was another matter. He couldn't help admiring Gunny's hardball gall, and although he loathed her being such a bitch to his mother, he sensed she would make a far better ally than enemy. She was napping on the sun swing, iPad in her lap on which a photograph of his mother's favourite herb trough was captioned: *All this mint and no Pimm's on offer? It would never happen in Kent!*

He settled beside her, making her start awake.

'Oh, it's you, William.'

'Everyone calls me Fitz.'

'Not everyone, William.' She smiled tightly. 'Have you finished whatever you were doing – er – upstairs?'

He shrugged. Now that he'd checked the app on the phone in his bedside drawer, he could see he'd triggered a bit of a Situation. As he'd suspected, his father coming home late had nothing to do with work.

'Now tell me, William, are you looking forward to your A-level studies?'

'Haven't really thought about it.' Not strictly a lie. A-level studies were no longer on this year's agenda.

From the far end of the lawn came the hard click of croquet mallet against ball and shrill squeal of protesting sister. Ed was loudly changing the rules so that the hoops were time portals into another galaxy, the balls transportation devices for Jedi masters and Rebel Alliance captains, and the mallet a meteor storm.

'I remember your father starting his sixth-form years,' Gunny was eulogising. 'Gunnpa and I were so proud of him, driving him there in the Jag, stopping off for lunch in the Cotswolds as usual – the smart end, near Stow.'

'How long ago was it Gunnpa died?'

'Gosh. Well, it must be, what, eight years?'

'Is it true you were getting divorced?'

For a moment Fitz thought she was going to tell him to keep a civil tongue in his head, but she'd always indulged him, especially when he did his Tom Hiddleston smile.

'Technically, yes, although we really didn't want to and it was all over a silly misunderstanding.'

'Because of his lady friend.'

'Who said that?' The eyes bulged in the stiff face. 'Your mother, I'll bet!'

He shook his head. 'I remember hearing Dad saying it. He said it was the last in a long line.'

'Gunnpa made lots of friends. He was a very sociable man.'

'Like Dad.'

She stared at him, eyes alert. Then, clearing her throat carefully, she asked: 'Is Daddy being... friendly, do you think?'

'I think Dad's being very friendly, Gunny.' Relief at sharing the fear washed over him.

'In London during the week, you mean?' Her voice stayed sing-song bright.

'Yes. And he was quite friendly in Switzerland a few months ago when he flew out for a case.'

'Come here.'

Fitz was pressed to a lavender-scented bosom. 'What do I do, Gunny?'

'Leave it with me.'

Part Two

HARVEST, HOLIDAYS
AND HOMECOMINGS

12

Pip had been up all night baking and googling, perfect insomnia pastimes as she'd long ago discovered, but she hadn't yet unearthed the detective trail she was looking for. She would have carried on searching for clues, were it not for the many early client calls for which she'd baked extra supplies.

Captain Jocelyn Percy's funeral was taking place at midday. Every time she thought about it, Pip felt a little shiver of excitement.

Her kitchen surfaces were rockeries of Tupperware containers filled with all the Captain's favourites: flapjacks, brownies, Bakewell slices and refrigerator cake, all cut into fittingly funereal coffin shapes. And her head was revolving with names, dates and clues that didn't yet match up.

Pip Edwards was the black widow of the world wide web, as merciless in pursuit of the perfect sponge recipe as a married neighbour's profile on discreet dating sites. Unafraid of its darkest underbelly, Pip could look up a hired hitman in less time than it took most surfers to check the news headlines. She often fantasised about setting up her own detective-agency-cum-bakery called Proof.

It was when she'd given up her job to look after her elderly parents that Pip had truly embraced the internet. In much the same way that Alan and Jean Edwards had once marked up the *Radio Times* on a Friday to plan their viewing week ahead, she now had a fixed routine. She had multiple social-media profiles and feeds, and was a long-standing member of manifold chat rooms. She occasionally trolled, but more often flirted, reviewed and advised; she watched lots of YouTube funnies as well as tasteful Tumblr porn GIFs, masturbating with quiet, secret pleasure. She had several dating profiles, none with her own name and a recent photograph attached. Her confidence online was in direct contrast to her diffidence off it.

She liked to think of herself as the village's Wizard of Oz. By day, she might occupy an antiquated world of servants' bells, game soup and afternoon tea in houses with no computers; by night she was on the superhighway in her high-tech bungalow hub, where she led a vicariously modern life through her alter-egos, like Epiphany_1983 on Mumsnet, who had imaginary DDs, DSs and a loving DH, or Piping_Hot_Babe on PistonHeads, who had a penchant for off-roading. She kept a laptop in every room, plus several tablets and two smartphones always at hand. Pip's second phone was what she thought of as her Dark Phone, a pay-as-you-go: she changed its SIM once a month, paying cash to top up at garages so the account couldn't be traced. It was like owning an alter-ego, a telecommunications sports-car that came out on only hot, naughty, top-down days. Not that she ever had those, but she liked to think she was ready.

Feeling unprepared made Pip extremely anxious, which was why she'd just spent a sleepless night digging around in everything from Blair's company records to historic Dutch warmblood pedigrees in search of a clearer picture of Ronnie. The clues still didn't add up, and she felt wholly unrehearsed, the intelligence she had acquired no match to the wit of the Compton Bolter, whose most devilish dog days – and Pip was sure there were many – had left not one tiny bite-mark of data. She still hadn't been able to piece together anything about Ronnie's life during the fifteen years between deserting her marriage and dealing horses in Germany, or much about her life since returning, and how Blair's mysterious older wife Verity fitted in. It was the first case she hadn't cracked in under a week.

Preparing for the sombre day in store, Pip felt highly agitated, her heart artificially palpitated by energy drinks and blue light. Bending down to shave her legs, blood rushing to her head, she nicked her ankles and the shower basin turned red.

With Google on her side, she'd kept track of all the Captain's closest connections like dots on a radar. They were all now converging. It was going to be a very big day. Only one remained under the radar.

Pip had a soap-addict's affection for funerals, especially those seething with high tension and family ill-will. Her parents' ceremonies had been lonely affairs, limp with misery and dulled by poor attendance, but Captain Jocelyn Percy's promised to be a green-and-pleasant-landing spot for the great, the good and the grudge-holders, an old-school roof-raiser. Nobody had told Pip what would happen after today. Lester remained tight-lipped as ever, and she suspected he knew even less than her.

Rubbing anti-dandruff shampoo into her scalp, she hardened her resolve to remain the stud's secret weapon. This week, with Alice texting about funeral arrangements, and Pax calling to check she was okay, Pip still felt part of the family firm, and that gave her consequence. Without the stud, she had very little tangible in her life. Internet chat rooms didn't resound with shouts, barks and racing commentaries or smells of wet dog and open fires. LOL, WTF and emoticons with colons and bracket mouths hardly compared to the triumph of real laughter, the unity of shared rage, or deep tribute of humble gratitude, like the day not long after starting work there when she'd taken Ann Percy her midday sherry and distinctly heard her say: 'What would life be like without you, eh? You are the most devoted and sweet of creatures.'

'Thank you!' she'd whispered joyfully, backing out, her constancy guaranteed.

Some time afterwards, it occurred to Pip that Ann Percy might have been talking to the Labrador at her side, but by then she was all-in for keeps. Right up until their last breath, she'd protected both Percys with fierce loyalty, welcoming allies and seeing off foes, helping Lester on the yard, even cooking Christmas lunch and Easter roast for the grandchildren and great-grandchildren, finding herself, to her delight, at the centre of a big, glamorous soap-opera family for the first time in her life. As soon as its new matriarch was sworn in, she was ready to renew her oath of allegiance. If only Ronnie wasn't so inscrutable, her loyal friends too discreet to speak out of school…

Jittery with caffeine overload, the answer finally came to her. Friendships tessellated. The friends would be friends of friends. There would be a repeating pattern. She stepped out of the shower and hurried to the nearest computer, dripping water and blood everywhere, already seeing the key puzzle pieces. The secret was to find a link between them other than the obvious one.

Pip's Facebook profile was a source of particular joy. Over the course of eighteen months, she'd targeted indiscriminate equestrian stars, media-friendly toffs and local celebrities with requests and now boasted three hundred influential Bardswolds-set friends, only a handful of whom she'd ever met. Getting more big-hitting village friends was her new goal. Some, like novelist Petra Gunn, were tough nuts to crack, with private personal profiles, the open pages produced by a publicist.

At least she *had* a profile, which was more than most of the Percys. Only Pax was on there, and she had just thirty-one friends with nothing posted on her wall for almost a year.

Fingers flicking this way and that on the track-pad, she called up Blair Robertson's groom, whose Facebook posts regularly appeared on her feed along with a lot of inspirational quotes. She scrolled slowly through her friends.

Verney. The family name! A son from Verity's first marriage by the look of it, all checked shirt, big smile and dark glasses. His profile was private, but he had friends in common with Pip. She'd click on to find another corner of the jigsaw.

Several gregarious event riders were very lax in their privacy settings. As Pip scrolled fore and aft through friends' lists, more Verneys appeared. Blair had stolen the queen of a big dynasty, it seemed. Cousins in Kent and Scotland, an uncle in Kenya. One fierce-looking niece – Roo – was particularly high profile, with an army of friends and followers. Here was another Verney. Was this one Verity's daughter? The dates added up. Like Pax, the avatar was a white silhouette with no recent activity and only a handful of friends, all laid bare by an amateur's mishandling of Facebook.

Of those friends, one stood out, her thumbnail a photograph of the most beautiful horse Pip had ever seen.

Verity Robertson.

13

Hoofbeats rang out on tarmac as the Saddle Bags trotted past Compton Magna's small church in the low morning sunlight. Most village alarm clocks had yet to go off, but the air was already heavy with steamed-off dew and warm pollen. The heatwave was now in its third week. High in the VIP zone of the graveyard, matting had been laid out around a deep, open rectangle, an artificially green carpet compared to the drought-bleached grass.

None of the women needed to ask who was being buried. The Captain's funeral was a Bardswolds headline event. Rumours had been flying all week that royalty would be there.

'Anybody else going to the actual service?' Gill asked sombrely. 'Do you think we should wear hats? One doesn't want to look too much like a principal mourner, but I do have a rather splendid black fascinator that's only seen one wedding. What do you think?'

There was a sticky silence, the other Bags uncertain how to react to an NFI to a funeral.

'From the sound of it, a crash helmet might be best.' Petra longed to be a fly on the wall for research purposes.

'And riot shields,' huffed Mo, hurt that her elderly parents had also been left off the guest list, despite farming and hunting alongside the Captain for a lifetime.

Bridge just smelt the free booze. 'Worth it if the Life Hackers are there to get the after-party going. I'm going to disguise myself as a pallbearer.'

'You've always said you can't bear Paul,' muttered Petra, winking.

'Genius!' Gill's funny bone was tickled enough to abandon the pious face. 'Paul's driving me *mad*. He's so excited about rubbing shoulders with the Windsors, I almost convinced him to shave off the Schnauzer' – it was her nickname for her husband's much-loathed beard – 'but all he's done is trim it with my ruddy nail scissors. He says it's Shakespearian, but he just looks like Noel Edmonds.'

'Ew.' Bridge gave her a pitying look. 'Is that why your scarecrow was a seventies throwback?'

'The checked flares were proper *George and Mildred* vintage,' chuckled Mo.

'Mum got decades of dog-walking out of those golf trews,' Gill insisted. 'Never throw out anything with wear in it, and certainly not to village jumble. You never know where you'll see it next.' She gave Petra a told-you-so look. 'What was it your mother-in-law said in her blog?'

'*A murder of crows could not have been louder than the patterns on show in "Open Wardrobe Week" as it was known in the Gunn household*,' Petra recited, her unwanted impulse buys having found their way from the summer fête's nearly-new stall onto half a dozen exhibits in the village's hotly contested scarecrow parade.

'Brilliantly evil.'

Gunny had been as remorseless as anticipated, her most recent blog a predictable metaphor for her disappointment in her son's marriage, much of it devoted to veiled suggestions that her daughter-in-law should make more effort physically.

Petra gave a gallant smile. 'My favourite was: *When a woman calls the weeds in her flower-bed "organic", you can guarantee she's not a regular at the waxing salon.*'

The Bags lined up in front of the winning Open Garden Week display, still on show at Wishing Well Cottage, crafted by enthusiastic weekenders. It featured the entire royal family, including George, Charlotte and three dorgis, all in flat caps or knotted headscarves.

'If an HRH really is coming to the village today, d'you think they're quite the thing?' Mo fretted.

Gill looked aghast. 'They should jolly well get rid of them.'

'The Webbs are in Corsica for the rest of the summer,' said Petra, who knew the family.

'Second-homers on third holidays, lucky things,' Bridge grumbled. 'I get a week's camping in Wales with Poland's most argumentative tent constructor.'

'More than I get,' sniffed Mo. 'If I take more than a day off, Barry hands me a dust sheet and a pot of paint. Gill's going on a cruise.'

'It's a narrowboat on the Norfolk Broads, and it's hardly luxurious. Not like Petra's fortnight in a Tuscan villa.'

The other three Bags levelled accusing looks at her.

'With four children and no WiFi,' she reminded them, receiving a round of unsympathetic hums. 'And Charlie.' The hums softened in commiseration.

Passing the Old Almshouses, with its wide, pretty face and tall barley-sugar twist chimneys, they all looked out eagerly for signs of life. Kit Donne's was among the prettiest façades in the village.

'He's taking his play to New York soon,' Gill said. 'We saw it on National Theatre Live at the cinema. *Very* way out and political.'

Petra suspected Gill found most comedies not set in the Home Counties and starring Celia Imrie way out and political.

'That garden is distinctly stripped back.' Gill tutted at the withered brown grass and weeds surrounding the house. 'It was so pretty when Hermia was alive. Hollyhocks as tall as Maasai.'

'Let's *please* not try to lead this whore to culture again.' Bridge groaned. 'I don't do flowerbeds, just flowers then bed, preferably with a romantic movie and a three-course meal in between.'

Gill laughed. 'Hermia would have approved of that. Before the accident she was the bubbly, hospitable one. Their old house – now yours, Petra – was always awash with visitors. She loved her parties and plays. Terrible waste of a life.'

'Were her injuries very bad?' Petra asked. She knew very little about the woman whose death had coincided with the Gunns' arrival in the village, except that she'd been invalided in a traffic accident while riding several years earlier.

'That's the awful thing about head injuries.' Gill's usually stern face twisted with rare compassion. 'Her body was still capable of everything it had done before the accident. It was her brain function that was impaired. She had to learn to walk and talk all over again. She had a bucket list that the Austens were always banging on about – I think they came up with it, actually – run a mothers' race at school, perform a Shakespeare speech on stage and ride a horse again. It should have been heroic, but she didn't manage any of it. Some people who've had very big brain traumas like hers can change personality completely. It's like a having a stranger in your midst, not like an amnesiac who simply can't remember, but somebody who sees things totally differently. Old friends found it very hard being around her. She became a complete recluse eventually.'

'How awful.' Petra couldn't bear to think of her own family enduring that. 'So hard on her children.'

'And on poor Kit,' Mo chipped in. 'Seven years, he cared for her. Totally ran out of money. When Hermia died, her brother, Sandy, had to pay for her funeral.'

They clattered on, the clang of hoofs on tarmac soon softening to hollow thuds on hard turf as the riders slotted their horses single file through the narrow opening by the gate to the church meadows.

Trying to stop the Redhead racing, Petra was still thinking about Kit Donne, her *Black Beauty* storytelling reflex starting to twitch, pity heightened. The man who'd once owned her family's home always cut such a lonely, romantic figure, perfect for a fictional reinvention as a widowed Squire Gordon, intensely intelligent and soulful.

'*Fuuuuuuck oooooooooff, yooooooooou waaaaanker!*' Kit shouted at the rear-view mirror, head bobbing to the CD Orla had bought him, a band called Chairlift, which he hoped wasn't a subconscious dig at the decades he had on her.

On the fast lane of the M40, he was being flashed repeatedly by a dusty green Range Rover as he stuck rigidly to the speed limit, slowly creeping past a long line of middle-lane hogs.

'*You* might not have twelve points on your licence and a magistrates' hearing next week to determine whether you'll be banned or not,' he told the rear-view mirror furiously, 'but I do, so BACK OFF!' The last time he'd driven into the Bardswolds, a Gatso camera had caught him overtaking a horsebox and maxed out his driving endorsements; he had no intention of upping the ante by doing a ton on the fast lane days before his court date.

Losing his licence, a lawyer could argue, would make Kit's professional life untenable. But Kit saw no point in fighting a ban. At the precise moment his case was due up in court, he would be flying to America for several months, his need for his own car non-existent. A short driving ban was immaterial.

And he hated driving. It brought out the passive-aggressive in him. As did synth-pop. He turned up Chairlift and thrust his middle finger up as the Range Rover filled his rear window with its snarling grille and dotty rows of cartoon-eye Xenon lights. 'I *said* BACK OFF!'

Today he was late lunching with old friends in Stratford, detouring first through the Bardswolds to visit Hermia's grave, as he'd promised their children he would, his Lughnasa quarter of the year. His heart plunged as he dropped through the Chiltern Gap. His two worlds had never been further apart. Early this morning, when he'd peeled himself away from Orla's naked body to undertake this journey for the second time in as many weeks, torn between booty call and duty call, he realised the love affair, while still secretive and far from cerebral, was starting to bed in, her hotel room barely slept in, her stay in the UK extended so they would travel to New York together to start rehearsing. Kit was mainlining testosterone.

'Taking the elixir of youth from a woman in search of a father figure is *so* Roman health spa!' Ferdie had laughed, when Kit reported how high his energy levels were.

His diet of coffee-shop paninis had gone overnight, his after-theatre life of early hours salons in boozy private members' clubs had been traded in for unprecedented amounts of sex, her sense of humour siphoning helium bubbles to his head. They laughed a ridiculous amount.

The moment they parted company, that balloon popped. Driving on his old home run now, the placebo of physical infatuation melted on his tongue leaving a bitter taste. No matter how he sugared it, she was closer in age to his children, their life stages decades apart.

He switched the car stereo gratefully to Radio Four.

The crowd he was meeting at the RSC today were all his generation, old friends who had known Hermia well, and for whom a new relationship so clearly led by the groin might seem like a betrayal, if not to the wife he'd mourned for half a decade, then to the peer group he now looked beyond to find sex and companionship. To his relief, Orla had shown no interest in coming with him, claiming Chekhov's sentimentality left her cold. Kit was grateful she matched his desire to keep their relationship under wraps, its novelty best eaten from one bowl with two spoons.

Theirs was a love affair tailor-made for New York, where he could bury himself in work and young company, his focus on inspiring her to pull out the performance of a lifetime. Threading his way through motorway traffic to the Bardswolds and his long-since empty nest for a Celtic anniversary had started to feel more staged than his work. His need for patterns and ritual was an addictive prop like the cigarettes he'd recently quit. Samhain, his autumn's end ritual, would come bang in the middle of his New York run. He was already debating whether to fly back for it.

Lights flashed behind him, the Range Rover harrying him on. Still steadily overtaking a long line of middle-lane traffic, Kit glanced in his mirrors. Behind its wheel, he could just make out the driver's crisp white shirt collar and a glint of dark aviator glasses, the passenger's blonde hair alongside.

He stamped repeatedly on his brake to make the bastard back off. It inched aggressively closer.

Kit raised a hand in despair at the stupidity of it all. He wasn't about to get hurt at high speed for the sake of principle. Flicking on his indicator, then sliding across into a small gap between cars in the middle lane, he glared out of his side window as the off-roader drew alongside. The blonde in the passenger seat glared back. Kit did a double-take and her blue eyes widened in recognition.

It was the harridan whose horsebox had probably cost him his licence. Not content with parking on his keys afterwards, here she was again, hollow-cheeked, cigarette in hand, black pearls at her ears and throat, travelling in a car that was trying to drive him off the M40.

The Range Rover swept past. Countryside Alliance, horse trials and Game Fair window stickers taunted him from the tailgate.

'Tis in my memory lock'd and you yourself shall keep the key of it. It could stay locked there.

*

Kicking down the brake on the double buggy, Carly looked at her split old Dunlops, which she'd bought with Ash to go to Glastonbury the first year they'd been together, now as worn down as bald tyres. They'd seen more action in the last year than they had in the decade before it.

Her sixteen-year-old self, striding through the mud to see the Manic Street Preachers, had walked so tall beside her handsome sex bomb soldier with his Daniel Craig body, mile-wide smile and eyes fixed only on her. A decade on, Fusilier Turner still lit Carly's touch paper, but having kids meant her thumb was always on the fire extinguisher, and Ash kept the dynamite deep inside, his body thrown over the grenade to protect his family. He was sleeping less and less. Having gone to bed alone the previous night, Carly had awoken before five to find herself a hot sandwich filling between husband and elder son, both of whom had crept silently in to join her in the early hours, one small, naked and smelling of baby-wipes after a bad dream had made him wet the bed, the other in the same joggers he'd worn all week, having sat up half the night with his console, focus as unswerving as it had been when crossing Helmand Province at night in an armoured personnel carrier.

She handed her smartphone to Ellis. 'Stay here with the pushchair and play Crossy Roads for five minutes. I want you where I can see you.' Not that spotting him was hard these days. He'd become so attached to his 'Splorer Stick that it went with him everywhere. A small boy carrying an extendable multi-coloured fluffy duster was easy enough to track.

Carly squeezed through the gap in the hedge and sidestepped her way along the narrow divide between it and the paddock fencing until she reached the place where the lower rail was broken and she could slip beneath it, staying crouched low to avoid the electric wire that ran around it to keep the horses' noses off.

He was at the far end of the field, huddled up with his older brothers and cousins beneath the shadow of the big cedar tree there, all eyes watching a quartet of distant horses being ridden through the wildflower meadow where the stone circle was.

If any of the army wives had suggested to Carly when she'd moved here that she'd get a crush on a horse, she'd have told them

Jake Gyllenhaal would need to grow two extra legs and a tail. Now she counted down the hours to her breathless secret mint liaisons. She visited him almost every day, a clandestine meeting with the one living being that quickened her heartbeat more than any other.

'Hello, beautiful,' she breathed.

Recognising her, the colt threw up his golden head with a shrill whinny, tangled, pale-tipped forelock sliding across his blue eye. He flicked it away, like a boy-band member irritated by his on-trend hair, sauntering over to thrust his nose at her pockets. His siblings no longer crowded in, accustomed to being chased away by their dominant thug of a baby brother.

'Hello, Spirit.'

The colt dropped his head blissfully as she scratched around his ears, pushing his poll against her hands, demanding more.

'YOU!' a voice shouted behind her, making the colt shy away. 'This is private land!'

She turned slowly. It was the tweedy little man she'd seen buzzing around the stud's fields on a quad bike or riding past the Orchard Estate in a flat cap. Striding towards her on foot, he was barely five feet with a pronounced limp, but no less ferocious. A little dog raced ahead and stopped to bark at her. Behind her, the colts all moved forwards, snorting with interest.

'What are you doing here?' he shouted, his eyes tiny dots in raisiny creases beneath the brim of his cap.

'There's no harm,' she said, boldly enough to let him know she wasn't a lowly serf about to throw herself at his shiny boots – and they were *very* shiny. 'I like seeing the horses.' She reached back, feeling Spirit's nose butt straight into her open palm, a warm breath blasting across it.

'You're trespassing.' Under his flat cap, he had the deepest dimple grooves and wrinkles she'd ever seen, a very white moustache, and those dark, crease-framed eyes had a milky cataract gleam. He obviously couldn't make her out clearly, limping a lot closer before the wrinkles tightened into a squinting frown. 'I might have guessed. I recognise you from the estate. You hang around the field gates here. Are you a Turner?'

'I'm Carly.'

'Carly, you're trespassing.' He sounded like Alan Sugar's country cousin.

'I just came to see Spirit. What's the harm?'

'If you're referring to that little wall-eyed dun, the harm is that Compton Magna Top Gun is a very valuable young horse.'

'Is that his name, then? Bit of a mouthful.'

'Tom for short.' He bristled, clearly not wanting to engage, but too polite not to answer a direct question.

'I get it! Like the old movie? *Top Gun*, Tom Cruise.'

He was shooing back the other yearlings and two-year-olds, all crowding closer now. 'It's a modern film about pilots, I believe.'

'I wasn't even born when that came out.' Like Social Norm, the old boy thought all movies after *Where Eagles Dare* were modern. 'It's proper vintage, trust me.'

'If you say so.'

'Watch my lips.' Grinning, she mouthed *So*.

The man glared at her impatiently. 'Watch for an apology, I hope. Now these colts aren't handled, so for your own safety I suggest you walk very slowly towards the gate while I keep them here.'

Carly stood her ground. Behind her, Spirit – a.k.a. Tom – rested his whiskery black chin on her shoulder and let out a long sigh, regarding the tweedy man with his wall eye. 'I usually talk to him for a bit. Tell him stuff.'

She could hear a drone flying somewhere nearby, although she couldn't see it.

The rest of the colts edged towards her for safety. The old man looked at her for a long time, the milky gaze moving from head to head in the little herd, finally settling on Tom again, his white face watching him from under Carly's arm now as she scratched along his scraggy mane.

'How often do you come here?'

'Once or twice a week, maybe.' She played it down.

He nodded tersely. 'Stop feeding them and I'll turn a blind eye.' He trudged off to check the water trough, terrier at his heels.

'Not much choice there,' Carly muttered, feeding Tom a mint.

'I saw that!' the man shouted, not turning around.

She grinned.

'Tom.' It didn't really suit him, this leggy golden athlete with his odd eyes and shock of highlighted black hair. Carly thought he was more of a Ronaldo or a Nadal... or Spirit.

She pocketed the rest of the Polos as she crossed back over the field with him marching alongside, chatting to him about her day, unafraid of him dancing around her, like Billy Elliot, all heels and spins, head-bobbing, nipping at her sleeve and demanding more mints. Carly knew he was just as much a kid as Ellis. He tried to block her way as she reached the broken rail, like a bouncer.

She laughed, shooing him aside and climbing under. 'I've gotta get my wages. Buy you more mints. Take these kids to see a very special dog.'

She gathered them now, pushing the buggy back onto the lane and on towards Manor Farm, riding out a tantrum from Ellis, who was furious to be separated from her phone, a bad night's sleep making him hugely crabby. The 'Splorer Stick was thwacked angrily against verges and hedges.

'We're going to see Pricey this morning,' she reminded Ellis, to cheer him up.

The 'Splorer Stick was waved triumphantly in the air, his foot-stamping, air-punching dance of pure joy making her laugh afresh. Life always seemed so much better after seeing Spirit. Or Compton Top Gun, a.k.a. Tom.

A drone buzzed around overhead as the Saddle Bags crossed the last flat stretch of the church meadows at a brisk trot, sending up butterflies.

'I bet that's Bay Austen's.' Gill looked up at it disapprovingly. 'It's supposed to be helping him catch poachers.'

'He'll tire of it quickly enough,' Bridge assured her. 'The one Aleš bought off eBay to check out gutters and chimneys, he listed again a month later. Let's face it, ladies, all men are the same with flying robots, toy cars or beautiful women – if they can't get inside it, they soon get bored.' She waved up at the drone. 'Bay's probably spying on Petra.'

'Don't be daft,' Petra scoffed, tossing her head with a self-conscious flourish, like an eighties Timotei advert.

Mo kicked her cob to keep up with them, her tell-me-more voice breathless: 'Didn't I see you and Bay being *very* friendly at Pony Club Camp this week?'

This was news to Petra, who'd dropped off Bella and pony at indecent speed, her week an even more complicated taxi-run of family assignations than it was in term-time.

'Now I think about it,' Mo closed one eye, remembering, 'Briony, who runs the game cookery school over Broadbourne way, has a look of you about her. Awful laugh.'

'At least she sees the funny side of life,' Petra said snappily, convinced Bay had already tired of her, wishing she felt more relieved. He hadn't texted her in almost ten days. Meanwhile her husband had sent her just three short messages from London this week, which read: *Have you remembered my BASC sub?* followed by *I'll need my prickly heat ointment in Italy* and *Don't forget I need a new strap on*, which had caused a brief flurry of drama until he'd added my *prescription goggles. Sent too soon.*

The wildflowers in the church meadows had burned to sepia, jewel-headed and adrift with dandelion clocks, its hedgerows bloodshot with red poppies, the track cracked. Even this early in the morning, the colts that had been turned out in the shorn hayfields crowded in the rotating shadow of the huge Percy family cedar. Beyond the almost-dry brook, grain was being volleyed into trailers as a combine harvester shaved Manor Farm's wheat. The Bags waited until the huge convoy were at the furthest end of the field before taking the track that ran along the far side of Lord's Brook down to the sweet chestnut woods, breaking into a bargy race to get there before the machinery turned.

'Slow trot!' Gill ordered, alert to the concrete ground and the deafening haze of harvest. 'Wasn't Briony the one whose husband ran off with the male au pair? Or was that Leonie the caterer? She's another favourite of Bay's. All the locals get her in for parties now. I best she's doing the funeral.'

Petra was illogically peeved that so many cooks were muscling in on her Safe Married Crush. He obviously had a food fetish. She eyed the stubble hopefully, calling forwards, 'Pipe-opener?'

'Ground's like concrete.' Gill held up her John Wayne hold-hard arm. 'We'll canter in the woods.'

Bay Austen's deep dark woods, Petra reflected as the Redhead danced in anticipation on Bay Austen's track in Bay Austen's field, the spectacular views ahead his children's inheritance, along with those devilish blue eyes. He was the classic philandering village cad; her most adored fictional heroes were his forefathers, their quick wit and cruel charm deflowering virgins and making married mistresses swoon. Theirs was no more than the silliest flirtation, but Charlie's cold shoulder was so much easier to bear when her phone chirruped with a throwaway joke and a *Bx*, especially in a heatwave.

Italy will make it all better, Petra told herself firmly. She and Charlie always relaxed and made friends on holiday. Gathering their children close would be a bonus too. They hadn't sat down together as a family since Gunny's censorious visit, during which Charlie had returned from London to race round Open Gardens Week faster than a gadfly. He'd been devoting himself to an alumni cricket tour ever since, the annual fortnight of uninterrupted family holiday time highlighted in his diary like a rare foreign assignment.

As the Redhead cantered sideways, desperate to go faster, Mo and the cob jogged to keep up, both steaming now. 'You all packed for the holiday?'

'Next on the list.' Too late for the beach-body diet now. Petra hoped her tankini would still roll on.

'Still pretending you have an 'usband?' The *Carry On* chuckle. 'You can take mine if you like.'

Petra rolled her eyes. Like cantering, Italy couldn't come fast enough.

Like gazing at a Magic Eye book to see the hidden pictures, Pip could discover a lot about Ronnie by studying Verity Robertson's historic Facebook profile. Hair still wrapped in a towel, she scrolled down through a decade of Wiltshire country life in the spin of a mouse wheel.

Blair's wife had once been a regular contributor, posting all manner of silly shares, family snaps and horsy high jinks. Once deeply involved in the upper echelons of eventing she, like Ronnie, owned horses and the two knew each other socially, becoming near neighbours in Wiltshire after Ronnie's return from Germany. At the time, Verity had uploaded regular pictures featuring an unruly middle-aged group at parties or in sponsors' tents, Ronnie invariably at the side of handsome men in bright trousers. Craggy sexpot Blair occasionally smouldered in the background.

Pip quickly deduced from her status updates that Verity had a drink problem, her detective eye spotting the increasingly random thoughts, clumsy typing and forgetfulness, the way she often repeated herself. This grew worse as her timeline progressed, misspelling names, taking offence at innocent jokes and posting long, rambling reflections on her glory years, accompanied by photographs scanned upside down. A sudden about-face on foxhunting had caused great upset from almost all quarters of her country-set crowd, apart from Roo Verney the fierce-looking, media-savvy niece in the Cotswolds, whose flat-nosed avatar pic cropped up regularly to entreat Verity to join her in direct action.

Three years ago, having apparently barely ridden since a broken back a decade earlier, Verity had announced to Facebook friends that she was looking for a horse *for my seventieth year!* Then there had been a muddled gush about why old horsewomen should never hang up their boots. The post garnered a forget-me-not bed of blue 'likes' beneath it and plenty of suggestions of nice steady hunters.

Stop sending me plods! she'd beseeched. *I want to sit astride the world.* She ranted at all but the likers. A flurry of excited posts followed shortly as the perfect beast was identified. *When a dealer doesn't want to sell me a horse, I know it's good!*

That dealer had been Ronnie and the stallion in question was a world-beater on paper. His pedigree was German royalty, Verity reported delightedly to her friends, his track-record ground-breaking before injury had side-lined him to stud where he'd never settled. Cast back into a quieter working life now, he'd come sound in body if not mind.

This chap's the one!!! In UK already. Pract next door! Unwanted gift!! Verity had written, exclamation marks and sobriety in inverse proportion, it seemed.

Ronnie had clearly driven a hard bargain, Verity's many updates grumbled that the horse was being aimed at professional studs.

Then, *As ev one here nos, am marred to stud. Thanks to Blair deal done!!!* Cue more blue likes and plentiful good-luck comments. Her profile picture then changed from that of a florid-cheeked ageing beauty to a horse.

The stallion, who was called Beck, was supermodel photogenic, as his dedicated album on Verity's timeline proved, whether the photos were glossy studbook shots taken in Holland or the ones his indulgent new owner had snapped on her iPad when he arrived one snowy day in February, jumping straight out of his stable, charging off and ending up in a field of lambs where he stayed happily for five months. A tableau of idyllic field shots ensued until the lambs went to slaughter.

The photographs on Verity's increasingly scant timeline had then switched to injury close-ups – bite-marks, bruised ribs, blackened legs, a broken nose, all wonkily snapped on her iPad and accompanied by occasional self-deprecating one-liners so cryptic Pip guessed she had to be permanently pissed. There were no likes beneath these. Beck was a psycho. Concerned comments from friends ranged from *Send him back* to *Sue the dealer!*

Verity hadn't replied. All she'd shared in the past two years was one John Lewis Christmas advert. There had been nothing for the past six months.

All of which led Pip to one conclusion.

Ronnie Percy had sold her lover's ageing, alcoholic wife a horse assassin.

14

Ronnie rarely entertained second thoughts, but looking across at the man driving her too fast along the Broadbourne road, his profile Easter Island stone, she felt the rare frisson of uncertainty she experienced on riding a horse whose track-record was full of Fs and Ps for falling or being pulled up. Hers was a wildcard choice.

'I booked the best suite this time.' Blair swung the big car into Le Mill's grand entrance.

'I told you I'd rather to go straight home after the funeral.' She'd need her dogs and horses.

Despite many offers of an arm to lean on, today was one Ronnie had set out to tackle alone, the escort who had stepped into the fold at the last minute not entirely of her making, a very single-minded man for a married one.

'You need me more than anybody right now,' he'd told her.

She couldn't deny it. But she didn't want to make a hotel stay of it. 'I need a getaway driver, not a spa break,' she said, as they parked in front of the neat lavender borders.

'You'll be shattered afterwards.'

'I'm toughened glass.' She'd need her own door to close on this, her dogs and horses, nobody there to witness the cracks.

Bowie's *Low* was playing, and Blair let the engine tick as the final track reverberated with saxophone melancholy. One chocolate eye was on her. 'At least give yourself the option, Ron. It's your dad's funeral. Trust me, it doesn't pay to hard-arse it.'

Blair had lost his own father young, Ronnie remembered. She could imagine the flinty Aussie kid refusing to cry, bottling it up, so like her own children watching Johnny's coffin lowered. The neap tide of grief was already rolling back in, a moon-mad force of nature.

'Full fathom five thy father lies,' she looked out across a flat blue millpond, 'his aqualung was the wrong size.' The silly reinvention of a beautiful couplet, first told her by Hermia, had once delighted Ronnie. Yet today she could see only the pearls that were the Captain's eyes, her heart anchor heavy.

'*Our little life is rounded with a sleep.*' Blair's bone-dry voice was more suited to whooping a horse over a fence, but he knew Bard and Bowie were her comforters.

Ronnie tilted her face to look at him gratefully. 'Daddy had no truck with Shakespeare, although he enjoyed the battle scenes in Olivier's *Henry the Fifth*. "Once more into the breeches" was the family hunting-days motto for years, and *to horse, you gallant princes!*' Her eyes rested on the pond, hearing her father's sharp bark, the elevation of horse above human. '*When I bestride him, I soar, I am a hawk: he trots the air; the earth sings when he touches it; the basest horn of his hoof is more musical than the pipe of Hermes.*'

'Beats Whyte Melville.' Blair's strong hand encircled hers, his thumb pad deep in her palm, a lover whose touch went into her soul on days like this, but Ronnie sensed it was wrong to have brought him along.

'I don't think you should come to the church, Blair. I can't make this any tougher on my kids than it already is. Alice has a hound's nose for infidelity.'

'I'm not letting you go through this alone.'

'We'll only set tongues wagging.'

'They've always wagged, mate.' His dark eyes were indignant, face all angry angles. 'We've known each other almost forty years and I'm your jockey, so let them say what they like. Your dad never held back.' A defiant smile broke cover. 'Told me once that I ride like a gaucho and design cross-country courses for race riders. He always insisted you couldn't build a decent track without a coffin, so the least I owe his is a nod of respect.'

★

Riding into the loamy cool of the woods, the Saddle Bags scaled the steady, humus-carpeted slope up to a run of old jumping logs.

Gill cantered alongside Petra, their horses jumping abreast. 'I have a favour to ask before you get too embroiled in flip-flop finding. Can you use your charms on Pip Edwards at the stud do later? She'll have the heads-up on what's happening there.'

'I hardly know her. And gate-crashing a do is not on my to-do list.'

'Think of it as your duty to the village. Everyone's invited. If you're worried, you can be my plus one.'

'Given the number of hunting and shooting boffs who'll be there, you should have plus fours.'

'Love it! But you're the only Gunn I need,' Gill insisted. 'The Percys are terrible blockheads. If the family decide to sell up, developers will be crawling all over the buildings in no time. Pip was in the Captain's confidence and we both know she's still dying to chum up with Compton's writer in residence.'

'I am not your Mata Hari.'

As sweet as the baked goods she was perpetually gifting, Pip had zealously pursued a friendship with Petra the previous year, her sights set on writing a Cotswolds-based erotic detective mystery, featuring cake recipes and an alien-abduction ending. Too kind to say no, Petra had spent a long time extricating herself from the alliance.

'I've only just shaken her off,' she grumbled, as they pulled up at the top of the rise, both riders determinedly hiding how breathless they were. 'Please don't ask me to be a fake friend.'

'It's an act of kindness.' Gill dished out mints. 'You're good at reassuring people. Pip's bound to be worried. The stud's future is everything to her, as it is to us all in Compton Magna. She'll know what's going on – she's cleverer than she makes out and always has her finger on the digital pulse.'

'Charlie's coming back on an early train to get in the holiday mood.' Petra fed a mint down to the Redhead as a shout behind made them turn to look back along the forestry track to see Mo's cob still stubbornly refusing to jump the first log while Bridge had careered off into the trees.

'It'll all be over long before then. Funeral's at noon – a few of us are meeting up beforehand in the Hare to raise a toast.' Gill pressed harder. 'Bay will be there.'

'You warned me off him!'

'Only because he so obviously fancies you.'

Petra was shamed by the rush of joy she felt.

'Consider the warning lifted for twenty-four hours. What harm can it do? You're hardly going to get off together at a funeral.'

Oh, how sexy would that be amid the starchy, black-tie formality?

'Absolutely not.' She straightened up, focusing on the Tuscan pool that was waiting tomorrow, as blue as a Lothario's eyes, sun hotter than his lips on her cheek. She envisaged cicadas, cypresses and the Chianti-fuelled annual marital-sex lifeline, a fortnight of rest and happiness and feeling just slightly desirable. Her Safe Married Crush on Bay, a strictly term-time distraction, could travel safely as light luggage. Figures moving along the path just beyond the trees made the Redhead shy back.

'Sorry,' a voice called.

Recognising Carly and her buggy jogging back from the farm shop, small boy charging in their wake, Petra waved. 'Hello!'

Carly waved back shyly and hurried on, while her son came crashing through the bracken to take a closer look, brandishing a fluffy duster.

He stopped at the tree line. 'You have big arses!'

'I beg your pardon?' Gill gaped at him.

'Are they race arses?' His accent was strongly shires.

'No, they're pleasure arses, I mean horses.' Petra leaned down to him, loving his *Just William* thatch of black hair, silver eyes and scattering of freckles. 'What's your name?'

'Ellis Peter Turner. I'm four. I like your arse best. Can I pat him?'

'Her. Yes. Best put the duster down first.'

'It's a magic 'Splorer Stick.'

The Redhead patiently endured a battering of small palm against shoulder, chest and nose.

'Hello there.' Gill addressed Ellis from on high, her kindliest tone so authoritarian it made him cower against a tree trunk, like William Tell's son with the apple on his head. 'And what are you up to?'

In the woods, his mother called him back, shouting that they were going to miss the bus if he didn't hurry up.

'We're going to see Pricey! She's beautiful. Best day ever!' He picked up his fluffy duster and crashed off.

'Amazing how popular Katie Price is,' Petra marvelled, as they waited for the others to catch up. 'I'd kill for her book-signing queues. *And* she's horsy.'

'She's a dog,' Gill said dismissively.

'Don't be such a snob. She's one of us.'

Gill cast a withering look. '"Pricey" is a bull-lurcher that boy's mother pulled from a hedge. Nasty business.'

'Of course,' Petra remembered guiltily. 'Carly told me. She wants us to adopt it. Charlie says no.'

'Don't,' Gill warned, glancing up as the drone buzzed its way back into sight. The other two Bags, ambling up deep in conversation, broke off to look up at the drone too.

'Bloody Bay! I hate the things.' Gill shook her fist at it, then checked her watch. 'Gadzooks! We have to ride like the blazes or I'll be walking in behind the coffin.'

Petra loved her for 'gadzooks' and 'ride like the blazes'. They did just that, crackling along the woodland tracks at full tilt, outstripping Carly jogging along the lower path with her son now on her shoulders, dappled tree canopy protecting them from the ever-hotter sun and the fish-eye of the little drone that buzzed in their wake, even after Gill had waved farewell at her driveway gate.

It buzzed above the fields alongside Plum Run, making Bridge's pony spook. When Petra peeled off into her own driveway it lingered over the orchards.

Imagining Bay at the controls, monitoring his camera footage, Petra whipped off her helmet and raked out her hair.

Surely he had far better things to do than chasing her with a glorified, battery-operated Frisbee-cam? She gave it a withering look and mouthed, 'Go away.' Gill was right: the ruddy things were as ubiquitous as swallows now. Charlie had been desperate for one last birthday but, like Aleš, quickly tired of it, handing it down to their sons.

Narrowing her eyes, she looked up at an open attic window,

calling, 'Fitz! If it's your drone out here perving round the village, can you land it *now*?' Brother Ed was already on a warning for flying it over the manor's walled garden when its owners were sunbathing in the nude, although he'd claimed to be following a hawk in flight.

There was no reply. It hovered closer, dropping lower, its rotor tone changing.

Then, as she tied up the Redhead, the drone whizzed across the road, listing dramatically, and crash-landed on the stable roof, skittling down the gulley and into the gutter like a coke can from a vending machine.

There was a rose Sellotaped to it, along with a note: *From your secret admirer.*

As soon as she'd peeled it off, the drone's rotors started up once more. With great effort, it took off, battery at a low ebb, and buzzed away.

Petra watched it in wonder, the eighties adverts back with vengeance. Giving her head another Timotei toss, the rose a Jane Seymour Le Jardin sniff and the note a Milk Tray card trick slide between her fingers, she danced back to her house for a Flake advert waterfall moment under the power shower.

There was a bus stop not far from the rescue centre. The last time Carly had visited Pricey, she'd been alone, the dog still weak from an infection she'd picked up at the orthopaedic specialist's, dull-eyed and institutionalised. Ellis had badgered her to let him come this time, although she knew the centre staff wouldn't let him into the run or kennel until the dog had been assessed for rehoming once her health improved. They'd already explained to her that a dog trained as she'd been might find it hard to cope with life as a pet.

Today, the bull-lurcher was a ball of irrepressible energy, bright eyes creasing up with joy to see Carly, lips smiling, entire brindle body wagging in delighted pirouettes, one leg stiff and cumbersome, with its brightly coloured Vet Wrap, like a baseball bat, almost knocking them both off their feet. Watching, Ellis bounced up and down with his little sister outside the enclosure. 'Can we take her home, Mum? Can we? Can we look after her?'

'That's not going to happen right now, love.' Carly felt her heart crush tight, knowing that Ash was set against it and the cost would cripple them.

Her hands were burning hot again as she cupped Pricey's smiling face, laughing at the kisses coming up to meet her.

'She's still very weak and she's been through a lot of trauma,' the kennel maid explained to Ellis kindly. 'She's going to need a lot of specialist care.'

'How long until her leg's better?' asked Carly.

'It's another four weeks until she starts hydrotherapy. Before that, we'll keep doing as much as we can to work through her aggression issues.'

Looking at Pricey now, Carly found it hard to believe she was anything but sweet-natured, but the nurse told her in an under-tone, out of Ellis's hearing, that they were seeing more examples of dysfunctional behaviour now she was stronger, especially around other dogs.

'We're pretty sure she's been regularly starved to bring out her fight instinct, probably beaten too. She bites herself when she's stressed, and she still won't sleep in her bed, just walks the kennel until she drops on the spot from tiredness. If we knew a bit more about her circumstances, how she was trained and worked, it would be easier. She's not at all territorial, which is unusual. She's watchful – she sights and attacks. She's great with you, but there's one poor volunteer, a young lad, we can't let in here because she just goes for him. Not many want to take one home like that.'

Carly took a photo of that smiling, happy dog face with her mobile. 'I'll keep asking round.'

Ellis kicked up a stink when they left, overtired and inconsolable. He was still at the noisy end of a tantrum when they clambered into Ash's truck, ten minutes late. The cab smelt of shower gel and vending-machine coffee as he accepted her perfunctory kiss, his eyes predictably evasive, eager to get going.

The screams and kicks from the back seat demanded otherwise. 'Why can't we have the dog, Dad?'

Ash was already low-browed and defensive, as though she'd set him up. He'd never taken any interest in Pricey.

'Just button it, Ellis.' His voice was an army order, his word always law in the pickup.

The 'Splorer Stick hit the back seat. Sienna started crying.

'I'll burn that bloody thing if you do it again!' Ash roared. He loathed the 'Splorer Stick.

'*Why* can't we have the dog?'

'She's a big old bitch who eats too much. Plenty of those in the gym.' He glanced across at Carly. 'Place is rammed with lard-arses on holiday diets. This time next year, we're minted.'

Carly gritted her teeth, hating it when he spoke like that. She blamed his Compton mates, the Tinder-swiping bachelor pack, along with the misogynist Turners. Ash had been no sweet-spoken angel in the army, and women were rarely admired for their wit, skill or career success in the mess, but they *were* admired.

She'd have called him out for macho-bantering in front of the kids, but she needed him sweet while she put Pricey's case. 'Could someone else in the family take her on? What about Norm? He lost one recently, didn't he?' She wasn't always sure of Norm's sanity, but he loved his dogs.

'I can ask.' He shrugged. 'At least it's not a bloody foal.' He cuffed her shoulder, grinning. 'You saved much yet?' Her Spirit tin, kept on top of the fridge, amused him no end, currently amounting to about a fiver in loose change because they were increasingly cash-strapped and constantly had to raid it for phone credit and groceries.

'I'm working on it. Got the pole-dancing-club job starting next week.'

'Me too.' He overtook a Bentley way too fast – another bad habit he'd picked up lately was chicken-running flash cars. His eyes burned into the rear-view mirror as rows of Xenons flashed furiously behind him. 'Don't tell me it's the same place?'

She appreciated the old dry Ash humour, albeit delivered in a snarky voice at twenty miles an hour over the limit. 'Polo-mint Rhino,' she dead-panned. 'It's a special Cotswolds version.' He didn't laugh.

'Nah, this one's called Transaction. The clue's in there. Lots of big feet in high heels.'

She let out a snort of amusement. 'That's a good one.'

They were wisecracking almost like they used to, edgier and darker these days, but the old magic was there. Ash was always at his most communicative after the gym, Carly's snorts soon turning to laughter. That stopped when they came up behind the funeral hearse crawling towards the stud's drive.

'Do *not* overtake it, Ash.'

'I wasn't going to!' The swaggering attitude doubled as he eyed the coffin in the hearse with its discreet lily wreath. 'Good riddance to the old bastard. If our lottery numbers come up we're going to buy his house and I'll turn it into a tank-driving centre. There's a lot of money in tanks.'

'And fat women.' She strained to catch sight of Spirit as they passed his field. 'Just not in horses.'

15

'Get a wriggle on, Carl, love. I've got good news.' Janine was already waiting at the end of the path for Carly when she'd dropped her kids at her mother-in-law's maisonette ahead of Feather Dusters' weekly cleaning assignation at Upper Bagot Farmhouse. It was a gig they now tackled together, along with a teenage Turner niece on 'work experience'. Ahead lay three hours in which Janine would eye up the Gunns' collectables, the niece fold pretty triangles in the loo-roll ends and Carly do the rest of the work.

Janine's long talons drummed a marching rhythm on the gate she was holding open for Carly, nail art currently featuring summery surf boards and sunbeds. 'We're on,' she whispered, as they hurried to the van. 'Jed and Mark say you can come along tonight. Easier to see now the wheat's cut. Should have some good sport.'

Her throat tightened. She'd always considered Janine's promise to take her lamping with the Turner boys to be a hollow one. 'I'm busy.' She knee-jerked into retreat.

'No, you're not. I've checked. Ash is good to look after the kids. I told him we were having a girls' night out. Didn't he say?'

'First I've heard of it.'

Janine's thick, sculpted brows lowered over Turner wolf eyes, alpha to omega. 'You not interested in coming no more, Carl? It took a lot of persuading to organise this.'

Carly had absolutely zero desire to watch animals get hunted down. Whatever the Turners did wouldn't be on the brutal scale Pricey had been trained for, but there would be lurchers galore, that lean and fast band of trained thieves to which Pricey belonged.

She thought about the dog's smiling face snaking into her hot hands that morning, all the damage deep inside her head still unhealed. Starved to be aggressive, the nurse had said, beaten too.

'You up for it or not, Carl?' Janine demanded.

Carly shrugged assent, the pack outsider adopting her customary submissive pose, mind whirring. She'd asked, she'd got. But she'd wanted tell, not show.

It played on her mind as they cleaned the Gunns' house, keeping her head down in a frantic whirl of vacuuming and dusting. She found the place soulless without Petra, who'd dashed out to the supermarket leaving an apologetic note. Springer spaniel Wilf followed her around, his dark eyes mournful, alert to suitcases open on beds. She hugged him in quiet corners as she plugged and unplugged Henry Hoover.

'Good job his coat's waterproof. Mum's always sobbing into it too.' The oldest Gunn son caught her with her forehead pressed to the dog's ruff on the attic landing.

'I'm not crying,' she muttered, starting to dust again.

'You still haven't messaged me.' He was watching her from the doorway, all golden tan in faded Hollister shorts and a vintage The Smiths tour T-shirt.

'Funny that.'

'You'll find me under F for Fitz.'

'And I'm B for Busy, mate.'

He slid down the wall beside her to a sitting position, head tilted against the end of a bookshelf. Carly had never seen so many books except in libraries. This landing had floor-to-ceiling shelves, from which the teenager now pulled a hardback novel.

'Mum's friend Pearl.' He held it up so she could see the name on the cover. 'She used to house-sit while we were away.' His posh-boy voice was redeemed by its faint echo of Petra's *Emmerdale* curl of laughter. 'She's my badass godmum. Wilf has her number, so the vet bills were off the scale. We've got pros coming this time. It'll be like gundog boot camp.'

'Sounds good.'

He picked another book from the shelves beside him, flipping it open. '*Love in the Time of Cholera*. Sound like good holiday reading to you?'

'Maybe.'

'What are you currently reading?'

'Elwyn Hartley Edwards's *The Complete Book of the Horse*.' Her village-fête buy was her bible. Over forty years old, well-thumbed and foxed with a first page inscribed 'Hermione Austen 1973', she'd read it from cover to cover all summer.

'At least it's not one of Mum's. If you like horses, have you met ours?'

'I always say hello over the gate.'

Grinning, he jumped up. 'I'll introduce you properly. The Shetland's badass. Come on.'

'I'm working.'

'Take a break. I insist.'

'You're all right.' She waved him away.

'I know I'm all right. I'll put the kettle on, shall I?'

'If it makes you happy.' Grateful to see him go, Wilf bounding downstairs in his wake, she took her vinegar spray and started at the little casement windows, looking out across the orchards to the valley, the sky as perfect hot blue as any she could remember.

When Kit arrived in Compton Magna, cars were parked to either side of the Old Almshouses. His drive gates were blocked, and more cars were arriving to double-park along Church Lane. A scattering of mourners were standing about, looking hot and uncomfortable, some making their way into the church, others admiring his garden where the remainders of his children's Donald Trump scarecrow topped the bonfire ready for autumn.

His summer visit was usually his favourite, the start of harvest drawing the skin and pith from the hills as its crops were cut and roots lifted. This should be Hermia's Lughnasa. But his body now experienced a *déjà vu* so wintry that iced water might have been injected straight into a vein.

Kit was very bad at funerals. Bloody-minded. Selfish. Grief-stricken.

Hermia had left no script, no stage plan. It had all been left open to interpretation, her husband's wishes wholly different from those of her family.

He had no desire to remember the day they had buried her.

He drove straight on, almost flattening a wizened couple zimmering across the lane in front of him. In his blinkered haste, he missed the turn beside the Green and found himself shooting out onto Plum Run, driving straight past Upper Bagot Farmhouse, barely recognisable as the place he'd moved into with a young wife a quarter of a century earlier.

He looked straight ahead, the memories still too painful. His children had been born there. His wife had lost her liberty there.

It took all his effort to stay on the road and drive to the Jugged Hare car park where he holed up in the far corner overlooking the orchards, a storm raging in his head, blood drumming through his ears like rain. The pub was taking a delivery, beer kegs rolling down into the cellar in great thunderclaps. An unfamiliar landlord collecting a tray of bottles from the delivery lorry cast a suspicious glance across the tarmac at the ashen-faced man parked in the far corner by a Cotswold Way map and dog-poo bin.

The view back across the vale through the fruit trees soothed Kit, the drystone wall rebuilt with new honeycomb nuggets, the orchards mown, the county boundary sign dug out of the undergrowth and repainted – Gloucestershire and Warwickshire companionably sharing one of the best views in the Cotswolds. It had been the view from his and Hermia's bedroom. On a clear day, you could see past the Malvern Hills to the Black Mountains.

Kit put his head into his hands. A confirmed atheist who had no truck with superstition, he didn't believe in ghosts for a minute, but whenever he came back to the village, he could hear Hermia speak as he did nowhere else, that emotionally infused voice stolen from her in the accident, its soft lilt of kindness telling him off for 'overthinking everything, like Wordsworth', her Cumbrian husband with a poet's soul and a mathematician's logic.

The storm in his head was passing, his senses picking up fine details again, the tick of the engine cooling, the scent of the roses he'd brought to put on the grave, the buzz of his phone on the dashboard.

Messages had queued up, most of them from Orla, out sightseeing with friends. There were selfies featuring Admiralty Arch, the Mall and Buckingham Palace, all copied to her Instagram and Twitter accounts, garnering thousands of all-important likes.

Uncomfortable with the blurred lines between her public image and private life, their love affair too acquired a taste to feed the masses on social streams, he took a photograph of the most beautiful valley in the Bardswolds, stretched out in front of him, and sent a direct text, captioned *Land thrice racked*, a favourite line from the play, referring to excessively high rents.

To Kit's consternation, she immediately shared it with a million followers, many of whom – thinking she'd taken it herself while sightseeing in London – asked if it was Hyde Park.

'It's Jekyll and Hyde Park,' he muttered. To him, the Cotswolds had always summed up the hypocrisy of country life, all outward respectability and inner lust, a duality he was all too aware he bore like a native.

The smell of the roses was overpowering, their association embedded with loss. He could no longer tolerate lilies, narcissi or sweet peas for the same reason. Soon all flowers would be lost to him. Maybe he'd move on to plastic windmills, like the Turner family graves. That it would infuriate his in-laws was a very satisfying prospect.

Turning to buzz down his window to dissipate the scent he found a big slab of a face staring in at him, teeth bared and nose creased, like a shark's.

'You spying on me, pal?'

'No.' It had to be the Jugged Hare's landlord, a tenure that lasted about as long as a pomegranate's shelf life in the sanitised, smoke-free, fifty-covers-a-night gastropub.

The once-popular village institution changed hands every few years, each time with a new food angle, the prices always too high and the food too fancy to win back villagers. In the pre-Millennium glory years, the Jugged Hare had been run by a retired footballer, who had slept with all his barmaids and fiddled the books. Kit had treasured that decade of beer-battered cod steaks, raucous live music and smoky lock-ins before their host whisked his prettiest waitress off to run a beach bar off the Costa Blanca.

'You're here from the council about the noise, aren't you?'

'No.'

'If you're CID about the chef's tantrum, I fired him.'

'Absolutely not.'

'Selling agent?'

'Kit Donne.' He stepped out to offer his hand. 'I hope it's okay to wait out a funeral here.'

The man glared at him suspiciously. 'This car park's for pub clientele only.'

'Are you open?'

'Licensing hours are eleven a.m. until eleven p.m.,' he parroted. 'As it happens, we have a small party of locals gathered in the skittle alley for a sharpener before the funeral. None was served until the hour.'

Kit glanced at his watch. It was just before a quarter past. Looking across at the signs planted in the verge in front of the pub, boasting FOOD ALL DAY and LOCAL CRAFT ALES, he spotted one offering morning coffee. 'Espresso?'

The paranoid landlord closed one eye distrustfully. 'You from *The Good Pub Guide*?'

'No. I just want a coffee.'

'Hmm.' He reluctantly led the way. 'Big turn-out down at the church, is it?'

'It's not small.'

The landlord looked somewhat mollified. 'Might get a lunch crowd in.'

'Who are they burying?'

'Old boy from the stud. Customer for coffee, love!' he shouted, as he swung open the pub door, much as an air-raid warden would announce a Luftwaffe squadron. Kit spotted a woman behind the bar hastily hiding the cash-and-carry firewater she was funnelling into a craft gin bottle. 'Espresso for the coffin-dodger.'

'You're not here for Captain Percy's send-off then? Left a mountain of gambling debts, they reckon. Place'll be up for sale inside the year. The daughter's a right fly-by-night.' The landlady called to her husband, as he headed into the kitchen, 'What's it they call the Captain's daughter round here? The Bald Bowler or summink?'

'The Bardswolds Bolter,' Kit remembered. 'Veronica Ledwell.' He recalled the thick cream personalised stationery, letter after letter piling up in his wife's keepsake box. *You will love her.* How often had Hermia said it? Enough to render it meaningless. The evidence wasn't convincing.

'That's the one! You know her?'

'Only by reputation.'

'She's certainly got one of those.' The paranoid landlord chuckled.

'*One can survive everything nowadays except death, and live down everything except a good reputation*,' Kit quoted Oscar Wilde wearily.

'I knew it!' The landlord turned to him, white-faced. 'You're the new *Sunday Times* restaurant critic, aren't you?'

Carly loved vacuuming with her earphones in, music blaring.

It was only when she turned off the power switch that she heard Janine squawking up the stairs, 'Carl, you'd better get your arse down here! The kid's just brought a pony in over our clean kitchen floor. Says he won't take it out until you've met it.'

Soon enjoying a surprisingly good espresso, Kit perched on a barstool, buried in Paranoid Landlord's *Daily Mirror*, a newspaper he hadn't read for years.

He was deep in the sports section when his peaceful hideout was invaded by village mourners crowding in for last-minute sharpeners, complaining that the skittle alley was too hot and the complimentary craft-gin shots had tasted like floor cleaner. He barely had time to look up before they'd surrounded him and, in an instant, he went from avoiding the action at the theatre bar to centre-stage improvisation.

'Alice is in charge of the spread at the stud, so it'll be a pipette of sherry and weak intravenous tea at the wake,' said a tall, rakish woman, whose shock of iron-grey hair supported a fascinator as unlikely as a telecom tower sprouting from a heather moor. She plonked a handbag on the open newspaper. 'Hello there, Kit. Gill Walcote, to spare you the effort of remembering. Tie Cross Cottage, just across the Green from you. Are you coming to the Captain's funeral, too?'

'No.' He slid quickly off his stool, already planning his getaway.

'My *God*, it's Kitten!' One of his late wife's nephews strode up to the bar now, a wide-shouldered tower of blue-eyed Austen bombast. 'Hello, stranger!'

Kit raised a thin smile. 'Bay.'

'I thought you never came here any more.'

'Very rarely. Just to visit the grave. It's Lughnasa.'

'Lunacy indeed! What a day to choose! Half the county's here.'

'Pure happenstance.' Getting away wasn't going to be as simple as throwing down a fiver and nodding farewell. Taking your leave in Compton was a contact sport.

'By God, this is splendid.' Bay gave Kit such a man-hug he almost swallowed his tongue. 'What are you drinking? I insist it's forty per cent proof and at least ten years old. Malt whisky, isn't it? That's what we could all do with.' A nod already had Paranoid Landlord reaching for the top shelf.

An ability to remember such things, to play host and take charge socially in any situation had put the Austen family in control in this village. Kit might be able to recall whole pages of dialogue, but he had absolutely no idea who drank what, not even his own children.

He'd always rather liked Bay for all his over-charming swagger. Hermia had insisted he had the talent to act, and he certainly looked the part, upright and handsome, tailor-made to saunter on screen in a big-budget Trollope adaptation.

A bottle of ten-year-old Islay was placed on the bar.

Kit held up a hand apologetically. 'I'm driving to Stratford. In fact, I should have set out already, so if you'll—'

'One quick drink won't hurt.' Bay unplugged the top. 'We're all on the hoof. You must at least toast the Captain with us. Aunt Hermia was a great favourite of his.' He turned to bark over his shoulder. 'Guy! Fizz! Uncle Christopher's here. Dad, Mum – come and say hello to Kit!'

They appeared on all sides now, tall handsome athletes, Kit's white-haired brother-in-law, Sandy, several years his senior but still enviably loose-limbed and fresh-faced, with a handshake that could dislocate a shoulder. 'How the devil are you, Kit?'

He heard his voice claiming good health, like an automatic pre-record, his eye on the door once more. 'You?'

'Absolutely bloody marvellous!' He'd forgotten how hammy Sandy was, another loss to the theatre, far out-luvvying any actor in his acquaintance.

A glass was pressed into his hand, more pats on his shoulders.

Austens surrounded him now. They were so easy to warm to, so genuinely happy to see him, so bonded together and easy-going. So terribly like Hermia had been. How could he have forgotten that?

'To Captain Percy!' The entire bar raised glasses as one.

Lifting his too, fully expecting cash-and-carry siphoned hooch, Kit's lips were kissed by the most complicated, familiar of old Islays. Without warning, he had a deep, nostalgic kick of being back home.

'Get him back outside!' wailed Janine as, feet skittering on the flag-stones of the Gunns' kitchen, the Shetland careered into the glass orangery, greedy eyes fixed on a potted fig. Having slipped out of his head-collar, he'd already demolished an orchid and taken bites out of two potted aspidistras and a kaffir lime.

'Don't you just love him?' Fitz couldn't stop laughing, sagging against a wall, lead-rope still in hand.

'Why'd you bring him in here?' demanded Janine. 'My robot vacuum's in peril over there somewhere.'

'He comes in all the time.' Fitz wiped his eyes as the Shetland unpotted the fig. 'Being a house pony is his big gig now nobody rides him. The 'rents get him in whenever they have friends over.' The Shetland moved on to a spider plant and Fitz finally went to retrieve him. But before he could buckle up the head-collar, the robotic floor cleaner whizzed out from behind a wicker sofa making the pony shy back. Breaking free, he clattered off into the kitchen again.

'Oh, shit! The larder's open!'

Within seconds, Petra's beautifully organised, well-stocked pantry was total chaos, the pony covered in flour, rice and cereal, one foot in a wicker basket of meringues, the other in an old panettone tin. Reaching up to get his nose on a shelf of icing goodies, he knocked down tins and jars, herbs and spices so that he was coated in bright colours like a cow at Holi festival.

Still laughing, Fitz swaggered in to try to drag him out, determined to show off his heroics to Carly. The Shetland aimed a small hoof accurately and efficiently into the centre of the teenager's groin.

'Little sod!' Pulling on two pairs of rubber gloves to protect her nails, Janine then tried to pull him out by the tail, only to receive a long, insulting volley of flatulence as up close and personal as a deodorant application. The pony refused to budge. The teenage niece suggested calling the fire brigade.

'I could have a go?' Carly offered.

'What do you know about horses?' sneered Janine.

'She's read a book,' Fitz pointed out.

Sneezing repeatedly from the curry powder, the Shetland had already decided to come out of his own volition. But as he tried to turn round, he got stuck between the shelves. Losing his footing in his fight to free himself, the pony fell into the narrow space, thrashing amongst the wicker, eyes rolling furiously.

Carly picked her way in past the spilled food.

'Don't risk it Carl!' cried Janine. 'Think of your children. You have no idea how dangerous the little ones are!'

Ignoring her, Carly stooped down beside his thrashing head and flailing legs.

16

'You must come down for a spot of shooting this autumn, Kit,' Sandy insisted, 'or a day out with the hunt.'

'I don't ride.'

'Neither do half our mounted followers, eh, Bay?'

Still trapped under a relentless family charm offensive, Kit had started to remember how much their bonhomie had once irritated him, and why he'd deliberately dissociated himself from his wife's family. The Austens, self-appointed village grandees, had an evangelical zeal to get everyone involved in social events and country sports. Kit, who at best was uninspired by hanging about in cold fields killing things to eat, and radically opposed to slaughtering things for fun, had never been easy to recruit into the family firm. That they still counted him as an insider showed their innate, ridiculous cliquishness.

The other mourners were straightening ties and looking at watches, but the Austens had always treated time like cocaine: the finer it was cut, the better the high. 'Got a good half-hour yet. Another round!'

'We bloody miss you, Kit.' Bay topped up his glass.

'You have a funeral to get to,' Kit reminded him, setting it aside, remembering that he was driving. 'You're not here to toast me.'

And yet it felt like that. Days like this were nostalgic to them, joyful even, harking back to an era when Kit had been the academic malcontent in their midst.

'You do the toast, then,' Bay insisted.

Today in the tiny Jugged Hare side bar, locals who knew Kit of old – and there was a surprising number – had greeted him as a long-lost friend too. He remained a clansman and comrade. What the hell?

'To Captain Jocelyn Percy!' He raised his glass, not at all certain if he'd ever met the man.

The woman in the fascinator trapped him in a beady stare. 'Does this mean you might get involved in village life again? Only the parish council desperately needs committee members. Some I shan't mention are very half-hearted.'

He shook his head. 'I'm away for the rest of the year.'

'What a shame. If you don't mind me speaking out, you could look after your place a bit better. It's an historic building. Your garden's jolly wild, and there's something of a plague of rats living in that old greenhouse of yours. The Boswell Boys offer horticultural services locally – I can give you their number – and Vic Phipps's your Fosse Hills rat man. And if it's as bad inside the house as it is out, I hear Carly Turner is an excellent char, although you have to go through the ghastly Janine at Feather Dusters to get her.'

'Thank you.' Kit bristled. His children should take responsibility for all this, given they refused to let him sell the place. 'All very useful advice.'

'A pleasure.' She grabbed a business card from the bar-top plastic display of local traders and taxi companies, and wrote several numbers on the back. 'Mention my name. I've added it here because you've forgotten it again. Gill Walcote.' Two fierce ursine eyes fixed on his. 'We thought your play was a bit odd, but we liked it.'

'Thank you. By coincidence I feel much the same way about this village.' He took on the forceful gaze and held it, then looked sharply away as it threatened unexpected mutual warmth.

The village mourners were starting to troop out now, thank goodness. The Austens were still at the bar, having an animated conversation about a piece of land they wanted to buy from the Captain's estate: 'Ronnie won't let it go cheap. Last I heard, she was a blue-chip bloodstock agent in Germany. Or was it a blue-blood one?'

'Chip off the old block either way. Drives a hard bargain, I'll bet.'

'It's not just her decision, it's all the trustees. The agreement has always been that we have first refusal.'

'That'll be a cool million around here at current market value.'

'Rubbish. Half that. The land's in poor heart.'

'With a big sward. Percy family are no fools.'

Poor hearts and big swords sounded all very medieval to Kit.

'Ronnie Percy doesn't know what she's up against.' Bay emptied the whisky bottle into the glasses of the few remaining drinkers and caught Kit's eye, his eyebrows ironic lions rampant.

The name again reverberated in Kit's head. The embossed stationery had read Veronica Ledwell, but Hermia's memories another: Ronnie Percy a.k.a. the Bardswold Bolter. She'd made contact after years of lapsed friendship, when the Donnes' lives had been whirlwinds of London Theatreland and Cotswolds nesting. Kit hadn't paid much heed at the time, only aware of the pages of bold, round handwriting Hermia had devoured and how much it always lifted her mood. Years of postcards, letters, birthday and Christmas cards and gifts. A riddle of a symbiotic friendship, rekindled then abandoned in an hour of need.

He banged down his glass. 'Ronnie Percy's a bloody cow.'

Bay Austen turned to him in surprise. Then, with a lot of approving guffawing the stragglers lifted their glasses.

'To the bloody cow!' Bay proposed.

Finding his glass had been refilled once more by Paranoid Landlord, brandishing a suspiciously orange Glenfiddich, Kit calculated what he'd drunk, wondering if three espressos cancelled out any part of it. He knew he really shouldn't have any more. But in need of analgesic and shocked by his own sourness, he sank it.

'Come along!' Sandy Austen urged Kit. 'You'll be among friends.'

'Thank you, but I'm running late as it is.' If it came to the toss, he'd rather lie under his greenhouse catching rats.

Detouring to the Gents, grateful to be alone, Kit knew he had to do something about the house. It had been bad enough in May when he'd dived inside for all of ten minutes to collect a pile of books and plays and some old CDs.

He reached into his pocket for the card the woman with the fascinator had handed him.

Home (from) Home Comforts
All-inclusive domestic package for second homes!
Want to arrive to a clean and aired house, freshly changed beds,
still warm baking and a freezer full of home-cooked food?

That would do.

Lester wanted the funeral over with. From the onset, the grand-children had squabbled about the order of service, the music, its readings, invitees, nominated charity. The Captain's life had been lost to the detail long ago. But the devil in him spoke loud and clear now. *Tell them all to go to Hell, Lester!*

He slotted a handkerchief into his top pocket, neatly folded with the monogram showing – a gift from Ann twenty years earlier, still carefully starched and ironed after each use – then put another fresh one inside his wallet pocket to offer to Pip later.

She'd arrived this morning in a flurry of tearful efficiency, although whether her tears were for the Captain, down to her all-night baking marathon, or because she was going to miss the service was unclear. Alice insisted that Pip must stay at the house while everyone was at church, a Cinderella in mourning.

'Somebody we trust has to oversee the domestic side,' she'd told Pip, amid much protest, determined to keep the Captain's unruly housekeeper in her place. Deeply hurt, Pip had bustled across the courtyard, with a brace of Bakewell fingers, to complain about it.

'If she only knew the extra mile I went to for that man! I knew the real dirt on him, the bad things he did, and I forgave them all.'

Lester had given her a very sharp look, then realised she was just talking about the Captain's bad habits, such as shouting obsceni-ties at the television, stuffing used tissues down the side of the sofa cushion and his refusal to bathe. Pip couldn't possibly know the seven-magpie secret. Nobody did.

But she did seem to know something. The last time he'd seen that fevered, sleep-deprived look, Pip had just learned that a cele-brated author lived in the village and had spent two nights reading absolutely everything she could find online about the woman's life, loves, family, house extension, mother-in-law and financial affairs. Just not her books.

Thankfully, she'd pushed off soon afterwards to do her morning round of pensioners. She was now late back – deliberately so, Lester was certain. He wouldn't be at all surprised if she was already waiting in church, saving a space on the front row for Ronnie. The thought made him fish in a pocket for his inhaler.

There was a light knock on the door. He braced himself. But it was just the funeral director.

'Ready for you, sir.'

Lester checked his reflection, then went out to let his old friend lean on his shoulder one last time.

One step out of line, and he'd tell them to go to Hell.

'Morning, Mrs Hedges! Sorry I'm late! I saved the best until last!' Pip hurried into the little cottage on Church Lane to find the old lady watching *Homes Under the Hammer* in the gloom, still in her nightie, her thin white cotton-wool hair over a baby pink scalp, like a Westie's stomach, a hungry cat curling around each swollen ankle.

'You're a welcome sight, dear.' Mrs Hedges didn't look away from the screen where rival bidders were winking and nodding to win a Bexhill maisonette.

With her uncomplaining smile, television addiction and unlimited 4G WiFi, the frail old lady was one of Pip's favourite Home Comforts clients. That her little cottage was opposite the church lichgate meant Pip had deliberately timed her final Home Comforts call of the morning so that she could watch the funeral guests arrive, still prickling with indignation that she wasn't attending the ceremony.

'They're burying the Captain today,' Pip reminded her, with a martyred sigh, as she went to open the curtains, poised for the gratifying moment when Mrs H told her what a treasure she had been to the old man, as all her other clients had been saying all morning.

But Mrs H just squawked at her to leave the curtains closed so she could see the television better, and waved her towards the kitchen. 'Put the kettle on, dear. There's an unrenovated semi in Cheadle coming up.'

Pip regrouped as the tea brewed. Eager mourners might like to come early and claim a good spot with a handbag on a pew so they could look round the graves, but the main players were a way off. Pip's aunt had arrived for her sister's funeral so early that she'd helped arrange altar flowers, then sat through a christening first. Pip knew she must be patient.

Mrs Hedges was soon washed and dressed in a velour jogging suit, watching *Bargain Hunt* with a cup of tea and a coffin-shaped slice of chocolate brownie.

Pip eased the curtain aside.

'I've left you a light snack in the fridge for later,' she told her, as she watched mourners passing the window. It was a big turn-out. She hadn't yet seen Ronnie. That was who she was waiting for. That, and anyone at the big house acknowledging the Captain's loyal, grief-stricken housekeeper was missing.

The mobile phone in Pip's right pocket rang.

'Is that Piped Wards?' Deep voice, lovely northern accent.

She was nonplussed. 'Sorry?'

'I picked up a card in the Jugged Hare. Home from Home Comforts. Piped Wards.'

'That's me! I'm Pip Edwards. It was a printing error. How may Home from Home Comforts help you today?' Aimed at village weekenders, the second of the little entrepreneurial side-lines she'd started after her parents' deaths had never really taken off. She'd designed a website and printed flyers: *I keep your second house your forever-ready home.* Nobody had ever responded to it. Until now.

'Would you be available to look after a house for me? Tidy it up a bit?'

'Whereabouts are you?'

It was the theatre director three doors along Church Lane. She couldn't remember his name.

'How much do you charge?' he asked now.

Pip had never thought out a price structure. The amount she charged her oldies barely covered her costs, but she liked to feel needed. He was bound to have lots of famous friends visiting. She'd happily tidy and snoop around it for free. She named a temptingly low figure, adding, 'Plus expenses.'

'Are we talking parliamentary expenses?' He laughed. 'That's incredibly reasonable.'

'Just cleaning materials and any groceries you need getting in.'

'Can you provide a reference?'

Untrusting bastard. She was practically offering to do it for *free*. 'Sabrina ffoulkes-Hamilton from Glebe Farm.' She reeled off a number.

'Thank you. I'll call you straight back.'

Almost as soon as Pip put one mobile phone back in her pocket, its twin on her other side rang.

The Dark Phone was coming into its own at last.

Beaming at Mrs Hedges, who was hushing her so that she could hear the hammer price of a Clarice Cliff teapot, she mimicked Gill Walcote's bark. 'Glebe Farm!'

At that moment, the teapot doubled its estimate amid much cheering. Pip moved into the kitchen as the red team jumped around hugging one another.

'Sounds like you have a houseful,' Kit Donne's lovely voice said in her ear. 'I'll keep this quick. Is Pip Edwards worth getting in?'

'Absolute treasure!' Pip's impersonation of Gill told him. 'Couldn't live without her.'

'Is she as inexpensive as she makes out?'

'You *must* pay her more than she asks. Worth her weight in gold. Just don't steal her from anyone. We guard her fiercely round here.'

'Can she be trusted?'

'With your *life*. And your gundog's life. And your gun. That's how good she is.'

'Thank you.'

Pip rang off, feeling pleased. A moment later, the first phone was sounding.

'Hello!' She realised she was still talking like Gill. 'I mean, Home from Home Comforts. *I keep your second house your forever-ready home!* How may I help?'

'Me again. Thanks for that number. Can you come round for a chat now?'

'Now?' She peered out of the tiny kitchen window at the lane and saw a green Range Rover gliding along it, looking for a parking space, a familiar blonde in the passenger seat. She thought about the uppity caterers and Alice treating her like casual staff, about Lester being too tightly buttoned to stand up for her. Let them wait. 'It'll have to be quick,' she said, ringing off and hastily calling up her search engine, keeping half an eye on the window as the Range Rover cruised past again, still hunting for a space.

Pip was on Kit Donne's Wiki entry in seconds, scrolling too quickly past all the theatre stuff to read much of it, although Awards, Television/Film and Personal Life held her attention longer. High culture wasn't really her thing but he'd worked with lots of actors she'd seen in *Midsomer Murders* and the Harry Potter films, so he had to be good. She scurried outside.

To her right, the Range Rover was making its third approach, the driver's face a thundercloud. She recognised Blair Robertson's craggy good looks from his internet profile. Ronnie was missing, so she must have got out to hurry into church.

To Pip's left, the coffin was making its way slowly up Church Lane on the shoulders of six pallbearers, the big off-roader standing in its path. Blair started to reverse.

Pip's little blue car was parked directly outside Mrs Hedges' front door.

Waving at him to wait, she leaped inside and, revving wildly, drove out of the prime parking spot, mounting the pavement to let the Range Rover into it, then careered along the lane to dump the car around the corner by the No Parking sign on the Green. None of the village busybodies were likely to complain. They were all in church.

She ran back to the lane to find that the funeral procession was through the lichgate and halfway along the path. Blair's Range Rover was parked outside Mrs Hedges' cottage, its driver gone.

Following the Captain's coffin came the three grandchildren, their spouses and children, a scattering of other close friends. Nobody noticed Pip watching from beneath the horse-chestnuts at the far end of the lane.

'Goodbye, Captain,' she breathed, as she saluted him. She waited for the tears. They had to come now. But, instead, she found herself wondering if she'd baked enough for a sell-out crowd. She glanced at her watch. She had at least an hour, probably longer. Easily enough time to get a new job, pick up fresh ingredients from home and run off some quick contingency supplies in the stud's kitchen. It was important to keep busy, they always said.

She trotted up to the path to the Old Almshouses. She was expecting the door to be opened by a wild-eyed, open-cuffed Ian McShane type, but he was smartly turned out in checked shirt and dark cream trousers, thick brown hair neatly trimmed, only a hint of silver fox lining the temples and ears. He looked like an army officer on leave.

'Come in – Philippa, isn't it?' He beckoned her quickly inside, glancing warily across at the church.

'Pip. From my father's nickname for me.' She fed him the customary Pipsqueak line as she stared in astonishment at the mess.

'Right. Take a squeak – I mean, seat.'

'Find a seat, you mean!' she joked, handing him a plastic container of coffin cakes. 'These are for you.' She'd been going to leave them for Mrs Hedges, but felt her own cause was greater. In any case, the old lady's daughter had asked her not to leave choking hazards after a recent episode with a fruit scone.

'Thank you. That's very kind.'

'Pleasure.' She moved a pile of books and newspapers from a nearby chair. The one on top had turned yellow with age.

Pip's mother had always maintained that the *Guardian* was read by clever lefties with filthy houses and the evidence was all here. Kit's weekend house, while incredibly pretty, was a total tip. As well as thick dust, there were mugs growing mould, smeared glasses, spilling ashtrays and a forest of empty wine bottles.

'I haven't lived here for years,' he apologised, standing with his back against the chimney breast to outline his plans for the immediate future. His eyes, a tawny hazel, were extraordinarily penetrating, the sort that seemed to read your mind.

Kit's grown-up kids came here with friends, he explained. There had been a regular cleaner once, but he'd lost her number and she didn't appear to have been in for a while. Hearing the name, Pip was hardly surprised. She'd moved away two years ago. 'Do you not stay here very often yourself?'

'Not at all. But I might come back here to write at some point.

I need space to work.' As he said it, his face changed, as though the idea had only just occurred to him and was a welcome one.

'Tidy house, tidy mind,' Pip enthused, liking the scale of this house, so much smaller than Percy Place with its impenetrable attic rooms, eave-high with family clutter. Let *them* deal with that.

'Oh, I'm not at all tidy.' Kit smiled. 'I just don't like other people's mess.'

It was a lovely smile, with deep dimples on each cheek. It was a father's face, wise and somewhat cynical, but full of compassion and kindness.

'I've a fridge magnet at home with the quote *If a cluttered desk is the sign of a cluttered mind then what is an empty desk a sign of? Einstein.* That's quite witty for a scientist, isn't it?'

The smile was joined by an appreciative laugh. 'He was infinitely quotable.'

'My favourite is *A balanced diet is a chocolate in each hand.*'

'That's Einstein?' He looked surprised.

'No, it's a fridge magnet.' Pax had given it to her last Christmas. That big family Christmas at which they'd all told her how irreplaceable she was, the capricious Percys.

'Are you feeling all right?'

Maybe it was lack of sleep or the heat, the emotion of the day, but Pip was indeed starting to feel very odd. 'I'd love a cup of tea.'

'Of course. How rude of me.' He headed into an open-plan kitchen at one end of the room. There were more books and papers littered all over the surfaces, but not a Delia in sight.

The Captain's books were about horses, sportsmen and occasionally politics, but Kit Donne's were about the theatre, along with poetry, critical commentary, novels and biographies. She picked up one, blowing dust off the jacket to read the author's name. 'Is Siegfried Sassoon related to Vidal?'

At the sink, the checked shoulders lifted a little, kettle wobbling under the tap. 'Not to my knowledge. Siegfried was a very interesting, complicated man. I've been trying to write a play about him for over a decade.'

'It's good to work slowly. I always go a bit fast. This place could take a while to put straight, mind you.' It might be small, but she didn't relish the amount of cleaning involved, or the loneliness, real and virtual. There was precious little phone signal at this end of Church Lane, and no sign of a modem in the house. Nor could she see a television – the Captain had turned her into a racing addict. 'How long did you say you're away?'

'A few months, but my kids will be coming here.'

How incredible to have a dad so successful that he could more or less forget about a holiday cottage. The Percys were already squabbling over every bale of straw the Captain had left in their trust.

'They're lucky having you.' The hot pressure behind her eyes was joined by a pain in her chest. Her jaw ached too. Please don't let it be anything serious, she panicked. Or if it is, let me get back to the stud first so I collapse in front of the ungrateful Percys and see their guilt-ridden faces.

She stood up, panic gripping her. What was she doing here? She should be there, fighting for her place, for the Captain's wishes.

Kit was too busy looking through cupboards for teabags to notice her cross the room behind him. 'It'll have to be black, I'm afraid,' he said. 'There must be some here somewhere. All we drank for seven years was fucking tea.' Bang, bang, bang, went the cupboard doors.

Pip faltered. For the first time since arriving, she realised he was on edge too. That angry tone was far more beguiling and familiar than his modulated theatre-director voice. The Captain had been angry constantly after Ann's death. The familiar, passionate timpani of slamming objects was music to her ears.

'I hire in third-party cleaners for my clients, if that's acceptable. I use a very reputable local firm.'

'There are lots of cleaning things here in the cupboards.' Kit opened one to demonstrate and a desiccated mouse fell out.

'You need a cat,' she said, crouching beside him to peer inside. It was full of droppings and trendy eco-products. Her oldest tabby, Shane – named after her favourite Boyzone member – would love it here, with his all-seeing feline eyes and fondness for decapitating vermin. That would give her an excuse to pop in every day. It would give her something to look after other than inanimate objects.

A deep-clean by Janine Turner and her Feather Dusters was called for. She'd charge it to expenses, along with Rentokil, fresh flowers, new bedding and a few fridge magnets as a personal touch. He must be able to afford it if he had a play transferring to Broadway.

He'd picked up the mouse by its tail, fascinated. 'It looks a little like a leaf, doesn't it?'

Spotting a roll of plastic bags in the cupboard, Pip peeled one off and tugged it open. 'In here, please.'

'*Heaven is here, where Juliet lives, and every cat and dog and little mouse,*' he placed it in the bag, '*every unworthy thing, live here in heaven and may look on her, but Romeo may not.*'

'Oh, I loved Leonardo Di Caprio in that.' The hot, hurty eye pressure grew overwhelming as Pip remembered the movie with its deeper than deep love, cool music, dusty Cadillacs, goldfish and devoted parents. Daddy Montague had looked just like the Captain.

Kit's penetrating gaze was on her again, this time at close range. 'Are you quite sure you're all right?'

'I'm fine.' Eyes, chest and now throat burning, she glared into the cupboard beneath his sink. It blurred in front of her eyes.

As Pip knotted the bag around the mouse, a big tear plopped onto it.

A warm hand covered hers. 'It's just a mouse.'

Plop, plop, plop. So, so late they came, these tears for the Captain, that she was embarrassed to admit their cause. 'I like mice.'

'That's very admirable.' He patted her hand.

Plop, plop, plop, plop, plop, plop, plop. The tears were raining now. The Captain had been no mouse. He'd been her entire hard-drive and cloud memory.

A fierce body-flash of pride gripped Pip, and she cast off the hand. 'I can't stay. I promised Sabrina I'd drop three caramel cracknel cheesecakes into Grange Farm for her weekend guests.' She marched to her handbag, dropped the mouse inside, plucked out her diary and mopped up the tears with a tissue. 'Now, I'm technically fully booked, but I can see you're desperate so I'll do it if you want me to. I'll need my own set of keys and the alarm codes.' She turned to face him, chin high.

He looked so amused that Pip knew he'd rumbled her.

'I liked Mrs ffoulkes-Hamilton. You overacted it, but you have great comedy timing. She lived in Glebe Farm earlier.'

Pip didn't know what to say, scrabbling around for something clever, her voice shrill with embarrassment. '*The best-laid schemes of mice and men often go awry*, to quote Shakespeare.'

'And Robbie Burns agreed wholeheartedly.' The laughter was back. 'Let's give this a go, Pip.' He held out a hand to shake on it. 'The keys live under the boot-scraper in the porch. I'll pass your number on to my son and let him take it from here. And, by the way, I'm allergic to cats.'

Outside, Pip looked up at the pretty face of the house again, noticing a carved wooden plaque above the door, a theatrical one with the masks of comedy and tragedy on it. Kit Donne switched between the two so lightly it was hard to know which fitted best, but she decided she liked both.

It was a beautifully peaceful summer's day. The big congregation were silent inside the church, no doubt praying sombrely. Pip was now grateful that she wasn't with them, cooped up amid scripture, moth-bally suits and a lingering smell of horse. That wasn't how she would remember the Captain at all. To her he would always be shouting for his *Racing Post*, cheeks bulging with gingerbread, belligerently unsociable.

Hearing the church clock strike the quarter, she let out a bleat and set off for her car. *The best-laid schemes of mice and men might often go awry, but women always have a contingency plan.* It was another of her favourite fridge magnets.

17

Lester sat at the very back of the church as the funeral service got under way, gratefully aware that he was now too deaf to hear much of the bishop's address or the Percy grandchildren's readings, and too blind to see the expressions on their faces. Cocooned from others' grief, he looked back in quiet reflection, running five decades in reverse, from life's finishing enclosure full of congratulatory connections, to its quiet saddling stall where the Captain's long equestrian career had been a mere battle plan, an officer and his emissary.

Beside him, stud vet Gill Walcote and her small, bearded New Zealander husband were discussing Ronnie in an undertone, her arrival deliberately last minute through the church side door, followed a few minutes later by a dark-haired companion.

'It's Mr Sit Tight.' Gill lowered her voice further: 'Blair Robertson. It's a bit blatant bringing a lover, given half the horse world's here.'

'It's all just rumours, surely.'

'They said that about Bergman and Rossellini.'

'Names are familiar. Are they three-day-eventer riders?'

Lester tuned them out again, back in the Household Cavalry days once more, the affinity he found with his charges a revelation. The Captain had spotted it straight away. 'Stick with me, Lester, and I'll see you right.'

He'd been true to his word. Not once had their fellowship disbanded. Until now.

The tears rose again, but he was accustomed to beating them back now, eyelids faster than a row of sandbags.

A neat, square tissue pulled from a travel pack was thrust at him. 'Bad day for hay-fever,' muttered Gill.

'Indeed. Thank you.'

As they all stood to sing, he waited for the organ to strike up to blow his nose as quietly as he could, then hastily dab his eyes.

He couldn't see Ronnie through the coalfield of black shoulders and hats, but he knew exactly where she was from following the gazes of those around him. All eyes were upon her.

Many still vividly remembered how scandalised the village had been almost thirty years ago, when adorable Ronnie Percy had run away with a lover, leaving her six-year marriage and three young children behind, along with her heartbroken parents.

'Now you mustn't worry yourself about any of this, Lester,' Jocelyn had growled. 'She'll come back.'

'If you say so.'

'I say so, Lester.' The crack in his voice had given away how upset he was. 'And what I say goes. Until she does, best not mention her name, eh?'

The two men hadn't spoken about her again from that day until the Captain's death.

'Do you really think she'll come back to run the stud?' Gill whispered to Paul, between verses.

'Definitely. Your old Brit families are bred to sacrifice personal ambitions for the sake of the family name, aren't they?'

Lester thought about the seven-magpie secret. He'd need a very steely nerve to see him through.

Pip bustled proprietorially around Percy Place plumping cushions, straightening pictures and monitoring the caterers, an uppity gaggle of Sloaney women headed by waspish finger-clicker Leonie, who had moved Pip's cakes to the back ranks of the sweet treats trestle. Her date and walnut slices, sombre as sarcophaguses, were hidden behind high-rise displays of cupcakes topped with helter-skelter butter icing.

'Mrs Petty paid for a very generous spread.' Leonie threw a few paper napkins across Pip's lovingly baked burial mounds. 'There's really no need for home-made.'

'I bought all the ingredients with my own money. I've been up all night making them.'

'Not meaning to be unkind, but it shows.'

'*I'm* in charge here.'

'Mrs Petty hired me. We have a professional reputation to protect.' She whisked off and Pip removed the napkins and rearranged her food, replacing the business cards the caterer had discreetly fanned around the table with her own. Determined as she was to stay on at the stud, it did no harm to spread the word, and she'd been encouraged by Kit Donne's approach, planning to distribute more around the village. Now she'd cracked another Ronnie clue and put the wronged wife into the picture, she was tempted to print off some Proof ones offering her detection skills, too.

She ate one of the caterer's cupcakes, pleasantly surprised by its lightness, her imagination fired by her discovery of more pieces of the jigsaw puzzle that morning, although they had slotted stormy clouds into all her blue-sky thinking about Ronnie. Gazing up at the portraits of Percy horses, she struggled to see one as beautiful as Beck, the grey stallion in Verity Robertson's Facebook avatar.

What was it Verity had written on her timeline when she'd first set her heart upon having him? *In UK already. Unwanted gift!*

Pip slotted another piece of the puzzle into place. Of course! Ronnie had originally intended the stallion for her father's stud. Who else needed to be thrown a lifeline and bloodline that good?

'Magnificent beasts.' Leonie the caterer stepped in beside her, also looking up at the portraits.

'I'm more of a cat person,' Pip said, feeling something being pressed into her hand and looking down to find a neat stack of her own business cards gathered up and returned.

'There's more than one way to skin a cat,' Leonie hissed. 'If I find these on my tables again, fur will fly.'

Glancing over her shoulder, Pip saw her cakes beneath white blankets once more.

The sugar rush spiked again. Pip marched to the gun room and rattled through the drawers and cartridge bags until she found her ammunition. It was time to take the caterers down and show Alice she wasn't to be messed with.

★

Being an object of fascination was nothing new to Ronnie: she'd adopted the chin-up approach often enough to scrutinise many a ceiling, but dealing with tears was a rare call. Brought up by parents who believed the only acceptable public displays of grief were those of swans and elephants, she was determined not to cry.

It was looking in the direction of her children that threatened to crack her resolve, and some part of her brain she couldn't control had her eyes hostage.

In the front pew at the side of the church, where the Percys traditionally sat, Alice had slotted in her wide-shouldered offspring – the trio a head taller than her now – along with her wide-shouldered husband, all with their heads cocked the same way, as though listening for mice. Across the aisle Tim, a slick Italian greyhound of a man, sat alongside his second wife, Giselle, young and elegant in a black cloche. Ronnie had met her only once, her son's love life already as chequered and colourful as her own. Sitting close beside Tim, her plain black dress at least a size too big, Pax was rigidly self-controlled and pale as bone beneath her freckles, eyes red. Ronnie noted the space between her and her husband, Mack, a span of clear air that spoke volumes.

The congregation stood to belt out 'All Things Bright and Beautiful'.

Ronnie gripped the seat ledge of the pew. Beside her, Blair's little finger lay against hers, as comforting as an arm round her shoulders, every nerve ending radiating reassurance.

She was grateful for his self-containment, his entire focus on her, which meant her entire focus was on not crying.

'He *loathed* this hymn,' she muttered.

The order of service for Captain Jocelyn Percy's funeral was nothing if not predictable: Bach had seen them in, 'Abide with Me' sung first, Corinthians fifteen after the Collect, and once they'd intoned the prayers of penitence, there would be tributes from an oleaginous young Fosse and Wolds MFH and a pithily witty showing judge, renowned for her after-dinner speeches and hatred of straight hocks. If that hadn't sent the older mourners off to sleep,

Psalm Twenty-three would, and finally 'Praise My Soul the King of Heaven' would prod them awake before Bach was played as they followed the coffin out for the Committal.

Where was her father? Ronnie wondered. That angry, witty, irreverent martinet, who valued good horsemanship above humanity. The gambler, the wine lover, the secret *Casualty* enthusiast and hater of John Humphrys. The Gershwin addict for whom 'Rhapsody in Blue' played three times in a row was not obsessive, purely beautiful. There was no sign of him. No sign either of the devoted if irascible husband, father and grandfather, who had learned compassion for one generation by scorning another.

And there should be horses outside. Daddy always needed them close enough to hear whinnies and squeals.

It was as though her children had picked a one-size-fits-all ready-made country-church funeral package. Jocelyn, who had enjoyed an ambivalent relationship with religion, would undoubtedly have preferred a Tennyson poem or Raleigh quote, had disliked the self-congratulatory showing judge intensely, found Bach dull, and the MFH was too young to have hunted alongside him.

'Hold on to your hats, it's another reading,' she murmured, as they all sat down. 'This one will test my mettle.'

Tim, as small, blond and handsome as his Percy forefathers, stood at the altar and drawled out a few verses of Ecclesiastes three. He looked bored, his coping mechanism in stressful situations, another thing common to Percy men. Jocelyn had looked half asleep when they'd buried Ann, and she'd strongly suspected he'd been at the Scotch all morning.

'*A time to keep silence and a time to speak...*' Tim droned.

Ronnie's eyes refused to look up at the ceiling. Instead, they were drawn again to Pax, her fingers pressed tight to her mouth. It always cut deepest to lose life's champions, and Jocelyn had adored his calm, fearless younger granddaughter.

'*A time to love and a time to hate...*'

As Pax's shoulders started to shake, husband Mack swung his big arm around them. Shrugging it off, she slid into the space recently vacated by her brother so fast she shunted sister-in-law Giselle.

She despises him, Ronnie realised in dismay, unable to look away.

And now, as though afflicted by the same optical trick, Pax turned, catching her mother's eye, her startled hare's gaze luminous with unhappiness.

'... *a time of war and a time of peace.*'

Pax was Ronnie's peacemaker in name and nature. How hard they'd both tried to rebuild the broken family bond. How spectacularly they'd failed.

Tears brimmed. They looked hurriedly away. Beside Ronnie, Blair's finger slid over hers, one knuckle tight to another, as profoundly comforting as a hug. She could see Mack mouthing, 'You okay?' at Pax, who slid yet further away from him. When Tim resumed his seat, he was crammed in like an economy traveller on a bucket flight.

As the bishop launched into the prayers of penitence, Pax's gaze drifted over her shoulder again and found her mother's, the hare's eyes caught in headlights, tears welling once more. Mack glanced back too, his expression dispassionate.

With heart-bursting certainty, Ronnie recognised a marriage frayed at the seams, the love having fallen out of it. She saw her own past in her daughter's present and wanted to clamber over the seat-back to that cold, lonely space between them, reassuring Pax that she was there for her, that she understood exactly how it felt.

Sensing her distress, Blair moved his hand over hers, fingers interlaced, his wedding ring pressing hard into her knuckle.

She slid her hand away, her eyes still on Pax. They had both married in this church, although she hadn't been invited to her daughter's ceremony, her exile at its peak.

'*O keep my life, and deliver me,*' intoned the bishop, '*put me not to shame, for I have put my trust in you.*'

'Lord, have mercy,' Ronnie murmured, her gaze sliding to the coffin.

Her father had set no great store by religious supplication. His legacy had delivered a lifetime trust to her, not God. And it was very much there to put her to shame.

Racing back into the farmhouse, Petra was on fire with multi-tasking, pre-holiday energy. Dumping her canvas shopping bag on the island, she sniffed her secret admirer's rose drooping in its little vase, grabbed a basket of the girls' clean washing and hurried towards the stairs.

Janine was rushing the other way, carrying a mop and bucket, eyes wide. 'I can explain about the larder!'

'Say again?'

The pale Turner eyes blinked. 'You haven't put your shopping away yet, then?'

'No. Sorry, Janine. I'd make you and Carly a cup of tea but I'm in a mad dash to change for this wake at the stud, then I *must* come back and pack. And the house-sitters are turning up to be briefed at some point.'

'Relax. I'll put your groceries away, Petra. You go on up.'

'You are a star. Have you seen Fitz?'

'Outside with Carly, talking to the ponies.'

'Sweet. I'll be back in an hour.'

Reassured, Petra went in search of something suitably funereal. Excuses not to go to Percy Place kept bubbling up – but that morning's Milk Tray moment still filled her with wilful recklessness.

A text from Charlie came through as she rattled through the black end of her wardrobe: *Tied up here, so usual train after all. 7.18 pick-up. C c.* No apology. A mis-hit kiss. 'Tied up' again. The familiar Chelsea-basement bondage image flashed up.

Her finger hovered over her phone screen's reply button as she thought through her response: I'm packing for everyone, I have three lots of washing still to do, half a dozen emails to fire off, bills to pay and flights to check-in online. The cleaners are working round the piles of mess I haven't got round to tidying up. The house-sitters will get here to be briefed soon. I'm collecting Bella from camp at four, Prudie from dance club at six, Ed from his train half an hour later and you from yours later still. The fridge needs clearing, the pets worming and the field poo-picking. *And* I've just agreed to attend a complete stranger's wake in order to chat up his mildly stalkerish housekeeper. Now you tell me you're going to roll up at gin o'clock to find it all done.

Without warning, Petra found herself smiling.

And so it would be: the Gunn family would be in holiday mood even if she had to sing 'Quando, Quando, Quando' with a *gelato* in one hand and a bottle of Chianti in the other. *No worries,* she typed, *see you at 8 x.*

Sensing her hall pass had been stamped, Petra wriggled into a subtly figure-hugging black dress, curled her hair up into a clip, then applied a dab of blusher and dash of mascara that she'd no doubt sweat straight off.

It was now positively Mediterranean outside, Petra's holiday mood irrepressible as she struck a pose. The dress wasn't quite so subtly clingy across her tummy roll, and exposed far too much bare upper arm with its horse-rider's T-shirt tan, but it was nothing a pair of Spanx and a silk shrug couldn't transform to pure unadulterated J.Lo sultriness.

Having pulled on her best shapewear and added a wisp of vintage Jigsaw, she dashed downstairs and put a fresh wash on, then stuffed low heels into her handbag and stepped into her FitFlops to hurry to the stud. She planned to stay just long enough to toast the legendary Captain, have a quick, supportively nosy conversation with Pip, clock Bay, and then she'd come straight back. She would *not* drink too much or flirt.

But when she walked along Church Lane and passed a small crowd in the graveyard, she realised that they were only just lowering the Captain's coffin into the ground.

Petra sloped across the road to linger respectfully behind a large black car – could it perhaps be a royal one? – watching as a clergyman in a snazzy mitre and purple cloak threw earth into the grave and invited mourners to follow.

She recognised Ronnie Percy straight away, the blonde hair and upright stance unmistakable. At the same moment as Ronnie stepped forwards to take a handful of earth, a statuesque redhead did so too. They performed a strange, courtly after-you dance, soil in hand, before throwing it in together and embracing tightly.

'For goodness' sake, not now!' snapped a tearful voice, as a small, dark-haired woman muscled past them to lob in a few sods, like Carol Klein hastily backfilling a newly planted rose.

Still the two women clung to each other. Petra watched Ronnie reach up to wipe tears from the younger woman's freckled face, their foreheads tipping together now.

The tiny, dark-haired woman – she had to be the other daughter, Petra realised – stood her ground, growling like a terrier. 'This really isn't the place for reconciliation.'

'What could be more fitting?' Ronnie reached out her arm to include her.

'Absolutely not!' She recoiled. 'I'm not about to forgive you, and neither is Tim, are you, *Tim*?' Her voice rose shrilly.

The small, rugged blond man she was addressing looked round from talking to fellow mourners. As soon as he did, Petra spotted Bay among them. With a startling sixth sense, he fixed his gaze straight back at her, smiling widely. Then, pulling his phone from his pocket, he turned away just as swiftly.

A chirrup sounded deep within Petra's handbag.

It had to be a text from him.

Leave it there, she told herself. Leave it. *Leave it!* A man who sent drones bearing roses across fields in pursuit of fun was more than capable of sexting at a funeral, and she must not go there. A shout went out from the graveside that could have been aimed at her: 'You're an embarrassment, Mummy!'

The raised voices grew louder, accusations flying now.

Cutting through them all came a man's voice, as gravelly and Aussie as the Hunter River. 'Don't any of you *dare* speak like that to her!'

Everyone started talking at once, his voice loudest and angriest of all.

A moment later, Ronnie charged across the lane, blue eyes livid as she jumped into the passenger seat of a Range Rover where she sat glaring out of the window, making a furious phone call. A craggily handsome, dark-haired man in a grey three-piece suit stalked in her wake now, eyes like burning peat as he climbed into the driver's seat. Petra watched their jaws moving with wasp-chewing intensity. Moments later, Ronnie jumped out and slammed the door. Starting the engine with a deep diesel roar, he drove off.

'Bugger!' she hissed, turning to Petra as though it was the most natural thing in the world to find her brief farm-shop ice-cream acquaintance malingering behind an undercover royal vehicle. 'Don't you hate sensitive types?'

'Depends if it's my sensitivities at stake or theirs.'

'He'll come around.' The blue eyes were over-bright. 'I don't suppose you have a taxi number? And a phone I could borrow. Mine's still in the car.' She was pure Lady Penelope and totally irresistible.

Petra fished in her bag for her phone, swiping in the screen code, finding the number for S Express Cabs and handing it across.

'Thanks. Hello? Can I book a – hello? Blast, cut off.' She marched further along the lane to try again, oblivious of the other mourners milling about now, almost all eyes on her.

Petra gave chase. 'The reception's lousy here. I'm on my way to the stud too, so perhaps you could call from there.'

'The reception's going to be lousy there too. I'm going to the family tree. Keep me company.' She started striding away with the phone pressed to her ear again.

There was something so compelling about Ronnie Percy that Petra felt as though she'd just been invited on the most tremendous adventure.

'Hello, is that the taxi firm?... What?... Sorry, I think I must have misdialled... No, Bay, this is not "the sexiest writer in the Bardswolds" and I don't want to come to the pub...'

It didn't matter that Petra's to-do list was as long as the *Mahabharata* or that she was wearing a push-up bra, clingy dress and FitFlops, she was soon scaling the stile into the church meadows and battling to keep up as her small blonde companion, in pearls, loafers and shift dress, marched onwards, navigating her way around Petra's smartphone as she tried to relocate the taxi number. 'Why do they make these things so fiddly? Don't forget Pony Club Camp finishes at four not five today,' she reminded Petra.

'How do you know?'

'There's a text here from "Tilly's Dad open brackets, might be Guy close brackets". I'm glad someone else can't remember names.'

Ronnie, lightning-thumbed, was back through to S Express Cabs. 'The Comptons, that's right... Can't you come any sooner than that?... No, no, it's fine. Outside the Jugged Hare, in that case.' Her blue eyes met Petra's, the soul of old friendship. 'I bet bloody Blair's drowning his sorrows in there. What? I'm going to the station, yes.

Veronica Percy.' Ending the call, she held out the phone to Petra. 'Thank you. I knew we'd be allies. I'm just sorry we won't be acquainted long enough to be chums.'

Petra was uncertain how to interpret this, but it smacked of all too short a lease. 'You never know when you need an ally. Text yourself from my number anyway.'

'That's sweet.' She smiled, doing it. 'And don't trust Might Be Guy. If a man who's not your husband puts kisses in a text, he's either batting for the other team or he wants to sleep with you. My friend in the Range Rover is a man of few words but a two-kiss texter, which speaks volumes.'

'Have you been together long?'

'We're friends,' she said over-quickly, then smiled slowly.

'I hope you patch things up soon.'

'We always do, although he's not exactly helped my cause here. Men are so ridiculous, aren't they, the way they leap to our defence?'

Petra couldn't remember Charlie ever leaping to her defence, and he was a practising barrister. She nodded vaguely, increasingly out of breath as she raced alongside.

'My elder daughter, Alice, is terrified I'm going to barge my way into the stud to start throwing wild parties full of kinky country types doing obscene things on the George the Third button-backs, but I'm not intending to.'

'What a shame. It would make a change from pheasant casserole at the Austens'.'

'Do they still do that?' She flashed her charming smile again. 'Isn't it *awful*? Daddy used to say it was full of game-droppers and name-droppers.'

'Charlie, my husband, gets furious when I call it the Well-hung Party,' Petra confided, although she kept quiet about the fact they'd never been invited. 'Where do you live now?'

'Wiltshire. My landlord's family have some land where we run a horse trials. It's a terrific day out. You should come. The Pony Clubber will love it. Do you ride?'

'Yes.'

'Good for you. *Four things greater than all things are, Women and horses and power and war.*'

'Rudyard Kipling.'

'Clever you for knowing that. The first two putting as much distance as they can between themselves and the others if they have any sense, I've always thought.'

Ronnie Percy was no standard-issue kick-on countrywoman; she started firing out questions with relentless, husky cheer: 'Have you lived in the village long?'

'Seven years.'

'An old-timer! Do you like it?'

'Yes.'

'Come on – truth. It's horribly insular, isn't it?'

'It's a beautiful spot.'

'That accent's not local. Yorkshire Dales, yes?'

'Hawes.' Crikey, she was like the speed-walking Gestapo. Petra would need to put her hands on her knees and pant in a minute.

'Oh, lovely, I've always thought Hawes very underrated.' She gave a ghost of a wink as they swung through the kissing gate onto the stud's unimaginatively named Sixty Acres.

The bachelor pack of yearling and two-year-old colts and geldings, who had been playing sundial with the cedar's big shadow all morning, charged off in all directions with tails fanned as the women approached.

While Petra watched in awe, Ronnie's gaze was more critical. 'Nice-looking bunch, but nowhere near enough elasticity in the joints for top-end competition. I know just the stallion to add it. My goodness, he'd put Compton Magna back on the map. Owner would never sell him, so all pie in the sky, of course. And this lot will make jolly decent hunters.' She eyed a golden-coated, long-legged foal trotting in their wake. 'Now *he's* quite different.'

The foal made his way across to one of the older colts, a fellow yellow dun, still snorting with suspicion at the trespassers. Trying to interest him in a game, the foal bounced around him in a spring-loaded trot, nipping and teasing.

'He's much younger than the rest, isn't he?'

'Seven months at most.' Ronnie started to walk slowly towards them. 'Daddy always gets Lester to send the hotheads straight to prep school. If they think they're big boys, they come across here to live like one and get taken down a peg or two. It's not how I'd do it. I like a sharp, brave horse, and wouldn't want to blunt that for a moment.' Unable to get his startled brother's attention, the foal marched up to her, pushing and nipping at her pockets. She laughed, tapping his nose away firmly. 'He's already got fans, I see. He knows all about titbits, and that won't have come from Lester.' She clapped her hands over her head to send him on his way and the little foal returned to his bigger doppelgänger, who had retreated further and resumed his white-faced, blue-eyed efforts to engage him.

'Terrible racists, horses.' Ronnie watched their black manes and honeyed bodies snake and twist. 'Take any big mixed herd, and they'll inevitably divide up and hang out with the same colour. Prejudices aside, that little man's my guess at a future superstar.'

'*A woman's guess is far more accurate than a man's certainty,*' said Petra, and they watched the colt get his playfellow at last, the two racing off across the field together, squealing and bucking, little and large.

'Oh, I like that.' Ronnie marched onwards. 'Is it Shakespeare?'

'Kipling again. Sorry for sounding a swot. I studied him at university.'

'Never apologise for knowing things. It's heaven. A childhood friend of mine was just like you, always quoting something fascinating, then making a joke of it. She was adamant Kipling couldn't write women.'

'He's also accused of being a terrible racist, although plenty of scholars disagree these days.'

'Daddy was a great admirer of *The Jungle Book*. He read it aloud to me when I was little, doing all the voices: *Now don't be angry after you've been afraid. That's the worst kind of cowardice.*'

They'd reached the Percy family tree where the Captain's horseshoe had been painted black to match his wife's.

'Now I am going to cry.' Ronnie smiled tightly. 'It won't last long, but it's probably best you go on.'

Petra hesitated, feeling that rare heart-swell of finding someone she longed to know better. 'I know you want to be just good allies, but I can't turn my back while you weep. I'll stay if you'll let me.'

'Oh, you are golden.' Blonde head ducking, Ronnie's arm nudged gratefully against Petra's side, the blue gaze brimmed up into hers for a moment. 'I can't tell you how much that means. But, really, best you bugger off.' The eyes were blinking furiously, determined not to have a witness to sorrow.

'You have my number.'

Turning to walk back to the church meadows, she saw the herd of youngsters had regrouped in the shadow of the tree as silently as Grandmother's Footsteps, the dun colt and his sidekick in the front rank, nose to fly-swatting tail. This time, they didn't skitter away when she FitFlopped past them, immobile as the standing stones, all eyes on Ronnie. It seemed she had the same effect on horses as she did on humans.

18

'I almost broke a bally tooth on this!' barked a furious old crony of Jocelyn's, holding up a half-eaten smoked-salmon tartlet full of lead shot.

Emptying the contents of two twelve-bore cartridges into the waspish caterer's little vol-au-vents and mini pastries had, briefly, made Pip feel glorious. Her pot-shots hadn't been blasted from the barrel of a Holland & Holland in the grip of passion, however. They had been as meticulously inserted as microchips.

Prising her way into a brace of Eley Hi-Flyers from the crimp ends with a kitchen boning knife had been a challenging undertaking – Pip had had no idea shotgun cartridges were so impenetrably well engineered – but she'd nevertheless managed to pre-load several items from Leonie's finger buffet with the little lead balls, and it gave her a terrific avenger's frisson when the complaints started coming in.

'Since when did we shoot salmon?' the man with the tartlet demanded.

Unfortunately most of the grievances were directed straight at Pip. Leonie, an eager hunt foot-follower who knew half the mourners, was behaving more like a guest now, platters of food her passport to drift between friends for long chinwags. Meanwhile her two willowy teenage waitresses, ninjas in black and white, sprang up with plates of salted toffee mousse cups and frangipani tuiles, if Pip left the sweets table unmarked. Staying close to the food, keeping guard on her own cakes, she was in the front line.

The mourners were all treating Pip as though she was in charge, which under normal circumstances she'd take pride in, but having been excluded from the funeral service, she refused to preside over prissy food she had sabotaged. She was exhausted; nobody had offered her a drink; her feet ached in the expensive court shoes she'd bought especially and her scalp itched from doing her roots. When she discovered that Ronnie Percy wasn't even *coming* to the reception, it was the final rosemary and fennel cheese straw.

'I'm afraid I can't take responsibility for any of the bought-in food the family has organised,' she told tartlet man, in a high, tight voice. 'As the Captain's *personal* cook and companion, I baked some of his favourite cakes in his honour. Please, do have an almond slice and a sponge finger to make up for your *distress*.' She pressed them on him like daggers. 'I'm Pip, by the way. He was devoted to me. Did you know the Captain long?'

'Fifty years.'

'It's such a shame we saw so few of his old friends here in his last years, but I'm sure you've been terribly busy. He was so lonely by the end. Broken with unhappiness.'

'I... um... Yes.' Discomfited, the man bit into the almond slice. 'Most tasty, Pippa.'

'The secret's in the jam. And it's Pip. My dad used to call me Pipsqueak, you see. This is me.' She pressed her Home Comforts card on him. 'I also run a detective agency called Proof. Complimentary artisan baking with every client meeting.'

After he'd beaten a retreat to the safety of fellow black ties braying about British sports-horse breeding, Pip patrolled her table, murderous thoughts raging. Cramming the caterer's delicate little fancies into her mouth when nobody was looking – what better way to get rid of enemy supplies than eat them? – she loaded plates with a selection of her finest baking and thrust her Home Comforts business card at anyone passing close by. If this was how the Percys rewarded loyalty, they would have to fight to keep her.

Leonie stalked up just as Pip had stuffed three iced macaroons into her mouth. 'Have you heard? Lead shot has been found in the food.'

Unable to speak, Pip shrugged.

Leonie's eyes narrowed. 'We must be vigilant. And I'd be grateful if you let guests choose their own cakes. People are saying it's like an episode of *The Apprentice* over here.'

You're fired, Pip thought murderously, eyes streaming, a macaroon crumb caught in her throat.

Leonie's long, thin face softened. 'You miss him, don't you?'

She nodded, furious that the tears were streaming for all the wrong reasons – the macaroon mix was so dry and almondy, Prue Leith would be appalled – but she couldn't hope to speak.

The next moment she was clasped in a lobster-claw embrace, the hiss harsh in her ear, 'I've warned you once. Don't cross me. I *own* the Comptons' social catering.'

'Excuse me one moment.' Pip retreated to the observation tower to leave one-star reviews for Leonie's catering company on every site she could find. The Captain, a big fan of revenge and hater of macaroons, would have surely been proud.

'I won't ever forget you,' she promised, letting the tears come freely at last, a glorious *Titanic-Bambi-Lion King* purge, until she realised she didn't have a tissue, at which point she stopped and settled down to watch the Austen family sizing the place up, sherry in hand, as she waited to calm down enough to go back.

Petra quite forgot to swap her FitFlops for the heels in her handbag. Close up, the house was every inch the Birtwick Park beauty she'd dreamed it would be. The family were welcoming guests in the grand entrance hall, its black and white floor beckoning Petra in to navigate the tricky chessboard of commiserating with a line of close relatives to a man she had never met.

'I'm terribly sorry for your loss.' She started with the tall, elegant redhead granddaughter, whom Ronnie had hugged in the graveyard.

'Thank you.' She looked at Petra with sad, kind eyes. 'Forgive me, you are?'

Here we go. 'Villager. Petra. Have a horse. Upper Bagot Farmhouse.'

'Oh, gosh, of course, you're the writer. I love your books! How kind of you to come. I'm Pax.' She whisked Petra down the line, like a VIP, introducing her to her siblings, small rugged Tim, who thanked her cleavage for the sympathetic words, and even smaller and more rugged Alice, nerves fraying in black Aquascutum, who told her to hurry into the main drawing room before the food ran out. 'Didn't expect this many to turn up, but the village always loved a freebie. Did you know Grumps well?' She eyed Petra beadily.

'We shared a great admiration for Kipling.'

Alice smiled briefly, whispering, 'Try some of Pip's cakes. They really are jolly good. Such a shame we'll have to let her go.'

'No, we won't,' Pax corrected, 'Grumps would want her to stay on.'

Her sister's eyes flashed. 'Pax, do your bloody...' Alice's narrow Cupid's-bow mouth formed the word '... maths.'

A rosebud mimed back: '*I am.*'

Realising she was party to a private argument breaking through grief's formal surface, Petra smiled politely and moved on.

She was dying to have a quick look around before she tried to penetrate the chattering black throng, but Gill was already lying in wait by an enormous carved bear, her fascinator at forty-five degrees, like a party hat after one too many congas: 'Where have you *been?*'

'Holiday stuff.' Loyalty is a fickle thing, Petra reflected, finding herself holding on to her encounter with Ronnie Percy and the family tree like Mary Lennox to her secret garden, reluctant to break the spell just yet. 'I can't stay long.'

'You *must* talk to Pip. When I tried, she just thrust a huge stack of flapjacks at me and told me to steer clear of the vol-au-vents. It's wall-to-wall hunt buttons and blazers in there, and they're serving oloroso by the barrel. Nobody knows what's going to happen to the stud and we're all pretending not to care, like cocktail hour while the *Titanic* listed. You must get the heads-up. The atmosphere's horrid. There was a frightful ding-dong in the graveyard earlier. Alice accused her mother of crocodile tears and Blair Robertson – you know, Daniel Craig in breeches – leaped to Ronnie's defence. The next thing you know, he and Alice's husband are like two bare-knuckle boxers rolling up their sleeves graveside and Ronnie has bolted as usual. That's probably the last we'll see of her.'

Petra looked at her watch again, knowing her to be in the village for at least another half-hour waiting for her cab. It was hard to make a dramatic exit from the Cotswolds by private hire unless you booked well in advance.

'Bay's convinced the family are keeping just the stud business and some land and selling the rest, but my guess is nothing's been decided.'

'*A woman's guess is far more accurate than a man's certainty.* Is he here?' Anticipation curled in her belly.

'Somewhere. I think a bunch of them went to look at this year's foals in the hope there's a Badminton winner going cheap.'

Nowhere near enough elasticity in the joints for top-end competition. Petra remembered those over-bright blue eyes, the tough kindness.

They made their way into the drawing room, hung with so many horse portraits it resembled an old-fashioned zoetrope: if you spun it, they would gallop round and round. Double length, it had a false-panelled wall that had been folded back to reveal its mirror sitting room, creating a ballroom-length space that had once hosted legendary parties.

'You will never *guess* who was in the pub earlier.' Gill had grabbed them some sherry. '*Kit Donne.*' She breathed it like a state secret. 'And he was in a horrid mood. I'd forgotten what a miserable bugger he is.' They'd made it to a table covered with Pip's business cards and a well-plundered cake selection. 'I told him he should smarten his house up.'

'Gill, you didn't!'

'The village comes first, Petra.' She helped herself to one of the last chocolate brownies. 'Which is why you must talk to Pip. Where on earth is she?'

'Fondant French fancy?' A tall, thin blonde in expensive leather trousers thrust a plate of brightly coloured little cakes under their nose. 'If you're looking for Pip, she took herself off for a comfort break. Bit of a runny tummy. I'd leave that brownie if I was you. Said she'd be back soon.'

'I don't have soon, Gill,' Petra apologised. 'I have to go now.'

'Nonsense. Have another sherry and let me give you a guided tour of the house and stables.' Gill waved Leonie's French fancies away.

For a tour around Birtwick Park, Petra would fly to Italy with nothing but a bikini in hand luggage.

'Who's he?' was the first thing she asked, as they admired the mosaic of framed hunks on horses, one man featuring more than most, long-thighed and furnace-eyed.

'Johnny Ledwell. Handsome, isn't he?'

'And some.' Petra admired the bone structure and perfect horseman's seat. 'I'd put him in a book.'

'Not a man of many words.'

'I can make up for that.'

'I doubt it. If rumour's to be believed, some things are best left unsaid.'

In St Mary's pretty churchyard, Jonathan Selwyn Ledwell's grave was as far away from the Percy plot as Croydon is to Chelsea on a London map. In life, the family Johnny had married into might have stayed fiercely loyal, but in front of God they'd turned him out to grass on high pasture, the rumours of suicide and other misdemeanours banishing him to an isolated plot close to the perimeter fence. Ronnie had always thought it served him far better than the Percys' dingy yew-sentried corral. From here, the glorious view stretched straight down across the meadows to Sixty Acres, where the herd of young horses he'd had direct influence in breeding took afternoon naps, tails flicking, heads occasionally curling back to nip at an itch. The little dun, far smaller and more golden than the others, was still chummed up with his bigger mate.

'You'd like that colt,' she told Johnny, taking the dead flowers from his grave and setting one of her father's floral tributes there, a delightful ring of sweet-peas from the hunt that she was certain the Captain would have been happy to pass on to his son-in-law. For all their emotive words, her children hadn't been to their father's grave in a while. It was so drought-parched that only a few thin stinging nettles drooped near Johnny's narrow resting place, the ground hard as concrete, a fitting barrier between her winged feet and his clay ones.

It was only after their marriage had ended that Ronnie had realised Johnny Ledwell's cold, polite retreat from her, one child at a time, was a way of dealing with his overwhelming guilt and depression. Living with a man who wouldn't look her in the eye had felt utterly hollowing and bewildering, single parenthood within a supposed marriage of equals. With each pregnancy – none conceived soberly or lovingly – he'd become more detached, and Ronnie had felt shut out from the stud, annexed with her mother in domestic crèche HQ, planning her solitary competition career around childcare while her husband and father played God with bloodlines. She was just the baby-incubator and travelling sales rep, whose best horses were always sold out from under her.

Johnny, who had started sleeping in the dressing room while Ronnie was nursing Alice so he could be up early for autumn hunting, had never entirely moved back, drunken conjugal visits made through the adjoining door. After Pax was born, even those had stopped.

Like the Captain, Johnny rarely looked to female company for conversation, intelligence, knowledge or even laughter, but for more practical and prosaic pleasures. And he had looked to Scotch long before that. By the end, he was drinking so heavily that a bottle of Johnnie Walker was just the daily starting point, like Ronnie's first strong mug of tea.

'Our elder daughter has serious control issues,' she told his headstone, 'our son remains a flake on the make, and our baby girl is about to call time on her marriage. It goes without saying that none of them wants my help.' She winced away the urge to cry. 'But they need someone. If you can break out of here and rattle some chains, it would be appreciated.'

'Or you can ask God,' intoned a deep voice behind her.

'Christ!' Ronnie whipped round.

'Him too. We can ask them together, if you like. I'm the Reverend Hilary Jolley.' A large hand was thrust out of a cassock to shake. 'Shall we pray together, Mrs Ledwell?'

Ronnie smiled warily, reluctant to offend God, yet always astonished that his representatives on earth were so universally odd. The Reverend Hilary Jolley was very hard to sex, a tun barrel of waistless godliness, mid-length hair, broad shoulders, a short neck and the sort of soft features that smacked of two genders divided by a common duty; there was an argument for both sides. The eyes, however, were as kind and lively as the name.

Ronnie, who had fallen in and out of love with the Church a few times in her life, had never needed Him onside more.

'I'd love to.' She smiled gratefully. 'I just need to have a quick chat with an old friend first, if that's okay?'

Lester dealt with the Captain's wake as he did any large gathering – he retreated into a corner, like a guardsman into his sentry box, and stood dutifully still, eyes front.

He'd found the funeral service surprisingly comforting. The Captain would have criticised it like mad for dullness, no doubt, but Lester preferred his operas uncut and his tests of endurance long format. The piece of graveside theatre at the burial, while regrettable, had at least seen Ronnie away as sharply as a fox from a gunshot. Now the crows had all descended on the stud to pick over the cheeseboard, showing no sign of lifting off again soon. *Tell them all to go to Hell, Lester.*

The Captain would have been a terrible warmonger had he served through conflict. Lester, always far more phlegmatic, stood guard, daring the battle to come to him.

Pip had been too busy waging her own cake wars with the caterers to bother him, for which he was grateful.

Pax checked on him more than once, kind-eyed as always, her voice as soothing as those of his favourite contraltos. 'Lester, such a hard day for you. Can I get you anything?'

He shook his head each time. He'd urged her to sing when she was younger, told Johnny and the Captain she must join a choir, could still never listen to Handel's *Rinaldo* without imagining her in the title role. But then he'd always had ambition for them all.

Tim offered him cigarettes, even though Lester had quit when the boy was a teenager. 'How d'you do it? Giselle keeps encouraging me to vape, which sounds ghastly.'

'You stub one out and you don't light another.' After Johnny's death, Lester's sudden sense of his own mortality had brought many changes. Johnny's son had his father's predisposition to addiction and his mother's wanderlust, which in combination made it all too easy for him to run away from responsibility, already checking his watch to countdown to departure.

Alice, by contrast, was a stayer, like Ann Percy, immensely resilient, with a streak of terrier obsession from Johnny's side, which meant she wouldn't stop worrying away at a situation until she was satisfied with the result. He could see her charging from group to group now, making sure every guest had been spoken to, every polite commiseration acknowledged and recollection shared, although she wasn't really listening to any of them, merely ticking off a list in her head, like Johnny counting hounds. It was why he had made a far better huntsman than master, his people skills awkward. The better master by far would have been the mistress.

The familiar faces of the Fosse and Wolds Hunt, out in force here, all knew Lester of old and understood that the man who had followed their hounds three days a week for decades rode his own line and never talked at point. Today they were united in support, a big field of associates that would be the first to step in with help if he needed it, but had the sense to leave him alone when he did not.

It was only the Austens who inevitably ventured too close to his sentry position, trying to flush him out with a lot of back-slapping, but Lester had already anticipated the Percy family rivals baiting him, and he held hard. One of the best lessons Johnny had taught him was that wilful hounds and horses learned better from a good example than bad discipline. They only wanted reassurance after all, just as the family did.

'Lester, you'll have a jolly good hunch what Ronnie intends to do with this place.' Sandy Austen fixed him with the hypnotising look all Austen men shared. 'You two were always thick as thieves.'

'Long time ago.' There was honour among thieves. Seven for a secret never to be told.

'Educated guess?'

'I didn't have much of a formal education, Mr Austen.' They'd lost one for sorrow today. That left six. Ronnie had always possessed a Midas touch with horses. 'But I've learned that it never pays to underestimate Mrs Ledwell.'

19

Kit let himself into the churchyard through the kissing gate opposite the Old Almshouses, appalled at how thin-skinned being in the village made him feel. Not content with indulging in too much whisky, nostalgia and name-calling in the pub, he'd just offered a woman a job purely on the basis that she'd burst into tears. He'd probably come back from New York to find Pip Edwards had stripped the place. Then again, wasn't that what he wanted her to do?

He pushed the gate closed, looking up just in time to see a blonde figure walk behind the yew trees in the distance. For a moment he felt as though a ghost had taken hold of his hand. Hermia had moved like that once, light and slight, a will-o'-the-wisp beacon far ahead.

Making his way around the back of the Austen family mausoleum – cause of the great upset when they had wanted to put Hermia into it – he drew close enough to catch sight of her again. She was standing in front of his wife's grave, square-shouldered and slim-waisted in tailored black linen. He couldn't see her face, but he could already guess her identity. She was reading the inscription, ten of Shakespeare's sweetest lines, her stage-namesake's first speech in *A Midsummer Night's Dream*, swearing every lovers' emblem she can conjure that tomorrow truly I will meet with thee. Kit had been inconsolable with the need for that promise at the time, demanding the entire speech be engraved, not just its final couplet.

Everyone got so fraught around death and its remembrance, he reflected bitterly, much as they did with movie credits. His experience of directing films had left him shocked at the self-indulgent narcissism of the industry; his experience of organised remembrance had left him eager to die before anyone else he loved did so. He'd not let them carve a generic job description and cast list on Hermia's gravestone: beloved wife of, mother of, daughter to, sister to. She was his to love and cherish in death as in life, and he'd refused to surrender that love to convention. It was a small rebellion, given the Austen family had buried her among their own, marked with the Christian name that had never been his for her. Kit hadn't known Hermione, just his own sweet Hermia.

The woman standing at that gravestone was hugging herself tightly, staring fixedly at the inscription. His sinews hardened. He could hardly march up to his wife's childhood friend on the day she'd buried her own father and accuse her of letting Hermia down but, right now, it was the thing he wanted to do more than anything. He'd never quite shaken off the rage of his Donne forefathers, notoriously loud-mouthed, brawling farmhands, known for picking fights all over Cumbria.

As he moved forward to speak to her, divine intervention came in the form of the vicar, emerging from the church porch, all moist-browed androgyny in voluminous black robes, beckoning the woman inside.

Seeing her in profile before she disappeared into the church, Kit let out a hollow laugh of recognition. She was the horsebox blonde. His nemesis twice over.

The mourners showed no signs of leaving, still milling about talking horse and country, the Austens' voices loudest while the Percy grandchildren stood together, pale-faced and deep in conversation.

Returning from her loo break, Pip noticed with satisfaction that there was nothing left but crumbs on her plates and stands. Her cakes had proven a lot more popular than the caterers' frothy little meringues, Florentines and macaroons, which were still on show.

'I'm afraid we had to throw your home-baked bits and bobs out.' Waspish Leonie appeared beside her. 'It seems somebody deliberately sabotaged the buffet with lead shot, can you *imagine*? Yours were *riddled*.'

'Goodness, how terrible.' Pip's competitive spirit flared, an experienced online game-player unfazed by dirty moves like this. 'What a good job I baked plenty.' She dived beneath the trestle, relieved to find her extra supplies untouched. 'I'll check these over personally.'

'I can't allow you to put more out, I'm afraid. Health and Safety.'

'The Captain loved my baking,' she flared. 'I was closest of anybody to him in his final years, and this would have been his dying wish.'

'My dying wish would be to live a bit longer,' said a friendly voice and a glass of sherry was offered to Pip. 'You look as though you could do with this. Goodness, you've worked hard. I love the coffin-shape theme going on. I'll have one of everything made by you, Pipsqueak. How are you bearing up?' The greeting was as full of warmth as a hot-air balloon.

Pip felt a flush of delight. Although they'd not spoken much lately Pip still counted Petra as a friendly face in the village.

If Petra weren't always so approachable and kind-hearted – and *Last of the Summer Wine* northern – Pip might have resented her beautiful house and family, her handsome husband, hourglass figure and oh-so-perfect life. Today she was swathed in glamorous Kate Bush retro and moreish scent, the kind brown eyes set in a filigree of mascara-perfect lashes, dark hair swept up in a chignon. The flip-flops were super-cool. Standing with her, Pip instantly felt like an insider again.

'It's certainly been busy!' She beamed, raising her sherry glass. She never normally drank, the taste making her think of Christmas with her parents, each bottle of Harvey's Bristol Cream taking three years in the drinks cabinet to finish.

'How completely *Flambards* is this?' Petra whispered. 'Have you spotted royalty yet?'

About to admit the only royals here were the Worcester serving plates, Pip stopped herself and adopted a not-at-liberty-to-say face. Then Petra's delicious scent filled her nostrils as she leaned into Pip's ear, the voice an intimate undertone: 'I've just been round the yard with Gill and I was convinced I saw Charles and Camilla, but it was just the Protheroes from the Gables admiring an antique trough. Very similar bottoms. Excuse me.' She turned as a couple interrupted her to take their leave with a kiss and wishes of *bon voyage*. 'Sorry about that.' She returned her rich treacle gaze to Pip. 'We're going on holiday tomorrow and you'd think we were emigrating.'

'No worries.' Pip glowed in reflected glory. 'You must know everyone here.'

'Not quite.' She clinked sherry-glass rims with a generous smile. 'I don't know you nearly well enough.'

Pip felt as though she'd grown a foot in height. 'Ask anything about me you like,' she offered eagerly. 'You write books and I'm an open one!'

Despite her assertions, Petra already knew quite a lot of biographical detail about Pip, who talked non-stop, so even their few short encounters had been a confessional *tour de force*. *Bake Off* addict, serial lonely-heart, blog-lover, animal adopter and befriender of village pensioners, Pip was generous to a fault, but her loneliness and neediness often made her relationships short-lived despite her devotion. She lived alone in what had been her parents' bungalow on the outskirts of Bagot, binge-watching box sets and devouring library thrillers faster than most women read their horoscopes (Petra had tried not to be offended by Pip's excited announcement that some of her own books were 'my absolute favourite sort of trash'). She had five cats named after Boyzone, three surviving Take That chinchillas and a goldfish called Johnny Depp.

Petra didn't feel there was a lot more about Pip that she needed to have on record, but meeting the legendary Bardswolds Bolter had inflamed her researcher's curiosity, and Pip clearly thrived on attention. Trying not to dwell on her hypocrisy, Petra grasped the opportunity to quiz further. 'What do you make of Ronnie?'

The eyes bulged enthusiastically. 'As soon as we met, I knew we'd be super-close. She's an expert in her field, of course, and very classy. I was practically her dad's PA as well as running this house, and I'm sure Ronnie will expect the same service, although I'm getting job offers every day.'

'I'll bet you are. You must be sorry she's not here.'

'It's a very emotional day for her,' Pip said, in a reverent undertone. 'She knows everything is being taken care of.'

Remembering Ronnie's joke about a very poor reception, Petra glanced across at the three grandchildren whose huddled conversation seemed to be hotting up. 'I heard she and Alice don't see eye to eye?' She looked back at Pip.

'Ssh!' A glint of wickedness crossed the pug-like face. 'Alice is very sensitive about her height.'

Gill's right, Petra realised. She's sharper and sassier than she makes out. 'C'mon, Pip, spill the beans. What do *you* think is going happen with this place?'

From Pip's wide-eyed silence, she worried she'd pitched it far too intimately. But she realised that the other woman was looking in wonder at something behind her, just as her own eyes were covered with hands smelling of Imperial Leather and chocolate brownie.

'Exactly the same question that's on my lips,' said a smooth voice. 'You must have left it there when we kissed in my dreams last night, Mrs Gunn.'

'Trust me, I'm a rubbish kisser and have a cold-sore.' Petra laughed as she swung round to face Bay, six feet two of beefy charm, his navy-blue eyes, sparkling with delight, inviting all who crossed them to get utterly lost there.

'Leave my dreams alone,' he grumbled. 'I can kiss who I like in them. Besides, I've been secretly following you round all week.' His voice was as low as a lover's tyres rolling quietly up to the back door.

Petra thought about the drone and felt a frisson of shared secrecy, all a bit terrifying, but she didn't want it to stop. 'Amazed you found a place in Waitrose car park.'

'I revved my engine in the click-and-collect zone.'

'I'm not that easily bought. I only popped in for Marmite to pack on holiday.'

'Lucky Marmite, going on holiday with you.'

'Ed can't live without it.' Petra's eyes seemed to be having an entirely different conversation with Bay's than the prosaic nonsense her mouth was spouting. 'I'm more of a marmalade fan.'

'*Voulez vous coucher avec moi ce soir*? Coarse cut?'

'Seville, shredded.'

Watching them, Pip felt as though they were Dex and Alexis, Rhett and Scarlett, Leia and Han Solo. She could hear Lady Marmalade soul-sistering in her head now, saw Nicole Kidman and Ewan McGregor cast in jewel-bright colours in *Moulin Rouge*, Tom Cruise and Kelly McGillis with blue sky and cumulus reflecting off their sunglasses in *Top Gun*.

Marching back along the Plum Run from Compton Magna's grave-yard to Bagot's pub to collect the Saab, Kit still had enough residual Islay fire and Colombian caffeine left in his belly to turn and face his old home. Upper Bagot Farmhouse, despite the developer's face-lift and division, wasn't a whole lot different, still a busty Georgian front with a saggy Tudor bottom. A pretty young blonde was wiping the windowsill of what had once been their dining room.

Kit hurried on. Pitching back into his car, checking a message from Orla – a glorious pop-art tourist-spot selfie, complete with emoticon and exclamation marks – he was grateful that she kicked ass in urban confinement.

And yet, as he looked out across the orchards once more, he felt a curious sense of not wanting to leave.

His phone rang: Ferdie complaining that he was late. 'We said one o'clock. Donald wants to talk to you about *Lear* before the others get here.'

'*The tempest in my mind doth from my senses take all feeling else.* Sorry. Still in the Comptons. Leaving now.'

'Of course, you've been to the grave.' Ferdie's voice softened. 'My turn to apologise, dear boy. I know how uncomfortable you find it there.'

'Actually, I'm toying with the idea of coming here to finish the Sassoon.'

'Have you been drinking?'

Having rung off, sitting in front of the best view in the Cotswolds, Kit closed one eye and tried to remember the way to Stratford.

He called up Google Maps on his smartphone for directions, but it insisted that he was looking for the Stratford East theatre in London. 'No, no, no!' he yelled at it furiously, after several attempts to correct it failed. He now tried Google Microphone, enunciating, 'The RSC, Stratford-upon-Avon.'

'Finding NCP car park near Stratford East Theatre, E15,' the app promised.

'YOU BASTARD THING!'

Somebody wrenched open the back door, breathing hard. 'Thanks for waiting.'

Kit looked into the rear-view mirror in alarm. The ghost was sitting right behind him now, buckling up a seatbelt.

'I've only got twenty in cash.' She was digging around in the neat little pockets of her black jacket. 'Will it be enough?'

'For what?'

'Broadbourne station.'

'You think I'm for hire?'

'Didn't I book you?' She looked at him impatiently, then bit her lip in surprised recognition. 'Oh, goodness, it's you.'

As Kit opened his mouth to reply, his phone demanded that he turn left out of the car park, still hell bent on navigating him to Stratford East theatre.

'Oh, God, I'm so sorry!' In the back of the car, Ronnie suppressed involuntary laughter, the inconvenient absurdity of graveside humour striking her afresh. His face was so perfectly, furiously indignant. 'I was expecting a taxi to be waiting and I thought you were it – forgive me.'

'Turn left,' intoned a recorded voice.

'Oh, shut up!' Kit threw the phone onto the seat beside him. 'I'll forgive anything if you can tell me the best way to Stratford.'

Ronnie's amusement vanished as abruptly as it had surfaced. Kit Donne smelt of whisky. 'So, you've been to the pub?'

'Just a coffee and a quick drink.' He turned back to the wheel, checking the car clock with horror. 'I'm running stupidly late. I know the station's en route. Let me give you a lift; we can introduce ourselves on the way.'

Ronnie very rarely experienced a deep pinch of fear, but its fingers were beneath her ribs already. Her father and Johnny had both driven drunk – one into almost every ditch in the vicinity in an era when it was acceptable behaviour, the other to his death when it was not.

'Are you sure you should be behind a wheel? There's a whiff of the distillery in here.'

'Is there really? It was only a couple. Maybe three.'

'You could still lose your licence.'

'I have lost it, all bar the rubber stamp.' He stabbed the key into the ignition slot on the second attempt. 'Overtaking horseboxes too fast.' The eyes caught hers in the mirror. 'They can't ban me twice.'

'They can do worse than that if you cause an accident.' She didn't know if he was over the limit or not, but she didn't want him driving anywhere to test it. Hermia had once described her husband in a letter as 'a man whose thoughts are his own, his conscience universal'. But the universal conscience was late for lunch. The engine started. Looking over his shoulder, his foot stamped on the accelerator. Instead of reversing, they shot forwards, only just stopping short of making a leap into the orchards. 'Shit!'

Ronnie didn't pause to think. Looming between the two front seats and reaching for the ignition key, she was practically in his lap.

'What are you *doing*?'

'I should ask you the same question.' She tugged the plastic fob deftly from its slot. 'Stop and think, for goodness' sake.'

'I'm meeting friends for lunch.' His hand flailed for his keys.

'You'll meet your maker first.' She tried to retreat to the safety of the back seat, but her dress belt was caught round the handbrake, making it impossible.

Pip was no great moraliser, despite her parents' long and extremely faithful marriage. Her early *Dynasty* imprinting – along with a teenage addiction to Jackie Collins and Danielle Steele – had lent her faith in the glamour of infidelity; her own very brief marriage had by contrast given her a decidedly low opinion of the institution. Pip, who told very few people about Algerian language student Ali and their whirlwind wedlock, was only grateful that she'd taken the Vale over the veil.

Until now, she'd been disappointed by the vanilla tameness of the village's many long marriages, which she knew from scrutinising unguarded Facebook pages were lifeless unions. *C'mon, Compton!* she'd wanted to cry to the zombie domestics. *Get yourself an avatar,* find a chat forum for marital infidelity, and get sexy! You have no idea how much fun I have as Mrs Jolie-Smith_1975. But, as it turned out, the Compton elite had the potential to be every bit as exciting flirting in the flesh as her covert virtual world.

'We need more deaths in the village, Mrs G.' Bay was a consummate flatterer. 'That black dress looks disturbingly good on you.'

Petra's laughter was full of charming indignation. 'If the locals start dropping like flies we'll know who's behind it, hey, Pip?'

'Yes, totally. Don't mind me.' Pip stepped back to rearrange her cakes, eager not to break the spell.

Bay was happy to oblige, lowering his voice to a stage whisper close to Petra's ear. 'Promise you'll show me your tan lines the moment you're back.'

'That's a line we'll never cross, Bay.' Her eyes signalled to Pip for help.

'More cake?' Pip offered half-heartedly, remembering Ann Percy claiming all Austen men started by winking a blue eye at the midwife when they were born.

Bay claimed a sponge slice, then whispered to Petra, 'Spoilsport. I'll show you mine.'

Pip would have swooned had she been Petra, but the object of his attention stayed super-cool. 'That's a dare every quadcopter owner round here cheats with a dusk fly-by. One followed me for ages today. Landed on my stable roof.' She'd gone very pink, Pip noticed. Probably the heat.

Bay looked impressed. 'Bloody good piloting. Mine's been stuck in a big oak canopy in Lockes Wood since Wednesday, which is a total sod because we've got seriously nasty poachers around now the crops are being cut. Coursers mostly.'

'A whole new course cut,' Petra said drily as Pip offered round more sponge fingers.

Taking one, Petra felt profoundly deflated, not to mention disconcerted. If Bay's drone was up a tree, who had sent the rose? It struck her as a faintly creepy gesture now, as well as disappointing.

Bay was still talking about poachers: 'This lot are evasive buggers. We're getting a lynch mob together to try to catch them tonight, and there's no point going out half cocked. They're hard bastards.'

Petra thought about the poor lurcher Carly had found left for dead.

'Will you be armed?' Pip was gazing at him, like an eager mastiff at a sausage.

'Waving a shotgun about in the dark isn't much use in trying to round up half a dozen urban fantasists and dogs trained to kill. It's a far cry from Eddie Grundy taking one for the pot, these days. It's all camo gear, night-vision goggles and instant messaging. We're pretty sure the lot we're after tonight use old pay-as-you-go BlackBerrys of all things.'

'How business retro,' Petra said, then felt very silly when Pip nodded knowledgeably and started talking like Lisbeth Salander.

'Of course, that way they're all linked with an untraceable messenger like hoodie looters,' she deduced. 'Any downloadable GPS tracking app can be brought into play so they know exactly where each other is while the authorities haven't a clue. Add in high-level mapping and they're the SAS of poaching, basically.'

'Er... quite.' Bay flashed an on-off smile.

'Where do you learn this stuff?' Petra gaped at her, astonished.

'I read a lot online.'

'Bloody cunning, though, eh?' Bay helped himself to a Bakewell slice.

'So will you be taking any other weapons?' Pip asked, bulging, hyperactive-thyroid eyes stretched wide. 'Taser? Mustard spray? Tranquilliser gun?'

'Only this and these.' He tapped his head, then pointed at his eyes. 'It's about flushing them out and scaring them off, not flogging them with bike chains. That's why we need that drone back.' His eyes found Petra's again.

Caught in a gaze as bright as any flashlight, she perked up.

'Our tree man's windsurfing off the Costa de la Luz this week,' he went on, 'so I've put the word out for a cherry-picker.' One half of the double-entendre act sought out his comedy partner with playful blue eyes. 'Do you know anyone with one, Mrs G?'

Petra wished she wasn't so easily led, but his smile was too tempting, and she felt stupidly happy to find the Lady Marmalade flirtation back on, albeit with a change of fruit. 'What exactly does a cherry-picker do, Bay?'

The smile widened, the blue eyes darkened. 'I'll be delighted to give you a demonstration sometime.'

'You know, I haven't had a cherry for ages.'

'Actually, there are cherries in my Bakewell slices,' Pip pointed out.

'People pick them too early.' Bay ignored her, eyes fixed on Petra. 'The taste is sweeter the longer you wait.'

'So you'd recommend well-grown wood?' Petra fought laughter.

'Indeed.' His smile widened. 'A decent cherry-picker can reach spots never accessed before.'

'Good head essential for heights, I imagine?' Petra asked.

'Going down is far more fun.'

Pip's jaw had dropped.

Stepping closer to Petra, Bay lowered his voice so only she could hear, the eyes scorching with intent. 'Do you want to go for lunch somewhere quiet before we collect the girls from Pony Club Camp, Mrs G? Let me show you how well I handle a Gunn.'

Her body was shamefully quick to prickle with an all-over blush as she laughed this off, awash with panicky piety. 'This is a wake.'

'Up call.' He smiled easily. 'Micklecote Manor serves a splendid deconstructed *meggyleves*. That's—'

'I know what it is.' Petra had eaten the chilled sour cherry soup in Hungary.

'Delicious washed down with kirsch.'

As he said it, Petra became aware of something black moving behind him, like a dreamcatcher glued to a robotic arm. Gill, in her fascinator, was listening in.

'I can't,' she bleated. She turned to Pip urgently. 'So what *do* you think Ronnie will do about this place? You never did say.'

'You should know, Petra darling,' Bay cut in, amused. 'You were the one spotted having a long walk and talk with the Bolter earlier. I knew I recognised the voice.'

'Was *that* Ronnie?' Petra had never been good at lying. Her body blush deepened as she feigned shock, acutely aware of Pip's betrayed pug eyes and Gill's *j'accuse* fascinator. Of course it would have been noticed that Ronnie, setting off across the church meadows in full view of the funeral congregation, had had Petra Gunn in hot pursuit. Yet she felt a profound, protective loyalty to the little blonde.

Pip was agog. 'What did she say to you?'

'Just horse-talk,' Petra bluffed. 'We only cut across a field together. She needed to borrow a phone. She told me about a stallion she rates.'

'Is it grey?' Pip demanded.

'I have no idea. It has flexible joints, which sounded like a bank account to me.' Petra was uncomfortably aware that the fascinator in her peripheral vision was now pointing at her like a jousting lance. 'She said it would put Compton Magna back on the map.'

Pip's eyes bulged, as though she could visualise that map glowing in front of her, *Dad's Army* arrows pointing at the stud.

'Surely she's not planning to run this place as a going concern.' Bay snorted sceptically.

Petra shrugged. 'You're asking the wrong person. But she said it was all pie in the sky because the stallion's not for sale and she has a horse trials to run in Wiltshire.'

'That horse is wasted where he is!' Pip piped up furiously.

Before Petra could ask for more detail, a shriek went out from behind the trestle where Pip had stashed her empty Tupperware and handbag. A moment later, Leonie emerged with a plastic food bag held at arm's length.

'As if the lead shot wasn't enough, just *what*,' she thrust it at Pip, 'were you intending to do with this?' Inside it was a very flat, desiccated mouse.

20

In the Jugged Hare car park, an undignified tussle was taking place between the seats of a Saab as Ronnie and Kit fought for possession of the ignition keys.

'I am not over the limit!'

A saloon with S Express Cabs decals on its sides was pulling up beside them now. Still wrestling, Ronnie and Kit inadvertently elbowed the indicator stalks and dashboard, setting off hazard lights, windscreen wipers and sporadic bursts of the horn. The ignition key had dropped somewhere into the passenger foot well along with Kit's phone.

'Get out of my bloody car!' he thundered at Ronnie.

'I'm bloody trying to!'

The belt of her dress was still snagged in the handbrake mechanism. When she finally managed to undo it, she discovered it was sewn into the dress, keeping her firmly tethered to the central console. She sat up as best she could, mustering good grace.

'Please take my taxi to Stratford with my blessing,' she offered. 'You can come back for the car tomorrow.'

'I want to drive it now!' Kit was apoplectic.

'I'm afraid I'm going to have to ask you to get out first.'

'What are you going to do? Arrest me?'

'I need to take this dress off.'

'I don't bloody believe this.' Kit wrenched open the driver's door beside him, realising too late that Paranoid Landlord had marched out of his kitchen once more and had his nose up against the glass. His big square face took the full force of the Saab door opened at speed. Leaping out in shocked apology, Kit caught his leg on the rim and fell face first onto the tarmac.

'I have this all on CCTV!' The landlord had his fingers pressed to a split eyebrow. 'That was assault!'

Sitting up, spitting grit and tasting blood, Kit was gripped with a brief paranoia that he *was* over the limit. He felt fine. He'd always kept carefully below his ceiling, admittedly a vaulted one, but mathematics was on his side, the logic of units, time and dilution easy to calculate compared to the illogical need for Dutch courage. Kit had been an appallingly disorganised – and bad-tempered – driver all his life, regardless of alcohol intake. Putting the car in the wrong gear was a common occurrence as its battered bumpers bore witness.

Lowering her window, the female taxi driver called, 'Anyone here called Ronnie Percy?'

Kit turned impatiently back to the Saab and was faced with a glimpse of black lace and creamy skin as the funeral dress was hastily removed and detached from his handbrake.

'She'll be right with you,' he told the cab driver, putting some distance between himself and the car to give her more privacy.

As he did so, a green Range Rover screeched into the car park, pulling up in a cloud of dust. A furious-looking man in a *Peaky Blinders* suit jumped out. He had the broken-nosed face of a prize-fight champion, the body of a cavalryman. Kit recognised the Australian who had picked falling horse tack off his head a fortnight earlier.

'Is Ronnie here?' His dark eyes assessed Kit's grazed lip, then the landlord's cut brow.

'If she is, tell her the meter's running!' the taxi driver shouted.

The Australian had spotted a flash of blonde hair in Kit's car and hurried towards it. 'Ronnie? I'm sorry, okay? I've been a— What the fuck are you doing stripping off?'

The window buzzed down a fraction. 'Bad as this looks, I'm not the one who needs tearing off a strip.' She pulled her dress over her head, an apologetic smile disappearing into it.

Blair turned around in angry bewilderment, homing in on Kit. 'Don't I know you?'

Before he could answer, they heard the Saab engine flare and both men turned to see Ronnie at the wheel, back in her neatly tailored black dress, not a blonde hair out of place.

'*Now* what's she bloody well up to?' Kit fumed.

She reversed up to him. The window buzzed lower.

He crossed his arms in front of his chest. 'What are you doing with my car?'

'Please, do take the taxi as my gesture of apology.' She thrust the twenty-pound note at him. 'I know where you live. I'm more than happy to park this outside your house and put the keys through your door. You can pick it up tomorrow.'

'I can't let you do that.'

'It's honestly no trouble. Neighbourly gesture. I can't let you drive. You might hit somebody.'

'If you weren't a woman, I'd hit you.' Defensive as well as affronted, his normally slow fuse was pure gunpowder. 'How *dare* you assume to judge my sobriety? Who made you moral guardian of this parish? You don't live here.'

'I was brought up here. Now I'm back. And I love this village.' She looked surprised to admit it.

'So do I.' He was shocked at himself too, competitive now. *'Tis in my memory lock'd.*

The blue eyes didn't blink, and he felt his hypocrisy curdling in his veins. His judge and jury stood before him. He had to prove his innocence. 'Do you sell breath tests?' he demanded of Paranoid Landlord.

'There's a machine in the Gents.'

'Let's settle this.' He stalked into the pub.

Thirty seconds later he stalked back.

'I need three pound coins. There's change in the glove compartment,' he told Ronnie icily, watching as she fished it out and reluctantly handed it over, blue eyes alight with contrition. They both knew this had gone too far. They hadn't even introduced themselves yet.

'You know, you're every bit as bloody-minded as I imagined you'd be,' she told him.

'As are you.' Kit stormed back inside.

★

'How could you say *nothing* to me about meeting Ronnie?' Gill lectured Petra, through the lavatory door. 'I don't believe for a moment you didn't know who she is. And the way you're behaving with Bay is absolutely *awful*. It's like watching an old *Carry On* and it's plain to see it *will* carry on until it gets a lot messier, if you keep fanning the flame. I suggest you take a good long look at yourself in Italy, Petra, because this Safe Married Crush thing has gone far too far.'

Petra could only agree, grateful that she was going away. She knew she sought out flirtation and laughter from Bay as surely as a sweet-toothed binge-drinker with a bottle of Baileys. Or maybe that should be cherry brandy.

The Percy Place downstairs loo was a seventies time-warp. There was no mirror. Instead the peeling walls were crammed with faded old framed photographs of people holding horses and trophies, sitting on horses with trophies, or grouped awkwardly together with trophies shaped like horses. Drying her hands, she recognised a few faces from sixties and seventies equestrianism, including royalty, in the days when show-jumpers were never sober and eventing was full of army officers riding across country in ribbed polo-necks.

'Bay's our village teaser stallion, you know that,' Gill was telling the door. 'He flirts with wives. But anything more than that is strictly *verboten*. Don't be the one to take it further, Petra. What about the children and Charlie? Monique and Bay's children?'

'We're not setting up a blended family, Gill.' She peered at a picture of handsome Richard Meade. 'We had a silly flirt and he asked me to lunch, that's all.'

'That way lies madness.'

'And Hungarian soup.' Her gaze moved on to a very pretty freckle-faced girl about Bella's age, red plaits suggesting a young Pax. '*You* were the one who used him as bait to lure me here.'

'Do you want to be like Ronnie, is that it? Abandoning your children, breaking two families?'

'The jump jockey was married too?' She hadn't stopped to wonder who he'd been until now.

'Engaged. He's in there with you.'

'Where?'

She unlocked the door and Gill crammed inside, glancing around the pictures.

'Here.' She started wiping off a thick layer of dust, a figure appearing of such hollow-cheeked, heavy-lidded sex appeal that Petra whistled. 'You wouldn't throw him out of bed, would you? He's Jean-Claude Van Damme in a Tattersall shirt.'

'Don't be silly. That's Lester. Angus Bowman's the one holding the horse.' Gill wiped more dust away. 'Devastatingly handsome, isn't he?'

.It was a group photo from the early eighties, faded to pastel, featuring a mud-splattered horse with an even muddier rider in an orange bib, smile as wide and white as his stock. 'Now *he* looks like a young Robert Redford. I'm amazed they didn't burn this.'

'That horse had just won the Melton Hunt Club Ride for the third year running. The Captain bred him. Ronnie could have run away with everyone in that picture and it would still have stayed framed on a wall.'

Petra peered at the other characters, the men timeless in tweeds and flat caps, the women with bad eighties hair, Princess Diana pie-crust collars and Puffa gilets. One, scowling beneath an impressive *Neighbours* mullet, had a familiar bear-like stare.

'Gill, that's you!'

'I always liked that hairdo.'

'*You* were his fiancée?'

'God, no! I was barely twenty and swotting away at veterinary school, although I admit Angus Bowman was my first big crush. His fiancée was Lucy here, in the trilby, one of Daddy's shining stars at the equine practice. They made such a lovely couple. She was utterly heartbroken when he ran off with Ronnie.'

'What happened to him?' She looked at the handsome face, all class and cock, that yesteryear James Hunt sex appeal lethally attractive even in faded sepia. 'Are he and Ronnie still together?'

'God, no. She's with him now.' Gill pointed at another eighties shot, higher up on the wall and featuring a familiar eventing pin-up in his lean, white-smile youth lounging on top of a Burghley winner. 'He's married to her.' She pointed to one of several figures in a nearby picture. 'Although when this photo was taken, she was married to him,' she pointed to another figure in the shot, 'and rumour's always had it she was shagging him at the time.' Her finger tapped a very familiar face, destined to grace postage stamps one day.

'But that's...'

'Quite. I've no idea what became of Angus. When Ronnie bolted, they went up north somewhere and dropped out of view. Ronnie got back into eventing after a few years, but I never came across his name again. He had no family connections to speak of – I think he'd been born in what was then Rhodesia. Hunts can be very insular, so my guess is he's somewhere in the fells being a latter-day John Peel.'

'The legendary disc jockey and champion of new music?'

'Now you're just teasing me. Angus was the Bay Austen of his day.' She tapped the sexy vintage smile with her finger. 'All the Bardswolds village wives were in love with him in the Abba years, his sports car always parked outside houses of husbands who worked away a lot. When this was taken, he was probably thirtyish, ready to settle down and have a family. He'd have done that perfectly happily with Lucy, but instead he got caught up with the one village wife no man could ever resist.'

'I bet Ronnie did far more than thinking up cherry-picking innuendos,' scoffed Petra, secretly and shallowly flattered that Gill had bracketed her with a wife no man could resist.

Somebody knocked politely on the loo door. Putting the picture back, Petra and Gill squeezed outside together to find a small queue had formed, headed by Pax's husband, a tall terse Scot flying on one too many sherries, as he told the legendary little show judge beside him: 'Sensible thing to do wi' an old wreck like this is empty it and auction it.'

The judge looked appalled. 'Surely that's not what the family intend.'

'There's a lot of legal stuff ta get through before anything's decided.' He shrugged. 'They'll give it until Christmas.'

'To do what? Put decorations up?' Gill laughed incredulously. 'That's not enough time to change anything here. The next crop of foals isn't due until March.'

'There are a lot of horses to sell.' He disappeared into the loo.

'Never known a bad Percy horse,' sniffed the show judge.

'Make jolly nice hunters,' Petra said brightly, hurrying past to take her leave. She was appallingly behind schedule.

In the lunchtime heat of the Jugged Hare car park, Kit finally marched out with a breathalyser test to be witnessed by Paranoid Landlord, an impatient taxi driver, the Australian with the Range Rover and the temperance zealot who had hijacked his car.

After another hiatus, because he needed his reading glasses from the car to make sense of the miniature print instructions, he snapped off the plastic end of the tube and breathed into it.

They all watched the crystals turn green in a rising tide towards the red limit line. They stopped a few millimetres short.

'You're legal!' declared the publican happily. 'That calls for a drink.'

'Fair dos, mate.' The craggy Australian offered Kit a handshake. 'Now can we all fuck off home?'

Kit ignored the hand, indignation still boiling in his head. 'I'm not your mate, and I'm already fucked off without fucking off anywhere else. Now I am going to Stratford to be immeasurably cheered up by civilised company.'

'You do that, *mate*.' The Australian's tar-black eyes were murderous.

Chastened, Ronnie took the key out of the ignition and stepped from the car. 'I owe you a big apology.'

Kit was struck afresh by how tiny she was, her blonde head barely level with his shoulder. The indignant fury went out of him almost instantly, finding his ghost to be no more than a small, blue-eyed stranger, whose face was pinched with sadness beneath the apologetic smile as she held out his keys. 'This was a bad day to pick a fight,' he muttered, the victory hollow. He had no real desire to drive the car any more, just the principle. He still couldn't remember which road to take to Stratford. 'In fact, I might leave it here, after all.' He looked at the keys in her hand. She had very small neat fingernails, he noticed. 'I'd be grateful to take you up on your offer of the taxi. Do what you like with the Saab. You yourself shall keep the key of it.'

'Safer leaving it here than in London.' She looked at him curiously, the wise warmth in her eyes too generous to deny, its ability to burn right through his bluff painfully familiar. They must have been an incredible childhood duo, Hermia Austen and Ronnie Percy.

'I hope New York makes you happy.' Getting back into the Saab, Ronnie restarted the engine, poking her head out of the window to tell her Australian friend to follow, then looked up at Kit again, the blue eyes still all too wise. 'It certainly can't make you any more miserable.'

'Who does she think she is?' Kit raged, as she drove off. 'Insufferable bloody woman!'

'Isn't she just?' Blair gave him a quick, unfriendly smile, then got back into his car. 'But she's the best mate you could dream of, mate.'

Climbing into the taxi, Kit remembered his overnight bag was in his car. It hardly mattered. He'd been a toothbrush and T-shirt nomad for so long, he knew they were as easily bought in transit as carried.

Hermia would have found a way to make him laugh amid his predicament, the man who'd been taken for a ride by her best friend, now valet parking his car for him. He checked the time on his phone, noticing a raft of new messages from Orla. As the taxi belted away from the village, he didn't look up, his future in his hands, two thumbs taking charge.

The wake had thinned to hardened locals as Petra hunted for a family member to say goodbye to. The Compton old guard always loved a party. Finally she spotted a cloud of red hair as Pax headed into a side room carrying a fresh bottle of oloroso to top up glasses. Following, Petra put her head round the door just in time to catch Pax necking the sherry straight from the bottle, tear-reddened eyes softening with relief.

'This is all your bloody fault, Pax,' a small voice snarled out of sight.

Trying to back away, Petra found herself pressed up against six feet two of hard-riding muscle. Bay put a finger to her lips, breathing 'Ssh,' into her ear.

'Grumps wouldn't want us divided like this!' Bottle in hand, Pax moved across the room, all quivering Tennessee Williams beauty and high tension. 'I know it's a tough day, but we have to face facts.'

'You should have thought of that before you started offering concessions!'

Appalled to be witnessing something so private, Petra shrank back, elbows digging into Bay's ribs, trying to catch his eye over her shoulder, but his handsome face was immobile, hands gripping her shoulders, watching Pax as she swayed by the back of a small chintz settee, her voice lowered to a theatrical bass note when she spoke. 'Mum will only come here with your blessing, Alice.'

A plume of smoke puffed up from behind the chintz with a smack of disapproving lips. The smaller sister's voice was high with indignation. 'She's a curse, not a blessing! Today's service was a farce, lover-boy muscling in on it all. He'll have his Konigs under the table here before you know it. First Angus, then Lion, Henk and now old Mr Sit Tight. She sure as hell chooses the bad boys.'

Despite herself, Petra found the mysterious quartet thrilling, bad boys being an object of desire for any child of the eighties.

'She knows more about running this place than any of us,' said Pax.

'Tim has fifteen thousand hectares of vineyards under his jurisdiction, I oversee a big mixed farm, you project-manage large-scale renovations. We're *so* on this. I still think we're wrong not contesting the will.'

'No!'

'The stud is *this* close to bankrupt.' A hand appeared above the sofa now, pinching thumb and fingers together. 'Just because you're stressed out by your marriage going through a—'

'That does *not* affect my decision.'

Bay was straining across Petra to see into the room better, his hands sliding down her shoulders as he did so, taking her dress straps with them. She wrestled them back up furiously, hearing a quick 'Sorry' breathed into her ear.

Pax was staring in the direction of the door now.

They both froze, then realised she was looking at something above it. If she glanced a few inches lower she'd see them spying through the gap. Bay's lips were still up against Petra's earlobe, motionless, breath held until Pax turned away again, swigging the sherry bottle before addressing her sister: 'I just want us to do what Grumps asked for. He'd have been so upset to see us fighting like this.'

Alice's dark head popped up over the chintz sofa back, eyes white-rimmed with fury. 'He *loved* fights. And I will fight until my knuckles are bare bone for my children's futures!'

'He always did have a cruel sense of humour.' Another voice joined in the argument now, cool and drawling, as Tim stepped through the open French windows. Ronnie's pocket-sized rugged son fixed his blue gaze on his younger sister. 'Remember, if Ma steps out of line or screws up here once, even slightly, we're straight back to the lawyer. It's a trust, remember?'

'Hah!' Alice laughed scornfully.

Petra felt Bay look round before he drew her aside to duck behind the folded panelling of the false wall. A moment later, a small figure in neatly tailored tweed stormed past, pulled open the door and marched into the study.

'If I may speak?' Lester stood at his five foot five full stretch, poker-backed and shiny-booted, small black eyes set fiercely in his gnarled face. 'With respect to all of you in your hour of grief, your grandfather made his intentions very clear so there's no point squabbling in here like whelps.' The rhythmic round vowels, which were rarely ever raised in anger, old-fashioned and monotone as a Home Service broadcast, might have been addressing them from the centre of the jumping paddock where he'd taught them to ride as children with a relentless, repetitive, perfectionist discipline that made all three now flex their fingers to their palms, pinkies out, and put weight in their heels without noticing. 'Save your arguments for another day. The Captain might not have been one for airs and graces, especially towards the end, but the funeral guests are all leaving, and he would have expected somebody other than myself to thank them for coming and bid them farewell. So bloody well get out there and show some good manners.'

It was the longest speech anyone had heard Lester make in decades, not since the stud's last great competitive era when he'd walked cross-country courses with young-rider Pax, talking her through the best routes and strategies, that soft burr of a voice hypnotising her and calming her nerves.

Guilty tears sprang to her big, vulnerable eyes. 'Christ, how thoughtless of us all. Stand with us, Lester, will you?' Reaching out her hand, which he took awkwardly, hobbit-small alongside her, they left the room, Alice and Tim stalking sullenly in their wake.

Pressed against the cool plaster beyond the door frame, concealed from the rest of the room by the folded panels of the false wall, Petra and Bay looked at one another in horrified amusement.

'I have to go,' she bleated.

'Of course. And Lester's right. It's only good manners to say farewell.' He kissed her directly on the lips, softly and swiftly, pulling the Chianti cork on a hundred poolside fantasies. '*Ci vediamo presto*. Three o'clock for camp awards don't forget. You get Sexiest Pony Club Mum.' And he was gone.

Petra closed her eyes and groaned very quietly. She'd forgotten they were both due to sit through an hour of small girls receiving rosettes, medals and cups. The Safe Married Crush was very hard to steer round gigs like Pony Club Camp when it got as dangerous as this.

21

Ronnie insisted on driving back to Wiltshire, content to hack home on a long rein after a hard day, re-riding each obstacle in her mind as she went. Blair, who never missed a minute marker, was already clock-watching by the time they climbed out of the Fosse Vale. 'This car has two more gears and a turbo, you know.'

'It's a steep hill.'

'And learning curve. I had no idea until today what a headstrong lot you Percys are.'

'Not any more. The name just died out.'

'As will this clutch imminently. Where in God's name are we headed, Ron? The motorway's in the opposite direction.'

'We're taking the scenic route. Slowly.'

'Are you moving back to run the stud?'

'I haven't entirely decided.'

'Where does that leave us?' he snapped. 'You can't just abandon your horses mid-season!'

'There are plenty of stables there.'

She'd bedded into Wiltshire so seamlessly, Blair barely a valley away, friends all around. But her rootstock was wide and shallow as heather. Her feet had itched for a long while, her work–life balance devoid of family ties, and reliant upon others' grace and favour. The prospect of taking over the stud might nail iron horseshoes to her soul – and losing Blair melt that iron into it – yet the opportunity to make amends to her children was burning all before it.

Blair knew her well enough to appreciate there was no stopping her once she had made her mind up about something, and it infuriated him enough to throw practical problems under her slow-moving tyres. 'The place is close to bankrupt.'

'I'll come up with something.'

A moped was overtaking them.

'We'll start going backwards in a minute.'

'That's how I roll.'

'I like how you roll.' He turned to her, eyes dark with unease. 'Where are we rolling?'

'Through the Cotswolds, of course.' Ronnie's fingers rapped on the wheel, tilting a fleeting smile in his direction. 'It's a beautiful day. We hardly ever get to be alone together, rarer still on a day like this. Let's just enjoy the ride.'

'I want to keep the ride.'

They listened through *Diamond Dogs*, each country corner taken as slowly and precisely as a dressage test.

'I've had one idea that might work, but you won't like it.'

'Try me.' Blair rubbed his face, then raked his hair which stood up, a silver-fox Ziggy Stardust. 'Anything to glue our shit back together, unless it's buying back the stallion. You know I can't ask that one.'

'I know.'

The mention of Beck stalled them, as it always did. Not talking about Blair's marriage also encompassed never talking about the horse she'd sold them, which infuriated Ronnie. Beck was being wasted, just as in her darker moments she knew Blair was. It was a constant static between them.

That Blair wouldn't leave his wife was sacrosanct. That Ronnie would never ask was stubbornness.

She took a deep breath.

'Don't talk about Vee,' he anticipated.

'I'm not. Unless you want to.'

The silence between them ticked.

'If I stay in Wiltshire, we have to talk about it at some point.'

'I'll make a note in my diary. Are you staying?'

'I could bring in a manager to run the stud.'

'Good idea.' His eyes slid aside to meet hers, bright at the prospect of things staying unchanged. 'Who did you have in mind?'

Her fingers rapped faster on the wheel, little hoofbeats galloping away. 'He's one of the O'Brien family.'

'Show-jumping O'Briens? Talented buggers.'

She nodded. 'They call him the Horsemaker. He's exceptional. I first met him on a dealing yard in Germany, and the way he could turn a raw youngster round in no time was something else. By the time our paths crossed again a few years later, all the studs there wanted him. He can triple a stallion's fee, add ten per cent to a grading and put a zero on the end of a foal's price-tag. He's in Canada now.'

'Why would he come to Compton Magna?'

'If I ask, he'll come.'

There was a long pause. As he sucked in a deep breath, it was obvious Blair knew precisely what that meant.

'Don't ask.'

'Is that your Saab parked outside?' Petra asked Janine, when she dashed back from the wake.

'No, just the blue van, love.'

'Oh, God, don't tell me the house-sitters are here already?' Petra fretted, fishing the post from the cage behind the letterbox, a set of car keys among it. 'I haven't finished their list.'

'Nobody's called in.' Janine hovered, blocking her way. 'I tell a lie. The old boy next door came around with some courgettes and spuds.'

'Maybe they left it here and went for lunch at the pub.' Petra looked through the side window at the sleek black Swedish car, as out of place on the Gunns' very British gravel carriage circle as an Ikea wardrobe in a costume drama. Which reminded her. 'I must, must pack.'

'Um, you might want to go out to the horses first.' Janine was holding her feather duster up like a pike.

'Why?' she asked anxiously. There was no time for a crisis.

'Fitz can explain.'

Outside, Fitz was looking sheepish as Carly sat in a stable with a snoring Shetland's head on her lap.

'Mum, the *fleekiest* thing's happened,' he explained. 'When the little hairy beast got stuck in the larder—'

'Not my larder?'

'It's all cool. Janine tidied it up. Thing is, he was *seriously* stuck in there. We had to take the shelves out.'

'My larder?'

'Yeah. And he was kicking shit out of everything, me included.'

'This is my larder we're talking about?'

'And your firstborn child. The thing is, when Carly put her hands on him, he just lay there like he was drugged. After that, he did everything she asked, moving his little legs exactly where she told him, and when we'd got him out and he started to look a bit ill and kick his stomach—'

'He colicked?' she gasped. 'I'm calling Gill.'

'He's fine now,' Fitz insisted. 'Look at him.'

The Shetland had one eye open, watching Petra warily, expecting a telling-off. He did look remarkably contented.

'I did what it says in my book,' Carly explained. 'I walked him round a lot and he perked up no end. It's not rocket science.'

'She's being modest. She has a *serious* gift,' Fitz insisted. 'He was really sick. And Carly *healed* him. How amazing is that? She's a healer.'

She hadn't heard Fitz so animated about anything since *Thunder-birds* when he was ten. Not that she believed any of his tosh about healing miracles. Her Shetland had the constitution of a waste-disposal unit.

'Gosh. Well, that's great. Thank you, Carly.'

'It's cool.'

'You could use it in a book, Mum,' Fitz urged. 'Make Carly the heroine.'

Petra was nodding automatically, trying to remember if she had any swimwear that would leave minimal tan lines. 'Mm, yes, I might. Well done, Carly. Now, Fitz, I need to talk to you about drones.'

'Why?' Two dark red spots appeared in his cheeks, which, had she been in a less distracted frame of mine, Petra might have ascribed to more than just the hot weather.

'Does yours have night vision?'

'No.'

'Damn. Bay Austen needs to borrow one – his is up a tree – but it must have night vision. He's got a problem with poachers. They're going in with a small army tonight to see them off.'

'When you say army,' Carly said coolly, 'what do you mean?'

'Oh, shotguns and walkie-talkies and lots of the hunt heavies charging around on quad bikes with flashlights, I should imagine. They're terrible thugs under all that tweed.'

Carly chewed her lip and pressed her face to the Shetland's mane. As Petra whisked off she hugged his solid bulk tightly, grateful for her get-out-of-jail-free card.

Fitz lingered awkwardly. 'Sorry about Mum. She's got a bit of a thing about the local toff farmer. Embarrassing.'

'I like her.'

'She means well, and she never stops. Not like Dad, who's a total slacker. I must take after his side as they're about to find out.'

Carly watched his face twist this way and that, unable to hold on to a truth. 'Spit it out.'

'What my parents don't know is that I wrote my name at the top of every GCSE paper I sat this summer, and not a lot more. Hardly a word in fact.'

'More than I did.'

'Yeah, but I'm supposed to be a lawyer or an accountant or something one day. You're married to a war hero.'

'That's not actually a job,' she pointed out wryly. 'Although there's nothing stopping you marrying your own war hero yourself one day, if it makes you feel better about having no qualifications. It's all legal.'

'I'm not gay!'

'I wasn't saying you are. Plenty of war heroes with vaginas, these days.'

He moved to sit beside her on the straw, far too close, lowering his voice so it croaked. 'I'm sixteen. It's all legal.'

'So show a bit of maturity.' She stood up abruptly. 'Tell your parents you had mind-freeze – talk through your options.'

'I might join the army.' He gazed up at her, lounging artfully in a pool of dusty sunlight, all golden youth, floppy hair and big dark eyes.

'Don't. War fucks you up.'

'So does being a middle-class underachiever.' He lay back against the Shetland now. 'If you put your hands on me, perhaps my brain-freeze will thaw. It's that or soldiering.'

She grinned, touched by his posturing. 'You could start a war with your charm.'

'You could put an end to one with those healing hands.'

'Get out of church!' she scoffed. 'Common sense is what I've got. Comes from being common.'

Janine was pacing the kitchen with a duster. 'There you are! Petra bloody loves you. Gave us a huge tip for helping get that pony shifted – look.' She pulled two twenties out of her tabard pocket that Carly already knew she wouldn't see again. 'You did good, Carl.'

Carly was hailed even more of a Turner hero when she broke the news of Bay's vigilante poacher-catching mob. 'They'll have to cancel it, won't they? We won't be going.'

'Too bloody right!' Janine was straight on her phone, telling Jed and the boys to call it off, insisting Carly should get all the credit.

'When the boys go out again, you'll be guest of honour,' she told her afterwards. 'Welcome to the family, Carly girl. Now you really are one of us. No argument, I'm doing your nails with my best jazzles and sparkle transfers. My treat.'

In the Bulrushes late that night, her bedroom lit by a glowing screen, the Comptons' only baking sleuth was on a mission to keep herself in employment and the stud's horses in oats.

She'd started out by writing a Facebook direct message before realising that a woman who hadn't updated her status since #bingate was trending almost certainly needed an old-fashioned letter.

Dear Verity, she typed.

Pip's mother, Jean, would have been appalled at the informal approach, but Google wasn't very helpful on how to address the remarried former wife of an earl.

Finding a YouTube version of 'Land of Hope and Glory' to listen to for inspiration, she launched straight in:

Please forgive the unexpected nature of this letter, but the future of British sports horse breeding depends on you...

Part Three

SCHOOL UNIFORMS,
BLACKBERRYS AND
RAT-CATCHERS

22

The final ball had been bowled in the village cricket league and the jam judged in the Compton Bagot Show, ploughs were being fixed to tractors and blackberries ripened in hedges. Today's early-morning hack marked the season's change for the Saddle Bags. It was the week the schools went back. Book bags and sports kits had been unearthed, names stitched, glued and Sharpied into uniforms, and from tomorrow onwards the wake-up alarm would be ringing in ever-darker starts to school runs.

Chins determinedly up, the riders sped through the Comptons at a brisk trot, chasing shadows cast by a rising sun, which blazed on and off, clouds as fat as unsheared ewes barging across it.

Petra, already regretting showing off her fading tan in short sleeves, was willing the day to heat up as Gill led the way up onto the most windswept flank of the valley, navigating the bridle-path that cut a barren brown stripe through Sanson Holdings' newly seeded rape towards the old windmill on the ridge. Up here they were far from the hammering hoofs and hound cry of the Fosse and Wolds Hunt, who had met at dawn at Manor Farm and were drawing coverts all over Austen land. The Bags were consequently one woman down, Mo taking advantage of the free farmer's cap to join the field on her steady cob and treat daughter Grace to one last holiday blast on her pony.

'I don't know how she can bring herself to do it,' complained Bridge. 'Poor Grace subjected to that cruel, archaic bollocks.'

'Mine loved it,' Gill reassured her.

Carried by a light breeze, the huntsman's horn was faintly audible as unruly young hounds were called to order.

'Kids should be watching *Power Rangers* and eating sugary cereal at this hour,' Bridge grumbled.

Petra shot her a sympathetic smile. Bella had spent all week begging to be taken along because friends Grace and Tilly would be there, the latter's father Bay field-mastering that day. But Petra had refused to be talked into it, her feelings about hunting ambivalent, those for handsome MFHs less so. Both pursuits were old-fashioned, romantic adrenalin rushes best viewed at a distance through a lens that filtered out morality, she felt – something of a career requirement for a historical novelist.

Last year, Charlie had badgered her to do it as a part of his campaign to be invited to the Well-hung Party, a brace of dawn starts amounting to nothing, followed by several white-knuckle rides once the season proper started, expensively complicated to orchestrate with grandparents *in situ* babysitting and work days lost. None of it had won him a peg. Petra had been too awestruck by Bay to wish him more than good day and good night back then, let alone make lewd small talk. She'd also run horribly over deadline, writing night and day over Christmas to make up for it.

This year, determined to deliver her book before her goose was cooked, Petra needed to hibernate, not develop an unhealthy new addiction. The Redhead's coat was already thickening its velvet pile, and she felt every tiny hair on her skin prick up and cluster in sympathy, the stove and biscuit tin in her garden office – affectionately known as the 'Plotting Shed' – a tempting prospect. The sun had lost its heat days after their return from Tuscany, like Charlie's smile. She'd always hated the slow autumnal cool-down that stole holidays and horseplay while softening the ground for tills and tines.

Like teacher and farmer, Petra's working year started in September, writing a book each school term to re-create an epic historical romance in three easy portions. It was a far cry from her early career in which one full-length novel would be meticulously planned and researched for more than a year before she wrote a single sentence, but that was a privilege she could no longer afford.

'I remember thinking, as a child, that cubbing was very dull,' Gill was saying, horn signalling far below, shrill as a curlew.

'It's autumn hunting now,' Petra corrected, reeling out the reins as the Redhead stooped to scratch her nose on one knee.

'Just plain cruel whatever you call it,' Bridge muttered, as her grey pony trotted impatiently on the spot, like a jogger at traffic lights.

'Yes, all that standing about and being told to keep quiet is terribly harsh on little ones.' Gill was defiantly old school. 'If there was a big breakfast afterwards it made up for it. The stud one was always the best – Ann Percy knew how to put on a spread.'

'Maybe Ronnie will resurrect it,' Petra suggested.

'If she comes back. Dickie Carter's just done the probate valuation on the stud and he said Alice showed him round in a distinctly proprietorial fashion.'

'No breakfast muffins at Percy Place this year, then?'

'The Austens have that gig now. Dickie seems to think they're definitely buying the land by the church meadows – there are two legendary Wolds coverts in there, Scorpion Spinney and Compton Thorns, where Shakespeare and some cronies were supposed to have been caught poaching deer as young bloods.' She gave Petra a downcast look. 'I knew the stud would be broken up.'

'At least it's safe from hobbit houses.' Petra tried to emphasise the bright side.

'Just not prats in red coats chasing poor foxes,' Bridge grumbled.

'They follow a pre-laid scent, these days, Bridge,' Petra reminded her.

'Yeah, like I follow the one-way path in Ikea when my every instinct tells me I can break through sofa-beds straight to the meatballs and lingonberry? I think not.'

'Paul is very fond of Ikea,' Gill said glumly. 'He always forgets the horror of flat-pack.'

'It's a true test of a marriage,' Petra sympathised, the Redhead starting to dance as the bridleway widened to grassy tractor track, 'self-assembly furniture.'

'Especially if it's one's marital bed,' Gill muttered bitterly. 'Thank goodness John Lewis was there last time to stop Paul wrestling with a bent Allen key in our bedroom for hours on end.'

'A relief to Alan Key too, I should imagine,' Bridge murmured, as Petra was gripped with giggles.

'Apparently one in three Britons are conceived in an Ikea bed.' Gill hadn't noticed.

Bridge's brows shot up. 'That's amazing, considering those places are really well lit.'

Petra's giggles were giving her a stitch. 'Wow!'

This saw the Bags into all-out canter, the view across the vale beneath them as wide as a tapestry. Like a sprinter in a jumper, the woolly Redhead forged in front of her newly clipped companions. Wind in her ears and on her goose-bumps, Petra tried not to dwell on the coat change ahead of her from riding jacket to book jacket. She was hanging on to the holiday glow, those warm embers of summer fun. The Gunn brood might be disbanding – Ed had been delivered to boarding school last night – but the farmhouse still burbled and banged with family noise. The girls had three days' grace before the long daily run began.

'Fitz looking forward to a new start this week?' Gill asked over-brightly, as she drew alongside, compensating for the fact that her rebellious, volatile daughter, Dixie, had defied expectations and achieved nine GCSEs while smart, level-headed Fitz had reversed predictions by totally bombing out.

Petra counted down to a gracious smile, knowing that Gill meant well. 'Very much.'

It was under a starry Tuscan sky that a penitent Fitz had finally admitted his forecasted sweep of A stars was *molto esagerato*. That their bright, confident son had kept schtum about the awfulness of his exam flunk until the last possible moment had come as a horrible shock to Petra, who counted it a personal failure that she hadn't spotted the signs of stress. Charlie had accused Fitz of idleness and arrogance, of drug-taking and porn-bingeing, unable to believe it possible that he wasn't being rewarded with a full house of A stars after all the years of school fees.

Fitz waved away his mother's suggestion of counselling or teen therapy, equally firm in his refusal to attend the crammer Gunny was prepared to pay for. Instead he'd asked if he could retake the entire academic year locally – 'I won't let you down, I promise,' he'd told his shocked parents and Petra had persuaded Charlie it was a very grown-up solution, playing down her own selfish motivation for wanting her firstborn living at home in term-time.

Tomorrow he would start at the local academy in Chipping Hampton. She only hoped she was right to trust him. He'd retreated into his own world more than ever since Italy, which didn't bode well for a new start, the big confession doing little to dissipate the sullen tension that buzzed round him. He endured his mother's over-jolly attempts at making family time with stiff-jawed discomfort and had been particularly prickly around Charlie. Petra found it a strain to be in the same room as them, worrying that the atmosphere would get a whole lot worse once her working hours put her out of play. As a final straw, Gunny had rung last night, inviting herself for autumn half-term ('I know you're putting together one of your racy romances, but it's the Shakespeare Book Festival and I'm hoping to see Hilary Mantel in conversation. Now, she really *can* write history').

Compton Windmill came into view now, a grand seventeenth-century limestone domed tower on pillars, which always reminded Petra of an elephant. As they cantered towards it, unexpected rain began spitting into their faces. The Redhead, humping her back disapprovingly, snatched at the reins and dropped her head lower to race for shelter. Bridge's little grey kept pace, and they charged across unploughed stubble, making their riders whoop. Ignoring Gill's protests, they covered the final few hundred metres at Cheltenham speed.

Driving her little open-top car along the die-straight, narrow lane that led up from the Fosse Way to the Comptons, Lou Reed blaring and the dogs on the parcel shelf, Ronnie broke cover from the wooded tree tunnel and high banks to coast between familiar golden stone walls with mile-wide views to either side. Beside her, Blair started awake and lifted the rim of his baseball cap. 'We here?'

'Almost.'

Everything was achingly familiar, none more so than the sight that made her curse under her breath as she slowed down to edge past hunt foot-followers' cars banked up on verges and in field entrances, binoculars glinting across to nearby woodland. The Fosse and Wolds were autumn hunting.

It wasn't yet nine. The mounted field would be circuiting the valley for at least another two hours, which meant Lester would be spared crossing her path again today.

The Australian was looking up at the woods, dark bruises beneath his eyes from a sleepless night spent making love between arguments. 'Uncle Fester is out with them, I take it?'

'Don't call him that.' He'd taken against Lester in the same way he'd set himself against her children. That was the way love affairs went, she'd found. Protecting your little bubble against the outside world inevitably made it explode.

They'd stayed at Le Mill, their battle of wills temporarily calmed by intimacy and the prospect of horse-trading. Their stolen hours together had, as always, pragmatically coincided with a legitimate task – Blair taking an overnight detour on the way from Burghley to stop off and look at the stud's youngsters, she visiting Compton Magna this morning for the paperwork the solicitor needed to account for the stud's stock.

'So how many three-year-olds do I have to buy to keep you in Wiltshire?'

She waved away the question without answering, both knowing it would take more than selling off a few youngsters to lift her obligation to her father's estate. A near-bankrupt stud was not given away to one's children easily, its assets still frozen and tied up in legalese. Having seen the size of the debts, Ronnie no longer had her sights set on signing everything straight over, and a quick fix looked impossible. If she'd thought on the day of the funeral that she could ride back on her white charger and make everything right, she had been mistaken. The place was in far too much of a mess, and white chargers were a rare commodity. She'd sold the one with the breeding to turn around the stud's fortunes.

'How many?' he pushed.

'The lot,' she said, to shut him up.

She slowed to pass a closely bunched gaggle of hunt-followers' trucks and off-roaders, at the midst of which two small, defiant figures with cameras were surrounded by an army of camo, donkey jacket and tweed. Everyone was shouting at once.

'God, they're bullies.' Ronnie pulled up and switched off the car stereo, leaning across Blair to address one of the camo men. 'Leave those poor women alone!'

'Be a good girl and bugger off.' An ancient bulldog of a foot-follower in a flak-jacket turned to wave her car on while the women carried on shouting and filming. In their forties or fifties, one was marathon-runner thin with a pink fringe, the other a stout blonde in a checked Puffa and Hermès scarf.

'Shit!' Blair sank instantly out of sight, reaching back between the seats for the checked blanket kept there to pull over himself.

Taking no notice, Ronnie called at the women, 'Are you two all right?'

'I thought I told you to keep your nose out of this,' the wizened bulldog growled, then did a double-take. 'Begging your pardon, Mrs Ledwell. Didn't recognise you there.'

She identified the wolf eyes and Popeye chin as belonging to a Turner family elder. He tapped his walking stick on a threadbare waxed-cotton shoulder nearby. 'Barry, tell the lady here what's what.'

Another follower turned, much younger, florid-faced and broad-beamed in moleskin and checked cotton, thrusting a weathered farmer's hand into the open top of the car to shake. 'Barry Dawkins, hunt supporters' committee.' He had a Gloucestershire accent as broad as the River Severn. 'Good to meet you. These women are known troublemakers. With respect, we've got it covered.'

'Well, uncover it – your boys are all over them!'

'You of all people should know the nuisance these people cause to a good day's sport.'

'Barry, we both know the hunt has nothing to hide.' She gave him a wise look. 'These ladies should be encouraged to film as much as they like.'

'Stop stirring,' a voice muttered from beneath the blanket, as the pink-fringed woman stepped forwards.

'Thank you, sister!' Her soft Brummy voice was laced with a smoker's crackle. 'Are you Liz from Evesham? We heard you'd been delayed.'

'No, I'm Ronnie Percy from the Compton Magna Stud. And I'm very happy to help if this lot's bothering you, but set one more foot on my land and I'll have you arrested for trespass.'

A quad bike shot out of a field entrance further up the lane and whizzed to their gateway, its driver shouting to clear the way for hounds.

Ronnie reversed, watching the seething stream of speckled white, tan, yellow and black cross the road, huntsman shouting at individual hounds to keep them in order, the hunt staff's long whips trailing, red coats standing out brightly from the tweed of the field. The names were all too familiar and historic – 'Cornet, hoic! C'm*ere*, Chasuble! Careless, Cupid, over!' Johnny had used the same names many generations ago, each year's puppies christened with successive letters of the alphabet, like storms, his rolling Worcestershire burr a country anthem. He'd been such a dashing huntsman, his pack devoted to him, working hounds in an era when he was deemed a local hero, not an elitist criminal. She'd fallen in love with Johnny Ledwell so fast, she should have joined the Tumblers Club, the ignoble band of mounted followers who paid a cash forfeit when they parted company with their horse. She'd fallen out of love again so soon afterwards, the landing far harder.

The monitors vigilantly filmed the hounds pass, although the three hunt staff in their scarlet coats were just moving them on between coverts and letting the master give his mounted field a pipe-opener.

Those riders crossed shortly afterwards, led by Bay Austen, cream shirt showing off his tan, his bowler brim down on his nose. So arrogantly, anachronistically handsome. And he knew it, winding up the monitors with a charming 'Good day, ladies,' and a devilish smile, before turning to look up the road. 'Good morning, Ronnie!' The air-force-blue eyes gleamed. 'Call me back soon, will you? We have a deal to make.'

Ronnie raised an index finger from the steering wheel in acknowledgement, muttering, 'Bloody man.' She remained furious that her father's trust was obliged to sell the land he was riding into now, its coveted coverts full of adders and fox, metaphors for the battle between the two families.

Midway back, Lester looked fit for a show championship in

bowler hat, houndstooth check and the shiniest brown boots. He didn't glance in Ronnie's direction as they passed.

This was ridiculous. He had to face her soon. None the less, she intended to get this morning's task over with as swiftly as possible.

As the autumnal cavalcade followed the huntsman's lead like leaves blowing along behind a rolling red windfall, Ronnie put the car into gear, frustrated to see the foot-followers intimidating the monitors again. The two biggest bullies were deployed to obstruct their path while the rest jumped into their vehicles to race to a better viewpoint.

'Back off and let them past!' Ronnie tried again. Then, when they ignored her, she yelled, 'Bike! Get back to 'im! Bike!' in the same way that a huntsman would order hounds to back off.

They took a reluctant pace back.

There was a bronchial laugh nearby as the old bulldog climbed into portly Barry's battered Land Rover, waggling his walking stick. 'Ronnie'll be master of foxhounds within the year, lads, you wait and see!'

'She's always preferred being a mistress,' muttered the stowaway.

Ignoring him, Ronnie shouted back, 'I'd never put up with behaviour like this from you lot if I was in charge.'

'Just like her father.' The old Turner guffawed, as Barry started his engine, rattling away in a plume of diesel fumes.

'That's my cover blown,' she muttered as she pulled away, raising her hand to wave.

'Mine too,' said the blanket.

'The Fosse and Wolds won't have a clue who you are.' She lifted it. 'Besides, you have a perfectly legitimate reason to be here.'

'It's not the hunt I'm concerned about, it's the ruddy monitors.'

'They're hardly going to film *you*.'

'The blonde's Roo Verney.' The blanket was cast to one side as Blair sat up. 'Mad as a box of frogs with a dingo thrown in. Used to be a full-on balaclava-and-wire-cutters sab.'

'That's the rebel niece?' Ronnie glanced in her mirrors. 'A chum of mine says she's the bane of every huntsman between Warminster and Warwick.'

'She's none too keen on me either. The Verneys play her down, but Vee always had a very soft spot for family outlaws before she got too—' He stopped. Blair never wanted to say it out loud, especially not today. The smile flashed up again, bright as a shield. 'You okay?'

'I'm fine!' she said over-brightly, switching the stereo up so they racketed on to the village outskirts accompanied by 'Satellite of Love'. 'We're here to count horses.'

Both were pros at pragmatism.

They turned up a drive as deep as Moses' divided Red Sea. While the paddocks surrounding them were neatly shorn and well-tended, the poplars along the verges were sinking fast in a rising green tide. The lawned borders ahead looked fit to be cut and baled, Nature all too quick to reclaim her territory. The grass must have grown a foot in a month.

Ronnie parked beside her father's old Subaru, thick with dust. She jumped out, Blair's pointer and her younger Lancashire heeler springing from the back like synchronised divers. The old heeler waited patiently to be lifted down.

Blair unfolded himself from the tiny front seat to climb out too, turning to admire the clock-towered archway into the first of the Victorian stableyards. He strode beneath it, his pointer bounding ahead.

'Everything's in the barns and home paddocks just beyond the watchtower,' she called after him. 'See what you think of the herd.'

An advantage of the hunt meeting in the village was that all the broodmares and young stock had been brought in to minimise their stress. Unhappy with the auctioneer's valuation of the stud's stock as a job lot, the probate team had insisted that each horse must be individually itemised as a matter of urgency, but the Captain's record-keeping had become increasingly eccentric in his final few years. The task of cross-checking so many horses against their passports and covering certificates had been somewhat reluctantly delegated to Ronnie ahead of today's solicitor's meeting. Asking for Lester's help to do this might have been politic but he knew as well as Ronnie did why it might also bring down the house of cards. In a very starchy email to her mother, Alice reported that Lester – who could identify each horse in his care blindfold and recite its pedigree through five generations – had developed sudden amnesia, no doubt fearful that his favourites might be sold.

It's just a straightforward headcount, the email had instructed. *For God's sake, get the cheap vets from Ludd-on-Fosse to scan the microchips, not Gill Walcote who'll charge a fortune.* Alice had forgotten that her mother was a canny operator, having lived on a shoestring for years. Borrowing Blair's microchip scanner meant they could cut out the vet entirely. And once Ronnie learned her daughters weren't intending to be there, borrowing Blair with it made the task much more bearable, especially if he took a few youngsters home with him. The stud was horrifically overstocked with winter approaching.

'You coming?' Blair was watching her over his shoulder, unaware of how big a deal coming back again was for her. It was threatening to rain, dark clouds moving across the sun.

'I'll just grab the paperwork from the house.' How carefree she made it sound, how prosaic. She hadn't stepped into it for more than a decade; her father had died alone in it; her toxic marriage had almost suffocated her and her children had grown away from her here.

She leaned into the car to grab the house keys.

His hand on her back made her jump. Then she turned and pressed her forehead into his chest, grateful for the arms that locked around her and the silence that went with it. He knew exactly how hard she was finding this. Of course he knew.

Fitz pulled out his earbuds and fished down the side of his bed for the lightning cable, cursing the iPhone's ever-shortening battery life. It had already been on its last legs when he'd inherited it from his mother who never upgraded anything until it was knackered – which she called Yorkshire common sense and he called being a tightwad – so it took a lot to keep it alive, but he still didn't want to swap over to his dad's old BlackBerry. He now picked that out of his hoodie pocket to switch on and check out the app. What he saw made him look away, shuddering.

He'd been at home on study leave the first time he'd stumbled upon the innocent-looking messenger service among the unfamiliar icons. It had been a few days before his first GCSE and Fitz had struggled to make sense of it. With his father in London, he'd almost asked his mum what it was about before realisation dawned.

Charlie Gunn was having an affair. He and 'Lozzy' had been messaging each other using the app for months, sometimes several times a day. When he'd upgraded his phone and given his old handset to Fitz, he'd signed out but never deleted his account, inadvertently leaving the conversation record for his son to stumble upon, the password pre-stored, new messages appearing daily. If Fitz added a message himself – so far *test* and *you bastard* – it showed as coming from his father. Neither Charlie nor Lozzy had noticed, but the conversation – which rarely got above crotch level – was hardly Sartre and de Beauvoir.

Since Italy, Fitz had taken to carrying the phone with him at all times, like a loaded gun.

Before finding the messages, Fitz had thought he was pretty wised-up, and certainly more street than his parents, his porn-viewing sophisticated, sexting skills advanced, and his sexual learning curve on a progressively upward parabola, thanks to Dixie Wish starting him off at fourteen on her parents' sofa while they were out at the hunt ball, then finishing him off at fifteen in the back of her mother's horsebox. He'd then taken long-distance-girlfriend Sophie through the same moves when they were on their Duke of Edinburgh gold award. Fitz was da boss.

Now he felt differently. This thing was way beyond his scope, and he was monitoring the situation for self-preservation's sake. Nothing new had been added while they were in Italy, but it was full throttle again now.

'FIIIIIIIIIIITZ!' Prudie was outside the door. 'Mummy left you in charge, didn't she?'

'I have my webcam trained on your every move.'

'Bella's just dropped her cereal spoon down the waste disposal and it's making a funny noise. And Wilf's been sick. And there's a woman at the door with a cake-tin, saying she's Mummy's friend.'

The woman at the door had mad eyes and a mouth like a piranha. Dressed from head to toe in startling pink, she had a food container cuddled in her arms with a sheaf of papers on top. 'Hello, William. Is Mummy in?'

'Out riding.'

'Of course! Silly me. Shall I wait inside? It's starting to rain.'

'She won't be back for ages.' He stayed in the doorway, not caring if he was taking his anger out on her. Nobody called him William and was forgiven, apart from Gunny, and she was on borrowed time with her hollow promises.

'I've got plenty to be getting on with.' She held up the printed papers as evidence.

The top sheet was a registration form for a Civil War re-enactment society, which she'd filled in. Under 'Occupation', Fitz spotted she'd put 'Detective/Researcher'. 'Do you have ID?'

'Don't be silly, I'm Pip! Mummy's friend. You're William Peregrine...'

This was even worse. She had used his middle name.

'... Alan.'

Both middle names. Had she seen a copy of his birth certificate or something?

'We're not allowed to let anyone in without ID,' he insisted. 'I'll tell her you called. Thank you for these.' He reached out to take the box.

'I'd better not give you them.' She hugged it tightly. 'They contain lots of caffeine and a splash of alcoholic liquor. Mummy might be angry.'

She'd be angry with Fitz for being rude to one of her village friends, but he'd take that one for the team. 'I'll tell her you called, Pauline Lesley Edwards.'

Her piranha jaw dropped as Fitz smiled sweetly and closed the door.

23

'Are you really getting the Redhead's shoes taken off this afternoon?' Bridge lamented, as the Bags sheltered beneath the tall arches of the familiar windmill, black cloud emptying fast, a rainbow arching across the vale and ending in the Comptons, which were still still bathed in sunlight.

'That's the plan. I have to devote myself to bed-hopping Roundheads.' Petra hoped there was a crock of gold at the end of this book. It had been a long time since she'd opened a royalty statement without breaking into a cold sweat, the figures shrinking each time.

'Bloody waste,' Gill said, doling out the mints. 'A horse should stay in work.'

'She *will* still be working. From now until half-term, her job is to prance around the field with her little chums, motivating me to get a first draft together. She's my muse.'

The other Bags could never understand why Petra insisted on mothballing her riding gear for weeks on end to write.

'You're not wriggling out of the Goose Walk this year,' Gill insisted.

Petra kept quiet, fully intending to wriggle.

The Goose Walk was a Compton tradition in which a flock of geese was driven through the village on the eve of Michaelmas Day. The drovers, calling at each house in turn, would gather ingredients for the following day's harvest festival feast in return for a song and a sip of strong local grog, all ending up in the pub for a raucous sing-song.

'It's just an excuse for a drunken night out,' Bridge pointed out, crunching her mint.

'It dates back five hundred years.'

'Yeah, like all Compton village piss-ups – carol-singing, wassail-ing, May Day, trick-or-treating.'

'Not trick-or-treating, Bridge, no.' Gill gave her a withering look.

'Try being married to a man from Małopolskie.' Bridge grinned. 'Village revelry's in his blood. The wodka is kept permanently by the door.'

'Paul's bicycle clips and electrolyte bottle live by ours,' sighed Gill.

In her pocket, Petra's phone picked up a rare signal and produced a drumroll of incoming messages and different app notifications.

'They're playing your tune, screen queen,' teased Bridge, who, like all the Bags, regularly gave Petra stick for checking her phone so often. 'I bet that's Bay telling you it's not too late to lob on a rat-catcher and join in the murderous fun.'

'More likely Pip offering to come round with a fudge cake and more research notes,' she said, glancing at Gill with martyred eyes, groaning as she read the first of three messages from Pip. 'Correction, she's just this minute *been* round. This is your fault, Walcote.'

Pip had proved very hard to shake off since the Captain's funeral, posting on Petra's social-media timelines far more consistently than she did herself, then becoming a text pest once she returned from holiday. In recent days, having discovered that Petra's upcoming trilogy was to be set in Cornwall during the English Civil War, she'd taken it upon herself to become a voluntary research assistant, sending endless links to Wiki pages usually very late at night. The latest flurry had arrived in the early hours that morning: *Wd make great romantic story!*

Pip had fixed on a swash-buckling Royalist, whose bad temper and ill-fated marriage Petra knew well. She'd already replied: *Thanks everso, but Daphne du Maurier got there first! My general's on the other side with a v. feisty wife, and I already have the plot worked out. I'm all set to go.* She hoped it would stop Pip wasting her time, although she didn't have much of a plot at all, just a heap of messy research notes and a growing crush on a historical figure, which was always her starting point.

Great minds think alike! Am I right? came a reply now, along with a thumbnail of a rare portrait of a seventeenth-century noble-man looking gorgeously like a long-haired, bearded Adrien Brody.

Unnerved, Petra pocketed her phone. Only her agent and publisher knew he was her next hero. Pip was alarmingly good at second-guessing things.

'Is she still stalking you?'

'More sprouting enthusiasm than full-formed stalk,' she conceded. 'I think she means well.'

'And Bay?' Bridge's eyebrows nudged up.

The Bags had been very low on high drama on their past few hacks, but Petra knew better than to bring her Safe Married Crush into play again, their funeral kiss fading all too swiftly on her lips in Italy to leave a bad taste.

'Petra's parked that, haven't you?' Gill's voice was pure iron.

'Absolutely,' Petra said firmly, having ignored every message he'd sent in the past week. 'In a parking Bay, in fact.'

'Genius.'

'And how's the true blue male member doing, Gill?' Bridge switched target, although the others had always considered Gill's prudish SMC on their local MP to cover darker desires.

'Still an upstanding mouthpiece for his female constituents?' added Petra, catching Bridge's eye.

'Yes, he's back in the Commons for a mass debate on the Finance Bill, I believe.'

At this, Petra and Bridge got silent giggles.

Rain over, they headed out into searing golden sunshine.

'What will you do for a safe crush now Bay's parked?' Bridge rode alongside Petra.

'Tom Fairfax.' Petra's next fictional hero was sexy parliamentarian 'Black Tom', the rider of the white horse, a raven-haired Yorkshireman, who had led the New Model Army to victory. Already more than a little in love with a man whose heroic fairness was the stuff of legend, she hoped being alone in a room with him for a few weeks would make up for her withdrawal from the village.

She had no need of Bay. Two weeks in Tuscany might not have mended the splintered wood of her marriage, but it had oiled the grain. After a few glasses of Montepulciano, the Gunns had enjoyed unusually adventurous sex, Charlie coaxing Petra into trying out all sorts of new things with the aid of a sarong and a bottle of after-sun.

If she let herself think about it too hard, though, she fretted that he'd been watching far too much porn in London during the week or, worse, spending time in a BDSM massage parlour.

When they next pulled up for a breather, she caught herself checking her phone again, secretly bucked up to count how often Bay had texted since she'd been back from Italy, less so to find Pip had outnumbered that total in just one morning, along with tweeting on her timeline, pasting on her wall and tagging her endlessly in pictures of— was that Sir Thomas Fairfax? No! Not only was she giving away the plot before it was written, she was claiming part-ownership. *Very proud to be Petra's new researcher on this*, she'd posted an hour ago. *Taking cakes round to celebrate our Civil War hero!*

Pip drove at her customary full pelt through Compton Magna, telling herself it was probably illegal to serve walnut caramel coffee cake oozing with Tia Maria to infants, especially rude ones.

She'd hoped to catch Petra with the offering while she breakfasted, imagining an idyllic tableau of children in boaters and blazers drinking freshly squeezed orange juice. She'd even rehearsed her own breezy apology that she couldn't stop, anticipating the warm smile and a flood of thanks for all her hard work. Instead she'd been made to feel like some wicked witch touting apples by the two suspicious pyjamaed daughters with chocolate-spread beards, who'd told her Mummy was out hacking, backed up by a teenage son with a gravity-defying fringe, who'd taken a snapshot of her on his phone and demanded to see her ID. There was definitely something not quite right about him.

Pip's need to please was dented but undefeated. Her baked treats would be perfect for Lester to come back to after autumn hunting.

She'd already packed the ingredients into her boot to bake some scones for him – it was the perfect excuse to let herself into Percy Place, via the boiler room, the only lock that hadn't been changed, and reclaim her favourite kitchen. The Aga had been switched off, mice had moved in, and the ancient electric back-up oven infused everything cooked in it with the smell of oxtail, but the Captain's house is where she felt happiest. In its abandoned state she was its secret custodian, checking its many rooms while Lester's treats baked.

As Pip rounded the last bend out of the village, a young hound standing in front of the stud's entrance made her brake hard, mount the verge and skitter to a halt, missing it by inches. It came and smiled through the window at her. Pip wasn't a fan of dogs – especially hounds – but Lester would be furious if she left a lost one loose on the road so far from the pack. She reached for a cake from the tin on the passenger seat, fed a bit out of the window and inched the car off the grass, dropping lures at regular intervals as she set off very slowly, her crumbly trail leading him towards the distant sound of the horn.

Lester banged his crop against his boot at point, rolling his tongue and whooping, 'Ay, ay, Charlie!' along with fellow mounted and foot-followers, the trusted Fosse-and-Woldsers encircling the little coppice. It was a hunting ritual that involved making as much noise as possible to keep a fox in his covert, turning him back if he tried to escape into open country.

Just as quickly, at the sound of a long, plaintive horn call to stop hounds, the followers fell silent.

'Why do we do all this if we can't kill the foxes, Mr Lester?' asked a bright voice at waist height, and he turned to see the Stokeses' granddaughter Grace Dawkins, looking up at him from a small hairy pony.

'Ssh!' He glared down at her. 'Get back with the others.'

Undeterred, she smiled at him expectantly, speaking in a whisper: 'We can talk like this if you like.'

'Ssh.' He breathed it even more quietly, ears cocked as he heard the hounds regrouping at the far side of the covert, the whippers-in cantering round to reposition there, another sharp sound of the huntsman's horn preparing the pack to draw again.

'My friend Tilly's dad's the field master,' came the whisper. 'He says you know more about horses and hunting than everyone else here put together, Mr Lester. You must know the answer.'

Lester gritted his teeth. 'If you say so.' He glanced down again.

She was a pretty thing with a ferrety snubbed nose and a decent little riding position.

'It's obedience training,' he muttered. 'We're teaching the hounds *not* to chase Charlie Fox.'

'Are the terriers learning that too?' she asked, as hounds drew again and the terrier-men charged around on their quads to stay close, camouflaged and flat-capped, standing up on the pegs, the big boxes strapped fore and aft, whimpering and yapping, as little black noses tried to prise the lids off.

The hounds started to sing almost straight away this time. Hearing the horn call doubling, Lester thumped his boot-tops with his crop's bone handle.

Little Grace watched him impassively. 'I like your horse.'

Coat gleaming like a newly minted copper coin, freshly hogged and standing as four square as a Horse of the Year Show champion under the judge's eye, Lester's little cob was by far the best produced conveyance of the day.

'Seen this lad bred, born and broken,' he couldn't resist boasting.

'Did you mate his mum and dad?'

'In a manner of speaking.' He spotted a streak of chestnut fur in the undergrowth and snapped, 'Now buzz off back to your mother.'

Waiting until she'd trotted off, he put his all into his saddle-thumping shouts and *brrr*s as the hounds sang their way closer, undergrowth snap, crackle and popping. 'Ay, ay, Charlie!'

A buzzing noise made him look up, and he spotted the drone just above the trees. The sabs all had drones these days. It was filming them all, capturing the riders grouped around the wood, looking to all as though they were holding up, a strict no-no under the Hunting Act.

The chestnut shape snaked past again, a lead hound little more than a wicket's length behind. Lester watched the fox falter at the wood's edge. It was young, barely more than a cub, every instinct focused on survival. He stopped thumping his boot-tops, transfixed.

Pausing for a split second at the mesh stock fencing between woodland and pasture, the little fox glanced back, then forward and straight up to meet Lester's eyes, animal to animal. With a bound, he made a bid for freedom, but instead of streaking away, he twisted back with a frantic cry and flurry of scrabbling ginger fur, the wire snagging and trapping him.

Hounds bayed. The drone hovered lower.

Lester slithered stiffly off the cob and scooped up the little fox, arthritic fingers struggling to free its thrashing leg from the twist of loose wire before hurrying back to the cob to pull the sandwich tin from his leather saddle bag, toss it away into the undergrowth, thrust the stunned creature inside and buckle it closed. A split second later, three hounds broke cover.

They bounded around him, noses and tails thrashing. Then, to his blessed relief, they homed in on his tin, which had burst open spilling bloater-paste sandwiches everywhere. If there was one scent guaranteed to turn a hound it was fish paste.

'Good man, Lester.' Bay didn't spot the marauding trio as he thundered past to join the huntsman, who was drawing ever faster on his horn, keeping the rest of his young pack's attention on the job. Behind him, the whipper-in shouted at the unruly breakaway squad attacking Lester's sandwiches, leather thong tapping backs. They teemed beneath the cob's legs.

Lester's saddle bag went very, very still.

Moments later, the horn let out a long call ending in a tremolo. Deep in the covert, the rest of the pack sang victoriously.

Leading the cob to a sturdy fencing rail, Lester clambered onto it with effort to remount. He glanced down at his saddle bag uncertainly. He'd never done anything so reckless in the field. It was against everything he'd ever been taught. He'd have to hang back for a quiet moment when they moved on to the next covert and feed the fox back in. He lifted the flap a fraction.

'Lester! Isn't this exciting? Cake?'

Lester almost fell off in shock, swinging round to find Pip in her bright pink fleece thrusting a spotty tin up at him.

'What are you doing here?' he hissed. The master would be apoplectic. 'You can't hand those out now.'

'I brought a hound back,' she announced proudly, pointing at a liver and white dog gambolling happily into the woods.

'That is no hound.' He watched it disappear. 'That's an English pointer.'

24

Ronnie had been given twenty-seven mortice keys in unlabelled bunches for the stud farm. The twenty-seventh she tried opened the shiny new lock to the swollen, dog-scratched back door and she found herself rooted to the step, head pressed against its peeling paint. For a moment, she was leaden with loss, shot through with the inescapable loneliness of grief.

She wanted to hold Blair's hand very badly now.

'Bugger it.' She shied away from the door and lit a cigarette, needing someone to chase her inside, like a horse up a ramp. Alice and Pax should have been there with a lunge whip and a bucket of carrots.

Her daughters had embraced their roles as executors with extraordinary efficiency, Alice orchestrating probate valuations of the estate and its contents, while Pax spent long evenings assimilating lists of her grandfather's cash assets and debts. They'd kept their mother updated with concise, bullet-pointed emails, copied to Tim in South Africa and the expensive Leamington solicitor. The pedantry exasperated Ronnie, who had stopped opening emails about the market value of elderly tractors or three hundred round bales of oat straw. Yet the stud's precarious finances made the need to get past the legal process a pressing one. The list of creditors who couldn't be paid until probate was granted was very long.

Her children were carefully avoiding another confrontation, the safe cordon marked out around Ronnie making her feel like an unexploded bomb. They'd been the same in childhood, her heart-breaking trinity raised by their grandparents and led by the fierce eldest sibling, whenever their mother arrived to visit, politely lining up to greet her, leaving only the family dogs to bound forward in unbridled welcome. For years, Ronnie's open arms had fallen to her sides in defeat until she'd finally given up trying.

Throwing the barely smoked cigarette into a flowerpot, she hugged herself now. Too many bloody memories here. She checked them with every stride as she went through the back door at speed, her little dogs at her heels. All three of them marched through the vestibule where the family's hunting boots had stood for six generations in military formation beneath thick layers of coats on pegs, then out along the back passageway hung with stable name plates from favourite horses over a century of Percy breeding. For a moment Ronnie paused, eyes clamped shut, her nose filling with a smell that wiped out four decades in a breath. Horses and hunting days, their scents breathed at the run along echoing corridors, feet sliding on beeswaxed floorboards, dust dancing, pursued by a pack of hearth-warmed dogs.

This was a house filled with equine, not human, memorabilia, she recalled with relief. The photographs and paintings that lined every wall were of four-legged subjects. The few with family members in the saddle largely pre-dated recent generations because there had been precious little space to hang anything since the early 1950s. Only the drawing room, where the Percys had entertained guests, had been redecorated in living memory, and that had been minimal: the oak-panelled walls and marquetry floors were sensible wash-down Victorian interior design for the professional horseman. Ronnie's parents had rarely replaced anything that had life left in it. As such, there was very little evidence that they had ever been there, beyond clothes in wardrobes, dog scuffs on doors and her mother's carefully kept stud records.

That was what she went to gather now: passports, covering certificates, studbooks and grading records. They were already laid out in archive boxes on her father's desk where they'd recently been shown to the auctioneer who had valued the estate's assets.

Traditionally an explosion of brimming ashtrays and paper piles that nobody was allowed to touch, the room had been cleaned and sorted, and Ronnie experienced another rib pinch of anti-climax.

She'd anticipated feeling as though the Captain had just walked out of each room into the next, but instead he'd been unceremoniously tidied away with a squirt of Pledge.

Carrying the paperwork outside took several trips. Blustering clouds were playing hide and seek with the sun. She could hear Blair calling his dog somewhere beyond the stallion paddock. At a greater distance, the hunt was moving between coverts on the opposite side of Lord's Brook. She'd jumped that brook countless times as a child, Hermia hot on her heels, both girls whooping and congratulating their ponies and one another.

Could she live here again, she wondered, even for a short while?

Going back into the house to fetch the final box, she cut through the kitchen to fetch a glass of water.

The smell was wrong. Comforting, it was the burned-sugar warmth of home-baking, sweet enough to take the bitterness out of the many arguments with her mother she remembered being waged there.

The scratched, heavy-based Ravenscroft glasses in the cupboards hadn't changed, impervious to Ann slamming them down to empha-sise a point, and the sink mixer tap was still loose. When she and Johnny had lived in the old servants' quarters, this kitchen had been a daily meeting point for mother and daughter.

Ann had been a splendid cook, despairing of teaching newly married Ronnie to cater for her husband or host big country dinner parties: 'When I married your father, we had six staff, but a young wife must learn to run her own house these days.'

The kitchen, too, was uncharacteristically tidy. A state-of-the-art food processor looked out of place on the worn wooden worktop, and Ronnie wondered what had become of the peculiar, pug-eyed housekeeper.

In the breakfast room, the mantelpiece was laden with her mother's loathsome Staffordshire china dogs. One rainy summer's day, aged about nine, Ronnie and Hermia had finger-knitted little scarves for them all and staged *The Sound of Music* in canine pottery. Twenty years later, picking up one of the dogs to hurl at a drunken Johnny, she'd found one of the little scarves trapped dustily behind it and stopped herself, pressing its cool head to her hot cheeks instead. Ronnie had been brought up to possess steely self-control. Instead of making a scene, she'd swung round to face her husband with an upper lip so stiff she might have been a bisque doll. 'Tell me, Johnny, what have I done to offend you so much?'

He'd once told her Ledwells never argued. Percys loved a scrap: Ronnie battled with her mother daily, occasionally and explosively with her father, regularly with stewards and dressage judges. But with her husband the silences stretched on for weeks.

'We're fine as we are,' he'd insisted, a man far happier dealing with overwrought mares than with his unhappy wife.

'You haven't touched me in months, Johnny. You behave like I repulse you, like you're forcing yourself to touch worms.'

'I've been busy. I get tired.' The whisky had anaesthetised all warmth from his voice. At the time, it had come across as cold arrogance.

Ronnie wished she could have seen the truth of it back then. Reliving the conversation, she remembered only her mounting sense of frustration and isolation.

'Johnny, talk to me,' her twenty-five-year-old self had entreated. 'You can't tell me you're happy with our marriage.'

'You're a good wife.'

'So why do you walk out of a room when I walk in? We have no joy in each other, no conversation, no physical relationship.'

'Plenty of that in the lorry park.'

'What are you suggesting?'

'It's no secret what goes on.'

'Is that what you really think?' She'd laughed in amazement. 'That my knickers drop faster than the ramp when I'm away competing?'

Johnny had always used silence to underline a point, sometimes for days.

'It's *you* I share my bed with, Johnny, you I want. I never take any notice of anyone else.'

'They notice you.'

'That's their problem. If it bothers you, I'll hang up my boots.'

'Absolutely not.' It was the first time he'd looked animated.

'I could work more with you on the breeding side. That way I don't have to leave the children so much while they're little.'

'The stud is their future. Its reputation rides on you.'

'What about my reputation? There's no truth in any rumours.

You can't suffocate our marriage because of them. That's not a reason, Johnny. That's looking for an excuse.'

She had been within reach of the truth in that moment, had she known it, but again her anger had flared too brightly. 'Do you really hate me that much?'

'I don't hate you.'

'Then what?'

'I just don't...' He'd hesitated, the sentence committed, suspended in animation, as though he'd taken off at speed over a blackthorn hedge on a horse he realised couldn't land the leap, the barbed spikes coming up in slow motion.

'... love me?' she'd suggested hollowly.

Their eyes had met in the mirror, all too briefly and honestly. His were dark, bloodshot caverns in that hopelessly romantic face.

'I just don't like this conversation,' he'd said eventually. 'We won't have it again. I need another drink.'

After he'd left the room, Ronnie had set the dog back carefully on the mantelpiece and tied the scarf around its neck to combat the chill. Not long afterwards, she had started her affair with Angus Bowman. If Johnny was looking for an excuse not to love her, she gave him one.

Ronnie's middle-aged face staring back at her from the breakfast room's speckled mirror now struck her as out of place, like the shiny Kitchen Aid next door. This house belonged to another era of her life, a cosseted childhood, an ill-judged marriage, early motherhood, adultery.

'You don't belong here any more,' she told it firmly.

Throwing open the door to the drawing room, quite another smell overwhelmed her. Sherry. The Percys had been big on sherry.

They'd held an annual autumn breakfast here when the Captain and Sandy Austen had been joint masters, one a five-generation traditionalist, the other a sociable pretender twenty years his junior, back in the day when the stud's land had stretched right down to the Fosse Way, its holding twice that of the Austens', the rivalry between the two families never more ridiculous than when one's kedgeree took on the other's home-bred black and white puddings, Patum Peperium versus smoked mackerel pâté, sherry versus champagne, old versus new. When Johnny had taken over the mastership from his father-in-law, those breakfasts had become legends of hard-drinking endurance, often lasting late into the afternoon.

It was at one such marathon that Angus Bowman had stood beside Ronnie and said, so quietly that only she could hear, 'You do know I'm totally in love with you, don't you?'

Bowman was a garrulous, daredevil amateur jockey, who occasionally hunted with the Fosse and Wolds, always flirting shamelessly with Ronnie if she was in the field. A blond, blue-eyed, smooth-tongued demi-god, he was all too easy on the eye and ear.

Going to bed with unhappily married wives was Angus's forte. Bit between his teeth, he'd quickly stepped up the ante, introducing her to a group of friends who wanted to buy several young event horses for Ronnie to compete and had very deep pockets. It was a big coup for the stud. The Captain encouraged the deal: 'Do whatever it takes to screw the most out of them.' She and Angus duly negotiated and flirted.

Soon three of Ronnie's top string belonged to the syndicate. Each time she went away to compete, Angus seemed to find an excuse to be there to help and cheer. Finding her old form, Ronnie started winning big competitions, her name back on the lips of team selectors. She left the children at home with their jolly nanny: campaigning back at top level took her further afield, regularly camping overnight in the lorry park. The rosettes and points piled up. She and Angus celebrated. She won her first three-day event in seven years. The next morning, she woke up with Angus.

He was a total revelation in bed. Ronnie couldn't believe her body was capable of such persistent pleasure, exhausting and addictive, shamelessly decadent. An adept and confident lover, Angus made her laugh, come and crave non-stop. As their affair took off, it spiralled into high-risk hedonism, their encounters conducted breathlessly in the back of horseboxes, borrowed cottages on estates hosting horse trials, motels near race courses and, one legendary autumn morning, beneath the picnic-table fence at a three-day event while everybody was busy at the pre-course walk briefing.

She was leading two lives. While the village and family saw only the ever-smiling, hard-working wife and mother they adored, the eventing world knew precisely what was going on, and counted down to the inevitable explosion.

Angus, thirty-four when the affair started and ready to settle down, was already engaged. Ronnie was almost ten years his junior, but life as Captain Percy's daughter meant a full dance-card from cradle to grave, marriage tethering her young, her greatest duty already dispatched in mothering three children. Johnny Ledwell's animal husbandry skills would see the stud into the next century. Meanwhile Ronnie struggled to see beyond the next week.

'I want you to leave him,' Angus had whispered in the drawing room that morning after autumn hunting. 'Run away with me.'

'I won't leave my children.'

'They come too. That's the deal.'

It was another six months until breaking point, the affair warming them through a bitterly cold hunting season and bringing Angus within dangerously close quarters. The temptation to flee grew almost overwhelming. She was certain Johnny hated their sour, atrophied marriage as much as she did, yet he remained icily indifferent, drinking to blot out all feeling, caring more about his studbook than the writing on the wall.

Ronnie had spent sleepless nights forming a plan. Johnny would do the honourable thing and move out, surely. He could rent somewhere in the village to stay close to the children. They had to come first. She and Angus would need to move slowly. Once the divorce was final, they could get to know each other better away from the adrenalin rush of adultery. The children were already big fans of 'Gangus', and her father rated the jockey highly. Her parents would come around eventually.

She'd longed to talk to Hermia, but her friend was on a theatre tour, and Ronnie had hidden her unhappiness for far too long to spill it all to a pay-phone in a dressing-room corridor. Eventing friends were all pro-Angus, but she needed balance and compassion. Johnny wasn't the one having the affair; he was the father of her children; he didn't get angry and didn't argue even when blind drunk. He just didn't love her.

Had Ronnie ever stopped to question why he drank, and whether that had anything to do with love, she might have stumbled on the answer sooner. But by that point she was already hurtling towards the door.

One of Ronnie's dogs let out a shrill bark. She heard hoofs trotting briskly up the drive.

'Oh, hell.' Was Lester coming back early?

She knew she must go straight out and get the reunion over with. Far worse to let him stumble across Blair evaluating youngstock. She hurried to the study to collect the last of the stud-files boxes then back through the house to the courtyard. But coming through the gate to the stables, she found no sign of Lester or his horse. Abandoning the archive box on the car bonnet with the others, she went through the archways in search of him, but he'd vanished. The stable awaiting his hunter remained open. She wondered if she'd imagined it.

A step behind made her spin round. Blair was emerging from the shadow of the clock-tower, his face breaking into a shrewd, crease-eyed smile. 'You knew I'd bloody love them, didn't you?'

'I thought they'd be your stamp.' She was relieved.

'They're the whole package – FedExed, air-mailed, signed-for Robertson tough types.' They walked together out to the modern barn where the long faces of the oldest unbroken homebreds were lined up like piano keys, watching them eagerly. 'They're like little Aussie cattle horses with more timber.'

'And they're cheap,' she reminded him. 'Which is why you like them so much.'

Blair's craggy smile widened as he put his arm round her and pulled her under his chin to tousle her hair. He was an alchemist when it came to turning base metal into eventing gold. He'd never bought an expensive horse in his life. Apart from the birthday present for his wife.

'I'll take the lot. And you'll stay in Wiltshire. Deal?'

'Let's not go there.' She held up her hand, breaking free to turn and call her dogs away from sniffing around Lester's cottage door, his little terrier barking inside. As she did so, she realised Blair's wanderlust pointer was missing. 'Where's George?'

'Gone rabbiting, I should think. He'll be back.'

'Anything you especially like the look of?' Ronnie cast her eye over the homebreds.

'The little buckskin colt turned out over there.' He pointed at a small flurry of action in the nursery paddock.

'Not for sale.' She went to check on him. Furious to be separated from his new best friend, the foal was storming up and down the far side of the hedge, pink nose in the air. 'And he's a baby. You want ones you can start straight away.'

'C'mon, Ron, that's not fair. He's the best of the lot by far.'

'Which is why he's not for sale.'

'You're Ronnie Percy.' He grinned. '*Every*thing's for sale. You'd sell the shirt off your back for profit.'

'Not if I didn't have a decent bra on.'

'You'd sell that too if the money was right.'

She looked over her shoulder disbelievingly. 'You think that?'

'Take it as a compliment. You don't give a shit. It's what I like about you. That and your arse.'

They shared a kiss to stop another row bubbling. His mouth tasted of strong coffee and sweet tobacco.

Ronnie had always been attracted to competitive, unreconstructed men who knew what they wanted and took it, which in the horse world made for rich pickings. Selfishness was easy to read, and highly driven men like Blair never took their eye off target. Triers like Ronnie never stopped racing to ride the faster line.

'I know you say that Vee won't let the stallion go,' she said, watching his face adopt its customary visor-down look of a knight preparing to gallop towards a jousting opponent. 'Hear me out. The horse is totally wasted. Why not loan him to stand at stud here for a season? That way you know he's safe. Vee's safe. We're safe.'

The dark eyes burned into hers, the conversation over before it started. 'Not my decision, mate.'

The do-not-go-there shutdown was the rule she broke most often. 'You know it is, Blair. Don't hide behind her.'

'Nobody hides behind Vee.'

'Think of the horse.'

'There are lots of horses out there. I only have one wife.'

'And one mistress.'

'Let's keep it that way.'

She held up her arms.

Blair's way of riding across country betrayed his tactical nature, a man seemingly utterly committed to one line yet able to change course at speed, a quick-thinking maverick whose ability to stay in the saddle through every twist and turn was legendary.

He changed course now, pressing his forehead to hers, the bitter-chocolate eyes intense. 'If you live here, you're making it impossible for us to carry on as we are.'

'I know that.'

'I can't just slip out to walk the dog and come to see you. I'm not ready to let us go, Ron.'

'We agreed we could walk away from "us" at any time.'

'So you want to walk?'

It was very hard to resist that Aussie magnetism, as rough-hewn and pure gold as a chunk of Mount Carlton. He was fiery and non-conformist, immensely practical and knowledgeable, unstinting and a fantastic lay. Ronnie wasn't ready to lose 'us' either, even if it had to adapt to survive.

'I think driving's the better option between here and Wiltshire, don't you? *If* I decide to live here, you're just going to have to collect these youngsters one at a time in a single trailer. But there's a lot to sort out before that happens.' She looked back to the yards for Lester.

'Yeah, like finding my bloody dog.' He turned to holler up at the fields. 'George! George, c'mere!'

Ronnie's two little heelers were snorting furiously at the door in the wall beside the tack room that led through to the little garden at Lester's cottage.

'Could George be through here?' She strode towards it. Beyond it lay his walled private plot, a miniature sanctum immaculately laid out with soft fruit, cold frames and geometrically planted vegetables. The thought of it made her hands shake, but she refused to let in the memories.

'Doubt it.' Blair wandered after her. 'Uncle Fester rode in there a little while back. Didn't you see?'

'But that's his garden.' She went to hammer on the door.

'He didn't look like a man who wanted to be followed,' Blair warned her.

'Lester, are you there?'

A horse whinnied.

'Now's not a good time, Mrs Ledwell,' came a firm voice.

'Is everything all right?'

'Perfectly, thank you. You get on with whatever it is you're doing. I'll not bother you.'

'If you're sure?'

'Perfectly sure.'

'Lester, you and I do have to talk at some point.'

Apart from the jangle of a bit and the sound of a horse snorting, all was silence.

Raking her hair back in frustrated bewilderment, she turned to see Blair watching her, brows lowered. 'You heard the guy. We'd better press on. Where's that scanner?'

She headed back to her car to fetch it, then held it out for Blair to take.

He crossed his arms. 'What's the deal here, Ronnie?'

'There is no deal.' She grabbed a roll of livestock stickers, which she dropped into the box of equine passports, balancing the scanner on top, then picked it all up and turned to him. 'If you sticker the ones you like, I can check the breeding on those first.'

Taking the sticker roll from her, he peeled one off and placed it on her chest.

'Past her prime,' she muttered, removing it. 'Unreliable sort. Doubtful lineage.'

Faster than a shop worker with a label gun, he applied sticker after sticker all over her until, laughing, she snatched back the roll, losing her grip on the heavy box.

Fifty passports fell to the ground as his hands reached for her face, drawing it to his, lips on hers. 'That's all I bloody want right now. Stay in Wiltshire.'

25

Petra bade farewell to the Bags at her gates, saluting them. 'I'm trading Redhead for Black Tom, but I'm only a phone call away.'

'Good luck!' Bridge saluted her back, eyebrows at sad angles. 'We'll miss you.'

'I'll call you later, then.' Gill dismissed Petra's theatrical curtain call with a disparaging look. 'And we'll all see you at the Goose Walk.'

Petra and the chestnut mare crunched up the drive just in time to see a quadcopter swooping over her house roof.

'Fitz, just what are you up to with that drone?' she shouted towards his open window.

He appeared around the corner of the house, croquet mallet in one hand, a bag of carrots and marrows in the other. Petra was shocked to see him dressed and outside before nine.

'Just setting up a game for the girls.'

'Wow. Isn't it a bit early for croquet? The lawn's still wet.'

'You said give them breakfast croquet.'

'Croquettes, Fitz. Bacon and avocado croquettes. In the bottom oven. No sugary cereal.'

'On it. Oh, Mr Thing next door just handed me this.' He gave her the bag of vegetables. 'Plus that weird woman who posts crap on your Facebook page came to the door earlier, but I didn't invite her in. She took the tin of cakes away. Major fail.'

'You did good.'

Wondering how Pip knew the code to the electric gate, Petra fed the mare the carrots and turned her out, then hastened inside to face the consequences of her negligent mothering.

Being overseen by their big brother inevitably turned Prudie and Bella to pre-teen monsters. In pulled-up hoods, hot-pants and neon Crocs, they were fighting over possession of their brother's iPhone with which they were taking selfies, its low-battery warning beeping.

'Enough. Give that to me.' Petra confiscated it. That the sisters were dressed, at least, lifted Fitz's childcare skills greatly in her estimation.

She turned the phone over in her hand, hot as a brick, its screen cracked. 'Didn't Dad give you a newer one than this?'

Fitz snatched it. 'I like this one.'

'You need something better if you're bussing it to school and back, not to mention your social life there.'

'I won't have a social life there.'

'Of course you will.' Fitz had always made friends easily. 'Fetch the phone your father gave you. I'll help you set it up, if you like. Does it take the same SIM card?'

'It's already set up.'

'Dad'll be pleased. He was asking me about it last weekend.'

'Say what?'

'Just if you were using it,' she remembered vaguely.

'It has its uses,' he muttered darkly, and Petra guessed the latest model iPhone would be on his Christmas list this year. 'When do you start your new book?'

'This week.'

'Cool.' He scowled at her and patted his hoodie pocket as he slouched out, grabbing his mallet. 'I have a match to run.'

Ronnie and Blair made light work of matching each horse to its stud record, assessing them as they went along. That they always found it so easy to team up together and get a job done was an irony not lost on them.

'Bring them all back to Wiltshire,' Blair suggested. 'You can rent this place out. I'll produce them and we'll split the profit.'

She threw him a blue-sky smile, knowing he was much better at high-flying optimism away from home. That was why he spent so much time on the road competing. They both hated standing still, thinking aloud or looking back. Sometimes Ronnie wished their love affair could remain as one endless road trip from event to event.

Having scanned half the horses, she made coffee in the tack room while Blair took a cigarette break and went in search of George again.

She left the kettle creaking towards boil and returned to Lester's garden door. Listening carefully, she could hear a horse cropping grass and a soft, reassuring voice: 'You'll be all right, boy. Just you settle in there. You can smell the ferrets, eh, Charlie?'

She chewed her lip, wondering if the customary bloody-minded eccentricity might be touched with a trace of senility, these days.

'Everything's fine, Mrs Ledwell!' his voice called through the door. 'You just get on.'

Ronnie sprang back in guilty surprise. 'Would you like a cup of tea?'

'No, thank you.'

'Lester, we must talk.'

Silence.

'I have no idea how you're coping here with nobody to help except Pip, but it's Herculean. You can't keep it up once the horses come off grass. When did you last have a day off?'

Peering through the slot of the Suffolk latch, she couldn't see him. She knew better than to try the door. As a child, she'd loved sneaking through it to the fairy-tale garden, but as adulthood had layered sensibility over curiosity, she'd learned to appreciate Lester's privacy, his world moving further out of reach, his secrets still haunting her today.

The old broodmares watched her over their doors with limpid eyes as she turned away. No ghosts here, they said. Drawn by their reassurance, she crossed the yard.

By the time her marriage was at its ragged end, Ronnie had stolen in and out of this yard like a thief. It had been Johnny's domain, her competition horses confined to a run of old timber boxes around the back of the straw barn, battle lines drawn. His alliance with her father and Lester had been absolute, her adultery an unspoken secret.

Breaking point had come during Cheltenham week. Confiding in her mother was, Ronnie later realised, totally foolhardy. Ann had refused to empathise with her daughter's despair.

'Don't be so wet,' Ann had snapped impatiently, when Ronnie told her how unhappy her marriage was. 'Johnny doesn't hit you or the children. He simply avoids you. And he's jolly good with horses. Many women I know would love a husband like that.'

Then, almost luminescent with excitement, Ronnie told her about Angus, too close to personal happiness to step back and see the picture as others did, especially a matriarchal traditionalist like Ann Percy. She'd broken the spell that had kept her daughter happy for months. 'Your father must be told.'

Jocelyn's reaction was swift and uncompromising. 'How long's it been going on?' he'd demanded, his voice full of approaching thunder.

'Almost a year.'

Ronnie would stop seeing Angus Bowman immediately, he insisted. Johnny would be protected from the truth and the stud's reputation safeguarded. Then, almost as an afterthought, 'You must put your children first.'

'I am. I have. They'll come with me.'

'Come with you where?'

'I'm leaving Johnny.'

'You are going nowhere!'

It was then the lightning bolts were loosed, Zeus putting his foot down on Mount Olympus, straight through the floor. Ronnie had never heard her father rant so angrily. He refused to allow her selfish, grubby love affair to compromise the long-term future of the family and stud, he stormed. The Percys would stand by Johnny. If Ronnie did not do as she was told, she would lose her inheritance as well as her marriage. If she took the children, Jocelyn raged on, he would cut them all out of his will, too, and Ronnie would deny her own blood as well as herself the birthright that six generations of Percys had enjoyed. Seeing him lost to the red mist, Ronnie had half expected him to threaten to shoot the horses, but he lit a cigarette and announced he was going up to change for supper. 'We will say no more about the matter.'

'Discretion is the better part of valour, Ronnie,' her mother hissed, after he'd gone. 'Have an affair but, for God's sake, don't bloody blab or blub. You should take a leaf out of Johnny's book.'

'What do you mean?' she'd gasped, his emotional sclerosis cast in a sudden new light.

But Ann waved her away. 'Go up and say goodnight to the children.'

With her secret out, Ronnie's get-out plan had gathered speed. Upstairs, the children were already asleep. Kissing their peaceful faces, she'd made a silent promise that she would do everything in her power to keep them safe. She had no choice but to confide in the jolly nanny – a close ally, quietly aware of how bad her employers' marriage was – who promised to help if things blew up. They hurriedly packed three little getaway bags to stash in the wardrobe just in case, then shared a tearful hug.

When Johnny had come in from the yard later that evening, already half a bottle of Scotch up, Ann and Jocelyn had acted as though nothing whatsoever had happened. The decanter circulated, the new foals were discussed. For a while, Ronnie's one hysterical thought was that she should call Hermia after all and tell her that her parents had turned out to be the Laurence Olivier and Joan Plowright of Compton Magna.

Instead she said, very loudly and clearly, 'I want a divorce.'

Shooting her a withering look, her mother went to check on the cottage pie while Johnny poured himself another Scotch and her father muttered, in a stern undertone, 'For God's sake, Ronnie, go up to your room and lie down.'

If she hadn't heard Pax crying upstairs, Ronnie suspected she might have walked straight out of the house there and then, too blind with anger to care about anything but escape. Instead she went and rocked her youngest child, her own tears sliding silently into that beautiful curly red hair.

Much later that night, Johnny came to her room, crashing round drunkenly offering her sex, kissing her with such aggression he cut her lip, so incapable of giving affection or wanting it that he passed out at the end of the bed, the first time he'd slept in it for four years.

'Whose affair started first?' she asked, but he was out cold. She could guess the answer. It hardly mattered. The marriage was irreparable.

At dawn, while her children still slept, she crept to the phone in the kitchen and rang Angus. He was riding in the Foxhunter at

Cheltenham that day, already up and expecting her call. She'd wished him good luck in the race brightly.

He heard it in her voice straight away.

'Forget that. What's the hell's wrong?'

'It's all blowing up with Johnny.'

'I'll come straight over to get you out of there.'

'Please don't. I'll deal with it. Win that race for me.'

Afterwards, Ronnie had lain in a hot bath while the house still slept, teeth chattering. She had to speak to Angus again. He needed to know her crisis wasn't his crisis: he had to focus on the race; she couldn't leave her children, even for a night.

But when she'd hurried downstairs in a towelling robe, every phone in the house was being marked by breakfasting or newspaper reading or ironing, so she stepped into wellies and raced to the village phone box. His line rang unanswered. Eventually she was forced to give up because somebody was tapping impatiently on the other side of the steamed-up glass.

It was Angus. He was smiling widely, blood on his chipped teeth. 'I've just told Johnny I love his wife.'

'Oh, Christ, what has he done to you?' She'd rushed out, arms around him. His nose was broken.

'Actually, he was very decent about it.' He'd laughed. 'It was your father who did this when I told him I'm taking you away.'

'What about the children?'

'They bit my ankles and set the dogs on me, but we'll win them round.' He started kissing her, his salty sweet blood against her lips. 'A friend's offered me his holiday house for the month. He's also offered his divorce lawyer. You *won't* lose the children, I promise. Now, for God's sake, run away with me, Mrs Ledwell. We'll sort all this out.' Their mutual laughter was as infectious as being tickled, unstoppable, almost painful.

At that moment, she'd loved him like no other. Being offered such a simple solution to such a horrid mess was deliverance. She was twenty-five and felt as if her life had restarted; she'd grown wings. She would be back to claim her home and her children the instant the dust settled, but right now she was flying all the way to the Lakes, the wind in her hair.

Just days later, Angus took a chance ride on a foggy afternoon at Whittington Races that changed everything completely.

Ronnie pressed her cheek against that of one of the stud's oldest mothers, a dulcet-eyed former hurdler, with a dappled brown coat the colour of coffee beans.

It was a safe bet that her love affair with Angus Bowman would have passed the finish post far sooner, had it not been for his accident. That day, in a blistering, rotational fall that had sent him crashing into the turf under half a ton of fast-moving horse, his spine had been crushed like thyme beneath a pestle.

Angus had no close family, no insurance and nobody to fall back on. He'd abandoned a fiancée for her, forsaking his closest allies. All he had was Ronnie, as honourable as she was compassionate.

Caught up in the wheels of deep shock, Percy pragmatism saw Ronnie through, stubbornly refusing to lose all sight of her children, yet unable to desert Angus, at first staying in a bed-and-breakfast close to the hospital, then renting a cottage nearby and, as the weeks stretched to months, taking secretarial work to make ends meet, applying to the Injured Jockeys Fund for help as she oversaw his agonisingly slow recuperation. Before they knew it, they had a new life tethered in a tightly knit tangle in Cumbria, and Ronnie's punishingly long drives to Gloucestershire to see the children tore her apart, her bouncy, happy-mummy show protecting them from the darkness of true mother love, a torrent of lava in her veins that missed them every minute of every day.

By the time she and Angus were settled enough for her to seek a formal shared-custody arrangement, her parents' forceful arguments against it had gained considerable purchase: the stud provided the idyllic childhood she had enjoyed; Jocelyn could fund educations for his grandchildren, which she could never hope to afford, and Johnny was laying the foundations for breeding lines that would see them take over from six generations of Percys at Compton Magna. It was the only home her children had ever known, surrounded by family and animals they loved, with a jolly nanny they adored, and they didn't want to leave. Most damningly, Ann had pointed out with vitriol that Ronnie already had one dependant to care for. It had been made clear early on that a wheelchair would always be part of Angus's life. Her children didn't deserve an accidental stepfather coasting bitterly through life. Leave them at home where they belong.

Ronnie turned away from the mare, whose breath stayed warm against her shoulder. In almost thirty years of absence, she hadn't lost her sense of belonging here. And yet her lesson in love had come at such a price, she wasn't sure she could ever earn it back.

Mitch, the chatty postie, was at the gate of Upper Bagot Farmhouse with a signed-for parcel and obligatory weather talk: 'Bit blustery today,' he called, as Petra crossed the gravel to sign for a parcel. 'Trees'll be turning before you know it.'

'Every leaf speaks bliss to me, fluttering from the autumn tree,' she quoted Emily Brontë.

'My missus likes Simon and Garfunkel too.'

Putting the post under her arm while she signed his proffered screen, Petra's phone began to ring in her pocket. She swiped it without looking, waving a thank-you to Mitch.

'Hello?' Propping the phone to her ear with her shoulder, she flipped through the letters, hearing a deep chuckle and a hunting horn.

'What are you up to?' Bay's voice was laced with sloe gin and cheer. 'Fancy breakfast?'

Stay calm, Petra. You're parking him. 'You're three hours too late.'

'Call it lunch, then. Bring the girls. Tilly's desperate to see Bella before school starts.'

'We've got plans.' Hacking, shoe-shopping, binge-watching *The Next Step*. Anything but seeing you and feeling sixteen again.

'I've been bloody texting you all week. Why didn't you come out with us today?'

Beneath the parcel – which was for Ed – were the usual window-faced reminders and a stiff cream envelope addressed to Mr and Mrs Charles Gunn, which she guessed was a wedding invitation. 'I've decided I'm not a hunting fan.'

'Nonsense. Those thighs were made for tight breeches,' he coaxed, voice going croakily sexy.

'I have a book to write, Bay.'

'And I can't wait to read it. But before you get started, I do think you need some help with your descriptive accuracy. I've been reading through your oeuvre, as you know. And all the sex is terrific – do keep it coming, them coming – but your heroes miss quite a few tricks.'

'Go on.'

'I'd need to demonstrate.'

'Demonstrate?' Suddenly feeling hot, Petra fanned herself with the thick cream envelope.

'Yes. I think we should arrange a demonstration as soon as possible, don't you?'

'What sort of tricks had you planned to demonstrate?'

'Very hard to describe. Can't put my finger on it without the books and the author in person. But once I have it all at my fingertips, I guarantee it'll come to me terribly quickly.' His voice was positively pornographic.

Petra closed her eyes, envelope fanning madly, parcel dropping from her grip with an ominous crack on the gravel. She wasn't entirely sure all the insinuation wasn't just in her head, but it was doing things to her body her sixteen-year-old self would have written straight in her diary.

She thought determinedly about her long marriage, about the sexy Italian moves, the desire to put the S back in SMC and about her need for writing space. 'Bay, this has to stop.'

'What has to stop?' He laughed incredulously.

'You know exactly what I mean.'

'Really, darling, I don't. Shit! Gotta go. Charlie's turned up.'

'Charlie?'

'Little red chap, not your big—' The horn sounded close by and Bay shouted. The next moment the line went dead.

Huffing, Petra opened the cream envelope.

Sandy and Vivien Austen cordially invite...

It wasn't a wedding invitation. It was the sacred stiffy her husband had coveted for so long. The Manor Farm Pheasant Supper, a.k.a. the Well-hung Party, hosted by Bay's parents at the beginning of November. With it was an invitation to a private shoot on the farm a few days beforehand.

Petra felt her hot cheeks drain to clammy embarrassment, appalled at herself for doing an awkward, bumbling *Brief Encounter* number on Bay. He'd sounded so surprised.

She looked at the invitation again, knowing Charlie would be beside himself with joy. Her bluster would be forgotten by November. She had a book to draft full of inaccurate sex before then. And if she removed the biscuit tin from her office, she might get down to a size twelve while she was doing it.

Petra dialled Charlie's mobile, but it was on voicemail. At chambers, his direct line rang out before diverting to an unfamiliar clerk in Property Law. 'Has Charles Gunn come in yet, in Commercial Law?'

'Let me check, madam.' There was a pause for Muzak, then, 'He's not here this week, madam.'

'I'm sorry?'

'Mr Srivas says Mr Gunn is not expected to come into chambers until next week, and then only on Tuesday.'

'Put me through to Deepak. Tell him it's Petra.' Deepak Srivas was the other junior barrister working under silk Henry Baliol, Charlie's old-school-tie crony, who had been instrumental in encouraging him into law. Deepak was a defiantly state-educated over-achiever, and often a probing thorn in Charlie's side. Petra liked him a lot.

'Ah, Petra. Long time!'

'Am I missing something, Deepak? I didn't think Charlie was in court this week.'

'That's because he's not – at least, not a legal one.'

'That sounds very loaded.'

'Unintended. Squash court,' he said. 'Cross-chambers tournament.'

Of course! Charlie and Henry loved bashing small balls around manfully. Did that usually justify being out of the office for so long?

'I'd forgotten he's not in this week,' she fudged.

'The official line is working from home.'

Petra picked up an edge in Deepak's smooth tone. 'What's the unofficial line?' There was an adversarial pause.

'I'm his wife, Deepak. You're not being paid to defend him. Yet.'

He sighed, but she sensed the wry smile. 'Okay, you didn't hear it from me but things got a bit hot after he slipped up at the big offshore-trusts trial, so when Charlie came back from annual leave, Henry suggested a lighter load.'

'Is he being investigated by the Bar Standards Board?'

'No, no! Henry's got his back, and the clerks are soliciting. They're looking for a nice straightforward case to ease him back in.'

Petra tried not to panic. Charlie obviously hadn't said anything because he was embarrassed. It was like Fitz and the GCSEs. Like father like son. She must try to react with the same sympathy, not the urge to find the nearest blunt instrument and hit him with it. Nor must she give in to the urge to change into her sexiest skinny jeans and rush to Manor Farm for a bacon sandwich and Demonstration of Tricks behind the pheasant coops.

'It's good of Henry to be so supportive,' she said carefully.

'Hmm.' Deepak clearly didn't think so. 'Anyway, how are you and the children in the shire? Happy as hobbits?'

'Indeed. But we draw the line at second breakfasts.' She cast a wistful look at the Well-hung invitation before stomping inside to take a shower.

26

Compton Magna Primary School always reopened after the summer break with a day in which only the teachers and new reception children attended.

To help them settle, each child was allowed to bring a favourite toy. This autumn term there were trolls and Olafs, Disney princesses and Buzz Lightyears, plush animals, teddy bears of all description, and a large fluffy duster.

'Why'd you let him bring it?' Ash hissed at Carly as they lined up in the playground to shuffle to the classroom door where the reception teacher and her assistant were peeling tearful four-year-olds away from their parents' legs.

'He wanted to,' she said simply. Ellis needed his 'Splorer Stick more than ever today. She'd given it a good wash and tried to puff it up.

Between them, Ellis held it proudly, like a ceremonial sword.

It was rare for the Turner family to have less than a brace of offspring starting each academic year, but this time there was just one, Ellis Peter Turner, hollow-eyed and mute, clinging to his beloved 'Splorer Stick, staring at his newly fitted Clarks shoes.

Carly and Ash formed a protective arch around their firstborn and hung back behind the pushy middle-classers accustomed to addressing teachers as equals rather than higher beings. The Turners had missed the reception parents' meeting that week because Carly had been working at the restaurant, and Ash had forgotten he was supposed to go. She'd imagined she'd find a gaggle of working mums in the same boat. Looking at them now, they were almost all a decade older, a pay scale higher and several social circles wider. They also

all seemed to know one another already. Trying to imagine them as
Petra, Carly caught a few eyes with a sympathetic smile, but found
herself blanked. Ash, by contrast, was being openly gawped at, the
triangular gym body and lean hips as hypnotic to yummy-mummies
as a copy of *Fifty Shades*.

His college course started next week and he'd been getting himself in shape. Carly hoped college would mean fewer late nights,
and regular school drop-offs together. Ellis needed the family team.

When it was his turn to go into class, Ellis set his chin heroically and didn't look back, waving the 'Splorer Stick at them over
his shoulder as he marched inside, determined to show his dad he
wasn't scared.

Carly was too choked to speak, walking back, pushing the double
buggy while Ash trudged, head down, alongside. She imagined he
felt the same as she did. After a while he sniffed and looked up at
the scudding clouds. 'Got to get rid of that fucking duster.'

'Let him have the dog,' she snapped. 'He'll surrender it for the dog.'

Passing Upper Bagot Farmhouse, which she'd be cleaning with
Janine later, she spotted the Gunns' teenage son in the garden with his
two sisters, hammering coloured balls through hooks on grass so
damp with dew they left great snail trails.

Wilf had bounced up to the garden wall, recognising her and
wagging himself in circles.

'Come here, you!' Fitz called, then saw Carly and Ash. She waved
and he nodded, suntanned cheeks streaking deep red.

'Carly!' Petra bounded out of the house, hair wet from the
shower. 'Just the person! I have Flynn coming this afternoon and
I've got to take these smalls for shoe fittings and Fitz for his new
uniform. Is there any chance you can spare me an extra hour to hold
the ponies and the mare for him if I bung you some cash? They'll
probably be fine tied up, but a cup of tea and another pair of hands
go a long way.'

'No worries.'

'Brilliant! Come back at midday.' She beamed at her over the wall.
'This is Ash.'

'Great to meet you at last! I hear you're going to be a personal
trainer? God knows, I could do with one of those!'

He flashed a half-smile, eyeing her muffin top with professional interest.

'It's Ellis's first day, isn't it?' she asked. 'How was he, going in?'

'Yeah, he's cool,' Carly said proudly.

'What a star!'

Ash was already swaggering ahead, hands deep in his pockets, head low, scowl lower.

She caught up with the buggy. 'Petra's a nice lady. I like her. You should have said hello.'

'Flynn says she's a flake.'

'Then she deserves a farrier who shows her a bit more respect.'

'Like you with your little hammer and nails?'

'Don't take the piss.' She wished she'd never mentioned it was something she'd like to do. She'd looked it up and been disheartened to find there would be a year at college before she could start as apprentice to a master farrier like Flynn. The nearest City and Guilds course still had places, but it cost more than they could ever afford on top of Ash's PT training – her part-time jobs were barely covering costs as it was. Carly was resigned to being patient. She would win Ash's support, save up her college fees and earn Flynn's trust somehow.

Her phone beeped, its screen showing a selfie of a sleepy-eyed boy with a strange fringe, added to her contacts as Fitz. He'd done that the day she'd first cleaned the farmhouse, she remembered.

Just checking you haven't deleted me?

Another kid about to start at a new school, Carly thought. Feeling sorry for him, she sent a wink emoticon.

You look very beautiful today by the way, he replied.

Ash turned to tell her to hurry up and she quickly pocketed it. The son of a Gunn was stringier than Where's Wally, stroppier than Horrid Henry and barely shaving yet, but she didn't trust Ash not to overreact if he read a message like that. She'd delete him later.

But when her pocket pinged and she checked it again, she knew she wouldn't have the heart. *Could use your wise advice on an open line. Bad stuff going down here. Might need a fairy godmother. (Helps that you're fairy godmilf.)*

*

Pip panted out from the undergrowth of Compton Thorns covert in which she'd half expected Bear Grylls to pop out from behind a bush with a tinderbox and a hammock, telling her she'd never escape. There were 'Adders Keep Out!' signs everywhere. Her breathing shallow, hoarse from shouting, she gulped what oxygen she could into burning lungs.

The hounds had long since moved on to the next wood along. Pip was disappointed in Lester, who she'd thought might help retrieve the stray dog, but he'd ridden off at speed as soon as the huntsman called his hounds out. The overexcited stray pointer had stayed in deep cover, rolling in fox poo between flushing out pheasants. He now reeked.

Pip had finally managed to bribe him onside by laying a Hansel and Gretel trail with the rest of her cakes. Dragging him back up the hill to the lane, she found a harassed-looking woman in a Puffa waiting by a lop-sided Citroën Cactus, her camcorder trained on the far distance.

'Fucking foot-followers let down one of my tyres!' She sounded like a posh Adele. 'I didn't manage to get anything useful on camera. How about you, bubs?'

'I beg your pardon?'

'Shagtastically smart thinking, pretending to be a dog-walker and letting him loose in there. They had a kill, didn't they? Did you film anything admissible in court, bubs? Fucking bastards.'

'I saw one of the terrier men taking a wee behind a tree, but I didn't think to catch it on my phone. Shame, really. I could have sent it to *You've Been Framed*.'

The woman gave her a wide-eyed death stare. 'You're not Liz from Evesham, are you?'

'Pip from the village. I work at the stud,' she said proudly, waving an expansive hand. 'This is our land.'

'Bloody bugger, you're one of them!'

'No, I am not. I'm a cat lover and a pacifist. Are you an AA member? I always get them out if I have a puncture.'

Pip had often seen the hunt monitors when she'd taken the Captain round the lanes in pursuit of action. The old man had delighted in shouting offensively at them but Pip had always admired the feisty band of middle-aged women standing up to big, burly foot-followers. This one looked remarkably familiar, with her flat nose, close-set cobalt eyes and shock of blonde Boris Johnson hair. 'I don't suppose you know who this dog belongs to?' she asked her.

'No shagging idea. My aunt has pointers, all bloody loonies.' Hounds were drawing the covert out of sight, the horn echoing across to encourage them. 'Bugger blast! I'll have to try to get there on fucking foot.' She set off along the lane at a jog, then stopped beside Pip's little blue run-around. 'Is this your car?'

Nodding, Pip studied her features again, realising exactly where she'd seen that striking masculine nose before. Facebook. With over three thousand friends and a very active profile, Lady Roo Verney was a self-styled animal-communicator, anti-cruelty activist and vociferous social media-ite. She was also the last person Pip knew to have had contact with Verity online.

'Would you like a lift?' she offered eagerly.

'That makes you the fucking love of my life right now. I'm Prunella Verney by the way.' She shook Pip's hand so firmly that Pip could hardly feel it to put the key in the ignition. 'Call me Roo.'

Setting off, dog on the back seat, gulping loudly and smelling rancid, Pip excitedly made the connection: 'You're Verity's niece!'

'You know Aunt Vee?' She was filming out of the passenger window. They could see the red coats of the hunt staff moving in the valley, charging along a track beside the woods, the horn blowing long, repeated notes. 'Hounds are on the wrong scent.'

'How *is* Vee?' Pip asked, adopting her best caring tone.

'She has her good days. Old age is a finger up the backside, isn't it? Especially when you're, you know, fucked.'

Pip didn't entirely understand but she nodded, with a sympathetic hum, wondering if Roo had some form of Tourette's. She certainly had no volume control. It was like being in the car with a female Brian Blessed.

'How's her horse?' she asked.

'That bloody psycho doesn't help one bit. The family would have shot it, if it wasn't so valuable. All Blair's fault, of course. Bloody buggery man. Brake! I need to film this.' They shuddered to a halt and she leaned out of the window to pan across as a quad bike zoomed over the stubble, switching between commentary and conversation: 'And here we see a terrier man going in...Vee dotes on them both unfortunately... The terriers will dig a fox from earth to shred it limb from limb... Of course the horse is totally wasted on Vee.'

Pip had to play this carefully. The camera was rolling so she didn't want anything incriminating recorded, but it was too good an opportunity to waste. 'She could always sell him back to his dealer, couldn't she?'

'Unlikely. Most horse dealers are total fucking crooks. Loathsome bunch. How do you know my aunt again?'

'I... was researching a book,' she improvised quickly. 'For my best friend Petra Shaw. She's an—'

'I know who she fucking is! *Love* all that Regency lesbian eroticism she rocks off. *Is* she gay?'

'No.'

'What a bloody shame. She knows her way around scissoring.'

'She does all her cutting on computer, these days,' said Pip, misunderstanding.

Roo put her camera down. 'Bugger! I've pissing well lost them behind the wood. Drive!' she ordered. 'Yes, I'll bet old Vee gave you lots of shaggingly good stuff. Even when she can't remember her own name, she can still recite the bloody story about being related to Katherine Ferrers, the Wicked Lady herself. I bet all that casting off one's corsets to disguise oneself as a highwayman is right up Petra's alley. Is that what the next book's about?'

'It's a loose retelling,' Pip said vaguely, making a mental note to cross-check dates. 'I wrote to your aunt very recently but I heard nothing back.'

'Was it typed?'

'Yes.'

'Then of course you bloody wouldn't. She thinks anything typed is a bill and it goes straight in the bin, always has. Worse than ever, these days, of course. What are they fuck-meisteringly *doing*?' She lifted the camera again and filmed as Pip racketed along to the stud entrance, in which the car-followers' muddy convoy was parked up. 'Here we see deliberate obstruction,' she told the sound recording.

The bulldog man was trying to block their way, standing in the middle of the lane, arms out.

'Keep twat-buggery driving!' Roo hissed to Pip.

Doing as she was told, Pip put her foot down. Bulldog Man stood his ground then, eyes bulging, screamed. Covering her own eyes, Roo screamed too. The dog threw up the remains of twelve cupcakes on the back seat. Pip banked the verge, bounced past him and pelted on.

Roo peered out from between her fingers. 'Did you fucking well run over him?'

'Of course not.' Then she started to giggle. 'Sorry, did you want me to?'

Roo was gazing at her in wonder. 'What did you say your name was again?'

'Pip.'

Joining in the infectious laughter Roo thrust her head out of the window and looked back at the fist-waving foot-followers, flicking up two fingers. Then she collapsed back in her seat and whistled. 'Ever thought of becoming a hunt monitor, Pip?'

'I'd lose my job.'

'Ah, yes, at the stud, you said. Aunt Vee asked me to communicate with that loony stallion of hers once. Brain-fuckingly mixed up, poor chap. Told me he wanted to be called Moon and live a natural barefoot life running with mares on high pasture, but Vee was having none of it. Silly old bird's so frightened he'll end up in the wrong hands. Stop the chuffing car!' she demanded, as they passed the gate into the church meadows. 'I'll go on foot from here. Thank you *so* fucking much, bubs. Here are all my taglines.' She fished in the Puffa for a card striped with social-media addresses. 'Friend me and I'll friend you back. If you want to be more than friends, I'll take you out to fucking dinner sometime.' The blue eyes softened and then she was gone.

It took Pip a moment to realise she'd just been propositioned. Her first lesbian date offer. The first time she'd been asked out by anyone, in fact. Ex-husband Ali following her to Tesco Metro after work every day for a month didn't really count.

'I like sexy men with tattoos!' she told the dog, in the rear-view mirror. And yet it felt so nice to be asked to dinner. She tossed her hair back and drove on into the village like Portia de Rossi in a drag-racer.

Anxious not to encounter the hunt foot-followers again, Pip took the puking pointer to the Old Almshouses to wait it out until they moved on. It was the ideal opportunity to check the place over as part of her Home from Home Comforts service, she decided, and she had a new Tinder profile half composed in her head.

Sleuth with a sweet tooth seeking missing link with inks. Show me your stamp collection, big boys...

It had a nice romantic ring about it.

Until now, Fitz hadn't investigated the phone his father had given him much beyond the messaging app. As soon as he'd discovered that, it had transformed into a portal to an adult world, a handle to a twisted dystopian place beyond the safety net of weekend leave and school holidays. It was a magnifying glass that showed up every flaw in his mother's over-jolly pretence that all was well. His father had unwittingly handed him a weapon that could destroy them all, and he could see straight through its sights, like an assassin.

Leaving his sisters playing an elaborate *Fort Boyard*-themed game around the climbing frame, he slipped inside his mother's Plotting Shed, her workspace more like a messy undergraduate's digs than a romantic garret. There were fairy lights and disco balls, mementoes from student holidays, postcards, a cinematic lightbox over a window hung with Orla Kiely curtains, and a lot of *Black Beauty*-themed ephemera. It wasn't a historian's ivory tower, it was a time capsule dating back to her happiest era. Petra Shaw BC. Before Charlie.

Fitz had figured out that his mother's career had been in decline pretty much from the day she'd married, however brightly she spun it. She'd had two bestsellers before he was born, another shortly afterwards that was later adapted as a movie. While he was at prep school her minor celebrity kudos had made him a popular play-date for children whose mums wanted to get to know her. By boarding school he'd been too embarrassed about all the sex scenes to tell people what she did, and now that he was old enough to be proud of her, nobody knew who she was.

He slumped in her creaking office chair. Would Petra Shaw be better off without Charlie Gunn? The jury was out. But Fitz was absolutely certain they'd all be better off without Lozzy on the scene. His mission to bring that one down hadn't got going yet.

Petra no longer went to launch parties or on foreign tours. She'd once told Fitz that writing kept the wolf from the door, but as far as he could tell the wolf had climbed through the window while she wasn't looking.

He pulled the phone out of his pocket, starting it up. Deliberately ignoring the app, he set about getting to grips with the way it worked. Nothing he saw improved his opinion of his father, from the multiple gem-based games to the reactionary news feeds. He'd also left a media card in it with lots of photographs. Holy shit. How many pictures of his own penis could a man take?

Hey, old man. He texted one to Charlie now to wind him up. *Who were you pleased to see?*

When the device pinged, he thought it was his dad replying, but instead it was the moment Fitz Gunn felt himself turned from boy to man.

Carly's WhatsApp avatar was a photograph of a foal with a white face and a blue eye.

Don't like Godmilf.

Too Oedipal for you? he replied

Just fucking rude.

I'm Perseus not Oedipus.

I don't care if you're Maximus Decimus Meridius, don't you ever milf me again. This is strictly platonicus, poshboy. Here for advice if you need it. Anything else – random texts, sexting, selfies or telling me I look good – you're b-a-d, banned and deleted.

Fitz smiled, suddenly feeling a whole lot better than he had in weeks. He might still need to slay Lozzy the Gorgon, but the fiercest goddess in the village had his back.

27

Petra had plugged her earphones into her mobile and was listening to her eighties playlist as she walked. She wanted to clear her head totally, marching up the track that ran around the side of the big crop field behind the farmhouse to the top of the stud's land.

But her head refused to clear. Talking to herself was a writer's madness she'd suffered for years. Imaginary conversations were her mainstay.

First she rehearsed an altercation with Charlie: 'You can't keep things like this from me! Why didn't you talk to me about it? But, of course, we don't talk about ourselves any more. Just other people.'

In her ears, Cyndi Lauper started shouting that money changes everything.

'And money. We know the overdraft's not getting any smaller. We can't afford for you to live in London all week if work's so thin on the ground. Should we let the flat? Or sell it? Oh, God, then I'd have you home all week again. No, let's not do that. I'll just write a bestseller. I'm on it. This conversation never happened.'

She skipped music tracks to some mellower Cocteau Twins, imagining she was driving to have that lunch with Bay in which he showed her how well he handled a Gunn. She was magically transformed into Rachel Weisz, her voice cracking with intimacy: 'You know exactly what I mean when I say this has to stop, Bay. This flirting thing, this mutual attraction. We both feel it, and nothing can happen. The heaven is in the temptation, not the submission. But, my goodness, I want to submit. A novel,' she laughed under her breath, 'a bloody good novel full of amazing, life-changing sex.

Lie-back-and-take-it, seduce-me-now pleasure. The sort of sex I want
to have with you but can't.'

'GEORGE!'

'Jesus!' She pulled out an earpiece and swung round.

'GEORGE!' A woman's voice was shouting just the other side of
a field hedge jewelled with brambles. Unmistakably Ronnie Percy's.

Petra felt a little spark of cheer. Then she heard a man's voice,
deep as a stag's bark. 'George! Where the fuck is he?'

'Not here!' she called out helpfully, although she supposed George
could be a pet hamster for all she knew.

Nevertheless she heard a cheery 'Thanks!' come back.

Feeling like a good citizen, she checked Wilf was happily stalking
rabbits in the stubble up ahead and plugged her earphones back in.

As Petra marched on, she found Ronnie and her companion
were inadvertently keeping pace on the opposite side of the hedge,
repeated loud cries of 'George' penetrating Adele. Then she heard a
hearty 'Hello there! It's my ally!'

On the far side of the hedge a rise had lifted Ronnie into sight,
her blonde head turning in delight. Behind her, a brooding Indiana
Jones type was casting dark eyes across the horizon.

'Oh, hello!' Petra feigned surprise, pulling the buds conspicuously
from her ears. 'Sorry! Loud music. I was just—'

'Are his balls still on?' Ronnie interrupted urgently, as Wilf came
bounding over.

'Sorry?'

'The spaniel.' She cocked her head towards frantic yapping in the
hedge line further ahead. 'Here come my girls. Olive's on heat.'

'No balls,' Petra reassured her, as one of Ronnie's small black and
tan dogs shot out through the hedge, shrill barks ringing out. While
Olive and Wilf launched into an elaborate body-wagging, jumping
dance, like a pair of sixties groovers, the very elderly, grey-muzzled
dog Petra remembered from the farm-shop encounter also lumbered
out of the undergrowth.

'That's Enid,' Ronnie introduced her. 'She and Olive are great
rounder-uppers, hopeless picker-uppers. I had a terrific spaniel like
yours once, softest mouth in the world. Softest head too. Remind
me, is he working?'

'Actively job-seeking. My husband shoots. Wilf usually eats and leaves, but Charlie's determined to get his gundog boot-camp investment back.'

'Of course, the man who wants to get in with the Name and Game Droppers. This is Blair, by the way.' She introduced Indiana Jones. 'Blair, this is... Don't tell me, I'll get there...'

'Petra.'

'Petra from the village, a good ally of mine.' She gave Petra a grateful wink.

Indie nodded broodily and headed away towards the woods.

'Don't mind him. Lost his dog. Have you seen an English pointer out here?'

'Sorry, no.'

'GEORGE! Super to have around on a rough shoot, but I wouldn't trust him at one of the Austens' seven-pillars-of-tweed jobs.'

'We got an invitation to one today.'

'Your chap must be overjoyed. I should have guessed from what you were saying on the phone just now. Such good manners to tell the host you can't have sex with him.'

Petra looked at her, wide-eyed.

'We couldn't help overhearing.' Ronnie grinned. 'You were rather shouting. I'm glad you've taken my advice about Bay Austen. Madness to mess around with a man like him and twelve-bores in the house.'

'There's just one bore at home when he's not in London.' She felt her face prickle. 'He's not the best shot.'

'I'm a bloody good one, so you can always call on me if Bay's misbehaving.' She gave a naughty chuckle. 'Or your husband, come to that.'

Petra laughed nervously.

'*Never* shoot a hare,' Ronnie said, in a stage whisper over the brambles, blue eyes confessional. 'They haunt you. The Austen boys used to take me out coursing – Sandy and Robert were my generation. Their younger sister Hermia and I *hated* it. Hares are such beautiful creatures, the wildest of the wild. Bay Austen is altogether more cunicular.' The eyes twinkled.

'I wasn't speaking to— That is, there's really nothing going on. I came out to walk off a bad mood. I talk to myself a lot.'

'We all do that.' She strode off.

Keeping pace, heeled by all three dogs now, Petra listened to her as she stalked along the opposite side of the hedge line for a field's length, chattering good-naturedly in her hypnotically husky voice about shooting. She stole glances at her, enthralled. The legendary village prodigal daughter, scarlet harlot, bolter, child-deserter, and her unexpected ally.

'Do your children shoot?' Ronnie asked.

'The boys do.'

'How many do you have in total?' It sounded like she was asking about a farm herd.

'Four, two of each.'

'My God, you're a superstar.'

At the field corner, the hedge thinned between double rails over a trough and Ronnie climbed onto them, scanning the horizon. 'I bet he's back on the bloody yard.' She looked down at Petra, the big smile doing its magical thing of lifting Petra's spirits. 'What ages are your children?'

'Sixteen, thirteen, ten and eight.'

She clambered down, blue gaze neon bright. 'Then you *definitely* don't want to mess around with Bay. Take it from one who's been where you are – not in the same boat, but in the same white water. They are *never* interested in your children. GEORGE!' Jumping back down, she marched off, disappearing with a cheery wave as the ground dropped away.

At first Pip thought that nobody had been in the Old Almshouses since her last visit. Tying the dog to the gate, she started by cleaning out the back of her car, flicking the regurgitated cake onto the drive, then vacuuming the seat with Kit Donne's flashy Dyson, spraying the interior liberally with a dusty Molton Brown room scent she'd found in his downstairs loo.

The dog watched her with interest, whippy tail waving cautiously, pong carrying in the breeze.

'You're not getting back in my car wearing that aftershave,' she told it.

The downstairs wet room in Kit Donne's holiday house was much better suited to washing a large dog than her parents' disability-adapted walk-in bath. She was sure Kit wouldn't mind: he seemed a very laid-back sort, sending her occasional absent-minded texts to check all was well and ask if he needed to pay her.

Showering the dog was a messy business – it kept wriggling around and drinking the water out of the nozzle attachment. Pip's trousers and socks got so soaked that she was forced to peel them off and put them into the tumble-dryer.

Dressed in just her pants and pink fleece, she gave the dog a wide berth, taking a photograph with her smartphone. 'Who do you belong to, then?'

Its collar had a brass ID tag so worn all she could make out was GEO and 711.

Pip made herself instant hot chocolate while the pointer hared around the house, shaking vigorously and running its back along all the sofas before settling into an armchair, gazing at her with big, mournful eyes.

On her previous visits, Pip had discovered that if she sat in the oriel window and angled herself left, she could pick up Mrs Hedges' unsecured broadband, which she did now to post a Stray Dog Found notice on her Facebook wall, tagging in all the villagers she was friends with. She then updated her Tinder profile with its new tagline and a super-flattering selfie achieved by holding the phone directly overhead and looking up into it, as if she was in a dentist's chair, cheeks sucked in and eyes wide, then fading the contrast and applying a sepia effect. It was almost pretty. She swiped right on a few new local profiles – the heavily tattooed 'JD', profile just 'hard-core countryman' looked exciting: all his pics were of his torso, a full bodysuit of colourful Gothic-work.

The Old Almshouse still made her slightly uneasy – it was dark, cottagey and far too cluttered – but now she'd mastered the double oven, and found an internet sweet spot, she was an increasingly regular visitor.

She'd had a basic tidy-up straight after getting the job – recycling the leftie newspapers, laying mouse traps, retuning and dusting the little television she'd found in a cupboard, wiping down the kitchen and trying out its gadgets – but there was no rush to deep-clean for Kit Donne's return as far as she could tell. She liked to think she was getting a feel for the place, earning her fee by keeping it lived and baked in.

Now she spotted an *Evening Standard* dated three days ago in the basket by the wood burner and felt a flash of embarrassed irritation: one of Kit's children must have been here. Further investigation revealed two beds had been slept in, one by a disposable-contact-lens wearer, who'd tossed the packaging into the bin, the other by a fan of dental floss and face wipes. No evidence pointed to sex having taken place.

Pip, who had researched Kit's family extensively, knew that the daughter, working as a junior stage manager, was doing a season at Pitlochry, the son rehearsing in Manchester, and their father in New York. Having thought of the Old Almshouses as her own personal bolthole, she felt peeved that the client's family might swan in at whim when she had a professional mandate to bake in advance, call in Feather Dusters and now also get rid of any strong smell of wet dog. A quick check of the daughter's Instagram feed confirmed that she had been to a music festival in Cornwall, so she must have called in on her way through. She eased open the window a fraction.

The pointer was still watching her from the armchair, curled into a tight ball, eyes mournful. Nobody had replied to the Dog Found post on her wall. Pip checked out Roo Verney's Facebook profile again while she waited.

A red dot started flashing. A moment later, the South Midlands Hunt Monitors was broadcasting live.

'So here I am in the heart of bloody Cotswolds hunt country, although I might have got my *c*s and *aitche*s muddled there,' Roo reported, in a breathless undertone with a close-up of her large chin and pearls, like a mutant Clare Balding. 'Let's see if they're legal or not, shall we?'

Amid lots of camera shake, swearing, panting and foot-shots featuring muddy paths, the khaki chests and gloves of country-men, Roo did an impressive bit of reportage from the footpath. 'Hear that? That's the huntsman's horn calling away. They're on the sod-twatting scent and you can bet it's a virgin one: never been laid. And here's a pissing foot-follower. Bloody bugger me!'

Pip's eyes widened as she saw Blair Robertson's handsome, craggy face home into lop-sided focus on her phone screen, then heard Roo's breathy posh-Adele voice laughing: 'No fucking way! *You*'re here! I know you're a shit, but this takes the soggy bloody biscuit, this does.'

'Roo. Hi.' His deep voice was urgent. 'I'm looking for George.'

A deep bark at close quarters made Pip drop the phone in alarm.

The pointer had bounced across the room and was now sniffing the phone, tail wagging and head cocked as Blair's voice shouted, 'GEORGE!'

Then Roo's yelled, 'They're coming this way!'

Pip made a nervous grab for her phone but the dog growled, making her recoil and knock it under a side table holding a bust of Shakespeare dressed in a dusty flat cap. The phone had started reverberating with the sound of hounds and Roo in full cry.

'Get out of my way, Blair. I need to film this.'

The horn trilled. Blair was elbowed aside. 'Christ, that bloody hurt!'

George bounced and barked.

A moment later he was wearing the flat cap and Shakespeare was in bits.

Roo's breathless voice was still talking from somewhere beneath the debris. 'You shouldn't have got in the way. That's a lot of blood. Oh, shit, I think my battery's about to—' The live feed stopped abruptly.

George crept behind the coffee table and looked at Pip guiltily. Retrieving her phone, she took a photograph of cowering dog and bust as evidence, then strode to the front door and, holding it open, whistled as heartily as she could. 'Here, boy! Your master's hurt. They're three fields that way.' She pointed, shoved him outside and slammed the door.

Satisfied that she had done as much as she could, Pip cleared the bust into a bin liner, then put on a big striped apron to hide her bare legs from passers-by as she took it outside.

The dog was leaning against the front door. He fell gratefully against her when she opened it and heeled her to the bins. When Pip changed her mind and took the binbag to the car – her parents' voices in her head telling her to superglue the bust at home – he jumped into the back seat.

'Out! Three fields that way!' she ordered, tugging her fleece hem over her bottom as she saw him off the premises. Then, remembering the ingredients she'd packed into the boot to make scones, she perked up: she could make them here while she waited for her trousers to dry. The Almshouses oven was far better than the stud one.

George was waiting in the porch, wriggling beseechingly.

'Shoo! Just go away!' She aimed a kick at his backside, missed and fell among the wellies, dropping a box of eggs. Thoroughly wound up now, Pip slammed the door so hard that a picture fell off the wall beside it.

Lester watched the fox cub settle in the old ferret hutch, circling like a puppy on the frayed towel he'd put inside after the animal's first hour of pacing and scrabbling. He was an exquisite little thing, white bib and tail tip crisply laundered, infancy still gifting him the charm of vulnerability. He fell asleep almost immediately, the rise and fall of his ribcage just visible through the dry, leafy bedding Lester had lined it with from his bonfire pile.

The chestnut cob was also resigned to his strange surroundings, tack off, belly full of close-cropped sweet lawn grass, legs full of hunting. Having rolled extensively on Lester's freshly dug brassica bed, he was nodding off in the suntrap by the high wall of the stableyard, the skin on his shoulder twitching as a fly landed there. His lower lip drooped. Stubbs dozed on the back doorstep.

Only Lester was wide awake. While by nature solitary, he resented lying low when there were horses to care for.

He started pulling up the old bean canes to keep busy, stacking them against his little greenhouse and throwing the withered plants onto the compost pile. He'd often thought of his garden as an oasis, a place he could survive through a war if he kept the gate locked and the beds tended although he had only ever cultivated the garden to produce gifts for Ann Percy.

He stopped to listen beyond the wall, hearing a distant shout. These days Ronnie sounded very like her mother, whose smoker's voice had been Ovaltine comforting, despite her no-nonsense briskness. When first at the stud, Lester had developed an adoration for Ann Percy that had threatened to break him, but he'd been little more than a lad in those days, with no sense of who he was or where his feelings would lead him. It was easier with animals. You knew you hadn't long to wait to win their trust. As Johnny used to say: 'With horse and hound you have straightforward loyalty and instinct. Love is a human invention.'

The mother of all invention, as Lester had discovered just once in his life.

'George!... Blair!' Her shouts drew closer. 'Christ, I'm going to miss this bloody appointment. Lester, are you still in there?'

Instinct and loyalty might tell him not to respond, but he was already walking towards the door in the wall. As he did so, he heard the opening notes of Elgar's Cello Concerto, a phrase of music so familiar it almost took him down. He stopped in his tracks, asthma already rattling in his chest. It was an anthem to his sorrows, played so often all those years ago that the vinyl had worn down to crackles. Where was it coming from?

It took him a moment to realise it was her phone ringing, the music snatched away from him as she answered it just beyond the door.

'Where *are* you? Have you found him?... We have to go... Yes, I can check there again.' Her voice moved away.

Breath shortening by the second, Lester hurried inside for his inhaler.

28

Baking always calmed Pip. Ignoring the whining outside the door, she sifted and crumbled, shaped and cut out. Eventually the whining stopped.

When she'd put the scones into the oven, she checked her Facebook messages by the window. Several people claimed to have spotted pointer George in the village in the last few minutes. To her frustration, he was heading completely the wrong way – chasing a cat through the churchyard, then lifting a leg on the vicarage gatepost.

He gave me the slip! She posted hastily to cover her back, adding, *Knocked me over* to sound a bit more heroic, along with a sad face.

Nobody replied.

Feeling hurt, Pip vacuumed around the table from which the bust had fallen, then searched for something to put on top of it instead. There was a pretty mother-of-pearl-inlaid writing box buried among the books on the big desk that she dusted down and placed there, peeking inside. It was crammed with hand-written letters, all in the same round, bold hand, all addressed to Hermia Donne.

She plucked one out. It was dated 1992.

My darling H, it started. She cast her eye to the end where it was signed off with just *R xxx*.

The contents spoke of horses and theatre, lovers and dogs in a chatty gush. Definitely not a man unless he was professing that *Lion has a terribly bad back again, which means making love with me astride on top is our only option. Is it terribly wicked to admit I rode the intermediate dressage test for Floors Castle in my head last night? He loved counter canter.*

Pip flipped through a few more, fascinated. R was *very* indiscreet, funny and no moral crusader: *Lion's wife is on the sniff,* confided one. *Time to cool our heels again, L says, which means Paris is off. Secretly not displeased as it clashed with Appleby and you know how I love a gypsy. Tell me, are the Turners still causing havoc?*

It had to be Ronnie. This was her secret history, or part of it. Pip scrabbled for the rest. There were more than forty letters written through the nineties and into the mid-noughties. They contained a lot of boring detail about the children's milestones and sporting triumphs, which Pip speed-read without much interest, deciphering the nicknames – Tim's being 'Mothy' and Alice's 'Rabbit', both long since shaken off, unlike 'Pax' – and sussing that Ronnie visited them at various boarding schools or took them on short breaks in the north while she remained exiled in Cumbria.

She put them all in chronological order and speed-read again, piecing together the missing years she hadn't been able to access online.

The written correspondence had struck up when Ronnie was based in Cumbria, Hermia in Islington, by which time the old friends had drifted apart to such an extent they'd not communicated in several years. In London to see a critically acclaimed theatre production, Ronnie had witnessed her childhood chum wowing audiences in a Greek tragedy and been so blown away she'd written to her afterwards. It was an ecstatic reunion, a mutual sense of humour and deep trust in one another making for jubilance on the page. In those early years, the letters came thick and fast, the gaps easy to fill.

After the Bardswold Bolter had left Compton Magna, Ronnie Percy had lived with the jump jockey in the Lake District, Pip deduced. She'd worked as a PA in Keswick, funding a return to horses and eventing. Her boss – Ronnie referred to him as Lion – had become a lover. A fellow theatre fanatic fifteen years her senior, he'd taken her on overnight trips to London to see West End plays, glibly palmed off as business trips. Ronnie was unapologetic: *There are limited opportunities for women in my position, fewer still for men in his; we simply adore each other.*

Moving back to the Comptons to live at Upper Bagot Farmhouse, Hermia was soon writing back with everything she could find out during school holidays, which Ronnie fell on gratefully: *The only*

decent news I get of the children from home is from you, darling H,
she wrote in 1994.

In another, she thanked her friend for winkling out of Alice the
reason she was in trouble for bullying at school, a battle to be top
at sports to impress her father: *I'm so grateful you're Rabbit's godmother and always have the low-down. There's too much pressure
to buck up and be grown-up at the stud. Daddy absolutely won't let
them come here even for a night, although it's a truly peaceful spot
and Angus is a big kid at heart, who would love to get to know them
better.* Angus sounded like a dashingly sporty type from what Pip
could tell, all rock-climbing, hunting and power bikes: *He's marvellous – abseiling in and out of bed, whizzing around on the demon
wheels – you should see him flying down the ramp like a hunter and
off up the lane to the pub, sparks flying. When I think back to that
awful day five years ago... we were both in such hell afterwards.*

Reading on, Pip got an impression that wheels-obsessed Angus
wasn't an easy man to live with, despite Ronnie's light touch at
painting him. With Ronnie away working long hours he spent
time on friends' boats and partied hard. Infidelity featured a great
deal, not only her own with married boss Lion: *Angus constantly
in Homespun Neighbour's cottage admiring her making jam et al.
I wish he'd just get on with it and make a pass at her. She's even
bribing my dogs with Bonios now. Only Black Dog is loyal to me.*

That Black Dog was her constant companion for a long time after
Johnny's death. Ronnie's guilt was marrow-deep, and the Captain's
determined efforts to keep her at a distance had been devastating:
*I screamed at him on the phone so much tonight I've lost my voice.
They will never know the truth of it all. I won't betray Johnny's
memory for them, and I can't wreck their childhood yet more.*

Pip knew her brief tryst with Ali hardly compared to Ronnie's
legendary bolt, but she had suffered the bigotry of her parents
through it, and felt a fierce and angry bond of unity.

*Daddy told me the day I left that I would never be able to come
back,* the letter went on. *I should have listened, but he was so unfor-
giving, so full of anger it just made me run faster. He said he'd make
sure I suffered for what I was doing. I sometimes think he set the
black dog on me. Lester was its kennelman.*

Pip was enthralled. She'd guessed Lester had been involved somehow.

She read on, the pieces falling into place faster now, although there were infuriatingly long gaps, sometimes six months or more going past without a letter. One such break must have coincided with the end of the decade-long love affair, Angus departing next door to live with 'Homespun', a betrayal Pip found baffling, particularly as Ronnie had written, *She never tires of pushing him around*, which seemed harsh.

The addresses at the tops of the letters changed as she moved between various idyllic-sounding remote rural rentals, eventually landing in the Dales to be closer to her children's schools and run a saddlery, which Lion helped her set up, their relationship a constant for more than fifteen years. She always seemed sociably busy and upbeat, even when the long affair was forced into deep ice as Lion's political aspirations necessitated total discretion. He had won a parliamentary seat in the early noughties.

As she reached for the next letter, her phone popped with another Facebook notification. Someone had spotted George being almost flattened by a white van on Plum Run.

Thanks! Am looking everywhere! Pip posted straight back, along with another sad face and *Still seeing stars TBH*. She cast a cursory glance out of the window, ducking as she spotted Blair Robertson stalking along the lane. He was even craggier and sexier in the flesh.

She stepped back quickly as he turned to look at the house. The Old Almshouses was so pretty that everybody admired at it.

On her phone, the wiggly dotted line was moving with the words 'a friend is typing'. Her heart skipped when she saw Petra's name. About time! *Dog belongs to a visitor at the Percys' stud. Just found him on my drive. I'll run him over.*

Was that it? Not even a kiss or a 'hun' or a smiley emoticon? Having had no thanks for all her Civil War detective work, Pip was beginning to feel just a little bit used. Petra was taking all the credit, and now for the dog too. So much for friendship. A red mist descended.

Shows how much you care! Pip replied furiously. *And am I mistaken or are you threatening to RUN HIM OVER?! WTF?* She slammed her finger on the Return key.

A comment had crossed with hers. *Sorry – pressed 'send' too fast. I'll run him over there now. Are you okay, Pip? Are you hurt? Pxx*

Deleting her previous outburst, Pip posted a row of hearts and a photo of George, realising too late that it was the one she'd taken of the dog with the broken bust.

She was about to delete it when Petra posted, *OMG, he killed Shakespeare!*

The comment immediately attracted several likes. Petra always got likes whatever she said, whereas Pip had to work hard for them. Perhaps she could turn this to her advantage.

She could smell the scones burning, but she ignored them for now and typed: *Scene of the crime. He trashed a client's house. Will repair from my own pocket. Shows what happens when you try to be a Good Samaritan. Like helping writers who don't appreciate it.* Sad face. No likes.

Ouch! Blushing face. Two likes in five seconds.

The dog is dangerous, Devil face. *So watch out.* No likes.

This is the Cotswolds. I'm used to handling badly behaved gundogs, horses and men! Face with halo. Four likes in ten seconds, plus a comment from a reader about her hunky heroes.

No doubt based on Bay Austen, fnar. Pip typed beneath that. Winky face.

Silence. No likes.

Pip felt briefly vindicated, then immediately very glum. She'd over-stepped the friendship tape again. She couldn't even take her a plate of scones to apologise because they were ruined.

The burning smell was really bad now. She hurried to the kitchen to drag them out, plonking them on the work surface and fanning them with a tea towel. On the peninsula in front of her, she spotted an envelope addressed to Mrs E.

Inside was a pair of theatre tickets and a pretty, arty card, the writing inside in purple pen. *Thank you for making the place look so beautiful!* Kit's daughter had written. *Hope you like theatre. These tickets are for a touring production a friend of the family's in, which comes to Oxford in October. (They're a gift for Dad's birthday, but he'll be in New York so they're going spare – enjoy if you go, if not give them away!) Hope to meet you soon, maybe when Dad's back for Samhain. xxx*

Pip fluffed up proudly. What a lovely girl. It helped that these festival-going student types had such low standards in cleanliness that she saw stacking a few books in size order as a home makeover. Glancing at the date on the tickets, she realised it was also Lester's birthday, the two men unlikely astrology twins, although they had a certain diffident testiness in common.

Demanding knuckles rapped on the door.

'Yes?'

Still bare-legged and sockless, she reached quickly down to the tumble-dryer to fetch out her trousers. The plastic handle snapped off in her hands.

'I've just been told my dog might be here?' rumbled a deep Aussie voice.

As he said it, the smoke alarm went off behind her.

'Upper Bagot Farmhouse!' She flapped her tea towel at the alarm and hauled at the rim of the dryer door, but it was locked shut. The wailing overhead continued.

'Where's that?'

Pip longed to offer to show him, to be the sharp-eyed female village sleuth who reunited Ronnie's lover with his dog. She just couldn't do so wearing nothing but a polo shirt and flesh-tint pants.

'Big house on the lane with the orchards,' she shouted eventually, covering her ears. 'You can't miss it.'

Petra was barely across the lane from the farmhouse when she spotted Indiana Jones striding along Plum Run towards her. A split second later, the pointer had broken free from her and lolloped off to hurl himself deliriously at his master.

'Thanks!' He unclipped the trailing lead and carried it back to her. 'I hear there's been a big search shout-out online.'

'You can thank Pip Edwards for that.'

His craggy Marlboro-man face broke into a smile that should have come with a health warning for middle-aged women. 'I'll do that.'

Petra beamed at him. No matter that he was Antipodean – and she suspected highly adulterous – the black hair and soul-dark eyes were spot on, the sex appeal undeniable.

She had her Black Tom.

Wandering inside, feeling bad that all Pip's efforts had been unwelcome, she unlocked her phone screen and quickly posted: *You delivered my hero to my door, Pipsqueak!* Let everyone reading it think it was George the dog.

It was only then that she read the comment about Bay Austen.

Fitz, in the kitchen eating cheese straight from the block, glanced round to see her white face. 'You okay, Mum?'

'I... um...' He was the only technical person in the house. 'I've just read this thing on my phone I want deleted.'

He was at her side like a shot. 'Whatever it is, it's probably not as bad as you think. We're all here for you, Mum. I've known and Gunny knows.'

'You read it?' It made sense. Fitz and his grandmother were both Facebook friends. They must have all seen Bay's name fnar-ed at her. 'There's no truth in it.'

'Of course not. Dad's a major fantasist, we all know that.'

'What's it got to do with your father? Oh, God, do you think he's read it? We're not even *friends* on Facebook.'

'Let me see.' He wrestled her phone out of her hand. 'You have twenty-three likes already. They all think you mean the dog,' he assured her, deleting it. 'I can't get rid of Pip Edwards's comment about Farmer Giles, I'm afraid, but everyone knows you've got a bit of a thing about Bay, so no harm done. If you need it, I have a mate who can hack her account and flood it with boobs.'

'That won't be necessary.' She gave him a grateful hug and he sloped off to his room.

Petra patted her red cheeks and blew out. The humiliation of her son knowing about her SMC was deeply embarrassing.

Her phone rang with the theme tune from *Black Beauty*, Charlie's handsome face smiling at her. How had he found out so soon?

'You... are... *amazing*.' His voice was mohair in her ear. Charlie had an effortlessly sexy phone voice.

'Mmm?' she hedged.

'I just picked up your voicemail about the Austens' shooting party. Been in court all morning, sorry.'

'Squash court?'

'That's right, yes! Squash.' He was too quick, too glib. She smelt the lie. 'You phoned chambers, I take it?'

She thought about Deepak's revelation that Charlie was in disgrace. *Not now*, a voice in her head told her. *Not now*, fresh from an unseemly Facebook moment. *Leave this one well alone.* After all, he wanted to go to the party precisely to make good work contacts. 'Yes. It's great news, isn't it?'

'Good morning, Mr Donne! It's Pip Edwards in Compton Magna. How's New York?'

'Waiting for the sun to rise.' He yawned. 'It's five-thirty in the morning here, Pip.'

'Sorry about that. I'll be ever so quick. All is super-good with the house. I just wondered if you knew what make the tumble-dryer is and whether there are any instructions anywhere? Bit of a stuck door crisis here.'

A female voice in the background asked sleepily who it was. Pip's ears pricked up. *Interesting.*

'I had no idea there even *was* a tumble-dryer,' he said crankily.

'Oh, it's very smart, one of those trendy Dysony types that looks like a space-age filing cabinet. I've tried googling but I can't see a manufacturer's logo.'

The woman in the background at Kit's end was telling him in a seductive voice to get off the phone, which Pip thought very unsympathetic, given her crisis.

'Try the dresser,' he told her, yawning again. 'Is this really why you woke me up?'

Pip gave a tight laugh, hiding her pique. *I'm looking after your house for pocket money*, she wanted to point out. *Kind words cost nothing, such as: 'Anything nice planned for your birthday?'*

'I'd settle for eight hours' uninterrupted sleep,' he said, with effort.

There was a burst of muffled laughter in the background, the purry female voice goading.

'Okay, and a weekend away,' he covered the phone briefly, amid rustling noises and more muffled laughter. 'It's only fair that everyone in the production gets a break before a long run. Which reminds me: Samhain.'

'Sowing?'

Mobile reception threatening to cut her off, Pip pulled open the overstuffed dresser drawers, from which old pens, wrapping paper, lightbulbs, phone chargers and theatre programmes jack-in-the-boxed.

He spelled it out, the same word she'd seen in the daughter's card: 'Celtic festival day – it marks winter beginning, the dark half of the year. It's a bit like the Mexican Day of the Dead.'

'Hallowe'en, you mean?'

'No pumpkins or sweets, just a big fire. It's the most important one of the four feast days.'

'I'll decorate the cottage.' She brightened at the thought. 'Skulls and red roses, a few glow-in-the-dark bones, maybe.'

'Please don't.' There were tell-tale kissy mming noises at the other end of the line now.

'At least let me bake. I'm sure I saw a Pan de Muerto recipe on the Paul Hollywood fansite.'

'It's unlikely I'll make it back. I'll call and let you know closer to the day.'

'You're the boss.' Digging through the dresser drawers, Pip started chattering happily about the lovely note and the tickets his daughter had left when she realised he'd hung up on her. How rude! Wasn't it supposed to be the city that never slept? And she hadn't even found the manual.

She attacked the tumble-dryer door with renewed venom, eventually springing it open with the help of a fish slice and a pizza wheel.

As she gathered the rest of Ronnie Percy's letters together, Pip remembered she had an old-fashioned one of her own to write. The future of the stud was depending on her. She stripped the beds, tidied any last signs of George's rampage, threw away the burned scones and wheeled out the bins for collection, then locked up.

Reversing out of the drive, she almost flattened Blair, who was walking back along the lane, now reunited with George.

'Watch where you're going!' he snarled.

Pip knew exactly where she was going; she was going home to write to his wife.

Her phone pinged: Tinder notifying her that she had a match.

Hearing voices in the arrivals yard, Lester stole in through his back door and upstairs to observe from the window, taking his asthma inhaler with him.

The good-looking event rider was back again. Lester had to hand it to Ronnie, she had a fine eye for a man, although they usually belonged to somebody else.

They were getting into the open-top car, three dogs lined up on the back seat, argument raging. Ronnie was obviously furious that she was going to be late for a solicitor's meeting. The children would be furious if she let them down, she wailed.

Lester thought it thirty years too late for that. Outside, the birdsong was drowned as the sports car accelerated away. Only the magpies were audible, taking off from the drive and chattering noisily to the horse-chestnuts.

He didn't need to look outside to count the piebald birds.

'Seven for a secret never to be told.' Lester looked down at Stubbs, snaking his bearded nose against the rug to scratch it. The fox cub in the ferret cage was yet another secret, his little enemy on the inside.

'The day I set that little bugger free, I'll be ready to tell her,' he promised Stubbs. 'But I'll bet she's bolted off again long before that.'

Do U Want 2 meat up, babe?

JD was not much of a conversationalist.

Let's have a chat on here first, Pip suggested, trying to think up some questions to ask.

He was on his tea break, he replied to her opener. *Strong and milky three sugars*, came his second reply, then *KitKat* followed by the affirmation that he liked cake. The fact that he was a labourer was his biggest revelation. She told him she was manager at a stud with a side-line in baking, research and property maintenance. He seemed quite taken with that and asked if she wanted sex.

Not yet. I've got scones baking. She wanted to extract enough information out of him to google him, but he told her he had to stop because his break had ended.

Catch U l8r yeah, babe?

While Pip's second batch of scones was baking, she remembered to check out the freebie theatre tickets she'd been given.

Her mouth fell open as she read them properly. *Poldark the Musical.* Who could resist tap-dancing in a tricorn hat? Its headline star was a pop legend. Its wizened patriarch, Charles Poldark, was being played by a *Midsomer* regular and one of the Donnes' oldest friends. He'd been around so long even Lester would have heard of him.

Pip buzzed, feeling sprinkled with celebrity stardust. It certainly beat JD and his KitKat.

Casting her tablet aside to take a tray of perfect golden scones out of the oven, Pip decided to leave Lester to his own devices this afternoon and watch all three series of *Poldark* in anticipation. He'd only want help turning all the horses back out, and she always found that terrifying. Plus she wanted to keep her head down in the village for a bit.

Pip checked Facebook quickly. Still no reply from Petra, who had gathered dozens more likes for her comments and a few replies accusing Pip of being monstrously rude.

Hurt, she couldn't resist looking at Roo Verney's wall again.

Roo had posted more evidence of that morning's surly countrymen and stroppy hunt-followers, along with a message: *I must thank my secret saviour, whose job I won't jeopardise by naming her. You know who you are. A gutsy woman and a Wicked Lady (I hope!). Friend me. Follow me. Call me. Xx* Pip 'liked' this, then upgraded it to a heart and just as quickly downgraded it again: she didn't want to give the wrong impression.

Friendship was a much-prized achievement in Pip's life. She clicked the request. The acceptance came almost straight away. Flushed, she navigated away without leaving a message. She didn't want to get into the whole dinner-date thing: she had JD's feelings to consider now.

He messaged again at lunchtime: *On dinner break. Do you want sex l8tr or not, babe?*

Staying in to write a letter, sorry! Maybe a drink sometime?

He sent an emoticon of a row of beer kegs and googly eyes and they left it there, anticipation hanging excitingly in the air.

Pip settled down to reread the original letter she'd posted to Verity. No wonder it had gone straight into the bin. It read like a marketing flyer. She found an old Basildon Bond writing pad in her father's desk and slotted a cartridge into one of his beloved fountain pens, then made her handwriting as bold and round as the one she'd seen earlier in letters to Hermia. The best way to talk to a drunk was very directly, she decided. No beating about the bush or buttering up.

Verity,

Please let him go. He will want for nothing. He will have lots of sex. He will be happy. He will feel young again. He will live in the most beautiful surroundings, on high pasture.

Surely you can't deny him that?

I await your call.

She signed it *P*, adding a little tail that was open to interpretation. If it was mistaken for an R, then so what? The erstwhile Lady Verney was bound to take the entreaty of someone from a long line of horse-breeders more seriously than the daughter of a machine-parts-factory payroll accountant. Pip felt gripped by positivity and purpose.

In the mood for reaching out, she worked her way through more Basildon Bond writing a letter to her one surviving family member, her mother's unmarried sister who lived in a care home on the Isle of Wight, and with whom relations had long been strained: *I know we had our differences after Mum and Dad's funeral about the Copeland tea set and opal necklace, Auntie Sylvia, but I hope it's all forgotten. Would you like a visit soon?*

Then she called Lester.

He answered after fifty-three rings. 'Stud.'

'Pip here! I'm so sorry I can't help today. Unavoidable. All okay?'

'Of course.'

'Good morning out with the hunt?'

'Fair.'

330

'Sorry about the dog thing. Genuine mistake.'
'If you say so.'
'Are you pissed off with me?'
He said nothing. Pip gritted her teeth.
'I'm taking you on a treat for your birthday.'
'There's no need.'
'*Poldark the Musical.*'
Another silence.
'It's in Oxford. You like Oxford, don't you?'
'It's pleasant enough.'
'Help me out here, Lester. Be excited.'
'If you say so.'

Part Four

MICHAELMAS GOOSE
AND HIGH WINDS

29

'Stud.'

It had taken eighty-four rings for Lester to pick up the phone.

'Happy birthday!'

'Pip, it's not yet six in the morning.'

'I know! But you're always an early bird. I'll be over in half an hour to help you muck out. I've made special breakfast pastries and a cake for later. We're on the eight o'clock train. I thought we'd go to the Ashmolean first, or Pitt Rivers if you prefer.'

'There's a hurricane blowing in. I'm not coming.'

'You *must* come, Lester. It's *Poldark the Musical*. There's horses and cliffs and waves.'

'I'm not happy leaving the place.'

'The media always exaggerate these things, and Alice is going to be at the stud all day.'

'She's only a slip of a thing.'

'She'd beat you in a fight.'

She could tell from the silence he'd conceded the point, but he wouldn't budge on his desire to remain here. Refusing to be defeated, she played her trump card.

'Oh, and Alice texted me last night to say that Ronnie is calling by the stud this morning. She's especially eager to talk to you apparently.'

'I'll come to Oxford.'

Pip smiled. Best not to mention why Ronnie was coming. It was to do with her selling some of the horses. He definitely wouldn't want to leave if he knew that. She'd promised Alice she'd pass on the message, but had decided it was best to break that bit on the train coming home. She didn't want Lester stressing about it today. She'd be sorry to miss Ronnie – the second time this month – but she'd baked a huge batch of ginger biscuits to leave in the tack room for her, with fresh milk and the best tea mugs, as she told Lester proudly now.

'Pip, have you slept?' Lester asked warily.

'Oh, you know me. Cat naps. See you in half an hour!'

Pip picked up her other phone and admired a new picture message of a large, pierced penis artfully resting against novelty Union Jack underpants with KitKat crumbs on them. As well as baking, she'd spent a lot of the night swapping selfies with Tinder match JD, who turned out to be a fellow night owl and, also like her, was a big fan of binge-watching box sets and online role-play gaming. They had a lot more in common than she'd first imagined. She'd now given him the number of her Dark Phone and they communicated regularly on WhatsApp. He'd sent lots more shots of his tattoos, and other exciting parts of himself – this was the fifth dick shot for her collection – and she'd sent him some intimate pictures screen-grabbed off random Tumblr NFSW pages.

Nice one! she messaged now, uncertain what the correct reaction was.

He sent a smiley face and a love heart.

JD liked her describing her baking, and he was very interested in her work at the stud, which she'd bigged up.

U really not free 2nite? Want you to sit on it babes.

Poldark the Musical!!! She reminded him. She was taking Lester to The Grand Café for high tea afterwards. JD knew all about it.

He sent a row of crying emoticons and love hearts.

Pip hugged the phone. She had quite a lot of weight to lose before she met him, not to mention the intimate waxing, but she had a very warm, fuzzy feeling inside her about this one. She might just have found her very own Shane Lynch at long last.

Three weeks into her new trilogy, Petra had gone off the hero. She'd barely got beyond her first description of Sir Thomas Fairfax's long black hair and piercing, warmongering gaze before her crush withered on the branch, unable to shake off the mental image of Russell Brand. Each time she faced the page he leered out at her, all teeth and eyes in skinny jeans, saying, 'I tells ya!' and talking anarchic politics.

The real Black Tom had been a brave and noble general, intoxicatingly in love with his fiercely loyal wife, but the man Petra had invented was evangelically pious, manipulative and pompous, and Anne Fairfax a possessive control-freak. Petra no longer wanted to spend time with them. It was like being trapped in a coach with Neil and Christine Hamilton and three weeks of a silent house by day, alone with her reimagined history, had already given her cabin fever. Her mind drifted continually, stewing everyday worries and finding a hundred unnecessary domestic chores to occupy herself until her five carefully planned day shifts shrank to nothing. She had to jump over the edge and commit to her characters soon. That Friday feeling was no longer a good one. The end of the week not only spelled her failure to write as much as she'd planned, it also brought Charlie home.

Their weekends together were once again neatly topped and tailed with 'How was your week?' and 'Have a good week!' with platitudes traded in between, and the intimacy of Tuscany already felt a lifetime ago, a mere holiday romance.

They hadn't had sex since Italy. Lurking in the back of her mind was an unpleasant suspicion that she couldn't write about a devoted, passionately connected marriage because she wasn't part of one.

It was Friday again, birdsong insisting dawn was about to break. Having set her alarm for the early shift, and stolen out to the Plotting Shed before five, thermal mug of tea in hand, her determination to make Thomas smoulder puritanically from the page was again foiled. She dragged herself away for breakfast and the school run with barely a word written.

'How are we feeling today? Happy, happy, happy!' She bounced into the kitchen, like a children's party entertainer.

Hedge-haired and sleepy-eyed, the girls carried on watching *Newsround*, the presenter excitedly warning that the first big storm of autumn was on its way today. Standing over the toaster, mod cool in his black blazer and loose tie, Fitz cast his mother a withering look from behind his fringe. 'Nobody's convinced, Mum. You're always completely squippy at the beginning of a book.'

'Am I?'

'Like majorly.'

'Oh.' Petra wasn't sure whether to feel relieved or not.

'It'll be brilliant,' Fitz reassured her, disappearing into the larder for peanut butter.

Having Fitz around was the one big plus point this time. He didn't communicate much – less than Charlie, in fact – and remained a room-cave dweller, almost totally invisible at weekends, but it was lovely to know he was there. He was knuckling down and getting on at the academy, his home time eaten up with study. Petra needed to take inspiration from him.

As soon as she got back from dropping off the girls, she hurried around the shortest of her morning dog walks with Wilf. It took them across a big ploughed field behind the farmhouse as far as the woods that marked the stud's boundary. The high wind that had been rattling the sashes all night was shaking out conkers from the horse-chestnuts. Trying to dodge them, she jogged along the track beside it, which turned into a hedged tunnel of waving sloes and blackberries, leading down to the old walled orchard with its ancient stone stiles behind the cottages on the Green.

Wilf charged ahead, quickly disappearing from sight.

It was a familiar tactic, but Petra had his measure. All she had to do was move out of sight and wait. As soon as Wilf realised she wasn't accounted for, he'd belt straight back to her side. If only it worked as well with husbands, she reflected, as she moved behind one of the bigger bramble bushes and crouched against the drystone wall of the orchard, grateful to be out of the wind.

She checked her phone. She always kept it switched off when she wrote, and no longer obsessed about texts from Bay. Since her 'This has to stop' warning, he'd sent her just one message: *I miss 'this', Bx*

She missed it too. Desperately.

Helping herself despondently to a handful of fat blackberries, she heard hoofbeats and familiar voices. The Bags were out, hammering along the Green, the wind carrying their voices towards her. Petra elected to stay hidden. She had no desire to face the cheerful 'How's the book going?' interrogation while sporting a malcontent's bad mood, mad hair, unflattering glasses and stress spots. Squatting as low as she could and finding a large thistle jammed against her rear, she realised they were talking about her.

'... and, let's face it, Charlie's a social animal,' Gill's voice rang out over the wind, 'whereas Petra's a lot more introverted than she looks.'

'She's so bubbly,' Mo protested.

'She's changed a lot in the past year or two. When they first moved here, she was always throwing parties and hosting girls' nights in.'

'It must be hard when your husband works away all week.'

'If he comes back at all...' Bridge put in. '"For years, mild-mannered Petra Gunn lived with the secret of the body under the lavender border..."'

'She should have buried him under the rose bed. Jolly good ferti-liser. And it's a lot harder when they're under your feet all the time, drying their Lycra cycling shorts on the Aga, trust me,' Gill said darkly. 'Charlie's practically moved out of the family home – that's my idea of heaven.'

'Ohm of the week!' announced Bridge. Pronounced 'Ohm', like a Buddhist chant, the 'Off-putting Husband Moment' was an old Bags favourite. 'Mine is Aleš lining up his toenail clippings on the bedside table in perfect size order.'

'Air guitar to Genesis while sitting on the loo of our en suite,' Gill muttered, 'door wide open.'

'Twenty-minute masterclass straight after sex on how to mix the perfect plaster skim,' sighed Mo.

'You had sex?' Gill was shocked.

'It was his birthday.'

'I still reckon Petra's got the worst deal of all of us,' insisted Bridge's cheery, sardonic voice, as they clopped ever closer. 'Yes, Paul's a prod-rock wimp on two wheels, Aleš has OCD and anger issues, and Barry would rather drain a diesel tank with a drinking straw than show emotion, but none of them's a sleaze, are they? Charlie's such a bloody dog.'

Scowling, Petra shifted on the thistle.

'Petra loves dogs,' Mo said warmly. 'She's got a knack.'

'She does seem drawn to them.' Gill's voice was still as clear as that of a yacht skipper in a high wind. 'What was it on her Facebook page you read about baying hounds, Bridge? Or was it hounding Bay? The one that got the village tittering. Has that calmed down?'

'It was just a snidey comment from Pip Edwards.'

'That bloody woman. God, this wind's hell.'

'You don't really think Petra's hubby's got someone else on the go, do you, Bridge?' Mo said anxiously.

'Well, he's got form, hasn't he?'

Shocked, Petra dropped lower in her prickly lair. She was appalled to hear them talking about Charlie like that. What did they know about his form? That had been years ago, before they'd left London, when she was pregnant with Ed. Blood curdling with the toxic shock of betrayal, she tried to remember what she'd said to the Bags. Not much. Over a decade later the fault-line still ran through their relationship. She pictured Charlie hurrying towards his train the previous Sunday evening, remembered her own sense of relief at the end of two days in which dissatisfaction hung between them.

The wind picked up with a sudden squall so violent that the trees all groaned and apples pelted down in the orchard around Petra.

'She's called Claudia, apparently,' Bridge said, with authority.

Charlie and... *Claudia*? Who was she?

'Over here from the Caribbean,' she went on. 'Force to be reckoned with.'

How did Bridge know Charlie was involved with this Claudia woman?

'Oh, yes, I read all about it in Mum's *Daily Mail*,' said Mo, in a worried voice.

It had made the *papers*?

'There's going to be one hell of a mess when she turns up tonight,' Gill said darkly. 'The Met boys have warned northerners to stay inside.'

Claudia was coming to Compton Bagot? And what did she have against northerners to worry the Metropolitan Police? Petra racked her brain for the last time she'd heard a news headline.

'We've got the sandbags out,' Gill went on. 'Last time Lord's Brook flooded it was halfway up the garden. Watch out, Bridge! Plastic bag at nine o'clock.'

Hurricane Claudia, Petra remembered with relief, watching a stray supermarket carrier flying past overhead. They'd been talking about the big storm on *Newsround.*

On the other side of the wall, voices whoa-ed and hoofs skittering on tarmac, Gill yelling, 'Right rein, right rein!' and Bridge laughing.

'You're doing super!' Mo encouraged. 'Wayta go, girl, wayta go!' *An Officer and a Gentleman* was her favourite movie, and she never missed an opportunity to raise the cheer.

Just at that moment, Petra missed the Bags' camaraderie with a heartburn that made her want to stand up. But she mustn't: she had a seventeenth-century Yorkshireman in need of a sexy makeover waiting at home, and the sight of her appearing would finish off Bridge's pony totally.

The Bags had drawn level with her hiding spot, the horses so close she could smell them.

'Will they cancel the Goose Walk in this weather?' Mo asked.

'We *never* cancel the Goose Walk,' Gill said sternly. 'And bloody Petra is being winkled out of that house for it, whether she likes it or not. It's not healthy being cooped up like that. She needs fresh air.'

Petra had no intention of taking part in the village's Michaelmas tradition.

'Won't the goose be scared in this wind?' Bridge was saying.

'It's an old pro. It's done it before.'

'Does it get eaten?'

'Purely ceremonial. The goose is a pet, from Vintner Cottage. We're serving Chris Hicks's home-made chicken pie.'

They were still beside Petra's lair. She could smell the extra strong mint fumes as they were circulated and crunched; Mo's cob was eating grass immediately on the other side of the wall, bit jangling. Bridge's pony was snorting furiously, sensing something hidden there.

To prove her right, Wilf broke from cover with a great crackling of twigs, and there was a frantic clattering of hoofs. Wreathed in smiles, he bounded straight for Petra, the wind turning his ears inside out. He had company. Two short-legged, prick-eared black and tan raiders appeared, barking first at Petra, then up at the riders.

Petra shushed them with frantic silent mimes.

Then, as she resigned herself to the mortification of being sprung, Ronnie Percy strode out from behind necklaces of blackberry-beaded bramble, stopping short as she saw Petra crouched, like an SAS commando, finger pressed to her lips.

When Carly went to see Spirit and his bachelor-herd friends after dropping Ellis at school, she found his field empty, hoofprints tracking across the road and into the field opposite where the old man had driven them up to the yard. She'd seen him do it before, amazed that one diminutive, wizened character could command a dozen flighty young horses so effortlessly.

'No horsie!' Sienna mewed, as Carly spun the buggy in a U-turn and headed back into the village, past the school again, the yummy-mummy four-by-fours all gone now, her elder son sharing carpet time somewhere beyond those tall windows dotted with paper butterflies and alphabet letters.

Defying Carly's expectations, Ellis loved school. While some of the little Alfies, Phoebes, Georges and Chloës still clung to their mothers' legs, weeping piteously each morning, Ellis broke free to run inside his classroom, book-bag knocking against the back of his knees. He came home each afternoon happy, exhausted, starving and with shoes like mini Saharas from the sandpit corner. His 'Splorer Stick had been abandoned somewhere in the garden, his Octonauts lunch box the first thing he now looked to grab each morning.

Carly was proud of his fortitude. He was her steadfast, aloof little loner, who didn't entirely fall into step with the group of grazed-knee bruisers who charged around together at break time in a boys-only mob – his closest friendship so far was with a girl called Jazmin – but he was sleeping better, talking more and seemed to have been accepted. The first birthday party had been clocked up, the slice of cake carried home in a Disney Cars napkin. Carly found it just as hard to relate to the other mothers, away from the hug and dash of drop-off and pick-up. She sensed they looked straight past her as much as she did them, those competitive wives who talked about house, hair and nail extensions. While they boasted of careers and devoted their weekends to taking their kids to swimming lessons, music, karate and football, Carly worked back-to-back shifts at Le

Mill and the farm shop, her weekdays spent cleaning with Janine's team and keeping on Ash's case to get to college on time.

To Carly's consternation, Ash's late-night boozing and insomnia hadn't stopped when his course had started. If anything he was worse. Ash flew as rebelliously close to the wire as possible, pushing his body as far as he could, testing its limits and powers of recovery. It seemed to be the only way he could make the adrenalin still pump.

She'd been doing a lot of reading about animal behaviour in recent weeks, seeking answers to why Pricey behaved as she did, and what made Spirit so different from the rest of the stud's herd even as a baby. What she'd discovered had given her as much insight into Ash as into dogs and horses.

She'd borrowed a book from the library about retraining dogs. One chapter described the symptoms of working dogs that had undergone intense trauma, abuse or near-death experiences. They could be aggressive, changeable, unco-operative or even devious. They had trouble sleeping, were prone to obsessive repetitive behaviour and some simply shook uncontrollably, often for hours on end. So like Pricey. So like Ash. Their rehabilitation had to be taken slowly and patiently, according to the book. There was no quick fix, just as the sanctuary kept telling her. Cognitive therapy helped, finding positive associations. Pricey's handlers were taking her out for more walks in open spaces, after dark as well as in daylight, and she was being carefully introduced to more male handlers and other dogs and animals. Carly didn't know how to help Ash get over what he'd seen in Afghanistan and Iraq. He was taking himself back into the war zones in his games, finding the camaraderie with his friends, but it didn't seem to be helping. Last week he'd suffered one of the worst nightmares she could remember, waking screaming beside her, drenched in sweat, but when she'd gently suggested looking into some sort of counselling for ex-servicemen, he'd bitten her head off, demanding to know why she thought he was some sort of wimp who couldn't handle it.

He'd stormed off to take a shower. Afterwards he'd wanted sex. It had always been his pacifier.

Last night, on an equine web page, Carly had read that geldings were passive-aggressive and mares were dominant-aggressive, but that nothing would stand between a stallion and the thing he wanted:

he would fight to the death to get it. Ash could lose perspective just as quickly. When he wanted to game, you walked in front of the television at your peril. When he wanted to large it with his mates, he'd climb through a window to get out and join them if he had to. When he wanted sex, he made it hard to say no.

Last night he'd woken her up with his hard-on already gloved up, manoeuvring her into position like a sandbag. It wasn't the sort of love-making Carly craved, the languorous, sensual connection between husband and wife, lovers and parents stealing an early night. It had been a long time since Ash had had the inclination to give her clitoris more than a quick thumbs up during sex. She could date it back almost to the day he'd left the army. He'd always been one of the lads, and soldiers weren't saints, but here in the Comptons there was no code of conduct, no garrison order around them, just a small village containing a gang of Ash's single and divorced bad-lad friends and a male-dominated family with a bad reputation.

Colts and young stallions run in 'bachelor packs' until they are mature enough to break away and take on the herd stallion in a fight for mares, she'd read on the equine website. It said nothing about them returning to that pack years afterwards.

Pushing the buggy homewards, Carly's resolve hardened. She was going to make Ash fight for this mare again.

You left for work yet? she texted him.

Going now! Get off my back, gorgeous. x

A positive flipside of being flipped over for sleepy sex was that he was always chipper the next morning, even if he overslept.

She scrolled through her other messages: Janine on her case, her waitress mate from Le Mill checking lifts and the Son of a Gunn asking advice: *Hey, fam. Going into German class AF. Slaflosigkeit over puma out of my league, ikr? B-a-d me.*

Carly had no idea what he meant. She didn't bother replying.

He messaged again as she rolled the buggy alongside the Green. *Ignore that. Someone here hijacked my BB, bastards. Bitte verzeih mir.* He'd attached a funny GIF of a guilty-looking dog.

She bit a smile, guessing he was being given a hard time. *You shouldn't be using your phone in class, poshboy. Are any Turners giving you grief? Shout out if you want them sorted.*

Reaching the Green, she passed three riders talking to a woman in the orchard. One of the horses, a small grey, boggled at the buggy.

'Horsies!' Sienna was thrilled.

Nah. We're good, read the incoming message. But if you know someone who can take out my dad…

She snorted with laughter, making the grey horse rattle backwards on the opposite side of the lane.

Ronnie wasn't entirely surprised to find her dog-walking ally hiding from Gill Walcote behind a wall. She could remember the vet's pushy daughter as a girl, always barging ahead at hunt jumps and roping villagers into sponsored charity hikes to raise money for African orphans, a classic do-gooder who made everyone feel rather bad for disliking her. Ronnie would be tempted to jump out of sight too, but Gill had already spotted her.

'Good morning, Ronnie! Trying to beat the storm too, I see. Windy day!'

'Yes!'

'Lucky my chap's hurricane proof.'

'Always had a good eye for a horse, Gill!' She admired the rangy warmblood, then glanced down at Petra. An apologetic smile flashed up at her.

Gill was introducing the other riders. 'We ride out a few days a week, usually early doors,' she went on, howling wind flapping the rim of her old-fashioned crash helmet silk. 'You must join us sometime.'

'Jolly kind offer.' Ronnie nodded hellos at the two other women.

'Isn't that Petra's dog?' Gill leaned down to look at Wilf, rolling around just inches from Petra's foot. 'Is he lost? What *is* down there? Not another dead sheep?'

'Just taking him home. Remind me, Petra lives where?' Ronnie smiled easily.

'Upper Bagot Farmhouse.'

'Kit Donne's place?'

'The Donnes moved out years ago, not long after Hermia's accident. Surely you know that.'

Ronnie didn't for a moment betray her surprise, but her sense of being a time traveller hurtling along on the wrong bus returned. She should have known – perhaps she had and had filed it away during that painful termination of a friendship. Her foolish mistake struck hot flint sparks deep in her chest.

'Right-oh, leave it with me.' She waved the Bags off and called the dogs sharply as she waited for the three riders to trot out of earshot. 'It's safe to come out. They've gone,' she said eventually.

Petra hadn't felt so gauche and idiotic since being caught with her taffeta hoicked up at a May Ball, weeing behind a marquee to avoid queuing for the Portaloos. 'I'm truly sorry about that. I don't normally hide.'

'Wise move, I'd say.' Ronnie was still gazing after the Bags, eyes creased against the wind. 'Gill's a well-meaning bully, the girl with the nice Connemara can't ride for toffee, and all Stokes women would knit while the rest of us lose our heads.'

'They're my friends!' she said, hypocritically affronted.

'And I only do allies.' Ronnie clicked her tongue, watching her stretch. 'Are you injured?'

'Stiff. That was cowardly.'

'Nonsense. I love hiding from people. We're the cats who walk by ourselves.'

Petra, who knew the Kipling story well, bucked up a little. She might be mortified and in a tearing hurry, but that feeling of big adventure was back, as surely as Kathleen Turner swinging in on a jungle vine.

'Are you in the village long?' she asked hopefully.

'Flying visit. I'm on my way to the Moreton Morrell. Last comp of the year for my younger horse. Hope he stays upright in this. Bloody jockey's in mutinous mood, which doesn't help. Don't suppose you want to buy a nice little eventer to compete with a pro? Blair's dying to keep the ride. He'd love you as an owner.'

'Can't afford it, sorry.'

'Shame.' Ronnie smiled briefly, then set off for the stile to the track. 'I'm fond of that little horse. I'm jolly sorry about abandoning a car in your drive by the way,' she called over her shoulder. 'I thought Kit Donne still lived there. Shows how out of date I am!'

'That was *you*?' Petra laughed, as she gave chase, apples cannoning down.

'Was he very mad when he picked it up?'

'It's still in our barn. When nobody came for it, Charlie had it traced, then decided to keep it safe once he discovered who it belonged to. We assumed a garage had delivered it back to the wrong address – Kit's away working in New York.' She had a nasty suspicion Charlie planned to use the Saab as social leverage, Kit being on his VIP-villager hit list, in the hope of scoring good theatre tickets and meeting Patrick Stewart.

'I must have sent letters to the wrong address for years,' Ronnie muttered.

'It was empty for a long time before it was developed,' Petra said breathlessly, already struggling to keep up. 'There was a huge wrestle over planning.'

'I can imagine.'

'We bought it from a hedge-fund manager who had it as a weekend party pad before us which is why the whole place is teched up like a Bond hide-out. Charlie loves it. I'm still trying to find the button that opens the floor hatch to reveal a shark pool beside the wine cellar to drop him in— Oh, shit, sorry!' She remembered too late that Ronnie's father had died falling in his cellar. 'That's so crass of me.'

'It's fine, honestly. Shark pits are the must-have gadget for the Cotswolds wife.' Ronnie's blue eyes were merry with empathy. 'Is it that bad?'

'Gosh, no!' She gave an over-bright laugh. 'Storm Claudia in a teacup.'

'It's only when one's slung the entire wedding-gift dinner service at him that one needs to release Jaws and the gang, eh?'

They'd reached the end of the track already, a gate leading into the woods, another to the ploughed field, their paths ahead split. Ronnie turned back. 'Good luck riding out the storm. *Ego procellosa sumus.*'

'We're full of wind?' Petra translated, delighted to unearth her latent Catullus-lover, untested for years.

She laughed. 'We will storm. We all have the tempest in us.'

'Did you throw a dinner service, then?' she asked, and a split-second flicker in Ronnie's smile told her how presumptuous she was being, too chummy too fast as usual.

But the blue eyes were bright with amused empathy again. 'There wasn't much left after my parents and grandparents had worked their way through the Percy creamware. I was more of a door-banger.'

'Oh, me too. And bin lid.' Petra looked up at the squally sky. 'And keyboard, but that's because work's not going well, which is probably why I'm an angry Cotswolds wife in search of the shark-pit button.'

'Do you ever just come out here and have a scream?'

'Not really.'

'Oh, you must. It feels terrific. Go on – have a roar.'

'I can't. I'd feel silly.'

'Nobody will overhear you. I don't care – I'll roar too. Always blows off the cobwebs and clears your head. I could do with one, frankly.' She climbed two rungs up on the gate into the woods and hollered into the wind. 'Arrrrrrrrrrrrgh…'

Deciding it would be slightly less embarrassing to join in than to stare up at her, Petra hopped onto the bottom rung and had a go. 'Eiiiiiiiiiiiiiiiiiighhhh!' It felt surprisingly good. Wonderful, in fact. 'Aaaaaaaa!'

Side by side they roared and wailed, throwing their arms out like two Roses on *Titanic*'s prow, letting the wind blast in their faces, until their breath ran out and they were hoarse.

'Morning. Gusty out.' A village dog-walker in a red Pac a Mac yomped past, raising his hiking cane, his West Highland terrier casting a worried look their way.

The two women folded over in silent laughter.

Jumping down, Ronnie rolled and lit a cigarette expertly in the wind, squinting at the horizon, the big life's-good smile coinciding with a low sun blazing between scudding clouds.

'Claudia has nothing on the Percy family.' She lit it. 'My older daughter's at the stud right now, gathering what little Wedgwood is left.' She looked over her shoulder in its direction. 'Stupid of me to come today. We're collecting horses later. And it's Lester's birthday, so I brought a hatchet to bury and a peace pipe to smoke, but I might have guessed Daddy's groom savant would out-manoeuvre me again. He brought all the horses in first thing and has swanned off to Oxford with Pip Edwards to sightsee and watch a musical, can you believe?'

'Blimey. Is he... you know... with Pip?'

'What?'

'Nobbing her.' Where had that come from? Her twelve-year-old self trying to impress the older girls with street-wise cool. Petra blushed. It was *so* Yorkshire.

But Ronnie found it hilarious. 'You sound like Blair. And I very much doubt it. I suspect he's still avoiding me. Lester was quite the Bardswolds bachelor catch once.' That husky laugh revved up again. 'Farmers' daughters and hearty horse-riding girls from all over the county would queue up with game pies, jams, cakes and cider, believing the way to a man's heart is through his stomach. But Lester's appetite is bottomless, and he never puts on an ounce of weight. Nobody lasts the trip.' She looked at Petra, blue eyes vexed. 'Can one trust Pip, do you think?'

'If she's onside, yes. The thing she wants more than anything is to please, but she's utterly ruthless in going about it. My husband's cut from the same cloth. They have eternal optimism sewn into their bulletproof linings.'

Watching Petra Gunn's lovely dark eyes offering all the fun of friendship, Ronnie was entranced by the clever depth of them, like wells into which one could cast every secret wish, knowing they'd be safe there. She gave her confidence so generously, her quick wit a valuable weapon. Ronnie had long ago learned that a sense of humour between women was a universal language, its hidden truths as precious as its shared laughter. Petra couldn't hide her emotional rawness, another Cotswolds wife perched guiltily on the edge of depression. Ronnie had seen too many to count. She'd been one herself.

'Have you been married long?'

'Almost twenty years. He'd just come out of the army to train as a barrister in London. Commercial law. The boring bits.'

'And is he boring too?'

'No, he's supremely suave. Very witty. Very contained.'

She still loves him, Ronnie realised, watching her face closely. But there was a deep cleft. It was little wonder Bay Austen was sniffing around. Relighting her roll-up, she listened to Petra talk about her husband, a loafing Hooray from the sound of it, explaining that he stayed in London all week. 'We have a little flat there, my old nineties bachelorette pad. We let it when we first moved here, which helped with school fees, but Charlie found commuting such hell, and once the boys both started boarding, the female domination at home was a bit too much. You must come round for a drink some time. Charlie would love to meet you. I promise not to press the shark-tank button.'

'I'm still living in Wiltshire, but let's hold that thought,' Ronnie said noncommittally. 'Now I must go.' Friendships were so much harder to find than love affairs, Ronnie had always found, and yet they fitted together so simply when they were unearthed. She needed to bury this one again quickly in case she became too attached to it.

'And I must get back to work,' Petra said, pulling a plastic bag from her pocket that she started to fill with blackberries, alternately bagging and eating in rapid succession.

Ronnie watched her in amusement. 'Is foraging part of your job?'

'This is displacement activity. It won't last long.'

She whistled for her dogs before asking: 'What is it you do?'

'I'm an author.'

'Oh, what fun. I must read you,' Ronnie held the gate open for her dogs, who trotted through to sit to either side of her, gazing up loyally. 'Please don't tell me they're huge political biographies everyone at dinner parties pretends to be reading while they're really guzzling up the latest Jilly Cooper. What name do you write under?'

'Petra Shaw.' She smiled gratefully. 'And they're steamy bodice-rippers.' If only she could build up steam on this one.

'You *are* clever. I could give you plenty of racy stories.'

Looking at her exquisite face, imagining how irresistible she must have been to red-blooded men from infancy, Petra had no doubt she could. *That*'s where I'm going wrong with the Fairfaxes, she realised. Her protagonists were far too wholesome to be exciting. If Anne Fairfax had Ronnie's firework charisma, maybe she could turn the whole tangled plot round. That would keep Black Tom perpetually on his toes, dashing heroically back and forth from battle to claim her all for himself.

'Do you put people you know in them?' she was asking. 'Gill Walcote in crinoline having a rampant affair with the church verger? Old Norm Turner squiring village damsels in his Romany days?'

Uncomfortably aware that she'd been using Ronnie's 'friend' Blair as inspiration, Petra felt her face colour. 'Sometimes. The characters are usually an amalgam of people. I'm a bit stuck with my new hero.' Russell Brand was bouncing around in her head in his skinny jeans, crying, 'The swines!' again. 'He won't behave himself at all.'

'The most exciting ones never do. Who wants their bodice ripped by a crashing bore?'

'He's a happily married man.'

'They can make the best lovers.' She winked naughtily.

Petra had clambered onto a bank to reach the juiciest fruit. Ronnie was disturbingly upfront, but she found her company addictive. 'Adultery's always far more fun to write,' she confessed. 'Giving in to forbidden lust is a terrific aphrodisiac.'

The husky voice dropped to a hush. 'Remind me, are you having an affair with Bay Austen?' She asked it so sweetly she could have been trying to remember whether she'd met a mutual friend at a party.

Flustered, Petra slid clumsily down the bank. 'No! We're – friends. I had a bit of a crush, but I've put it firmly to bed. Alone. I don't mean I'm doing anything in bed alone with it. It's just on ice. Over, I mean. Gone.'

'Ah.' Ronnie gave her a wise smile. 'So he's not in this new book?'

She could feel the red spilling into her cheeks. 'I'd probably get thoroughly carried away if I did that.'

The bluest eyes in Gloucestershire were on her, sparkling with devilry. 'There's your answer.'

'Bay's all wrong for Thomas Fairfax.'

'I didn't say he should be the hero. Cast him as a libidinous sidekick.'

'Is that wise? I'm trying to cool that fever.'

'It's a great way of getting rid of all the pent-up frustration.'

'It needs re-penting.'

'Make him a priest! My best childhood friend went to a convent school. Her reports would make your hair curl. Father Willy was a total rogue.'

'Tell me that wasn't really his name?'

'It was. Looked like Warren Beatty and ran off with one of the sixth-formers. There was a terrific scandal.'

'I'm not sure where I'd fit Father Willy in,' she apologised, thinking about her Cornish battle scenes with erotically charged encounters in sea-lashed caves.

A moment later, they were both gripped with laughter.

Ronnie was first to recover, the echoes of schoolgirl giggles from forty years ago disconcertingly close. She reminded herself firmly that she didn't need the ties of a friendship in the village, but she knew she'd been right to ally herself to Petra Gunn. The warm-eyed brunette had an unpretentious truth about her that would always find a way to an air pocket.

'Thank you so, so much!' Petra was bright-eyed with enthusiasm. 'You've bucked me up no end. I can't wait to get back to it. *Ego procellosa sumus!*' She held up her blackberry bag triumphantly, buffeted in the wind.

'*Ego procellosa sumus!*' Ronnie saluted her, turning away.

30

Ash was late again setting off for college when Carly got back to the estate, still revving the pickup in front of the house, having a loud conversation through the window with one of his cousins, Jed. Carly tapped her watch at him as she passed. He blew her a kiss and roared off.

'You still up for coming out lamping some time?' Jed called. Low-browed, with eyes like razorblades, he was among the Turners she mistrusted most, renowned for dirty deals, misogyny and poaching.

'Bit windy, isn't it? What about the dogs?'

'The secret is to lie low and wait until it's just passed over,' he explained, pale eyes distant. 'The minute it's calm, Bambi and his mates all come out from their hidey-holes. Rich pickings.'

There had been a storm the night before Pricey was found, Carly remembered. Janine had insisted Jed wouldn't be out in it, that it had to have been townies, but the opposite was true. He loved nothing more than waiting out a storm, like a looter after a riot.

'Count me out.'

'Scared of storms?'

'Terrified.' She gave him a sideways look. 'You just ask Ash to go?'

'Not his thing, is it? Never was.'

'No.' Carly smiled to herself as she turned back up the path. She'd had a niggling worry that the late nights with his mates might be taking in some less than legal detours, but if they had, no off-roading, guns or lamps had been involved.

Ash had left his phone on the shelf in the hall when he was putting on his coat. The battery-low warning was beeping. She plugged it in to charge for him, the screen lighting up as she did so, a photograph of herself greeting her, an old pouty one with take-me-to-bed eyes. She wished he'd put the kids on there instead. She hardly recognised herself without dark under-eye bags and a nagging remark on her lips.

'What you two need is a date night,' Janine told her, half an hour later, as they Cif-ed the glossy black kitchen of one of the flashy new builds on the Broadbourne road. 'It's drink-the-bar-dry at the Jugged Hare tonight. They're closing down at the weekend. VAT dodgers apparently. Ash and the lads are going. You could tag along.'

'Thanks, but that's not a date, that's a piss-up.'

'You're a Turner now. They're one and the same. C'mon, Carl, you've got to make an effort.'

'*Me* make an effort? Your brother hasn't taken me anywhere since we moved here. He hasn't flossed his *teeth* since we moved here.'

'He's still fit, though, isn't he? Look at you! No make-up, roots as wide as the Fosse Way, and you've broken those lovely nails I did for you already. Give him the girl on the phone again, yeah? He misses her. I'll babysit.'

Wishing she'd never shown the picture to Janine, Carly stomped off to clean the marble-tiled bathroom, checking out her reflection in its mirrors and groaning. Janine was right. If she was going to use animal behaviour to help Ash back up to alpha stallion, she had to look like a dominant mare.

Ronnie scowled at the sight of Bay Austen's Land Rover parked between her little car and Alice's Mitsubishi, his dogs barking at hers from the back. She whistled the two heelers onto her back seat and went in search of Alice, whose pony trailer was crammed to the roof with paintings, ornaments and furniture. 'Just gathering a few keepsakes. I don't want to get into a fight about it,' she'd told her mother earlier, clearly very much steeling for a fight. Ronnie had told her she could have what she liked, then taken her dogs out.

It's all set dressing, she thought sadly. After our final curtain call, a lifetime's props and costumes are shared out. To make a fuss was just scene-stealing.

Now Bay had rowed in like a pantomime villain. She wasn't sure she could face him. Funerals aside, their last encounter had left a catastrophically bitter taste, although being Bay he would throw enough sweets to the audience that nobody would notice.

Lester had been quite right to take himself off to see a different show.

Three steps into the vestibule and she hesitated. Even with the wind rattling every window, she could hear Alice's sharp little bark coming from the kitchen.

'We're as frustrated as you, Bay. Mummy's so ruddy maddening.'

'All she has to do is sign the interim transfer documents for the land, then the money will be there for you to pay HMRC.' Bay's drawl had deepened from how she remembered it.

'She says she doesn't want a penny of it and it's all for us, but she's obviously stalling,' Alice confided. 'I thought she'd be back with the dogs by now. That's why I called you so we could make sure she signs the ruddy thing. I told her to come and find me.'

'She brought Marlboro Man?'

'Who?'

'The Aussie eventer married to old Vee-Vee.'

'No, thank God, although he'll be here later. She's already sold him some horses. She came here this morning to pull them out from the herd. They're picking them up later.'

'Always could sell a horse, Ronnie.'

'Just hates selling land. Granny was the same.'

'Especially to Austens. Especially, in your mother's case, to me.'

Too right, thought Ronnie, marching towards the kitchen.

'Hardly matters, given the whole place will be up for sale soon enough,' Alice said.

Ronnie stopped.

'So you're planning to dispose of the lot?' Bay sounded surprised.

'The idea was to sell just this house initially, but a couple of estate agents recommend putting the farm up as a whole. We'd first have to find a little yard to base Lester and the mares – not so much retiring to stud as retiring *the* stud – but otherwise there's nothing to stop the sale once Mummy's signed her claim over.'

Ronnie put her hands to her mouth. The very thing her father had dreaded.

'The village all seem to think she's coming back. Barry Dawkins and his band of supporters are already rallying the hunt committee to offer her a joint mastership next season.'

'Don't be silly, Bay. Pax insisted we give Mummy a chance to step in and run it, but she'll never do it.'

'I'm surprised Pax is happy to see the place sold.'

'She's outnumbered. Don't get me wrong, we'd all *love* to keep it – my oldest wants to be a National Hunt trainer and this would suit him perfectly in a few years. Tim's dying to set up his own British winery so would like to annex some of the south-facing hillside for vines. And God knows Pax deserves to get back in the saddle more than any of us – she knows her breeding too – but it's just not practicable.'

Ronnie's hands tightened across her mouth, hearing the very thing her father had wanted.

'We're not the Waltons,' Alice went on, with her shrill laugh. 'The brutal truth is it costs far too much to run an old pile like this. We'll talk Pax round to selling. Mack's completely on side already.'

'Good old Uch Aye Ganoo.'

'He's a smart cookie. Made a better job of being husband to her than you ever would have.'

Ronnie's eyes narrowed, remembering the Scot's cold detachment at the funeral.

'Better *first* husband,' he corrected idly. 'You don't think Ronnie's going to try to move Marlboro Man in, do you? He must be looking to trade up to a younger cougar now. Suit him nicely, the set-up here.'

'Over my dead body!' The shrill laugh rang out again.

Ronnie had heard enough.

She marched back out to her car and took off down the drive.

She would not see the stud sold.

If they couldn't trust her, she must put up somebody too trust-worthy to doubt.

Abandoning her car in the gateway to Sixty Acres, she walked her dogs to the family tree, its branches slapping and cracking in the wind. Uncle Brooke was upside down as usual, as were several cousins.

Pulling out her phone, Ronnie scrolled through her contacts. At the end of the Ls was the most dependable man she knew. Seeking Luca O'Brien's help risked infuriating Blair who believed a man that could be relied upon to drop anything to come to her aid was not one a lover should trust, but Ronnie knew Luca better than that.

It must have been eight or nine years ago when she'd first encountered the young horseman from County Kildare, mentioning him in a letter to Hermia – *I've just met my first centaur!!!* – one of many letters sent to the wrong address, a one-sided correspondence doggedly maintained for years. She'd been living in Germany at the time, writing excitedly of a talented work rider who possessed a truly extraordinary gift. Like her, Luca had been born into an old equestrian dynasty, his family Italian-Irish show-jumpers. They'd sparked off each other from the start, and been friends for more than a decade now, his skills transferred from competition riding to breeding, his knack for producing winners taking him to some of the best sports horse studs in the world. His methods were unconventional and his feet just as itchy as her own, but he was so undeniably effective he'd become known as the Horsemaker.

Blair had always borne a jealous streak, but she'd deflected one rather charming pass years ago and had no intention of allowing a repeat performance. He was far too angelic to be her type. But he was perfect for Compton Magna. The moment she'd met him, she'd known she must introduce him to Pax. This was her chance at last. He was her peace-offering to her daughter and to the whole village.

He picked up her call in two rings, the soft Irish voice a lullaby even across two continents. 'How are ya, Ron?'

'You were asleep.'

'If this is a dream, don't make my teeth fall out.'

'Luca, I want to offer you a yard to run.'

'There they go. Tooth Fairy just made me rich man. Is this for real?'

'Yes. How soon can you start?'

'Jesus, what's it been – three years? You could at least ask how I'm keeping.'

'You can tell me when you get here.'

He laughed, a gorgeous, rumbling sound. 'Where is here?'

'England. My family's stud. We spoke about it.'

'Beautiful place, so it is. But I'm in contract to the end of the year. Then I was planning on going back to Ireland for a bit.'

'Stop off here on the way.'

The rumbling laugh again.

'When do you need an answer?'

'Now.'

'I've got six months to play with at most. I'm working in France from July.'

'That will be perfect. Long enough for all the mares to foal down, and break in and sell the surplus stock. So you'll do it?'

'You can break the news to my mammy.'

Carly redid her roots while she was cleaning her own house that afternoon, painting on the gunk from a cheap supermarket kit, washing it out ten minutes early because she had to collect Ellis from school.

To her horror, it had turned her dark parting Honey Monster orange. There was no time to do anything more than cram on a hat before belting out to the school. The wind was even stronger now, hurling more wheelie-bins around, several trees down in the orchards along Plum Run, the children's artwork whipped out of their hands as they emerged from their classrooms.

Typically, today was the one on which Ellis's new best friend's shy young Hungarian mother chose to offer Carly a cup of tea in the workers' caravan she shared with her husband at the Austens' farm.

'Children can play, yes? We have girl talk.'

Carly craved girl talk, but she'd left the house half cleaned, the other two kids with her mother-in-law and she wanted to be alpha mare for Ash. Apologising that they'd have to do it another time, Carly refused, the mother scuttling away.

Ellis kicked up a fuss, refusing to touch his beans on toast at home, then charging out to kick a ball at the shed with such force his light-up trainers glowed constantly like little furnaces.

Cutting his first two lower teeth, Jackson was bawling constantly. While Carly was trying to soothe him, Sienna waddled unnoticed into her bedroom and spread her mother's make-up everywhere.

'Stick, stick!' she said proudly, holding up the stub of red lipstick that was now all over her face and the walls.

Hearing his mother's wails of horror, Ellis reclaimed the 'Splorer Stick from under the stairs and took it outside to whack against the shed instead.

When Ash came home, he walked into a house of howling, kicking, bleach-smelling discontent. Carly hurried downstairs, roots still orange. 'Hello, bae. I've got all this covered. You just chill. Good day?'

He was holding his phone. 'You moved this?'

'I charged it for you.'

'I don't like you messing with it.' He noticed Ellis in the garden, horse-whipping the clothes-airer. 'Why's he got that fucking duster out again?'

'Missed out on date night. Unlike us.' Carly struggled to sound enthusiastic.

Ash looked equally unimpressed by the idea. 'Won't be your thing, bae. The only booze they're giving away is the shit liqueurs and alcopops they can't sell back to the wholesaler. You know the lads will be there.'

'Great!' She feigned delight. 'Any port in a storm. About time I got to know them better.'

Petra hardly noticed the storm building, her mind possessed by craggy Sir Thomas and his ravishing wife Lady Anne – puritanical zealots with an insatiable lust for one another – and dastardly Father Willy, a younger Fairfax son from the Catholic side of the family infatuated by a joyful taste for womanliness.

Fitz staggered in, like a Sherpa from a blizzard, shortly after four, battling to close the door behind him.

'Sorry to interrupt, but it's pretty wild out there. Should we do anything?'

Sixteen, sporty and with an addiction to action movies, Fitz needed a daring deed. 'You could put the chickens away.'

She returned to Father Willy, his first conquest, a curvaceous young widow, writhing under his firm-fingered touch. Bay's fingers – tanned and square-tipped and deep-knuckled – were vivid in her mind's eye.

When the girls were dropped off, Petra's mum-run friend reported roads closed due to fallen trees and power lines. She saved her work and brought her laptop inside, trailed by a relieved Wilf. The girls occupied in the playroom, Petra sneaked open the laptop at the dining-room table and carried on writing.

Sir Thomas Fairfax was returning from battle to see his wife for the first time in many weeks, their reunion rapturous, her bodice ripped by his teeth while her tongue and teeth worked on his ripped body. As she wrote, Sir Thomas quickly metamorphosed from a craggy Indiana Jones to a young Charlie, reunited with his hair and erstwhile lusty sexual appetite. Anne was no longer a minxy blonde, but Petra herself in her twenties, described with the wisdom of her forties, now seeing the ravishing young raver she had been then, not the gawky, fat-thighed wallflower she'd imagined. She and Charlie had been *hot*. Black Tom and his wife had that Friday feeling.

The house phone rang just after five o'clock. She ignored it. Let it go to messages. But Prudie trotted through with it a minute later. 'Daddy says the trains are all over the place because of the storm so he's not coming back tonight.'

Petra took it, horny as hell, voice drenched with pheromones. 'Can you really not make it back? I have a special treat.' Blackberry champagne, the shag of your life.

There was nobody on the line.

'He said he didn't need to speak to you,' Prudie lingered, 'but he wasn't sure you'd got his text. What's an areola, Mummy?'

'Sorry?'

'It's on your computer.' She pointed at Petra's laptop, reading from the screen. '"He took her whole areola into his mouth and rolled his tongue around the—"'

'It's a type of sweet.' She quickly shut the lid.

31

The storm-clouds over the Comptons were blackening fast. It had been dark as twilight since teatime. Commuters rushed home early. In Compton Magna, the cottages alongside Lord's Brook started sandbagging their doors; in Compton Bagot the houses near the millstream bridge did the same.

Nobody noticed the white van parking at the entrance to the bridleway near the stud.

Fitz opened the door to the villagers on the Goose Walk, severely depleted in number this year, its feathery star being carried in Gill Walcote's arms because it had sensibly refused to cross the Green in the high wind.

'Are you the only one in, Fitz?' Gill asked cheerfully, from beneath a waterproof hood.

'Mum's working. She's totally, like, obsessed. D'you want a carrot or something?'

'We expect a bit more than that! You're supposed to give us a drink and harvest produce in exchange for a song and a seat at the Michaelmas table.'

'Wait there.'

He found a bottle of Moët and a big bowl of blackberries in the fridge.

'There you go.' He thrust both at them.

'The devil spits on blackberries on Michaelmas Day,' one of the mob told him, a gnarled elder with a know-it-all smile.

'He spat on mine months ago.' Fitz closed the door on them as they started to sing a diddly-dee folk number about apple gathering.

Leaning back against it, he took his phone out of his pocket and checked the adulterous app.

His father and Lozzy were busy tonight, the hurricane stirring everyone up. They'd had a row, it seemed.

He could hear the Goose Walkers moving on, debating about whether to go straight to the pub or not.

The argument seemed to have started with a cancelled liaison and escalated from there, Lozzy accusing Charlie of neglect, indecision and hypocrisy.

'Not the only one to level that charge.'

Fitz's thumb twitched over the screen, tempted to play the hand of God and join in, storm raging in the background.

He swiftly pocketed the phone as he heard his mother dashing along the corridor. 'Don't tell me I've missed them! There's a big basket of greens and ginger wine waiting.'

'I gave them some stuff.'

'You're a star. Sorry I'm a totally flaky mother, love, but it's finally writing itself. Are the girls watching a movie? I must run them a bath.'

'Reading, I think. They've already had showers.'

'My God, today couldn't get any better!' She clapped her hands together, dancing off to her daughters.

Fitz looked at his phone. 'It could. Believe me, it could.'

Carly rescued what make-up she could from Sienna's raid to give herself rock-chick eyes and lollipop lips, prised herself into her tightest jeans, then found an up-do that hid the orange roots and just about withstood the wind under her big fur-lined coat hood on the short walk to the Jugged Hare.

The Best Rock Anthems... Ever! belted out from the stereo, the vacating publicans in good spirits while giving away all their bad ones.

'It's a relief to be getting out of the pub game,' the landlady told Carly, as she handed over a WKD and a large amaretto. 'His blood pressure's been through the roof.' She nodded at her husband, and they all looked up at a crash overhead. 'Roof might not last much longer.'

She and Ash were the first of his gang to arrive, enjoying a brief date as they claimed the big sofa in front of the wood burner. Carly curled up against him, soft sofa back behind her, hard muscle alongside. 'Check out your guns!'

'What's with all the lovey-dovey stuff? This about that dog?'

'No!'

He grinned. 'Cos I think I've sorted that. Jed's gonna take her on.'

'Jed does coursing.'

'Ssh! Keep your voice down. It's what she's bred for.'

'No *way* is she going back to that life. The sanctuary won't let her go to someone like Jed.'

'It's a private home. He's got his girlfriend and her kid living there. They all know their lurchers. Think of the dog, Carl. And Ellis. The kid loves that dog. He can see him every day if he's living a couple of roads away.'

'Her. Pricey's a girl.'

'Jed's called her Killer.'

'You what?'

'Picked her up this afternoon.'

'You're winding me up.'

'Gotcha!' He laughed at her horrified face, eyes creasing in delight as he cuffed her. 'Had you going there, didn't I?'

'Jesus, Ash.' She rubbed her face, almost tearful with relief.

'No, he's actually called her Tequila – Te-killer, get it?'

She stared at him fixedly. 'He really has got the dog?'

'He really has.'

Carly thought about Jed's flick-knife eyes earlier. Had he been the poacher targeting Bay Austen's deer herd that night who had left his dog for dead, and was now reclaiming the fiercest of fighters and survivors?

'I can't let this happen.' She shook her head. 'He lamps on Manor Farm land. She almost died there. He's going out there tonight after this storm blows over.'

'Fucking shut up, will you?'

'Ash, there's nobody in here.'

'He's got six dogs,' he breathed. 'No way will he take the new one, okay? He's not trained her or anything yet. I thought you'd be pleased.'

His phone rang. He spilled her sideways and went to answer it by the door. She watched him anxiously. Something was bothering him this evening, beyond the usual titanium-clad aloofness.

'Let's not talk about the dog again, okay?' she said, when he rejoined her.

He put an arm round her and flashed his big armoured smile. 'You look dope tonight.'

'Is something up, bae?'

'Nothing's up.' He traced his fingers along her jawline and dropped his mouth to her ear to murmur, 'But my cock will be later.' He kissed her mouth. She could always taste a lie on his lips.

When the lads turned up, Carly grew even more suspicious. There were furtive looks, eye shrugs and gestures that told her they'd be talking about something else if she wasn't around. While Flynn was telling her about the 'nutcase' horses he'd been trying to shoe that day in high winds, she could hear Ash talking to Ink behind her, words hissed loud enough for her to get the gist of something going ahead that night. Ash didn't sound happy. 'It's shitting on your own doorstep, isn't it?' Was he talking about the lamping or something more?

His phone rang again and he did his dash to the door, Ink and Hardcase headed to the bar for another free round.

'Alone at last, sweetlips.' Flynn was being ultra-attentive, his double denim eyes taking a tour of her push-up bra and tight trousers.

Carly leaned forwards and whispered, 'What's the fuck's going on, Flynn?'

'Search me.' He made it sound like a genuine invitation.

'Spit it out or you'll be spitting out your teeth.' She gave him her best death stare.

'God, I love it when you talk rough. But seriously, sweetlips, I haven't a clue. I just know, whatever it is, this storm's fucking it right up.'

*

The Marylebone train had been almost an hour late into Oxford, where Lester and Pip had got on. They almost made it to Banbury station when they lurched to a stop again.

Pretending to sleep opposite Pip – who hadn't stopped talking – Lester was still in shock. The whole day had been a sensory overload, a nightmare that never ended. Nothing had prepared him for the crowds, the wind, and the sense of being swept along by both from point to point. Pip had followed her phone map everywhere as she ticked things off her list: gallery, open-topped bus ride, restaurant, theatre. She might as well have been shopping in Asda.

Poldark the Musical hadn't been as Lester was anticipating at all. He hadn't seen the most recent television series. He remembered the one forty years ago with Angharad Rees and Robin Ellis, and recalled rather enjoying the spectacular scenery and high drama. Today's stage show bore no resemblance to it. He was still trying to work out how all those men with oiled torsos waving scythes about fitted into tin-mine closure and smuggling. Then there were the swirling lights, trampolines, strobes, high wires and the sheer noise. Lester had used up an entire asthma inhaler.

'Just popping to the loo.' Pip rattled off along the aisle and he opened one eye to check she was out of sight before sneaking a look at the programme.

He must try to be more grateful. Pip had tried so hard, even getting their names on the stage door to meet some of the cast after the show – she said one of the lead actors was a friend of a friend, but he didn't come out of his dressing room – then treating him to an old-fashioned black cab. Oxford was starting to look post-apocalyptic, the driver telling them somebody had been knocked unconscious by falling debris in one of the college quads. They'd both agreed to skip tea at The Grand Café and come straight home.

He was worried sick about the horses. Pip had called Alice several times from her mobile phone with no reply. He should never have left them, never caved in to his own cowardice avoiding Ronnie. Glancing at the programme, he also knew he'd done something he would never have done while the Captain was alive: he'd been selfish. He hadn't had a day off since June, when the Captain had laid off the weekend helper. Once the horses came off the pasture for winter, Lester had no idea how he would cope, but the only person who seemed to have noticed this was Ronnie, and he'd rather muck out the foal barns single-handed than prod his pitchfork into that hornets' nest.

He looked up as Pip returned, white as a sheet.

'Kit Donne's in first class! With a nun.'

'Who?'

'The theatre director – you know, he was married to Sandy Austen's sister. He's supposed to be in New York.'

'Probably visiting his wife's grave. He's a good man.'

'He could at least have called ahead. His house is still filthy! His daughter definitely said Hallowe'en, and Kit was even iffy about that. Now it seems he's found God and come back early. It's his birthday too. He's supposed to be soaking in the sun in Puerto Rico or wherever New Yorkers go for tropical weekends.'

Lester closed his eyes and wished he was somewhere tropical too. He'd always dreamed of retiring to a little beach shack with coconut palms and clear blue ocean.

'As soon as we're at Broadbourne station,' Pip went on, 'I want you to distract them and I'll drive straight up there for a quick whip-round and bed-make. Oh, God, I've only glued half of Shakespeare's head back together.'

'We're going straight to check the horses,' Lester said emphatically. 'Try calling Alice again.'

Kit had never had a birthday like it. He'd always known Orla had a kooky imagination but bringing him back to the UK for a weekend was madcap enough. Booking a weekend in the Cotswolds was veering on a psychedelic trip.

'You're a grumpy Brit,' she'd told him, when revealing her surprise at the JFK check-in desk. 'You're only happy somewhere wet and cold. I want to see you happy, so I'm taking you back to your birthplace on your birthday.'

He hadn't the heart to point out he'd been born in the Lake District.

'I sorted it through this amazing agency called Fairytale Fantasies, who find castles and shit to stay in. We're in this *totally* princess tower on a hilltop. Look.' She'd shown him a Gothic folly he recognised with a painful lurch as the one at Eyngate Park. 'We get a butler and a Michelin chef. And they meet us from the train with a horse and carriage. How d.a.f. is that?'

'What is DAF?'

'Dope as fuck.'

'And that's a good thing?'

'You're so funny!'

The nun thing was even weirder. She'd cooked it up with the play's costume designer, the whole company apparently in on it.

'You kinda remind everybody of Captain von Trapp, so I thought it would be cute to be your Maria.'

Orla's disguise had been intended as a short-term measure to see them through the train journey anonymously so that she wouldn't be bothered by passengers wanting selfies, a kinky private joke. Who would guess the middle-aged man in a country coat and newsboy's hat travelling with a nun in tinted nerd glasses, a wimple and dowdy knee-length habit was secretly on a Fairytale Fantasies mini-break with a former A-lister?

The normally hour-long train journey had already doubled in length, thanks to Hurricane Claudia. Having started off out of Kit's comfort zone – the flirty footsie beneath the table, a stockinged sole sliding up his leg to massage his crotch – it was now out of Orla's, and she was coming thoroughly derailed.

Wimple slipping, glaring at the rain lashing against the window, she was close to tears behind the tinted glasses. 'I hate this shitty country.'

'A sentiment shared by regular users of this particular commuter line.'

'Don't do the Alan Rickman sardonic thing on me. That grumpy Brit thing isn't working.'

'I *am* a grumpy Brit.' He emptied the last of the bottle of duty-free vintage Ruinart into their plastic cups.

'I knew I should have gone with the Austrian schloss,' she hissed. 'Or Vegas. Everybody loves Vegas. There's loads of castles in Vegas. And lions. And we could get married. Joke.' She thrust her tongue beneath her lower lip.

Across the aisle an elderly couple were eyeing them suspiciously. Kit wished she'd chosen anywhere else, but kept quiet. It must be costing her a fortune. She still behaved as though she was earning movie rates, taking cabs all over Manhattan, flying business back and forth to LA just to have breakfast with friends. He knew exactly how much Orla was earning, which was no match to what he'd seen her spend in the past month.

Her phone rang. Sister Maria's expression was not one of serenity as she listened. 'They've cancelled the fucking horse and carriage.'

Kit sighed with relief.

The couple across the aisle looked over their *Evening Standard*s in alarm.

Cracking open the second bottle of Ruinart did little to improve her mood, especially when the phone rang again, her eyebrows like two matador daggers now.

'The roof's blown off the fucking fairy tower.'

Riding on a wave of good champagne and old-fashioned British spirit, Kit found this far more amusing than he should.

'I'll excommunicate you if you laugh,' she snarled, eyes on fire behind the metal frames. She glared at her phone screen. 'What do we do?'

'Have they offered alternative accommodation?'

'A yurt. We still get the butler, but there's a short walk to the john.'

They glanced out at the rain-lashed gloom. The train carriage rocked in the wind.

'We'll book a hotel,' Kit said, unlocking his phone screen.

'I hate hotels.'

Her face was pale and clammy, her hand trembling as she lifted the cup to her lips.

'Have you checked your blood levels?'

'I'm fine!'

'You need to eat something.'

'I said I'm fine. I know my body.' She reached for the bottle. 'What about your cottage? That's near, isn't it?'

Kit's two worlds briefly collided in his head. He could no more bring Orla into the house he'd shared with Hermia than he could take her to his old school in Grasmere and sit in a classroom reciting from the Brecht play that had first given him his love of drama. That was his inner life. 'We'll book a hotel.'

He chose Le Mill because he thought she'd like all the overtly obsequious boutiqueyness, then arranged for a cab to pick them up from the station. He was rather looking forward to the face of the pompous reception staff when he checked in to a king-sized suite with a nun.

'I'm sorry I ruined your fucking birthday.'

He looked at her, this beautiful strange creature, whose mind he was as far from working out as Cyrillic script, yet whose body he'd devoured like airport reading. He adored her on stage and in bed, but out of context they had yet to write the script. Like all the affairs he'd had since Hermia, theirs was a production romance, one based around the same play repeated again and again, night after night, in a company that disbanded as soon as the run finished; a self-contained, repetitive, live-for-the-moment relationship. If Kit shared his past with someone, he did so because he believed they would share a future. He wanted Orla Gomez to be an absolute superstar night after night in New York, no more.

The train started moving again and he raised his glass. 'Nothing's fucking ruined when we have Ruinart and fucking.'

Across the aisle, the *Evening Standard*s were lowered in outrage.

'You sure?' A smile stole up to him from under the wimple.

'Sure I'm sure.'

The foot slid back up his leg.

The train shunted to a stop again. The voice on the Tannoy announced there would be a further long delay. The foot stayed put and the smile widened. They might not be soul mates, but Kit liked what her sole was doing.

He dialled the cab company. 'This is Kit Donne again.'

'Who, love?' said the broad Bardswolds accent at the other end.

'Kit *Donne*. I booked a cab from Broadbourne station to Compton Magna just now? The train that's delayed?'

'They're all delayed, love. Haven't you noticed there's a storm? We've called all the drivers back. Too dangerous out there. There's a fatality on the Fosse Way. Trees are coming down all over the shop.'

*

Ronnie's day had gone from bad to worse. At Moreton Morrell, in driving rain, her brave young horse had been disqualified for an error of course – his clean record marked, his rider refusing to take responsibility. It was the weather. It was lack of sleep. It was Ronnie asking the Horsemaker to run the stud.

She'd never had Blair down as a bad loser before, but he'd behaved like a surly, sour hothead, slamming his way into the horsebox to change out of wet breeches and shouting that they'd changed the course at the last minute because of waterlogging. 'They should have cancelled. There's more diversions out there than the A1. Now we've got to get this lot back to Wiltshire in this weather.'

'We're picking four up from the stud,' she'd reminded him.

'Forget that. I want to get straight home.'

Rain had drummed on the roof so loudly they'd given up shouting at each other.

She'd brought her own car, but it had got stuck in the mud, its engine dead after it was pulled free by a tractor. Abandoning it to a tow truck, she was forced to share a ride on the lorry after all, sitting beside silent, livid Blair. Another horsebox broke down in the entrance to the lorry park, which held them up for a further hour.

Hugging a dog to each side, Ronnie turned to his fixed profile. It was the end of the season, the final competitions inevitably cold and muddy. He'd been on the road all week, competing and hosting seminars, delivering horses back to their owners. She could tell his old back injury was killing him. He was worried about Verity, of whom they so rarely spoke but who sat like a dark shadow between them. Tired, notoriously short-tempered and resistant to change, he could probably be forgiven for bad temper.

'Sorry.'

He tipped his head in acknowledgement. He didn't offer any apology back.

They raced the storm along the Fosse Way, but a long snake of red tail-lights leading to flashing blue lights far ahead made them both groan. Cars were turning around.

'A tree's down – landed on a van!' someone yelled up at them from their car window.

There was no way to turn Blair's lorry. They had five horses on board. The wait could be hours.

It was just after six, but it felt much later, the sky already dark as night.

'If we can get as far as that turning on the right, we can take the back roads.' She pointed a hundred yards on. 'We can hole up at the stud until this passes. Pick up those horses.'

'Vee's got nobody with her tonight. We haven't time to swan round there.'

She gritted her teeth.

The radio reports warned of floods across the road ahead. More cars were turning back. They crept forwards, almost within reach of the turning, air brakes hissing.

'There are plenty of stables, a warm house. Let's make peace and go there, Blair. Think of the horses.'

'I *am* thinking of the horses.'

The wind was rocking the big horsebox more aggressively, gusts smacking against it. Ahead of them a branch fell across the opposite carriageway with a loud crack. Nobody could turn back now.

Without another word, Blair took the turning into the lane, clouting overhanging branches and taking out a signpost. 'There'd better be a drink there.'

Remembering seeing Alice stashing the decanters and the best wine in her car boot that morning, Ronnie said nothing.

32

The stud's bachelor pack was sheltering along the Yorkshire boarding in the furthest open barn from the stableyard, close to what had once been the old back entrance to the stud, its hoggin track still used to access the paddocks. They looked up in surprise as headlights came bouncing along it, then were abruptly extinguished, the engine rolling past to park by the tack room, doors banging, unfamiliar voices and flashlights moving about.

One light came bobbing back towards them.

Already spooked by the wind, most of the herd clustered to the corner of the building, snorting suspiciously, but the little dun colt stayed with the big pile of hay that had recently been left there, watching with interest as the shadowy figure approached and stood waiting on the track, the flashlight clicking off and a phone screen lighting up.

'I'm in position, yeah. I can see the road from here. Nah, nuffink. Yeah, I'll shout if anything turns up the drive. Be quick.'

The foal whickered for attention. The flashlight went back on.

'All right, mate?'

He bobbed his head.

A hand covered in tattoos reached out and patted him, quickly retracted when he nipped it in search of treats.

'Little bastard.'

The other colts started to creep forwards, but quickly retreated when his phone lit up again and he spoke.

'You're kidding? There should be tons of kit in there. What do you mean all old shit? Nah, forget saddles and all that. Can't sell

372

the bloody things— Well, *unload* it. Just chuck it in a stable and get back here.'

When the van rolled back, the voices were angrier. They seemed to blame the man who had been waiting on the track. He was blaming someone else – 'Stupid bitch made it sound like bloody Sandringham here.'

Suddenly a shout went out.

'Bloody big wagon coming down the road! Looks like it's turning in here. Get going!'

'Let the nags out first! Quick. They'll be too busy running round catching them to notice we've been here.'

The gate to the barn was wrenched open with a clank. The bachelor pack melted back. The dun colt barged forward.

'This little sod bit me.' The man with the tattooed hand brought it down hard on his backside as he shot out. He kicked back with both hind legs.

'Ow, fuck! Now he's bloody kneecapped me!'

'Get the others out!'

The bachelor pack charged round in terrified circles in the barn.

'Forget it! Let's just fucking get out of here.' The gate was let go and clanged shut.

As the van engine roared, its lights turned on briefly to sight the exit route, the foal illuminated trotting along the track towards the fields, paddock rails to each side. He looked round, eyes gleaming like a deer's in a gun's lamplight.

A moment later, a van was on his tail.

He jigged left then right, but the rails were all stallion height, the gates all closed. The van was gaining on him, his kneecapping victim intent on revenge as part of the getaway.

The colt accelerated, sighting the gap in the rails and hedge ahead where no gap had been before, old carpet thrown over the bank to enable tyres to get grip across it. Catching a hoof on it, he stumbled, flailing, all four legs going in different directions, the van bouncing up onto the carpet behind him.

'Fuck! You're going to hit him!'

The wheels spun, the engine roared.

He scrambled up, the smell from its radiator in his nostrils, the heat of the van against his skin. Jinking right he charged along the track towards the road, wind sharp in his eyes. Ahead, dark as a watchtower in the distance, was the big tree in the field he knew best.

The van turned onto the track behind him, accelerating in his wake.

'Now's your chance!' Pip hissed to Lester, when their train finally ground to a halt at Broadbourne station, Kit Donne and his nun stepping out onto the platform ahead of them when the doors slid open. The nun looked a bit unsteady on her feet.

'With respect, Pip,' Lester muttered, 'I think the state of his house is the least of his worries.'

Kit was shouting into his mobile phone. 'I need a taxi to the Comptons! I'll pay double!'

'Mr Donne!' Pip stood beaming in front of him. 'You should have said you were coming. Are you going to the house?'

'Le Mill. My – er – companion is dining with me there. And staying. There.'

The beam brightened. 'Would you like a lift?'

'I would like nothing more. This is – my good friend Orla.'

'Sister.' Pip bobbed, uncertain how to address a nun.

The nun scowled at her, struggling to light a Marlboro in the wind. 'I'm here to bless the Costwolds.'

'Cotswolds,' Kit corrected, smiling uneasily at Pip. She'd forgotten how distinguished he looked with his Professor Higgins eyes and deep cheek dimples.

The stud was deserted. The horses had been hayed and watered, a note from Alice flapping on Lester's cottage door, the writing almost illegible after a soaking.

Lester. Gone back to the farm. Our fields there are flooding – all hands on deck! Mummy may turn up and take away some horses. Keep notes. Happy Birthday. A

Ronnie was always efficient in a crisis. Beds went down in the driest of the outside stables, the only ones unoccupied, nets and water containers swiftly filled. The horses were unloaded, stabled, checked over and rugged to keep the chill of the wind off them. Then she hurried around the stud horses, doing the best headcount she could manage.

In an outside barn, a gangly dun two-year-old was drenched in sweat, running up and down the Yorkshire boarding, his constant companion gone.

'The foal,' Ronnie realised. 'The foal's missing!'

The road up to Le Mill and Compton Bagot resembled a river, water gushing up to the rims of Pip's little blue car's wheels as it struggled to keep going.

In the back seat, the nun was like a maddened rally co-driver. 'Left, left! Foot down! Hard right. Fucking floor it, baby.' Her voice was slurred.

'Can you please not smoke?' Pip lowered her window, then hastily raised it again as the wind almost took her head off.

'Or swear,' Lester muttered.

'Which order do you belong to?' asked Pip, brightly.

'The Holy Church of Lawless Fucking Disorder.' She flicked the cigarette out of her own window, wimple blowing off as a flash of lightning lit them all, thick black curls springing out with a distinctive red streak over the left eyebrow. Thunder crashed in its wake, so loud Pip's ears popped.

In the back, Kit disappeared rapidly from sight. 'Nobody said it was going to be an electric storm!'

Almost within sight of Le Mill, a big yellow JCB was parked across the road in front of the narrow stone bridge over the millstream. Pip recognised Polish builder Aleš Mazur standing guard over it in a high-vis jacket. Built like an American football quarterback and tough as a Cold War border guard, Aleš, fluorescent collar up to his ears, made them all want to put their hands on their heads as he marched forwards pointing his high-watt torch at them like a Kalashnikov.

'The wall is come down. Not safe to cross. Only way into village is to go around by Priors Compton and intersect through Manor

Farm back drive. The Austen family have opened private road. They have many good men keeping that way clear. We talk on mobiles.' He held his up with a toothy smile.

'We'll walk over the bridge on foot.' Kit's head popped up, scrabbling for a handle and not finding one.

'It's a three-door car, remember, honey,' Orla pointed out. 'So cutely British.'

'I forbid it!' A hand banged on the little car's roof.

'You heard Aleš. It's not safe.' Pip put the car into reverse and swung it round, warming to the nun, whose voice reminded her of a television character she couldn't place.

'But the hotel is just there!'

Taking no notice, Pip whitewater-rafted the little car back along the Broadbourne road and cut left.

As Aleš had promised, the back drive to the Austens' farm was being manned by one of the Czech farmhands, in an orange tabard, who waved Pip through. 'Claudia, she is a bitch, yes?' He grinned, then did a double-take when he saw the wimple-free nun. 'It's Greta the sexy vampire!'

'I'm Orla the pissed-off American. Greta's so history.'

'OHMYGODITHOUGHTIRECOGNISEDYOU!' Pip shrieked. 'I *loved* you in *The Vampire Chronicles*! I have them all on DVD.'

'Thank you.' Orla lit another cigarette. 'You can lend them to Kit. He's not seen any.'

Pip chattered happily about her favourite parts of the blockbuster film series as they skidded and bounced along the concrete Manor Farm machinery drive, eventually finding their way onto smoother tarmac to the main public gates and out onto the home run, spirits lifting at the sight of the Compton Magna village sign.

Someone with a torch was standing on the lane by the stud entrance, waving them down. Looking craggily heroic in a stockman's jacket and bush hat, Blair Robertson marched up to the driver's door. Rain-lashed and wild-eyed, he was devastatingly sexy.

'Have you seen a horse? A foal?'

'I work at the stud. I'm Pip.' Her voice was a Penelope Pitstop squeak of excitement.

'Which one is missing?' demanded Lester.

'The buckskin colt foal. Gone a while, we reckon. Could be anywhere. Ronnie's bringing the quad bike down.'

Lester was out of the car like a shot. 'You check Sixty Acres, Pip,' he barked through the door, as he zipped up his coat. 'I'll go up to High Pasture. Hop to it!'

'I can't abandon the car here!' she bleated, reluctant to get wet. 'I have passengers!'

'They can help.'

'One is a Hollywood movie actress.' She wasn't budging.

'That never fucking stopped me having an adventure.' Orla flipped the front seat forward and jumped out too. '*Now* I'm starting to enjoy myself. I knew there was a reason to wear practical shoes.'

'Those are not practical shoes.' Lester glared at the dainty flat lace-ups.

'There are wellies in the boot!' Pip stayed glued to the steering wheel. 'I think I'd better wait up at the yard in case he comes back there. Somebody needs to be on site.'

'I agree,' Kit muttered, from the floor in the back. 'Ideally two people.'

Lester waved a hand dismissively and headed towards the bridleway.

Orla pulled on the wellies and an old coat from the boot, then raced after him.

As Pip turned the car into the drive, she almost crashed into a quad bike flying in the opposite direction.

In the back seat, Kit's head slammed against the central console. He bobbed up in time to see his nemesis swerve to the driver's side, a blonde Mad Max on a throbbing Honda.

'Oh, Pip, I'm so glad you're here!' That husky voice, accustomed to hailing neighbours across country estates, could project round the NEC arena without needing a mike. 'We need everyone we can get. Do you want a lift on the back of this?'

'I'll follow. You go.'

'You're an angel!' She whizzed off.

'Sod it.' Pip stopped the engine. Ronnie Percy had every measure of the Captain's charisma and a great deal more charm. Her loyal heart swelled, the family calling her to arms. 'I'll have to do this even in my best wool coat and pixie boots.'

'Can't you at least drop me off?' Kit demanded.

'Go up to the yard. Key to the tack room's on the top of the door sill. Put the kettle on and call for back-up.'

'Call who?'

'There are numbers on the board,' she said vaguely. 'Neighbourhood Watch, maybe.'

There was another crackle of lightning and a crescent of sparks from a nearby telegraph pole.

Kit cowered lower.

'Power's blown. Forget the kettle. If you're staying in the car, can I borrow your coat? This is M&S Limited Edition.'

In the Jugged Hare, the log-burner roared, the rock anthems blasted, and a large Embden goose was waddling round the tables picking up dropped crisps.

The departing publicans were in defiant mood, despite that night's drink-the-bar-dry marathon turning out to be something of a damp squib while Hurricane Claudia was terrorising the village. The elite gathering's weather-beaten exclusivity made it feel surprisingly jolly, a hardy clan of regulars in high spirits. Those who were there had no intention of leaving while the storm was still hurling thunderbolts outside.

Propping up the bar, the bedraggled Goose Walkers had bailed early, and were drowning their sorrows in free liqueurs, having been blown from door to door for little reward, that evening's haul barely enough to fill a Bag for Life.

'This pub is like the old days tonight,' said Brian Hicks, the parish council chairman, Shakespeare beard still dripping storm water from its point.

'Isn't it just?' agreed Gill Walcote, limoncello in hand.

Beside her, Paul had forsaken the *digestifs* for mineral water – paid for – so as not to break his cycling training programme. 'You'd think they'd have laid on food other than kittle crusps.'

'Nibble a carrot.' Gill pushed the Goose Walk booty his way, fed up with him whingeing all evening.

'I'm disappointed Petra couldn't see her way to coming out with us tonight.' Brian sniffed, deprived of an opportunity to leer at his most elusive and shapely council member.

'She's busy writing,' Gill said tightly, disappointed too.

'And suxting her favourite farmer,' Paul chuckled.

'I told you that in strictest confidence,' Gill hissed at her husband.

'Come on, love, it's only a bit of fun.'

'What is "sucksting"?' Brian leaned forward eagerly, unfamiliar with Paul's New Zealand accent, and even more so with what 'sext' meant.

'I'm sure you can work it out, Brian.' Paul winked, thrilling Brian with a notion that something far more physical was going on.

'Are we talking about Bay Austen? I sensed a *frisson* at parish meetings.'

'It's been blown out of all proportion,' Gill insisted. 'Although Petra's an absolute sucker for rogues.'

Brian's eyebrows shot up. 'Really?'

'I've warned her, it's like a strong-willed horse. If you give him his head whenever he wants, he'll run away with you.'

'Has it gone as far as that?'

Gill sighed sadly, 'I'd give Bay a piece of my tongue given half the chance.'

Realising both Brian and her husband were staring at her open-mouthed, she drained her liqueur. 'What?'

With Blair now pillion behind her, Ronnie raced across Sixty Acres. The family tree loomed dark ahead of them. Behind it, they saw a tail twitch.

'He's there!' She dropped the throttle – she didn't want to scare him off – and coasted up in a big curve. The colt's eyes glowed in the quad's lights. Soaked through and shaking, he stood his ground defiantly.

'You'd be brave enough to go to war, wouldn't you?' She laughed, turning back to Blair. 'This little horse is going to make the stud famous again when he grows up.'

'I thought the Horsemaker was going to do that.'

'Don't start.' She turned to run her hands along the foal's legs.

Blair moved closer, leaning against the tree trunk and lowering his torch. 'If you already knew you were going to call him in, why'd you write what you did to Verity?'

'What are you talking about?' she asked distractedly, feeling heat in the foal's knee, a raw welt of a graze there.

'You know I'll never leave her.'

'I know that. I've never asked you to.'

'She got your letter, Ron.'

All three of them jumped as lightning forked directly above Lord's Brook, lighting up Blair's face, his dark eyes tormented.

'What letter?'

As she straightened up, there was a noise like a bomb exploding.

In the car, Kit swung round in time to see the huge cedar tree split clean in two, its upper branches bursting into flames. Silhouetted beneath it, the horse, the quad bike, Ronnie and her companion disappeared as the canopy crashed to the ground.

Kit searched frantically for his phone before remembering it was in his coat pocket.

He clambered into the driver's seat, almost weeping with relief to find Pip had left the keys in the ignition. Who cared if he was banned right now?

Spinning the car around, he belted into the village to fetch help.

33

'**O**hfuckohfuckohfuck.' Pip squelched and slithered across the field, pixie boots wedging into hoof holes as she raced to the tree, or what had been the tree moments ago, now a smouldering split totem with its branches collapsed around it. As she ran, she fumbled her phone from her trouser pocket with shaking hands, the fingerprint unlock not working in the rain. A clout of thunder made her duck, the phone slipping out of her grip.

'Ohfuckohfuck.' She cast around for it desperately, but it must have landed screen side down. Rain dripped in her eyes. Where *was* it? She stepped back. Something crunched underfoot.

'Ohfuck!' It was completely dead.

She ran on, approaching the wreckage, a twisted and impenetrable coppice. Close to, the acrid smell of bonfire hit her full in the face.

'Hello! Can you hear me? Hello!' she screamed, into the tangle of foliage towering over her. 'Hello!'

She heard branches cracking, the Australian shouting, 'Ronnie! Shit! Ron.'

'I'm fine!' came that calm, carrying voice. 'I'm with the foal. We're trapped and he's badly cut. Are you hurt?'

More crashing around and wood splitting. 'I can see you. Hang on. I can't move this branch. I can only reach through. See my arm here? I'll get the flashlight on you. Jesus!'

Pip lapped her way round the fallen branches, unable to see a way in. She got as close as she could to where she could hear their voices. 'I'm out here! It's Pip. Hello! What do I do?'

'Get fucking help!' The Australian's deep whip-crack voice was urgent. 'The foal's in a bad way. There's a ton of timber on top of us here. Christ!' A huge severed branch collapsed further.

'Still okay?' Pip asked tremulously.

'Stop asking and get going!' he shouted.

Ronnie's voice was more soothing. 'You need to get someone with a tractor, Pip. And the vet. Hurry!'

She must have nerves of steel, thought Pip, admiringly. 'Um, do either of you have a phone I can borrow?'

'If we did, don't you think we'd be using them?' growled Blair.

'Right-oh,' she called, turning to race for the gate and finding her pixie boots wedged so deep in the mud they might have been set in concrete. Her legs just twisted and she keeled over into the grass. 'Ooof.'

As she struggled up again, losing one boot, she felt a stabbing pain in her ankle. 'Ow! Ow, ow!'

Behind her, the urgent voices continued as Ronnie and Blair helped the injured foal.

'We have to tourniquet it!' he was saying. 'He's losing a lot of blood.'

'No – just keep pressure on it. Keep your hand right there. Whoa, ssh, it's okay, little one. Press down harder.'

'Christ, you're hurt too, Ron.'

'I'm fine. Let's focus on this chap.'

'You're bloody bleeding everywhere! It's *your* blood, poor darling.'

'Not all of it. I'll keep my hand on this, you keep yours on that.'

'That's what you said the first time we went to bed.'

Pip cocked her head, listening with interest as she groped around trying to locate her lost boot.

'Hey, gorgeous. It's okay. It's all going to be all right.' Blair's rasping voice softened, so intimate and so loving. Pip felt hopelessly moved. She could imagine him holding Ronnie as she wept silently into his wide, manly, waxed-cotton chest. He really loves her.

'You heard him,' that husky purr told the foal, shattering her illusion, 'it's all going to be all right.'

The foal let out a shrill whinny.

'Ssh, whoa, it's okay, I know it hurts.' Ronnie's reassurance soothed

Pip too as she felt her ankle. It did hurt and she was sure it was swelling. Cautiously, she made it up onto her knees. A massive fork of lighting stabbed down over Compton Magna village, leaving a red streak on Pip's field of vision. Great. Now she was blinded too. More thunderclaps made her flatten herself on the ground, briefly adding deafness. She must overcome adversity and get help. She closed her eyes, psyching herself up for the pain.

The conversation behind her moved on through the thunder, their voices cracking with emotion and volatility, star-crossed lovers *in extremis*.

'Are you asking that because you think I'm about to bleed to death, leaving my regrets on your conscience?' Ronnie's voice broke with a dry laugh.

'Might as well be frank before you croak.'

What had he asked her? Pip wondered, as she tried her weight on her foot and winced.

'In another lifetime, yes.'

Yes to *what*? Pip wanted to shout as she tried a few limping steps.

'Is that why you don't care if Verity rumbles us?'

'She won't, we both know that. Ssh, sweetheart, whoa. Keep your hand on the wound, Blair.'

'I told you she got your letter, Ron.'

Pip let out a small bleat, lost to the wind.

'I didn't write a letter.'

'I bloody saw it. You asked her to let me go.'

Pip limped closer again, falling over her lost boot. No, no, no! she wanted to shout. It wasn't Blair she'd asked for, it was the stallion. She should have guessed drunken Verity would get the wrong end of the stick.

'Why'd you do it?' Blair was demanding, sounding more sad than angry. 'You know what she's like. She didn't understand all of it, but she got the gist. She wouldn't stop beating herself up about it. It took me all my powers to talk her down, and by then she'd made her mind up to do something about it. She's quite adamant.'

Ronnie's husky voice was incredulous. 'I don't understand anything you're saying right now.'

Pip hopped around, pulling on her boot. She didn't want to stay to find out what terrible threat Blair's aged and alcoholic spurned wife had issued. It was bound to be bad. But her boot, sodden and muddy, refused to go on.

Blair's voice was sawn through with mistrust: 'I was going to storm round and call you out about it straight away, but I had to drive six horses up to Yorkshire and I needed to get my head round it. You've always known I won't ever leave her and I've always known you don't want me to, so why do this? Why now? Verity got that letter two weeks ago, and I know we've not been alone until today, but I've waited all fucking day for you to say to my face what that letter said to her, and you've said precisely nothing.'

Pip got the boot on at last, backing away.

'Is this why you've been so insufferable?' Ronnie was laughing in disbelief.

'Yeah. Because I figured it out today, when you told me you'd asked the Horsemaker to run the stud.'

Hang on. Pip stalled. What's the Horsemaker when it's at home?

'It's a bloody clever way to get what you want, I've got to hand you that.' *Now* he really sounded angry. The sort of muted, murderous, back-of-the-throat fury that usually signalled a silhouetted hand and dagger poised to plunge in a television whodunit.

Ronnie was still laughing incredulously. 'What *do* I want, Blair?'

'The stallion.' He said it very slowly. 'And guess what? You got him. Verity wants you to have the fucking horse back. That's the trade. She keeps me, you get your stallion back.'

There was a long pause.

Pip tilted her face up into the rain in gratitude. Result!

'Blair, I think we're losing the foal.'

In an inner pocket of Pip's borrowed coat, a phone rang with the 1812 Overture.

'Is somebody there?' yelled Blair. There was a huge crash as leaves and branches fell aside, a steel-hard shoulder slamming against the biggest one trapping him.

Pip hurried out of earshot, lifting the phone to her ear.

The voice at the other end was slurred: 'I am so going to fuck your brains out later, Kit Donne. This is sensational! Get your arse up here! And bring me food, for Chrissake. I feel kinda weird.'

★

Up on high pasture, Orla Gomez was embracing her search with gusto, loving the storm.

'C'mon, Leicester Square!' She laughed. 'What are we looking for again?'

Lester ignored her, marching on with stiff-hipped dignity. It was like searching with that blue fish in the film Pip was so fond of. Dory, that was it. She was plainly drunk and had no appreciation of the urgency of the situation. He was starting to suspect she might not even be a nun.

'Hey, do you have any candy?' she called.

He limped along the hedgerow looking for signs of the foal, his thickening breathing making it hard to concentrate. His inhaler, sucked frantically through *Poldark the Musical*, was empty.

'Some juice, maybe? A biscuit?'

'Now is not the moment for snacking,' he wheezed, his weak eyes following his torch along the hedge to the paddock rails, blinking in confusion as the hedge disappeared where it was supposed to carry on. There was something lying on the ground there.

'You are one tight-lipped little dude, aren't you? I could get quite seriously mad at you in a minute.'

He turned around, furious, and realised she was gone.

Then he looked down. She'd passed out on the grass.

'Get up!' he ordered.

She groaned.

'Get up! You're intoxicated.' His voice was little more than a gasp now, the shallow clag of his lungs stealing his breath.

He reached down to pat her face, finding it icy cold. Taking her wrists to pull her up, he felt her pulse racing. There was a bracelet on one wrist, the little hard disc of a medical emergency tag on it. He had one for asthma – Pip had insisted. He fumbled for his torch, his lungs barely able to draw a breath.

'Hi,' she slurred.

'Yes, hello.' He angled the torch, squinting. Damn. The writing was too small. 'Now wake up.'

'Hype.' She slurred again. 'Hypo.'

Squinting, Lester focused hard on the bracelet tag, the crossword clue half-filled now. 'Hypo' as in hypoglycaemia. It read *Diabetic*.

'Bother.' His chest tightened more.

He found her phone in her coat pocket and dialled 999. The emergency services were clearly overrun, but the operator who told him an ambulance was on its way was calm and helpful. 'Do you have any sugary drinks to hand?'

'I'm in the middle of a field, madam,' he wheezed, with the effort of being heard over the wind noise.

'Can you locate an insulin pen about her person?'

He felt in her coat again and found several old tissues and a set of keys on a Boyzone keyring. Pip's. The nun's habit had no pockets. 'No.' Throat blocked, he tried to cough, just making a rattling whistle.

'Are you all right, sir?'

'Spot of asthma,' he croaked.

'We'll get a team out to you as soon as possible, sir. Where exactly did you say your location was?'

'The highest... field on... Compton Magna... Stud. There's a... bridleway track... alongside.' It appeared to have a large new gateway hacked through its hedge, he wanted to add, but he felt too ill.

In the Jugged Hare, Carly fed crisps to the goose. She was seriously fed up with Ash and his gang. The lads had now drained every alcopop in the place and moved on to Drambuie and Coke. Taking the piss out of each other, trying to remember the order of the *Rock Anthems* playlist on its third loop and telling rude jokes the main thrust of conversation. They were all finding themselves hilarious.

'So, Ink, right, so, Ink,' Flynn was waving his vape stick around with a waft of blueberry fumes. 'This guy goes into a tattoo parlour, right, and he asks for a tattoo of a fifty-pound note on his dick, yeah, and...'

'Guns N' Roses, "Sweet Child o' Mine"!' Hardcase shouted, just before the intro struck up, then stood to take a bow.

She caught Ash's eye. He gave her the ghost of a wink.

His old crew weren't so different from soldiers, she realised. But it was a lousy date night, and while Ash might have stopped leaping up to take phone calls by the door every few minutes, she could see the huge difference in him from the old days of Fusilier Turner out on the lash with his mates from the base. The long, louche lounge lizard who would once have taken up half the sofa with his big shoulders and big smile sat forward, elbows on knees, feet bouncing. His hands needed to play with something all the time – a bar mat, a folded crisps packet, a coin, turning and flipping and spinning. He couldn't relax, and he was talking a lot less than he used to, the drink hardly touching him.

He has no more fun when he's out than he does at home, Carly thought sadly.

The others were laughing raucously at Flynn's punchline. Then they were off on a free-for-all of best lines from movies.

Carly bit her lower lip and tried not to think about Pricey. It was still hammering down outside, lightning strobing the windows. She hoped she wasn't terrified as the storm rampaged round her strange new home.

She glared at Ash, hurt that he'd found a solution he must know she'd dislike. He winked. Then the loudest thunder of the storm so far made him flinch, silver eyes bleached with pain.

It reminds him of tank fire.

Catching her watching him, he flashed the armoured smile. '"Ye'd best start believin' in ghost stories, Ms Turner."' He gave his best Captain Barbossa caw. '"Yer in one."'

Behind them, the door to pub swung open, carried by the wind to bang hard against the wall, making everyone turn. Lightning lit the windows. It was the perfect dark-and-stormy-night moment.

A bedraggled stranger marched in. He was wearing no coat, his sweater soaked through, a black hat making him look like he was from a time gone by. 'There's been an accident! Tree struck by lightning! Two people trapped! A horse too, I think.'

At the bar, wiry-haired vet Gill Walcote spun around on her barstool, complimentary glass of Taboo in hand. 'Whereabouts?'

'Field below the standing stones.'

That was Spirit's field. Carly was on her feet. Ash and his cronies looked up at her in surprise. 'We've got to help!' she said.

Ash rolled his eyes. 'We'll just get pissing soaked, Carl.'

She gaped at him in shock. 'You're trained for stuff like this, Ash.'

'Not any more.' His knees bounced up and down, fingers moving a fifty-pence piece around. 'They won't want Turners.'

'"The Boys are Back in Town"!' Hardcase announced, taking another bow as the chords were struck.

'Well, I'm going!' Grabbing her coat, Carly ran across the room, her hands ablaze.

'Sssh, little one. Whoa. It's all going to be all right.' Ronnie kept pressure on the foal's wound, although he'd stopped whinnying and protesting or trying to get up, stopped lifting his head too now. Bending low over him, she could just make out his breathing through the noise of the storm, an ominous gurgle to it. His blood was still trying to pump past her fingers as she held in place the makeshift pad she'd fashioned with her detachable coat hood. She wasn't letting go for a moment.

She swapped hands holding the pressure pad and shook her numb right arm. The space they were confined in was claustrophobically small. If she tried to move more than a few inches, the sharp broken ends of branches caught her, stabbing at her. She could see almost nothing. 'Sssh, little one. Whoa. It's all going to be all right.'

Like a solitary Samson, Blair was trying to pull away the wood and foliage to get to her. It was a hopeless task without machinery, his roars of frustration louder than the thunder, refusing to accept the old cedar had him beat , the amputated branches wide as barrels and now tangled like a vast game of Pick Up Sticks.

'Fucking bastard tree!'

He was angriest with Ronnie, of course, but they would say no more on it. The love affair was over. They both knew it. 'Sssh, little one. You'll be all right.'

Dripping water everywhere, Kit abandoned Pip's car at the pub and shared the cab of a Land Rover back to Sixty Acres, driven at breakneck speed by a rough-hewn, red-faced oil drum of a man in moleskins.

'Know you!' He beamed, as they set off, rain lashing the windscreen. 'Actor fellow from the Old Almshouses, am I right?'

Kit didn't bother correcting him, but the wiry-haired female vet crammed between them could mainstream pedantry even in any crisis. 'Kit's a theatre director, Barry. That's like being a huntsman as opposed to a hound.' She turned to Kit. 'It's Gill, by the way. I know you've forgotten again.' He had.

'Emergency services and the Austens are on their way,' Barry reassured them, as though the two were synonymous. 'Got a tractor and chainsaws coming too. Your hubby's fetching the horse ambulance – am I right, Gill? All we need's manpower. Might have guessed that rowdy Turner lot drinking in the Jug wouldn't put their hands up. Hardly got enough in here to lift a twig.' He peered in his mirror at the back of the Land Rover where several villagers and a goose were sliding around on bench seats. 'Bay will rally his team, I've no doubt.'

Kit peered out as the horizon lit up again, concerned about Orla, cursing himself for being such a coward in storms, and for lending Pip his coat with his phone still in it.

'Do you know who it is?' Gill was demanding, as they racketed past the Green.

'Who what is?'

'The two people you saw by the tree in Sixty Acres?'

'Ronnie Percy, I think.' Whenever he saw that woman, bad things happened. 'And the Australian man she's friends with.'

'Good God.'

Act of God, more like, thought Kit, glaring through the windscreen.

They swung into the field.

'Fucking hell!' Barry's mouth dropped open.

It certainly looked biblical. The long fissure through the trunk of the cedar tree glowed with burning embers, damp smoke billowing, a lone figure pulling branches away from the collapsed canopy that towered over him. As they drew closer, Kit recognised the Australian, coat shredded, face and hands covered with scratches.

'Thank Christ!' His voice was hoarse. 'There's a woman and a foal under this, both injured. Be bloody careful. I got out, but it's not stable. Has someone called an ambulance and a vet?'

'*I'm* a vet.' Gill strode forwards. 'Can I get close enough to them to check him over?'

'Not until we move a load of this timber.'

'Then we must get as much of the fallen tree away as we can. Ronnie, it's Gill! How's he doing?' she shouted in.

'Hanging on in there. I can't stop the bleeding, though. And he's weak.'

'We can't wait for the fire brigade!' Barry took charge, an eager Gloucestershire Falstaff in his prime, bursting out of his Tattersall checks. 'They'll be overrun tonight. Everybody grab a branch!'

Carly joined in the effort to try to move the smaller branches away while they were waiting for the chainsaws. Her hands were soon splintered, the nails Janine had redone that afternoon snapping off, her palms hotter and hotter. She could hear the red-faced man in moleskins shouting orders, but the voice that stayed with her was Australian. She could hear him talking to the foal that was trapped in there.

'You'll be fine, little fella, we're coming to get you. Hang on in there. You have Badminton to get round in a decade's time.' He was clearing debris faster than all the other men.

Another Land Rover roared up, the bearded vet at the wheel, a horse trailer with a green cross on it hitched behind it. It was followed by more pickups loaded with chainsaws and a tractor, two lads from Manor Farm, a smattering of villagers with hand saws. A man who announced himself as the chairman of the parish council in a brief speech nobody listened to was marching around with a clipboard and a waterproof pen drawing up a plan of action. Soon they were all sawing, felling, heaving and hauling.

But it was torturously slow work. The chainsaw men, struggling in the rain, kept breaking off to cool chains, fiddle with bolts and talk timber, amazed the lightning-struck trunk was still burning.

'Cedar's a high-resin tree, you see. Like your pines. Good for kindling. Very hot burning, but smokes and spits a lot.'

'Like a Turner,' cackled one of the others.

Carly lowered her brows, hearing Ash's parting comment: *They won't want Turners.* It's no wonder they got bad PR. She was mad at him for refusing to help. She understood he had big problems, but that wasn't the man she knew.

Get some muscle over here pronto or you won't see my vajayjay between now and Christmas, she texted him furiously, knuckle-flicking between words to try to shake off the buzzing heat.

'Bloody cheek, I know, but could I borrow your phone?'

She looked up to find the dark-and-stormy-night stranger looking deathly pale beneath his hat, his wool sweater stretched by the rain, the V plunging too low on a chest dusted with hairs.

'Just one sec.' *PS Bring a spare coat. You have 5 minutes.* 'There you go.'

'Thanks.'

She went back to work, dragging out great leafy cedar fronds, glancing over her shoulder in delight when she heard a big engine driving up like a bat out of hell, but it was only Bay Austen in his Land Rover, dressed for dinner. He leaped out and surveyed the scene, shrugging a big coat on over his suit to talk to Moleskin Man.

Kit was grateful the storm had moved far off enough to stop him dropping to the ground with every lightning flash. Sheltering behind Barry's Land Rover, he dialled his own number, trying to hear above the buffeting wind and Bay's loud bonhomie nearby.

'My lads working hard, I hope, Barry? Wish I could stay. Genuinely. Got the in-laws over from Holland and we're off to the RSC to see a Korean version of *Hamlet*. I'd hoped they'd say it was cancelled, thanks to this weather, but you know fucking thespians. The show must go on, eh, Uncle Kit? Our *Tempest* in the tithe barn on a night like this was hilarious, wasn't it? Still scared of storms, I see.'

Kit did him an on-the-phone gesture. But when calling his own number brought no joy, he was forced to catch Bay as he was getting back into his own car. 'Do you have Pip Edwards's number?'

Bay's eyebrows curled contemptuously. 'Hardly.'

'Do you know who might?'

He sucked his lower lip, a roguish smile breaking. 'Actually, I do. Hang on.' He pulled out his phone and sent a lightning text.

A lightning one came back. 'There you go.' He held it up for Kit to copy.

'Thank you, and thank...' he read the name off Bay's screen '... P kiss kiss, from me too.'

'With pleasure. Been looking for an excuse to do just that. You need a coat.' He took off his huge one, threw it into the back of his car and drove off with a cheery wave.

Kit retreated to Barry's Land Rover again, sitting inside it this time to call Pip, but there was no answer. He tried his own number again.

There was a tap on the window. It was the broken-nosed Australian, carrying a big roll of rope gathered from a nearby trailer.

'Hey, mate, it might have escaped your notice, but we need all hands on deck out here. Can the Snapchatting wait, maybe? There's a foal bleeding, and I'm not sure Ronnie's too clever either.'

'I won't dispute that,' he muttered.

The dark eyes flashed. 'You're the dill who abandoned his car, arncha?'

'One and the same.' He flashed a humourless smile, the macho posturing irritating him.

'Well, you can make up for that now, can't you, mate? Get those soft London hands dirty.'

Kit looked at him levelly, not sure why they disliked one another so instinctively.

Blue lights spilled across the field and both men turned to watch them racing along the Manor Farm drive, having cut through from the top lane, strobing in and out of the trees.

'About bloody time!' Blair barked.

But when they bounced away behind the hedge line and disappeared from sight, they didn't reappear again, clearly not intended for them.

'I think it was an ambulance,' Kit said.

'Might need one of those yourself if you don't lend a hand, mate. C'mon, have a fucking heart. We're busting our balls out here.'

Nodding a truce, Kit climbed out. 'There's someone else missing. The woman who was here when the lightning struck, Pip Edwards.'

'She went to get help.'

'Well, she didn't find it.'

'Shit.' He rubbed his face with battered hands, and strode back towards the rescue.

'My girlfriend's unaccounted for too,' Kit kept pace, dialling his own number again, 'along with the old guy from the stud.'

'That's all we fucking need,' the Aussie gave a hollow laugh, 'that and an alien invasion.'

They both swung round as they heard a buzzing, like an approaching hornet swarm, an arc of lights appearing on the horizon.

34

'Keep him chipper, Ronnie. I think the cavalry's arrived!' Grey hair covered with sawdust, Gill dashed out from the gap being cut through the cedar debris just in time to see the Turner family arriving over the rise of the hill, a rogue army in convoy. Ancient Discoverys, pickups and Isuzus with raised suspensions and roll-bar frames, rows of halogen lamps glaring above the windscreens and on the bull bars, dog guards and gun racks in the back, rifle mounts on the roofs.

The big off-roaders parked in a line, lamps like stadium lights. A man's silhouette appeared through them, long-legged and Adonis-chested, a coat over one shoulder, a soldier's upright stride. Spotting Petra's pretty blonde cleaner standing nearby, arms folded and smiling, Gill hurried across to her. 'How did you get him to change his mind?'

'The usual.' She shrugged. 'Sex ban.'

'Works the opposite way for me.' Gill sighed. 'No time to lose, let's get them to work.'

'You want some help?' Ash gave Carly an ungracious scowl, handing the coat across. It was one of Flynn's leather rocker jackets.

'Do what she tells you.' She pointed at Gill, taking the jacket to go and find the man with her phone.

'Now there's an offer I can't refuse.' Gill beamed at him. 'How many of you are there?'

There were tens of them, a positive cornucopia of long hair, olive skin, body art and beer belly – Ash was definitely blessed with the best of the family's genes – and while putting them to work was like herding cats, they could certainly graft once they got going.

Having tasked them all with clearing the debris, Gill hurried through the work-team to check on the foal. 'How's he bearing up?'

'Not great.'

'We'll have to get an IV bag in there somehow.' She called the chainsaw team forwards. 'I just need to be able to crawl in to get a catheter into him.'

They cleared a mouse hole of a gap for her to wriggle through. 'Can't make it any bigger.'

'I'll never fit through that.' Thinking fast, she went in search of Carly Turner. 'How do you feel about small spaces and big needles?'

Carly didn't need asking twice.

Ronnie had cramp almost everywhere it was possible to have cramp, and her right arm was now so numb she couldn't use it to hold the pressure pad in place. Her left arm had to twist like a contortionist's in the confined space to keep it there. The space filled up even more as a torch made its way through the maze of branches still caging them in, a soft Wiltshire accent saying, 'I'm Carly, budge up.'

For the first time in an hour the foal lifted his head and let out a shrill whinny.

'Hello, Spirit.'

Ronnie watched as she reached out to touch him, ringed fingers threading through the blood-matted gold coat. The tail twitched, the foal's head settling back with an audible sigh of relief. 'Spirit?'

'The Disney horse. It's just a nickname. I know he's got a fancy one.'

'I like it.'

'All okay there?' Another torch gleamed as Gill started issuing brusque instructions. 'Now, Ronnie, Carly isn't a qualified veterinary nurse, so I need to know if you're happy to let her attach the fluid drip under instruction.'

'I've seen almost every episode of *The Supervet*,' Carly reassured her kindly, still stroking the foal. He lifted his head again, this time turning it to look at her, bobbing his pink nose.

Ronnie stared in amazement. Minutes ago she'd thought they were about to lose him. 'You do what you have to,' she said, feeling dizzy now.

'Just don't tell Paul,' Gill hissed. 'Stickler for rules. I've sent him to look for Pip Edwards with your – with Blair Robertson, Ronnie. His attitude was aggravating some of the Turners a bit.'

'He can be rather abrasive.' She felt a deep stab of regret that they couldn't have been abrasive together a bit longer, but his rant about the letter had been like Othello raving about the handkerchief.

'Right, Carly, first rule of veterinary practice is what?'

'Sterilisation?' she suggested.

'That'll do.'

Torch between her teeth, carefully doing as she was told, Carly sterilised and swabbed, clipped, then took out a very large needle, which she stared at nervously.

'Now, the jugular's a socking great vein in the groove of the neck,' Gill shouted down the tunnel. 'You need to aim for cranial third and jab it in.'

'You what?'

'We don't jab, obvs. Turn of phrase. Slide it in. That's the easy bit. The tough bit's keeping it in and attaching the rest of the gubbins. We'll get to that in a bit.'

'What's the cranial third?'

'You know – the *cranial third*.'

The foal's head lifted again, white face shooting up this time, looking round in alarm, his wall eye suspicious. He nickered. Carly rubbed his face and he nudged her hand, almost making her drop the needle. He nudged again and she dropped the torch from between her teeth.

'He wants a treat.' Carly's voice was shaking as much as the needle.

'I think,' Ronnie said gently, 'that we'd all be happier in here if we forget the drip for a bit and you just stay here with him until these big branches are cleared, don't you?'

'I'd like that,' Carly said, in a small voice.

'Gill, we're going to hold off a bit!' Ronnie called out. 'He seems to have rallied.'

Ronnie would have liked to talk to Carly, and tell her about somebody else she knew who had the same remarkable touch with horses, an almost magical way of reassuring them and helping heal. She wanted to ask if her hands got hot like his did, and if she could sense it for hours, sometimes days at a time beforehand. But the chainsaws started up again too loudly for conversation, and she was feeling stupidly tired. Carly would get to meet the Horsemaker in person before long. 'Spirit' would too. Letting Carly take over the pressure pad, she leaned back and closed her eyes.

'Ohbuggetybuggetybugger.' Pip chewed her knuckle as she perched on a pile of old pallets, wondering what to do. Her house keys were in her car and she wasn't sure where that was. She could go to the stud, but she needed to think up her alibi first. It didn't really cut the mustard to say she'd been on her way to the Austens' farm when her boot had come off again, and her ankle really hurt, and she'd heard rescuers arriving anyway so she'd decided to shelter in the old barn at the end of the field.

Pip had watched events unfold from her vantage-point, anxious and conflicted. She knew she should have gone back to help long ago, but she'd always had a phobia of blood, and it had sounded like there was a lot of it.

To keep herself distracted, she'd found Kit Donne's mobile phone an object of profound fascination, its security swipe code an easy-to-crack H. His contacts list read like the credits of a BBC costume drama. His messages were hilarious – who knew he was so dry-humoured? – the ones to his children especially, a loving weekly banter that all involved seemed to relish. The ones from Orla Gomez made even more riveting reading. Pip thought wistfully of tattooed JD and her broken phone.

Kit was also very popular. The phone had rung so many times, she'd turned it to silent, especially when she'd heard voices shouting for her, although they'd gone away again now.

If they came back, she had a plan. If they didn't, she needed one too. But for now, Pip navigated her way to the app store to download Tinder on Kit's phone so she could sign in and say hello to JD.

At last the biggest cedar branch was cut down enough for a small army of tattooed Turners to lift it away, the colt finally freed, his golden coat drenched in red. He struggled straight to his feet, trembling and weak but determined to show his mettle.

Ronnie did likewise, enormously relieved to be liberated and amazed to see the large army of helpers who had achieved it. The field was lit up like a football pitch by a big row of battered four-by-fours with off-road lights, the storm loitering on the far horizon.

'Deep spike wound but pretty clean entry.' Gill examined the huge gash in the colt's shoulder, having put the jugular catheter in with deft professionalism. 'Nicked a big vein, which is why he bled so much. Good job it wasn't arterial or we'd have lost him ages ago. We'll get it cleaned up at the clinic, then see how best to go about patching him up. I'll call you from there, or you're welcome to come along, Ronnie. Ronnie?'

'Oh, yes, absolutely. Thank you.' She was finding it hard to focus. She turned to Carly. 'And thank you too. You have a gift.'

'He really going to be all right?'

Before either woman could answer, a voice shouted from the rank of off-roaders, 'Carl! Come here, bae.'

'I'd better go.' She flashed a quick smile and stooped to say goodbye to Spirit.

He whinnied furiously when she walked away, struggling to follow her.

'Wait there a minute!' she called over her shoulder, and sprinted off, returning as he was being half loaded, half lifted into the trailer, Gill's bearded husband holding a fist of Gamgee to staunch fresh bleeding.

'Can I travel with him?' she asked Gill. 'I can hold that for you, if you like.'

'That would be super.'

'Health and Safety,' Paul warned his wife. 'Best not.'

'Fuck that.' Carly was already up the ramp and taking over the task. 'I'll sign a disclaimer.'

'You heard her.' Gill waved him away, throwing up the ramp a moment before her husband stepped off it and propelling him into the darkness. 'Do you want to come, Ronnie?'

'No – you go on. I've got to get up to the stud. Call me as soon as you have an update. I must thank Pip for raising the alarm.'

She looked round again, the light disappearing as, one by one, the Turner vehicles roared off.

'It wasn't Pip.' Gill marched round to the passenger door while Paul started the engine. 'It was Kit Donne, bursting into the pub wet through. Quite the hero, and so lovely to have him back. Nobody knows where Pip got to – Blair's still looking, I think. I'll call.'

Turning away, Ronnie saw Kit, caught in the headlights of one of the turning cars. He was talking to a red-faced Barry Dawkins, and wearing a black flat cap and an absurd leather jacket. She'd never understood why arty, middle-aged men dressed twenty years younger than they were. Remembering how disagreeable he'd been in the pub car park, she braced herself, shaking her head sharply to stop it feeling so spaced, and headed over.

JD had deleted his Tinder account. Pip tried to convince herself this was a good thing but she found it unsettling. And she could hear her name being shouted again, much closer this time.

'Pip! Pip Edwards! Pip, can you hear me?'

She put her plan into action, hurrying out of the barn and back over the fence to the muddy path beside Lord's Brook, like an Olympic steeplechaser, then lying down and pulling off her still-caked boot. 'Here!' she croaked, in a whisper. 'Over here!' To add authenticity, she staged a dead faint.

Heavy footfalls, the sweep of a stockman's coat, the rattle of park railing as it was climbed.

'Pip!'

She recognised Blair Robertson's Australian bass boom with an inner smile. Now he *was* hero material.

'Pip! Where the fuck is she?'

He was almost on top of her. Was he *blind*? She opened one eye.

His silhouette passed directly in front of her and twisted back menacingly. A lighter sparked into a flame just inches away, cigarette end flaring. Two white-rimmed eyes glowed briefly, making Pip squeak. The eyes widened, the flame snapping out.

'Jeez! Didn't see you down there!' He crouched by her head. 'What happened? What hurts?'

'My ankle. I was running to Manor Farm to get help and—'

In her pocket, the 1812 Overture rang out.

She hoped he didn't recognise it as the same ringtone he'd heard by the tree long after she was supposed to have raised the alarm.

But he was feeling in her pockets. 'Let's use this phone, shall we? They're all worried sick about you back there. I think we might need an ambulance here.'

'No, it's fine!' She sat up quickly. 'I can probably—'

Too late. He'd got the phone in his hand. She snatched it from him. 'That's Kit's. I'd no idea it was there, but I'd best take this.'

'Sure.' Blair straightened up.

'Is that Mr Donne?' came a laboured wheeze.

'Lester, it's me, Pip.'

The wheezing sounded awful. 'Is he there?'

'Oh, Lester, there's been a lightning strike and Mr Donne lent me his coat and I went to get help and fell and hurt myself –' she glanced up at Blair '– *badly* and I have no idea where he is. Are you at the stud?'

'I'm in the Royal Infirmary,' he was coughing and spluttering, 'with Miss Gomez. You have to tell Mr Donne to—'

A voice interrupted bossily in the background, telling him to switch off his phone and put his oxygen mask back on.

'Oh, my God, Lester!' Pip bleated. 'Are you okay? I knew we should have taken a spare inhaler today.'

'Lot of fuss over nothing. You have to tell... Mr Donne to come. And there's... nobody at the stud so I... need you to—' With a cheep, the battery died.

Pip pressed its cool screen to her hot cheek. This was her call to arms, her invitation to re-enter the big village drama with no harm done.

She looked up to see Blair's hatted, long-coated silhouette towering over her, like Clint Eastwood in *Pale Rider*.

'Think you can walk?' Was it her imagination or did the deep voice sound just slightly sarcastic and possibly angry?

'With a lot of help, perhaps.' She held up her hand. 'I might need lifting over the fence.'

★

The decimated tree was lit by only a few dim Land Rover headlamps now, rain flecking in the beams, high wind still making its fallen branches creak and groan.

Kit zipped up his borrowed jacket with effort. It was at least a size too small and had a skull painted on the back, but he was immensely grateful for its protection. It was the best of gifts. Orla had gone to incredible lengths to create a crazy birthday round trip for him, only to prove that she barely knew him at all; it had been her fantasy, not his. This young woman, whose name he didn't know, had seen he had no coat and got him one. True generosity needed no luxury price tag or special date.

He'd decided his best course of action was to collect Pip's car, which had weekend bags in the boot, and return it to the stud in the hope that both women and the old retainer were there. He was waiting on a lift from Barry, who had marched off to talk to his chainsaw gang.

Spotting Ronnie Percy making across the field, he retreated behind Barry's Land Rover. But she called his name, that three-counties voice lacking its previous gusto. She was crossing in front of the headlights, and when Kit stepped out, the first thing he noticed was that her hands were covered with blood.

'Oh, you're there.' She sounded oddly muted. 'I owe you a very big thank you.'

'You're bleeding.'

'*A little water clears us of this deed.*' She smiled, truck headlamps like stage footlights lighting her high cheekbones. 'It's the foal's, poor little chap. Would have lost him wasn't for you.' She was swaying now. 'That was terribly kind, given how rude I was last time we met, so thank you again.' She was deathly pale. There was a deep rip in the shoulder of her jacket, the lining exposed.

'I think you're hurt.'

'A bit of a nick from a falling horseshoe.'

'May I?' Kit reached out and lifted back her jacket. The deep red stain stretched from collarbone to hip. 'Christ! We need to get you to hospital. Get in the car.'

'Do you think that's wise after last time?' She laughed, turning away and crumpling.

Kit caught her, surprised by how slight she was and how cold she felt. 'Need you to take her to hospital!' he shouted to Barry.

Within seconds, the red-cheeked farm contractor was back with his Land Rover, pulling out a blanket to wrap her in before Kit lifted her inside. A goose hissed at him. Ronnie groggily complained that she was fine. The goose started pecking at her hair and she sat up, ghostly white now. 'This is ridiculous. Oh, Jesus.' Her head tipped forwards and she put her hands to her temples, looking as though she was about to faint again.

'You'll have to come along and travel with her in the front,' Barry told Kit.

'Can't we just chuck the goose out?'

'Sybil's a village institution.'

Kit eyed the goose, then looked at Ronnie, her face in the half-light startlingly like Hermia's. *You will love her.* 'Fine,' he muttered, picking her up again and hawking her round to the front. She was protesting loudly that somebody had to go to the stud to check the horses.

Growing frustrated by over-exaggerating her limp – it really didn't hurt that much, and she could see more cars leaving Sixty Acres all the time – Pip shook off Blair's helping arm and started to run, one-shoed to the lightning-struck cedar. As a set of Land Rover tail-lights trailed away, she panted up to the remaining village rescuers and waved Kit's phone. 'Where's Mr Donne? Lester's had an asthma attack! Orla Gomez has taken him to hospital and needs a – lift back.' That sounded far too anti-climactic. 'Greta the Vampire, Hollywood, drugs, sugar daddies. *That* Orla Gomez. She was here in the village earlier.'

'Hardly the moment to share celebrity news, Miss Edwards,' snapped the chairman of the parish council. 'We've had an incident.'

'I know! I was first on the scene.' Pip adopted a martyr's pose, eyes wide. 'I went to get help, but I had a fall. I can hardly walk.'

Blair cleared his throat beside her.

'It's the adrenalin keeping me going,' she went on, rolling her eyes at him, 'like horses that finish races with broken legs.'

'Horses don't finish races with broken legs,' he muttered.

Pip wished he'd shut up with the Russell Crowe sarcasm. 'Anyway, *Orla Gomez*, the *Hollywood A-lister*, is here for the weekend with Kit Donne. I chauffeured them from the station through treacherous conditions earlier.'

'We see her!' cried one of Bay's farmhands. 'Greta Vampire dressed as nun. Sexy lady.'

'Would it be something the *Fosse Gazette* might be interested in?' asked the chairman.

'I think she and Kit are trying to keep the relationship a secret. I look after his house here. And drive for him.' She dropped her voice. 'He's banned, you know. Now I need to take him to the Royal Infirmary. Where is he?'

'Already on his way.' One of the locals was hauling a chainsaw up into his tractor cab. 'He went with Ronnie.'

Blair turned to him, craggy face tense. 'Ronnie's been taken to hospital?'

'She got hurt in the tree fall. Barry's driving them.'

'Shit!' Blair hissed. 'I should go there.'

'She was pretty stressed out that nobody's up at the stud. Might be better to wait there.'

'What did he do with my car?' Pip wailed. 'My handbag's in there with my house keys and everything. Not to mention the signed *Poldark the Musical* programme.'

A round of shrugs greeted her.

Pip felt tears welling.

'I'm going up to the stud to check on the horses,' croaked a deep, kind voice. 'Sounds like you need a cuppa.'

That deep Aussie voice sold a mug of tea like a massage, chocolate binge, hot bath and Top Ten Heart-warming Neighbours Moments rolled into one.

'You're right,' Pip conceded nobly. 'Somebody needs to look after the place.' The Portmeirion mugs were already laid out by the biscuit tin. And she knew where the tack-room key was hidden.

35

The wind was dropping at last, but rain had started beating down again, soaking Pip afresh as she trundled a wheelbarrow round the stud yards, head torch bobbing. She hadn't anticipated having to earn her 'cuppa' by checking the horses with Blair, haying and watering. He was a much harder taskmaster than Lester, telling her off for half-filling water buckets and leaving poo in stables.

'I thought you worked here?' He clambered up into his horsebox cab to fetch his phone afterwards.

'The stable stuff's voluntary. Lester's too old to do it all on his own. I'm the housekeeper, not the horsekeeper.'

'As long as you're not the Horsemaker, I'm happy,' he said cryptically, jumping down and pressing a fast dial. Above his head, Elgar's Cello Concerto rang out loudly from a phone on the dash. 'Which hospital are they going to?'

'Royal Infirmary.'

'Where's that?'

'Not sure. Birmingham, maybe?'

He lit a cigarette, sheltering beneath the first arch to smoke it. Stubbs yapped inside Lester's cottage. Dogs barked in the horsebox.

'I'll let them out in a minute and make that cuppa,' he muttered, dark eyes hollow as though reliving a traumatic memory, which Pip supposed he was. She remembered the conversation she'd heard between him and Ronnie, and felt an uncomfortable pinch in her belly as she thought about the letter she'd written, which Verity had drunkenly misunderstood.

'I'll make the tea!' Pip offered, switching her head torch back on. 'I baked ginger biscuits for you both.'

She felt around the sill beneath the ivy for the key to the tack room, but it wasn't there. The door was locked. She felt again, her fingers closing over it at the opposite end to where Lester normally kept it. That was odd. He was always very pedantic about its location, tucking it into a fissure in the wood so an opportunist running a hand across the top wouldn't find it. Who had she been talking to about hiding keys recently? Ah, yes, JD. His boss kept the site key in a storm drain. Might be a bit of a problem tonight, Pip thought as she let herself in.

The first thing she noticed missing was the biscuits. Her favourite Wrendale tin, left with a pair of heavy stirrups on top to stop mice investigating, was gone.

Then she noticed other gaps. The best saddles, kept under cloth covers on the long wooden tree in the centre of the room. The showing bridles, Lester's polished pride and joy.

Despite adding everything up faster than a maths prodigy, Pop was in denial about the answer.

This couldn't have been JD, could it? He called her 'babe' and knew her favourite cake recipes. He got a hard-on every time she messaged him – she had the photographic evidence to prove it. And she'd told him all about her job, told him about the beautiful horses she rode and the quad bike she drove and all the expensive tack she had to clean, how fond she was of the grumpy old stallion man who lived on site. JD had known she was taking Lester to Oxford today.

Had he targeted her from the start? She put her hand to her mouth to stifle a sob.

A step behind her made her scream.

'You all right?' It was Blair.

'We've been burgled.'

'Are you sure?'

'Yes! They've taken my biscuits! And some saddles and stuff.'

'Bastards.' He put a reassuring hand on her back. 'Best not go in in case there's fingerprints.'

'I think I know who did it,' she said, in a trembling voice.

'Okay. Let's have that cuppa in the horsebox and we can call the police.'

Hands shaking, Pip locked the door again and put the key back, the light from her head torch darting everywhere because she was nervously convinced that armed burglars were lurking in the hay barn, JD the tattooed master criminal ready to take her down if she named him.

'I bet that's how come the colt got loose.' Blair was striding away across the yard, coat tails flapping. 'Classic distraction tactic – let out a load of horses to cover your tracks. They'd probably only just left when we got here.'

There were piles of what looked like seaweed dotted around in one corner of the yard, Pip noticed. Hurrying to look, she found two double bridles and a martingale.

'They dropped some of it!'

He turned, his torch moving from focusing on her to fix on something behind her head. 'I think they left more than that.'

Another bridle was hanging over the door of an empty stable. Inside it, like a giant leather octopus with girth straps and reins for tentacles, was all the missing tack.

'Maybe they had a change of heart,' Pip suggested hopefully. 'Do we still have to call the police?'

'Up to you. You said you think you know who did it?'

'Local ne'er-do-well,' she said quickly. 'Sad story. Best I deal with it. If we put it all back, will you promise not to say anything to Ronnie?'

'I think not talking to Ronnie is supposed to be where I'm at right now. Let's put all this kit back, then have that drink.'

The horsebox living area was a warm, dry haven, lights glowing thanks to an onboard generator. While the kettle boiled, they peeled off wet outer layers to reveal wet inner layers that clung clammy as clay.

Blair was doing his moody tortured look again, Pip noticed. Then he peeled off his wet polo-shirt and all she noticed was the leanest, sexiest six-pack she'd ever seen in the flesh. Possibly the only six-pack she'd ever seen in the flesh, come to think of it. A moment later it had vanished inside another polo-shirt.

Blair let Ronnie's little dogs back in, clambering out to lift the old one, which couldn't make it up the fold-down horsebox steps.

'What did you mean about you and Ronnie not talking?' she asked, hoping the you-keep-the-horse-I-keep-the-man ultimatum Verity was offering didn't have and-you-can-never-see-each-other-again attached.

'Let's put it this way,' he said drily. 'Someone else will be riding her horses next season.'

'No! Why?'

'We fell out.'

'Can't you patch it up?'

'No.' His craggy face really looked terribly sad.

Pip chewed her thumbnail. He's thinking about Ronnie like I'm thinking about JD, she empathised.

Lightning flashed outside.

'My wife hates storms. I hope to God she's got someone with her...'

Carly paced the familiar veterinary reception, this time after hours. The television feed and coffee machine were switched off, the lights low. Nobody was manning the desk.

Spirit was in surgery, having his severed vein stitched up and the wound closed. Gill had offered Carly the chance to scrub up and go in to watch before her husband had vetoed the idea for contravening some veterinary oath or insurance clause. Carly had changed her mind about who was the nicer vet.

But it was Paul Wish who came through the door to talk to her, bearded face wreathed in smiles. The foal was back up and doing well, he told her. 'They heal quick at that age. He's a tough little fella, I'll hand him that. Gill's just settling him down.'

'Can I see him?'

He looked doubtful.

'Tell him she can come and see him!' shouted a voice.

The foal was in a box twelve tog deep with shavings. As soon as Carly went in, he let out his demanding belly whinny and nudged her into the corner demanding a withers scratch, then flumped down at her feet, chin hard on her instep. Carly dropped down beside him, pressing her face against his.

Gill's face appeared over the door. 'Super, isn't he? Now let us run you home.'

'Can I have just a bit longer?'

'Now why, when you have such a handsome hero for a husband, are you hanging round here?'

Because he'll be with his mates until three in the morning, then come and wake me up for sex. After that, if we're lucky, he'll sleep okay, and if we're not, he'll wake himself up screaming. Because when I asked him to be a hero tonight, and the alpha the Turners all want him to be, he hated me for it. Because when I go home, I'll have to face Janine sitting on my sofa in my house, like she owns it, and she'll want to hear all about what's happened and how Ash was a hero, and it's what she wants to hear but it's not how it was. Not really.

And because I know Pricey is now two streets away from where I live, chained to a kennel in a run that I can't get anywhere near, and the guy who now owns her will be out lamping Manor Farm's deer as soon as this storm's passed. And before long, Pricey will be out with him too. And she'll hate that, just like Ash would hate being sent back to war. Because it did things to their heads. And that's why I made Ash do what he did tonight. I made him be a hero to punish him.

She looked at Spirit. He'd gone to sleep with his face pressed against her shoulder, long, fluffy-centred ears flopping, as trusting as a child. 'Because I love him,' she said simply.

'Don't let me die, Leicester Square! You won't let me die!'

Lester disliked high drama intensely unless it was in black-and-white starring Richard Burton and Anthony Quinn. Orla was gripping his hand so tightly that the end of his fingers had turned purple.

He lifted his oxygen mask. 'You're not going to die, Miss Gomez. They say your blood sugars have stabilised.'

'That's not what I'm talking about. Aren't your NHS hospitals supposed to be riddled with norovirus and legionnaires' disease and flesh-eating bacteria? I can't stay here.'

'They're waiting to see if the registrar wants you kept in overnight.' Which, from the general air of excitement that had surrounded them since their arrival, he strongly suspected they might. This girl's celebrity rather than her medical status seemed of great interest to certain members of staff, who had swept aside the curtain that evening. Selfies had already been taken, autographs given. Lester, by contrast, had been posted on a chair in a corridor with a leaky wheeled oxygen tank, until Orla had asked for him.

Now she was treating him like her PA. 'I'll have to go to a private clinic. You can arrange that, can't you? I'll need some sleepwear and a few essential toiletries. My suitcase is still in – wherever.' She closed her eyes wearily. 'I feel so tired, so faint.'

Another emergency was being wheeled into the adjacent cubicle. The attending doctor was talking to a nurse, their quick-fire mono-tones indicating it was serious enough not to stop for a selfie. The patient had been assessed with radial artery laceration causing severe bleeding, she said. Fluids and blood were requested from the nurse, the consultant paged to determine whether it needed suturing or surgery.

Then Lester heard a familiar laugh and felt his own blood still.

'Oh, do please just stitch it. I've a yard full of horses to get back to.'

'We need to clean it up and see how damaged it all is in there first,' the female doctor told her. 'We've just pulled a very large nail out, remember.'

'We should have given Uncle Brooke a new one years ago.'

'Does this hurt?'

There was a sharp intake of breath, a catch of laughter. 'Imagine I'm sticking a needle in your eye.'

'Then I can no more stitch it than I would stitch up my own eye.'

The low chuckle reverberated, steel-edged with pain. 'You're the pro.'

Lester looked down at Orla. She'd drifted off to sleep, full-lipped mouth falling open to reveal teeth as white as fondant icing. Prising her fingers from his, he patted her hand and set it gently at her side. He then peeled off his oxygen mask, slipping from the cubicle and stealing hastily away, flicking his collar up like a spy as he passed wild-haired Kit Donne bellyaching at a reception nurse in flat northern vowels. 'I'd just like to know how long we might have to wait. Only there's somewhere else I really need to be. Hang on a minute. It's Lester isn't it?'

Lester grunted assent.

'Where's Orla?'

'Through those doors there, sir. I've just left her side and she's doing very well.'

'She's *here*?'

Lester nodded. 'If you'll excuse me.'

While Kit hurried towards the observation cubicles, Lester made his way to the pay-phone, where a host of taxi numbers were displayed on a board.

A hearty back-slap propelled him forwards. 'My very good man!'

It was the hunt's most loyal foot-follower, Barry. 'Can't abide hospitals. You here for Ronnie too?'

Lester cleared his throat. There was a lot to clear. 'Spot of... asthma.'

'Not sounding too good, I must say. Want a lift home later? I seem to be running a taxi service.'

'Need a lift home now, if you'd oblige. Horses to look after.'

'Say no more. She's got someone here, that's what counts. Bit of an oddball, that actor fellow. Seen how he's dressed? My Mo would call that flamboyant, which is a kindness, I reckon.'

Lightning flashed at the windows, like paparazzi at a celebrity's limousine. Pip found it secretly thrilling to be in the horsebox that must be the hub of the affair between Ronnie and Blair. It was unbearable to think of them never again sizzling away in the slide-out pod. It was patently obvious that the Aussie rider was too young to spend the rest of his days with a dipso wife twenty years his senior. Verity would probably peg out with cirrhosis of the liver soon enough, but meanwhile Blair's affair with Ronnie was obviously no threat to the marriage. It seemed ridiculous to Pip that her humble letter could bring an end to it all. The stud must come first, and the stallion had always been destined to save it, but Pip felt it was now her duty to save Blair and Ronnie too. There had been enough heartbreak today.

410

Blair set two mugs on the table and picked up his phone. 'I just need to make a quick call home, if that's okay.'

'Oh, yes, of course. Would you like me to...' She indicated the door. Rain was hammering on the roof, thunder rolling round.

'I'll just go to the other end. I won't be long.'

Pip picked up a copy of *Horse & Hound* and pretended to read it as he let himself into the horse area. He was as far away from her as he could get, his voice low, rain like static on the roof. Even so, if Pip stood up against the cut-through door and focused really hard, she could just make out his gravelly voice.

'Vee, it's Blair... Yes, Blair... How are you doing? Is anyone there with you?... Oh, that's good. She got my message then. I called her to say I'd be late because of the weather. Oh, Roo's there too?'

Pip's ears pricked up.

'Quite a party you've got going on,' Blair was saying, with a low laugh. 'Has it been bad there?... The storm, love. There's a big storm... Well, that's good. I'll be back as soon as I know the roads are clear... Yes, I know Roo... No, I'm not nearly home. I'm stuck here because of the storm. There's a storm, love... Yes, I know she's there.'

Pip's heart went out to him, imagining Verity three-quarters of the way down a gin bottle already, slurring and repeating herself.

'Let's not talk about the horse... I know you've got it written down in your book, but I don't want to talk about the horse. I'll get it all sorted, okay?... Good... Yes, I know Roo. She's there, is she?... That's good. Well, I'll call you when I'm on my way again... Okay. Love you too. Bye.'

Pip hurried back to her seat just as he emerged, his face forlorn for a moment before he summoned his craggy smile. 'Sorry about that.'

He sat down at the table with her. Ronnie's younger dog immediately jumped on his lap.

'How did you get on today?' Pip asked brightly, pointing to the body protector and number bib abandoned nearby.

'Not great. Should have withdrawn, really. The weather was always going to screw my chances.'

'Does your wife ever come along with you?'

His eyes were big and broody again. 'She's not been well.'

'Oh dear. I hope she gets better soon.' Which would take a long stint in rehab, she imagined.

'Yeah.' He stared into his tea mug.

Over-eager, Pip ran for the touchline with her big name drop. 'Prunella did mention something about it.'

'You know Roo?'

'Yes, she's an old friend of mine.' They were friends on Facebook and Roo must be close to forty, so it wasn't entirely a lie. 'Such a character!'

He was watching her face closely. 'She is that.'

'Roo says Verity has her good days?'

'So she told you about Vee?'

'Yes, it's a terrible illness.' She almost added 'alcoholism' to speed things along so she could get to the bit about him needing Ronnie's sexy sobriety in his life.

'Roo's good with her, doesn't seem to mind being called by the name of every Verney child until she gets there.'

Probably too drunk, Pip deduced sympathetically.

'Is she getting any help?' She took a swig from her mug.

'We have carers that come in every day,' he sighed, 'but Vee sends them away as often as not. She's used to getting her own way. Most of them are terrified of her. Live-in carers never last five minutes.'

Pip realised her powers of deduction might have let her down.

The rain was gunfire on the horsebox roof. 'Before Vee developed Alzheimer's, I always said I hoped someone would shoot me if I got it, but when it's someone you love, you just hope beyond hope they'll get better.'

Pip felt the tea cool in her mouth, unable to swallow. Her mother had suffered severe dementia. In the end, the only family member she remembered was the cat. It had almost broken Pip's father. 'It's a terrible illness,' she finally repeated, with total sincerity.

The ruggedly defensive smile was switched back on. 'Let's not talk about it. Let's talk about you. Is there anyone special in your life, Pip?'

She felt her lip wobble and with no further warning, a great sob rose through her.

'Hey.' He shifted round the table to put a hand on her back.

'What's all this about?' The craggy face was lowered to look into her eyes. 'Eh?'

Pip snorted and sobbed and wiped her nose, longing for the comfort of biscuits. She was crying a bit for the lost promise of JD and a lot for her mum, but she didn't want to tell Blair that. Most of all she was crying for him because he was lovely under the gruffness and she understood why he needed Ronnie, just every so often, to make him feel fifty-something, not seventy-something, and to help him forget the wife who was fast forgetting him. But she'd ruined it for them both.

'We have to go to hospital,' she told him, blowing her nose. 'Urgently. Ronnie needs you.'

He shook his head. 'Don't get involved in this one, Pip.'

'You two are so perfect together.'

'Trust me, we're not. We just understand where each other's at. I beat myself up for being a lousy husband to Verity, or, rather, not being a celibate one. Ronnie conducts every love affair with the stable door unlocked and her eye on the horizon, and that's fine by me. I'm glad she's bolting with Verity's horse.'

'She loves you,' Pip tried desperately. 'A woman knows.'

'A woman knows.' The sardonic smile was back.

'And you love her.'

He said nothing, just looked at her with his eyebrows at an ironic angle.

Pip changed tactic. 'Strikes me as a bit lacking in balls to leave her bleeding to death in hospital with Kit Donne and hunting-mad Barry for company.'

Slamming his mug down, he stood up. 'You got a car we can use?'

Delighted, Pip jumped up. Then she remembered her car was missing. She had no idea where the keys to the Captain's Subaru were.

'Don't they have height restrictions in hospital car parks?' she squeaked, as Blair clambered into the cab. 'You could ride a horse there instead?' She shivered happily at the idea of a heroic knight in shining armour clattering into A and E. Lucky Ronnie.

'Buckle up.'

36

In the observation ward, the nurse had recognised Kit from triage and waved him through the double doors. 'She's in here.' She held the curtain back and ushered him inside before he could protest. 'She'll be pleased to see you.'

'Ah.' He flashed an awkward smile.

Drips feeding into a cannula on the back of Ronnie's hand. She glanced up as he stepped into the cubicle, forehead creased with a combination of interest and pain. Her hospital gown had been tied round the waist to accommodate the big dressing on her shoulder, and he averted his eyes from a frilly blood-stained bra.

'How are you?' he asked bluntly, eager to beat a retreat and find Orla.

'Fed up. I hoped you might be the consultant.'

'Sorry to disappoint you.'

He caught her conciliatory smile in his peripheral vision, heard the husky little laugh. 'We've never formally introduced ourselves, you realise.'

'I know who you are.'

'It might help build bridges.'

'Is that necessary?'

'Hermia and I were friends for a great many years.'

'Hermia and I were married for a great many years. If the common denominator is missing, it doesn't correlate.'

Her eyebrows shot up questioningly.

'There is no need for a bridge.'

That amused blue gaze stayed on him. He could feel the hairs on his neck prickle with angry static. He'd always known she would be like this: wilful and capricious, tough as titanium, taking nothing seriously, a force of positivity pushing against his pessimism. Qualities all too painfully familiar because she shared them with the woman who had once been her best friend. But while Hermia's sense of self had been left on a country lane, lost to a car travelling too fast, Ronnie Percy still had her charm and quick wit.

'Well, I hope the consultant sees you soon.' He started to back towards the curtain.

The cashmere voice was infused with warmth: 'How do you do? I'm Ronnie Percy.'

Kit refused to play along, feeling along the pleated curtain to find the end.

'I always hoped we'd meet in better circumstances,' she went on. 'Hermia wrote of you so often, and so enthusiastically, I felt I knew you, but I can see that was terribly presumptuous. You're very different from how I imagined.'

'Really? You're exactly as I expected.' Where was the bloody way out? He was rattling curtains like a twitchy neighbour.

'I adored your wife. She was the sister I never had. We had years of barely racing off a birthday card to one another, but we always kept in touch somehow. Her letters are among my most treasured possessions – they got me though my very toughest years. I miss her terribly.'

'Likewise.'

'Extraordinary jacket.'

'Thank you.' Kit moved to the other end of the curtain to find a gap. As he did so, the side he'd just abandoned swished open with a rattle of rings and a waft of expensive aftershave. A large man in a suit strode in; before Kit could make a run for it the curtain swept closed again.

'Mrs Ledwell, I'm Mr Vane, the consultant vascular surgeon.'

Ronnie let out a snort of amusement, which she hastily turned into a cough.

Immaculately dressed in a navy wool pinstripe and lilac shirt, the consultant had a round, fleshy face and the sort of extravagant sweep of sprayed-back forelock beloved of American soap-opera actors.

'If you could sit there, Mr Ledwell, I'll just examine your wife.'

Kit swept a section of curtain aside victoriously only to find himself looking at the feet of the patient in the adjacent cubicle. He closed it and turned back. 'I'm not—'

'Sit!'

Kit did as he was told, wearily accepting that it was *huis clos* until he could follow Mr Vane out.

The consultant was annoyingly self-satisfied, eager to impress upon Ronnie the inconvenience of being called upon to look at something so trivial as her 'little gash'. The emergency team had done a very good job of flushing it out, he told her, and there was no requirement for his superior surgical skills unless she wanted an invisible scar, in which case she'd need a private consultation.

'I'm quite happy to have a scar.'

'What does Husband think of that?' Mr Vane looked at Kit.

'Fine by me.'

'Hmm.' The doctor cast his professional eye across the rest of her. 'Seems a shame to leave a crack mark on a piece of fine china.'

Ronnie let out a little rumble of laugher. 'Oh, I've been dropped and smashed more often than a farmhouse teapot.'

'You should take better care. One must treasure the best Spode. Exquisite lines.'

Is he flirting with her? Kit frowned. Wasn't that against the Hippocratic Oath?

'Do you collect?' Ronnie was asking politely, sounding like a royal making reception-line talk.

Kit rolled his eyes. Need she be quite so well-mannered? She had an open wound. Hermia had been the same. He glanced at his watch.

'I'm very fond of Limoges teacups.'

'I've always preferred mugs.'

'I can tell.' The surgeon's eyes flicked towards Kit.

Cheek! Supposing he *was* her husband, he'd be calling the man out. Kit eyed the surgeon's big hair grumpily. Ridiculous look for a man close to sixty. Standing up, he crossed his arms, leather jacket creaking. 'Is this going to take much longer?'

'You know, I might be able to sneak you into surgery after all,' Mr Vane told Ronnie, as though bestowing a great favour. 'I can make time.'

'I really just want to be stitched up and get out of here.'

'You heard her,' Kit growled.

'I'll get one of the seamstresses.' He swept out at such speed, Kit had barely turned to follow when the curtain clattered shut, casting them back in the blue lagoon. He settled back in the chair for a moment.

'How do you do?' he said quietly, 'I'm Christopher Donne. My wife adored you too. She talked about you a ridiculous amount before her accident. She lived for your letters. She wasn't such a good correspondent afterwards. She couldn't hold a pen for a year. She had to learn to talk again, and even when she did, only close family understood her. Until the day she died, she couldn't remember the word "toothbrush".'

As soon as he saw the blue eyes fixed wide on him, he realised she hadn't known any of it.

The curtain swept open. Ravishingly tousled and tearful in the skimpiest of hospital robes, Orla let out a hoarse sob. 'Kit, baby!' she cried. 'About fucking time! This has been like the worst fucking nightmare, and now I wake up and hear your voice and I know there is a God. Great jacket, by the way. They want to keep me in here. You have to get me out. And where's my fucking luggage?'

'Is that you, Carly, love?' Janine called sleepily.

'Armed burglar.' She found her sister-in-law prone on the sofa, a bowl of crisps propped on her chest, eyes glued to the television.

'I've still got three episodes of *Hannibal* to go.'

'Don't mind me.'

'What've you done to your lovely nails?'

'Long story. I need a bath.'

'You'll have to ask Ash to budge up. Been in there ages – I reckon he's been in a fight.' She straightened up, crisps tipping out. 'Shit, it wasn't you, was it?'

Carly hurried upstairs, grateful the lock on the bathroom door was broken. The main light was off, gloomy grey rays from the shaving strip meeting the orange glow of the streetlamp outside.

He was under the surface of the water, skin a muscular bone-pale canvas of distorted tattoos. 'Oh, Christ! Ash! *Ash!*' She stumbled across the room. His hair was long enough to grab and she yanked his heavy head up.

He loomed from the water with a great splash. 'What the fuck are you doing?'

'I thought you'd – I thought—'

'I was rinsing my bloody hair!'

'Shit! Sorry!'

Slicking his hair back with red-knuckled hands, he stared at her, silver eyes huge. 'You thought *what?*'

He had a cut beside his right eye and his lip was thickening.

'Have you been in a fight?'

'It's from clearing the tree earlier.'

'When I said goodbye, you didn't have all the facework.'

His tongue ran over his teeth as an ironic smile lifted his battered cheeks. 'You thought I'd topped myself, didn't you?'

'No!' She perched on the side of the bath, reaching out to touch his sore lip, her fingers numb with sudden warmth. 'I'm just worried about you, Ash. I know I pissed you off tonight. I shouldn't have made you do it, not like that.'

'Hey, bae, it's all good. You did me a favour.' He put his fingers over hers and drew them away from his face. 'I got these brands reading out some rules. Turners don't like being bossed around, but it's about time someone took charge round here. It's what Granddad wants.'

Carly swallowed. Just what had she goaded him into?

'Now make yourself useful and soap this.' He pulled her hand down below the water. 'I honoured the deal, remember?'

Whatever Carly had triggered, it had made him stand to attention more rigidly than he had in weeks.

Having been trapped next to the noisiest cubicle in A and E for ten minutes, then led to one of the treatment rooms to be stitched, Ronnie was well aware of the celebrity drama going on, but the nurse was eager to fill in the junior doctor stitching her, so she was forced to relive it again, summarised in a cheery Brummy accent.

'So Greta the Vampire demands to be taken to a private clinic and Dr Cameron is like "This isn't America, you can't just transfer healthcare provider like a hotel," because he wants her to stay here so he can show off to all his friends. But Dr Obeikwu says, no, it's cool, he'll just make a call because he knows the admissions guy at the Grove, and before you know it their ambulance is on its way here and she's telling her old rocker of a sugar-daddy to get her weekend bag from an abandoned car because there's a face cream in it that cost two hundred dollars. And Sugar-daddy says, "For two hundred dollars I'd expect it to have its own bloody chauffeur." Are you all right there, love?'

'Fine.' Ronnie gritted her teeth because it hurt like hell, but at least the commentary had a numbing effect, like white noise.

She tuned it out, too disenchanted by Kit Donne to want to remember his long-suffering acerbity as the smoky-voiced starlet called him her grumpy Brit and wrapped him round her little finger. It disappointed rather than surprised her that Hermia's latest replacement was barely in her thirties – she'd had enough experience of older men in her own thirties to know how that one worked. It was what he'd told her about Hermia that played over and over in her mind.

Ronnie and Hermia had regularly gone through long periods of not writing in their twenties and thirties. Her friend's accident had happened during one such uncommunicative phase, coinciding with the slow and demoralising end of Ronnie's relationship with married lover Lion, and Hermia being busy with her young family.

The first she'd heard of any accident was her father saying, almost in passing, that Hermia had taken a fall – a silly slip-up on the road, he'd called it – and been concussed. She'd sent a card commiserating. A few weeks later, having heard nothing back, she'd sent one of her customary catch-up letters, several pages long and full of months' worth of news, not all of it casting her in a good light. The short note that had come back from Hermia explained that she was very busy and suggested that their lives had moved on, so perhaps it was best their correspondence cease. Shocked, Ronnie had seen it as a judgement on her very ragged lifestyle, not for a moment imagining any personal struggle might lie behind it. She'd given things time to settle and written again, several times, but the only things to come back were the Christmas and birthday cards they traditionally exchanged, and which Hermia was always better at remembering. Eventually, those stopped too, Ronnie sending occasional rushed postcards promising letters she never had time to write. It was only when she'd come back to England five years ago that she'd learned of Hermia's death. A brain haemorrhage, her father had told her, in one of their rare, stilted telephone conversations, unapologetic that he hadn't thought to mention it at the time: 'Been a bit peculiar for years,' was his summary, 'nobody saw much of her.'

Now she knew the truth of it, she knew exactly why Hermia had written the note to her, and it was heartbreaking.

Reacquainted with her blood-stained clothes, which made her look as if she'd been in a shoot-out, Ronnie was discharged and sent back through a waiting room packed with Hurricane Claudia's battered victims. She stood despondently in a line for the pay-phone, hoping Blair was all right. He'd been so heroic trying to get her out. Did he even know she was here?

The line wasn't getting any shorter, so many smartphones waterlogged or out of battery that the old-fashioned wire was a life-saver and taxi-hailer. Feeling her tobacco tin in her pocket, she headed outside.

The sky was clear now, the faintest bright spot visible in the light-polluted city sky as Venus made her annual return. Ronnie gave her a grateful nod, in need of some love. She walked to the far edge of the waterlogged set-down area and perched on a wall to roll a cigarette. When she looked up from lighting it, she saw a skull and recognised Kit Donne impatiently scanning the cars coming and going. A taxi swept in through the puddles and he rushed forwards only to be shooed away by the Indian family who had booked it. Turning away furiously, he spotted her watching him and stalked across.

'I ordered a cab bloody ages ago.' He perched beside her, as though their brief acquaintance in adversity lent them a cantankerous camaraderie.

'Bad luck.' She didn't share the sentiment, just the crankiness.

'May I beg a cigarette?'

'They're roll-ups.'

'My favourites after Gitanes, Woodbines and crack.'

She rolled him one, handing it across with a lighter.

He kept it in his hand after lighting up, sparking it like a Catherine wheel. 'This was the hospital we came to after Hermia's accident.'

'That must be hard.'

'I've always been grateful to it. They saved her life. At least, I used to be grateful.'

He smoked like Hermia, that distinctive cosmopolitan pluck punctuating speech. It made Ronnie warm to him slightly, imagining him and Hermia sitting outside a London pub in the sun when they'd first got together, smoking Camel Lights and having animated conversations about Pinter or Stoppard.

'Her head injury was among the worst the neurologist had seen in his twenty-year career.'

'I had no idea.'

'For weeks we didn't know if she would live or die. Surely someone told you.'

She shook her head. 'Nobody from the village ever spoke to me, apart from Hermia. And my father, of course, but he probably didn't really take it in. He was terribly self-obsessed.'

Kit's eyes watched her face intently. 'Must run in the family.'

'Ouch.' She winced, taking her lighter back, the sparks irritating her.

'You stopped writing to Hermia.'

'She asked me to.'

'It took her ten minutes to write a side of A4 by hand before she had the fall, a day to type three lines on a computer afterwards. When you got a letter from my wife to say she didn't want you to write to her any more, it didn't occur to you that she might want just the opposite?'

'She meant it. There was a very good reason.'

'Enlighten me.'

Ronnie's eyes fixed on an ambulance setting off, the siren starting up as it joined the public road. What was she supposed to say? 'My God, what a coincidence! You'll never guess what?' Hermia, who had once read straight between the lines of Ronnie's jolly letters to the years of guilt and frustration living with Angus after his accident, had wanted to protect her friend from any repeat of it. Thinking back, a suffocating fist of love and anger pressed hard against her windpipe. You stupid, darling, stupid, kind, stupid, tender woman. I'd have come back. I'd have come straight back.

Saying nothing, she relit her damp roll-up and watched the cars coming and going.

When he realised he wasn't going to get an answer, Kit turned to glare at the building behind them. 'She was in here for months. Even when we did get her back – what little of her we got back – her personality had completely changed. She could learn to walk, to talk after a fashion, to write slowly and even very occasionally to laugh again. She absolutely loved *Father Ted*. But she couldn't learn to love us all as she once had. It's so hard on children to find that unconditional love has a condition after all. It's called TBI, traumatic brain injury. She tried her heart out, but she was so frightened all the time, and in such a dark place, that often she protected us by withdrawing. It was like living with a ghost. I used to be grateful to this hospital for saving her life, now I'm not so sure. Maybe she died that day after all and just haunted us.'

'She protected you by withdrawing.' Ronnie echoed the phrase quietly to herself. 'She didn't want to hurt me either.'

'Hurt you by what? *Needing* you? She loved those bloody letters of yours!' When angry, he sounded more Cumbrian. 'She reread them endlessly, and all the hundreds you'd sent from school. Those were the other times we saw her smile and laugh. She always looked out for more, but they came so rarely.'

'I didn't know you'd moved. I sent them to the wrong address. For years, I sent them to the wrong address.'

'She got every single letter, Ronnie. The postman brought the ones addressed to the farm. She asked me to send you things – poetry, photographs, always hoping for more. I could have told her a woman who abandons her own children isn't going to think twice about abandoning her friend.'

'I can't believe you just said that!'

'It's true, though, isn't it? You never came back to the village to visit your children, let alone Hermia.'

'I bloody well did, but that was before you moved there from London – and it was so awful always with Johnny that it was easier to do it around their schools once they all boarded. After Johnny died, it was a long time before my parents wanted to set eyes on me again. I came back once – it can't have been long after Hermia's accident. I was going to call to see her, and if I had, this awful misunderstanding wouldn't have lasted, but I made a stupid, stupid mistake. I had to leave.'

'And now you're still riding round with your married prairie cowboy when you should be coming back and facing up to your responsibilities.'

'Christ, where did all this come from?'

'It's what the villagers were saying earlier while we were pulling all that bloody timber off you.'

'I'm surprised you didn't just leave me in there and set light to me as a witch. And who made you my judge, dressed like Bon Jovi, shagging someone who wasn't even born when your illustrious career was taking off?'

'I'm so flattered you've followed my illustrious career and love life.'

'I used to take enormous pleasure in both because they made someone I loved very happy.'

'You didn't *love* her. People like you are emotionally impotent, Ronnie.'

'I'll love who I fucking well like!' She stood up furiously, noticing for the first time that they had attracted quite a crowd, several of whom were filming them with smartphones.

Pushing through it came a figure in a long, battered coat, two overexcited dogs on leads eyeing up ankles to bite. His voice was as deep as a dry well. 'Does that include me?'

'Blair!' She rushed to him, flooded with relief and gratitude.

'Let's not hang about. I'm parked across two lanes of the ring road. Pip's telling everyone there are police horses on board ready to guard the city shops against hurricane looters.'

Kit watched them go. *You will love her.* You heard her: she'll love who she fucking well likes.

As they disappeared through the ranks of cars, his taxi rolled up.

'Sorry, I'm late, brother. Some bloody div's brought a bloody great circus wagon into town.'

'Bring on the clowns.' He got in.

'Sorry about this, brother.' Ten minutes later the taxi driver was drumming his fingers on the steering wheel as they crawled along a B road behind a large horsebox. He flashed his lights and tooted the horn.

'Honestly, it's fine,' Kit muttered, sliding sideways into the door with a sudden jolt as the driver swung out and tried to overtake. 'Shit!'

The taxi pulled back just in time to avoid an oncoming car. 'Fucking cheek! You see that? Gave me the finger when he should've moved over. I'm taking this bastard on.'

'Really – just leave it. I've tried that one and you'll only regret it.'

Part Five

SHOOTING PEGS, TRICK
OR TREAT, BONFIRES

37

The trees were shaking out burnished leaves, a drift of gold and bronze butterflies through which the Saddle Bags trotted as they hacked along the raised spine of Drover's Wood. Last night's frost hung on the air, the spiders' silk strands across the track in front of them crystallised, like jewelled VIP ropes. The sun was rising behind them, their shadows long, outriders weaving between the trunks and dark hollows in which Hallowe'en monsters lurked.

The Redhead, unridden for at least a month, was on high alert. Petra struggled to sit out the spooks, soft-bottomed from long hours in a swivel chair while her imagination was the only active thing about her. Six weeks' antisocial labour was in cloud storage for half-term, full-on family life bringing her down to earth with a bump, her horse trying hard to join in.

'Oof!' She hung on to a hunk of chestnut mane as they leaped away from a pheasant rising out of the undergrowth with a squawking flap.

'One Charlie missed last week,' Gill pointed out.

'He missed most of them, didn't he?' Mo chuckled.

'Charlie's *alive*?' Bridge teased.

'He held his own at the Manor Farm shoot,' Petra said loyally. 'It was Wilf who held everyone else's. He picked up more birds than a lad's night out. Charlie's sending him back to gundog school.'

'What about your secret admirer?' demanded Bridge, laughing. 'Was Bay smouldering at you between drives?'

'Hardly secret,' snorted Gill.

'We didn't see much of him.' Petra said, breath pluming in front of her. 'His cousin was the one meeting and greeting. Bay and Monique looked in at elevenses. They were off to Newbury races.'

Accompanying Charlie shooting the previous weekend had been a labour of love, their neglected children farmed out to friends. 'Bad form on a neighbour's private day, if you're not there to help pick up,' Charlie had insisted, then ignored her throughout. Their absent host's kiss on the cheek and whispered 'You look good enough to eat, Mrs Gunn,' had kept Petra warm all afternoon, standing behind the guns with the fur-trimmed wives and girlfriends, grateful that her husband's peg was at the furthest end so she could avoid all the competitive muttering about charity balls and common entrance, and nobody could hear Charlie's unsportsmanlike whingeing about low birds. She'd daydreamed about what to do next with Father Willy, a warm brand on her cheek where Bay's lips had been.

Charlie returned to London bad-tempered, disappointed that his fellow guns had been eager locals, not legal eagles, his outing bringing no advantage to press home professionally. Now they were a day away from the Well-hung Party, and she'd given Father Willy the mother of all erotic epiphanies to round off her first rough draft.

'And did anybody mention what's happening with the stud?' Gill asked casually, as they single-filed out of the woods to cross the Broadbourne road into Austen land on the opposite side of Lord's Brook to the village.

'Nothing new. The Austens are still waiting on the land deal from what I could tell.'

It had been a month since the night of the hurricane, the Percy family tree just visible from their high vantage-point. There had been no more sightings of Ronnie. Predictably tight-lipped, Lester carried on as usual, and Pip still blustered back and forth twice a day in her little blue car.

'If I was struck by lightning, I'd think twice about coming back.' Bridge's eyes rolled above her scarf. 'Even insurance companies call that an act of God.'

'Lightning never strikes twice in the same spot,' Mo pointed out cheerfully.

'Balderdash,' scoffed Gill. 'That's an old wives' tale, like cows lying down when rain is on its way.'

'But they really do, don't they?' asked Petra, doubting years of basing her mackintosh selection on the behaviour of Friesians in neighbouring fields.

'Are you taking your kids trick-or-treating later?' asked Mo. 'There's a disco in the Bugger All afterwards for the little ones. Grace is hoping Bella will be there. They've set an age limit this year.'

At the previous year's Hallowe'en, the older Turner kids had terrorised small children and parents alike, one Edward Scissorhands in particular leaving his mark on most of the parked cars while a brace of ghoulish clowns ran rampage. A skeleton and a mummy were spotted having sex in full view of the CCTV by the bins.

Petra shook her head, grateful for an excuse to miss a frosty evening tramping round the village extorting Wilko sweets from cynical householders. 'Gunny thinks it's a consumer con and insists they all stay in so she can share quality time with her grandchildren. They're staging a spooky movie night instead. Wooooah!' The mare took exception to a flock of nearby sheep.

'Good job we've only got those two back for a week,' sighed Gill, watching the pair flying down the hill in giant cat leaps. 'Must be hard to write in a neck brace.'

A buzzing noise made them glance up and they saw a familiar drone heave into view, zipping after the Redhead, who flattened her ears and accelerated away.

'Or, indeed, a full-body plaster cast.'

The taxi driver eyed her fare in the rear-view mirror, her fingers drumming on the wheel to 'Thriller', the Hallowe'en tracks non-stop on the radio today. Her passenger looked like he'd already seen a ghost.

His phone was sounding alerts for messages every few seconds. He ignored them all.

She was sure she'd seen him somewhere before. She picked up a lot of celebrity fares from Broadbourne station, and this one could be a name-drop share with the girls, who were getting a bit bored by the number of times she'd ferried Alex James around. This one was an oldie with the brooding, good-looking confidence that hinted at film sets or recording studios. The newsboy hat and checked scarf were a touch of ironic spiv chic, and the wire-rimmed glasses were definitely ironic. The bouquet of peonies and winter roses he was holding must have cost a ton, and her car smelt of expensive cologne. But it was the red coat that screamed stardom. It was an Oscar carpet, reupholstered with plump down filling and designer kick-pleats.

She turned down the spooky anthems. 'Train journey good?'

'Uh-huh.'

'Staying long?'

'I haven't decided.'

His phone let out another flurry of alert tones.

'You're popular.'

'*O'er-prized all popular rate.*' Kit tipped the brow of his hat lower.

'Breakfast in bed, Gunny!' Prudie bustled into the guest annexe with a bowl of chocolate cereal swimming in milk, topped with a small bunch of grapes and two physalis onto which she'd sprinkled icing sugar to look professional. 'I got Fitz to carry the tea.'

'Oh, how charming!'

Fitz watched from the doorway as his grandmother hastily slid yesterday's *Telegraph* over the round of toast and marmalade she'd made for herself in the annexe kitchen, muting *This Morning*.

'So, Prudence, what are you calling this creation?' She picked up her iPad to share a photograph with Instagram followers. Prudie was by far the most photogenic of her grandchildren, bending her knees to twist sideways and strike a pouty pose.

'It's called *Coco Pops dans le Lit avec Fruit*. You have to get back into bed to fully appreciate it.'

'I'll have it here at the breakfast bar, thank you.'

'I'm practising my French because I'm invited to take part in the opportunity of a lifetime.'

'Oh, yes?'

'Dancing in Paris, Grandmère!'

Fitz sighed. 'Prudie's dance troupe are taking part in some Euro Disney thing, Gunny.'

'You get a free pass to the theme park!'

'Do you now?'

'All expenses paid!'

'Apart from travel, accommodation and food,' Fitz murmured. 'Mum worked out it would be two grand a pop and said no.'

'And you'd like me to pay?'

'Oh, *will* you, Gunny? Will you *really*? Please say yes!'

'No,' Gunny said emphatically.

'Or "*non*",' Fitz told his sister, smirking because he'd just won a bet.

Unlike her ultra-competitive siblings, Machiavellian Prudie never bore grudges, knowing there was more than one way to skin a cat.

'*Tant pis. C'est pas grave.* Enjoy your breakfast. See you later!' She danced off.

Gunny pushed the offering aside, picking up her newspaper and toast. As well as incredibly smooth skin, which she made up with full war-paint before anybody was allowed to see her each morning, her short blonde hair had less grey in it than his mother's. Fitz, who dreaded going bald like his dad, hoped he'd inherited her genes.

He perched on a high stool opposite. 'How's it going?'

'How's what going, William?'

'Things.'

'*Things* are very well. Do you still have eyes behind that fringe?'

He pushed it higher. 'Sorry it's a bit of a lame Hallowe'en. Dad's been busy in town. Seeing a *friend*.' He eyed the rejected Coco Pops.

She indicated for him to help himself. 'We had words about that in the summer, your father and I. It was made *very* clear that he must be more antisocial.' She ate a corner of toast. 'He promised to put an end to it, this...' The slice fanned expressively.

'Friendship.' Fitz started spooning up the cereal.

'Yes.'

'He's still being friendly.'

Gunny let out a sigh. 'I feared as much, which was why I wanted to come here to check.'

In fairness to his father, Fitz suspected he'd been trying to put an end to it throughout the autumn. But it wasn't proving easy, as the app bore witness. 'His friend wants to talk to Mum. There are lots of photos apparently. And a video.'

'Are we...' the toast went down the wrong way and he had to slap Gunny on the back '... talking revenge...' the slice waved around again '... porn?'

'No, not that. A confrontation. Phone ringing, strange voice on the line, "You don't know me, but I know your husband" type thing.'

'Or the doorbell rings.' Gunny shuddered, her eyes clouding. 'You answer it, babe in arms. Young woman. Striped Biba coat and knee boots. Blonde flick-ups. She's crying, mascara on her cheeks. "Let him go," she pleads. "He's only staying for the sake of the child."'

'Yes, um, that too.'

'That must never happen, Fitz.'

Kit's phone vibrated again. He should switch it off, but while it still beeped he knew she wasn't doing anything stupider than sending him abusive messages.

It wasn't as if Ferdie hadn't warned him: 'My dear boy, please don't seduce your leading lady again. It's getting very smold-smold, and I'm frankly bored of opening the *Standard* to see you papped by stage doors looking sleazy. What is it with you and last-chance saloon-girls?'

Not listening to Ferdie's advice was something Kit had turned into a speciality.

To do her credit, Orla had been the soul of discretion through their affair: 'This show's all about me,' she'd told him matter-of-factly on that first vodka-fuelled night. He'd laughed, happy to stay under the radar until the five-star reviews came in.

Kit had known it was curtains the moment the pleated blue cubicle divider had been snatched open in the Royal Infirmary, but it wasn't until they were back in New York that Orla had provided the costume change to play out their final scene.

The heating in the car was suffocating. He shouldered his way out of the huge duvet coat, the unwanted metaphor for the end of the short romance, a red rag to his bull.

Orla had marched him into a store on Third Avenue to buy it when the freak blizzard blew into the eastern seaboard the week before opening, blanketing Manhattan in thick snow. The unseasonal storm had caught everyone on the hop, killing five people in the state and drawing comparisons with the deadly fall of October 2011. Shrugging on the coat, he'd laughed at how much of a berk he looked in it, then laughed more when he saw the price label, but he'd been too cold to care.

It was a young man's coat. Beautiful, talented Orla was a young man's lover, too self-absorbed and capricious for the deeply entrenched ego of middle age. He understood her brittle shell, how it had thickened throughout her career, bulletproofing the vulnerability she'd first drawn upon to act before she'd sold her soul as a series vampire, now reinvented brilliantly in comedy. She needed every unbreakable inch of it for the role he'd cast her in.

Like Svengali and Trilby, theirs was an absurd mismatch. She'd hated the apartment he'd rented, the jazz clubs he hung out in, the street food he ate. She grew bored with him sitting reading; she couldn't understand why he walked everywhere. If he'd drunk a bourbon – and Kit drank a lot of bourbon – she wanted him to clean his teeth before they kissed. The sex had been too showy for lasting tenderness, her desire to pleasure him that of someone seeking applause, his own performance drawn unflatteringly onto her brightly lit stage when he preferred the dark, quiet intimacy of the back row of the stalls.

'Doesn't he look divine?' Orla had asked the cast later that day.

Kit didn't look divine. He looked like a cliché in a berk coat; he looked like an older director dating a young actress. Ronnie's deep, ringing upper-class voice had mocked him: *And who made you my judge, dressed like Bon Jovi, shagging someone who wasn't even born when your illustrious career was taking off?* He'd thrown the coat down furiously beside his stalls seat and made them run through the show twice, filling a new leather notebook with his most pedantic directions to date. On the back page, he'd written the one note he saved until the show was safely into its run to give Orla personally: *I think it's best we leave what we had together here.* A month's sleepless nights condensed into eleven words.

All lovers sensed the end coming, like dogs picking up on approaching thunder.

'Is it over?' she'd asked tearfully, the night before opening.

He'd kept his notebook closed. 'This is your beginning.'

When Kit's Broadway debut opened, beautiful, self-destructive, smoke-eyed Orla had brought the house down through the first fortnight of the run. Her reviews blew everyone out of the water, her well-publicised diva behaviour forgiven. The rumour that she'd only made it through because she'd been sharing a bed with the uncompromising sod of a director remained tightly under wraps.

Now the uncompromising sod had upped and left, and the diva was kicking off big-time. Kit, who had never lost faith that he'd cast the right actress, could have predicted Orla would turn a three-month love affair into a five-act play. Her ability to reach emotional top notes from nowhere was what made her so mesmerising on stage.

'I need you! I can't perform without you!'

Kit hoped the understudy was grateful: this was almost certainly going to be her moment.

She would soon play herself out. In two days, maybe less, she'd be back onstage stunning the crowds; it was her new drug. He'd just been the pusher. 'You don't need me any more,' he'd told her. 'We have nothing in common. My downtime is your doldrums, my uptime is your Mogadon. You want me to be a flamboyant British eccentric in a red coat and I'm a boffin in corduroy.'

'This is about the *coat*?'

'No! It's more than that. It's—'

'I knew the moment you bought it you hated it!'

'I didn't. I just—'

'Then the cast all laughed at you in it.'

'They did?'

'You look fucking great in that coat.'

'I look like a berk in it, but that's not—'

'You're dumping me over a *fucking coat*?'

It wasn't the coat. It was about the fact they really did have nothing in common apart from the play, the aphrodisiac that had thrown them together, which she had made magical. It was about the fact that however deep they were capable of being as individuals, it was a shallow grave of a relationship. It was about the fact he bored her. He'd been happy to be Henry Higgins, finicky in his demand for technical detail and repetitive precision, but that was what he was like offstage as well as on it, directing. He was intense, precise and he read books. A lot of books. It was about the fact that she put on a show twenty-four seven, while he didn't want the inconvenience of camera lenses and media scrutiny in his life. It was about the fact he *liked* drinking whisky – until he could barely walk sometimes. It was about the fact that he'd wanted to have sex with her more than he'd wanted to grow old with her – he'd had a head start there and had a lot less time to lose. It was about the fact he was still deep in mourning. It was about the fact that every three months since his wife had died he'd come back to visit her grave and cursed the very soil that surrounded her.

'Yes, it's over because of the coat.'

He tipped his hat brim back up as the car bounced over the familiar humpback bridge, and into the outskirts of Compton Bagot, passing the ugly 'pensioner bunkers', his son called them, bungalows with the best views in Warwickshire that developers now bought up a bereavement at a time. More had been replaced by the oak-framed faces of new money since he'd last taken the road. With their defensive electric gates and in-and-out drives for a quick getaway, these new fortresses now formed a guard of honour along to the ribbon development that garlanded the village Kit liked best in the Cotswolds.

While most visitors fell in love with pretty Compton Magna, Kit had always preferred Bagot for its lack of pretension and workman-like attitude, its long history boasting a castle mount and mottes, along with medieval barns and half-timbered cottages that sagged around its hilly lanes, like teeth sinking into an old jaw. It had taken a lot of dentistry over the years, packed with new housing and ugly extensions like cheap fillings. Recent expensive redevelopment had brightened the welcoming smile, and it bore a new, high-maintenance beauty, which saddened Kit somewhat. He'd seen too many fake white veneers in America; he craved uneven English teeth.

They passed the village hall, its porch fringed with ropes of light-up spiders and fake webs, a banner advertising a Hallowe'en Disco that evening flapping loose at one corner.

Kit could still remember the old Parish Rooms and British Legion being here, dens of iniquity housed in little more than two Nissen huts. In the eighties they'd been razed to make way for the Bernard

Ugger Memorial Hall, a then state-of-the-art amenity with a stage, kitchen serving hatch and disabled loos, funded through the philanthropy of the local coach-company owner from which it took its name. Better known as the Bugger All, it was a Bradstone monolith of no architectural sympathy, looking uglier than ever amid all the recent prettification.

At least it hadn't yet been converted into a house: the Old Post Office had stopped selling stamps and the Old Chapel hosting services since he'd first known the village. Very few gathering places remained. The butcher's was a holiday let rechristened Chateau Briand Cottage, and two new thatched cottages stood in the spot once occupied by a little garage. Jack-o'-lanterns were perched on doorsteps and windowsills everywhere, a witch on a broomstick attached to the large oak beside the war memorial.

As they passed the Jugged Hare, Kit saw a large 'Under Redevelopment' sign in front of it, his first irritable thought being that he'd now go hungry.

'That's been bought by the television chef that won *Strictly*,' his driver told him. 'It's going to be a raw, vegan and fruit-beer pub. She's already got one in Painswick. It's really popular.'

He glared at its car park, scene of his first battle with Ronnie Percy. On the stormy night he'd abandoned Pip Edwards's car there to summon help, those mocking blue eyes had seen right through his fragile, foolish shell. *You will love her* rang hollower than ever.

The car was climbing away from Bagot now. Kit's throat tightened as they drove past Upper Bagot Farmhouse. He looked away as always, but not quickly enough to avoid catching sight of children in the garden, the memory still sharp of his own two charging round it, Hermia in their wake, blonde ponytail flying. His kids had no idea he was back in Britain. He needed to cool off from Orla before he made contact.

He glared across the orchards, just a few red apples survivors clinging to the trees, all cast in sharp relief in a morning sun so golden it deserved God's finger at the end of it. It wasn't yet five in the morning in New York. Having left Newark airport early the previous evening, unable to snatch more than a fitful doze on the flight, his body clock's hands were spinning in confusion.

'Whereabouts d'you want dropping?' his driver asked.

'Just down the lane to the right.'

'It's so pretty here.' The driver sighed as she turned into Church Lane.

Compton Magna was putting on a predictably coquettish show, today seemingly hewn in pure gold, the stone luminescent in the amazing morning light. More pumpkins lined doorsteps and sills, a huge bonfire was already forming on the Green ready for 5 November and the horse-chestnuts were raining yellow leaves.

Today the most photographed village in the Bardswolds had even laid on a group of riders hacking towards them, a quartet of smiling women burnished by the sun. The taxi slowed and they all raised their hands in thanks.

'I love horses,' said their driver, waving back. 'Beautiful creatures, aren't they?'

'No.' Kit looked quickly away. 'That's it, ahead there. The one with the sweet-shop chimneys.' Hermia used to call it their Lebkuchenhaus, like the old witch's cottage in 'Hansel and Gretel'.

He picked up the young-man's coat and stepped out to fetch his case, its wheels rattling over the dropped kerb. The outside world could go hang. He wanted to be alone with his wife.

'Hang on, wasn't that your theatre man?' Bridge was looking over her shoulder.

Petra spun in the saddle, squinting short-sightedly as the taxi drove off. 'Not in that coat.'

'Must be the son.' Mo waited for them. 'He's one of them flares – no, bell-bottom... What do I mean, Petra?'

'Hipsters.'

'That's it. I knew it was a type of jean. Not like his dad at all.'

'I bet Kit cut a dash in the eighties.' Petra winked.

'He's always had a look of Martin Kemp from Spandau Ballet.' Mo sighed.

'Adam Ant,' Petra argued.

'You two are so old,' Bridge teased. 'He's a dad candy like Colin Firth, take it from me.'

'What's that?' Gill called back.

'Kit Donne,' Petra explained. 'Someone went into his house just now.'

'In which case I'm sure he'd appreciate *not* being talked about on his doorstep,' she lectured. 'And for your information he looks like Bryan Ferry.'

The other Bags caught each other's eyes, sensing the crush that dare not speak its name had a rival, and it wasn't the local MP.

'SMC,' Bridge mouthed.

'I saw that!'

'It's *all* over social media that Orla Gomez was sleeping with her British theatre director,' Pip told Lester, sweeping the cobbles around him as he leaned on the half-door, watching the foal plunging around on the fresh straw in one of the corner boxes on Big Yard. 'To think you *saved her life*. It could be really good PR for the stud.'

'I don't think so, Pip. We don't get many calls from round those parts wanting mares covered.'

'It's the silk-thread effect, Lester. You need to keep the metadata weaving its magic out there, let the web tighten.'

'If you say so. Needs sweeping over there.' He nodded to the archway in which a drift of leaves had gathered.

As she whisked off, Lester turned back to the foal. With so many horses coming into the stables and barns for winter, he wouldn't be able to cope with mucking out without her help, but his ears didn't thank him, Handel's Chaconne Variations in G barely audible from the feed-room stereo despite him turning the volume right up.

He watched the dun foal, racing from one end of the stable to the other, bubbling over with cabin fever. He was supposed to stay on box rest for another week, but Lester would let him have his run of the smallest paddock later. He'd healed well; it was a fine day. The scar on his chest needed old-fashioned fresh air.

The stud phone was ringing. Alice checking up on him, no doubt. He ignored it. She'd call back. Her reassurances that the future of the stud was a priority were starting to sound rather hollow.

'Cake break!' Pip bustled to her car for a tin of chocolate muffins and a can of gourmet dog food. 'I brought choice cuts of duck in jelly for Laurence and Stubbs to share.'

Lester gritted his teeth. Since she'd discovered the fox in his ferret cage – not difficult, given it was visible from his kitchen window – Pip had spoiled it rotten, naming it and bringing it daily treats. They competed childishly for its affections while Stubbs watched jealously.

The cub was beguilingly tame, easy to scoop out of its cage and happy to loaf around Lester's little walled garden pouncing on flitting leaves. Lester had meant to set the young fox free weeks ago, but he'd been waiting for the perfect day, knowing its chances of survival were bleak. Now Pip had thickened its waistline with lapdog food, they were practically non-existent. It was yet another four-legged creature in his care whose future was uncertain.

'Phone!' Pip called, as it rang again.

It stopped abruptly, and he realised she'd answered. Limping inside, he found her bright pink in the face, tongue-tied and tangled in flex as she hummed and hawed and giggled, which meant it had to be a male caller, either Tim or Flynn or at a guess—

'*Bay Austen!*' she mouthed at him.

He nodded, reaching out wearily to take the receiver.

'Okay, yes, I'll pass that on if I do. Bye!' She hung up. 'There! I got rid of him for you. He wanted to know if we've arranged anybody to clear the fallen cedar yet because his boys can do it this week. The horses would need to come off it while they do.'

'Not his land yet.'

Pip's mind was revving. 'It must mean the sale is moving forwards again.'

'Hmm.'

'He's a lovely man.' Pip sighed. She hadn't forgotten how deliciously he'd flirted with Petra at the Captain's wake, although she supposed that was rather unfortunate timing.

'If you say so.' Lester's wizened old face refolded itself from one disapproving expression to another as he fetched milk from the ancient, juddering fridge.

'Why don't you like him?'

'Not my place to like him.'

'The Captain obviously liked him,' she pointed out.

'He did *not*. Wouldn't give him the time of day for years, let alone sell his lot any land. "Over my dead body, Lester," he once said.'

'Well, I suppose it is!' she pointed out cheerily, stirring the tea in the pot. 'Now he's dead.'

'Had no choice in the end.'

'Better the devil you know than the devil you don't!' She poured two mugs. 'The afterlife's a bit of a blind date like that, isn't it?'

There was an awkward silence.

'Let the Austens clear the tree,' he muttered eventually. 'Never liked those horseshoes. Nailed the family ghosts in, Mrs Percy used to say.'

Pip felt this merited revealing her Hallowe'en-themed muffins with a flourish, their iced tops decorated ghoulish green to look like Frankenstein's monster with strawberry string scars and chocolate matchstick bolts. She liked to add a seasonal touch for her pensioners, although the food dye had come out brighter than she'd anticipated, making them look radioactive. When Lester ate one, his lips turned green.

'So do you think the Percy ghosts will haunt Bay for taking their tree away?' she asked.

'Lot of old nonsense.'

'Bay's bound to be a bit freaked, don't you think, to want it gone?'

'More so by Ronnie coming back to haunt him,' he said cryptically. 'He played a dirty trick there.'

'What trick?' Pip seized on this. It was all too rare for Lester to give anything away, but cake always loosened his tongue.

'It was a long time ago.'

'Was it when she came back to the stud to see Pax during the summer holidays, the first year she was in sixth form?'

His eyes appeared out of their folds, surprised. 'How d'you know that?'

Pip had now read every one of Ronnie's letters to Hermia Austen that she could find in the Old Almshouses and pieced together some of her missing story. There were big gaps, and Ronnie's predisposition for making everything sound as if she was having a riot, even through the gloomiest of times, made it hard to follow all the threads, but she had a fairly comprehensive picture of the year in question. Something had happened to make Ronnie leave again in a hurry. Whatever it was had driven a deep cleft between mother and daughter.

'The Captain told me about it,' she reassured Lester breezily. She had a shrewd suspicion what it might have been. Bay'd have been twenty-one and fresh from agricultural college, Ronnie about to turn forty. It had cougar paw prints all over it. She looked at Lester expectantly.

'Like hell he did.' He flashed a rare smile. Even his teeth were green. Pip hoped her pensioners didn't terrify the trick-or-treaters later.

Then Pip felt her blood run cold as she remembered. Hallowe'en! What did the Donnes call it? *Samhain*, that was it. The pagan Day of the Dead. She'd totally forgotten about Kit Donne coming back to visit his wife's grave. Now he and Orla Gomez were washed up, he might even be planning to spend a night in his house. She'd left all the beds stripped, and William Shakespeare's partially rebuilt pottery head was still mostly spread out on a tray in the Bulrushes like a thousand-piece jigsaw.

'I have to go!' She raced towards the door, then doubled back for the cakes, not noticing the relief lifting Lester's creased cheeks.

As Lester watched her tear off, the phone on his kitchen wall started ringing again.

'Stud.'

'Lester.'

The green smile vanished as soon as he heard that husky, melodious voice.

'I'm coming back tomorrow. Make up two stables again, will you? This time, I'm staying.'

38

'Carl, I need you! I've an emergency job on.'
'I can't, Janine, I've got a double shift at the farm shop. I don't knock off till six.'

'Okies, babe. I'll try Shell.'

One benefit of Ash taking over as unofficial Turner-clan leader on the estate, Carly reflected, was that she'd been elevated in status so Janine no longer bossed her about so much.

She stopped by the gate to Sixty Acres, eyes searching for Spirit. He still wasn't out with the others. She knew he was doing well, but that was nothing compared to seeing him. It was like Pricey, locked away from sight in Jed's run. He said she was 'grand' and 'training up nicely' but Carly had yet to clap eyes on her. It didn't help that Ash and Jed were currently stamping round each other, like a couple of sumo wrestlers.

The Turner family's war hero was locked in a battle with his lawless cousins, Jed among them, and he used as leverage his training as a killer to keep them all in check, not any diplomatic skills. It was rule by threat, and Carly sensed a big fight brewing.

At home nothing much had changed. The sex was as swift and untender as the day-to-day conversation. The detachment persisted, the insomnia and obsessive gaming to anchor his tremors and rages. He was more argumentative with her and the kids. They were all on eggshells. She'd bought Ellis a new 'Splorer Stick, orange this time. The hedges to either side of her were laced with orange threads from his walks to and from school the previous week.

Excitement about Hallowe'en had kept the four-year-old distracted through half-term. That evening Carly would go straight from work to meet Ash and Ellis out trick-or-treating with the big group of Turner kids who always went round the village. Ellis's costume was already with his nan for him to change into. She only hoped Ash remembered.

At Compton Manor Farm Shop, Bay's hollow-cheeked blonde wife, Monique, was stalking about in her tight breeches, hair scraped back. She looked like a ballerina in a wind tunnel.

'Just the person!' She collared Carly as she came in. 'Bay's parents are holding a party tomorrow night, okay? Our caterer cannot get enough agency waiting staff. I hear you have experience. You can do it, okay?' It was more of a demand than a request.

'I'll have to see if my other half can babysit.'

'Bring your children here, if not. My nanny can look after them.'

Carly nodded doubtfully, imagining her kids kicking off in the Austens' luxury barn conversion.

'Don't,' the manageress whispered, after she'd gone. 'The au pair's a teenager who speaks no English and is already threatening to walk out because their little monsters run her ragged and Monique never gives her the time off she's owed. It's their third nanny in six months. Monique's a bee-atch.'

'Nobody's born bad.' Carly felt her hands grow warm, thinking of Pricey and her snarling, defensive flip-outs. She hoped those weren't happening now. 'Maybe she's had a traumatic experience that makes her like that.'

'Yeah, being married to Bay.'

An extended family of mice appeared to be the only ones to have used the Old Almshouses since summer, but they'd moved on too. It was so cold, Kit suspected they'd frozen to death. There was no heating oil left in the tank or logs for the wood burner. He was grateful for the floor-length red berk coat, which reminded him comfortingly of a sleeping bag. The only thing he could see that Pip Edwards had done was finish all the crosswords.

Kit was profoundly, tearfully grateful. He could hear Hermia's voice clearly again. She would have crept inside this coat with him to warm him up, ordering him to stop navel-gazing and get his teeth into something more palatable than the bitter little pill he'd brought back. She could never tolerate self-pity, especially after her accident.

Wide awake, body clock making its first coffee and listening to *Morning Edition* on WNYC, he'd switched on the immersion and dug several elderly electric heaters out of a store cupboard, which he now arranged in a Stonehenge circle around the Eames chair beneath the arched garden window that they'd both loved sitting in because the light was so good. Pulling his reading glasses down from his head, teeth chattering only slightly, he'd flicked on his e-reader, battery flagging after the transatlantic flight. *Memoirs of a Foxhunting Man* was now a long way down his library list – it had been a year since he'd read it last – but his digital copy was already mosaicked with as many typed-in highlights as his broken-spined paper one.

'A script hasn't been Kitted until it looks like a Mondrian,' Hermia had always said.

As the minutes passed, Kit became too absorbed to notice the space heating up around him, too grateful for warmth and Sassoon's words to regulate it, the percentage he read racking up alongside the temperature. Forty per cent of the way through the book, his scarf was unwound, at fifty-five per cent the sleeping-bag coat was discarded, followed by his sweater at seventy per cent. At ninety-six per cent, he carried the book to the bathroom to have a pee, stepping out of his trousers and leaving them in a crumpled figure of eight to return to the chair, scuffing off his socks en route. Flexing his toes at one hundred per cent, he peeled off his T-shirt and unscrewed the cap of a bottle of duty-free whisky, lifting it to his lips. He paused, raising it in a toast.

'I miss you.'

For a moment, blood rushed in his ears, distorting sound, so that the house seemed frantic with voices, kindness and grief once more. The notepad on his lap had filled with his own handwriting, yet he couldn't remember picking up his pen.

Scrolling through the downloaded book list, page after page, he found *Memoirs of an Infantryman*, but its battery died before he'd got beyond the Preface. His own was lagging in sympathy, the heat rendering him soporific. He closed his eyes and reached out to put a hand on the comforting bald head of Shakespeare's bust, finding it on an unfamiliar hard-edged object instead, metal initials inlaid in the top. His fingers traced them, HA, then stilled.

What seemed like a second later, he heard a bright voice calling from the door, 'Mr Donne! It's Pip. Helloooo!'

Kit, disoriented, thinking he was in bed in New York, tried to get out of his usual side and found himself pressed up against the windowsill, cold wet condensation on his cheek.

Her voice chirruped on, footsteps closing in: 'I wasn't expecting you until later! I brought your designated cleaning team. This is Shell Turner. It's lovely and warm in here.'

Kit rubbed his face, which felt like a cushion that had been sat on too long.

'I don't want it cleaned.' He stood up, not realising the whisky bottle was still in his lap. It dropped to the flagstone floor, smashing in a wet explosion of glass, the smell like a punch in the face from a drunk.

'Oh, let us deal with that. Shell! Gosh, you're in your underpants.'

'Just get out!' he roared, reaching for the coat, knocking the box off the table where Shakespeare's bust had been. Envelopes spilled across the whisky and ice lake.

'I'll come back another time, shall I?' Pip said brightly. 'I'll just leave you with these cakes to welcome you home. Happy Hallowe'en – I mean Salmon Day.'

'Samhain.' He heard the door close and sat down again with his head in his hands. When he opened his eyes and looked down, the ink was running on a letter that had been left out of its envelope, one of the few Ronnie Percy had sent her friend after the accident.

The rules of the blame game aren't always fair, he read, *but if one doesn't play by them, one may never be invited back to the table to win back one's stake.*

Everything was a game to her, even guilt.

Animosity curdling, he went in search of a dustpan and brush to sweep everything she'd ever written to Hermia into the bin.

★

As soon as Petra stepped into her kitchen, Gunny swung round on a barstool with a Bond baddie lift of the eyebrow, immaculate in cream, Liberty scarf artfully arranged, expensive white veneers bared. 'I can smell horse from here.'

Petra managed a return smile and an offer of coffee. 'Or would you prefer I shower first? The girls are happy playing outside and the boys geeking for now.'

'It's fine if I sit downwind. I'm surprised Charlie never complains. Always had a very sensitive nose.'

'He and Wilf have that in common.' Along with overenthusiastic socialising, wanderlust and a strong sex drive.

Soon, coffee cup in hand, Gunny was firing questions, like an immaculately coiffed and powdered daytime television presenter given a ten-minute slot to interview Petra about her latest book, *Charlie and Me, Our Middle-Aged Marriage.*

Did they go out much, just the two of them, these days? When had they last had a grown-up mini-break? Were they planning to stay in the Cotswolds permanently? What plans did they have for after the children had left home and Charlie retired? 'I shouldn't let him leave it too late. Look at his father, heart-attack at sixty-four. He'd only just got his golf handicap down. Nigel and I had grown so far apart by then. It's not good for a man's health, a lacklustre marriage. A husband has needs into old age.' She gave Petra a penetrating look.

'We don't lack lust,' Petra insisted, and avoided adding, just not for each other.

'Well, that's good.' Gunny gave her a steely wink. 'I had hoped he'd take a few days off this week, but I gather he's tied up on a big case.'

'Yes.' Petra shook her head to dismiss the image of her husband's massage parlour dominatrix strapping him to a Samsonite. Charlie had finally been brought in from the cold to head up a dull and lengthy arbitration that would keep him out of trouble until Christmas.

'He works too hard.' Gunny sighed. 'High-powered men need lots of stimulation outside the workplace.'

'There's always things going on round here, the party tomorrow night for a start.'

Despite Charlie's sulks after the Austen family shoot, Petra had no doubt that he'd throw himself into the mêlée at the annual pheasant supper, the Well-hung Party. All of the Bardswolds' movers and shakers would be there, and Charlie wasn't above photo-bombing the *Cotswold Life* social pages in his village one-upmanship. The invitation, on the mantelpiece since September, was Petra's daily inspiration for Father Willy and motivation to stick to an alcohol-free, biscuit-free diet.

She thought guiltily about the dress she'd bought especially, egged on by Bridge, the village's fashionista insisting Petra wasn't too old for plunge necks and high splits if she kept everything wobbly taped in.

Much as Petra wanted to believe that all the vanity planning was for her self-esteem and to ensure Charlie's approbation, she knew that wasn't strictly true. Last night she'd caught herself fantasising that his case dragged on until Friday, that Monique Austen was away doing some emergency high-level horse-dancing thing, and that Bay plied her with champagne, then whisked her into one of the farm's luxury glamping lodges with a roaring wood-burning stove for a stolen night. She'd stopped herself, partly because she knew it was very wrong to think it, and partly because she was a bit woolly on the technical detail: just how would Bay get past all the tit-tape and shape armour under her dress? The Safe Married Crush still worked best in abstract.

Sitting in front of her mother-in-law she allowed herself a brief imaginary clinch in the woodland lodge. Gunny's iPad made a camera-click noise.

'I must say it is very endearing the way you smile when you think about Charlie.' Gunny typed a caption to the photograph she'd just taken before sharing it. 'I'm asking my ladies for colour-correcting foundation advice. You have a lot of eye bag and red tone.'

Petra was spared thinking up a crushing reply by Mitch the postie's horn sounding from the gates. She headed gratefully outside.

The most gossipy postman in Gloucestershire had turned to talk to a passing motorist, a parcel from Petra's favourite upmarket lingerie website under his arm. Just in time! She perked up, then balked when she realised the motorist was Pip Edwards, her flat-vowel voice carrying across the gravel: '... and, of course, there's the old rumour about Bay and Ronnie giving in to mutual attraction, so that might be why she won't sell him the— Oh, hi, Petra! Getting sexy new undies, I see!' she called.

'Lucky fella, that old man of yours.' Mitch chuckled, fishing for his barcode scanner.

'*If* they're intended for his eyes!' came a giggle from the car.

'Winter thermals.' Petra snatched up the stylus and signed the screen, doubting the latest high-tech waist-shrinking, bum-lifting miracle pants with built-in-breathability and camel-toe control would impress her husband at close quarters, but it was the overall effect she was aiming for, and they'd had rave reviews for taking inches off one's silhouette.

She was twitching to know what Pip had meant about Ronnie and Bay, but Mitch was still clutching her lingerie box, eyebrows at Breaking News angles.

'I've heard tell you village ladies who all ride together are a saucy lot.' Mitch was chuckling. 'Barry Dawkins says you get up to all sorts.'

'Oh, yes?' She handed the tablet back.

'Don't you run a chart of Top Ten Village Men? And you each have a favourite.'

'Gosh, no!'

'Oh, I bet I know who Petra's is!' Pip piped up.

Petra was appalled by her fellow Bags. So much for what's-said-in-the-saddle-stays-in-the-saddle. She'd long suspected Gill often betrayed them to Paul, but Mo was a turncoat too. Did Barry have any idea that lawless, lurcher-loving Jed Turner was his wife's secret fantasy?

'Barry said it's called the SMC League.' Mitch handed the parcel across. 'What's that stand for, then?'

'Small Male Cocks,' she said lightly.

He stood up straight, tugging down his fleece.

'We count pheasants,' Petra explained. Wherever there were pheasants, there were handsome farmers running shoots. She let her mind drift briefly back into the lodge with Bay, lights dimmed, *La Bohème* playing on a crackly wind-up gramophone. Her phone buzzed, its message lighting the wood burner by spontaneous combustion. *Trick-or-treat later? Bagsy me skeleton and you mummy. Bx*

Pip was gossiping breathlessly with Mitch about Kit Donne.

Leaving them to it, Petra wandered off to reply: *Are you going to village disco?* Was that too teenage-sounding? She inserted *and Monique.* Then, flushed with shame at her duplicity, added *and Tilly. Bella keen to know.* The SMC needed strength in numbers to keep it pure.

Regretfully not came the reply.

She felt a snub of disappointment and a twist of relief. Dragging her children and Gunny to the village hall just so she could ogle Bay was beneath contempt: she had all tomorrow evening with a husband in tow to do that.

He sent a GIF of Skeletor twerking that made her snort with laughter. *Think of me.*

Hearing a tap on glass and looking up, she saw Gunny and Ed peering out of the tall dining-room windows directly overhead and shuffled guiltily out of sight, then realised they were pointing at the drone, hovering over the orchards. She replied: *Touché.* She found a GIF of a sexy Ancient Egyptian and sent it, face prickling at her wickedness.

Tut-tut, Nefertiti. That'll keep me up all night ;-) Bx

Petra checked the GIF she'd sent, waiting for it to load properly this time, and saw that what had looked like a buxomly burlesque goddess Isis opening her wings with a shimmy was a lot more hard-core beneath the feathers. She'd need her reading glasses to tell for certain, but Isis seemed to be demonstrating how she'd conceived Horus. 'Oh, bloody hell.' She held it at arm's length and tilted her head.

'Interesting animation,' said a voice behind her, making her leap from her lair. 'I've always found Ancient Egypt fascinating. Is that a trailer for the new Mary Beard series?'

It was Kenneth, the kindly veggie-growing neighbour, holding a plastic bag over the fence, blackcurrant eyes glittering beneath white catkin brows. 'Two butternut squash and a large marrow for you, my dear.'

'Thank you!'

Hurrying back into in the house, she dumped everything in the kitchen and went off to pee. Her red-faced reflection in the mirror above the basins gazed furtively back at her. Gunny was right. She needed toning down massively.

In the kitchen, the big American fridge's double doors were wide open, radiating light. Fitz's skinny silhouette was turned away from it, bent over the kitchen island playing with her phone.

'Oy, boundaries!' She waved her fingers for him to hand it back, horrified that he might have found the sexy Egyptian GIF, worse still her mirror selfies of herself in tomorrow night's party dress, trying to work out if she looked fat. Not to mention the ones of her in her underwear, attempting to determine the same before she'd ordered control pants online.

'Just checking it out for when you upgrade and I get given this.' He slid it across the countertop. 'Dad's old BlackBerry sucks. I can't believe you still text. That's so quaint.' Oh, God. That meant he'd seen the Bay messages. Not that there was anything terribly incriminating in them, was there? She'd probably read far more into them than there was. Nevertheless, she made a mental note to delete their entire text thread later.

The fridge alarm was going off, like a car's seatbelt warning. Fitz turned back to survey it, head tilted to study shelves crammed with Petra's latest supermarket trawl. 'You heard from Dad today?'

'His case is a really tough one,' she fudged, watching him pulling out the big tray of party nibbles she'd been planning to park in front of Gunny on Scary Movie Night.

Using the party nibbles as a salver, he loaded on eclairs and a tub of salted caramel cream. 'You two are cool, though, yeah?'

'Of course! He's just a bit stressed with work.' Poor Fitz clearly craved his dad's company.

'Cool.' He sloped off.

'Hi, Bay, it's Pip!'

'Who?'

'Pip Edwards? From the stud? We spoke earlier about the tree that was struck by lightning.'

'Oh, yah.'

'You have the go-ahead to clear it. Just watch out for the ghosts!'

'Ha-ha, yah.'

'It'll be like *Sleepy Hollow* – you know, when the Tree of Death gushes blood and the trunk splits and the headless horseman gallops out intent on revenge.'

'Right. Look forward to that.'

'Enough ghosts and ghouls round here already, what with Hallowe'en! Even Kit Donne's back to do his funny pagan ritual, the salmon-sowing thing. Did you see he's split up with Orla Gomez? Greta the Vampire.'

'No, that one missed me.'

'I was just saying to Petra – you know we're chums – he really needs someone to look after him. He misses your aunt so much, you can tell. Sweet, really.'

'Yes, well, if you don't mind, I—'

'Petra has us in stitches about the SMC League. Your name was mentioned.'

'The what?'

'You're definitely top of it.'

'What is the SMC?'

39

It was dark outside when Kit woke, parched and hungry. All there was to eat were Pip Edwards's Frankenstein monster muffins. He scoffed three. They were delicious, and he felt a pang of guilt for rebuffing her attempt to welcome him and get the place ready. He should have called ahead, as he'd promised.

He checked his phone, but there was no signal, the screen clock telling him it was past five. He could hear teenagers cackling in the graveyard across the road, getting their kicks from Hallowe'en. Kit wanted to storm out and tell them to get the hell out of his wife's resting place, but remembered he'd been that Gothic teenager once. Hermia would probably appreciate the company. He had yet to visit her, the flowers a wilting reminder in the sink as he poured a glass of water, then another. His stomach rumbled.

He had no car. Where *was* his car? Not that he could legally drive it yet.

Pulling on his clothes before shrugging on the red coat, he headed outside and tried to remember the way to the farm shop. As soon as he had a signal, messages rattled in. He ignored them and called Ferdie.

The lecture was predictable, lasting all the way through the church meadows and onto the track through the fields. He'd forgotten how hilly it was, and was soon puffing hard.

'You need to take more bloody care of yourself, dear boy,' Ferdie berated him. 'You don't eat or exercise, you just drink and fornicate. You're practically sixty. That's a heart-attack waiting to happen. Take a sin break.'

'I *am*... taking a break... It's why I'm back... early. I'm walking... to the farm shop. It's sub-zero and pitch dark out here, I'm talking to you on my only source of torchlight, and the going is very – shit – hard underfoot.' He picked himself up from tripping into a rabbit hole.

'How gloriously *Withnail*. Where are you?'

'The Comptons. The bloody pub's closed and I need food.'

'Do farms sell Jack Daniel's?'

'Ha-bloody-ha. I haven't eaten since New York.' He didn't count the muffins.

'Humble pie wouldn't go amiss, Kitten. I told you Orla was a loose cannon. She's just made a terrible fool of you, I'm afraid. You're plastered all over social media looking like a camp sofa, but she's *la vie en rose*. Last night was her best performance to date, I'm told. Ten-minute standing ovation. She's tipped for a Tony and they're talking about extending the run.'

'My work is done,' he muttered.

'What are you up to now, apart from planning the most brilliant production of *Lear* ever staged next year?'

'I thought I might head back to London, have another crack at Sassoon.' Kit's dream to turn Siegfried Sassoon's fictionalised memoirs into a stage production was a long-running family joke, his many attempts piled up on a high shelf in the Stoke Newington flat.

'Ah.'

'Is that a good "ah" or a bad "ah"?'

'You're the director. What's my inflection?'

'Inflexibility.' It was an old joke.

Kit had reached Compton Magna Farm Shop at last, tracking down the pumpkin-decked food hall full of overpriced condiments in gingham-lined baskets. Saint-Saëns was being piped through loudspeakers. It was empty, apart from a man in a suit by the home-cooked meals and a pair of leggy women dressed in Joules who were wandering about muttering loudly that Daylesford was far better.

'We're in Stratford most weekends,' Ferdie was saying, as Kit plucked up a basket. 'Let's all meet for a drink.'

'I might not be here long. This is just a quick stop-off. Better in London.'

'You're far too prickly in London. You should stay in the cottage for a while, Kit. Focus on Sassoon there.'

'I can't afford the corner shop.' They stocked Teapigs, not Tetleys. He lobbed a packet into his basket, adding several tubes of artisan crackers, and moved on to a fridge of Bardswolds Dairy Cheeses in bright wax jackets, like colourful ice-hockey pucks, selecting a few at random.

The dark walk alongside Lord's Brook to the farm shop had lifted Kit's spirits so much he could forgive the silly prices. It was a pretty play emporium for a little empire. The Cotswolds never changed, its stunning green terrine of hills still interleaved with crisp new money, old-school ties, hunting stocks and glossy magazine lifestyles. That the shop was owned by Hermia's family made total sense. The Austens had always lived very richly off the fat of their land and the lean profits of their suppliers.

'*We fat all creatures else to fat us, and we fat ourselves for maggots.*'

'*Hamlet*,' Ferdie recognised. 'Always a good diet mantra, not that you need one. You look very gaunt in those photographs. We'll see you at the weekend. Donald's going to make you up one of his herb tinctures.' He rang off.

Kit made his way to a crammed drinks section. Ferdie had underestimated Bardswolds' answer to Fortnum's. There was a trendy single malt from Cornwall that came in what looked like a perfume bottle.

Looking at the price, he almost put it back, but his need was too great. With a mental apology to Ferdie – he supposed he could start cutting down on his drinking by dabbing it on his wrists – he headed for the tills, where the girl serving told him the forecasters were predicting hard frosts. He recognised the Cs tattooed on the soft sides of her wrists, but not from where. She said politely, 'Coldest winter for years ahead, they say. We'll be snowed in soon enough, I reckon.'

That suited Kit. Nobody knew he was here, apart from Ferdie. His children weren't expecting him back on home turf until Christmas, his mobile phone had no reception in the house and the landline was out of service. It was the perfect place to reread the Sherston trilogy. Maybe Ferdie was right. He should stay here longer – he could use it as a base to work on the project.

'Uncle Christopher! I heard you were back! You *do* know you're now a local hero only two legs short of Lassie?'

Kit quickly amended his thinking. In a village, *everyone* knew you were here.

Dressed in a waistcoat and shooting breeks, flamboyant red sock tops poking out of his country boots, Bay back-slapped him into the counter. '*Rock* that Hallowe'en look, Kit, old man. Staying long?'

'A short while.' He wondered what 'look' Bay was talking about.

'You must come to our little do tomorrow night. Ma and Pa's usual shooting-season opener. Eight for eight thirty. I'll add your name to the table plan and rustle up a pretty widow.'

'That won't be necessary. I already have—'

'See you there!' Bay was marching off, bottle of craft gin in hand, grabbing a lemon from a display crate as he passed.

'— plans.' Kit turned back to the girl with the C tattoos to enter his PIN.

'You're the stranger from the dark and stormy night.' She smiled at him.

Looking up, he caught sight of his reflection in the mirror over her shoulder and realised his lips were Incredible Hulk green. 'Just how I want to keep it.'

Nevertheless, as he walked back to the Old Almshouses, taking the lane this time, he grew more enthusiastic about the idea of knuckling down there to put the Sassoon script together at last. Flying into Heathrow as dawn broke that morning, seeing green fields below and longing for Hermia, he'd instinctively needed to come here. Her memory faded with each visit, shrinking into the shadows. If he didn't hold on to it this time, it would move further away.

She'd helped him work on the idea in the early days, those frustrating hours of head-scratching a narrative structure, books and notepads open amid teenage homework and washing-up, Hermia trying – and usually failing – to hide her exasperation at being unable to articulate her thoughts clearly, knowing it just slowed down her mercurial-minded husband with the wife whose 'brain had a limp'. Her words. They took so much longer coming, but he loved her words. Now he no longer heard them in his head unless he was here.

In London, Kit had stepped too far away from the man he sought to dramatise. Sassoon had been a devoted horseman, which Hermia had sought to help him understand about the man whose compassion had sprung from the hunting field as well as the battlefield, an idea Kit still struggled with, his view deeply clouded. He would listen to her now, but he would be keeping horses firmly on the page and out of his life while he was here.

As he speeded up, desperate to get home and resume reading, there was a loud clank and one thin handle of the plastic bag gave way, depositing his overpriced groceries on the lane in front of a row of thatched cottages.

A gaggle of children dressed as witches, ghosts and luminous skeletons were coming the other way making 'whooooo' noises.

'Hell!' Kit stooped to collect his shopping, cramming teabags and cracker packets into his coat, relieved to find the bottle was unbroken. Two of the cheeses had rolled under the garden gate of one of the cottages. He swung it open with a creak to retrieve them, suddenly floodlit by a security light, which helped him track down an ale and mustard truckle under a frost-tipped lavender bush.

'Wooooaaaaaa!' A small ghost behind him made him jump.

As he straightened up, the door of the cottage was thrown open. 'Hello!' An elderly man in a checked shirt with a cardigan, beamed at him from the step. 'Our first trick-or-treaters!' He sprang along the path in welcome. 'My goodness, it's Mr Donne, isn't it? Compton Magna's very own impresario! Brian Hicks, chairman of the parish council.' He claimed a handshake and looked around the children. 'You brought some young theatrical talent, I see.'

There was a lot of giggling and a few 'Wooooooaaaaa!' and 'Arrrgh!' efforts, torches under chins. Kit would have liked to tell his impromptu minstrels to put a bit more bloody effort in. He had a reputation to protect.

But Brian was enchanted. 'Marvellous! Christine has prepared some warm blackcurrant squash and home-made bonfire toffee. One moment and I'll fetch some.'

'Fuck that,' said a small zombie, as Brian disappeared inside. 'Let's go round the holiday cottages. They give out London sweets and hard cash.' They whooped off, torches swinging.

Hurriedly, Kit retrieved the second truckle, but Brian was back outside before he could beat his own retreat, his small wife carrying a tray behind him. 'Now, making children disappear is a new one on me!'

'Smoke and mirrors.' Out of politeness, Kit took a piece of the bonfire toffee being offered and found his teeth glued together by bitter asphalt.

'If you're moving back, can I interest you in joining the council? We've a seat free so we can co-opt you straight in. Your late wife's family have always been most generous with their time.'

'Hmmaaaaawff.' He had no intention of socialising with villagers, and certainly not with Hermia's family, whom he still blamed for her accident.

'That's wonderful! I'll drop off the old minutes and details of the next meeting. The committee will be delighted.'

Teeth still stuck, Kit rolled his eyes, waved a farewell cheese and marched for home. It was absolutely typical of Compton Magna to pop out for teabags and find oneself coming back with invitations, new commitments and loose fillings.

On a whim, he went to the churchyard. The teenagers had gone. He could hear an owl hooting close by. 'I'll bring you your flowers later,' he told Hermia's headstone, sucking the last of the toffee from his teeth. 'I just wanted to promise you I'll finish Sassoon this time. And to apologise for Orla, and for not loving your friend *at all*. Jeez!' The barn owl screeched past so close he felt the air beat of its wings, caught its wide-eyed white face framed by a heart. The Tudors had called it a love owl, he remembered. Before that, it had been known as the ghost owl. He hurried back to the Old Almshouses.

The trick-or-treaters had all retired to the memorial hall by the time Carly caught up with them, squeaky trainer soles sliding around on the polished wood floors as small children threw shapes in the strobe lights to 'Monster Mash' and 'Ghostbusters'. Ignoring the age restriction, older Turner children dressed as terrifying half-deads drank beer and cat-called for thrash metal so they could throw themselves around in self-styled moshing.

Ellis was on a hyperactive sweets overload, trainers constantly alight as he charged around, the 'Splorer Stick flailing. He refused to come home with Carly when she finally caught him by the Batman cloak, fighting to be free. There was no sign of Ash.

'Where's your dad?'

He shrugged, jaw set in taciturn loyalty.

'Who's looking after you?'

He pointed his duster at one of the teenage half-dead, currently sharing a long face-eating kiss with a voodoo witch-doctor in a top hat. Then, pulling away, he tore off to rejoin the under-tens, by far the smallest and most aggressive of them all.

'I'll bloody well kill him.' Carly thundered outside to try Ash's number, but he was either switched off or ignoring her call. She could hear a dog howling. Her hands tingled and stung.

'Pricey?'

The howling stopped briefly, then resumed. Carly looked up at the dog star, Sirius, walking to heel beside Orion the hunter, and wished on it that she was okay.

Back in the hall, Batman had disappeared. She searched, asking the beer-drinking half-deads if they'd seen where he'd gone, the response zombie-shrugging indifference.

Outside again, she heard the dog howl and felt the back of her neck prickle, wondering whether Ellis had heard it too and followed.

She knew that Jed Turner kept his many dogs in a run behind Apple Rise on a neglected building plot. It was impossible to see or access from the estate, except through his own side gate and out of his rear garden, or via an overgrown farm track that ran through the thicket beyond the allotments and was shut off by padlocked metal gates. Having cut through the villagers' long strips of veggie patches often on the way to and from school, Carly knew a small, dextrous Batman could probably wriggle under them. There was a way into the allotments from the memorial hall car park.

She hurried through it. A drunkenly listing Frankenstein's monster was taking a pee beside a garden shed, lurching round in alarm as she raced to the gates.

Fluffy threads of brightly coloured 'Splorer Stick were caught in the sharp wire at their base.

Carly was slim, but there was no way she could fit under, and the gates were six feet high. 'Oy!' she called back to the monster. 'Give us a leg up!'

'That's private land, love,' came a muffled reply from beneath the rubbery mask.

'If you don't help I'll tell Psycho Pete you pissed against his shed.'

'I *am* Pete.'

'My four-year-old's gone down there.'

'You should have said.'

A moment later she was being propelled over the gate like a pole-vaulter.

'Ellis?' The track was covered in uneven hard-core. As she stumbled over it, the howling stopped and she heard whimpering and yelping, then her eldest child's laughter.

A dim bulkhead light illuminated all of Jed's dog runs, the shadows of six lurchers criss-crossing them as they barked, raising the alarm. The seventh was hard against the fence with Ellis, both overjoyed to see each other.

His face was pressed to the chain-linking through which it was being covered with excited kisses, Pricey's back end wagging frantically. When Carly approached, the dog positively twerked in the gloom, a rush of throaty warbles coming from her mouth so like Scooby Doo that she laughed.

'I found her, Mum!' Ellis laughed too. 'I found Pricey!'

'Well done.' She stooped beside him. 'Now, keep your voice down. We're not supposed to be here. She looks all right, don't she?'

The dog was in far better shape than she'd feared, her brindle coat glossy, her eyes bright. Yet the nervous energy that came off her made Carly's heart hammer harder, picking up on her distress. She pressed her hands to the fence, palms so hot she half expected the wires to melt like solder. Pricey pushed the dome of her forehead back at her, clearly willing the fence to dissolve.

The dogs in adjacent runs were barking their heads off. Someone would surely come out of Jed's house soon.

'We can take her home now, Mum!' Ellis raised his voice above the cacophony.

'Ssh. No, Ellis, we can't. She's not ours to take, love. She belongs to the man whose dogs all these are.'

'That's not fair! We only want Pricey.'

His anger upset Pricey, who tried to lick his face again, snaking her muzzle against the metal dividing them.

In the adjoining run, a huge black bull-lurcher, its slab of a head cross-hatched with scars, stopped barking and snarled at the strangers.

Pricey turned towards him, hackles drawn, that Scooby Doo warble now a deep and threatening warning. The black dog growled back. In an instant, Pricey was charging towards the fence and slammed against it, thirty kilos of hard, angry muscle making the wire mesh bounce and vibrate, like a giant snare drum. Moments later the dogs were trying to kill each other through the wire.

Terrified by the sudden change in his Pricey, Ellis broke into noisy sobs.

'Oy!' a gruff voice shouted, from the far side of the run. 'Quieten down, you lot! If that's you winding them up again, Tequila, your days are numbered, you mad bitch.' More bulkhead lights came on.

'We must go,' Carly hissed, tugging the tearful Batman back along the track, furious with herself for letting him stay long enough to witness the dog turning.

She was grateful to find Frankenstein's monster still hanging around in the allotments, now keeping company with several of the undead from the village hall, who pointed out a way of crawling through a gap in the fence at the side of the track to avoid climbing back over the gates.

'Fucking Hounds of the Baskervilles down there,' they cackled, as she hurried Ellis away.

By the time she'd marched him to his nan's to fetch Sienna and Jackson, got them all home, washed, changed and in bed, it was almost eight.

Carly wearily did the washing-up, emptied the overstuffed kitchen bin and carried it outside. An owl was shrieking from the big tree beyond the garden fence. Pricey was howling again. 'No creature's born bad,' she breathed. 'But some aren't give a chance to show they can be anything else.'

★

The text from Charlie came through first thing in the morning as Petra was tacking up the Redhead to hack out with the Bags. She read it in disbelief.

'Looking forward to tonight?' was the first thing Bridge asked when she joined them, tagging along at the back ready to pelt hastily around the ridge loop starting from Bagot, all four women on tight schedules, the lanes too icy to risk venturing further.

'Not going,' she called across, as they took the track behind the memorial hall, deflating balloons and stray spider's web string from last night's disco trapped in the branches overhead. 'Charlie's stuck in London with work.'

'*Shut... up!*' Bridge howled. 'Go anyway. That dress is sensational!'

'Yes, leave him tied up in the cellar tonight, Petra love.' Mo chuckled. 'We know that's where you really keep him.'

Charlie's text bothered Petra on a great many levels. Foremost, it bothered her because Charlie had lusted after this invitation and now seemed unconcerned that he couldn't get back. It bothered her that his case must be going very badly and he couldn't afford to be on the losing side again. It bothered her that his mother was here, blogging her every move and marriage blip, and this would merit at least two thousand words of vitriol, no doubt blaming slovenly housekeeping and inferior party nibbles. It bothered her that she'd miss out on wearing a dress and having a snoop inside Sandy and Viv Austen's grand farmhouse. A mosaic of Bingham-Percy architectural leftovers, it was rumoured to have oak panelling graffitied by Charles I and carved marble fireplaces from a Russian palace. It bothered her more than she was happy to admit that she wouldn't get to see Bay. Most of all, it bothered her that she could smell a lie in every word.

She was starting to think Charlie might be having an affair.

Work didn't seem to be motivating him at all, yet it was his excuse for being in London so much. He was looking incredibly good for a man who lost more cases than a cheap airline. In recent months, he'd started getting his hair cut in a sharply groomed Jude Law crop, lost weight and was running again. A new suit had appeared, the sharp-cut sort with a coloured lining, not the usual navy-blue conservatism. He'd even changed his aftershave. He constantly forgot social dates and parents' evenings. He was slow to return calls, defensive when he did. Their sex life was abysmal. If she was writing Ten Signs That Your Husband is Having an Affair, Charlie's behaviour would tick them all.

But if she just kept telling herself it was all in her imagination, her marriage would be fine.

'You *must* go tonight!' Bridge was still lecturing her as they cantered along the bridleway track. 'You're like the insider at the Oscars. We need the stories, the fashion low-down, the loo gossip.'

'I shouldn't think Sandy and Viv Austen's set are very fashion forward,' Petra pointed out. 'It's all game pie, gout and gabardine.'

Ahead of them, Gill held up her hand, indicating she was slowing down. 'Rider fore!'

'What's that mean again?' Bridge asked Petra, pony plunging as she tried to brake.

'Someone's riding towards us,' Petra explained, forced to turn a circle to take the speed out of the mare, while Bridge shot straight past her and disappeared through another hedge.

Eventually pulling up beside Gill on the brow of a hill and waiting for Mo and the fat cob to catch up, the three leading Saddle Bags watched a rider approach from the opposite direction, unmistakable in his upright posture as he trotted towards them on a tall thoroughbred, leading a glossy liver chestnut cob alongside.

'Good morning, ladies.' Lester raised his crop to his hat brim as he passed.

'How come he always looks so fricking smart?' Bridge whistled, as they watched him go, then set off at speed once more.

'Got to admire him,' Mo panted, kicking her own cob hard to keep up. 'He must be in his seventies now.'

'I hope I ride that well when I'm his age.'

'Why wait until then?' Gill muttered, quietly enough for only Petra. 'Did I hear you say Charlie's stuck in London tonight?'

'*Plus ça change.*'

'Worried?'

'Should I be?'

She sucked her teeth, looking across at Petra. 'No. If you had any suspicions, you wouldn't be able to stop yourself telling us. I know what you're like.'

'Absolutely.' Petra pulled out a brave smile. She had to confide in somebody soon or she'd explode.

That morning Prudie had brought Gunny *Les Cinnamon Grahams du Lait avec Cents-et-Milles et sprinkles chocolat* and left her with a Euro Disney brochure and a photograph of herself performing a tap-dance from *Matilda*.

Fitz placed the sweet tea on the annexe breakfast bar along with his BlackBerry. 'Gunny, I think we have a potential doorstep situation on our hands.'

'When?'

He showed her the most recent exchange. 'Tonight. They're meeting at the flat. Make or break talk. Dad says it's over. The reply threatens to call Mum and tell her.'

Gunny waved the phone away, refusing to look. 'You must get your mother out of the house tonight and confiscate her phone, William. I'll keep guard here.'

40

It was quite by chance that Pip spotted the horsebox driving past the Bulrushes. She was outside, disposing of the soiled cat litter, looking out across the valley at the frost. Then she saw the driver's profile slide past, recognising it immediately.

She hurried inside to throw together the fastest cupcakes of her life.

Petra phoned Manor Farm to explain that they would not be coming, speaking to an answerphone and gushing so many apologies that it timed her out before she made it clear who she was. She texted Bay to make sure the message had got through, their contact history on her phone blank now she'd deleted the thread with its disproportionate number of kisses, and its awful bonking-goddess GIF.

Come anyway! he replied. *I demand Mrs Gunn comes without her husband. In fact, it's my mission to make Mrs Gunn come tonight. Bx*

Petra decided to read this in a non-sexual way, but she deleted it none the less. Her conscience and her phone inbox were going to remain clean.

Leaving Gunny and the kids playing Carcassonne in the snug, she devoted herself virtuously to making butternut squash and marrow soup, arranging the vegetables only slightly suggestively to cheer herself up before peeling and chopping. Florence and the Machine were playing rebelliously loudly on the iPhone dock.

An incoming text beeped across the music. *Pip Edwards* announced the screen alert. She ignored it, turning as she heard the fridge door sucking open behind her.

Fitz took out a Coke, pushing the door closed and leaning against it to open the can with a hiss. 'Hey, you know you said you weren't going out to this posh old fogeys' party tonight after all?'

'That's right.'

'What if I'm your plus one?'

Petra tried to imagine him circulating among the Austens' stiff-jawed, stiff-upper-lipped and stiff-backed gathering of fossilised landowners, baronets and battleaxes. 'It would be terribly dull for you.' It would have been terribly dull for Petra too, if it hadn't been for the promise of Bay, with his charmingly predatory ways, the cool, controlling wife there to ensure it was all in the mind.

'I want to take you, Mum. I want you to be my date.'

'That's terribly sweet, but Gunny's here. We should make the most of it and have another night all together.' She felt obliged to make up for Scary Movie Night's failure to impress, the commentary on her grandchildren's dumbed-down cultural preferences scathing on @GunnPoint live streams, the big stain still drying on the tartan sofa from Gunny's red wine going airborne when Ed had done his Scream mask trick.

Fitz's mouth twitched into a half-grin, making her suspect Gunny was part of the reason for him wanting to go out. 'C'mon, Mum, you know you want to wear that new dress. You look beautiful in it. I saw the pictures on your phone. I want to show you off.'

Petra was quite choked.

'It could be useful for my future,' he coaxed. 'There are going to be some seriously well-connected seniors there. I scrub up. Teenage sons are where it's at socially – all the coolest parents use us as walkers. I promise I won't embarrass you.'

Having thought Fitz would be as much a fish out of water as her, Petra suddenly saw the value in it for him: her clever son, who always looked like he'd only just woken up, read *The Times* online while she read the *Mail*, had four times as many Facebook friends and, until the GCSE goof, had gone on skiing holidays with mates from school whose fathers were cabinet ministers and magnates. He was so startlingly tall and dishy nowadays, and teenage sons were indeed the ultimate accessory, if Liz Hurley, Madonna and Posh were anything to go by. Best of all, there was surely no better chastity-belt chaperone than a puritanical sixteen-year-old.

'You have to do something about the hair.'

He pushed it out of his eyes, which were blinking anxiously. 'Have you heard from Dad again today?'

'Not since first thing. He's in court. Why?'

'No reason.' He looked down, scuffing his feet. 'Gunny's just tweeted that you've abandoned her to a French board game and our fridge needs a good clean.'

Petra deliberately waited a few beats. 'It's lovely that you follow her on Twitter.' Then she laughed. 'We definitely have to get out of here tonight.'

'Cool. I'll keep her talking later so you have loads of time to get ready.'

Another text buzzed on her phone, this time from Gill: *Escape from your mother-in-law, Gunn! Ronnie Percy has been spotted MOVING IN. Let's walk the dogs past the stud. See you there. Bring binoculars.*

Petra scrolled back to check Pip's recent unread text. *Ronnie is here!!!!!* Any minute now there'd be tickertape streaming over the Comptons. She was delighted Ronnie was back, but liked to think their alliance meant she was elevated above spying.

About to text Gill that she was too busy – face mask, hair wrap, Gunny-baiting – she spotted her lingerie parcel on the kitchen table when she was sure she'd left it at the bottom of the back stairs to carry up. It had also been very neatly repacked whereas she'd left it spewing tissue paper after quickly checking the contents.

Petra looked up @GunnPoint's Instagram feed, an activity she'd been trying to wean herself off, like reading one-star book reviews whose creators seemed to have set out to destroy every shred of her self-esteem.

There in all their splendour, already shared several hundred times, was a picture of her reinforced, waist-pinching, bum-lifting, camel-toe-reducing miracle pants with the caption: *Do these live up to the hype, dear followers? Watch this space to see them in action on a mummy muffin top later.*

She had to get out of the house before she killed the woman.

*

When Ronnie swung the horsebox into the arrivals yard at Compton Magna Stud, she ground out the stub of the last cigarette she planned on smoking into the overfilled little ashtray. She stared at it for a long time. Her tiny roll-up remainders barely top-dressed its previous owner's filters. She'd given up Blair today, too. There would be no nicotine and no lovers while she was staying under her late parents' roof.

An impatient hoof crashed against the wall of the back of the lorry. Her old box would have rocked on its axis and splintered, but this one was a little armoured penthouse on wheels, built to cross continents.

In what Ronnie knew to be a rotten deal, she'd just swapped her two promising event horses for a seven-and-a-half-ton luxury horsebox and half a ton of horse trouble. This morning she'd driven away for good from job, home, oldest friend and lover. The lorry was both her pay-off and her fall-back – if this all went wrong, she figured she could live in the horsebox. She picked up her phone and sent a text to Blair to say she had arrived safely. She then went to her contacts and deleted his number.

Wincing, because doing it hurt a great deal, she glanced out of the window.

Lester was already standing guard on the cobbles, predictably dapper in tweed, the disapproving frown lines etched just as deeply in his face as Ronnie remembered.

Infuriated by the lump in her throat, Ronnie's gaze swept quickly around the frosted stone roofs, golden walls and archways through which corridors of flame-bright sunlight spilled across the cobbles. She'd hoped her daughters might be here, to protect their own interests and bolster Lester, if nothing else. All three children knew she was coming back today.

She swallowed a macerating blade of disappointment at her solitary reception committee, the very last person the Bardswolds Bolter would have chosen to greet her return.

We're both wise old owls, these days, she reminded herself. We know we must tough this out. As she wound down the window, though, her pulses were hammering. 'Give me just a minute.'

The flat cap nodded as he stepped back, and his fox terrier –
barking furiously at Ronnie's brace of heelers – was silenced by the
sharp rap of a leather cane against a polished boot, promptly sitting
and staring up at his master. Lester had kept the breed as long as
Ronnie had known him, each as loyal, fierce and disciplined as he
was. He was there to welcome her out of well-trained duty, every
instinct in his body undoubtedly wanting to snarl, bite and chase
her away again, just as she wanted to turn and run for the hills.

Lester eyed the horsebox with supreme distaste. He had no time for
these modern coach-built contraptions that looked like big camper
vans. The stud's old hunting box was all that was needed to get
a beast from A to B. But Ronnie had always been one for shiny new
things.

She was messaging on that phone of hers. The Captain would
have exploded at such bad manners. Lester's stupid old heart was
racing faster than it had in a long while, even when Pip told him the
Captain had died. Beside him, Stubbs started to growl, picking up
on his master's tension.

In the cab, Ronnie's fingers worked swiftly on her phone screen, deft
and agile as she stroked her way to her Personal Contacts, scrolling
up and down the many numbers, emails and addresses with one last
affectionate look before tapping Delete All. Her phone asked her
whether she was certain; did she want to back up her numbers first?
No, she didn't, she told it. She was perfectly certain, thank you. And
in an instant, a hundred or more fast friendships were gone. The
tension melted with them.

Ronnie had a plan. The past month had provided plenty of thinking time while she was dismantling her life in Wiltshire.

Twenty-seven years ago, when she had gone from receiving 250
Christmas cards to none, abandoning old bonds had been a far
more painful process, her departure leaving a bomb crater. Now
she knew how it felt to slip between lives, and coming home meant
travelling back in time. Memories had always made her edgy. She

kept only a very few in easy reach. Important phone numbers were among them.

She could remember them from years ago – Hermia's had been Chipping Hampton 410, Mr Walcote the vet 127, here at home 453. She had long since embraced ten-figure dialling, the digital age and messaging, but the numbers were among those etched as permanently in her head as the lines in Lester's face.

She knew the stallion man would approve of the first part of her plan, at least.

'Lester!' she greeted him now, landing beside him. 'Do you like my wheels?'

'It's very smart.'

'Goes like the clappers.'

Be British. Be polite. Be unremittingly upbeat. Just don't mention the war. They both knew the Percy rules.

With a lot of shrill barking, her younger heeler, Olive, goat-hopped down from cab to step to cobbles and went into a stiff-legged dance around Stubbs. Enid, as doddery as poor Lester, required lifting down.

'The younger one's a sex-mad virago,' she told him, watching her little dominatrix turn on the snarling scare tactics, Lester's dog rolling, supplicant-style, onto his back. 'But I can see she'll have no trouble from him.'

Lester bristled as Olive checked out his dog's scrotum. 'Should get her neutered too as she's a mongrel.'

'She's not a mongrel, Lester, she's a Lancashire Heeler.' She didn't seem remotely offended.

'If you say so.' He watched the little dog, which was a pretty thing, like a beefed-up dachshund with bat ears.

'It's a very old breed,' Ronnie told him, setting the second dog down. 'They were used to drive cattle. Tough as old boots. There you go, your boy has an ally now.' Elderly Enid had marched in to bark at her daughter to back off. Rolling over onto his belly, Stubbs scrabbled up to make formal, bottom-sniffing introductions. 'She's a very controlling mother and another terrible tart, but she does have good manners.' She shot him a sideways smile. 'And she'll be rounding up that herd of yearlings faster than a quad bike before you know it.'

Lester thawed a little. Dog talk soothed him, and he'd forgotten how indefatigable Ronnie could be, the sort of person who made everybody she met feel they were in on a terrific joke. Her mother had been the same. Earthy, unpretentious and refreshingly straight-speaking, they were a family of never-say-die ralliers. And Ronnie had an exceptional eye for a horse.

'You brought the same two as last time?' He nodded at the lorry container.

'Quite different. Take a look.'

Leading the way around to the back, Lester tried to hide how lame he was, but Ronnie had the Percy eye for conformation in man and beast. 'Had a fall?'

'Cold weather,' he muttered.

'Arthritic hips, more like.'

'If you say so.'

Ronnie felt an unwanted memory pull at her sleeve. She and Hermia had taken childish delight in concocting witty replies to Lester's catchphrase. It had driven him mad, especially when he was teaching them to ride.

'I say so,' she said now, the stock response. The Captain had been the only one allowed to add *and what I say goes around here.*

She could already imagine conversations between Lester and the Horsemaker, who habitually said 'so it is' in his soft Irish burr. It was a perfect match, but telling him that certainly wasn't part of the plan just yet. Getting him to look her in the eye was the first step.

'Had one of my linchpins replaced last year,' she told him, patting her hips fondly. 'Titanium. I'll give you the number of my consultant.'

He cast her hip a brief look of horror. 'I'm good for a few years yet.'

He looked so old and vulnerable that Ronnie was fighting an almost overwhelming urge to put a hand on his arm. But they would both be mortified by that. Lester and Ronnie had never once comforted one another, through a thousand humiliations, falls, triumphs, tragedies and the bitter secrets that had finally broken her marriage.

She didn't want to remember any of those.

'Got anything in here I'll like?' He watched as she pressed the button for the hydraulic ramp.

'You should know you don't need to ask me that, Lester.' She laughed. They were always on safe ground while four hoofs were standing on it too.

There was a loud whinny from inside, the unmistakably fierce, earthy scream of a stallion ready to claim new territory.

Ronnie caught the side of Lester's mouth twitching, then turning down. Was that a smile? As the ramp lowered and he looked in, there was no mistaking it. A toothy smile.

Everyone smiled when they saw Beck. He had the brightest, boldest head of any horse Ronnie had known. If bone structure could be patented, Beck's would be filed under Mythical. Also under Pain in the Arse, High Maintenance, Heartbreaking and Dangerous.

'I swapped two sane, well-mannered horses for this bastard and an Oakley,' she explained. 'He's my magic beans. What do you think?'

Lester's weak eyes strained to focus, but even misted, he knew he'd rarely seen a better-looking animal. Clipped out, his coat had the same luminescent shine as mother-of-pearl. Huge dark eyes blazed over the high partition, nostrils flared like hollow conches, ears like small sails tacking left then right, head bobbing and mane tossing. Like surf. He was a hippocampus bursting from the sea, a tsunami of a horse.

'Looks fair,' he muttered.

'Let's give him a moment to look round.' Ronnie clicked and soothed as the horse threw his head higher, glaring furiously out at his new territory, striking out in front and behind with such force the sides of the box bulged. 'He's bloody hard to handle.'

Lester knew he'd soon sort that. 'Breeding?'

'Ninety-nine per cent thoroughbred, the other devil incarnate. He's branded Holsteiner. Competed Grand Prix in Germany by the age of eight.'

'Dressage?'

'Show-jumper. Too screwed up to do the job now, mind you. He went to the Middle East for the price of a small oil well just before the London Olympics, but he hated it, put his leg through a wall and severed a tendon before anyone had sat on him. He was returned to Germany to stand at stud where his semen sold for a grand a straw. They should have left him there, happily shagging the dummy mare, but some bright spark thought it would be fun to bring him back into work.' She cleared her throat sheepishly. 'He was sold to Britain over the internet for mad money. I found out later a lottery winner had bought him for his new girlfriend. She was completely out-horsed, of course. He just got madder, badder and more highly strung. He was sold on to a local dealer, then pillar-to-posted from one end of the country to the other. A pro I know recognised him in an auction catalogue, and I picked him up for a song. By then his reputation for decking jockeys was notorious. He's been on a friend's yard since. He's very alpha, very messed up and *very* spoiled.'

The grey stallion had stopped head-throwing and screaming now. Turning to look at Lester, his huge eyes set beautifully against that wide silver plate of a forehead, he suddenly flattened his ears, neck snaking out like an eel strike.

Lester stepped calmly back on the ramp. 'Progeny?'

'Already competing in Germany. World beaters across country. Fearless.'

There was an indignant whinny from further back in the box. 'And that is Dickon, my old eventer, who is just as brave but slightly more accident prone.'

Lester's eyesight was too poor to make out more than an off-centre white blaze on a long dark face.

'Also from Germany. He earned his stable name because the first time I saw him at a horse trials in Holland he performed like a dream, despite having a complete dick on board. Young Rory Midwinter used to ride him for me. He was quite something in his day.' She let out a giggly growl, leaving Lester uncertain whether she was talking about the jockey or the horse.

They stepped back as Beck let out a screeching roar so loud the horsebox shook, head thrown back, black eyes bulging, nostrils cavernous. Dickon joined him with an alarmed whinny. Then they heard another roar behind them, squeaking and rattling, like a runaway gun carriage.

Ronnie swung round just as a familiar small blue car careered into the yard, seeing the horsebox ramp a second too late.

'Watch out!' She pulled Lester out of the way as it mounted the ramp, a fox terrier lost somewhere beneath it.

The picture of Ellis in his zombie Batman outfit that Carly had posted on her Facebook wall the previous evening was still making her phone pop every few minutes as a friend commented on how much he'd grown or how much they missed her, Ash and the kids. She was battling down a wave of homesickness for army life so intense she felt as though somebody had just punched her in the throat.

'You all right, hun?' Janine had let herself in through the back door and was unloading the contents of a large pink plastic toolbox on the breakfast bar. 'I've got some lovely new transfers to try out on you.'

As soon as she'd heard Carly was waitressing at the Austens' party, she'd insisted on applying a fresh set. 'Free advertising. I'm showcasing my Christmas selection.'

'Can I have reindeers?' requested Carly.

'You're getting Christmas puds.' She selected a dung-coloured polish and a plastic page of what looked like squished greenflies. 'I've got miniature frosted holly leaves.'

They could hear Ash thumping downstairs, big feet heavy on the treads. 'I'm going out,' he shouted from the hallway. 'I'll be back late.'

'Wait!' Carly turned, fingers clamped in Janine's vice-like grip as she was attacked with a big emery board.

He appeared in the doorway, short black Puffa coat making his torso look huge, like a superhero from a comic strip. 'I told you I'm out tonight.'

'You said you'd give me a lift.'

'Someone else'll do it.' He pulled a beanie down so low it almost obscured his eyes, reaching back to fish out his sweatshirt hood and pull that over too. All Carly could see of his face now was a stubbled jaw.

They'd had a furious row when he'd got in last night, his excuse for abandoning Ellis to trick-or-treating with his older cousins simply that he was 'sorting out a bit of bother'. He'd shipped too many beers to make much of an argument, just a lot of noise that had woken all three kids. In the end, Carly had banished him downstairs to the sofa, letting Ellis and Sienna crawl in with her, lying awake and fuming with unspoken indignation at his pig-headed unpredictability. They'd apologised over breakfast. At least, Carly had apologised, then asked him to apologise, and he'd grunted, nodded and agreed to drive her to the farm. Now he was doing it again.

'But you promised, Ash. Your truck's better in ice. This is good money. It could lead to more work.'

'Yeah, well, I might be working tonight too.'

'On your hangover.' Janine cackled.

'Doing what?' demanded Carly.

'Labouring.' The jaw was set in a determined line.

'At night? What sort of labouring?'

'Something Skulley's got on the go.'

'Illegal, then,' teased Janine, winking at Carly.

Ash's smile, so rare these days, flashed on and off. 'We're respectable old boys now, sis.'

'Ash, tell me it's not illegal,' Carly demanded. 'Which one's Skulley?'

'You haven't met him.' Ash dropped a kiss on his wife's head, ruffling her hair. It was the most affection he'd shown her all week, and Carly knew bringing money in would make him feel better about himself. She just wished he wouldn't spring things like this on her. He'd gone from career soldier to jobbing mercenary. His gym bag hadn't shifted out of the hall in a fortnight.

'Never ask a Turner man too much about what he's up to,' Janine advised, after he'd gone.

'Or tell a Turner wife what to do,' Carly snapped. 'So which one is Skulley?'

'Ink's brother. Sleeves of skull tattoos. He lives up near Coventry now, but sometimes still hangs around with the Compton boys.'

'And he's kosher, you reckon?'

'As a bagel, love. They've all seen their share of bother, but they're good lads. Look at Flynn. He earns good money.' She winked. 'It's a man's job, isn't it, putting shoes on horses?'

'Not necessarily,' Carly muttered, knowing Janine was deliberately winding her up.

'All the ladies love him. They love a hunky fitness instructor too, mind you. You'd better watch out there.'

'What do you mean?'

'You're always on his case, Carl. Lighten up a bit. Turner women don't nag. Not if they want to stay Turners.' Janine selected the white polish for the puddings' icing.

'He's not been going into college, Janine,' she whispered.

Janine gave world-weary sigh. 'I guessed as much. Tenner says he won't last until Christmas. I know my baby brother.'

'And *I* know my husband!' Carly snarled. 'He's got to get his priorities right.'

'He is.' Janine regarded her over the pot of lacquer, the wolf-pale Turner eyes narrowing between their thick black lines of make-up. 'I can't see Ash making fat Cotswolds housewives do star jumps in the back garden, can you? We're a travelling family. We make things, sell things, mend things, paint things.' She held up a decorated nail.

'He's always wanted to be a fitness trainer, even in the army.'

'You know your husband,' Janine said sarcastically. 'So you'll know he wanted to be a dental technician as a kid. Always tinkering about with people's teeth. Had Grandma Betty's dentures out that many times to clean them she looked like Joey Essex when she smiled.'

Carly hadn't known that. She glared at her nails, saying nothing.

'I'm making it up.' Janine cackled. 'Had you going there for a minute, though, didn't I?'

Carly forced a laugh. She wasn't sure she did know Ash as well as she'd once thought.

'What does Skulley do for a living?' She changed the subject.

'Gardening and ground maintenance and stuff. Typical jobbing Traveller.'

'Is it legal?'

'Depends whose rules you go by. He's usually got his fingers in the till or in his boss's wife. Nothing big. Flogging a few Christmas trees or turf rolls for cash, the odd garden statue or fence battery that's gone walkabout.'

Carly was appalled. 'Ash can't get involved with that! I've got to stop him.'

Janine kept a hand clamped round her wrist. 'You let him do what he wants, hun. You're not an army wife now.'

Carly thought of the friends currently reading and liking her Hallowe'en message, so full of saccharine happiness, not for a moment betraying how hard she found it here, how lonely she felt, how different Ash was. Another picture she'd posted that day had been of a horse in a witch's hat pulling a big, laughing face. Horses. Thank God for horses.

'I *am* going to train as a farrier, Janine,' she said firmly.

'Don't be daft,' scoffed Janine. 'That is *never* going to happen. You'd ruin these beauties for a start.' She admired her handiwork. Carly's nails looked like ten poisonous toadstools, the fingers that felt hot as branding irons when they sensed sickness and pain now all wearing comedy hats. The blonde woman from the stud had told her she had a gift when she was with Spirit the night he was injured. The bearded vet had said the same when they'd rescued Pricey.

Then it struck her, an idea so inspired it was as if somebody had just put their hands on her waist and lifted her overhead. 'I'm going to heal things.'

'Starting with what?' Janine snorted.

'My marriage.'

'OhmyGod, ohmyGod have I killed him?' Pip wailed, wrenching open her car door and stumbling out, realising too late that there was a four-foot drop because she'd come to a halt halfway up a horsebox ramp. Landing on the cobbles with a jolt that went straight through her, she crumpled into the arms of a concerned and astonished Ronnie Percy.

This shouldn't be happening, Pip thought wretchedly. Why hadn't Lester warned her? She'd have dressed up. She'd have put on the heating, aired the rooms, made up a bed and got some groceries in. She'd have baked more. She'd already marked up the Ronnie welcome recipes. Instead her cupcakes had sunk in the middle and she'd run over Lester's dog.

'He's fine,' Ronnie said, in her warm, no-nonsense voice. 'Isn't he, Lester?'

He was running a practised hand over Stubbs, but apart from a big fright and a loss of dignity in front of the bossy heelers he'd been trying to impress with his foxy charms, the little dog was apparently unscathed. 'If you say so.'

'I say so.'

Pip had come as fast as she could, not even stopping to put on her coat. Which was why she was still wearing her slippers. Hoping nobody would notice, she thrust a hand out to Ronnie. 'Welcome back to Compton Magna.' She adopted her best super-efficient power PA voice. 'We're so thrilled you're moving in at last! I've got everything ready for you, apart from a few last-minute preparations I need to make in the house, some of which I want to run through with you first if you have time.'

'I don't.'

'But I've baked cakes and brought my coffee pod machine.'

The occupants of the lorry were stamping and snorting furiously.

'I want to unload my horses.'

'I'll help!'

'Not in those slippers. Let's get these boys off, shall we, Lester?' said Ronnie. 'Can you move your car? I'm sorry, I've forgotten your name.'

'Pip Edwards. Pip. Your father's housekeeper.' She grew a little smaller. 'My dad used to call me Pipsqueak.'

'How horrid of him. Car!' she chivvied Pip.

Pip squared her shoulders, refusing to be defeated. 'I'll get it moved straight away and put the kettle on. I've no idea what we're all standing around here talking for.'

41

Petra hurried breathlessly towards Gill on the footpath that led along the boundary of the stud.

To her embarrassment, Gill had binoculars already trained on the stableyard. 'Isn't that an invasion of privacy?'

'Rubbish. I brought them out to look for my goshawk, but this is local history. Pip's straight in there.' Gill chuckled, handing her the binoculars. 'Looks like Ronnie's brought a couple of horses.'

'Does the village descend on the stud with pitchforks and flaming torches at any minute?'

'Give them twenty-four hours,' Gill muttered. 'The bonfire's already set up on the Green.'

'That's a nice-looking horse.' Petra admired the grey now exploding out of the box. He looked like he'd been chiselled from marble to stand on the fourth plinth in Trafalgar Square, dark eyes as huge and expressive as a silent movie star's.

'Give those here.' Gill grabbed the binoculars back so fast, Petra was almost garrotted. Looking through them, she took a sharp breath. 'My God, that *is* nice!' Then she gasped. 'Hold on, that's a *stallion*! You know what this means?'

'That Gill Walcote can spot gonads at two hundred yards?' Petra watched the horse throw itself into the air, body twisting up in a plunging almost vertical rear, grey legs paddling and head shaking, a blur of muscle, hoof and aggression that made her grateful there was a large field between her and it. Tiny Ronnie and wizened Lester clung on, coaxing the horse forward as soon as he landed, then marching him, doing a head-shaking jog, beneath the first arch and out of sight.

'Ronnie Percy's brought a new stallion in to stand at stud.' Gill fiddled with the binoculars' focus. 'And there's something else in that lorry – she might even have brought two stallions. This must mean she's going to run the place as a going concern. She can't possibly be selling up to developers or anybody else. The village is safe! Call Bay and let him know.'

'Why should I call Bay?'

But Gill was already on her own phone to husband Paul. 'Great news...'

Petra pulled her scarf tighter around her neck and watched Ronnie march back with her long stride, bounding up the ramp to fetch another horse, this one dark, rangy and long-eared.

Although faintly embarrassed to be gawking at the stud's legendary bolter, Petra was fascinated by the dynamic – Lester bustling, Pip lurking and the small blonde dynamo calling the shots.

'Have you called Manor Farm?' Gill asked, when she'd rung off. 'Bay's been like a caged tiger waiting for this.'

Petra fired off a slightly awkward text: *Will be at party tonight after all. Bringing Fitz. Hope okay. PS Dog-walking past stud and see Ronnie P is moving back in.* Something she'd heard Pip say to Mitch the postman had been bugging Petra. 'Is it possible Bay and Ronnie could ever have got it together?' she asked Gill.

'Hardly. She's not been back *and* he's nearly twenty years her junior. I know you credit him with superhuman powers of attraction, but I hardly think Ronnie would...' She hesitated, brows creasing.

'What?'

'No, it's nothing.' Gill shook her head, lifting her binoculars again. 'Oh... my... God.'

'What is it?'

'My goshawk! He's got a mate. They're sky-dancing, look! That is so rare.' She pointed at two tiny specks. 'Frightfully good luck.'

'Aren't they buzzards?'

'Oh, maybe you're right. Damn.'

Petra's phone buzzed. *I could love you very, very deeply, Mrs G. Bx*

*

'... and your dad used to say that if he needed anything he could just ask me and there it would be as if by magic. I do miss him – he was such a character and...'

Ronnie had already tuned out the little woman's voice. What was her name again? She couldn't concentrate on a word she was saying, her head splitting. She was sure Alice had said in an email that she had let her go.

'... make you some light lunch maybe? Your dad's favourite was my lasagne. He used to say, "Pip, you are the Comptons' answer to Fanny Cradock," and...'

Pip Edwards. That was it.

'... I'd like you to feel you can call upon me any—'

'That is *so* kind of you, Mrs Edwards,' she cut across her, 'but all I need right now is a paracetamol. Would you mind awfully seeing if you can find me a painkiller? Ibuprofen, aspirin, laudanum, anything.'

'Straight away!' She bustled into the house.

Ronnie rubbed her temples and went into the Small Yard where Lester had insisted her horses must be quarantined. Having taken over settling Dickon, whose kindness was in direct contrast to Beck's lack of anger-management, he was now rolling travel bandages proprietorially by his half-door like a jailer.

'Bit tucked up from his journey, this one,' he muttered.

'He's a worrier and a warrior.' She looked in at her favourite sidekick and heard a reassuring whicker, a rustle of straw bringing a big brown cheek against hers. She reached up a hand to rub the familiar path along the offset white blaze to the whorl on his forehead, then up into his frizzy black forelock, which always stood up like Bert's hair in *Sesame Street*. Now in his golden years, Dickon was a cavalry officer of a horse. 'We need to talk, Lester. Come in for some supper with me later.'

'I'd rather not, if you don't mind.'

'Don't be silly. We've got to try to get on.'

'I prefer my own company of an evening.'

'Still the same stubborn bugger.' She smiled, determined not to rise. Being with him was easier than Ronnie had feared, theirs a horseman's bond so deeply patterned through her infancy and to adulthood that she slipped back into it without thinking. Her plans could be drip-fed: she had time.

'Then we can wait.' She patted Dickon farewell and turned to face the old man. 'But I do want one ground rule in place straight away. We don't talk about Johnny or any of that business.'

'Agreed.' He couldn't say it fast enough.

Ronnie knew it was a cold day, but the sudden chill made the hairs prickle on her skin. 'Good.' She moved along to look in on Beck, box-walking feverishly and baring his teeth between furious bellows to announce his arrival. Polar opposite of Dickon, macho alpha muscle-man Beck was messy, paranoid and absolutely hated moving house. Lester had grudgingly put in the 'toys' he'd come with – balls, mirrors, licks and a giant dangling apple, all thrust upon Ronnie by Verity. She had no idea if they made a difference, but she was no more inclined to take them away from him than she was Lester's authority.

They went into Big Yard to see old Cruisoe, the grand old man of the stud, trumpeting pompously over his stable door at Beck. In the opposite corner, his wall-eyed son had his chin propped up on the V-bar trying frantically to see what was going on.

'Healing fine,' Lester told Ronnie, when she crossed to see him. 'Everything's in safe hands here, Mrs Ledwell.'

'I don't doubt it is. Call me Ronnie.' She forced another smile, head pounding, turning towards the arch.

'Brought the colts across from the Sixty Acres this morning,' he followed her, 'so the Manor Farm boys can clear the tree.'

'Well done.'

'Young Bay can't stop bragging when we're out with the Fosse and Wolds that Austens are buying that land.'

'That's right.' Stopping, Ronnie sucked her cheeks in slowly, the sour taste palpable. Clever Petra Gunn had very poor taste. Ronnie hoped she'd killed him off in her book.

'It's out of my hands, Lester.' She cast an apologetic look over her shoulder, knowing he hated the thought of the stud being stripped of land as much as she did. 'We need their money. If you excuse me, I'd better go and talk to Mrs Edwards.'

'You keeping Pip on?' The gruffness to his voice belied his worry. 'I'll think about it.'

She found the talkative housekeeper in the scullery, presiding over a large first-aid box filled with enough drugs to wipe out the entire village. Thanking her, Ronnie knocked back the two tablets she was handed – they could have been cyanide for all she knew. 'There's a letter that should have come here from the solicitor addressed to me. Terrible bore, but they've been on my case about signing some papers today. Do you know where it is?'

'There's quite a bit of post,' Pip said. 'It's one of the things I need to talk to you about.' She led the way into the main entrance hall, where generations of the Percys' best sires looked down on them from yellowing oil-paintings.

'Christ.' Ronnie came face to face with columns of post stacked in size order on the hall table. And the side table. And the floor. It was a Parthenon of post. 'Where did all this come from?'

'We hid it away in the big chest for the funeral, so I kept putting it there until it filled up.' Pip pointed out the ornately carved antique oak coffer beneath the stairs, big as a sofa. 'A lot of it pre-dates your dad's death,' she went on, in her breathless little-girl voice. 'He wasn't one for opening post by the end. Alice and Pax went through the important bills and bank stuff early on, and told Lester to forward anything official-looking to the solicitor, but they never wrote down the address and, anyway, Lester doesn't like coming into the house. It's mostly junk mail. I can collate it, if you like. I used to do that for the Captain.'

Ronnie picked up a thick wedge of hand-written envelopes.

'I thought it best not to open those ones without your say-so.' The voice rattled on. 'Isn't it awful people still sending things to your father even though everybody must know by now? I didn't have that problem with my parents, but then again they didn't really have a lot of friends. When Dad died I put a notice in the…'

Tuning her out once more, Ronnie set the letters down again. Nobody had cancelled the subscription to *Horse & Hound* or the *Field*, which made up the central tower, interleaved with the NFU's magazine and breeding-society quarterlies. Junk mail formed three piles as high as her elbow. Business-like rectangular envelopes were stacked in a paving-stone patio around all these, each block ten or twenty deep, sorted rather sweetly according to colour – white, cream, manila – as well as size.

'I could take the magazines to the vets' surgery and the junk mail to the paper bank if you like,' Pip was offering.

Ronnie didn't really want a housekeeper, and she certainly couldn't afford one, but she could see she needed help, and if that person knew the house, loved the horses and looked out for Lester, it was a head start nobody else could hope to match. It would be bad form to mention money, Ronnie felt, especially as she could offer none.

'It's terribly kind of you to help out.'

'As long as you need me.' Pip stood to attention in her slippers.

The landline rang and she picked it up proprietorially, addressing the caller with hushed suspicion. 'Compton Magna Stud... I'll see if she's available. May I ask what this is in connection with?.... Yes, this is the housekeeper speaking... Oh, I see... Oh, it's *you*...' She went very pink and giggled.

Ronnie smiled, warming to her. More Mrs Overall than Mrs Hughes maybe, but her father would have loved that she rushed over in slippers. It showed dedication.

She studied Pip as she listened to the caller, head cocked, the giggle like a cat's purr, blush creeping into her pale cheeks, like a raspberry juice stain through cotton as she listened. She'd be pretty if it wasn't for the drab clothes and that awful frizzy hair. Her eyes were big and startled, but there was secrecy in them. She reminded Ronnie of a favourite actress who stood on bleak Dorset beaches, solving murder cases. She sensed Pip Edwards was her secret weapon.

'One moment,' she told the caller now, covering the receiver and mouthing, 'Are you available?'

'Who is it?'

'Bay Austen.' The pink cheeks said it all.

She held out her hand reluctantly. It was better to get it over with. She was as disappointed in wily little Pip as dreamy Petra Gunn, but not surprised. Bay had been making women blush since he hit puberty.

'Bay.' There were very few people Ronnie spoke to without a ripple of laughter or a furnace of warmth in her voice, but Bay got a flat monotone so sharp that both her dogs sat down and looked up at her.

'Ronnie. I hear you're moving in. Welcome back!'

'Thank you. I take it you're calling about the land?'

'Can one neighbour not welcome another home?'

'Of course, and thank you.' She watched Pip start to wade through the piles of formal-looking envelopes to find the one she'd asked about, fast as a card shark separating a deck.

'It's been a long time, when was it – twenty years ago?'

'You know when it was, Bay.' She ran her tongue along her teeth, the bad taste back.

She'd known him as a boy before that, a little charm assassin hunting at the front of the field, always hanging about her at point, the merry blue eyes watching her flirt with Angus. He was just a couple of years older than Tim, his family a strong reminder of absent Hermia, the old feud between the Austens and the Percys enjoying a new era of friendship. She'd ruffled his hair, listened to his *Danger Mouse* impersonations and crashed into him a lot playing Marco Polo in the Austens' crowded swimming-pool. It had never occurred to Ronnie then that a boy under ten could have a crush, least of all on a mother of three in her twenties. After her marriage ended, she hadn't seen Bay for more than a decade. When they'd met again, the circumstances laughably awful, she hadn't recognised him. He had known precisely who she was.

'Now, the land,' he was saying, in the silken tones of a man accustomed to charming the opposition. 'My solicitor says you're the last trust signatory needed on the contract of sale. Then it comes across here for mine and we're away. If we're quick, we'll get it under the wire for completion before the Eyngate Park meet.' He started chatting easily about the plan to make an old-fashioned three-mile hunt chase from the grand old house on the Fosse Way across the farm's land to the legendary Compton Thorns. 'My band of supporters are on stand-by to fix up all the old hunt jumps. Nothing like galloping home to supper across one's own hedges, is there?'

She could hear the twenty-year-old in there still. Bombastic, flirtatious, easy to like, despite the bravura. She could imagine he was a hugely popular master. Confidence was such an aphrodisiac, especially in young men as beautiful and straightforward as Bay. Pax had been utterly infatuated by it.

'Bay,' she interrupted, another sharp command that made her dogs sit down obediently once more. 'I'm sure it will be a wonderful occasion and I appreciate you're spinning a delicious yarn to make me feel all this is meant to be but, frankly, I just have to find the bloody paperwork. It was sent here in error. I'll sign it as soon as—'

With a loud 'whoo-hooo!' Pip held up a thick A4 envelope.

'— I can find a pen.'

'That's excellent news! Why not bring it round tonight? Parents are having their usual do. We'll toast your return.'

'I don't think that's a very good idea.'

'It'll be a double welcome home. Hermia's theatre chap's back in the village too. Hoping he might come along. Hugely clever. Come on, Ronnie.' Bay's upbeat, growling voice was wagging its tail furiously. 'Isn't it time to let bygones be bygones?'

'Bay, when so much of your life has gone by in the blink of an eye, as mine has, you'll learn that letting things go is a very bad state of affairs. I'll sign the papers now.' She rang off.

Pip was hovering, holding out the solicitor's envelope.

'Would you like a cup of coffee? I've got lungo, intenso and decaffeinato. And cake.'

'A cup of tea would be heaven.'

'You know Bay well?' Pip hovered.

'Well enough.' Ronnie ripped open the envelope and pulled out a thick sheaf of papers, then leafed through them.

'They're having their party tonight. My friend Petra's going. She's a super-successful novelist.' She dropped her voice. '*Big* crush on Bay. Bought special underwear for tonight.'

Pretending not to hear, Ronnie held the covering letter at arm's length, struggling to read it without her glasses. It was instructing her to review the trust assets for the probate application and sign the sales contract for the land. 'Where would I find a pen?'

Pip disappeared on a quest for tea and a pen.

The light was fading fast as evening stole in. Ronnie flicked the switch on the wall lamps and stood directly below the only one with a working bulb, between two oil-paintings of big-boned hunters.

Running her eye down the page, she spotted the probate valuation beside the sixty acres of land. The figures couldn't be right. She started leafing furiously back through the sales contract.

By the time Pip returned with a tray of two different teas, milk, lemon slices, tiny fluffy cakes with slightly sunken middles and a selection of pens, Ronnie had gone.

Pip set her tray down dispiritedly. It was heaven to have someone back at the stud and to know her job was safe, but she missed the Captain who, you could fairly confidently guarantee, would stay in one place, especially when his gout got bad. Then Ronnie burst through the door carrying a suitcase.

'Tea. Heaven! You're an angel, Pip. Bring it upstairs and you can help me get ready. Are you any good at make-up? I'm hopeless.'

Pip's smile was so wide her earrings wobbled. The Captain had never needed a makeover.

42

This evening Carly wanted to prove herself to the Austens as a good worker. The farm shop would extend its hours for Christmas shopping, and there was talk of opening a café in the new year. With her waitressing experience at Le Mill, she saw tonight as an opportunity to impress. If she worked every job she could, setting some money aside, she'd calculated that she could afford the first term's college fees for the farriery course by September. Ash would have qualified as a personal trainer by then, so things would surely get easier.

Reluctant to be seen getting a lift with Ash's cousin, Mex, who drove a prehistoric van with rusted wheel arches and a cab waist-high in takeaway litter, Carly asked to be dropped at the end of the drive she normally used for work, not realising that Mr and Mrs Austen's home had its own private entrance. The closest she'd ever got to the big farmhouse was the old sheep yard at the back of the shop where she and the other girls shared cigarettes in breaks, and from where they could just make out its tennis court behind a tall topiary hedge. Baronial in proportion, the house was well shielded from the converted buildings that formed commercial units and holiday cottages. Climbing over locked gates and scrabbling around old glass houses and compost piles, Carly quickly discovered that it was no longer the back-door-always-open hub of the working farm.

Arriving ten minutes late, covered with leaves and mud, she made her way past a huge conservatory, glowing like a Moroccan lamp, to a side extension, where a harassed blonde beanpole in leather trousers was unloading big foil-covered trays from a van with This Most Excellent Canapé written in curly script on its side. A handsome olive-skinned youth in a suit minced back and forth in her wake. Mr Austen senior, in threadbare cords and tattered waxed jacket, was unloading boxes of hired wine glasses from his Land Rover.

'Reinforcements!' he greeted her affably, handing her a box and picking up another. 'Our pretty shop girl has arrived at last.'

Reminding herself he was old, posh and paying her, Carly apologised for being late and followed him inside.

She'd always imagined farmhouse kitchens as homely and welcoming places, with orphan lambs and dogs lying in front of an Aga and lots of waxed coats on the back of chairs, but this kitchen was footballer's wife state-of-the-art. Even though Mr and Mrs Austen were knocking into their late sixties, they had some seriously high-gadget wizardry going on.

'My son and his wife had all this put in when they had theirs done this year,' Mr Austen explained, as he showed her the drinks fridges – they had two. There were also two dishwashers just for glasses – the sort that pulled out like drawers – as well as an ice machine and a sparkling-water tap. 'It's all rather fun, isn't it? No idea how any of it works.'

The harassed caterer, who had handled parties for the Austens in their old kitchen for years, had no idea how any of it worked either, and was having a meltdown by a huge gumboot-green range cooker, as stone cold as a marble altar.

'It's log-burning,' Mr Austen told her proudly. 'Frightfully environmentally friendly. Rather wasted on us. Viv prefers that.' He nodded at a small combination oven just large enough to cook a meal for two.

'How long does this thing take to heat up?' the caterer asked, through gritted teeth.

'A couple of hours, I think. Is that a problem, Leonie? Oh dear.'

While a panicked discussion went on, the handsome waiter rolled his espresso-dark eyes at Carly and introduced himself in a softly camp Scottish accent as the Austens' groom. 'We're all being roped in tonight. The agency she normally uses for waiting staff has everyone on their books at this giga-wedding at Eyngate Hall.' An ageing pop princess was marrying her young old-Etonian actor – it was all over social media.

Carly liked the sound of the agency. She made a mental note to sign on.

They were eventually dispatched with trays of hot finger food to commandeer the range cooker in Bay's recently converted barn, its kitchen even more jaw-dropping than his parents'. The range was a hideous shade of easyJet tangerine.

'Bay had it custom sprayed Dutch orange for Monique,' the groom explained, trying to slide a tray into the warming oven and finding it didn't fit. 'He said he thought it might encourage her to cook. *Not very funny*.'

They could hear an argument raging overhead, a high, hysterical voice talking over a low, reassuring one.

'Do they do that a lot?' she asked in a whisper.

'A lot.'

They distinctly heard a shriek of 'Fuck you!'

A moment later Monique swept downstairs, a high-cheekboned, pale-lashed ice queen in a silk robe, helping herself to a glass of wine from the fridge. Remarkably composed for a woman fresh from a screaming match, she watched as her groom angled the big catering tray to tip the rows of neatly arranged choux pastry and filo wraps into a Le Creuset casserole. 'Nee, nee, *nee!*' She jabbed one slim hip to open a double-width drawer, taking out a baking tray and handing it across with a tut. 'The *groots* forgot to light the bloody oven again, didn't they?' Seeing their blank faces, she explained with the frustration of a teacher recapping the two times table to Year Threes. 'The grootouders – grandparents? Okay, has anyone turned the heating up? They are so mean with it.' She caught sight of Carly's Christmas-pudding nails. 'Ugh! Okay, those will *have* to go. Wait there!' She stalked back upstairs. There was another brief burst of argument overhead before Monique reappeared with a pair of immaculately white cotton gloves with grippy pimpled palms. 'Wear these. I don't have time to sort out anything else.'

Walking back to the main house, Carly felt ridiculous, like a historian on a television programme about to leaf through old births and deaths records.

'Dressage gloves,' her companion told her, snorting derisively. 'You might want to carry a whip too. There'll be a lot of dirty old leches at this thing.'

Looking down at her hands again, imagining them holding the double reins of one of the dancing horses Monique competed, Carly decided they looked quite stylish after all.

In the kitchen Leonie was lining up champagne flutes on circular trays. 'Mr Austen has asked that we pour the supermarket cava to give to guests when they arrive and save the Moët for refilling glasses.'

'Are you sure you want to go to this thing?' Petra asked Fitz's locked bedroom door, when there was no sign of him ten minutes after she'd told him they should set out. Charlie had just sent her a *Have fun tonight* text with a wide-eyed emoji and an unprecedented three kisses. She couldn't put her finger on it, but something felt very wrong about tonight, and it wasn't just her ridiculously tight miracle pants, which were bizarrely high-waisted, pulling up right underneath her boobs, like Wallace and Gromit's wrong trousers.

She could see her reflection in the tall sash window at the end of the corridor, chopped into twelve segments. Bridge was right. It was a great dress, a long-sleeved, low-backed curve-clinger, which was made from an absurdly flattering, sumptuously heavy fabric the colour of ripe Victoria plums. She was a bit hot in it, standing by the landing radiator, but winter drinks parties in country houses were often chilly, and Sandy Austen was notoriously thrifty.

The door opened a crack. 'Thank God it's you, Mum. Can we sneak out the back way? Gunny wants to photograph me for her blog on teenage public-school dropouts.'

'We'll go the back way,' Petra assured him, equally reluctant to star in the mummy-muffin-top Instagram feed.

When Fitz stepped out of the room, Petra whistled, trying not to tear up with pride and ruin her make-up. True to his word, he had scrubbed up beautifully. Dressed in impossibly tight skinny black jeans and his best cashmere jumper, fringe artfully arranged over his face so that his eyes showed for once, and smelling deliciously of the

Jo Malone aftershave she'd bought Charlie, which he never wore, her handsome son took her arm. 'You'll do.'

'So will you.'

They tiptoed down the back stairs and out through the boot room, Petra pulling on her big riding coat over her evening jacket so she could throw bedtime slices of hay in with the Redhead and the ponies on the way past.

'Best behaviour this evening, Mummy,' Fitz teased her in the car in a Perfect Peter voice, 'and please don't introduce me to anyone as William, "my gorgeous boy" or "little Willy".' It had been his baby nickname, for which he'd never quite forgiven his parents.

'These lips are sealed. Absolutely no Willies tonight.' Distractedly thinking of her fictional priest with his gifted tongue and magnificent rampant appetite, Petra didn't notice her son's agitated distraction.

'Do you want me to carry your phone?' he offered, as she parked the family's muddy Freelander among more prestige saloons and off-roaders two minutes later. 'You don't have any pockets.'

'Neither do you,' she pointed out. 'I have a clutch bag.'

'I'll carry that for you too.'

'Don't be silly.' She thought it was rather sweet that he was being so over-courteous. She just wished she felt more enthusiastic about the party.

In the end, Fitz took both her bag and her hand because her heels kept getting stuck in the matting path the Austens had laid out across the grass from the car-park paddock to the house.

'Hello, hello – so glad you could make it after all!' They were welcomed by Sandy and Viv, he as damson-faced and white-haired as she was alabaster and Titian, both gregariously accomplished hosts who swiftly saw guests' coats into the arms of a helper, beckoned for drinks and introduced them into a friendly group in a grand double-height entrance hall, already milling ten-deep with the braying of the well-heeled country set.

Charlie's golden ticket was very Cotswolds' old-school, signet rings glittering against champagne flutes everywhere, hardly anybody under sixty. Raised by principled socialist parents to believe everyone was born equal and died the same death, Petra always felt uncomfortable faced with proof that the privileged enjoyed a far better time in between, and that she'd married a man who aspired to that exclusive club. How easy it would have been a few months ago for Fitz to jump across his parents' self-made generation and gain entry now by answering the simple question, 'Tell me, young man, where do you go to school?'

The man who had asked it, a lantern-jawed rugby type in an Old Harrovian tie, let out a blast of delighted laughter when Fitz politely replied that he was seeing what the local co-ed academy had to offer that nine years at an all-boys boarding school had missed. 'The clue's in there.'

Petra's smile fixed slightly. Perhaps he was his father's son, after all.

Their hostess, utterly charmed, whisked Fitz off to introduce him to an old alumnus, while Sandy fed Petra into a trio of stooped old landowners by the roaring hall fire. 'This is Petra Gunn, Compton Magna's writer in residence – watch out or she'll put you in a book!'

The three, who made Petra think of the wise monkeys – one with thick glasses, another with a huge hearing aid and the third with a tracheostomy – asked the usual questions: 'Tell me, where do you get your ideas from? Have you had anything published? Would I have heard of you?' She dispatched swift, smiley answers, turning the conversation back to draw out an anecdote because people inevitably knew someone whose life they thought would make a wonderful book, and it was a good way of deflecting attention. As soon as people discovered how raunchy her books were, conversations could get very *Carry On*. Fitz was particularly mortified when social situations involving his mother descended to nudges, winks and gales of dirty-old-man laughter. Parents' evenings had always been a minefield.

While Hear No Evil droned on about an uncle in the navy who'd made replicas of civic buildings out of matchsticks, she sneaked a peep at her son standing amid an ever-growing crowd of admirers. He'd been right: the languid charm of a teenager was the ultimate Cotswolds party accessory. She'd have to start training up Ed.

'Got a chap lives next door to me who wrote dreadful nonsense about a nun in the Great War,' said the man with the thick glasses, mentioning a household name whose books were adapted into Oscar-winning movies. 'Awful poppycock.'

'Petra's are anything but,' said an amused voice behind her, and Bay stepped in to refill glasses. 'I've read quite a few. Startling absence of poppies. Petra, darling, how *are* you? I see you've brought a toy boy to scandalise the village.'

'My son, Fitz.' She accepted a delicious-smelling kiss on each cheek, trying not to feel downcast at the sight of his pretty, proprietorial wife beside him.

'You look quite ravishing, doesn't she, Moni?'

'Very good.' Monique flashed her freeze-spray smile and dropped a trio of cold kisses six inches from Petra's ears. With no need for wrinkle-smoothing make-up or lump-smoothing tit-high pants, Monique looked fashion-page chic in crisp, tailored shirt and slim trousers, making Petra feel like a cabaret act in her velvet and high heels. The house was incredibly hot.

It cheered her up that Bay looked faintly ridiculous in trousers that were probably Savile Row's finest but the bright blue of an exhaust-repairman's boiler suit. They brought out the colour of his eyes, sparkling mischievously as he poured champagne into her glass.

'Just half – I'm driving.'

'Don't be silly.' He filled it right up. 'We'll find somebody to give you a lift back.'

Just for a moment his eyes lost their sparkle – the comedian's glittery jacket shrugged off to reveal something darker and far sexier. Petra looked quickly away, resisting an urge to blow air up onto her hot face, grateful to spot their hostess bearing down on them as she made her way back to front-door duty.

'What a *seeuuper* young man. You must be so proud.' She turned to her daughter-in-law and Petra heard a muttered exchange in which she picked up 'struggling', 'kitchen' and 'hot', and Monique was despatched to sort it out.

Left unmarked, Bay wasted no time in whipping Petra away to a quiet corner under the guise of showing her a little William Etty painting he thought she'd like as inspiration for a book. 'God, I'm glad you came. Monique's been hell. She made me sleep in the spare bed last night. She thinks I've been a bad boy.'

'What makes her think that?' she asked nervously, hoping she hadn't seen the porny Egyptian goddess GIF.

'She can always tell when I'm having wayward thoughts.' His gaze moved in a slow, disconcerting triangle from her left eye to her right eye to her mouth, then moving lower to draw a triangle that made her feel even hotter. 'How she can't guess who those are about when you turn up looking as desirable as this, Mrs Gunn, I have no idea.'

'Bay, I've told you before this really has to stop.' She laughed nervously.

'Ssh, I'm thinking.'

Petra tried to peg the silly laughter. This conversation was dropping its knickers fast. Thank goodness hers were too tightly armoured to be lowered without the help of two shoe horns.

A couple had moved in behind them, also looking at the painting, and he stepped back, saying loudly, 'Seventeen dead stags feature in oil-paintings in this house and just one nipple, but what a splendid one it is, I think you'll agree.' The couple moved on and he leaned closer to Petra again, voice lowered: 'My wife's not a jealous woman. She's a controlling one.'

'Next you'll be telling me she doesn't understand you,' she muttered uncomfortably.

'She understands me, just doesn't like me very much.'

His fingers reached into her hair and drew out a long strand of hay. 'I'm just a boy standing in front of a girl asking her to flirt with him.'

Somewhere deep inside the miracle pants, miracles were rebelliously happening.

Not trusting herself, Petra turned away to look at another painting. God, it was hot. It was probably hell fires coming up to claim her.

'Flirt with your wife,' she said firmly, hurrying away to find safety in numbers before realising she didn't know anybody there, except the three old monkeys and Fitz, whom she couldn't see anywhere. The only familiar face belonged to Carly, her favourite Feather Dusters cleaner and occasional pony-helper, looking hot and pink against a white waitressing shirt buttoned up to cover her tattoos as she offered a platter of canapés around: 'Roasted artichoke tartlet with red-vein sorrel, or Parmesan and olive shortbread with oven-dried tomato and goat-cheese sprinkle.'

Petra took both with a grateful smile. 'Did your children enjoy Hallowe'en?'

'My boy did.'

'What are their ages?'

'Four, two and eight months.'

'Something looks delicious!' A whiskery old regimental type swooped in to claim a canapé. Petra saw Carly briefly stand on tiptoe before he moved away.

'Did he just pinch your backside?' she asked, shocked.

'He had a feel. Not the first one tonight.'

'That's outrageous!' It was like stepping back in time to an era when Ustinov, Niven and the Duke of Edinburgh had patted waitresses on the bottom in the Tuesday Club, thought Petra, glaring around at them all. 'Have you complained?'

'I need the work,' she muttered, shaking her head urgently. 'Please don't say anything.'

Monique swept up with an Arctic blast, and told Carly to keep circulating. She turned crisply to Petra. 'I think my husband's been boring you too long. Come and meet some friends I'm sure you'll get on with. You have lots in common, okay.'

The friends turned out to be a bunch of ageing and lecherous rakes from the hunt.

Petra was quietly grateful to find herself marked closely by Monique, who might make her feel like a well-fatted mother seal but was so ice cool it was like positioning herself next to an open window and kept Bay usefully at a distance.

Her bad mood was lightening at last, a sociable feistiness kicking in that she'd almost forgotten she possessed. She was reminded of the pre-Charlie publishing parties in London when knowing nobody had been part of the fun.

The hunting rakes turned out to be an entertaining bunch, flatteringly delighted to meet her, knowing all about her naughty books, several of which had found their way into their wives' bedside bookshelves with very pleasurable consequences.

Perking up even more, Petra found her party form, keeping them all in stitches as she described her latest plot, careful to ensure her description of Father Willy bore no resemblance to their most dashing

MFH. Then Monique drifted off to circulate, and Bay reappeared with champagne to fill glasses, his hand resting for a moment against the bare skin on her back, a gesture of ownership Petra wanted to find irritating, but instead made her feel stupidly special.

As he moved back past her, his mouth passed close to her ear and he whispered, 'I love you in that dress.'

I dressed up to make Charlie jealous, Petra recognised, with a pang of loneliness. I knew Bay would react like a hound with a scented rag dangled in front of his nose. What was the point without Charlie?

She found herself wishing she'd worn her trusty dull LBD. She was too hot and sober to scintillate for long, and had eaten far too many canapés for her long-starved stomach, which was being tourniqueted by her underwear.

'Pheasant casserole is served!' The call went up from Leonie, ladle aloft, steaming in her leather trousers as she presided over a cauldron of gamebird swimming in creamy, calvados-infused sauce.

As the guests began to queue at a long table laden with plates, cutlery and side dishes, it struck Petra as rather endearing that the most coveted Bardswold gathering served its statement dish like school dinners.

She wasn't remotely hungry. Neither, it seemed, were the boozy Fosse and Wolds roués, who hung back with her while the queue curled round them.

'You must ride out with us again this season, my dear,' one said.

The feisty streak in Petra wanted to point out that she really didn't approve – although she'd loved the galloping about bit – and she'd only ever joined in as part of her husband's quest to get him an invitation to this party. But, sensitive to her hosts, she settled for 'I'm afraid I'm far too busy.'

'Nonsense. Take a day off. Bay here will look after you. Terrific field master.'

Bay cleared his throat beside her. 'Petra's an anti.'

She looked at him in surprise, pretty certain she'd never told him that.

There was a round of good-natured chortles.

'Don't tell me you dress up in a balaclava and hide in bushes?'

'She does,' Bay insisted. 'Regularly spotted in hedges around the Comptons.'

'My dog runs off so I hide to make him come back,' she protested, 'and it's a snood not a balaclava.'

'*And* she pilots a drone.'

'I do not!' She couldn't entirely tell if he was winding her up or not.

'Always flies off in the direction of Upper Bagot Farm.'

'Bloody hell, she's a full-fledged anti.' The red-nosed roué roared with laughter. 'Like Pax Ledwell, hey, Bay?'

'Ronnie's daughter?' Petra asked, grateful for the change of subject.

Bay cleared his throat uncomfortably.

'Drove the Captain mad that she refused to come out hunting. You changed her mind though, didn't you, Bay?'

'Briefly.'

'Pax and Bay were love's young dream back in the day,' another of the rakes stage-whispered. 'Now, that would make a good story for one of your books. Very pretty girl. Lives over near Ludd-on-Fosse now.'

'Long time ago,' Bay dismissed.

Monique floated back from her friends, drawn to the amused guffaws. 'What was a long time ago?'

'Just an old girlfriend from the village.'

Her cool eyes didn't blink. 'What happened to her?'

'She went to London to work for an architect so it fizzled out.'

'That's not what I heard.' The most drunken of the hunting chorus had lurched forwards. 'I heard she ran orff because Ronnie came back and she and Bay— Ouch!' He leaped back as his foot was crushed under a size-eleven brogue.

'What is this about Ronnie?' Monique asked, in an ultra-bright voice.

Petra was keen to find out the same thing.

'Just giving Petra a few plot ideas,' he said. 'There's an awful lot of stories about Ronnie Percy that the hunt has dined off for thirty years or more, most of which are entirely fictitious.'

Monique, who thought Ronnie's reputation extremely overrated and Petra's books very silly, gave a thin smile. 'I think you need to soak up some of that champagne with casserole, don't you, darling?' She separated her husband from the group and herded him away.

The rakes' conversation had moved on to Ronnie Percy's return. 'Always was a bloody good-looking woman. Wouldn't mind having a crack if she's unattached.'

'Be good to see her out again. Prettiest sight in the Cotswolds, following her backside. I used to pray hounds wouldn't check for at least four miles...'

Petra escaped to the loo, now so hot that it took her several minutes to peel off the clammy miracle pants, which rolled down into a shrivelled truss around her ankles while she peed and stubbornly refused to go back up afterwards, no matter how hard she hauled.

In the end she was forced to step out of them, looking around for her clutch bag in the hope that she could somehow cram them in there.

It was only then she realised that Fitz must have kept hold of it.

Carly tried not to gape at the beautiful paintings and furniture around her as she offered hot canapés to guests not yet ready for casserole.

The house was sensational – she could have fitted the whole of number three Quince Avenue into the entrance hall alone. It was also boiling hot – underfloor heating and roaring open fires conspiring to give everyone flushed pink cheeks. Carly could feel her white shirt sticking to her back. Until tonight she had never in her life had her bum pinched by a stranger, but it was now happening so often it was seriously pissing her off, the same three culprits every time. If she'd been on a bus, she'd have shamed them loudly and posted photographs on her Facebook page. It was all right for the likes of Petra Gunn to take offence on her behalf, but she didn't have to count every penny coming in.

Mr and Mr Austen were at the front door greeting a late arrival as Carly dashed back through the entrance hall. Something about the sudden hush made her look back.

Tiny, blonde, conservatively dressed in tailored navy-blue silk, the woman walked in with no pretension, yet there was a bravery about her Carly sensed from across the room. Her eyes were blue and expressive, her smile burst out instinctively as she shook hands and kissed cheeks, a rumble of infectious husky laughter spreading to her hosts, then rippling on. Two small dogs marched in beside her and stood their ground.

'Do you mind terribly that I brought them?' she asked her hosts, as the dogs sat neatly beside her.

The moment she spoke, Carly realised who she was. She was almost unrecognisable as the pale, sodden woman covered with blood she'd caught in torchlight when they'd shared a mission to keep the foal alive.

'Any more of that lovely finger food?' Her bum was pinched again. 'Famished here and the stew's run out.'

'I'll just check, sir,' she said lightly, leaning into his ear to hiss, 'Do that again and I'm boiling your balls with the sprouts next Sunday lunch.'

'Good girl.' He patted her bottom again and she noticed his hearing aid was flashing its replace-battery warning.

The kitchen was deserted. The caterer and the Scottish groom had sloped outside on a cigarette break.

She could hear Bay and his wife arguing again in the utility room. A moment later, Bay thundered out, dripping with the glass of wine that had clearly just been thrown over him, and slammed his way through the back door.

Monique followed. 'Did you see which way my husband went?'

Carly shrugged. She wasn't about to get involved in a domestic. Monique thrust her glass at her. 'Fill that, will you?'

'Fill it yourself,' said a light, insolent voice behind them.

It was the Gunns' disconsolate teenage son, Fitz. With a bottle of champagne to himself, and a bad-tempered frown, he had to be plastered to speak to the ice queen like that.

But Monique's pale eyes glittered with mirth and she pressed her lips together in mock shock. 'I don't know who you are, okay, but you'd better grow up to be Mr Rochester.' Picking up a bottle, she strutted back out to the party.

Carly was open-mouthed. 'How the hell did you do that?'

'Basic psychology,' he told her. 'She rides big powerful horses all day long who do lots of little delicate things for her. It takes *years* of training to do that. Like her horses, she needs people to do precisely as she tells them when she tells them, and if they don't, she trains them and trains them and trains them some more until they do. Old schoolmasters who won't do it, like her husband, she fights with. Young, unbroken colts like me, who have a lot of spirit, she's happy to let mature.'

'You know much about horses, then?' She didn't remember him being too clever handling the family Shetland.

'I have no choice. I share a house with two and a half horse-mad women. I had to sit through a lot of dressage when the Olympics were on. I like your gloves.'

'What am I, then? In your basic horse psychology.'

'A beautiful wild mare corralled with a load of old cavalry horses.'

'I like it!' She laughed. She'd forgotten how sweet he was, all skinny limbs, big eyes and over-styled hair, with a crush on her that was misdirected but endearing.

He lifted the bottle to his lips, finding it empty, head tilting to one side, his smile mad-about-the-boy charming. 'May I please have another glass of champagne?'

He didn't sound drunk, she decided, filling it. 'Any kid who can carry off a clutch bag like that deserves a drink.'

'You're the first person this evening to notice.' He held it up, a tiny jewelled black thing that had been tucked under his armpit all evening.

'You're kidding?'

'Seriously. It's a generational thing. They don't see what they're not expecting. Take your bum.'

'I'm sorry?'

'The old boys that kept patting it.' His voice was persuasively articulate. 'It pissed you off. I noticed, but they didn't, did they? They mean no harm by it. The goalposts changed after they'd learned the game. To them it's like patting the dog as it goes past. The dog snarls, they laugh it off. The dog bites, they think it's a bad dog.'

'You can do one, mate!'

'They're just showing affection and approval. It doesn't make it *right*. It simply explains it. Classic case of can't teach an old dog new tricks, even when the pack order changes. That's why I rolled over, balanced treats on my nose and raised a paw out there tonight. You and I aren't dogs and we know it. Might as well use the fact they can't see it to our advantage.'

He reminded her of mentalists she'd seen on television, able to read and manipulate the way people thought by a combination of flattery and deception. He'd be devastating in a few years if he didn't go off the rails first.

'You saying I was right to let those old pervs pinch my bum?'

'I'm saying you know who'll be dead first.'

'You're bloody Malfoy.'

'Poor Draco. I blame the parents.' He opened the clutch and took out a phone with a flowery case, scrolled through the messages, then put it back, looking relieved. 'I don't suppose you want to come outside and burn one?' he asked, sneaking a thin tin from his pocket, eyebrows raised. They were disturbingly wise eyes, like his mother Petra's. 'It's good shit.'

Leonie the caterer and the Austens' mincing groom were coming back inside now, reeking of Marlboro Light.

Carly hadn't touched dope since she'd married Ash, but suddenly she didn't care if she stepped off the train. She'd done more than her fair share of the work tonight and had the bruises to show for it. She'd sign up with the waitressing agency tomorrow.

'I'm taking my break now. The casserole's run out, by the way,' she told Leonie, following the boy out.

As she did, wraith-like Monique flew back in, her shirt coming unbuttoned to show collarbones like ladder rungs. She filled a glass of water at the sink and, pinching her nose and turning round to lean back against the countertop, drank it in a series of tiny, self-controlled swallows.

'Ugh.' She handed the empty glass to the caterer. 'I always get bloody hiccups when I'm stressed. If you see my husband, okay, tell him his guest of honour has just turned up with a lot of papers and two bloody dogs, one of which has just bitten his bloody mother. I've told her to wait outside.'

★

Having spent a long time in the loo, trying to work out where to dispose of a sweaty flesh-tone tangle of Lycra and elastic that resembled something cut out of a colicking horse – the bin was minuscule and wicker and there was no way it would flush – Petra decided she had to brazenly whisk it outside and find a wheelie-bin. Slipping stealthily from the Austens' guest cloakroom she sped into the conservatory and out through its double doors onto the terrace.

Petra saw the small, elderly dog in front of her only at the last minute. She threw herself sideways, pirouetted out of balance, and – miracle pants flying into a rose bed – grabbed hold of a large stone sundial to stop herself falling flat on her face.

'Well caught!' gurgled a delighted, husky voice. 'I thought you were a goner.'

'Me too.' The bliss of cold air and no restrictive underwear was double heaven. Petra closed her eyes and just breathed for a moment, amazed at the sensation of blissfully cool lungs and backside.

She heard a light, high-heeled step in front of her. 'Are you okay?'

She knew that voice. 'Absolutely!' Her eyes snapped open with a bright smile. 'I'm sorry about that,' she said, looking round for Ronnie, but she'd gone.

43

Carly gave up after one toot of Fitz's skinny spinner of a spliff, knowing she'd lose control if she carried on and get paranoid about the kids, work, Ash and what a mother of three was doing getting high with a teenager.

As it was, she let her head whirl just slightly and listened as he got paranoid all on his own, talking between drags. 'So, my dad's been having this affair for months, maybe more.' Inhale, laugh. 'Mum doesn't know – she's had loads of affairs since they married, but they're make-believe, y'know.' Exhale, sigh. 'Dad doesn't see it.' Inhale. 'He's always been pretty self-obsessed and he feels majorly unloved, plus he's shit at his job.' Exhale, harrumph. 'He should be a politician. It's what he always wanted, but Mum's pretty left-wing and has an embarrassing job, which makes it hard to become Michael Gove reincarnate, and Gunny – that's my grandmother – grabbed all the Gunn family money, which makes it harder because going into politics is expensive, so he wants me to do it but I'm basically Lib Dem, which is as hard to admit in my family as becoming a Muslim, a vegan, a country-and-western fan or something.' Light up again.

'Your dad's having an affair?'

'Basically. The shit's really hitting the fan right now. His... um... girlfriend wants him to leave Mum. He's, like, "No way", she's, like, "If you don't, I'll tell your lovely wife what you've been up to." Mum thinks he's got some case going on in London this week, but he's just peeling "Lozzy" off the wall. Might not be a real name. Dad calls himself "Chucks".'

'How do you know this?'

'I've got Dad's old phone – he upgraded last summer. They use an instant messaging app that was still signed to his account on there. I'm a fly on the wall.

'I'm shit scared Lozzy might call his bluff. That would destroy Mum. She comes across as ballsy, but she's so easy to knock over and my dad's a good guy, but he's let Mum do everything for years.'

'That's familiar.'

'She kind of takes over like that. She has this way of doing loads of stuff at once and making the one thing you're doing feel really lame, you know?' He sucked the last glowing pip from the spliff. 'And now Mum's got some stupid sexting going on with a man from the village that doesn't help. I think she's sending him selfies of her in her knickers. Kids should never check their parents' phone. There are some things a son can't un-see. The Egyptian Henai will haunt me. Parents are fucked, aren't they?'

'Don't ask me. Mum's dead, and I haven't seen my dad since I was eight.'

'Bet *you*'re a good mum, though.'

'Yeah, sharing a spliff with a boy and his handbag when I should be working.' She grinned, hugging herself as her teeth started to chatter. 'My other half's God knows where and our kids are being looked after by a woman who's not stepped outside her front door in twenty years.'

'That's a dedicated childminder. Reliable. Not going anywhere.' He started to giggle.

Carly let him, understanding the silliness kick from dope, still close enough to the memory of herself at fifteen, high with mates, that it felt as though she'd fallen asleep then and woken up now.

'Shit, I'm over-sharing, aren't I?'

'Just a bit, but it's all good. This is the first meaningful conversation I've had since I moved to this place.'

'Then you're seriously underrated round here as a conversationalist.'

They looked out at the stars and Carly thanked a few at random that she had another friend. A psycho dog, a colt with a blue eye and now a boy with weird hair.

'Do your parents know you're gay?'

'Woah, I didn't know I was gay. Am I gay?'

'Sorry. That was shit of me.'

There was a pause. 'I've thought about it a lot. I haven't decided yet. I can't be a bisexual Lib Dem. That's *so* on the fence. Plus I'm in love with you.'

Something sneezed nearby. They both started as a small dog trotted past them, stopped to look up briefly, then trotted on.

Ronnie had no intention of hanging around after being banished outside by Monique – who she was certain had caused Enid to snap at Viv Austen by ankle-shoving the little dog directly into her path – except she'd lost Olive somewhere in the Austens' huge black garden.

'You could at least help look,' she chastised old Enid, who looked unrepentant, batwing ears pricked. 'How dare you nip the hostess?' Ronnie grumbled. 'I brought you here to growl at her son. And only on command, *if* required. You can growl at his wife as much as you like.' She headed into the dark garden again, pulling off her heels to carry. 'Olive!'

A second cauldron of pheasant casserole was being doled out at one table, old-fashioned treacle pudding at another, but Petra still had no appetite even though she'd been liberated from her organ-squeezing pants. She'd hoped to make her excuses discreetly and bow out with an early exit, but there was no sign of Fitz anywhere and she was starting to get worried. Nobody had seen him in over an hour.

She trawled the crowded rooms, searching, but her son had disappeared as surely as he did at home when his bedroom door closed on a three-day lie-in. The Austen house was dangerous territory now, amorous elderly drunks in tweed everywhere, some starting to bid farewell and demand kisses.

Passing a heavily carved gilt girandole, she checked her reflection. Her cheeks were now exactly the same dark plum colour as her new dress. She wasn't just hot, she was steaming, despite losing a layer. Her belief that the older generation's country-house parties were usually thrown by hard-core impoverished aristos, who made their guests shiver together by open fires, was shattered.

She sought refuge once more in the conservatory. It wasn't much cooler, but if she pressed her cheeks against the glass, she felt slightly less likely to faint. Pushing open the doors again, she breathed in the cold blast. The stars were extraordinarily bright on the horizon, Orion's belt as tight as the restrictive waistband on the undies abandoned in a rose bed to her left.

She scraped up her sweaty hair and let the cool creep round her neck.

'Moni likes a warm house,' said Bay's voice, behind her. 'Every time she comes over here, she turns up the thermostat. My poor parents can't work it.'

He was carrying two champagne flutes. He held one out to her. He looked hot too, dark hair tousled out of shape, shirt open a button too low so she could see a dusting of chest hair.

'I'm back-pedalling.' She shook her head, appalled at herself for finding him such an instant turn-on. How was it possible for years of sharp-witted cynicism to melt away at a glimpse of man-hair on a forbidden body?

'Rubbish. Freewheel.' He took her hand, put the glass into it and lifted his. 'To SMCs.'

She felt her sweat turn icy cold.

His smile widened. 'I'm very flattered.'

'Who told you?' Petra's mind raced. Then she remembered Mitch the postie gossiping with Pip, and her eyes narrowed, blood boiling.

'Who cares?' His eyes, ridiculously blue and amused, did their little triangle, big triangle thing. Eye to eye to mouth, breast to breast to—

She retreated behind a potted phormium, Boudicca without her armour now that she'd removed the miracle pants. 'The SMC is over. I've gone right off you tonight.'

'Shame – they turned the party lights on for us outside.' He looked upwards, inviting her gaze to follow.

Beyond the glass roof, the stars were out so brightly it was like a casino ceiling. Bay walked to the wall switch, turning off the big pendants so they were in near-darkness, the sky spectacular.

'Come here, Petra,' he said quietly.

Petra stayed behind the spiky plant, still fuming that he knew about her safe married crush. Her crush was private, only her flirtation available to him.

'Remind me, where is Mr Gunn tonight?' He walked towards her through the shadows.

'In London.' She retreated to a safe spot by a huge prickly cactus decked in fairy lights.

Bay followed. 'I told Monique last night that I'm hopelessly in love with you.'

'You did *what*?'

'I talk in my sleep.' The line was smoothly off-pat. 'Thankfully, she never listens to a word I say.'

'*Stop* with the cheesy chat-ups.' She crossed her arms, rolling her eyes furiously. 'I've told you, you're fired. You're no longer my safe married crush.'

'Is that what it stands for?' He laughed delightedly.

'You mean you didn't *know*?'

'Closest I could come up with was social media consultant.' He'd moved in beside her now, his glass clinking against hers. 'I prefer safe married crush, Mrs Gunn.'

'The only one of those things you still are is married.'

'That,' he ran his finger the length of her bare back, 'is something we have in common.'

Petra laughed, an embarrassed reflex rather than because she'd found it funny, because it wasn't funny at all when she thought about it. 'I think I should go home, Bay, don't you?'

'You're right. Kiss your host goodbye and go, Mrs Gunn,' Bay ordered, sounding reassuringly rakish, a deep sigh of resignation calling time. It was what Bay did, the cheering Noël Coward campery of the larger-than-life flirt playing out attraction in a public pastiche.

The kiss was supposed to be a joke – a 'mwah!' piece of curtain-falls acting that would make them both collapse with laughter before heading back into the throng. Strictly no tongues.

But it went very wrong, very fast.

Their lips tasted of champagne, of quick quips and slow smiles, of all the laughter and flirtation they'd shared, of strangeness and newness. They tasted each other and they liked it.

They stopped at the same time, quick breaths together, knowing they'd overstepped the mark. Bay's fingers were in Petra's hair, her hand on his neck, their bodies cleaving together, sex drives revving pedals to the floor whether they were at the wheels or not. They stood very still, momentarily stunned.

Their eyes found each other's, searching for the stop sign. There was no stop sign.

Then they found they couldn't stop kissing.

Carly tried not to let her teeth chatter too loudly as Fitz guarded his mother's phone, like a terrier at a rat-hole. She couldn't leave him. She'd be fired by now anyway. She was in this all the way to the sting.

When the theme from *Black Beauty* rang out, a dog barked somewhere near the conservatory on the far side of the house and they both jumped.

'Here we go.' Fitz held up the iPhone, its screen showing an unfamiliar number.

Carly watched him answer, so pale and self-controlled as he listened briefly to a voice screaming at the other end before hanging up.

'Yup, it's kicking off.' He barred the number, pulling his own mobile out of a back pocket to check the messaging app. 'I think they're both at the flat. My guess would be that now Lozzy's called Dad's bluff by ringing his loyal wife they'll shout and cry a lot, have one last night together, and call it a day in the morning.'

'How can you be so cool about it?'

'Because they're not,' he said, then his face crumpled. 'Oh, fuck, Carly. I can't handle this at all.'

She hugged him tightly, so whippet thin and sweet-smelling, shaking uncontrollably, his stupid waxed hair going up her nose. 'There's nothing you can't deal with in life, Fitz. *Nothing.*'

'Talk about sins of the father. This is way too much for a bisexual Lib Dem.'

'Ssh.' She held his face and wiped his eyes. 'It's okay, kid. Being clever and emotional just makes it harder.'

'There's nothing clever about this. I just heard Lozzy's voice.' He looked incredibly young. 'I can't be certain – it wasn't a great line. But I think he's a man.'

★

Monique was on the war path, freeze-spraying farewell kisses to the left and right of departing guests automatically as she marched to the kitchen to track down her groom, a close confidant and reliable sycophant.

'Where *is* Bay?' she demanded. 'I have bandaged his mother's leg and she insists we must invite Ronnie Percy in, okay, because half of the guests want to say hello to her – Viv is quite mad at *me*, which is illogical – but now I can't find Ronnie so she may have gone home, and I can't find Bay. Surely they could sign the papers another time. What have you heard?'

'Well,' he cocked his head enticingly, 'the hunt has *so* many stories about her I hardly know where to start.'

'Cut to the chase.'

'It's a rumour about Ronnie Percy and Bay. You're not going to like it...'

'Bay's with someone in the conservatory.' Leonie came in through the back door briskly. 'I just saw them while I was loading my van.'

'Doing what?'

She looked uncomfortable. 'I think you'd better see for yourself.'

Having retrieved Olive from the Austens' compost heap and shoved her unceremoniously back into the boot of her father's ancient Subaru, Ronnie now found that Enid was missing.

'Bloody hell.'

She jogged up the steps to the terrace, where her elderly bitch had last been spotted.

The double doors to the orangery at the top of the steps were open now, its lights switched off. Ronnie scoured its windows for signs of a small, grey-muzzled thief intent on slurping and licking abandoned food plates. Instead she saw a couple intent on doing something similar to each other's faces, illuminated by fairy lights, like Oberon and Titania in a glade. The man had his back to her, tall and wide-shouldered, shielding his partner from view.

Ronnie heard a low growl from just inside the door.

'Pssst! Enid.'

Ignoring her, the dog waddled stiffly inside.

As the couple broke off, teeth white in the half-light from wide astonished smiles, Ronnie caught sight of the woman's face and let out a cross sigh. Oh, Petra, you silly girl. It's so much better in books.

The kiss Petra shared with Bay lasted a minute at most, but it was immediately living memory, looped to replay again and again. She couldn't blame alcohol, and from the sweet, fresh taste of Bay's mouth, she guessed he couldn't either. Being drunk would have made them clumsy and guilty, it would have given them an excuse, but this was stealthy and deliberate. Knickerless and shameless, she free-fell for a long moment, unable to stop, too serious and dark-hearted for flirtation any more.

They sensed a presence behind them at the same time, jumping apart as though touched with a cattle prod. A small black and tan dog with bat ears stood watching and wagging its tail at them.

'Jesus!' Petra pressed her hands to her face. 'What were we thinking?'

'For my part, sex mostly,' he murmured. 'I want to take you to bed, Mrs G.'

'Don't be so stupid!' She stared at him in horror. 'This is madness.'

'My fault. Sorry.' Bay held up his hands as though she'd just turned into John Wayne with a sawn-off shotgun. She'd never seen his cheeks so high with colour. It matched his lips, which were now wearing a lot of Dior Rose Bonheur. It was all over his collar too, and his nose. His hair looked as though it had been backcombed by a cat's claws. Faced with the evidence of her own kissing technique, not much improved since her teens, she was appalled.

Petra found herself fighting giggles, a panic reflex because she had behaved so badly. At the same time, she wanted to scream and weep in shame. Her *son* was here tonight. His *wife* was here tonight.

'*Bay!*' On cue the distant cry of the wronged ice queen sledding in, two rooms away but closing fast.

*

Fitz lay on his back staring up at the stars, spotting the W of Cassiopeia. 'I used to think of that as my own personal star when I was William,' he told Carly, pointing up at it. 'Then I read that Cassiopeia was a queen so vain Poseidon put her there to stop her boasting how beautiful she was. Half the year she has to hang on because she's upside down. I feel a bit like that right now. Not the vain bit, obvs, although I know I've got bloody good bone structure.'

'Why did you change your name?'

'My grandfather's name was William – "Gunnpa", we called him. I hated him. He's the reason Dad's so repressed. I don't want to talk about it any more.'

They could hear shouting coming from the house.

'You want to go back inside?' offered Carly. Her teeth were chattering so badly she was shuddering on the spot, like a small pneumatic drill. If it hadn't been for the white gloves, she suspected she'd have frozen to death.

'Please.' Fritz sat up and reached for the clutch bag. 'Carly?'

'Yeah?'

'You won't tell anybody all this shit, will you? This village is the worst for dishing dirt.'

'I only talk to a horse, mate.'

'*Bay!*' Less than a room away now.

'Oh, Jesus.' Bay smoothed his hair, which sprang straight back up. He checked his reflection in the glass windows. 'How do I look?'

'Honestly?' Wiping her own face as best she could, Petra spotted that he even had lipstick on his ear, giggles threatening to spill over into hysteria. 'Like you've just eaten a tub of raspberry sorbet without a spoon.'

'Oh, fuck. I'll lose the kids.' He pressed his palms to his forehead. 'She'll take them to Holland. Charlie's a lawyer, isn't he? He'll whip your arse if this ends in divorce.'

'It was just a kiss.'

'Othello killed Desdemona for a handkerchief. You don't know Moni.'

The gravity of the situation was the ice-bucket challenge that finally dissolved Petra's giggles. 'Hide!'

'Where?'

'Bay!' Just seconds away.

Petra looked around desperately, spotting a small gap behind the cactus just big enough for one.

'You'd better do exactly as I say.' The voice was as husky as a Lambretta in a sunlit Italian piazza. With a blast of cold air and a rustle of potted fig, a small blonde figure appeared through the doors at the far end of the room.

'Ronnie!' Bay rictus-smiled in shock. He had lipstick on his teeth.

Petra swung round to their Pussy Galore saviour. Ronnie's Delft-blue gaze slid sideways: from where she was standing she could monitor Monique's approach through doors to the main house. The Lambretta dropped its revs to a growl. 'Your wife is ten seconds away. You,' she pointed at Petra, 'get behind that cactus. You,' she gave Bay a kind, weary look, 'say nothing.'

As Monique's shouts closed in, Ronnie walked towards him, arms wide, purring in her best throaty cougar gurgle, 'Darling, darling Bay! How *gorgeous* to see you!'

A moment later, her lips were on his and the mouth that had been so passionately and intimately involved with Petra's seconds earlier closed against hers. Part poleaxed, part thrilled, his eyes stayed wide open.

Petra cowered behind the cactus.

'Just what the *hell* is going on here?' demanded a shrill voice.

'Jesus.' Bay's voice shook as Ronnie hastily dropped the kiss.

Petra peeped round the bristles.

Bay was now wearing far too much fuchsia pink lipstick to give away the Rose Bonheur beneath.

Glowering in the doorway, Monique was apoplectic, her groom and caterer agog behind her.

Entirely unrepentant, Ronnie pressed her fingertips to a smile as wide as the snowy horizon. 'You caught us. All my fault. Forgive me. I was *so* pleased to see him.' As she turned with a defiant flick of her chin, she caught Petra's eye, gaze knowing.

'What is going on in here, Bay?' demanded Monique.

'Jesus,' Bay said again, running his hands through his hair. 'Sorry, Moni. Got a bit carried away there.'

'Bay and I go back a long way.' That crackling, deep-throat voice was incredibly endearing.

'So I hear!' Monique said shrilly. 'This isn't the first time you've pawed him, is it? He was only just past the *age of consent* last time.'

'I was nearer bloody twenty,' Bay blustered.

'It was a *lifetime* ago, darling, let's face it.' The smile was still wide. 'I apologise for still finding him irresistible, Monica.'

'It's *Monique* okay.'

The arrival of Carly with a tray to clear glasses made them all stop shouting. Monique glanced into the main house, grabbed her husband's arm and hissed, 'The Scott-Channings are leaving. For God's sake, wipe off your lipstick before you say goodbye. She's a list three dressage judge. *Je kunt me de kont kussen, lilijke dike oma.*' She spat at Ronnie.

'*Aanval is de beste verdediging.*' Ronnie had learned to trade insults in Dutch before she'd learned to count in it, thanks to long-term lover and horse dealer Henk. She held up a thick envelope. 'I just need five minutes with Bay. No more kissing, I promise. We have papers to sign. Hugh Scott-Channing's a very dear friend of mine and, trust me, he won't give a stuff if you say goodbye or not.'

Monique laughed hollowly. 'And his wife is a good friend of *mine*. Poor Samantha puts up with a lot.'

'Tough being a fifth wife, I imagine,' Ronnie said lightly.

Crouching behind the cactus, Petra watched Carly move closer as she gathered glasses. Eventually, reaching the small table in front of the plant, she spotted Petra hiding there. As Carly met her gaze, those young eyes so wise and weary, Petra fought an urge to mouth, 'Sorry!'

Her mouth still tasted of Bay's, lips plump from his stubble, her body thumping with a deep pulse that refused to go away, however much it had gone wrong. She wished she could take the last half-hour back.

She could see Bay pulling himself together with effort and squaring up to his furious wife. 'The land transfer needs sorting, Moni.'

'You're sleeping in the spare room again tonight, okay.' Monique turned on her heel and flounced out, clicking her fingers for her groom and caterer. 'I have witnesses.'

'I'll be waiting in Dad's study,' Bay told Ronnie, storming out too.

Ronnie whistled for her older dog and crossed the conservatory to Petra, spilling out of her prickly priest hole. 'Never contemplate infidelity during half-terms, holidays or Christmas. One has far too much to do. Save it for January, which is boring and sober.' Her face broke into its ravishingly naughty smile. 'And don't choose one with a Doberman Pinscher for a wife. You won't always have an old trollop like me hanging round outside to cover your tracks.'

'Thank you,' Petra said hoarsely, so overwhelmed with gratitude she could hardly speak.

'*Aanval is de beste verdediging*: The best defence is a good offence.' She sighed. 'She's got a filthy mouth for a pretty girl. Watch that one.' With a ghost of a wink, she turned away, passing Fitz, who had appeared in the doorway carrying a plate of leftover pigs in blankets, which he was motoring through, nodding politely at Ronnie.

'Cougar.' He whistled, scuffing towards his mother. Even with top-notes of expensive aftershave, organic chipolatas and Old Spot back bacon, he reeked of cigarettes.

'Do you want to go home?' she asked, trying to see past his fringe to his eyes, only able to make out the dark smudges beneath them.

'Yeah.'

'Did you have a good evening?'

'Three work-experience offers and a holiday job lined up. Have a sausage.'

Petra ate three, no longer confined by controlling underwear, although she felt as though she had a surgical strapping bound nauseously around her chest. I just kissed a man who was not my husband and I liked it.

'You okay, Mum?'

'Fine!'

'You look a bit flushed.'

'It's hot.'

'Is it the change of life?'

The phrase was so dated, it was easy to attribute. 'Just *what* exactly has Gunny been saying?'

'She said you were getting grumpy and sweaty, and that women your age go a bit mad.' Suddenly he sounded young and frightened.

My son's not here to avoid his grandmother, Petra realised, with a crack fissuring through her heart. He's here to check I don't mutate, sweat excessively and grow another head, like Predator. She wanted to march straight home and scream at her mother-in-law: I am only forty-four, Barbara! I attract thirty-six-year-old red-blooded Casanovas. I could still bear you another grandchild, if your son would deign to have sex with me.

'All is good,' she said, trying for a dyspeptic hug and managing an awkward shoulder pat over a plate of sausages. 'It's almost fireworks night. Now, finish those pigs and we'll go home. Where's my handbag? I want to see how your father's doing.'

'I lost it.'

'*Find* it, Fitz! The car keys are in it.'

He rolled his eyes. 'Okay, I'm on it. But I already texted Dad back. He was having an early one.'

44

Carly was shattered. She had been up since six and she'd eaten just three slices of toast and a Cup-a-Soup all day.

The bulk of the guests were finally leaving, a cheek-kissing and hand-waving ritual that took hours.

She took an empty tray along the wide inner corridor lined with display shelves, several of which were now topped with glasses to be harvested. She could hear raised voices in a far room.

An unidentifiable tiger purr: 'Bay, I am *not* signing the thing!'

'I'm paying the full probate value for that land!' It had to be Bay Austen, whose creamy *Downton Abbey* voice Carly couldn't take seriously.

'And what about the real value?' Even posher, deeper and a lot scarier. The dowager countess was Carly's favourite.

'Fuck off, Ronnie!' There followed a run of expletives that climbed the musical scale ending up with an indignant, high-pitched man-squeak of 'So there!'

Carly sighed, plucking up more dead glasses. Bay was no Hugh Bonneville.

'So many of your generation are still boys playing at being men. You have the morals of conker cheats.' The deep female voice rippled with tough-lesson kindness. 'Let's see how hard your nuts are, shall we?'

Enthralled, Carly edged closer.

*

Ronnie hated arguing in reading glasses. Habitually accustomed to removing them when looking up from a page to a face, they were now going on and off faster than a politician making an impassioned debut speech and she kept jabbing her cheek with the arms. 'The surveyor who did this valuation for the sixty acres is an old school chum of yours, isn't he?' Glasses off.

Bay was still wiping lipstick from his mouth. 'That's nothing to do with it.'

'Of course it bloody is.' Glasses on. 'We both know that particular block of land is worth twice as much as you're paying. This valuation is simply ridiculous.' Off.

'That's a matter of opinion.'

'Then I want another professional opinion.'

'Your father *stipulated* the Austens should buy it!'

She almost stabbed herself in the eye, sliding the frames up her nose to read the line: '"At *current* market value." And only because he hated Peter Sanson more. Why is the price per acre so much lower than the rest of the stud's land?'

'It's in very poor heart.'

The glasses came off slowly this time. 'I think the heart in poor order around here is yours, Bay. Haven't you screwed my family enough?'

'You tell me. You're the one who kissed the life out of me back there.'

She regarded him levelly. Jowlier and thicker set, laughter lines around his playful blue eyes, but still a handsome opportunist with a big ego. He thinks I really did jump on him for old times' sake, she realised in amazement.

'If you believe for one moment that I did that just now for *you*, to save *your* skin, or to make *you* look better, then you're a bigger fool than you look, Bay.'

'Oh.' Now he looked mildly affronted.

'Petra Gunn might be a prize idiot for succumbing to your charms, but she's not the first to make that mistake.' She gave a half-smile. 'Once bitten, twice shy – you've always been an out-and-out hound, which I suppose means your bay is worse than your bite.'

'I like that. I'm going to use it.'

She rolled her eyes. 'I got you out of a scrape this once, Bay, that's all. Petra has a lot more to lose than the Bardswold Bolter if word starts to spread she got caught with your hand up her skirt. *My* reputation can hardly take much more of a fall.'

'Yes, well, obvs we're very grateful for your help there. But it's just a harmless flirtation. Moni is ridiculously controlling.'

'Monique isn't the root of all evil, Bay.' She put her glasses back on, reached for a pen and started editing the paperwork. 'You haven't changed at all, have you? There are still so many blind eyes turned to your behaviour, I'm surprised your poor wife isn't handing out white sticks with the canapés tonight. What's sixty times ten thousand?'

'We're not paying that!'

'It's the market value.' She wrote in the amended figure. 'You'll need to initial this. And these,' she drew neat lines through the many ridiculous conditions, easements and entitlements his solicitor had added. 'I'm not trying to bankrupt you, Bay.'

'You're bloody well *blackmailing* me! What's the deal? If I don't pay through the nose, Petra gets shopped? So much for saving her soul.'

'That's your job, Bay.' Ronnie felt she could hardly spell out more clearly that she'd no intention of betraying Petra, but Bay rarely listened to women even if their words were accompanied by helpful phonetic aids. She was simply demanding a fair price, it was his guilty conscience paying it out as a ransom. 'You can afford to be a hero. I'm the village's scarlet woman, remember.' She held out the pen. 'But it's only the stud I want to get out of the red.'

He snatched it from her. 'I knew you were a selfish cow, but I never had you down as this scheming.'

'It's not for me, it's for my children. One moment. We need a witness. Can you come in here?' She raised her voice.

Carly shrank back as Bay's head shot out of the room and jerked for her to come in.

Walking in, Carly studied Ronnie again. She was tiny, and so glamorous when she was all made up. Ronnie turned and smiled, not recognising her.

'I didn't know anyone was in here,' Curly mumbled.

'Of course you did.' The smile was ravishing, the tone teasing. 'You know, it's terribly rude to eavesdrop, especially when somebody's being rather duplicitous.'

'You witnessed her say that! She is being *duplicitous*,' hissed Bay, signing the papers before storming out, cursing under his breath.

Carly signed where shown, writing her address in her neat hand.

'Thank you for this, Carly.' Ronnie read her name. Then her mouth opened, a smile stretching wide. 'My girl with the healing hands!'

'That's right.'

'Goodness, how wonderful. I'm sorry I didn't recognise you sooner. The foal's doing so brilliantly. Have you seen him?'

'I don't like to bother the old boy at the stud. He shouted at me once for going in with Spirit. I still visit his field, but he's not been there.'

'Not the stud's land much longer.' Ronnie held up the papers they had all just signed, her expression briefly filled with regret. 'But at least it's reaching a fair price.'

'I thought you were brilliant,' Carly told her.

'Oh, you are sweet. Now keep your trap shut about it. Blackmail's jolly bad form. Thanking somebody for their help in saving a life is not.' Five crisp twenties landed on the tray Carly had carried in. She wanted to protest, but Ronnie was already at the door, dog at her heels. 'Come and see the foal whenever you like. Don't mind Lester. He just takes a long time to adjust to change.'

At Upper Bagot Farmhouse, Wilf had managed to break into the larder, which contained the big beef joint Petra was marinating in red wine for Bonfire Night supper but – unable to figure out how to penetrate all ten layers of plastic bags, binbags, feed sacks and the upside-down dustbin Petra had booby-trapped it with to stop him stealing it – he was laying siege patiently, watching it with his head between his paws, willing it to break free of its own accord.

Having run out of things to blog and tweet about, Gunny had fallen asleep in front of a Jack Nicholson movie in the snug, snoring with her mouth open, the biscuit tin on her lap.

'We could post that on her timeline,' Fitz whispered, picking up his grandmother's iPhone and breaking straight into the pin code – his father's birthday – then flicking past received calls and messages.

'God, you're shameless.' Petra snatched it back.

'You have no idea,' he said sardonically, picking up the handset of the rarely used landline and dialling 1571.

'Is SMERSH on to us?' She laughed as her mother-in-law snorted awake with a disoriented moan, bug-eyed and puffier-faced than ever.

Gunny tucked the biscuit tin hurriedly under a cushion and looked round for her phone. 'Good party?'

'So-so.' Petra handed it to her, trying to remember the first thing everyone had looked for before smartphones were invented.

'Dad called, then.' Fitz put the handset back in its holster.

'That's right,' Gunny said brightly. 'Just for a chat. I think I'll turn in.' She stood up.

As well as puffy, her face was very blotchy and red round the eyes. Probably a reaction to so many cosmetic injections, thought Petra. Then she felt a pang of conscience. 'Are you feeling all right, Barbara? Do you want a hot drink to take with you?'

She shook her head, tapping her reddened skin with her fingertips and sniffing deeply. 'Fur and feathers. They get me every time. Your cleaners are dreadful, Petra. This house is filthy.' She blew Fitz a kiss, which he pretended to duck, and drifted out, waving goodnight over her shoulder.

As Fitz sloped off in her wake, with a grunted 'See ya,' and the biscuit tin tucked under his arm, Petra flumped onto the sofa and closed her eyes.

Tonight I kissed a man who isn't my husband.

It was after midnight at Manor Farm by the time Carly dried the last glass and put it back in the hire-shop box, the house silent. Mr and Mrs Austen had given her a generous tip and declared the night 'a total triumph'; the caterer had given her a less generous tip but taken her number; the bum-pinchers and a few other guests had left tips also.

Carly had texted Ash to see if he was free to give her a lift, but heard nothing. She tried calling him now, but he didn't pick up. Neither had Janine and Ash's cousins replied to texts asking if they could take her home. Only Ash's mum had replied, saying the kids were happily asleep in her kiddy room and to pick them up in the morning.

She was forced to walk, feet turning into ice blocks in their little black ballet shoes, teeth doing their pneumatic chattering again. The lane was an ice rink between sugar-frosted verges.

The lights were off in the house. She let herself in and hurried straight upstairs to have a bath, sinking into it and waiting for her blood and bones to warm before crawling to bed, already almost asleep.

An hour later she woke with a cry, certain she'd slipped into an unconscious sleep in a cold ditch on the way home.

But it was Ash, an ice block far colder than she had been, sliding up against her in bed.

'Where have you *been*?' she whispered.

'Nowhere.' He kissed her shoulder, teeth on her skin.

'I'm knackered, Ash.'

His hand slid between her legs. 'I need warming up.'

'Isn't it too cold and shrivelled?'

'You can help with that.'

They needed this closeness, Carly reminded herself, stifling a yawn and sliding under the duvet.

Just as she'd encouraged him into a much hotter, harder state, she heard him cry, 'Fuck me!' and he shifted away.

'I thought that's what I was doing?' She lifted the duvet canopy.

He'd spotted the cash she'd earned that night on the bedside table. 'There must be over three hundred here.'

'I got tips.'

'Think I'll take up waitressing.' He slumped back against the pillows.

When she returned to her task, it softened to her touch, more still to her lips.

'Your hands are too hot.'

'They're healing hands, Ash. Relax. I'll show you.'

'Leave it. I'm knackered too.' He drew her up beside him, kissed her head and rolled away, leaving her wondering what she'd done wrong, and what new secrets he was tucking under his pillow that he wouldn't share with her.

The ones that woke him up remained the same. That night, he cried out names, warnings, shouting words in Arabic telling civilians to get back. He called out for his friends who had died, his voice hoarse and shredded until, eventually, he woke himself up with a jolt, clutching his forehead briefly, then shouldering away the tears he thought she hadn't seen.

'Ssh, it's okay.' She reached across and pressed her hand to his temple, her lips soft to his back.

He ducked his head away, curling into a tight ball with his back to her again. 'Leave it, Carl.'

She pressed her hands to her chest, curling up too, feeling them burning to help, knowing they made no difference.

45

Lester was first on the yard, taking fresh nets round, his progress cautious because the hoar frost made the cobbles perilous underfoot, and cold hard thinking took time. He relished the solitude.

With Handel's Music for the Royal Fireworks blasting out defiantly, he guessed Ronnie took her father's hands-off approach to morning yard work these days.

She'd gone out last night. Pip, who had stayed late, had wasted no time in hurrying across the arrivals yard to inform Lester that 'Ronnie' was going to 'knock the Austens dead' looking 'a million dollars', to which he'd pointed out that they still had sterling as a currency and Mrs Ledwell had better not cause any deaths on her first night back.

He'd listened out for her safe return. She'd taken the Captain's old Subaru, which Lester used. He knew he had no right to feel proprietorial about the car, but he ran a hand over its frosted sides this morning checking for bumps, just as he did the horses, although it was already so war-torn from Jocelyn's many prangs it was hard to tell if there was anything new.

He didn't fancy running his hands over the grey German stallion's legs. The horse was now dancing a tarantella of stamping, kicking impatience as he waited for his food.

Lester studied him over his door, the horse marching round incessantly, stopping only to snake his neck out at speed and slam his teeth against the grille, rolling his white-rimmed eyes at his onlooker. He was a fine-looking beast, those cantilever hocks and short cannons good enough to reduce even the Captain's nemesis of a show judge to tears, and his head was extraordinary, its huge eyes mythical.

'We'll take none of that nonsense,' he told him firmly. 'You've got a job to do here.'

Ronnie might just have saved the stud, if they could only figure out how to calm him down.

He said a silent prayer and slid the bolt to carry in a hay net. The grey rushed to the back of the stable, dark eyes following him inside.

Anticipating attack at any moment, Lester swiftly tied up the net, untied the empty one and checked the water drinker was working before backing quietly out, straight into Ronnie, swaddled in a padded coat even thicker than her horse's, a white woolly hat over her blonde hair.

'His German yard trained them to stand at the back like that. It's more efficient with twenty or thirty stallions to handle. They're kept inside all winter. They don't turn out like we do.'

'You don't want him to go out?' Lester was torn between disapproval and relief.

'Of course he must, poor chap. Some of the well-meaning owners he's had over here thought he hated being cooped up, but he's terribly institutionalised. He feels safe in there, especially somewhere new. It'll take time. We'll do it together later, an hour in the round pen. I won't risk the stallion paddock yet. He's used to our kvazy Englisch vays, *nicht wahr*?' She moved forward to the grille, and the stallion turned back from munching at his hay net, flicking his ears forward, seeming to share the joke with a nervy nod.

Lester had forgotten the silly voices Ronnie gave them all, starting as a girl with her sing-song conversations, later awful Irish accents and silly upper-class ones for the thoroughbreds. Always a bit of an actress, like her friend Hermia.

'Let's get these stables done, shall we?' she said now, marching towards the barrows.

'You don't have to do that, Mrs Led— Ronnie.' It sounded all wrong. 'Of course I do.'

They took half the stables each – Ronnie licking through hers in no time – and Lester got increasingly irritated. While Pip did what she was told very slowly while talking non-stop, Ronnie had different ideas, briskly efficient, going at warp speed and then, when he was ready for a cup of tea, marching off to the barns to look over the young-stock and mares. 'Come on, Lester, show me what we've got. You know them best of all. It's fully light now.'

Lester prickled, following stiffly. Her familiarity, her jolliness should have been exactly what he knew to expect, but he'd lived cheek by jowl with the Percy family long enough to recognise their covering fire. Handel's Fireworks had long since given way to Water Music, but his wariness wasn't diluted for a moment.

Arriving at the stud earlier than usual to impress Ronnie with her helpfulness, Pip found both yards deserted and immaculately swept. She admired the new stallion again, standing at some distance from his door because he scared her.

Taking a tin of freshly baked almond thins to the house, she put on her pinny and rarely used rubber gloves to look the part, but the place was just as she'd left it. Even the kettle was cold.

Pip slipped through the house to the dining room, imagining her Christmas gathering. The mahogany table seated twelve. Her six lonely oldies, Lester, herself and – God willing – Ronnie would be a reasonable number to fill it. There were a couple of wheelchairs and a few oxygen tanks to occupy the gaps. It was going to be perfect.

In the Captain's study, there was an unfamiliar bulging leather document case on top of the desk, crammed with all manner of records, from passports and birth certificates to legal papers, banking and bonds, health records and old personal letters. Pip glanced out of the window to check nobody was around and pulled out a few, thrilled to find some of the matching pairs to the letters at the Old Almshouses. Beneath them, poignant in their sparsity and well-worn travels, were letters from Ronnie's children, with cards, pictures and postcards, the majority from Pax.

A movement caught her eye outside, one of Ronnie's little dogs scouting around the stableyard entrance. Pip put everything back, cursing as a large envelope marked with the solicitors' address caught and ripped. An official-looking letter spilled out, an interim summary account of the late Jocelyn Percy's estate. She slipped it back in, then stopped and looked at it again, sitting down very abruptly. She'd known the Captain died down on his uppers, but it came as a shock to see how little was left.

Ronnie pressed her gloved hands to her face to warm it, running her little fingers beneath her eyes and blinking, looking at the herd, winter coats already tarred and feathered with mud and straw, manes and tails dreadlocked. They looked their worst, pregnant mares, strapping youngsters, gangly adolescents and teasel-puffed foals all sharing winter quarters in constantly moving kettled throngs. They'd all sported just the first fuzz of a blackberry coat when she and Blair had checked the microchips in early September, a lightweight jacket compared to this thick astrakhan insulating them against the coldest months ahead. The clouds had chased the sun around that day, she remembered. She and Blair had kept the window open the previous night, listening to the millrace rush through the old wheel, making love and imagining they were behind a waterfall.

She turned away from Lester for a moment, tilting her chin up and composing her face as she sought to think about something other than Blair. He was threaded so intricately through the pattern of her life for the last few years that it was impossible to move around in her head without encountering him. It wasn't the memories that were difficult, but the big thump of loss and loneliness that came with them, the immediacy of not having him any more. She missed being held. She missed being guarded fiercely, even though she'd often hated it. She dearly missed his horse sense.

'There are far too many horses here,' she told Lester.

'If you say so.'

'And none of the four- and five-year-olds are broken?'

'You can start them off, Mrs Le—' He cleared his throat. 'Ronnie.'

'I don't do that any more, Lester.'

He nodded. 'Young man's game.'

'Or woman's,' she corrected, although she knew in this case it would be a man. Lester would approve of that at least, being a terrible old sexist. He was at his most curmudgeonly this morning, threatening their shaky *entente cordiale*. She doubted he was ready for Mrs Le

Ronnie to call the shots just yet, but as they started walking back to the yard – his once-rapid stride a cautious shuffle – she was reminded of the urgency. Lester was always going to be obdurate, the routine unalterable, the tack-room diary still filled in with neat copperplate logging each horse's care, the hunters all immaculately fit for the start of the season, as though her parents had paid their subs.

'You riding today?' He held a gate open for her, poker-faced and -backed.

'I've hung up my boots.' Ronnie had walked almost to the first archway before she realised she'd left him behind. He was standing holding the gate, small and hunched, glaring at her.

She walked back, Olive bounding ahead, Enid sitting grumpily in wait under the arch.

'Since when?'

'Last Wednesday. I'll let the pros do the work.'

'You're the pro, Mrs Le— Ronnie.'

'Back in the day.' She laughed as they walked on together and she quashed an urge to nip at his ankles, like her dogs, to speed him up. 'Not any more. Daddy gave up too, remember.'

'That'll be the black dog.'

'He didn't ever speak to me about that.' It made awful sense to Ronnie, amazed she'd never recognised depression in her father, or perhaps just never acknowledged it. His increasing withdrawal, his rages, his lack of forgiveness and reason. Lester had just revealed a corner of a paternal jigsaw that she'd never found, yet it matched her own perfectly. 'Poor Daddy.'

'Bloody big beast it was. Went straight under his horse. Labrador belonging to one of the guns on Sandy Austen's shoot. Killed instantly.'

'You're talking about a real dog?'

He glanced across at her curiously. 'That's what I said. Black dog. Never wanted to ride again after that. Lost his nerve like you.'

'I haven't lost my nerve, Lester. I've just stopped.'

'You'll come riding with me then,' he said firmly, whistling for Stubbs.

It was an order, Ronnie registered, hiding a smile. Her old horse-master was calling the shots, shouting at young Veronica to remount, sit up, kick on and never take a pull. For a second she was back in the glory days, almost feeling her ponytail bobbing and Hermia tight on her heels, shouting, 'Your line!' the fences coming thick and fast, clustering up for the dressing fence they had to jump together, knees clashing, like polo players'.

How badly she wished Hermia were still alive to talk to. She'd know how to break it to Lester that things had to change.

'Morning, all!' Pip Edwards was crossing the yard, carrying a bucket, sweet but ridiculous in fuchsia salopettes, coat and bobble hat.

'Hello! You look in the pink!'

'You are funny!' She laughed over-brightly, her face colour-matching her clothing as she trotted into a stable with a droopy-lipped black head hanging over the door. 'I'm giving Horace a dust.'

'It's what she calls grooming,' Lester explained, now so desperate for a cup of tea he was half-passing across the frozen yard towards the stable cottage like a figure skater.

Ronnie *pas-de-deux*ed with him. 'Oh, right. Which one is Horace?'

'Point-to-pointer. Came back from training in September because nobody paid the bill.'

'Any form?'

'Three wins last year.'

'We'd better sell him, then.'

'Break Pip's heart. Dotes on him. He's her favourite. This place and the horses are family to her.'

She glanced across at the pink figure flapping about in the bay's stable. 'We need to pull our boots up around here a bit, I think, Lester.'

The half-pass halted suddenly and indignantly. 'With respect, Mrs Le— Ronnie, you're the one who hung them up too soon, not me.'

'You need more help.'

'That's why you're here.'

'Yes, but I'm not planning to… That is, I want to bring in somebody more overarching.'

'What,' he cleared his throat, 'is "overarching" when it's at home?'

'Listening to *The Archers* broadcasts, repeats and omnibus!' a voice giggled.

They both jumped to find Pip alongside, holding a pink grooming kit.

'Just my little joke!' She bustled away to Horace's open stable. He was now standing halfway out, rug slipped round his neck, like a bib.

'Let's talk about it over a cup of tea.' Ronnie hadn't meant to bring it up like this, but the sight of so many unbroken horses made her jumpy, not to mention Pip Edwards in her pink Pony Clubber gear wielding a matching fuchsia body brush on the yard's best realisable cash asset.

'I'd rather talk about it now.' Lester had dug in on the cobbles.

'I have someone lined up to run this place. With you.' Oh, God, she hadn't mentioned Lester in her call to the Horsemaker. Why? 'Face it, we're neither of us young breakers any more. We need a fall guy.'

'If you say so.'

'I say so. He's super at starting them off. Jolly experienced in the covering barn too.'

'I do the stallion work. There's a lad from the riding school up the Micklecote road comes and holds the mares. I suppose he can help handle the grey bugger,' he added grudgingly.

Ronnie let this pass, reminding herself to drip-feed. 'You'll like him. He's very laid-back. And this place needs new blood.'

'You brought that. Best-looking stallion we've ever had in a stable here, that foreign horse.' He said it quickly, and she could tell how much it hurt him to admit it. Which would make it even harder to break it to him what she intended to do with Beck.

'Does the family agree to your over-archering plan?' His chin lifted.

'It's all to be discussed,' she said vaguely.

He'd side-shuffled as far as the door to his garden. 'The family has to agree to decisions like this, as I understand it, the stud being in trust.'

'I know that.' She eyed the door, remembering the awfulness of the day she'd thrown it open to reveal a heartbreaking truth.

'*Trust.*' He repeated the word darkly.

She caught his eye, suspecting they weren't talking about a new yard manager any more but a very old secret he guarded, like a dragon at a cave's mouth. 'You can trust me, Lester. I want what's best for my children. I always have.'

'You should have come back for them, then.'

'I wanted to and I tried. You know why I couldn't.'

He shook his head, eyes fierce. 'I kept my promise. You should have come back.'

They both looked away as Pip whisked past with a plastic shovel, laughing. 'He's just done a poo!'

Ronnie closed her eyes, realising how badly she'd judged this, how ridiculous it was to try to keep calm and carry on when, years earlier, they'd left things in utter turmoil, love flipped to hate.

'This place is my life, Mrs Ledwell,' Lester said quietly. 'You might think you know it all because you've jet-setted across Europe, and that I'm not good enough to run this yard any more but—'

'That's not true! When I said we have to pull up our boots, all I meant—'

'Let me *finish*, young lady!' Lester had only got angry a handful of times in Ronnie's memory. He was one of the most self-contained, self-controlled men she had ever met, but now he rose up six inches in his shiny brown boots and used every decibel of the army-parade voice that had once hollered at her to jump again, get on again, dry tears, kick on, live to ride another day. 'I do *not* need to pull my boots up! The Captain waited thirty years for you to come back. I pulled my boots on every day. He bred horses for you to compete on, too many horses. I pulled my boots on and worked them. He raised the children you left behind. I pulled my boots on and taught them to ride. He tried to stop the husband you left behind drinking himself to death. I pulled my boots on and carried his coffin. I carried your father's coffin too. I will die here with my boots on whether you overarch me or not.'

'Well put.'

'With respect, Mrs Ledwell, I am going to make myself a cup of tea.' The gate creaked open. 'Be ready to ride at nine thirty sharp. You're pulling your boots on too.'

It slammed behind him, the lid on the shared secret.

Ronnie wrapped her arms tightly around herself and looked down at the cobbles, counting down from high emotion. When she'd got to thirty, which was enough for her to be able to find a tiny gap for breath around the lump in her throat and the fire in her lungs, she looked up to find a pink, smiling face in front of her.

'I've got time for a cup of coffee before I go. I've baked almond thins. You look like you need a friend.'

'Thank you, Pip. That's very kind, but I must apologise to Lester.'

Pip scrunched up her face. 'Best leave him a while. Needs to simmer like a pudding to soften and sweeten.'

'Then I'll walk my dogs while he steams.' She had no desire to be annexed with Pip again, already wise to the Miss Marple curiosity and manipulative streak.

'Before you go, I should just mention Christmas. It's for Lester, so I know you won't mind.'

Ronnie half listened as Pip revealed her open invitation to the frail and lonely of the village, led by her elderly Home Comforts posse. Ronnie rather admired her unbridled enthusiasm. If, as Lester said, the horses were her babies – Ronnie had doubts – she had no desire to separate mother and children without a more careful audit: the stud clearly needed her help. But when she realised that Pip wanted to host her Christmas Day lunch here at the house – 'You will be guest of honour, of course' – she held up both hands.

'Absolutely not. Please don't involve me, Pip.'

'I can use Percy Place, though?'

'Absolutely not.'

She dropped her voice to a breathy pant. 'But I'm setting Lester up romantically. He's so lonely. He needs a companion.'

Ronnie stared at her in astonishment. 'Who with?'

'I've shortlisted half a dozen ladies, like a village *The Bachelor*, although Mrs Lane-Drew is probably a non-starter because she's allergic to horses, and the Misses Evans come as a double act, which might be a bit much for him – what do you think? Most men fantasise about identical twins, don't they? My friend Petra, the famous writer, wrote a scene once with identical twins doing outrageous things to Lord Byron.'

'Not Lester, Pip. And absolutely not the Misses Evans.' Petra was going down even faster in Ronnie's estimation.

'At least think about letting me cook Christmas lunch here. I'll let you mull it over, shall I? And I've some lovely gentlemen on my books if you'd like me to—'

Both hands went back up. 'Absolutely *not*.' She turned to whistle her dogs.

Pip scuttled after Ronnie, her plans crumbling. She'd been so looking forward to befriending Ronnie, to telling her all the village gossip, the portfolio of Compton secrets she'd pieced together on Facebook feeds or listening to her oldies talking, about Kit Donne, his messy house and love life, about Petra, her racy books and strange son. Most of all she'd been looking forward to Christmas all together at the stud, a new family emerging after the Captain's rule ended, making up for Ronnie's troubled relationship with her own kin, and the village's mistrust of her. Pip wanted to reassure her that she was onside.

'Think of the positive PR, what with all the rumours about –' she mouthed *Mr Austen* '– flying around.'

Ronnie didn't break her stride, tutting crossly. 'I suppose it shouldn't be a surprise news has spread already. This place never changes, and Bay was bound to dine off the Black Widow returning to kiss and make up. What are they saying? Actually, don't tell me. I don't care.'

Pip licked her lips, tasting fresh scandal. 'The party's all anyone can talk about this morning.' She tried to think *who* she could get to talk about it. Petra had gone very cold on her lately.

Already drawing ahead with her course-walking stride, Ronnie called over her shoulder, 'Getting caught wrapped round Bay Austen is the least that's expected of me, Pip. Tell the village I've hardly got warmed up.'

Pip hurried back to share this with Lester over almond thins, but he'd finished his tea and was strapping down the cob vigorously ready to tack up, Handel's *Ariodante* playing too loudly for her to get a word in edgeways.

Across the yard, a slim figure in ripped skinny jeans was leaning over the foal's stable doors, his pink nose tousling her trendy tangle of root-dyed blonde hair. Pip recognised her as one of Janine's Feather Dusters cleaners. 'Can I help?'

'He looks so well, doesn't he?' She turned, the foal's nose pressed against her arm. 'Ronnie said I could come and see him. Is she here?'

'Walking her dogs.' Pip marched across. 'I'm surprised you didn't bump into her on the drive.'

'Came over the fields. It's my shortcut to work.'

'Best you don't.' Pip thought uncomfortably about JD and the tack theft, and how easy it was to give information accidentally to criminals. The girl was a Turner after all. 'We're putting in new security measures – CCTV, more powerful electric fencing, guard dogs, that sort of thing.'

'What sort? I like dogs.' She turned to tickle the foal's neck. 'Those little bat fink things Ronnie has are tough little characters, aren't they?'

'That's Mrs Ledwell to you, and they're pedigree Lancashire Heelers!' a voice shouted across the yard, as Lester marched across to them, Stubbs at foot. 'I've warned you about this before. This isn't a petting zoo.'

'She said it was fine to see him any time.'

'That's as may be, but this is a professional stud and we can't allow people to just wander in when they feel like it. You are most welcome to call and make an appointment in advance, should you wish to see him again.'

'And you can do one.' She laughed.

'Do what?'

'It's a modern phrase that means "get lost",' Pip translated helpfully.

Two shiny boot heels clicked together, the voice a menacing hiss. 'Then I must respectfully ask you to "do one" also, young lady. I won't take impertinence on this yard from you or anybody else. *I* am still in charge here, and you are leaving. You have two minutes.' Stubbs snarled his approval.

Pip felt a shiver of gratification. Lester could be Field Marshal Montgomery scary when he was angry.

Kit marched across Church Lane, red coat flapping, and let himself into the graveyard, crunching across the white-tipped grass to Hermia.

The flowers he'd laid yesterday were already blighted by frost, their heads bent.

'I've read all three books, made a thousand notes and talked to you a lot, as you know,' he told her, lifting them from the vase, ramming them under his arm. 'I am now going to get into a bed for the first time in three days. Our daughter has dangled these confounded things all over the house.' He threaded a large dream-catcher through a ski pole he'd found in a cupboard and propped it in the vase. 'I can no longer sleep with you, but you walk through my head here all the time, my darling. Here's all my naps. I'll bring more tomorrow. Sweet dreams.'

He kissed his fingers, touching them to her stone before crunching away, head bowed, his vision slewed with the need to rest.

Someone was coming through the gate as he reached it. He stepped aside, watching eight short hairy legs and two longer booted ones march in. The gate was held open.

'Thank you.' He went through it, not looking up.

'My pleasure.' A familiar curl of dry amusement.

Already halfway across the road, Kit hesitated, grimacing as he realised who it was.

He turned slowly, bracing himself politely. 'I owe you an apolo—'

But she was already striding away across the graveyard.

46

Pip's disappointing morning got worse. Petra was out, the strange teenage son reported from behind the door chain, even though Pip had definitely seen her ducking out of sight of the kitchen window, and Kit Donne had barricaded himself in with all the doors locked and curtains drawn, jazz playing loudly, the parkin she'd delivered yesterday still on the porch shelf. She added the boxes of millionaire's shortbread and almond thins, shouting through the letterbox, 'Are you all right in there, Mr Donne?'

A tiny upstairs window opened above the porch. 'Is there a problem?'

She stepped back to look up. His hair stood on end, eyes baggy. 'Just dropping off some home baking! All part of the service.'

'Along with wake-up calls.'

'Were you in bed? You do know it's almost ten?'

'I was up all night.' He glanced along the lane at the sound of approaching hoofs.

'Were you at the party at Manor Farm? I heard it was wild.'

'No, I wasn't.'

'Oh, you missed a treat. Apparently Ronnie Percy was *all over* Bay Austen. They have history, of course. A Mrs Robinson-type thing when he was a student.'

The hoofs stopped.

Pip felt a sudden rash of nerves. Surely Lester and Ronnie had gone the other way, sticking to the tracks. She'd seen them set off as soon as the frost burned off.

But it was Gill Walcote's big ringside voice that called, 'Are you missing your megaphone and roller skates, Pip? I don't think they quite heard you in the vicarage.'

Pip scowled. She'd never liked her.

Above her, Kit tried to disappear through his little hatch window, but Gill had spotted him through the cherry trees. 'Kit! Welcome back! Are you staying long?' She trotted up to the driveway.

'I'm working, er...'

'Gill!'

'Gill, of course. I'm working. The aim is to *avoid all* interruptions.'

'Like housekeeping,' muttered Pip, under her breath.

'Oh, say no more! We have a friend who does that. Lives in your old house, in fact.'

'What a coincidence. Now, good morning to you all.' This time he succeeded in retreating, the window closing like a cuckoo-clock hatch.

Pip hurried to the pavement to greet the riders, realising disappointedly that Petra wasn't among the group.

Gill was giving her a Paddington Bear stare. 'What were you saying about Ronnie?'

'It's old news,' she said nonchalantly. 'She and Bay date back years.'

'My God,' whispered Gill. 'Petra suggested as much yesterday.'

'It's no wonder he's top of her SMC list,' Pip said smugly.

Three jaws dropped open above her.

'No!' Mo gasped.

'She wouldn't fecking grass, would she?'

'Pip, did Petra tell you about SMCs?' Gill asked tightly.

'We share a lot. Although I was surprised.' She lowered her voice. 'Bay's so tall and broad, you'd think he'd be in proportion, you know.' She waved a hand over the general crotch zone, wondering how close they got to the small male cocks on their chart to judge.

The jaws stayed open. Gill was first to recover her composure. 'So, how are things at the stud, Pip?'

'Very tense.' She used her best BBC foreign-correspondent voice. 'Ronnie's new stallion is too beautiful for words, but Lester says it needs better manners. They had a right old ding-dong this morning. She wants to make some overarching changes. Something to do with putting on boots for mating season, I think she said.'

'Covering boots are standard practice.' Gill nodded.

'Lester was furious. Told her he was the one who always wore the boots.'

'Sounds all very Freudian.' Irish Bridge on the grey let out a suggestive whistle.

'Dad used to say Lester burned a candle for Ronnie.' Mo Dawkins's eyes were wide. 'They were very close in the eighties when she was a pretty young eventing star.'

'Nonsense,' dismissed Gill. 'He's much older than her, a father figure.'

'That means nothing,' said Bridge. 'Aleš's uncle ran off with his best mate's teenage daughter.'

Although Pip often pondered Lester's love life – her whole Christmas lunch plan was an attempt to find him a lady friend, after all – she didn't like it being spoken about by others.

'Well, he's not enamoured of her right now, I can assure you,' she said possessively. 'He told me last night that Ronnie will introduce frozen semen over his dead body.'

'Definitely Freudian.' Bridge snorted.

'She obviously prefers toyboys,' chuckled Mo.

'She's a lovely lady,' Pip defended stoutly. 'She already says she doesn't know how she'd survive without me.'

Ronnie hadn't said this in quite so many words, of course, but Pip was certain she would, just as she would let Pip stage the ultimate heart-warming village Christmas for her.

'Where is Petra?' she asked.

'She claims she has to entertain her mother-in-law,' Bridge rolled her eyes, 'but we think—'

'That she has to entertain her mother-in-law,' Gill said firmly, waving the riders on, with a brusque farewell and a final glance up at Kit Donne's little attic window.

Ronnie was grateful that Lester preferred not talking when riding out. It gave them both time to climb down off high horses, crossing old turf in a bright wintry sun that threw their shadows up across the ridge and down into furrow, rising and falling with the grassy undulations like carousel riders.

They cantered twice round the Sixty Acres boundary while it was still Percy land, witnessing Bay's men chopping up the cedar to take away on trailers. Ronnie sensed this was a scene Lester deliberately wanted her to see and commit to memory, the Percy tree dismantled. Yet all that he had said in forty minutes' matching each other's pace was 'No good reason for you to give up when you still ride better than most of them.'

Clattering back up the drive to the yard, steam still rising from the cob's copper coat and Dickon's dark bay, the silence was considerably more companionable than it had been when they'd set out. Ronnie would have liked to explain she did have a good reason for not wanting to ride the old familiar tracks again, one that she couldn't ignore for ever, but she hadn't told anybody that yet, and his advice was probably right. To live at the stud and not ride was like living in a closed order and not praying. This was her religion, and she mustn't jump the gun.

'Thank you, Lester. I enjoyed that.'

'Likewise, Mrs—'

'Ronnie.'

He nodded curtly and limped to the tractor to take a round bale out to the covered barns, while she retreated inside to pick up the house phone.

Alice picked up in two rings, recognising the number as the stud's. 'Lester! At last. What's she up to?'

'Settling in well, thanks. How are you all?'

'We're fine.' Her voice went monotone. 'Did you sign the contract and title transfer for the land?'

'Yes.' When she explained the price change, she was met with mollified silence. From the background bleats and chanting Tannoy, Ronnie guessed Alice was at a sheep auction. 'Will you come and see me, Alice?'

'I'm very busy, Mummy.'

'I can come to you.'

'I don't think so. Really, we're flat out until Christmas.'

'What about then?' She refused to be deflected. 'Let's get together in the spirit of armistice. A Massty.'

Dating back to Major Frank's days, the Percys had gathered for an indulgent high tea of mince pies, Stollen, fruit cake, yule log, sloe gin, *Glühwein* and all things sweet known as 'Massty', a festive family tradition of which the Captain had been especially fond, usually hosting his on Christmas Eve, although it was a movable feast that had been known to take place at any time from Advent to Twelfth Night. 'You name the day.'

'We're totally committed.'

'Rabbit, I have something I need to tell you. I can't do it over the phone.'

'Put it in a Christmas letter.' She hung up.

Ronnie had expected no different, but it made her kick a chair.

She called Tim next, listening to his blustering apology that he was going to be overseas for the foreseeable future, the line breaking up appallingly. 'Sorry I've not been in contact since the funeral... Alice is very upset. We all are. It's all a bit bloody unfair, don't you think?'

'That's why I want to talk to you all. I'd hoped we could see each other at Christmas at least.'

'We're back in the new year.'

'I won't be – that won't be convenient.'

'Sorry, Mum. I'll try to call you over Christmas. Don't break the place, will you?'

Pax was hands-free in Buckinghamshire, late for an appointment, the satnav barking out instructions as they spoke. Like Alice, she pleaded a packed schedule. Unlike Alice, her regret and unhappiness were almost palpable, the cello chord pulling at Ronnie's heartstrings.

'Mum, I can't promise anything. Mack's parents only moved down from Scotland a couple of months ago so it's their first Christmas here. And I must think about Alice's feelings too – we're all going there on Christmas Eve. I'll call if we can make it work. I have to go, sorry.'

Remembering Bay's lips all over hers last night, she felt a wave of hot nausea that sent her to the sink to splash cold water over her mouth and face.

None of which put her in the best frame of mind to find Petra Gunn clanging on the front doorbell, dark rims under her kind brown eyes. Her waggy spaniel was the only one who looked pleased about the visit.

'I came to apologise,' Petra said shakily.

'I should bloody well think so. Come in.'

Petra's eyes had stayed stubbornly open all the previous night, her mind constantly reliving the moment she'd thrown her miracle pants into the garden and caution to the wind.

I kissed a man who isn't my husband and I liked it.

She'd girded her loins all morning to come here and apologise, determined to laugh it off, blame the time of year – and month – the booze and her host. She'd agonised about whether she should bring a present – what was the perfect gift for a combined welcome home/ thank you for pretending to be the one snogging a married man last night? – but it felt far too awkward. She was just slightly scared of Ronnie Percy.

'I take it you'd like a coffee?' Ronnie said sharply.

She followed her through the house. 'Only if you're making one.'

'I rather thought I'd make two.' Even when pissed-off, Ronnie had a tickle of mirth in her voice.

Now that she was walking back into Flambards, Manderley and Follyfoot all rolled into one, Petra felt even more vulnerable. She'd forgotten how grand the house was, mouldering magnificently beneath a heavy weight of tapestry, oak panelling and horse portraits. Although barely used in months, it was so infused with decades of open fires, hanging game and wet hunting coat, it smelt as though a raucous house party had just charged through the hallway, the echoes of their laughter just a room away.

It *was* Birtwick Park. She had known it all along. She could feel ringlets forming, the urge to canter Beauty around the orchard over- whelming.

The kitchen – so decked with old rosettes it felt like a twisted Pony Club version of the Great British Bake Off marquee – had faded buttercup-yellow walls and wooden surfaces branded with black burn scars, its cupboards as kicked, scratched, scuffed and split as the stable doors in the yards. It was precisely what Petra's ludicrously expensive 'distressed' kitchen was pretending to be.

'What a wonderful house,' she bleated nervously.

'You didn't come here to say that.'

'No. I wanted to say—' As soon as it was switched on, the kettle made such a rattling, shrieking racket it sounded as though someone was laying a road through the kitchen. 'I CAME TO SAY…'

'WAIT UNTIL IT'S BOILED!' Ronnie reached into a cupboard for mugs.

While the kettle did its gunshot-in-cement-mixer impersonation, Petra tried to relax and look at the many ageing photographs propped up on the dresser, not helped by Wilf going on an excited sniffing patrol around the room, letting out ecstatic, snorty little yelps and moans, brought into high relief as the kettle finally clicked off. *I probably sounded like that last night…* She took a deep breath.

'About what happened with Bay—'

'Stop!' Ronnie took her hand. 'Come this way.'

Walking at her usual ferocious pace, she led Petra into a narrow corridor and through a glass-sided lean-to crammed with coats, then outside into cold, bright sunlight where her dogs were waiting in a little walled yard. They greeted Wilf rapturously. Ronnie cocked her head and listened for a moment, then nodded as she heard a distant tractor and tugged Petra onwards, through a gate and around to the left, on through another gate into an overgrown walled garden.

'This'll do.' Ronnie stopped by a mossy Lutyens bench and climbed onto it. 'Let's scream.'

'Here?'

'Here.' She held out her hand to help Petra up. 'Ready?'

Oh, the bliss of letting out every decibel of shame, embarrassment, self-chastisement, guilt, lust, pleasure, thrill and pent-up frustration in an animal roar.

Beside her, Ronnie was stamping her feet as she screamed, the sound almost existential with anger.

'That's better,' she said hoarsely, when they both had no more breath. Calling the dogs, she marched back inside. 'Decaff or normal?' She cracked open a biscuit tin on the kitchen table. 'Almond thins, courtesy of Pip. Help yourself.'

'I'm so grateful for what you did for me last night, I can't tell you.'

'Then don't. It's such a bore being thanked.'

'But it was so noble, like Lady Windermere. I'm not normally that badly behaved.'

'Oh, I am.' The infectious laugh. Petra marvelled again at how youthful she seemed, optimistic baby boomer to her own pessimistic Generation X. Ronnie was of the generation for whom fifty was the new thirty in a life lived to the full; Petra belonged to one perpetually trapped in teenage angst, still mentally in their bedrooms writing their diaries. 'I've had a very naughty adult life, as you've probably heard, but I do have a few rules of conduct, contrary to popular belief, chief among which is that I do my utmost to protect my family.'

She settled at the table with the cafetière, indicating for Petra to sit.

'Let me tell you a story, which you're welcome to use in a book if you change the names to protect the innocent. In the early noughties, my mother had a little Bell's-palsy stroke and Daddy got in a terrible flap about it. My younger daughter Pax was living here – she wasn't far off leaving school and had her sights set on competing full time – and she asked me to come down for the weekend. I suppose I'd have been about your age. I was longing to spend time with Pax, who rode quite beautifully, and it felt as though I might just be finding my way home at last, my parents almost conciliatory. It was also a rather obvious ruse for Pax to introduce me to a boyfriend she'd been so coy about that Daddy was convinced he was Prince William.

'It transpired Mummy was absolutely fine and very put out to find me summoned for a reconciliation over her deathbed. I couldn't stay at the stud – there was still too much bad blood – so I'd booked myself into one of the out-of-season holiday cottages at Manor Farm.

'As it turned out, a young Lothario with a penchant for other men's wives regularly used the cottage I was staying in as a clandestine canoodling spot. Nobody had written me into the reservations book, so when he spotted the lights on that night, he mistakenly thought I was one of his inamorata *in situ*. I was in the bath at the time, ten minutes into "Rhapsody in Blue" on the radio when he sauntered straight in with a bottle of champagne, as beautiful as can be, already stripped off and about to get in with me. It was all terribly French farce and we ended up wrapped in towels sharing the bottle on the sofa and screaming with laughter. You can guess who it was.'

Nodding, Petra could also work out how the story ended but, like watching a car crash in slow motion, its inevitability didn't make its crumpling truths any less shocking.

Ronnie pushed down the coffee plunger. 'Don't you just wish you could go back and abduct your younger self sometimes? I can see I got a bit tight and was wired by being back, but the truth is I'd never gone to bed with a complete stranger before, and here was this strapping twenty-year-old with a cock springing from his towel like the Obelisk of Luxor ready to take me there. We were consenting adults, he was supremely desirable and, my God, it cheered me up. I genuinely had no idea it was Bay – we hadn't got to the name stage. Half an hour after we'd met, we were having the most sensational sex I'd had in years. It was very, very bad behaviour.'

She poured the coffee, looking up with a knowing smile, which made Petra flush because it was probably obvious she'd been think-ing about Bay, his Obelisk of Luxor and sensational sex.

'Did Pax – catch you at it?'

'Not *in flagrante*, thank goodness. She turned up later with a bag full of food and books and photographs to surprise me. We were finishing off the champagne and were dressed in some sort of clothes by then – not many – and she looked terribly pleased at first. I'll never forget her saying, "You've met!" then the look of horror crossing her face.'

Ronnie got up to fetch milk, deliberately turning away, taking a long time.

'We did full soap opera.' She sat down again, offering it across, the irony back in her voice. 'Pax was distraught. It didn't matter that she couldn't blame me for deliberately doing it, that I had no idea who he was. The fact was it had happened. None of us knew it was Bay she was seeing because Daddy would have put a stop to it. He hated all the Austens, apart from Hermia. Pax had desperately wanted me onside, someone who'd already fallen foul of my father's bad matchmaking. Instead I'd jumped on Romeo. It killed what little trust she had in me.

'Pax was doubly heartbroken to discover she was just one in a long line of Bay's girlfriends, most of them overlapping, whereas he was her first and only big love.' She frowned into her coffee. 'We might know Bay to be a complete player, but he was just starting out in those days, and he kicked up an awful fuss about Pax being different. They weren't even sleeping together – thank goodness he couldn't boast the full Alan Clark – but it was another thing he cited as proof of his honourable intentions.

'I left that night. My beautiful, fearless redheaded girl ran away not long afterwards. She junked in horses as a career and went to live with her brother in London. I don't think Daddy ever knew the full story, but you can imagine his thoughts on the matter. The rumours certainly did the rounds. First I'd broken Johnny's heart, now Pax's, the two people Daddy had hoped to entrust with his beloved stud. Both chances wrecked by me. I wrote Pax letter after letter, drove to London to see her, but she couldn't forgive me. We still barely speak fourteen years later.'

'Surely she can't still blame you for a genuine mistake.'

'She loved him. That sort of blame has a long tail. And Bay knew full well who I was that night. Which puts a big sting in that tail.'

'How do you know that?'

'Because he said my name out loud in bed, more than once. I didn't even think about it at the time. It was only afterwards it occurred to me I hadn't told him who I was.'

Petra, who had just helped herself to another biscuit, felt it melt in her mouth like a communion wafer as his badness sank in. 'The shit.'

'Bay can't help himself. He has an override switch that simply bypasses morality if he thinks he can get away with it. I did try to warn you.'

'I know. I'm sorry. You took the bullet for me last night.'

'I don't have a husband and young children.'

Now seeing Charlie, Fitz, Ed and the girls in her mind's eye, choir-like and haloed, Petra let out a nervous squawk. 'I couldn't bear them to find out.'

'They won't.'

'You saved my face by losing yours. I'm just so sorry.' Without warning tears welled and she heard her throat make that most shameful of all sounds, the turkey gobble. She tried to turn it into a self-effacing laugh, but the turkey just ran around more hysteri-cally, wattle waggling. Where in hell had all these tears come from? Bloody lack of sleep.

Sobbing, gobbling and snorting, Petra found herself being handed a tissue and hugged by someone as small, determinedly cheerful and reassuring as ten-year-old Prudie. 'Oh, you poor girl. Do you love him very much?'

Petra sobbed. 'Bay or Charlie?'

Two clever blue eyes shone up into hers. 'Asking that, I rather suspect you're not in love with either of them.'

The turkey wouldn't shut up now. Oh, what a shameful meltdown.

The hug tightened, the husky little voice as warm as mohair. 'You are deep in the poo, aren't you? Men like Bay are shits, and the Cotswolds are a sewer of them.'

Even in the mêlée of tears and gobbles and streaming nose, Petra felt a fresh dawn of mortification steal over her – not content with snogging one neighbour, she was now snotting on another. She had to pull it around.

'You... are... so... kind.' She managed to drag out something close to dignity.

'Rubbish. When you lose your reputation round here, you can never find it again, like your virginity or spare car keys.' Ronnie peeled away to fetch a kitchen roll, ripping off a hunk to hand to her. 'Now, mop up. I can't tell you how many times I've cried like that, and it really doesn't go down well in the office.'

Blowing her nose noisily, Petra managed to smile. 'Nobody sees me in my office, apart from Wilf. I can see I'm going to have to excom-municate Father Willy and big up Black Tom in the second draft.'

'Who's that one based on?'

Petra hesitated. 'Don't laugh, but I sort of imagined Blair Robertson with a beard.'

For a moment, the blue eyes looked terribly sad, then Ronnie summoned the ravishing smile. 'In that case, Father Willy has some serious competition, trust me.'

47

For almost a decade, chairman of Compton parish council Brian Hicks had opposed a public village firework display on safety grounds and been consistently outvoted. The Turners' dominion over the bonfire and guy was absolute, a duty handed down from father to son, the family's history of arson prosecutions common knowledge. This year the consensus was that they were in safe hands with Ash Turner, a former fusilier and war hero. Even his name fitted.

Nobody had seen a bonfire so big in the village since the Millennium, thanks to the volume of trees felled by the hurricane. It was as tall as a house, the guy slung halfway up wearing false breasts and one of Petra's more garish dresses.

'Good job she's not here to see that,' Gill whispered to Paul, as they tried to keep tabs on the daughters flirting with the Gunn boys, Boswells and Turners. 'She's terribly paranoid.'

'Jolly good of her to volunteer to sit with the nervous pets this year.'

'She's working, you dope. Her office is crammed full of them, like Doctor Dolittle. She's probably got that Shetland of theirs in with her.'

'That little bugger's scared of nothing,' muttered Paul, as the traditional anthem, the Prodigy's 'Firestarter', struck up over the speakers at the entrance to the drinks tent, a cue for the torch to be lit.

Excitement built when Ash stepped forward, looking like a beefy Olympic runner. He held it aloft to hear the cheer, then started to walk round the pyre igniting the petrol-soaked rags buried in the wood mountain.

*

Carly watched from a safe distance with the buggy, Jackson's eyes wide and excited below her, blue ear-warmers and beanie muffling him against the bangs in store later, his sister wearing matching girly pink ones. In his favourite orange to match his 'Splorer Stick, Ellis charged around with a group of smalls. Jed came to stand beside Carly with his lanky girlfriend who, with her sly eyes and long, pointed nose, resembled one of his lurchers.

'How's Pricey?' she asked, unable to stop herself even though she knew it had started to annoy them.

'Keeps running off,' the girlfriend sneered.

Jed shushed her as he cocked his head towards the bonfire. 'Shit, can you hear that?'

'What?'

'Barking. From in there. Really faint.'

'I hear it too!' the girlfriend gasped.

Could a dog have crawled in there, chasing something, then got trapped? She thought about Spirit under the tree, completely wedged by a great limb of timber. 'Shit! ASH! Stop it! Put it out! ASH!'

'Gotcha!' Beside her Jed and his girlfriend doubled up with laughter.

'You fuckers!' she screamed, as two of the snobbier reception-class mums brought back a wailing Ellis, who had fallen over, grazing his knees and bloodying his chin, his 'Splorer Stick bent.

The mums gave Carly's little group shocked looks, glancing pointedly at the buggy. 'Is everything okay here?'

'All good, thanks.' She glared at Jed, who was still laughing.

Ash thundered up with his flaming torch, caveman heroic. 'What is it, bae?'

He had a small, bearded man at his heels, barking like Fireman Sam: 'Brian Hicks. Do I need to implement the emergency procedures?'

'Ask them.' She pointed at Jed and the girlfriend, who set off cackling back towards the cider tent. Ellis was bawling louder than ever, Jackson starting to huc-huc-huc his way to tears of sympathy and outrage.

'I'm going to kill that man if he hurts Pricey,' she told Ash, reaching down to pick up Jackson.

'Not that again. Not now.' He stalked off, tension coursing through him. Fireworks, those loud explosions that echoed of battlefields, were his nemesis.

Huddled by the roasting-chestnuts brazier, fur-trimmed hood and jersey one close together, Gunny and Fitz discussed tactics.

'I think the friendship has stabilised,' Fitz told his grandmother. 'I checked earlier and there's new photo-shares.' He shuddered. His father had already caught the Sunday-afternoon train back to London, much of his weekend spent out shooting to avoid filial death stares, spousal neglect and maternal lectures. Gunny had skipped seeing Hilary Mantel *In Conversation* last night especially to corner him watching rugby in the snug while Petra and three of the children were vegging out in front of *Strictly* at the opposite end of the house.

'He knows what he must do,' Gunny said darkly. 'If the "friend" isn't completely out of the picture and barred from all phones by Christmas, he will have a week to tell your mother before we do.'

'Gunny, you don't think Dad might need somebody to talk to about this, do you? About why he needed to do it, and about Lozzy being perhaps not entirely... female?'

'Don't be ridiculous, William. She's just got a deep voice. Now do you want a sparkler? I can live stream it on Facebook.'

'They're banned, Gunny. You can video me eating a pork bap later, if you like. Excuse me a minute.' He spotted Carly pushing her buggy past and bounded up to her. 'Hey! How's you?'

She flashed her tightest smile, always colder in front of her kids. 'Good. Everything sorted now?'

'I messaged you to say so.'

'Sorry. Yeah. Course. Meant to reply.' She looked anxiously across to the bonfire where her knuckle-scraping hulk of a husband was joining the Turners throwing loose sticks in and muscle-flexing.

'Are you really okay?'

'I said so! My hands are hot, that's all.'

'You're kidding? It's freezing.'

*

In Upper Bagot Farmhouse, treating the house pets to a loud nineties medley to distract them from any fireworks, Petra was deriving
a certain dark satisfaction from turning Father Willy into a much
nastier character: *'My God is not a jealous one, He is a controlling
one,'* he told her, *hot breath and dry lips against her slender throat,
a fat tongue finding skin.*

Her phone buzzed with an incoming message. She picked it up,
still typing with one hand.

*I'll say it first, shall I? That should never have happened. I'm glad
it did. Bx*

Father Willy was threatening to get sexy again. She deleted the
message, casting the phone aside and starting to type: *'This shouldn't
be happening,'* he rasped into her ear, *the serpent uncoiling in his
cassock, 'but I'm glad it is.'*

*The hand stung against his face, like a small oar slapping the
water. 'No, it isn't.'*

'Ha!' Petra clicked her fingers over the keyboard, looking forward
to the battle ahead.

In the Old Almshouses, buried in notebooks filled with his thoughts
on Siegfried Sassoon, Kit looked up as the first fireworks went off, so
evocative of war that he returned to his page with a new percussion
underlining every word. When he finally paused to pour himself
a whisky, he glanced up at the dreamcatcher over the window.
Nothing would be trapped in its net again tonight, Kit predicted.
It was all far too wide awake in his head.

On the Broadbourne road, the Bulrushes was set high enough above
the lane to afford Pip an excellent view of the huge bonfire and
colourful little explosions.

She'd been on Tinder for more than an hour, right swiping
like a supermarket till worker, and still made no matches. In the
light of her JD experience, Pip was wise to being ghosted, bread-
crumbed, benched and zombied, but so far she'd only ever been
conned. Getting anyone to like her in the first place was her biggest

challenge. Despite everything, she missed her tattooed suitor, his love of KitKats and intimate selfies.

She gave up and looked at Facebook. A few villagers had posted firework shots. Petra Gunn's mother-in-law, who had recently accepted Pip's friendship request, was live streaming, commentating in a Penelope-Keith-visits-the-provinces voice that this was a quaint example of a community putting together a modest celebration, pictures cutting from close-ups of the Gunns' strange teenager, to long shots of a white-looking Ash Turner lighting fuses and sprinting away. Then, with a bang and screech, a streak of light would snake across the screen a few seconds after it had sparkled in the bungalow's picture window, thanks to the streaming delay. Which was why, when the window lit up, like the chandelier department of Laura Ashley, and the bangs made her jump even at this distance, she knew the footage was about to get interesting. On and on it went, explosions incessant, the screen action joining the window one, overlapping and echoing as every colour of the rainbow discoed. On screen, everything had disappeared into smog.

'Shit, that was loud! I dropped my bap. Are you all right, Gunny?'

'Fine. Weren't they splendid? That's much more like it.'

'I said no Category Four fireworks!' shouted a reedy voice. 'Who supplied that one? Stop the event!'

Losing interest, Pip clicked away and checked through other statuses.

Roo Verney was relaxing at the gym, posting a selfie taken on a bench press in Joules joggers, revealing an impressive flowered shoulder tattoo. Pip pressed like, then scrolled on.

Seconds later a private message popped up: *You still rally driving round that pretty village? Fancy getting together before Christmas?*

Pip wasn't sure if she was ghosting, bread-crumbing or benching, but she ignored it.

Carly had never seen Ash so glazed-over. It was as though he'd retreated far beneath the muscular man who now walked his family home, leaving a shell. They'd got the fireworks going again, the cider tent doing roaring trade, the bonfire still a giant tower of flames, but

Ash had stepped down at Brian Hicks's request. The officious little organiser blamed him for sneaking in a professional-grade firework that should have been set off by an expert at four times the distance, accusing him of doing it as a practical joke. Ash hadn't put up much of a defence. He was too shocked.

He was still pretending nothing was wrong, but his hands were jumping with shakes, his cheeks running with muscles, eyes hollow.

'Was it Jed, d'you think?'

He shook his head.

'It's one of them. They did it deliberately to get at you.'

'Leave it, Carl.'

'They don't like you being the hero, the family leader.'

'It was *orrr*some!' Ellis shouted, his new word, learned at school. 'You was *orrr*some, Dad. You are the bestest dad in the world.' He smashed the broken 'Splorer Stick into the verges. 'When I grow up I'm gonna be just like you.'

'Get the kid a new duster,' Ash told Carly.

Lying in a deep bubble bath talking to the Horsemaker on hands-free, while he ate his lunch on a derby bank admiring two thousand acres of Ontario stud farm, Ronnie tried to make Lester sound like an appealing proposition: 'He's been here for ever, a total grafter. Typical horseman, so doesn't say a lot, like you.'

'Think he'll mind me taking over?'

'He'll get used to it.'

'You can play matchmaker. You're great like that.'

'Thing is,' she sank a little lower in the bath, bubbles breaking on the nape of her neck, 'I won't be here.'

Part Six

CHRISTMAS CAROLS,
MINCE PIES AND
CRACKER PULLING

48

'et up. You have *so* bloody overslept! Look at that cold tea.'
G Kit jerked awake and looked round. Nobody was there. How often had she been his alarm clock? The bedside tea, frustrated laughter, a newspaper dropped on his face.

'Whisky, not tea.' He squinted at the dregs of the Scotch bottle in a glass on the coffee table. 'Sorry.'

He'd fallen asleep on the sofa again. He'd spent four weeks here now and he had yet to sleep on a bed for more than two consecutive nights.

As he sat up, photograph albums spilled from his lap. Kit had no recollection of looking at them. This was getting bad if he was having blackouts.

The pictures were old Hermia ones, dating back before his time, which was probably why he'd passed out, with no emotional hubris to jolt him awake still feeling the memory hurting him. She'd been Herm*ione* then, a name delivered with sharp upper-cut end, like eeny-meeny-miney.

Hermione on ponies. *Lots* of Hermione on ponies with her friend Ronnie.

'You will *love* her.' That increasingly painful paean, like the Bowie and Stones tracks she'd loved listening to, which had left him as baffled as his jazz left her.

She smiled up at him from dozens of different rectangles. Hermione as a bridesmaid, in her school uniform, laughing at tables crowded with Austens, on ponies and with her pony-tailed friend.

Hermione as puberty encroached, disturbingly desirable, the body

555

closer to the one he'd known, touched, loved and pleasured. Hermione smoking with you-will-love-her Ronnie, partying, sitting in a Mini with a gang of boys as cool as the Kinks – who were *they*? – a few more ponies, horses maybe, and the theatrical productions she'd regaled Kit with, rendering him in stitches. The Peter Brook-inspired *Midsummer Night's Dream* was a particular favourite – there were the two girls swinging on tyres over the church meadows pond, then dancing in and out of the standing stones, one sporting donkey ears and flares, and the other – Hermia by now, the girl he'd eventually met and fallen in love with – ravishing in a diaphanous kaftan.

He flipped the page. A close-up of the donkey pulling her ears across her eyes and poking out her tongue, holding up yet another cigarette.

'Kit, I promise, you will love her.'

He looked at the facing page. Hermia, wise eyes straight to the camera, obviously a bit pissed, leaning back against a tree.

'I bloody loved you.' He reached for the whisky, not caring that the church clock was striking two. Then he remembered the bottle was empty.

'A month in the country is about as long as a man can take,' he told Ferdie, as he walked to the farm shop, a journey he made regularly enough to be nicknamed Don't Look Now in the village because of the red coat, his antisocial excursions the object of much fascination.

'So the *Withnail & I* experiment is coming to an end, dear boy?'

'I haven't decided.'

Kit had started off so well, reading the Sherston trilogy within forty-eight hours of arriving, his first week spent making notes and mapping out scenes, his second sketching out sections of dialogue, reconnecting with a voice so wise and resonant it spoke inside his head as he slept.

But it wasn't Siegfried Sassoon's voice that stayed with him night and day. It was Hermia's, encouraging him, challenging him and constantly interrupting. He couldn't bear to leave it but she was seriously impeding progress. Her grave was now covered with dreamcatchers.

'Well, at least while you're there you're not chasing skirt in dressing rooms. About time you gave the old cartso some time off. Or struck up an acquaintance with the village panto's principal boy to tide you over.'

'The entire cast of *Mother Goose* orgy with me nightly.'

'Drinking much?'

'Not as much as I'd like, Big Daddy.' He adopted a southern drawl as Brick from *Cat on a Hot Tin Roof*: '*A drinking man's someone who wants to forget he isn't still young an' believing.*'

Pip Edwards had been ordering Kit's groceries online, a random selection of ping-meals that suited his needs perfectly, although there always seemed to be a lot left at the end of each week, whereas the litre of whisky and half-dozen bottles of red he put on the list were finished days before the next delivery. He supplemented the shortfall at the farm shop.

'What are you doing for Christmas?' Ferdie was asking. 'Donald's found a recipe for a superb five-bird roast.'

'Thank you,' he said carefully. 'I'll give it some thought. I want to try to get to see the kids – they're both doing rep in far-flung corners.'

'In which case they'll be Christmasing with the company, and you'll be free. There, your answer is a gracious "yes".'

He laughed, deflecting. 'I'll try to get to Stratford to see you, now I've got a car.'

His three-month ban had just been lifted, the Saab delivered back by a pompous local in whose garage it had been stored, trying to extort tickets for *Hamilton the Musical* as payment. Kit had let Pip deal with him. While she was something of a thorn in his side, her redoubtable eagerness came in extremely useful when he was trying to maintain hermit status. They had reached an understanding whereby he largely hid from her, leaving notes in the porch, and she didn't knock unless the curtains were open.

For the past three weeks, the farm shop had been gathering a Birnam Wood of overpriced potted Norwegian firs at its entrance, along with blackboards offering hand-reared gold crown turkeys and Toulouse geese. Two small dogs in quilted green jackets tied to one of these boards watched him beadily as he passed. Inside, it was decked in tasteful *hygge* reindeer bunting and Gisela Graham decorations, selling at twenty pounds a pop, speakers blasting out acoustic carols.

Feeling decidedly Bar Humbug, Kit went in search of his favourite tipple, then stopped in his tracks.

Ronnie Percy was standing right in front of his Scotch – the last bottle in the shop – her farm-shop wicker basket clanking against it as she swung it from hand to hand talking to Hermia's brother, Sandy.

'You *must* come for a Christmas drink, Ron. Viv and I count ourselves frightful hosts to miss you at the supper last month. Been stalking in Scotland since then, but no excuse now. Marvellous to have you back. Been out with the Wolds yet?'

'Awfully busy, unfortunately. Lester's had a few good runs.'

'Good man to have in the field. It's super having Compton Thorns and Scorpion Covert back with the farm. Must have been a wrench letting it go, but Bay's got a jolly good feel for land. He'll see it looked after.'

'Yes.' Ronnie forced a smile.

She'd been collared by the Austen patriarch on her way to the tills. These days, Sandy looked exactly like his late father, the original great hunting rival of the Captain, an old-school industrialist who had taken his family from shop floor to boardroom in a generation. White-haired, florid-faced, in ancient baggy green cords, checked shirt and a jumper that looked as though it had been lining a dog's bed for a year, Sandy was effusively affable as always. Nine years her senior, Hermia's eldest brother had always seemed very grown-up, their Famous Five's Julian.

'Do you really not have time for coffee? Viv would love to see you.'

'Another time. I have to get horses ridden.'

'Never could keep your feet on the ground long.' He let out an affectionate sigh. 'Can it really be nearly thirty years? You look marvellous, I must say.'

She was aware of a figure trying to sidle in behind her to get at the shelf, a huge red coat sweeping around, making her step away.

'Kit Donne, you rogue!' Sandy bellowed a greeting. 'Another one eluding my hospitality!'

'Hello, Sandy.'

As Kit straightened, Ronnie was startled by the bloodshot eyes and fortnight's beard.

'You know Ronnie, I take it?'

'Yes.'

They nodded politely, animosity crackling between them like static.

'Of course you do! Joined at the hip, Ronnie and my little sister. Hermione spent a long time trying to marry us off so we all had you for keeps, eh, Ron? How are you, Kit? Been beavering away on the next *Mousetrap*, I hear.'

'Something like that. Better get back to it.'

'Not before we all pin down a date for that drink. You must both come!'

Ronnie caught Kit's eyes and he looked quickly away, but not before she'd read the utter horror in them. 'I'm sure Kit's like me, Sandy, and never carries a diary with him to buy a pint of milk – or whisky, even. Why don't you call us both later? We'll try to set something up.'

'Good bally idea.' He beamed, not budging. 'It'll almost feel like old Herms is back with us. Still miss her like stink, especially at Christmas. She loved this time of year, didn't she?'

Ronnie could see Kit going rigid with the effort of not reacting to this, his gaze fixed on her basket. She could smell whisky on him again. Pip, who gossiped incessantly and kept them up to date on the director's eccentric working hours whether they wanted to know or not, was always eager to impart just how much of his Tesco.com order was liquid.

'Either of you going out with the village carol singers tonight?'

'I'm afraid not,' they said together, as perfectly synchronised as choir members.

'You must! Viv and I usually toddle along but we've got a drinks party to get to in Tetbury tonight. You two need to show what this village has been missing. Make Herms proud. Her "Hark, the Herald" descant was something to behold, eh?'

She glanced at Kit, glaring fixedly at her basket as though she was carrying Hermia's heart in it. She wondered just how drunk he was.

'Must be such a comfort to have each other to turn to,' Sandy went on, making it sound like they ate their meals side by side on lap trays. 'Terrible business, what with poor Herms never getting back to the full packet, and your chap Angus having that tumble racing, Ronnie. Poochie Dacre-Hoare is a mutual friend,' he explained, seeing Ronnie's frozen face.

Kit snorted with amusement at the name.

Ronnie stiffened. This was precisely the topic of conversation she'd wanted to avoid around Kit Donne. This, surely, was the reason Hermia had hidden the severity of her injuries from her friend. This was why the letters had stopped. The truth was glossed over. Hermia knew how one instinctive promise, one breathless pledge made in the back of an ambulance to stay and look after Angus, had impacted on the rest of Ronnie's life. Hermia had known the scale of the sacrifice, and it was why she'd had no intention of her putting her friend through any of it again.

Now Sandy was discussing Angus's accident and comparing it with his sister's as dispassionately as weighing up cattle infections versus crop blight.

'Not sure if I'd rather lose my mind or my legs, although there's many would say one's as empty as the others are hollow in my case! Only heard about old Angus years later, mind you, when Pooch mentioned he was in a wheelchair. Happened soon after you two got it together, didn't it, Ron? She said he went down in the pack and knew his fate while divots were still being kicked in his face. Not like Herms, who never knew what hit her. Tough on you two either way, a thing like that happening to someone you love. Don't envy either of you, holding it all together for all those years.'

Kit's hazel eyes were wide, his gaze on Ronnie's face now.

Sandy had picked up a bottle of Shakespeare Spiced Punch to examine. 'Just goes to show you can be hacking home or flying birch at speed, makes no difference. Why I stick to shooting, these days. This looks good. Fancy a tipple? You're a drinking man, Kit, talk this lovely lady into it.'

Kit looked as though he'd happily take the bottle and neck it now.

'No, I *must* go.' Ronnie stepped forward to kiss Sandy's cheek. 'Call me soon. Goodbye, Kit.' She nodded farewell without looking at him.

At the tills, Carly Turner was loading purchases into old vegetable boxes in a Santa hat. It was the first time Ronnie had seen her in weeks.

'How's Spirit?'

'Good. We've just put him back with the bachelor pack. *You* haven't been to visit him.'

Carly put the loaf in the box. 'I did, but the old man told me to...' Her mouth twisted. 'Anyway, I can see him in the field now.'

'Did Lester put you off?'

She shrugged. 'His sort hates Turners.'

'He has no right to judge.' Lester's campaign of quiet denial had become a loud noise in her head. He refused to break his routine or consider trying anything differently; every time Ronnie changed the way something was done, she found it gradually changing back, like memory foam. He was polite to a fault, tireless, and he loved the stud, but all the time, the unspoken truth hung between them like a hornets' nest, and days like today made her want to run in and kick it. She wasn't sure she was going to last.

Outside, she gathered her dogs' leads swiftly.

'Wait!' Kit caught up with her, striding out admirably for a sleep-deprived dipso. 'Did Hermia know what happened to the man you ran off with – Angus, was it?'

'Not at the time. Later, when we got back in touch.'

'Fast forward a few years to her fall, when she could no longer remember how to pick up a cup of coffee, and she brushed it off as nothing to spare your feelings? Told you she was too busy to write to you?'

'She was always ridiculously kind. She'd deliberately let me win gymkhana races so my father wouldn't shout at me, even though her pony was faster.'

'And she took the fall too.'

They walked along in silence, and Ronnie was unsure if he was appeased or not. He had a presence quite different from that of most men she knew, a quietness beneath which she sensed tempestuous activity, as though his mind was constantly being tidied, ensuring everything exploding inside was in chronological order and made sense. He started to quote:

'World-wide champion of truth and right,
Hope in gloom, and in danger aid,
Tender and faithful, ruddy and white,
Woman was made…'

Ronnie remembered sending him the little book of poetry after she'd found out about her friend's death. 'We used to recite Christina Rossetti to one another as teenagers, dressed rather pretentiously as Pre-Raphaelites and draping ourselves in the willow over there.' She pointed across to the pond where Sixty Acres met the church meadows, not wanting to point out that they'd both sneered at the line *Woman was made for man's delight* in the poem he'd just quoted. Perhaps he knew that. *Meek compliances veil her might.*

'How very *idyllic*.' There was a sourness to his voice.

'Are you jealous?' she asked in surprise.

'You think I secretly yearn to drape myself over a willow dressed as William Morris?'

'You'd suit our Brontë phase better. We used to sit in the attic at the stud in fingerless gloves reading out "No Coward Soul is Mine" in northern accents. You could be Branwell.'

'Thank you for that stereotype,' he snapped. 'Hermia was always telling me how much I'd love you. I trusted my wife's judgement in most things, but she was *way* off there.'

'She was cleverer than me, kinder than me and saw more good in me than anyone else did. I got her into trouble, flirted with the boys she liked, and only ever play-acted at all the big scenes and dramas she performed from the heart. I know how much you still miss her. I miss her too. She was one of those people who made you feel better just for knowing her.'

'And she would obviously forgive you anything.' The ironic note in his voice had hardened to heavy criticism.

Ronnie glanced at him. 'I don't think it's really my exoneration you're bothered about, is it?'

'*You* were the one who dropped out of her life for years on end.'

She stopped, waiting for him to slow to a halt and turn back with an angry flap of red coat tail. 'Perhaps I did, but when a friendship loses its day-to-day minutiae, its natural rhythm, it changes. It settles into a deep, safe well of affection. Its heartbeat slows in hibernation. It doesn't go away, but it lives almost exclusively in the past. Maybe that's where we wanted it to stay.'

He laughed bitterly. The smell of Scotch reaching her even from ten feet away. 'That's a load of self-justifying bollocks.'

She shook her head, her heart suddenly going out to him, this clever, lonely man who had loved someone so irreplaceable and lost her, not all at once, but head first and heart second. 'You were the lover who had to hold the past and the present together for years like a mismatched pair. That's hell. I know because I've done it.'

He marched closer, glaring. 'Don't you *dare* presume to understand how I felt!'

'I'll presume to have known your wife well enough to tell you that she would hate to see you looking like this, to know how much you're still suffering.'

'Only for my art,' he dismissed acerbically. 'Thank you for your concern but, rest assured, I only look a bit rough round the edges because I've been working.'

'The bits in between the edges are rough too. Drinking Scotch for breakfast can't be helping.'

'What is it with you and this fucking temperance crap?'

'I was married to a drinker.'

'Lucky for him you left him.'

She felt the white flash of anger rock her on her heels, too furious to speak.

Ronnie could no longer cut through Sixty Acres, the Austens having wasted no time in erecting stock fencing topped with barbed wire beyond the park rails the full length of the field. She was forced to march to the stile into the church meadows, Kit stomping furiously behind.

'I'm sorry, okay?' he called out. 'That was uncalled for.'

She held up a hand to shut him up, climbing fast towards the standing stones.

'I know he was an arsehole. Hermia told me.'

'Johnny wasn't an arsehole.'

'Not an arsehole then. I'm the arsehole. I come out with a load of— oof!'

Ronnie glanced round and saw he'd walked into a standing stone at waist height, and was hopping round clutching his groin. She hoped it had sobered him up a bit. Not pausing, she strode on past the little Church Lane gate he would take and along the hedge-line towards the bigger gates in the corner that came out opposite the stud's driveway.

Two children on ponies and a mother on a chestnut were hacking towards her, a familiar spaniel racing ahead to greet her two, reeking of fox poo, all waggy smiles.

'Wilf! Sorry! Wilf! COME HERE! Sorry! Oh, hi there, Ronnie!'

It was Petra Gunn, an occasional early-morning dog-walking companion in recent weeks, always reeling from lack of sleep with a head full of twisted plot, although never as rough-looking as Kit. Today she was back in the saddle and beaming.

'How are you?' Ronnie summoned a bravado she didn't feel. 'Do I take it you've finished?'

'Sent it off two days ago.'

'Well done, you! Hello there.' The daughters were ravishing little doppelgängers hanging off their ponies to greet her dogs. 'They're called Enid and Olive and I'm Ronnie.'

'We're Prudie and Bella,' the taller daughter piped up, 'and this is Comet and Harry, as in One Direction not the royal one.'

'And who's this nice-looking mare?' She patted the chestnut, which was pawing the ground impatiently.

'We're not on first-name terms,' Petra apologised. 'It's complicated.'

'Hello, Complicated.' Ronnie admired her pretty Whistlejacket head.

'Is that Kit Donne kicking one of the standing stones?' Petra was squinting at the figure above them.

'Typical theatrical type.' Ronnie felt anger spiking again. 'About time he cut out the Leontes mourning, quit all the Falstaffian seductions and found his Beatrice again, don't you think? Hermia was always complaining that he was hopeless left on his own. Egos need altars. And that man needs another wife.'

Petra was looking slightly startled. 'Any suggestions?'

'Someone very patient, fond of northerners and not bothered by living with an alcoholic.' She watched Petra's daughters as they rode on further up the hill, heads together and knees up on saddle flaps, and was reminded of Hermia with a sharp pang. Kit and his red coat had disappeared from view. 'Perhaps Pip should add him to her list of lonely village oldies to cook Christmas lunch for.'

'She's not still banging on about that, is she?'

'Daily.' She shuddered. 'I suppose you've got to admire her kind heart.'

'But that's the awful thing – none of them really want to go. Mo Dawkins told me that some usually get together anyway and have had a table booked at the Pheasant in Micklecote for months, deposits paid, and others have relatives they'd much rather go to. They're only doing it because they feel sorry for *her*. And because she's promised them a fantastically eligible mystery bachelor.' She raised her eyebrows.

'She's backed the wrong horse there.' Ronnie sighed crossly. 'Lester's spent Christmas lunchtime alone in his cottage with a large stack of Fray Bentos pies and Handel's *Messiah* for at least half a century.'

'Poor Pip,' Petra said guiltily. 'I mustn't bitch about her. She's terribly lonely and underutilised, and obviously desperate for parent substitutes. She gave up everything to look after her own.'

'She was jolly good to mine.' Ronnie felt a bond of responsibility for the fact they had clearly appreciated Pip. But she wasn't very easy to like.

'We should set *her* up!' Petra fixed upon the idea with delight.

'Who on earth with?'

'Someone older than her who likes baking. A sugar daddy.'

'Father Christmas?'

Petra giggled, her dark eyes shiny with mirth. 'Now we're both being bitches.'

'I've always preferred bitches.' Ronnie whistled for her dogs. 'Fiercely loyal, bold as brass balls and much less likely to wander. Join me bitch-walking soon. Wilf can be our beard. Must get on.' She set off for the gate with a brisk wave.

'Will we see you later?' Petra called after her.

'What?' She glanced back.

'Carol singing!' Petra had a gloved hand on her chestnut's rump, like a barmaid leaning over the counter. 'Tonight. Six o'clock on the Green.'

'I'm busy, sorry. I wouldn't bother coming up to the stud. You'll only be singing to the horses.' It was time, she decided, to tackle Lester.

'Mince-pie delivery!' Pip called through the letterbox at the Old Almshouses, but heard no reply as usual.

She hurried along to Mrs Hedges', grateful to find the daughter's car wasn't parked outside, and let herself in with her key, calling out to make sure she didn't startle her. The house was baking hot, *Storage Wars* playing at top volume on the television. As Pip bustled in, the old lady didn't stir from her orthopaedic chair, head lolling down, hands in her lap.

'Mrs Hedges? MRS HEDGES!'

Nothing.

She gave her a gentle prod and she keeled sideways.

Pip let out a deep sigh. She'd always known she would lose another client sooner or later – an occupational habit when catering for the elderly – but why did it have to happen so close to Christmas? And Mrs Hedges had been one of her top three romantic matches for Lester, being a fan of horse racing and classical music.

But she had three more mince-pie deliveries to make before helping Lester and Ronnie do the yard, then had more to bake for the carol singers. She couldn't hang about. She got out her phone to call the daughter, muting the television as it was answered. 'It's Pip. I'm afraid I have some very sad news about your mother.'

Mrs Hedges started awake. 'Who turned my telly off?'

The voice at the other end of the phone was demanding to know what was going on.

'Oh, sorry, I dialled the wrong number. Bet that's a relief!' She rang off. 'Now, Mrs Hedges, would you like a nice cup of tea while I'm here? I can't stay long.'

'I'm not letting you leave until I've heard all the latest, Pip,' Mrs Hedges insisted eagerly. The rolling soap opera Pip provided was guaranteed to keep her clients agog. 'How is the computer dating going?'

They settled down with the mince pies and a pot, *Storage Wars* still muted on the television, a couple of greasy bikers exploring a lock-up full of beauty-spa equipment on screen. Pip admired their tattoos with a sigh. 'Not well, Mrs H. I've been benched three times now.'

'Is that a sexual activity?'

Pip moved on to other news. 'Lester and Ronnie are so snappy with each other, it's ridiculous. She's being very stubborn about my Christmas lunch—'

'About that. My daughter would like me to go—'

'— and she's even suggested I hire the village hall, can you believe that? It's not like she's having her family over. She's got a horse whisperer coming to stay after Christmas, mind you. Lester's got the hump about it, bless him, but I looked the man up online and he is a *god*, Mrs H. Bay Austen had better watch out because his crown as village hunk is about to roll. The Stud Muffin is on his way. Ronnie's bound to be lining him up as her new toyboy, don't you think? Oh, and talking of Bay, Petra has finished her latest sexy novel, the one I gave her the plot idea for. She posted something on Facebook this morning. That means she's out of hiding so I think we'll have some action on *that* front again – are you all right, Mrs H?' The old lady was lying back with her eyes closed and her mouth open again. 'MRS HEDGES?'

She started upright. 'Would you mind telling me all that again, dear? You lost me after the bit about the village hall.'

Socked feet thundered upstairs in Upper Bagot Farmhouse.

'Girls! You forgot to put away your—'

Doors banged.

'— boots!'

The Gunn children's schools had broken up for the Christmas holidays less than a week ago, but Petra already had a One Direction earworm and Lego indents in the soles of her feet. Dropped coats and muddy wellies littered every doorway, and the fridge had been stripped of anything that could be eaten with a spoon. God, but she loved having them all back.

She picked up a quartet of jodhpur boots and crammed them into the overstuffed rack before shutting freshly hosed spaniel Wilf into the boot room.

Charlie was thankfully not around this week to criticise the tide of dropped books, clothes, toys, games consoles and dirty crockery closing in on his oblivious wife. Her kitchen was a mad scientist's laboratory of festive preparations, lists everywhere, iPad propped on the recipe-book stand, her phone streaming *Carols from King's* through Bluetooth. She sang along to 'Ding Dong Merrily on High' as a warm-up for the village carolling later, glancing out of the window at a frosty sunset. Last year, when it had been the Gunns' turn to host the kick-off drinks, had been a rain-lashed washout, pitifully few muddy footprints trailing out from the farmhouse's flagstone floors to embark upon the figure-of-eight loop around the villages of Compton Magna and Compton Bagot. Their merry sodden little band had shared so much mulled wine beforehand that they'd had a wonderful time, and the local badger community had feasted on the leftover mince pies on the compost heap for weeks.

Charlie's baritone would be missing from 'O Come All Ye Faithful' this evening: he was still in London finishing off a case – Petra suspected a wine case, not a legal one, given the number of parties in his diary – which meant she'd already tackled most of the social highlights in the village Christmas calendar alone. She'd hoped to lure Fitz along as her chaperone for the grown-up gigs but he'd refused to co-operate, claiming to be revising for his GCSE resits by completing a mountain of old exam papers.

Petra had turned off the WiFi once or twice to test the claim. The ping delay from power-down to teenager's primordial wail was less than a second, indicating that messaging, gaming and streaming were ongoing. But she had to hand it to Fitz: he'd got his head down and worked incredibly hard all term. They both had, her first ninety thousand words of the racy Civil War trilogy currently languishing with her publisher, out of sight and mind. Christmas would be a celebration.

She went to check the wall calendar, catching her reflection with a bleat of alarm as she passed the mirror – helmet hair, sallow-skinned, baggy-eyed and with a spot. The last frantic fortnight's writing to meet her deadline had taken its toll. Who got spots at forty-four? Being seventy was 'the new fifty', sixty 'the new forty' and so on, but being newly pubescent in middle age was not a good thing.

December's picture on the RSC wall calendar was a poster for an old production of *Twelfth Night*, falling apart after a busy family year. She cast her eye over it, wistfully remembering the early days when Charlie had rushed home for the holidays as soon as the decorations had gone up, demanding that she wear nothing but the light-up Santa hat in bed, an annual running joke between them, which had once driven him potty with laughter and lust. As well as missing the candlelit church service, he had missed the Hunt Supporters' Supper – ironic given that he was the country sports fan – and the village panto at which he traditionally hissed and booed loudest of all the Gunns because he thought the acting appalling.

Tonight, faced with the prospect of a slow march around the village, singing the low parts of 'Good King Wenceslas' and eating his weight in mince pies, the case in London had mysteriously dragged on, or been uncorked to breathe.

Petra secretly rather enjoyed going solo socially with her children. Charlie was very bad at small talk and a terrible clock-watcher. Their pews at last year's candlelit service had been treated to a disco show of his phone screen flashing on and off as he checked the time. This year had felt inclusive and unhurried by comparison, ten-year-old aspiring actress Prudie reciting her prayer so theatrically that the congregation hadn't noticed her younger sister Bella eating the sweets off her Christingle and pulling an I'm-so-embarrassed face, and Ed had played a jazzed-up version of 'Fairytale of New York' on his trumpet with such aplomb that the Reverend Hilary Jolley had danced in the aisles and sung along – even, Petra had noted with delight, belting out the 'your arse' line. Only Fitz – too cool for school – had stayed at home. Like most of Petra's friends' older teens, he had an incredibly busy, complicated social world that met occasionally, spoke more regularly and was in almost constant visual and messaging contact. He lived on his mobile, and occasionally on hers, which she suspected was when he ran out of credit. She found it irritating, although her iPhone was a fount of purity these days.

Bay had all but given up texting, which saddened her more than it should – she couldn't help dwelling on the magnificent Obelisk of Luxor she would never set eyes on, and the forbidden kiss that still woke her sometimes, her lips warm and swollen – but was a relief overall. Ronnie would never forgive her a relapse. She only wished Ronnie was coming tonight, but she was frustratingly antisocial for somebody with such a natural capacity for vivacity and friendship.

This year's pre-carol-singing drinks were being hosted by village do-gooders Brian and Chris Hicks, which meant weak rum punch and unheated Aldi mince pies, but she had a secret assignation for a very strong G and T with Gill first, a good catch-up long overdue with her favourite cynic, bad punner and tireless rallier of spirits. Petra adored Christmas in the Comptons, which made friendships feel all the lovelier, especially those on your doorstep.

Pulling on a padded coat, she went out to feed the horses. It was almost dark now, frost already hardening as she carefully carried hay nets across the slippery concrete. Heads bobbed and steamy breath rose, with deep, rumbling whickers and much door-kicking.

'Hello, you mad old bat.' She flicked on the lights, ducking as the Redhead swung round eagerly, already pulling on the net. Petra unbolted the door and squeezed inside as the mare barged forwards eagerly, and they both waded through thick straw with noisy sweeps to the wall ring.

Having harboured her *Black Beauty* daydream for so long, Petra never took it for granted. Even mixing feeds on the coldest, wettest mornings, she still counted her blessings on frozen fingers. Her daughters, who *did* take it for granted, were joyriders; Charlie, who grumbled that she smelt like a muck heap when she came in, would only help out if she severed a limb. The boys probably wouldn't notice the severed limb. But Petra didn't mind. The horses provided the closest to me time she got. And after she'd finished a book, it felt like the ultimate reward.

It always struck her as ironic that, when she'd finally earned enough to move her family from London to the country to buy into the lifestyle she'd always dreamed of, she'd found that juggling a young family with the long work hours required to pay for it meant she had almost no time to ride. Charlie didn't seem to have the same problem with shooting – just his marriage and his children. Petra pushed the thought away. With her fictional world taking over in recent weeks, there had been less space for day-to-day worries about her ever-cooling marriage, and she wasn't ready to let them back in. It was Christmas. There were log fires, mulled wine, molten mince pies and hot toddies to warm them both up again.

Petra watched the mare eat, foot stamping and ear twitching, the rhythmic grinding of her jaws a comforting beat. When she watched Charlie eat, equally greedily, equally ungrateful, she felt far less contented.

Earlier in the year, she'd scandalised a group of London girlfriends over lunch by explaining that neglected Cotswolds wives fell in love with their horses in inverse proportion to falling out of love with their husbands. Lots of rising trot hardened one's thighs for infidelity, she'd explained to shrieks of delight.

The Redhead was letting out similar-sounding squeals now, if less rapturous as she objected to the greedy Shetland raising his nose to the open grille between their stables, desperately trying to inhale her feed.

'*Squeeeee!*'

Petra looked at her curiously. 'Are you in season?'

'*Squeeeee… eeeeee… yip!*' A hoof slammed against the partition and then she turned her rear to the Shetland, flashing intimately like a speciality act in a Patpong hostess bar. The Shetland, who couldn't see over the grille, moved back and forth, tossing his head in frustration, like an excited tussock.

'You *are* in season.'

It had happened before. While most mares' fertility cycles took a break over winter, coming into season only between April and September, a few, like the Redhead, threw random winter heats that turned her into an obnoxiously predatory, coquettish Miss Piggy.

'You and me both.' Petra sighed.

Back in the kitchen, her phone was vibrating against the granite worktop of the island – which was odd because she was sure she'd left it on charge – and playing Mozart's Horn Concerto, Gill's long, stern, please-don't-take-a-photograph-of-me face on the screen.

'Can't come tonight.' She was on her car-phone, dogs yapping in the back. 'Colicking hunter near Micklecote. Been hammered far too hard today. They should have called off the meet in this frost. Ground like concrete and no decent scent.'

'Sounds like the Christmas party at Charlie's chambers.' Petra stood on tiptoe to stretch her calves, still aching from a long shift in heels making small talk with fifty inadequately aftershaved pin-striped legal clones whilst eating on-trend pickled finger food, so close to deadline she'd belted in and out of London on the train, only realising when she'd got home that she'd forgotten to speak to Charlie. 'Can't Paul cover it?'

'He's dealing with a ruptured tendon near Ludd-on-Fosse. There'll be a bun fight getting neds onto hoists for surgery when we get back. I'm following mine's horsebox to the clinic now.'

'I can't face it without you,' Petra pleaded, eyeing her spaniel in his basket. 'Wilf's wearing the furtive look of a dog that may have ingested more than one Christmas tree decoration. I may have to stay in and monitor him. And the Redhead's in season, can you believe?'

''Tis the season to be trolleyed.' Gill laughed, a sharp fox bark. 'I'll leave a stiff drink out for you when you drop the kids round with mine.'

'They're coming singing with me.'

'Don't be cruel. Carolling when Brian Hicks is in charge is hell on under-sixteens. Dixie's organised a pyjama party and a sleepover. She's been baking gluten-free cupcakes all day. Didn't Ed say?'

'He probably did, but I need a translator nowadays.' She sighed at the thought of packing overnight bags. 'Everything's sick, dope, lit and hundo-p goat in Ed's world.'

'Dix is hoping Fitz will come.' Gill had a wry smile in her voice.

'I'll pitch it, but I fear not. Don't tell Dixie, but I think things are hotting up with Sophie the pop-up girlfriend.'

She and Gill sighed in unison, the dream of being joint mothers-in-law to a star-crossed Fitz and Dix – which they'd agreed sounded like a trendy deli chain – fading for now. Poor Dixie's growing crush had gone unnoticed for a year and looked unlikely to be requited. As far as Petra could tell, Sophie – whom Fitz had met doing his Duke of Edinburgh gold award – was more of an Instagram flirtation than a serious relationship, but she still felt a pinch of maternal loss and a burning curiosity as her son read messages that made him blush and retreat from the room.

Spotting a dropped packet of blinis, she realised he must have been down for a fridge raid while she was feeding the horses.

'Now promise me you'll behave if Bay's there tonight,' Gill lectured.

'He won't be, will he?' She gulped, ashamed to find her first thought was what to wear instead of the warm velvet trousers that made her bum look like a two-seater sofa.

'Probably not, but it's best to be prepared.'

'I will,' Petra promised, wondering if she had time to wash and blow-dry her hair.

@GunnPoint No unusual activity to report. Friendship still active. Fitz sent the direct message to his grandmother's Twitter account. He was feeling increasingly sick at the shortening countdown to Christmas and the big reveal Gunny intended to stage, if his father did nothing about Lozzy. He checked the app constantly. The relationship was clearly in its death throes, yet it limped on, his father too cowardly and placating to change his ammunition from stun to kill.

Switching to Messenger, Fitz felt a degree of hypocrisy that he was doing the same to Sophie, replying only now to the bathroom-mirror pic she'd sent four hours ago. Things had gone a bit stale. They were down to exchanging a few scattered emojis and a selfie a day, neither wanting to break up with the other until after Christmas. He sent her a few random Santas and a quick abs shot.

He then spent twenty minutes searching horse GIFs while he ate his way through a packet of smoked salmon – the blinis had gone missing somewhere – a dozen Baby Bels, some cocktail sausages, crisps and cheesecake.

'You coming to the Walcote squad's tonight?' little brother Ed asked, opening the door. 'I think Dix will boinky-boinky again, if you ask. Can I watch this time?'

He threw a cushion, hard and fast, and Ed departed with a deep laugh. Having already boinky-boinkied on that sofa and been put off his stride when the Walcotes' three large dogs tried to join in, Fitz preferred a quiet night in.

Settling on a GIF of a horse bursting out of a Christmas cracker, he sent it to Carly.

She sent a thumbs up and a little x back. He hugged both tightly to his chest, which vibrated as Gunny replied. *@Fitzroving Thank you, William. I've sent a friendly reminder. Stop snacking in your room.* He looked round nervously.

49

Anticipating a good burst of body warmth from his gathered carollers, Brian Hicks had turned down the heating and the cottage was now so cold that steam rose off the weak rum punch.

'Better add another jug of water to that, poppet,' he told his wife, Chris. 'We don't want anyone tipsy. It's very icy underfoot out there.'

Number six the Green was one of a chocolate-box run of thatched cottages with leaded windows and much-photographed walled front gardens that were now almost all weekend or holiday homes. The Hickses had lived there for over forty years, proudly clinging to their woodchip, black-painted beams and chintz. They were the last of the old guard on the east side of the Green, refusing to sell out to a local property boom. Their house was worth at least a hundred times what they'd paid for it when seeking somewhere to raise their children close to Brian's accountancy firm in Birmingham. Now that he'd retired, Compton Magna was their world. Brian was a church warden, chairman of the parish council, passionate campaigner for more dog waste bins and outspoken activist against the Compton Magna Eco Village. Chris, who spoke little and only protested when told to, was his unswerving support.

Through the leaded window, a figure turning into the Hicks gateway was briefly stunned by his 1000-watt PIR security light that burst on, like a paparazzi flash. Brian – who never missed an episode of *Crimewatch* – clocked the large foil tray, determined chin and not unpleasing figure.

He threw open his door to his first guest. 'Welcome, Mrs Edwards!'

'It's *Ms*,' said a voice from behind a huge mountain of hot, freshly baked mince pies. Brian's mouth watered.

'Come in! Let me relieve you of this. You really shouldn't have.' He took the tray and handed it to his wife, nodding towards the kitchen. They'd keep the mince pies for their visiting children and their families: plenty of nibbles were already laid out on the sideboard, alongside photocopied song sheets and a discreet flyer about his anti-eco village campaign.

He turned back to Pip. 'Let me take your jacket, Miss Edwards.'

'It's Pip.' She started to take off her duffel coat, then clearly thought better of it.

Pip looked around the room eagerly. Her parents, who had never socialised, had been deeply suspicious of people like the Hickses, who came round every few weeks rattling tins or asking for tombola gifts – 'They'd bleed us dry, Pauline' – but Pip found them incredibly welcoming.

'Have some punch.' Brian ladled something that looked like orange squash into a plastic cup. 'You know my better half, Chris?' His small, mousy wife materialised behind him from the kitchen, like Debbie McGee popping out from one of Paul Daniels's magic cabinets.

'You have a lovely home.' Her heart lifted as she recognised the hallmarks of her parents' generation: the antimacassars, the G-plan furniture and the Worcester figurines crowding the mantelpieces amid the lovingly polished silver-framed photographs of children and grandchildren. She felt the same curious sense of homecoming as she did watching *Terry and June* repeats on Freeview.

The doorbell chimed, and the village started invading, loud voices, talk of snow, wine bottles whipped away into the unseen kitchen while more lukewarm, low-alcohol orange squash was ladled out. Eager to help, Pip offered round the trays of anaemic supermarket mince pies and distributed song sheets eagerly, but she'd never found conversational opening lines easy, even though she loved to talk.

She retreated to the corner with another beaker of winter punch, slugging it back and looking at the photographs again. There were more on the walls. There was a son and a daughter, both in possession of Brian's long nose and Chris's thin, mousy hair. They were clearly much loved, childhood, graduation, marriage and parenthood tiled between decorative plates and Welsh spoons.

Pip felt a pang in her chest. Raised by parents who had reacted to her sensitivities much as they did to the introduction of colour-coded recycling bins, by throwing everything in together and calling it dyspepsia, Pip assumed the three mince pies she'd crammed into herself had gone down the wrong way. She drained her plastic cup.

Then her heart lifted, the room seeming to spin and fill with glitter, like a snow globe, as Petra Gunn arrived, swathed in Emma Brown tweed and fake fur, wide-set eyes kohled and lips scarlet, as glamorous as a showgirl racing from the stage door to a Bentley for a weekend in the country.

'Pip!' She made a beeline for her, pulling a hip flask from her pocket. 'Isn't this house gloriously authentic? You have to admire the Hickses. One day soon Giles Coren will wheel in a television crew and an average family from Bedfordshire to live here for a week, mark my words. Have a top-up. Gill warned me the rations were mean.' She slugged a measure of something that looked like blackcurrant cordial into their beakers. 'Home-made sloe gin. Charlie says it's far too sweet, but so are we.'

Petra had swigged rather a lot of sloe gin before walking across the Green from dropping the children at the Walcotes', which was as warm as a tropical *cabana* from its bubbling Aga to its glowing wood burners. The Hickses' cottage defied science by being colder inside than it was out, the smiles that had just greeted her equally frosty, the headcount a familiar quorum of bearded, paunched, bald and dentally challenged village do-gooders and fellow parish councillors, turtle necks in abundance.

She wasn't sure how old Pip was – her guess would be a few years younger than her, maybe late thirties – which made them the youngest there by several decades.

Petra discreetly scanned the ranks for anybody who would fit the sugar-daddy-Father-Christmas bill for Pip, but they were a motley married selection.

'Carol-singing is usually a bit cheerier than this,' she reassured Pip in a whisper.

'I think it's perfect.' Pip beamed at her. 'I liked your message on Facebook today. You haven't been online in ages. We missed you!'

'As the message said, I've been writing a book, and have finished writing a book.'

'Yes, I liked your status.' Pip nodded.

Petra told herself off for preferring to be congratulated in person.

'Now you're back you must post more.'

'I want to catch up with my poor neglected children. Lots of Christmas trips. Now the girls are off school I'm trying to drag them out riding too, to justify pony nuts. I think Prudie's lost interest.'

'Is Prudie a pony?'

'Daughter. She's into bright lights and stretch Lycra, these days.'

Pip glazed over, as she always did when children were mentioned.

Brian bustled forward to plant a wet kiss on Petra's cheek, leaving pastry crumbs from one of Pip's mince pies that he'd just scoffed in the kitchen. 'Nobody told me our soprano had arrived! So good of you to come, Mrs Gunn. We might even overlook the parish-council meeting truancy.' He gave her arm a little squeeze to indicate it was a joke.

'Yes, I'm very sorry about that.' Petra knew from experience that some of the village old guard, like Brian, viewed a woman working from home as her excuse to dodge housework and community obligations, like arguing over the thirty-miles-per-hour limit extension along the Broadbourne road.

'Excuse me, Petra, but duty calls.' He clapped his hands. 'If anybody needs to take advantage of the lavatory, can they do so now? With the Jugged Hare currently closed, there will be no facilities en route, and I'd rather we didn't ask householders we're singing for if we can use their bathrooms, as happened last year when everybody drank too much before we set out.' Brian Hicks could de-energise a room faster than a power cut. He was soon pimping his economy mince pies again.

'We need Father Christmas, some reindeer and a mariachi band to liven this outing up,' Petra grumbled to Pip, eyeing a few late arrivals hopefully. 'Especially Father Christmas.'

'You're here and you're one of the loveliest people in the village,' Pip said, which bucked Petra up.

She felt guilty for always avoiding Pip and finding her so grating. With her unflattering reindeer sweater peering shyly between the toggles on her duffel coat, she looked harmless and sweet, her shiny face direct and expectant, first year to fifth-former.

The first year suddenly looked very pink. 'Don't look now but guess who's just arrived.'

'Santa?' she suggested hopefully, turning.

Six feet two of big smile, floppy hair and sex appeal in a shooting coat smiled back at her. 'Good evening, Mrs Gunn. I hope your safety catch is off.'

Lester had taken a bath, his hair still wet and combed back neatly. He was wearing the thick jumper that Pax had brought him from Scotland, which kept out even the chilliest draughts with which his cottage whistled.

He liked to watch the news at six o'clock, his routine timed to meet it perfectly, Stubbs and Laurence must be fed, his pot of tea brewed, and a round of toast just melting with butter. Routine mattered enormously to Lester. The Captain and Johnny had ribbed him for it, but it settled him.

Tonight the order of service was broken by a sharp rap on his door as he spooned a little tinned dog food onto Stubbs's dry mix and the rest into a bowl to take out to the fox.

It was probably the carol singers. Let them go to the house.

The rap came again, a distinctive four beat, an old familiar knock.

Hissing through his teeth, he went to answer it.

Ronnie was holding a large leather-bound photograph album. The blue eyes, bright with bad temper and Percy honesty, were resolute. 'May I come in?'

Lester hesitated, every urge to refuse, even though it went against his grain to be rude. Behind him, his toast popped up, making him jump. His fingers stayed, big-knuckled and bent, on the latch, longing to push it closed. Fingers that struggled to plait a mane these days, or open a jar of hoof oil. Fingers that could no longer easily tear the sack on a red birth bag or buckle up a bridle when it had been cleaned.

He stepped back and nodded.

She blew out a short, bolstering breath as she passed by him and he knew in that moment that seven magpies would have to fly.

Pip revelled in the chemistry between Bay and Petra, just as magical as she remembered it. Sparkier, perhaps, because Petra was refusing to rise to his bait, Katharine Hepburn to his Bogie. He obviously found the ice-maiden act hugely attractive.

'I hope Brian's got "O Come O Come Emmanuel" on his carol sheet.' He smouldered at her over a hip flask. 'It's our song, darling Petra.'

She stepped back, crossing her arms. 'I prefer "O Come All Ye Faithful".'

'"Ding *Dong* Merrily on High".' He did a mean Leslie Phillips impression.

'"Angels from the Realms of Glory".' Cold smile.

'Have it "Away in a Manger".' An eyebrow went up.

'"Go Tell It on the Mountain",' she hissed.

Pip was impressed. She was determined to be their Cupid tonight, come what may.

Petra was accusing Bay of spiking the punch now, both looking round at the carollers; Brian's elderly choir were coming alive a top-up at a time, cheeks as pink-tinged as the couple watching them. The two of them were beautiful together, she thought dreamily, holding out her own punch glass to be refilled as quiet Chris Hicks darted past.

Petra was sampling it, struggling to swallow as she took a gulp. 'Jesus, there's a lot of rum in this – how did you sneak it in?'

'A skill handed down from father to son.' His smile turned intimately to Petra's ear, but Pip heard the whisper. 'Your sloe gin is a far headier mix, Mrs Gunn, as are your eyes.'

'Stop it,' she scoffed, widening them at Pip, who grinned back encouragingly.

Worried this was already getting way out of hand, Petra was desperate to draw her into the conversation, Bay's hand running disconcertingly up and down her sleeve. She tried to beckon Pip over, but she'd retreated to the mantelpiece and was gazing dreamily at Bay's hand, which was now playing with the buttons on the back belt of Petra's coat.

'You look very pretty in tweed, Mrs Gunn.' He dipped his head and peeped at her through his lashes, a practised cliché of floppy-haired flirtation.

'You must remember Pip Edwards?' She reached out a hand and pulled the reindeer jumper towards them by its bobble nose. Pip's mouth was still hanging open.

'Of course.' He leaned down to plant a kiss on each of her wide pink cheeks. 'That jumper is most becoming. I'd love Rudolph's eyes to follow me round the room.' He caught Petra's gaze, as intimate as lifting a pillow on a lover's face. She looked quickly away, grateful to spot a fellow councillor beckoning her over.

She was soon listening to a long list of complaints about the village-hall committee and observing Bay from a discreet distance, village ladies fluttering in to land beside him, like aviary birds to a perch. She had to be very, very careful not to drink too much.

Bay caught her eyes on him and gave her a look so overtly sexual he might have been suggesting a quickie on the Hickses' couch.

'Do tell me more!' she demanded enthusiastically of her fellow councillor, who looked delighted.

At the door, Brian was banging a small dinner gong as he announced it was time to get going. 'Coats on, ladies and gentlemen, take a song sheet and check torch batteries.' Few had taken their coats off, so it wasn't long before they assembled outside, grateful for the frosty warmth. Their host was holding up a fisherman's lamp on a crook, which illuminated his bobble hat, and sounding like an SAS leader briefing a Black Op: 'We will proceed around Compton Magna clockwise from number one, the Green, then anti-clockwise from the Old Vicarage to the Almshouses before making our way back past the church and along Plum Run, calling in on the barn conversions.'

'Does he call out "left, right" when we're on the move?' Bay muttered, appearing at Petra's side.

'He gives a local history lecture,' she whispered, glancing round for Pip.

'We'll hang well back.' His voice was seductively hoarse.

A breathless little voice gushed, 'Isn't this great?' from Petra's other side and she sighed with relief to find Pip there, duffel coat buttoned up and scarf wrapped round her head.

'Once we reach Compton Bagot,' continued Brian, 'we'll proceed anti-clockwise again, along Back Lane and on to the Orchard Estate, emerging adjacent to the war memorial and looping past the old cricket field, which means we can take in some of the properties along the Broadbourne road, which the residents there always appreciate.'

'Otherwise known as Developers' Death Row.' Bay chuckled. 'Every time they knock down a shabby bungalow to build a glass-fronted gin-palace, Brian sees another crisp red fifty in the Santa hat.'

Petra glanced anxiously at Pip, who lived in one of the shabbier bungalows, but she was listening with rapt attention to Brian.

'The outlying farms are not practicable to visit,' he droned on, 'although we will make the effort to get to the Stokeses in Lower Bagot Farm out of respect to our community's oldest residents. Those with mobility issues can leave at any time. I have someone on standby with transport, should it be required.' He thrust the Skoda keys at Chris. 'I anticipate a finish time of approximately twenty hundred hours.'

Glancing at her watch, Petra imagined Charlie spilling exhausted into the Pimlico flat to shower and collapse in front of the television. Feeling full of bonhomie and spiked punch, she texted him a selfie to cheer him up and make him grateful he was still in London, then realised how tipsy she must be. She'd never sent Charlie a selfie in her life.

A warm arm threaded through hers. 'Let's sing, ladies.'

It was a big relief to see Bay slide his other arm through Pip's, and Petra was struck again with gratitude that she was there as chaperone.

'I have no desire to rake over the past, Lester.' Ronnie held the cup of tea he'd poured for her neatly in her lap, legs crossed at the ankle, her slender fingers supporting the bone china saucer, as though she were perching on a Regency sofa at a palace. He'd almost forgotten she could be ladylike, that she had been brought up to entertain the highest echelons, not just wield a pitchfork.

'If you say so.'

'I do. I brought the photograph album because I didn't know quite how to start this conversation, but I think we'd both prefer it stayed closed, don't you?'

'As you wish.'

'I want you to keep it. You and I are the only ones in it still alive, two- or four-legged. Put it on a shelf if you'd rather not remember.'

He nodded.

'You know I'm not staying, don't you?'

He stared at her, his eyes struggling to make out the exact expression on her face. He had always found that the pretty hid their feelings better. She had none of his folds and dewlaps, his deep shifting furls of skin that pinched together in pain or sagged low in tiredness, puffed up with sleep and sank back in grief. All he could see were the eyes. Still big, blue and resolute.

She was running away. It was what she did nowadays. He should have guessed when she turned up in the big horsebox with hardly any luggage. Pip had told him you wouldn't know she'd moved into the house from going in there.

'Where will you go?'

'Germany. My crossing's booked straight after Christmas.'

'But the new lad starts after that.'

'The lad is a man, Lester. A good man. He's going to try to get here sooner, but if not, I expect you to make him welcome. And he will be in charge.'

He said nothing and she let out that low, lovely laugh. 'We'll see about that, he thinks.'

'Don't read my mind, Mrs Le— Ronnie. You won't like what you find there.'

'You're angry, I know. You hated me coming back, but you damn well don't want me to leave now I'm here. And you certainly don't want the stallion to go.'

'You're not taking that stallion.' He shook his head. 'That's our future.'

'He could never settle here. You can see how damaged he is, how dangerous. He's been here a month and getting him in a round pen puts us both under threat. He was happy in Germany. He knew his job. He'll be better for going back there. It's all sorted out. We're both happier there.'

He put down his tea because the cup was rattling in the saucer. 'Old Cruisoe isn't what he was.'

'We'll buy in outside stallions via AI.'

'No! This stud has always stood sires.'

'And it will again, but not while we're re-laying the foundations. I can negotiate reduced fees once I'm over there. I have a lot of good contacts. I'm also going to look for a stud manager to take over next summer, after the Horsemaker leaves.'

'Let the lad sort the stallion.'

'No, Lester. I promised myself I'd take him back there and I will. I need to make amends.'

'And what about making amends here? What about what you did to us here? You should have come back twenty, thirty years ago.'

'I couldn't, Lester.'

There was a bark in the kitchen: Stubbs waiting patiently by the work surface on which his food had been put in his bowl and left.

'You had no reason to run.' He stared at his hands. 'All that nonsense stopped.'

'And I'm sorry for that. I don't think that was right at all.'

'It's not your business to think for me!' he shouted, shocking himself.

Her cup and saucer went down, her hands raking back the shock of blonde hair unchanged in half a century. He could feel the energy coming off her, the righteousness and disapproval turned back on him.

'I have no desire to rake up the past, as I said, but I will make one point. I've been a mistress several times in my life. It's not something of which I'm particularly proud – and I know you disapprove enormously – but it happened and I won't hide from its consequences. I have loved men who have made their marriage vows with other women. They had families and careers and friends and private lives quite separate from what we shared, some happy, others less so. One man in particular, Lion, was somebody I cared for very deeply. He's a secret that I've shared with very few people in my life. We were lovers for fifteen years, and remained close afterwards. Then, quite suddenly, Lion died. His family, those work colleagues, those friends, they mourned him. They were united in their love for him and their grief for him, and quite rightly so. He was a wonderful man, a very loved man. My mourning took place in another room, entirely separate, entirely unacknowledged. It was among the loneliest times of my life. I had nobody with whom to share my own grief. Nobody knew about us, you see. Just a few hoteliers and restaurateurs who called us Mr and Mrs Smith. And all I wanted, what I really needed, was just one person to say, "I know how much you loved him." Just once. Because it mattered. We mattered.'

Lester stared at the leather album cover. The mantelpiece clock ticked, Stubbs barked again in the kitchen, and he could hear the saliva in his mouth draw across his dry tongue as he swallowed. He waited, braced.

'I know how much you loved him, Lester.'

He looked down at his gnarled fingers, saw they were shaking.

He waited, braced for more. Like a terrier, Ronnie never held back when she was digging out a truth. That she had known about him and Johnny was never in doubt – she'd challenged them both before she bolted – but she had never betrayed them.

Unlike the other guests at the Ledwells' big white wedding, Lester had born as black a heart as a funeral guest. Ronnie had been led up to her marriage like an excited young mare straight off the track brought into a covering barn. The stallion did his duty. Johnny was a dutiful man, a proud father, a brilliant horseman and, at first, an exemplary buttoned-up drunk. He was a gay man following a long tradition of rural repression as he collaborated in a well-matched marriage. But Ronnie Percy saw truth in people as sharply as she saw honesty and good conformation in horses. She saw the love affair before they ever did.

'He loved you too,' she said now.

One ill-fated marriage, two men who had never found each other's like, three children born in quick succession, back to four-star eventing, five months as Angus Bowman's lover and she was gone. Knocked for six, Johnny and Lester had retreated into opposite corners. One closed his door while the other drank himself into an early grave.

For years, Lester had blamed Ronnie. But now she was the only one who had ever been brave enough to say it as it was. He had known what it was to love and be loved.

'Will you excuse me?'

In the kitchen, he put Stubbs's food down, spilling most of it. He took the second bowl outside, the cold air like a sheet of glass, his hands shaking even more.

The fox was curling to and fro against the wire, bold now, eyes gleaming, teeth smiling.

He couldn't get the latch open. These stupid, shaking old fingers.

Her warm hand closed over his, taking the bowl, then opening the cage to slip it inside. 'A fox indeed.' Her voice had its familiar husky bass note. 'You're full of secrets, Lester.'

She took his hands in hers, curling her dextrous, rein-callused fingers through his stiff, gnarled ones and raised them to her lips. And he knew the seven magpies were safe.

Pip was having the night of her life as they marched from house to house, Ding-Donging and O-Coming. She didn't usually drink spirits – she'd never liked the taste – but the sloe gin was no worse than cough medicine, and she didn't want Petra and Bay to think she was too juvenile. Tonight she was finally part of the village in-crowd, companion to two of its inner circle.

Outside number two, the Green, she watched them share a song sheet through 'Silent Night', all bass and alto, laughter and sarcasm. Pip had always thought it a very romantic carol. Elvis had sung it on her mother's favourite Christmas album. A teenage Pauline Edwards had closed her eyes and imagined dancing to it with Shane Lynch from Boyzone. She'd written Shane over three hundred fan letters until her parents put a stop to it because the stamps were costing too much. Grown-up Pip still held a candle for her favourite tattooed boy. Bay and Petra were Christmas-special pop-video stars, a soap-opera tryst in the frosty Comptons.

'You two look so good together,' she said eagerly, when the carol ended.

They cleared their throats and stepped apart, but Pip thought they looked secretly pleased.

Pip generally disliked physical contact, but she didn't mind Bay's arm hooked around hers, especially the laughter that rippled through him when Petra made a whispered aside, which she did a lot as they moved on and Brian delivered his village tour.

Pip thought again how perfectly suited they were, and despite her companions' derision, she was enjoying Brian's local history lecture, none of which she'd heard before.

'Magna means "great",' Brian explained, as they headed through open wrought-iron gates and along the Old Vicarage's grand drive. 'The Bingham-Percy family were great philanthropists and they asked the celebrated architect Richard Norman Shaw to design their model village full of his trademark quirks to make it look more historic.

'The cottages were for the estate's workers, plus the retired and the poor. Grander houses, like this vicarage and the stud, were built for Percy family members, thus a poor country curate was furnished with a house worthy of a canon.' He pulled the grand bell with a flourish and the singers launched into 'Deck the Halls'.

Inside, several lights were quietly extinguished. Nobody came to the door.

'It's owned by a Middle Eastern art dealer,' Petra whispered to Pip. 'I don't think he *does* Christmas. The first Sunday he moved in, he lodged an official complaint about the volume of the church bells.'

'He donated a mint to help stop the Travellers' village,' said Bay.

'My guess is he'd give even more to move the rest of us further away right now,' giggled Petra, singing louder.

The art dealer remained in lockdown, quite possibly wearing ear defenders. Eventually the carollers trooped off.

So far they'd collected less than ten pounds – the holiday cottagers had been a mean lot – but they were indefatigably full of Christmas cheer and spiked punch.

Still in the little garden of Stables Cottage, Ronnie stood beside Lester as they listened to the carol singers in the distance.

'I love this village when it puts on a good show.' She smiled. 'I told them not to come up here. I feel rather mean now. Daddy used to shout at them – do you remember? Told them he couldn't hear his radio.'

'You've got to stay,' he pleaded. 'You belong here.'

She shook her head. 'If things had worked out with the children, then maybe it would be different, but it's best this way. They'll start to feel they belong here again when I'm out of the way. I'll keep a close eye from Germany, and I'll come back to visit. I want to see that dun foal growing. He's our sire, Lester, wait and see. I'll find you others.'

'The grey stallion's a fine horse. Give me time with him.'

'You're far too precious.'

'Too old, you mean.'

'We both are. He's a young soul. He needs the same in a handler.'

'If you say so.' He eyed her wisely. 'You'd stay at the drop of a hat if the children asked you to.'

'That's not going to happen.'

He took a deep, unsteady breath. 'What if I tell them the truth?'

'No, Lester. Absolutely not. I won't do it to you, and it won't help. It's not about that any more. It's about me, their trust in me. Daddy knew that. It's why he left things the way he did. One earns trust.'

'You have my trust, Ronnie.' It was the first time since childhood he'd said her name as naturally as family.

'Good. Now let's have another cup of tea and watch some television soaps together, like we used to. You do still like soaps, don't you?'

'I should say so.'

50

Having forgotten her vow to monitor her drinking, Petra was feeling more spirited with every swig of a hip flask. They'd emptied hers and started on Bay's: it was something he took with him hunting three times a week nicknamed Sloe de Vie and practically a hallucinogen.

'I just want to warn you,' she told him between 'See Amid the Winter's Snow' and 'Joy to the World', quoting Prudie's favourite CBBC teen soap, 'that our "ship" is called *Friend* and nobody sails to Love Island on it, okay? Or Knob Bay, come to that.'

Bay seemed impressed. And Pip squeezed her arm afterwards, whispering, 'That was beautiful.'

'You heard?'

'I think most of us did. You said it quite loudly.'

Refusing any more Sloe de Vie, Petra sang lustily as they went from house to house, including the Walcotes' capacious and scruffy half-timbered cottage where they crowded in front of the porch and sang 'We Three Kings', three of her children forming part of a polite, yawning line-up, the youngest in pyjamas, the oldest wearing earphones.

'Mum's turnt AF,' Ed observed.

'Mummy's rather wasted,' Bella translated.

Around the corner opposite the church, one of Pip's 'oldies' distributed a tray of mince pies from the same batch Brian had stashed in his kitchen, kept warm on her Rayburn, as sweet and melting as Christmas kisses.

Petra ate two, keen to sober up.

'Turn over your sheets!' Brian rallied his singers. '"It Came Upon the Midnight Clear"!'

'Risky in this frost.' Moving closer to Petra, Bay brushed pastry flakes off her scarf. 'Did I spot your children having a sleepover?'

Petra's sheet fluttered to the ground.

Bending down to retrieve it as the others started singing, her head felt like a dropped bowling ball.

'... *from angels bending near the earth*...' Bay sang as he stooped, too, picking it up and handing it to her. 'Rare to have the place to yourself, I imagine.' He helped her up, gloved fingers threading through hers.

'... *from Heaven's all gracious King!*'

Singing the next two lines, Petra wondered if that had been a forbidden invitation to join her, the Obelisk of Luxor suddenly looming in her mind's eye.

'Fitz is home,' she told him cheerily, as the verse ended, sidling into a subgroup of Compton Women's Institute grandees for protection as they sang about angels flying through the cloven skies. Above their heads, those over Compton Magna held a capacity crowd of stars to watch over them this evening, the predicted snow clouds yet to draw their curtains across it.

Petra loved the village at night. It was a gingerbread-cottage metropolis, illuminating its sugary perfection through little mullioned windows, frost sparkling on stone-tiled roofs, no light pollution on the horizon to dull the glittering canopy overhead. They could have been extras in a Dickensian drama.

She found herself wishing again that Charlie was there.

At which moment, quietly and internally, Petra had the closest thing to an epiphany she could remember, her husband's beautiful balding head above her amid the stars, haloed in light, arms wide. The Obelisk crumbled, the SMC shrivelled, her head cleared and she felt overwhelmingly, ball-breakingly in control as they all filtered through the narrow gate to the beautiful Old Almshouses, now converted into one home, no welcoming lights on show, its walls glowing silver by moonlight.

'I bet he's gone back to London,' grumbled the WI chairperson. 'He's never here. Oh, he's left mince pies in the porch, look!'

'Kit was married to my late aunt.' Bay helped steady Pip, who was already swaying, unaccustomed to drinking anything stronger than a Bailey's at Christmas, let alone Sloe de Vie. 'Aunt Hermia was an actress.'

'*Tomorrow truly will I meet with thee,*' Pip quoted brightly, hanging off his arm.

'That's the inscription on her headstone,' Bay said in surprise.

'*Midsummer Night's Dream,*' Petra identified.

'I always like to stop and read that poem when I'm popping in on Mum and Dad.'

'Kit comes here occasionally to put flowers on her grave, but he never stays long. My cousins use the cottage sometimes.'

'Oh, he's still here,' Pip told them, nodding at the house. 'He puts dreamcatchers on her grave now, but he never sleeps much. He's like the Captain. Pays me not to clean.'

Brian had finished his informative talk on the Old Almshouses and they began 'While Shepherds Watched'.

The Angel of the Lord barely had time to come down when the door was thrown open and a shadowy figure dressed in what appeared to be a red sleeping bag and boxers thrust a tenner at them before slamming it shut.

'I'm sure he just said, "Bugger off,"' gasped one of the elderly do-gooders.

'Keeps himself in good shape,' said the chairman of the tennis club. 'I wonder if he wants to make up a mixed doubles next season.'

Bay leaned against Petra as he was briefly gripped by silent giggles, Sloe de Vie working like laughing gas. She had this covered now, stepping neatly away so that he almost fell over, and brushing down her coat. She was a mother of four, a parish councillor, and a lapsed Brown Owl. From now on, she would be filled with seasonal kindness, and no longer acting like a teenager trying to get off with the best-looking boy at a Christmas disco. Christ, were Bay's fingers threading through her hair now?

Reaching up to bat them away and finding it was just an over-hanging branch, she looked around for her chaperone. 'How are you doing, Pip?'

'Brilliant!' Pip was dangling off Bay's arm, hooking the other through Petra's and pulling the three of them together. 'This is one of the best nights of my life.'

'We need to get you out more,' Bay said, as Petra was drawn clumsily against him again, noses glancing off, eyes far too close. His held her gaze in the half-dark. Somewhere in a time capsule 'Last Christmas' was being played in a Yorkshire Dales village hall and he was asking her to dance. And while as a giggly fourteen-year-old she might have melted happily when faced with a teenage Lothario, her forty-four-year-old self had far too much to lose. She looked sharply away.

'I think Bay Austen *likes* you,' Pip said, in a loud stage whisper, as she clung to Petra. She was veering onto the verges more often than a speeding tractor now.

'He likes us both,' Petra said firmly.

'I'm really sorry to disappoint you, Petra,' Pip whispered, 'but I don't do threesomes.'

In the Orchard Estate, Carly was trying to get Sienna to settle, but the toddler was standing in her cot, dummy in mouth, lungs bursting with sobs. The sound was both heartbreaking and head-splitting. Carly had Jackson in her arms, crying too. He was due his bedtime feed – she'd been getting the milk ready when Sienna had kicked off.

A shadow fell in the door and she looked round gratefully, ready to hand the baby to Ash, but it was Ellis, cast into a giant by the low stairs light. 'Mum, I had another accident.'

Closing her eyes, temples tightening, she kept her voice low and calm. 'Have you wet the bed again, baby?'

'No! Promise!' His little voice was high and anxious. 'I climbed up to look at the people singing and the curtains fell down.' He burst into noisy tears.

Hugging him to her, Carly felt a flash of white-noise frustration. The curtain rail had been dangling by its Rawlplugs for ages and she'd asked Ash to fix it more than once. It had taken its final plunge while his neighbours were spreading tidings of great joy and Ash was on a crime bender. At least this time it was a virtual one.

Downstairs, the sound of handbrake turns and gunfire pounded out, Grand Theft Auto so loud Carly couldn't hear the carol singers, but she was determined to spread that joy in her children's teary bedtime world.

'Right, you lot.' She hooked Jackson under one arm, dropped the side of Sienna's cot with a skilful knee and lifted her with the other arm. 'Let's listen to the singers. What's your favourite Christmas song?'

'"Jingle Bells"!' Ellis cheered, reaching for his 'Splorer Stick.

Sienna stopped crying, excitement dawning. '"Dingle Bells"!'

'Then we'll Dingle all the way.'

Ash didn't even look up as she passed through the lounge into the little front hallway and threw open the door.

Built on the site of an old fruit farm, the small estate formed a large square, with a cul-de-sac leading off one corner. Viewed on Google Earth, it looked like a child's cartoon drawing of an old-fashioned television aerial. The carol singers had gathered on the scruffy patch of grass where Barry Dawkins parked his pickup. Known unimaginatively as the Triangle, it was a good vantage-point. An old bloke in a bobble hat was going from door to door asking for requests while his team belted out 'The Twelve Days of Christmas'.

Janine had already wheeled out Granddad Norm to park him in a prime spot and was summoning other relatives and neighbours, an exercise involving a lot of loud refrains of 'Get your fucking arses out here!' over the maids a-milking and geese a-laying. Carly could see Ash's mum watching from her front window, unable to bring herself to join them.

Bobble Hat Man was at Carly's gate now. She herded the kids to the end of the path to get away from the sound of gunshots coming from her house.

He introduced himself as Brian Hicks and claimed to have met her and Ash on the night of the hurricane, casting a nervous look at the front door. Ash had won something of a cult status in the village, as well as among the Turners, since that night, their local Gangsta Gypsy with his private army. As his moll, Carly had hoped she might demand new respect, but people like Brian still treated her as a slow learner.

'Any special requests, as they say on the radio?'

'I'd like you to sing "Jingle Bells",' she told him.

'I think you'll find that's not a carol,' he said kindly, holding up a song sheet. 'We can do anything on here. Our "In the Bleak Midwinter" is particularly fine.'

'Do I look suicidal? "Jingle Bells" is my kids' favourite.' She bounced Sienna on her hip.

'We don't know the words.'

'I'll find it on my phone. Hold him a sec.' She thrust the still-wailing Jackson at him and reached into her back pocket. A moment later she had a YouTube karaoke video cued.

Jackson, who loved strangers, had fallen silent and was gaping up at the man's grey-bearded face in delight, his gummy smile wide. Ellis had already charged off to the Triangle to join his older cousins, trainer lights flashing.

'Here you go.' Carly offered her phone to Bobble Hat. 'Use this.'

'I really don't think we can do this.'

'I'll get Ash.' She turned back towards the house

'There's no need to threaten violence.'

'To listen to it, you dope.' She smiled over her shoulder.

Being a Turner meant you had a certain degree of power, Carly was learning.

Pip was only vaguely aware that she was cannoning into people and kept pointing her torch into her own eyes.

Bay and Petra were star-crossed, she was certain, and destined to come upon a midnight clear, possibly multiple times.

Her new friends might keep sshing her like a child when she gave them the thumbs up, but Pip wanted them to know she wouldn't judge. She wasn't so naïve that she hadn't noticed the frisson mounting.

Too merry on Sloe de Vie and *eau d'amour* to appreciate that Petra was now putting a lot of Women's Institute regulars between her and Cupid, Pip stuck close to Bay. She was clinging tightly to his arm. Standing up was quite hard.

They were on the Orchard Estate now. They'd belted out 'I Saw Three Ships' along Plum Road and 'The Holly and the Ivy' on Medlar Avenue. As they chorused 'Once in Royal David's City' between Apple

Rise and Pear Close, Pip at last noticed Petra had moved to the opposite side of the group where she was hanging around with the oldies.

Brian was taking a vote on singing 'Jingle Bells' while Janine and her nieces handed round yet more trays of mince pies, these ones burned. Pip waved and whistled to get Petra's attention, then gave her a thumbs up with a questioning look.

A polite thumbs up came back, which made her pat Bay's arm and whisper, 'I think your luck's still in there, Big Boy.'

'I'm sorry?'

'Petra. Just saying.'

'Say no more, Pip. Please, say no more.'

'I've told her no threesomes, but I might reconsider.'

'That's more.'

She gave his arm a conspiratorial hug, pressing her cheek to it. He smelt lovely.

Pip recognised the pretty young Feather Dusters cleaner, a tot clutched to her chest, her shoulders engulfed by the arm of a tattooed hunk in a hoodie, who looked excitingly like Shane Lynch in his Boyzone heyday, front zip undone in that sexy way hard men did, defying the sub-zero weather.

'*Hello* there,' Bay said, in his most gravelly voice. He was directing his big, flirty smile at the wife with the baby. 'Don't tell me, I never forget a face...'

Pip snorted disapprovingly, muttering, 'That's an old one.'

'It's Carly, isn't it? Work in the farm shop?'

'That's right.' The blonde bounced her snotty toddler. 'This is Ash.'

'One hell of a wife you've got there, Ash.'

He'll be propositioning her next, like Robert Redford in *Indecent Proposal*, thought Pip, jealously.

'Had me run ragged saving that bloody dog from a ditch last summer. How's it doing?'

'She's okay, I think.' She gazed up at the Shane Lynch lookalike. 'Hey, babe?'

He shrugged.

'Ash came out of the army this year. He's going to be a personal fitness trainer.'

Lucky you, Pip thought wistfully, admiring the wide shoulders, intense silver eyes and Celtic tattoo on his neck. It looked very familiar. To think Carly the cleaner was married to this! How did Pip not know he was in the village?

'I could do with getting fit!' she told him.

Tattooed Ash ignored her, his pale eyes fixed on Bay.

'Of course! Ashley Turner.' Bay shook his hand affably, then winced as his was crushed. 'Our home-grown war hero.'

A born-and-bred Turner! The village's notorious rogues, Pip thought excitedly, all those wanderlust gypsy genes giving them a reputation for ferocity and fornication. Tamed by the armed forces, he was a caged tiger released back into the wild. Fitting that he had a big cat head tattooed on his chest, hiding colourfully among Maori inkwork and gladiator straps. That was familiar too, she realised, as she undid her duffel coat toggles and shook back her hair.

He looked extremely pissed-off, which was understandable with Bay Austen hitting on his wife on his own doorstep. 'You gonna sing for us or what?'

The voice was broad Gloucestershire and disappointingly nothing like Shane Lynch's.

'Like angels!' Pip promised, finding herself plucked away by her reindeer jumper nose and held firmly next to Petra in the gaggle of the singers now crowded round the mobile phone Brian was holding up. Thinking he was taking a group selfie, Pip struck a pose.

'He's showing us the lyrics to the song, Pip,' Petra muttered.

Reaching out to grab her arm for balance and missing, Pip lurched into Brian as he cued them into 'Jingle Bells', his thumb sliding across the screen. YouTube jumped to 'Let It Go' from *Frozen*.

'Oh, I love this one!' Pip started singing, turning out a performance that would be remembered for years to come. Putting her heart into it, she sang it for Petra and Bay, for the sexy Shane Lynch lookalike, and for JD, her beautifully built, inked and pierced heartbreaker.

As Pip sang, she realised exactly where she'd seen that tiger tattoo on Ash Turner's chest before. It was identical to JD's. As was the one on his neck. And if she pulled his joggers down right now, she was pretty certain the piercing would be familiar too.

*

Your friend's going totally tonto, Petra read on her phone as the rest of the group gamely tackled the complicated first section of the Disney classic. Being the mother of two girls, Petra could sing 'Let It Go' in her sleep and even – as now – while reading texts from flirtatious neighbours. *Plz take her home. Bx*

YOU *take her home, kemosabe*, she texted back as she sang, glancing over her shoulder at Bay then at Pip, who launched into the chorus like Janis Joplin at her last gig. Petra no longer felt sorry for her. She felt frightened for the village.

Her phone vibrated in her hand. *Pat's your friend.*

I hardly know her. BTW it's Pip.

Point proven! Bx

Singing the chorus with feeling, she didn't look at him again. That was such a Charlie-like comment. He was a total Charlie. He was from the same mould. All her Safe Married Crushes were men like her husband. That was what made them safest of all.

Her phone vibrated again. *Let's take her home together… Bx*

Fat chance! If they took Pip all the way along the dark Broadbourne road, that meant walking back alone together all the way to Compton Magna, quite possibly cutting across the village cricket field, past the old pavilion, cast romantically into a small wooden Taj Mahal in the moonlight, its lock all too easy to pick (she mustn't dwell on the detail, but Bay was bound to have learned skills like that in some misspent episode of youth, or maybe it was just unlocked). Inside there would be blankets and hurricane lamps and stolen conversations and the briefest shameful kiss – nothing below the waist – and they'd wish each other a merry Christmas while the Obelisk of Luxor stirred and rose, for ever forbidden to her.

You're on your own there, she replied, singing the chorus again and adding, *Let it go.*

Her fingers were like icicles. God, it was cold. Contrite and dizzy with Disney overload, she sent a text to Charlie, *I miss you. Xxxxxxxx* and another to her sons *Everything ok? xxx*

The song had reached its final crescendo. The Orchard Estate was all singing along, kids whooping, fairy lights glowing in windows and along eaves, at least one illuminated Santa climbing up a wall, and number ten glowing like a halogen heater under the weight of three lighting nets across its roof.

'Merry Christmas, everyone!' whooped voices young and old, a cloned mass of Noddy Holders, Comptons Bagot and Magna coming together in a communal mulled hug of socialising and good cheer.

Money clattered into the buckets. The estate was always the most generous and appreciative audience, a tight-knit community of families and neighbours, who feuded and celebrated with equal heart.

Petra's festive spirit broke its banks inside her, an unstoppable tidal wave of good will and nostalgia. Social Norm was wheeled closer to pour out home-made *poitín* into teacups to offer to the singers. Carly came up to say hello, baby on one hip, toddler on the other. Kind Mo joined them, taking the baby to cuddle and insisting Petra must come riding with the Saddle Bags the next day. 'We've missed you!'

'What's she doing to my Ash?' Carly was staring back at her house.

'I think somebody should take Pip home,' Mo said worriedly. They all turned to see her laying about Ash Turner with her duffel coat.

They hurried towards the little front garden of number three.

'You led me on!' she was screaming. 'You hustled me with your KitKats and dick shots. You never wanted to have sex with me at all, did you?'

'Get off me, woman. I have no fucking idea what you're talking about!'

'All that stuff you wanted to know about me was to plan a robbery. I know what happened the night of the hurricane! Did you get your mates to help? You thought you'd got away with it, didn't you?'

Poor Pip, thought Petra, pushing her way through the carol singers towards her. Her drunken state is my fault.

Then she stopped in her tracks as Bay strode heroically into the garden, arms outstretched, gathering Pip up. 'Let's get you home to bed, shall we, Pipsqueak?'

'And *you* want to get in Petra's bed, not mine!' She'd reached the argumentative-drunk stage.

Petra melted hurriedly out of sight behind a Transit van.

'That man *conned* me!' she was insisting tearfully, pointing at Ash. 'He sent me pictures of his erect penis in exchange for information about security at the stud...'

'That's fucking slander!' roared Ash.

'I can prove it! He's got a Prince Albert and he has a tattoo of a gecko walking out of his pubic hair.'

'Ew,' said a girl in the crowd near Petra.

'That's not my Ash,' Carly said decisively. 'He's got no piercings down there.'

'Fucksake!' Ash stormed indignantly inside.

Petra watched gratefully from behind the Transit van as Bay lugged a stunned-looking Pip quickly away.

Her phone vibrated. *Is Little Drummer Boy getting to you?* Charlie wrote with a weepy-faced emoticon. He knew her soft spots. *Case still dragging on. Hopefully sorted early tomz. Envy you not having to work this hard. x* And her sore spots. *PS Don't forget Mum's train gets in at 12.* And her sensitive spots.

The carol singers were heading out onto Back Lane to gather in front of the row of old cottages where the Mazurs and Flynn the farrier lived, and launching into an ambitious 'Coventry Carol'.

Polish Aleš Mazur, a bearded man-mountain in a Christmas sweater, who could be as hospitable when his front door was open as he could be red-mist angry when it was closed, distributed *nalewka* and sang 'Lulajże, Jezuniu', cuddling his infant son as a prop.

'It means "Sleep baby Jesus",' a tired-looking Bridge told Petra. 'Which that little guy had only started doing.' On cue, the one-year-old opened his eyes and bawled. Hurriedly handing his son back to his wife, Aleš joined in a raucous rendition of 'Rockin' Around the Christmas Tree' with long-haired, sleepy-eyed Flynn and a group of mates who had emerged from the farrier's cottage with him, all reeking of dope.

Brian, who was looking increasingly strained as mighty dread seized his troubled mind, ushered his choristers quickly away and embarked upon a detailed explanation about the medieval motte to their right as he herded them along towards Lower Bagot Farm, where the elderly Stokeses would be eagerly waiting.

Following at the back, Petra read replies from her sons. First Ed: *28 donuts, 2L Sprite, Level 38 of Splatoon. 0% tired!!!* Then Fitz: *Dog bin sick. Otherwise gud.*

Was that illiteracy, laziness or pretension? Whichever, it didn't bode well for his mocks.

There was a text from Bay, vanguard to a fresh flirtation.
Where does Pip live? Bx
One of the bungalows. Don't know which. Is she okay?
She's fine. Wants to build a snowman which she insists means
waiting for snow.

51

Having put the children to bed once more, Carly made herself a mug of tea and settled down on the sofa beside Ash's loud car-thieving game, her thumb scrolling her phone screen at speed, flicking through friends' Facebook posts, barely breaking in rhythm as she hit the thumbs-up of 'like' or typed *lol xx* or *I'm sorry for your loss* or *Congrats*. She then uploaded a picture she'd taken of the carol singers, with the caption *Luvin' our first village Christmas!* Duty done, she flicked across to her albums: pictures of the kids, the village, the horses, Pricey, army accommodation, girls' nights out, holidays. Ash on the beach, in the pool, on a lounger, in bed.

Getting up to fetch another beer, Ash crossed behind her chair, looking down. 'You got loads there.'

'Your inks have been shared more than a Domino's pizza, lover.'

'What bastard sent those to the crazy cat lady?'

'Whoever it is tried to rob her work.'

'They didn't take nothing, though, did they?' he muttered.

Carly eyed him suspiciously. 'How do you know that?'

'Heard it somewhere. They broke into the stud the night of the big storm, but there was nothing worth taking.'

'Then they let Spirit out to cover their tracks,' she said slowly. 'How do you know about this, Ash?'

'Pays to keep your ear to the ground in this family.' He wandered into the kitchen.

She thought back to the night of the hurricane – he'd spent most of it on the phone in the pub entrance.

Following him, she watched him rooting in the fridge. 'You knew the stud was going to be robbed, didn't you?'

'I heard rumours.'

'And you did nothing about it?'

'You can't just bulldoze around laying down the law in this family, Carl!' He glowered at her. 'Turners might want a leader, yeah, but it's a long game bringing order round here. I'm a non-commissioned officer, babe. I work my way up through the ranks. You had me commanding them all that night like bloody Mountbatten going in to battle.'

'I knew you hated it.'

'It got the job done. But I won't do any good in this family throwing my weight around. Where's all the beer gone?'

'In you, lover.' She smiled apologetically, turning and heading back to the sofa, calling over her shoulder, 'You drank it. There's half a bottle of Tia Maria in the cupboard if you're desperate. I'll join you. It's almost Christmas, after all.' The carol-singing had made her feel like it was really about to happen.

He carried the drinks through, stooping over the back of the sofa to deliver hers and clink it with his own glass.

She reached back for his free hand.

He took it, his broad palm and big knuckles enveloping hers. 'The lads are all at Flynn's. I said I'd go round there.'

She stopped herself snapping that it was the third time that week. She couldn't face a fight, knowing it would wake Ellis. She was well practised in the art of hissing, but Ash always just shouted.

Instead, she held on to his hand, stretching back to look up at him. 'Or we could just go straight to bed?'

Carly didn't feel randy yet, but she knew she would. Their bodies had the conversation in bed that they couldn't have anywhere else.

He was so tall, standing above her, that she couldn't see his expression, just the tight set of his chin.

For a moment his fingers gripped hers, then slipped away. 'Later, bae.'

Carly threw back her sweet coffee liqueur and returned irritably to her albums, remembering how much easier it had been when he was in the army.

She texted Janine: *So who in the family has a Prince Albert and a gecko?*

The list that came back was extensive. It seemed the pierced-dick-lizard thing was something of a Turner brand. Of the half-dozen names on there, one stood out a mile: *Jed.*

'Are you sure we haven't gone past your house?' Bay stifled a yawn as he herded Pip along the Broadbourne road. 'Do you recognise any landmarks?'

Pip managed a valiant 'onwards' gesture with her hand. She was having difficulty speaking, let alone remembering where she lived. The effect of Social Norm's *poitín* – the sensory equivalent of dental anaesthetic combined with a blow to the head – hadn't fully kicked in until they were halfway home, and now she couldn't entirely recall where home was.

They made it to the bus stop, a splintering wooden hut beneath a weeping willow, so Pip knew they were close. She'd caught her bus to university from there for three years. Those were the days.

'What are you doing?' Bay asked in alarm.

She was sitting inside the bus stop, mentally travelling back in time. 'Youcanleavemehere.'

'Of course I can't,' he said. 'What's the name of your house?'

'The Bulrushes.'

'I'll go and look for it. Don't go away.'

'Petrahasnthadsexforages.'

Bay sat beside her. 'I think she deserves a bit more discretion from her friends.'

'I'm only trying to help her.' She picked the words out with effort, then corrected herself carefully. 'Help you. You're both lovely. Shpeshly you.'

'Thank you.' He pulled out his hip flask. 'Now tell me what Ronnie Percy is up to.'

'I can't. Client confidentiality.'

'Percys are overconfident.' He held the flask out of reach as she tried to take it. 'Especially Ronnie.'

'Lester says she's beyond rodent – redunt – hope,' she said

dismissively. The stud's stallion man hadn't quite voiced that sentiment – he rarely spoke – but she knew he thought it.

'Old Lester thinks we're all beyond redemption,' Bay said, his
phone screen glowing as he tiredly tried to identify her house on
Google Maps.

'Especially Ponnie Rercy.' She closed her eyes to stop the stars
swirling about. She could hear Bay's flask top unscrewing again, the
clink of its hinged top.

'Ronnie was my first pin-up,' he admitted. 'Everyone in the
Comptons was in love with her. She'd hack round the village, all
blonde hair, cigarettes and laughter, stopping to talk to everyone.
She owned these lanes. Then she was gone.'

Listening, Pip imagined one of the soft-focus vintage clips played
on BBC2 retrospectives, all headscarves, clipped English and village
cricket. 'How old were you?'

'Eight.'

She snorted with laughter.

'I had an eye for women and horses from an early age.' He yawned,
stretching back. 'C'mon, where do you live, Pip?'

In Bay's mind, the two sentences were entirely unconnected. Pip,
floating somewhere between total incomprehension and second
wind, added them together, drew a heart around them and added
today's date as surely as the graffiti celebrating teenage trysts on the
bus-stop walls around them.

It was another perfect moment. This was the sort of evening she'd
dreamed of fifteen years ago, waiting here to catch the bus to lectures.
Laughter, friendship, intelligent conversation, unbridled no-strings
sex. In the absence of Shane Lynch, Bay was a very hot option. Petra
wouldn't mind, surely. Pip was younger and unattached; it would
be a straightforward physical exchange, like a game of ping-pong.

Pip preferred her men muscled, inked and wearing at least two
items of leather that weren't shoes and a belt, whereas Bay had that
posh thing going on with the Dominic West voice, bright trousers
and gold signet ring, but he was seriously good-looking and very
gentlemanly.

'Do you want to have sex with me?' she asked.

'That's a generous offer, but I have to get back to my wife.' The reply was so effortlessly polite, he might have been declining an extra-strong mint.

The matter-of-factness somehow made the rejection okay. When Pip had been married – not a relationship she ever cared to dwell on much – her husband Ali had accused her of divorcing sex from emotion. Pip didn't see that as a bad thing. She found emotions a lot harder to understand than sex.

'Now, stand up. I know where you live.' Switching on his phone again, Bay showed her a red teardrop point on Google Maps. As he did so, a new message came through with a bright trill.

Hope Pip got home okay. Thanks for proving me wrong. God rest ye. Px

They could hear the carol singers further along the lane now, offering tidings of comfort and joy. Pip really didn't want to be alone.

'We can sign a disclaimer,' she offered.

Petra bailed from carol-singing after they'd done 'God Rest Ye Merry Gentlemen' for the Stokeses at Lower Bagot Farm, always the jolliest of the calls, old Sid and Joan laying on hot toddies and piles of sausage rolls. She walked part of the way home with Mo. Muffling yawns with gloved hands, they chatted about visiting in-laws, then Mo passed on hunt-supper gossip and the latest *Archers* plot. Inevitably, the conversation turned to Pip Edwards.

'Do you really think she was targeted by a hustler?' Mo was shocked.

'In her dreams. She's a fantasist. Bay's probably strapped to the wall of her punishment dungeon in a gimp mask right now,' Petra predicted bitchily.

'That's awful!' Mo stifled a shocked laugh.

'I was going to set her up,' Petra added, 'but she's certifiable. And she's far too old for Tinder which is how they hooked up I hear. Nobody gets swiped right over thirty. She needs one of those agencies with a real person behind a desk who can see how vulnerable she is. And if she takes them cakes, they're bound to give her the best dates.'

'Barry has a very peculiar cousin down Andoversford way who

makes the prettiest little ornaments carving eggshells. Pip must use a lot of eggs.'

'It's a match. Tell him to line up the dick shots.' She sighed. 'I'm going to have to find a new SMC.'

'You can't have Jed.' Mo was very protective of her own crush on the village's darkest Lord of Misrule. 'Kit Donne's back. He's a good-looking man.'

'Gill's already staked her claim, although she doesn't know it yet. I think I'll focus on Charlie. If you can't appreciate your husband at Christmas, when can you?'

Mo's jolly, smiling face – which always made Petra think of a golden retriever – pulled back, chin disappearing into her neck, soft eyes full of cheer. 'You're not feeling yourself.'

'I'm married to Charlie, Mo. If I don't feel myself, nobody will.'

They hugged goodbye beside the memorial hall and Petra headed home to her unusually quiet house. She tracked down her teenage son in his darkened room, screens glowing, toast plates and mugs littered around him, grumbling that she was getting between him and the television when she stooped to pick them up. Downstairs, she unloaded the dishwasher, made up a bed for Gunny in the annexe, folded armfuls of the children's laundry and then, collapsing gratefully onto the kitchen sofa with Wilf, called Gill to make sure all was well with the children.

'Any gossip?'

'Edited highlights include spiked punch, Kit Donne in his underpants, Bay on the sleaze, and Pip's been scammed by someone with tattoos and a pierced penis.'

'Usual village jollop then. Let's debrief out hacking tomorrow. Early one okay?'

'I'll pass. Got mother-in-law arriving at eleven and the mare's stroppily hormonal.'

'All the more reason to come out and blow off the cobwebs before the widow spider trains her eight eyes for dust and dirt.'

'Thanks for that, but no.'

'Suit yourself. We'll call past at eight anyway, just in case. The kids can all stay here until we're back.'

Little Drummer Boy's majorette is home, Petra texted Charlie.

What train are you getting back tomorrow? Xxx He got extra kisses because it was Christmas.

Wilf rolled over with a squeaky yawn, presenting his freckled belly for rubbing, head cocked to one side, eyes ringed with playful white, tail thumping. Petra obliged him distractedly. She and Charlie stroked the dog more than they did each other, vying to be the one he loved most. He was loyal to Petra because she fed him and took him for walks – the marriage; he was loyal to Charlie because he took him shooting – the love affair.

She tried to picture Charlie asleep on the sofa now, television glowing, snoring with his mouth open, shirt gaping at the buttons, like fledgling beaks, rucked up over his slight hairy paunch. An unwanted image superimposed itself, like a strobe show, of Charlie in a bar, tie and tongue loosened, smile widening, telling an attractive woman that his wife didn't understand him. Now he was in the familiar massage parlour bondage room.

'Stop it,' she told herself firmly. Sitting down with nothing to do was always fatal.

She went out to check the horses, throwing each another slice of hay. The Redhead was still flirting with her small out-of-sight neighbour, tail fanned to one side as she presented an open invitation to the grilled glory hole.

'He's a gelding and he can't reach,' Petra pointed out gently, as the mare squealed to the frustrated tussock.

Clouds were shuffling in overhead now, heavy and menacing.

She sent Charlie another text: *It's going to snow. You might want to think about catching an earlier train.* The strobe image was playing again. Charlie. Bar. Loose tie. Sympathetic woman.

Did he have the same suspicious mind, she wondered, waking groggily on the sofa, lonely and shattered, reading his wife's messages, his own strobe playing? Petra. Carol-singing. Pissed. Flirting. Entire village witnessing.

Petra felt an involuntary smile steal across her lips. She'd seen Bay off. The Obelisk of Luxor was something she would never again dwell on. Apart from now, obvs.

Restlessly, she made a posy of pine and holly to put in the annexe for Gunny.

As she did so, Charlie replied: *No way case will fish tomz. Back Fri. Pols to Mum forme. Cx*

He only texted that badly when he was drunk. The strobe played ever faster, the gimp mask tightening.

She took her best reed diffuser and fluffy towels to the annexe. He'd be out with chambers, she reassured herself, drowning his sorrows as the case from Hell dragged on. Poor Charlie. It was mean of her to imagine him partying every night.

Poor you. Love you. Xx

Love you too. You aremy beatiful clever wife and im soluckyto have youi and ouir beautifukl childrenm xxxxxxxxxxx

Well, that was a turn-up for the books. She hadn't had one of those since England retained the Ashes.

Aw! Smiley face and love heart.

The phone vibrated again: *God rest ye too. Bx*

Bay. Her pulses rocketed. Her noble intention to devote her undiluted wifely love to Charlie this Christmas wasn't starting well.

'You all right, Mum?' Fitz sloped in, his dark hair all pointing left as though he'd been standing sideways in a wind tunnel.

Was that fashionable or had he been asleep? Petra wondered. 'Yes! Fine! You?'

'Yeah, hangin', y'know.' He eyed her phone. 'Can I – um – borrow that a sec?'

'Why?'

'Ponkers says the iPhone has an Easter egg I have to look at.'

'Fitz, it's Christmas not Easter.'

'It's a nickname for a hidden app.'

Quickly deleting the Bay texts, she handed it across.

He played with a few settings, curled his mouth down, unimpressed, then handed it back. 'It's pretty lame.' A moment later, he'd disappeared behind the fridge door.

'Your father won't be back tomorrow. He's stuck with this case until the weekend.'

'No shit.'

'Gunny will be here, though.'

'Shit.' The door swung closed. He was clutching most of her

Waitrose deli counter purchases to his chest. 'You're not feeling paranoid, though, yeah?'

'Paranoid about what?'

'I dunno. You're always paranoid.'

'I am not!'

'Cool.' The dark eyes smiled into hers, as rare as a double rainbow.

'Fitz, everything's all right, isn't it? With your love life and stuff?'

'My love life's good, Mum,' he said without hesitation, turned towards the door to the hall.

Petra closed her eyes with relief.

'It's everyone else's that's fucked up,' he added, as he exited, dropping a packet of sausage rolls.

Petra put it back into the fridge and took herself upstairs for a long, candlelit bath.

@GunnPoint *Friendship is OFF. Repeat, friendship is off.*

@Fitzroving *Good news. Have you taken the measures?*

@GunnPoint *All calls forwarded from landline and Mum's phone has unknown number bar. Electric gates closed.*

@Fitzroving *Good boy. Be vigilant. See you tomorrow.*

52

Lester was no longer so wary when he took the grey stallion his hay net first thing in the morning, familiar with the way the horse flew to the back of the stable to wait.

As soon as he was back out of the stable, however, before the bolt was even slid fully across, the stallion would resume his circular march, head snaking, teeth bared, as he slammed the bars, attacked his mirror and snatched at his hay.

This morning, Lester took his time to tie up, watching him over his shoulder. Ears back, the horse snorted with rhythmic, feverish pent-up fear and fury.

'Trust old Lester,' he breathed gently. 'You're staying here.'

The text came through before seven.

Just tried to call but can't get through. Case postponed because of snow. Coming home today after all. Not sure when – Christmas shopping first. Lots of treats for my beautiful wife!!! Will call from train. Love you. C xxxxxxxx.

The spelling was better than the previous night, but another unheard-of line of kisses made Petra jumpy, as did the early hour, the compliment and the fact it hadn't yet snowed any further east than Cardiff.

Yet it was so lovely to know he was coming back, and she wouldn't have to endure a night alone with Gunny after all, that she didn't want to dwell on it, just sending him back an equally long line of kisses and a hooray before hurriedly pulling on some clothes to take

Wilf out in the hope of bumping into Ronnie. She had an urge to scream on a gate.

But there was no sign of her walking her dogs. As dawn's steel gleamed brighter, she could feel the snow heavy in the air.

It started falling just as the Bags rode past her drive. Petra was still mucking out the Redhead, dodging her coquettish tail-lifting attempts to engage in flirtation. It reminded her of herself with Bay. Thank God all that was over.

'Lightweight!' the friends all goaded her, as she waved them past.

They didn't hang about, barely dropping below a trot. Gill had appointments that morning, Bridge had childcare only until ten, and Mo had to pluck turkeys and cut Christmas trees.

And Petra had her mother-in-law, who had already posted on her many social feeds that this year she would be uploading podcasts, vlogs and live streams from her son's house entitled Christmasculine, or 'A Man for All Festive Seasons', insisting commuters like Charlie felt strangers in their homes and needed to reassert themselves.

'Can Tilly and Gracie come here today?' demanded Bella an hour later. 'We can take the ponies out riding in the snow.'

'Not today,' Petra said. 'Gracie only breaks up from school this afternoon and Tilly's parents are…' in a very unhappy marriage and I'm avoiding the father '… busy. Gunny's train gets here in a couple of hours, and Daddy's coming home after lunch.'

'He's coming back *today*?' Fitz's eyes gleamed in the shadow of his hoodie.

'That's right.' She watched as he swung round and bounded into the boot room. 'What are you doing?'

'Closing the electric gates.'

'Why?'

'Gunny likes to see them closed.' He glanced out through the window at the lane. 'A man's home is his castle and all that. Think Christmasculine, Mum.'

'No wonder you two are getting on so well. You must *charm* her, Fitz. I thought she enjoyed being here over half-term, but her blog write-up was awful. She even posted photographs of the dust on top of the wardrobes. She could have done herself an injury balancing on a chair.' She tried not to enjoy the idea too much.

'She uses a selfie stick,' he explained. 'You should see her pictures of the cupboard under the stairs. That thing goes back miles. There could be bodies in it.'

'There might be soon.'

Having dropped Ellis off at school for his last day of term, Carly pushed the double buggy to the bachelors' field to see Spirit. It was empty, its snow blanket pocked with departing hoof marks. The old tweedy boy must have moved them. More snow was forecast later that day, the sky overhead lowering its hammock of clouds ready to let drop.

She'd have liked to take Ronnie up on her offer to go and see him on the yard, but she had to get back to clean with Janine's team all day.

She took out her phone, looked up Fitz and messaged: *U ok?*

The reply made her grin when she finally worked it out: *A ok. B ok! C U soon ok?*

She cracked a yawn, picked up Jackson's kicked-off shoe and Sienna's jettisoned drinking bottle from the road and wheeled around to trudge home and leave the kids with Ash's mum again.

The second fall of snow – thicker than the first – made it slow going into Broadbourne, and Petra was twenty minutes late to meet her mother-in-law's train, a lapse for which she knew she would be punished.

Gunny was waiting in the coffee house opposite the station, wearing an oversized fake-fur hat and camel coat that made her look like a cross between a lion and Boy George, her fingers flying across her iPhone as she spread news around her social circle of her abandonment. Now she snapped a photograph of Petra as she hurried inside, tripping on the step.

'At last!' She deftly shared it with her followers before tossing her phone into her Kelly bag and standing up to accept a kiss on each hollow cheek.

'Barbara, you look *wonderful*.' More Botox, she noticed. Gunny's face had now tipped over the balance point where mother-in-law had fewer wrinkles than daughter-in-law.

Petra gathered up Gunny's cases – more than she'd pack for a family week in Cornwall – and led the way outside.

'How *are* you, Petra dear? You look tired.'

'Never better!' she said tightly. 'Good journey?'

'So-so. I looked out for somebody reading one of your books as usual but, d'you know, in twenty years of regular train and plane travel I never have?'

'What a disappointment for you.'

'I'm reading the latest Philippa Gregory for my literary circle. Have you?'

'Not yet.'

'You must. Now, she really can write history.'

Plucking out her phone, she fired off messages as they drove – 'Isn't social media wonderful? Did you know I'm followed by Samantha Cameron's mother?' – while also keeping up a chirpy stream of snide comments as they drove back to the house. While they waited for the gates to open, she caught sight of the fairy lights in the centre of the turning circle and she gave a stiff laugh. 'I suppose that was the children's idea? You shouldn't indulge them, Petra. I'd have nipped that in the bud. Looks awful. Next thing you know you'll have a neon Santa climbing up your walls. Poor Charlie.'

'The lights were my idea,' Petra said touchily. 'The neon Santa's round the back.'

That shut her up until they got inside.

'I always forget how cluttered this kitchen is.' Gunny looked around conspicuously for somewhere to put her handbag. 'It's already terribly battered, isn't it?'

'It was hand-distressed by the designer.'

'I'm not surprised he was distressed. It looks as though you bought it second-hand on eBay. It's never quite worked, has it? Now, make me a cup of tea. You have bought in decaffeinated Earl Grey, I hope.'

*

'Sorry I didn't make it this morning!' Pip hurried into the tack room to find Lester filling in his diary. 'I had a lovely lie-in, then watched the snow. Isn't it beautiful?'

Lester looked up in surprise. 'You feeling all right?'

'Fabulous, thanks for asking. I didn't bake anything, sorry.'

Pip had, in fact, been so monstrously hung-over that morning that she had spent most of it eating every carbohydrate she could find in the house, which was rather a lot. Two tins of biscuits, an entire rum bundt intended for Mrs Bentley – which might, on reflection, have been hair of the dog – and a refrigerator crumb cake. Later, she'd felt stable enough to take a long bath, then lie on the sofa watching daytime television until the residual weary weakness passed.

She wasn't quite sure what had happened last night – it all went a complete blank after the bus stop – but whatever it was it had involved Bay Austen and she felt certain that it had been distinctly womanly. She'd woken up wearing her most sophisticated nightie, which had lace panels and a plunging neck, and she had a rash on her face, which, when she'd googled it, was consistent with stubble rash. (It was either that or acne rosacea, which she didn't like the sound of.)

'So, do you need anything doing?' she asked Lester breezily, swinging her leg over the long, central saddle rack in what she felt was a lover-of-Bay-Austen way.

Lester was looking even more surprised. He seemed happier today, though. Everything was happier today, especially with the snow. Pip loved snow.

'Nothing for you to do here until afternoon stables,' he told her, glancing up at the clock. 'I've got to get Cruisoe in and turn the other one out for a bit, then walk Horace in hand.'

'I can do that!' She did some imaginary rising to the trot, wondering if she should ask Lester to have another go at teaching her to ride while he was in such a chatty mood.

'Best you go see if Ronnie wants anything doing in the house.'

Something about that sentence had sounded wrong. 'What's Ronnie doing in the house?' That must be it: she normally spent all day on the yard.

'Christmas cards.'

'Oh, I'm good at addressing envelopes.' She did a flying dismount. 'I can hand-deliver them for her. Do you think she's sending one to the Austens?'

Jocelyn and Ann Percy had been keen photographers of horses and dogs, far less so of humans. As far as Ronnie was aware, her late husband Johnny hadn't taken a photograph in his entire life. Apart from ancient rolled school photographs, in which she appeared as a boatered dot, there was almost no visual record of her without a dog or a horse in it; even her wedding had involved two Jack Russells and a Burghley winner. The same was true of Alice, Tim and Pax.

The three grandchildren had taken photographs of each other growing up, though. Born to the snapshot generation, theirs were photo-booth selfies and Polaroid legends, their coming-of-age captured on 110mm film with flash cubes that burned a bulb with every moment they immortalised. Their adolescent albums weren't a thousand near-identical moments stored up in a cloud or on micro-cards the size of almond flakes, shared on social media. They were physical things one could run a finger across to trace a long-forgotten smile.

Ronnie had stumbled on them quite by chance, searching for the Christmas decorations, and she found them so heartbreakingly fascinating that she couldn't stop looking at them. These were the three childhoods led in parallel to which she was only ever a satellite, the birthdays and Christmases to which she'd never been invited, the backdrop familiar and unchanging. Being raised by pragmatic, disciplinarian Jocelyn and Ann Percy was something Ronnie had in common with her own children, but of course they had had each other to share the experience with, and she was enormously grateful for that, for the three faces pressed together and beaming into disposable cameras.

She could hear Pip stomping about upstairs, unimpressed to be tasked with finding the missing Christmas decorations that Ronnie doubted had seen the light of day in a decade but which featured extensively in the backgrounds of her children's photographs. She wasn't planning to put them up but she'd decided to send one to each of her children with their cards, giving them a little bit of shared memory.

Having grown up envying Hermia her big family Christmases, Ronnie hadn't entirely given up hope that she would one day be the sort of annoyingly adorable granny who raked the sports car in on the gravel on Christmas Eve, inappropriate gifts spilling from the back.

'Would you like a spot of lunch, Ronnie?' Pip appeared at the door. 'I can start looking in the attics after that. I know I've seen them somewhere.'

'You're an angel, Pip.'

'You wouldn't have said that last night.' Pip giggled earthily, and skipped off.

53

Within hours of welcoming her mother-in-law to the Comptons, Petra had already knocked back an illicit daytime gin and tonic, run into the paddock to scream and texted Gill half a dozen times. An expensive lunch at Le Mill had been deemed 'very ordinary' and Gunny's main course sent back twice while she kept up a live stream of @GunnPoint comments to followers – doubly embarrassing because their waitress had been Carly from the village. The children's table manners had been criticised – 'You can tell their father's not here much. Charlie could have dined anywhere from an early age' – and Fitz's hair had come in for particular stick: 'Is that supposed to look attractive or is it some sort of social comment?'

The awful thing was that Petra had grudgingly agreed with her on all points. The food had been disappointing; she was always hauling the kids up for shovelling food into their mouths with just their forks; and Fitz's hair did look weird. But did Gunny have to put it all online?

Leaving her to write up the restaurant on Trip Advisor – she was, she boasted, one of their top reviewers and, like Michelin, never gave anywhere more than three stars – Petra had escaped to the dining room to write a few last-minute cards to London friends.

Instead she found herself gazing out at the snowy scene, a robin sitting on the branches of the magnolia in the centre of the farmhouse's turning circle around which she'd trussed the LED Christmas lights. Their merry glow cheered her, their very own live Christmas card.

Petra forced herself to return to her latest batch of afterthought Christmas cards. Why did people she'd just struck off the list always insist on sending theirs at the last minute? It was the annual festive face-off, a chicken run that went right down to the last posting day wire. Now, when she should be charming Gunny, brining ham, delivering the neighbours' cards, adding last-minute items to the online grocery shop and calling her own mother, she was folding yet more round robins, adding names at the top by hand and signing off with a personal message.

It didn't matter that she saw so many old London friends on Facebook each week, liked their holiday snaps, Sunday lunches, baby scans and pets. A letter in a card was a physical thing, something she'd held in her hand. And for old acquaintances not on Facebook – Fitz called them 'masks' – this was the only contact they ever made to mark a friendship that had once shared so much more, an ever-decreasing circle of city friends, neighbours and school mums that dispersed a little more each year, only for a few to whirlpool back at the last minute.

Petra stacked her pile of envelopes together, ready to add stamps, and looked out of the window again, the farmhouse's grand gate-posts framing their glorious view across the narrow country lane, over orchards filled with snow-bent trees, across cats' cradles of hedgerows sketched on a broad white canvas of fields, the lines narrowing into the far distance as they swept up into the milky Malvern hills, all crowned by a sky the same deep blue as Bay Austen's eyes.

Where had that come from? She'd been deliberately not thinking about him. Her eyes narrowed as she spotted Gunny sidling towards her magnolia with a pair of secateurs. A moment later and her merry LEDs all went out.

Lester opened the stable door and Beck – moments earlier a threatening hydra – shot to the back of the stall. He shut the door and the stallion lunged forwards, ears flattened.

Open. Back.

Shut. Forwards.

He'd never known a horse like it. The poor fellow needed to let off some steam and kick up some snow. He needed a couple of acres to work up some speed, roll for fun and snort through the snow.

'Just got to figure out how to get you out of here first, handsome,' he muttered.

Open. Back. As soon as he picked up the head-collar, the horse charged towards him, ears flat to his head.

Lester only just made it out of the door in time. The bared teeth crashed against the bars and raked down them.

'I've got all the time in the world, friend.' Turning away from the lunging head, Lester went to fetch a bridle. He hoped Ronnie had a lot of cards to write.

The Redhead had plunged around in the snow in her paddock for an hour and was now squealing furiously at the gate to be brought in, hormonal frustration raging. Her only suitor, the entirely unsuitable and not entire Shetland, called lovingly from the stable.

Petra abandoned the snowcat she was helping the girls build and fetched the mare in. But she wouldn't settle, pacing her stable and taunting her tussock sidekick through the grilles.

'You'll get over it soon,' Petra assured her, with more conviction than she felt. 'I understand just how it feels. You need to do something to take your mind off it. Like ironing.'

Excited by the snow, the girls were desperate to go out riding in it. Petra, who remembered feeling exactly the same in her *Black Beauty* heyday and found it hard to say 'no', tried not to think of the mountain of things she had to do – there were yet more piles of the children's washing, presents to sort, and she'd have to go shopping again to cover the weekend because the kids – mostly Fitz – had yet again gone through the fridge like locusts.

He was loading up again when she went in to change into her riding gear. 'You've only just had lunch.' She felt her own stomach rumble. Le Mill portions were tiny.

'This is twosies. Gunny asked for a Nespresso Decaffeinato and Monty Bojangles chocolates in the annexe by the way.'

Mozart's Horn Concerto rang out from her mobile.

'I have gossip.' Gill was on her car-phone. 'And I have ten minutes to get to a laminitic pony in Micklecote in which to share it.'

Petra glanced across as her children piled in from the garden and started noisily discarding snowy layers, dispersing in all directions. Wilf was bounding about, spreading snowy paw prints. She shut herself into the larder, breathing, 'This had better be good.'

'Karen, our veterinary nurse, was driving past Pip's bungalow in the early hours on her way back from a Christmas party and saw a man coming out.'

'You're kidding?' She cracked open some Digestive biscuits and started scoffing.

'You'll never guess who it was.'

'Oh, let me try.' The doorbell was ringing now. She covered the mouthpiece, calling, 'Will somebody get that?'

There was no reaction.

'It'll be an Amazon delivery!' she shouted enticingly. 'Pressies!'

Feet thundered towards the hallway. Then Petra heard an altercation as Fitz, hurtling down two flights of stairs, shooed his younger siblings away, insisting he was the only one responsible enough to answer it in case it was an axe murderer.

'Still there?' Gill checked, followed by '*Wally!*' as she took umbrage at somebody's driving.

Petra bit into another Digestive. 'Brian Hicks.'

'Not even close.'

Petra nearly jumped out of her skin as the larder door flew open and Gunny stood in front of her, her iPad live-streaming a guided blog tour of the house.

Mouthing 'multi-talking', Petra smiled, crumbs everywhere, pretending to be scanning the shelves for baking ingredients.

Gunny grabbed the Choccy Stoffy box from the shelf and shut the door again.

'One of the Turners? Pip likes tattoos and she made quite an impression on the estate last night.'

'Stone cold no.'

'How about Flynn the farrier? He's an indiscriminate shagger and looked wasted last night.'

'Nope. But you're getting warmer with indiscriminate shagger. Do you give up?'

'Yes, I give up.'

'Bay,' Gill said, with insensitive relish.

'Really?' Chest tightening, voice climbing, Petra almost added, 'My Bay?' and stopped herself. 'Is this a wind-up?'

'Karen's sure it was him. Looking pretty furtive, she said.'

Petra managed a dismissive laugh. 'Bay walked Pip home when she got drunk. He probably held her hair back over the puke bucket. She was pretty much out of it.'

'What time was that?'

Hours earlier. 'Got to go, sorry! Door!'

Finally emerging from the larder, she found her daughters standing with their noses three inches from the television screen to get a better view of *Airmageddon*.

Ed had his feet up on the table, eating a bag of Kettle crisps. 'Fitz just told someone on the doorstep to fuck off. Gunny's taken the coffee pod machine into the annexe. Said she couldn't wait any longer.'

When Petra opened the front door, she found a bag of vegetables on the step.

She took them up to Fitz to demand an explanation, finding herself talking to a locked door. 'Why did you tell Kenneth to fuck off?'

'Who's Kenneth?' came a muffled reply.

'One of our neighbours, Fitz. He's handed you veggies over the fence in the past. He brought these sprouts and some kale to the door just now and you told him to fuck off.'

'He's the creepy one that flies the drone around.'

'He used to be an airline pilot. I'm not sure he has a drone.'

'He does. Big military one, always hovering outside your bathroom window or following you out riding. We call it Domdrone – Dirty Old Man. It was buzzing around out there when you had a bath last night.' The door opened a fraction. 'So I told him to fuck off.'

Petra remembered with a shudder the Milk Tray Man rose, which had been delivered by drone in the summer and she'd thought was from Bay.

'Trust nobody, Mum,' Fitz was saying darkly. 'There are weirdos out there with all sorts of delusions. You're in the public eye. You're bound to be targeted.'

He'd definitely been streaming too many violent conspiracy thrillers. She'd have to fiddle with the parental settings on the router again. 'It's very sweet of you to worry about me, but don't be rude to Kenneth,' she said. 'Next time he calls round, tell him I'm... out jogging or something.'

The laughter coming from the other side of the door told her that at least she'd cheered him up briefly – he really was stressing out over the revision. She'd never known him behave so oddly.

Getting a bridle on the stallion was a lot easier than Lester had anticipated, as long as one had the dexterity of a young man. He'd seen Ronnie slip the Chifney ring bit on with the double ropes they normally used to lead him, and knew that Beck's disciplined German training meant that as soon as the reins were looped over his neck, he dropped his mouth for the bit. The secret was to be ready. One had only a split second, and if you messed up, he reared back.

More by luck than deftness, Lester got the bit in first time, hooked over the headpiece and led him away before the big grey could fathom out what was going on. They were across the yard in seconds, between the hedges of the stallion paddock gate and he was loose.

Breathless and slightly giddy, hips aching, Lester watched the stallion race away, astonished by the movement. He'd never seen him fully loose before, the round pen only allowing a few strides. Here he could high-step through the snow for a hundred yards in all directions. The hind leg was magnificent – high-hocked, far-reaching and extravagant. The horse floated. His progeny would be something else.

'You are staying here, Beck,' Lester breathed.

The grey snaked his head, charging through the snow in the high-hedged paddock, dropping his nose to plough through it and then, huge eyes glowing, crumpled ecstatically to roll and roll.

Kit pressed himself into the oriel window-seat to get a bar of reception on his phone. Outside, white flakes drifted off the eaves and trees. Last night the Cornish whisky bottle had remained unopened and he'd slept for eight hours solid in his old bed, plagued by a nightmare in which he was on stage playing Lear's final scene, naked except for the red coat. There were no dreamcatchers left hanging in the Old Almshouses to stop it.

Kit felt purged, a fresh perspective forming in sobriety. It was time to admit that he'd ground to a muddled halt on the Sassoon project, the need for trance-like inspiration overtaken by the requirement for clear-headed technicality. To stand a chance of finishing it, he must clean up his act and his house, and put a stop to insular self-obsession.

Shoulder against the cold window frame, he called his children to arrange to visit them before Christmas.

'Are you sure you should drive all this way?' his daughter fretted. 'You're always a bit random in bad weather. Do you want me to look up trains?'

'I am not random in bad weather!'

'If you come by train you can have a drink on the way.'

'I don't need a drink on the way. Or beforehand. I'll be fine.'

'Let me look up trains anyway.'

Having thought them oblivious to what Ferdie called his retreat into 'blues, booze and muse', Kit had overlooked the fact that his children were close to their Austen cousins and had the heads-up on their father keeping his head down.

'Heard you flashed at the carol singers last night.' His laughing son was unconcerned, obsessively wrapped up in a play in which he was cast as a young Victor Hugo. 'Great way to get Sassoon done. Hugo used to strip off to force himself to stay on task. Only wore a wool cloak. Sis thinks you're finally grieving for Mum, but she always overanalyses things. I told her you'll have seen everything at the RSC by now and got the bar bills to prove it. Am I right?'

Grateful to be reacquainted with his modus operandi, Kit called Ferdie to arrange to meet in Stratford before he left the Bardswolds.

'Oh, good! We can bend your ear about Christmas. Donald and I have hatched the five-bird plan.'

'I think I'll stay in London for a bit. I need noise.'

'The first siren you hear will bring you back, mark my words, dear boy. Always knew you'd bed back in there eventually.'

Having taken a month to sleep in his own bed, Kit doubted it. He messaged Pip Edwards to say she could finally arrange to get the house cleaned in his absence.

Do you want me to pop round to discuss any special require-ments? she replied eagerly. *At stud now sorting Mrs Ledwell's Christmas decs.*

No, thank you. Kit imagined a twenty-foot tree in the hall and festoons of wreaths dripping with blood-red berries. *Just don't let anyone touch the notes on my desk.*

The box of Percy family decorations was finally unearthed in the cellar, which Pip had left until last to search, the image of the Captain's upended bulk all too vivid in her mind. She carried them up to the office where Ronnie was on the phone.

'Kind of you to think of me, but I'm having a very quiet one,' she was saying firmly, that laugh ever-present in her voice as she glanced at Pip, her face lighting up at the sight of the box. 'Let's catch up early next year… Yes, isn't it just?'

'My offer's still open to cook Christmas lunch here,' Pip pitched hopefully. 'I've lost Mr Thorne and Mrs Bentley, but I've still got the others on standby. Please let me do it.'

'I'm sorry, but it's still no. Let's see what we've got here.'

Pip was shocked by the battered metal reindeer and chipped glass bells. Ronnie's children were hardly going to thank her for giving out a few moth-eaten felt robins while she was languishing amid the stud's riches.

'Would you like me to pop into Chipping Hampton and get you some book tokens to go with those? I'm going there to stock up on stationery for Mr Donne.' Three filing boxes should keep his play safely out of harm's way; she'd have a little read while she was put-ting it in. 'He's going away to visit his children. They're a theatrical dynasty, like the Foxes. *Very* clever man. Tricky to please, mind you. Theatre types are very eccentric, aren't they? And writers are even worse. Look at Petra. Completely scatterbrained.'

Petra hurried downstairs with a laundry basket full of her and Charlie's stripped bedding to find one eager daughter in jodhpurs waiting impatiently by the back door, staring forlornly out at the snow falling, the other draped in front of the television. 'Has Daddy called with a train time? I left my phone down here. Where is it? Has Fitz got it again?'

The girls looked at her blankly.

'Can we go *now*, Mummy, *please*?' begged Bella. 'I've been waiting *ages*.'

'It's snowing.'

'It's stopping again – look. Just round the village block? It only takes fifteen minutes.'

'Oh, all right. I'll just go and change. Where's Gunny?'

'Lying down. She says this place always gives her a headache for the first twenty-four hours and that you need a mother's help.'

'I have four mother's helps. You're called children.'

Fitz was incommunicado behind his door, making no answer when she demanded to know if he had her phone. In her bedroom, pausing between pulling off one set of clothes and putting on another, she tried Charlie's mobile from the landline to see if he was on a train yet, but instead of a dialling tone heard crackling static. The snow must have taken out the line.

As she replaced the handset, she caught sight of her reflection in the full-length mirror, for once not posing with her stomach held in. Oh dear. A sedentary autumn in a desk chair had taken its toll. It was time to swap her usual wrinkle-bottomed pull-ups for the mustard-yellow breeches bought for her hunting forays last year, uncomfortably thick and stiff, but guaranteed to flatter and flatten bulges. Petra heaved them on with a few high side kicks, relieved that they still did up with effort. A fleece covered her muffin top. If she stood at the right angle, Salma Hayek smouldered back from the mirror.

'You probably need to see those from this angle,' said Gunny, from the door. 'Do you have a spare iPhone charger?'

The dreamcatchers on Hermia's grave held several inches of snow, the vivid imaginary journeys that Kit had been on while napping and day-sleeping all month already forgotten.

He dusted them off and gathered them in his farm-shop Bag for Life, abandoning the idea of trailing across to the Austens' overpriced emporium to buy a Christmas hamper for Ferdie and Donald.

The snow was a lot thicker than he'd realised and there were no gumboots in the Old Almshouses without big holes in them. Nor did he want to risk bumping into his brother-in-law or, worse, Ronnie Percy again.

'I'm afraid you got that one quite wrong,' he told his wife, stepping forward to dust off her stone and feeling something snap beneath the snow under his foot. He pulled out another dreamcatcher.

'*Tread softly because you tread upon my dreams,*' he murmured, shaking the snow off it.

'Very well quipped!' chortled a voice, and Kit turned to find the vicar beside him in a coat even more voluminous than his own, witch black with a matching hood. It was like meeting his Maker. 'Would you care for a cup of tea? I'm just about to put the kettle on in the vestry.'

'Thank you, but no.' Kit peered closely at the soft, androgynous face, trying to determine a gender.

'We do not judge a man on his faith here, just his need for succour,' the vicar droned. 'I see you so often and you always look so very troubled. Tell me, was Hermione your wife?'

'Not when I knew her,' he said stubbornly. 'She was Hermia.'

'And does her passing into God's arms still vex you?'

'Well, he dropped the catch the first time,' he muttered. 'Now if you'll excuse me, I have a lot of dreams to catch up on.'

'Come here, old fellow, I won't ask twice.'

'Won't ask three times then.'

'Come here, boy.'

'Fifth time and this is final, you bugger.'

'Twelfth time, you bloody sod. Don't you dare… Come back here! *Beck!*'

The stallion, Lester had discovered, was a nightmare to catch.

Lester had been played by enough horses over the years to know all the tricks. Quietly impressed by his athleticism and sheer ingenuity, Lester pretended to find it completely uninteresting.

'You got bored yet, boy?'

When bribery didn't work, the bucket rattled for minutes on end in a hopeless battle of wills, he switched to the old faithful waiting game, walking to the middle of the little enclosure and standing with his back to him, playing Grandmother's Footsteps.

He had all the time in the world.

Beck snorted and circled him, trying to see his face. Lester turned away. The horse drew closer. Lester drew away. Round the paddock they went, the stallion getting ever closer. Lester could feel his breath warm on his back now. Any... second...

With a rev of engine and toot of horn, the post van came up the drive. Beck spun away, shrieking at the top of his voice to let the rival on the other side of the hedge know this was his territory.

'Blast and botheration!' Lester gritted his teeth in frustration. His outburst wasn't a great display of aggression – registering slightly below that of a crown green bowler missing the jack – but it was enough for Beck, who turned to face him.

Lester saw the horse's eyes harden, his ears flatten, his head drop low. A hoof stamped in warning, the nostrils saucered.

He knew he had ten seconds at most. He was right in the middle of the paddock, the rails too far away to outrun a fit horse, especially with his stiff hips. There was an old oak halfway to the gate, a disintegrating spiral staircase wrapped around its trunk leading up to the long-condemned treehouse from which the Captain's grandchildren had decades ago trained binoculars on the village. It was his only hope.

As Kit hung the dreamcatchers back on the old beam pegs and herb hooks where his daughter had originally strung them, he wondered if it wasn't time to rethink the hippie student vibe. He would probably find it easier to work more sociable hours if it didn't feel quite so like a Brighton incense store.

A horse whinnied directly outside, so loudly it might have been in the room with him. Going to the window, he saw a woman with her children riding through the snow. Was she *mad*?

A ghost's shadow ran through him. Hermia's voice was in his

head again. 'You worry too much, Kit. I'm only going to the farm to use the sand school.' The last words his wife had spoken to him without a slur or a shake impeding her voice.

He hurried to fetch his coat and pull on the nearest shoes.

Lester had been up the tree for twenty minutes and the stallion was showing no sign of losing interest, circling, ear-flattening, warning off the tiger that had dared to come close to his mares. It was snowing on and off. He was extremely cold. At last, help came.

'Lester!' He could hear Ronnie running along the drive towards him. 'Are you all right? Pip spotted you in trouble from the house.'

'I've brought the first-aid kit and a blanket!' Pip panted along behind her.

'I'd rather you'd brought a tranquilliser shot and a ladder,' Lester muttered, as the stallion reared, pawing at the branch he was crouching on, almost catching him.

'Hurry up!' he demanded.

Beck threw up his head and sniffed the air, eyes fixing on a distant point. The roar that came out of him was so loud Lester's tree shook, a large slab of snow falling from a higher branch onto his flat cap.

Far in the distance, they heard a shrill returning call from a mare.

Spinning round, tail pluming up behind, Beck headed for the far boundary, almost seven feet of dense beech with rails to the fore.

'Sweet Jesus!' Pip dropped the first-aid kit.

At the gate, Ronnie covered her eyes. 'There go my magic bloody beans.'

Lester watched, open-jawed, as the stallion propped and jumped so perfectly over the hedge that the topmost twigs barely touched his hoofs.

'Not just a pretty face,' he breathed, as he dropped stiffly to the snowy ground and called, 'You follow on foot – I'll fetch the quad and catch you up!'

'This is *just* like *Frozen*!' Bella said excitedly. 'Elsa has fled Arendelle and Anna rides into the blizzard on her white horse searching for her! You be Christian, Prudie! Mummy, you can be Sven the reindeer.'

'The forecasters definitely said it would stop snowing by three,' Petra complained, as they rode round the village in thick-falling flakes. She was appalled at herself for her irresponsibility, too willing to indulge in childish adventure and eager to escape Gunny to check the latest weather satellite.

'We're fine, Mummy. We all have high-vis, flashing lights and reflective stripes. They can see us from space.' Petra always overdid the Dayglo.

'Well, if they don't see us coming, they'll hear us,' she pointed out, as the Redhead let out another shriek, no doubt calling for her little tussock chum, who was most put out to be left behind in his stable.

'People rode out in weather like this all the time in the olden days when you were growing up, didn't they?' said Prudie.

'I rode in snow,' Petra conceded. Little legs kicking like billy-oh across the Yorkshire Dales, chasing imaginary Edwardian criminals in cape-shouldered coats and flat caps through Birtwick Park.

A delivery lorry was coming towards them, wipers struggling against fat flakes being blown into them. Petra ushered her children into the gate to the church meadows to let it pass.

Now she couldn't get the Redhead to go forwards. Stubbornly, the mare planted, then started running backwards.

'Mum, stop riding like a pleb,' complained Prudie, who wanted to get back in front of the television.

The more Petra urged the Redhead on, the more she twisted and cow-kicked. She let out another loud whinny, her whole body vibrating.

Somewhere beyond the Green, a dragon-like bellow replied.

'Get going, you daft bat!'

The mare sat right down, depositing Petra bottom-first in the snow. Casting her mistress an apologetic look, she charged across the church meadows, squealing and bucking towards the standing stones.

'I'm fine, no need to panic! Don't get off,' Petra assured her daughters.

When she didn't immediately stand up, Bella looked down at her with big, anxious eyes. 'Are you really all right, Mummy?'

'My breeches have split.'

It was home time at the village school, the last day of term bringing high spirits and children weighed down with cards and artwork, mums huddled in duvet coats and fluffy hats outside, hands in armpits, excitedly anticipating a white Christmas.

Standing to one side, her coat not nearly thick enough, cleaning tabard still beneath it, Carly felt her phone vibrate in her pocket.

It was a picture message from Fitz of the Gunns' small Shetland pony peering murderously out from a hole he'd just kicked in his stable wall. *Nothing stands between a man and the woman he loves, however little he is. Not feeling v. gay today. x PS Dad coming home. Lozzy is history. Happy Christmas.*

Smiling, Carly sent a thumbs up and stuffed her phone back into her pocket.

They could hear hoofs clattering on the tarmac road, far louder than a small Shetland in pursuit of his stablemate. Children were grabbed and shielded. A woman screamed.

Then Carly gasped as, white as the snow billowing round it, a horse charged past, mythical in its beauty. The children started to cheer and shriek.

Grabbing Ellis's hand, she joined the excited procession of mothers, children and teachers surging out along the pavement to give chase.

Following some distance behind, whinnying furiously, trotting as fast as his short legs would carry him, came a lovelorn and very hairy Shetland.

Hurrying along Church Lane, Kit had seen the lorry coming towards him, driving too fast, heard the horse shrieking, the little girls screaming and now, heart in his throat, he saw the woman on the ground in the entrance to the church meadows, her two daughters looking forlornly down at her.

As he dashed to help, thundering hoofs overtook him from behind.

'Watch out!' screamed one of the girls.

Kit threw himself into the ditch between the lane and the church meadows' railings just in time to avoid the big silver horse flattening him as it jinked right to take off over the fence, careering up the rise to the mare waiting there. With a delighted squeal, she twirled round and presented her best De Wallen peepshow at him.

Beck didn't need asking twice.

'Children, come back here right now!' instructed the headmistress. The little crocodile of under-tens, who had been charging along the pavement to see where the beautiful white horse had galloped to, swiftly about-turned. 'You don't learn about this until year six!'

'Are they mating, Mummy?'

Petra struggled upright, only vaguely aware that the Redhead was now partaking in a very public sex act beside the standing stones, far more acutely aware of her bottom hanging out of her split breeches, wet snow in some very uncomfortable places. 'They're playing together. Avert your eyes, girls.'

'Mummy, we've seen it all on YouTube,' said Prudie. 'We know they're making babies.'

'I didn't mean avert them from the horses.' She covered her bottom as best she could with one hand, fumbling to unzip her coat with the other so she could take it off and tie it around her gaping breeches. As she did so, she stood on tiptoe to see through the billowing snow, up across the meadow. 'Although perhaps you should.'

The X-rated debauchery of the scene was taking place in full view of the village as a very willing chestnut mare was brutally and eagerly pleasured by her priapic silver suitor after an acquaintance briefer than a Snapchat share. Positively crammed back against the big white chest, head bobbing as though saying, 'Up a bit, down a bit, that's the spot!' the Redhead didn't seem bothered by the rough treatment.

Even my horse is getting no-strings sex, Petra thought testily. Her zip had got stuck to the lining now.

'Aren't you going to rescue her?' Bella asked in shock.

'I don't think that would be very wise.' Damn the zip! Her backside was absolutely freezing and half the village seemed to be coming out to gawp at the standing-stones action.

Then she felt something being wrapped around her shoulders, a warm, safe hug of a huge, squishy duvet coat.

She turned to find Kit Donne with his oaky hair on end and reading glasses still dangling round his neck.

'Oh, thank you so much!' Her cheeks prickled as she knotted its sleeves to stop it blowing away.

He was looking absolutely furious, newly bearded cheeks slamming with an angry tic, now dressed in nothing but a threadbare shirt, old jeans and odd shoes. 'What damn fool rides out in—' Before he could say another word, he let out a surprised 'Oof!' as he was head-butted sideways by an indignant Shetland, who then muscled his way in through the gate and roared uphill to break up the lovers.

'Oh, Christ, he'll get mullered.' Petra started to give chase only to find herself hoicked back.

Kit had hold of the red coat by the tail. 'Do you want to get mullered too? You don't go up there unless you know what you're doing.'

'Nothing stands between a stallion and the thing he wants. He'll fight to the death to get it,' said a wise voice, in a creamy Wiltshire accent.

Petra recognised Carly a few yards away, observing the action in the field through a gap in the hedge, small boy at her side.

The stallion, having taken his fill, slid off his conquest and turned to find himself under attack from a small, snow-covered equine tussock.

'Same goes for Shetlands,' Petra muttered nervously.

They all turned as a quad bike came snarling at speed along the lane. Pip was bouncing on its front rack, a first-aid kit and blanket on her lap, and Ronnie clung onto its rear with a lunge line. Lester was at the handlebars blinking away the snowflakes.

'Out of the way. Emergency!' Pip shrieked, rather unnecessarily, at Bella and Prudie, who had already ridden away from the gateway so Lester could drive into the church meadows.

Letting the quad bike pass, Petra hurried after it to catch the Redhead.

Beck was looking quite benign, the high ground affording a terrific view of his new prairie, a dominion stretching from Ludd-on-Fosse to the east to Broadbourne to the west, Micklecote to the north and Chipping Hampton to the south. He politely ignored the assault from the wronged little husband who was now gazing up at him in awe.

Beck lowered his black velvet nose. A hairy orange one lifted to meet it. A moment later, bromance sparked.

The Redhead was bored with them both. Saddle under her belly, she trotted back down the slope to her mistress, like a raver after a quick knee-trembler behind a nightclub.

'Exhibitionist.' Petra caught and checked her over, immensely relieved that she was safe.

Higher up on the field, a ship's figurehead on a fast-moving quad bike, Pip was aware that this drama had commanded a significant crowd of local spectators. This was her moment to be heroic, her chance to make up for the night of the hurricane when her pluckiness might have been slightly exaggerated. As they closed in on the action, she eyed the big grey stallion out enjoying his freedom. He was best left to the experts. Her gaze shifted down, her landing spot targeted, her audience expectant.

Eager to impress, she made a flying dismount from the quad bike. 'I'll get the Shetland!'

In the billowing snow, she didn't spot the three standing stones. Tripping clumsily over the first, she ricocheted off the second and knocked her head on the third, shouting, 'Ow! That bloody hurt!' before swooning to the ground.

'Oh, shit.' Ronnie hopped off the back of the bike and hurried across to her. 'Pip, can you hear me?'

Pip groaned and sat up, muttering that at least she had nice knickers on, so Ronnie was fairly confident she'd survive.

Villagers were running up to offer help now. Having charged off to a safe distance, the stallion watched them all, head high, snorting furiously, his diminutive new acquaintance at his knees. Lester was squaring up to them both with a head-collar, looking small and frail.

'Can someone look after Pip?' Ronnie called. 'We need to catch that one before he heads off again.'

A figure stooped down beside her and Kit Donne's profile drew level, tilting to look at her, the angry eyes generous for once. 'Leave her with me.'

'Thanks.' Ronnie nodded, grateful that he was at least capable of being gallant in a crisis. She leaped up to help Lester.

Kit kept an eye on Pip Edwards by the gate while they waited for the ambulance, walking slowly around with her because she said she felt sick if she sat down. She had her phone out to share events with Facebook friends,

'Are you sure that's wise?' Still dressed in his shirt sleeves, Kit's teeth were chattering almost too much to speak, but Pip's calm worried him. He seemed to recall you had to keep people talking after a head injury and make sure they knew who and where they were. 'Who's the prime minister?' he asked now.

'I know you read the *Guardian*,' she said kindly, 'but I'm really not interested in talking about politics.' She flicked her screen as her phone bleeped with a fresh notification. 'Oh, good! Someone's enquired about the box sets I'm selling on Gumtree.'

'How is she?' a husky voice asked anxiously behind Kit.

Turning, he found he couldn't answer. All week, he'd been encountering Ronnie's face in his wife's photographs, trying to fathom what it was he didn't like about her, what infuriated him so much. And, in an instant, he knew. Forthright, practical, clever and beautiful, hers were the health and vitality Hermia still deserved.

'You look cold, you poor thing,' she said now. 'Did you not bring a coat?' Those eyes were the same bright speedwell as his wife's. No wonder they had been mistaken for sisters. But while Hermia had radiated compassion, Ronnie seemed constantly on the verge of sharing an irreverent joke.

He shook his head, then jumped forwards as something snorted against his neck. She was holding the lead-rope of the huge white sexual protagonist himself, now the equine equivalent of a man lying back against the pillows, ears floppy, eyes soft.

'Don't worry, he's a pussy cat after a shag.' Ronnie grinned. 'Plus I've slipped him a Mickey Finn of ACP – that's basically horse Mogadon – while we wait for Lester to bring the horsebox.'

'Petra's horse will have a beautiful baby.' Pip sighed, looking up from the Gumtree app.

'Unlikely.' The blue eyes shared the joke with Kit. 'It's jolly rare he does the honours with his own flesh and blood. He prefers the dummy. He's a bit of a serial wanker, frankly.'

'I've got a friend online like that,' nodded Pip. 'Three times during one episode of *Homeland*.'

'Concussion,' Ronnie mouthed at Kit, with an amused wink.

He took another step away, the evidence disputing his wife's *you will* love *her* claim now stacked extremely high.

She was looking at him intently. The blue eyes had clocked his chattering teeth, the shivering chills running through him. 'You are an absolute superstar, but we really can't expect you to walk around freezing to death any longer. Go home.'

'I'll stay,' he said belligerently, not wanting to be bossed about by her.

'Go home.'

He glared at her, looking for compassion, but the only thing he could see was withering, bemused impatience.

Not saying goodbye, he turned and walked as fast as he could back to the photographs of another Ronnie, not this supercilious woman with her smoking-room voice and smut but the infectiously laughing girl Hermia had always insisted he would love when he met her.

'What a sour-tempered man,' said Ronnie, watching him go.

'Arty-farty leftie,' Pip told her. 'His house has mice. I told him he needed a good mog, but he came up with some gobbledygook about mice shunning rascal budgies or something.'

'*The mouse ne'er shunned the cat as they did budge from rascals worse than they,*' Ronnie quoted delightedly. '*Coriolanus.*'

'Oh, yes, she's one of my favourite characters.' Pip nodded.

54

'I should never have taken a fare up to the Comptons,' the driver from S Express Cabs muttered into her Bluetooth to her mother, as she steered around snow drifts on the steep wooded lane from Chipping Hampton. 'I'm calling it a day after this,' she whispered. 'I've got a right one here, Mum. Call you later.'

Her passenger had spent the entire journey having a fraught conversation on his mobile, which the driver pretended not to hear. 'It's not "all right for me"… I *do* know how much this is hurting you. She *doesn't* have "it all on a plate"… I have to think about my children… I *know* I should have thought about them before… No, it *wouldn't* help if she knew about you – or if you just didn't exist…'

The driver sighed. It wasn't the first time she'd heard the same one-sided conversation. The Broadbourne commuters were an unscrupulous lot. She turned up the Christmas songs on the radio. 'I Saw Mommy Kissing Santa Claus' was playing.

She glanced in her mirrors. He was a handsome bugger, had those soulful blue eyes few women could resist, matched with the hard-honed masculine body that looked like a loaded gun holstered in a sharp suit.

As they reached the village, she slowed to a crawl. There were people in the road. And horses.

Now she could see the blue lights of an ambulance in her rear-view mirrors. She pulled to one side.

'Christ alive!' came a cry from the back seat, as somebody in what appeared to be a padded red Superman cape led an excitable chestnut horse across the lane, carrying the saddle. 'That's my wife.' He wrenched open the door and leaped out.

'What about my money?' she wailed, lowering the passenger window. He thrust a handful of notes in and dropped them on the seat. 'Keep the change. Merry Christmas.'

Glancing across, she saw there was more than enough of a tip to justify calling it a day. It was only when she was halfway home, trying to identify the tinny voice she could hear undercutting the radio that she realised he'd thrown his phone into her car too.

Heroic in a pinstriped suit and long wool coat, arms full of expensive boutique bags crammed with guilt presents, Charlie Gunn raced up to his wife. 'Darling, are you all right?'

'Yes, fine. Hello.' She kissed him as automatically as she would if she was collecting him from a train. The more extreme a drama, the more normally Petra behaved, Charlie had found. It was that or helpless giggles. He'd been bracing himself for helpless giggles a lot lately. 'Bit of a drama to welcome you home.'

'What's going on?' As Charlie looked around at the crowd milling about, a horsebox parking behind the ambulance now, it occurred to him that this was the perfect homecoming, a chaotic scene to distract Petra from any suspicions she might have about his recent behaviour. 'Can I help in any way?'

'Hello, Daddy!' His favourite daughter hung eagerly off her pony nearby. 'We just watched a horse having sexual intercourse with the Redhead.'

Better and better, thought Charlie. A village sex scandal.

Petra's amused eyes widened apologetically. 'Like I say, there's been a bit of an episode. Pip Edwards took a knock.'

'Is she Pussy Galore from the stud you mentioned?' he asked, as the ambulance doors clanked open.

'Pip works at the stud.' Petra turned as someone shouted something behind her. 'I don't think she wants to go to hospital, but she took a fair old clunk to the head.'

'She needs to get checked out,' Charlie insisted, dismissing an evil thought that it would have helped his cause more if his wife had been the one with the bump on the head. 'You're probably in shock too, darling. I'll need to keep an eye on you. Trauma can make you feel very confused for days, weeks even.'

Petra was grateful for her husband's solid good sense. He'd taken his fair share of concussions in the rugby field. She had to admit a frisson of excitement at seeing him with all his Bond Street bags, like Richard Gere in *Pretty Woman*.

'Is anybody going to hospital with her?' called one of the paramedics, as Pip, listing and staggering like La Dame Aux Camélias playing out her last scenes, was led to the steps.

The crowd hastily started to disperse, coughing and looking away.

'Somebody should go with her.' Petra looked around helplessly.

Lester and Ronnie were wrapped up with the stallion, now refusing to be parted from the Shetland. She had the Redhead, two daughters and three ponies to get home.

'You could go!' she told Charlie. 'You have lots of experience in A and E.'

To her total astonishment, Charlie squared his broad wool shoulders and nodded heroically. 'Absolutely. Leave it to me. I'll call.' Patting his pockets as he kissed her cheek, he added, 'Best lend me your phone. I've mislaid mine.'

'Not on me. It's all right, Pip has two.'

'Love you.' With another kiss, this time firmly on the mouth, he strode to the ambulance, still carrying the designer shopping bags.

'Daddy is *so cool*,' sighed Prudie.

'And he didn't notice your bottom hanging out, Mummy,' Bella added happily.

'That's a comfort.' Petra licked her lips uneasily. There was definitely something odd about Charlie's behaviour.

Pip loved the drama of her ambulance ride, the concerned paramedics asking her what day of the week it was, warm hands checking her pulse and fitting a blood-pressure monitor.

She did feel pretty spaced and her head ached, but she hammed it up a little more to make sure she was getting the best possible attention.

Charlie Gunn was so smiley and well-mannered. Okay, so he was a bit stuffy and bald and chummy – she could see why Petra flirted with Bay – but he was her hospital hero, and once they were in A and E, he sat with her, fetching cups of tea to her cubicle, and making her laugh with stories of his rugby accidents over the years. In return, she told him lots of village gossip, careful to let nothing too incriminating slip about Petra and Bay's *frisson*, although she was feeling so groggy she might have made the odd passing mention, not that it mattered now that they'd both moved on. He was very interested in the Small Male Cock League. 'There was me thinking all my wife's friends talk about out hacking is their horses.'

When the medics told them she could go home, they gave Charlie the lecture about keeping her monitored for a few days and looking out for signs of double vision and nausea, as though he were her husband. It felt lovely.

'Have you got anybody at home to keep an eye on you?' he asked, as they waited for Petra to come and collect them.

Pip's eyes gazed at him mournfully. 'I'm usually the one keeping an eye out for everybody else.' She sighed. 'I'm a wraparound carer, you see, Charlie. I look after my clients' needs in a holistic way, whether it be baking a cake or personal protection. I also have a little sideline in private detection. *Very* discreet. Called Proof. It's my affair to know your affairs.'

'Oh, right.' He swallowed uncomfortably.

'Do you remember the television series *The Equaliser*, Charlie?'

'Vaguely.'

'I am the Equaliser of Compton Bagot. With better baking skills.'

'Gosh.' His eyes gleamed. 'Well done, you.'

Lester was not given to apologies and Ronnie saw no gain in seeking one, although she was seething that this should have happened.

They did final stables in silence, Ronnie working three times as fast as him, as usual. They finished swiftly, Lester retreating cautiously across the frozen, snow-scattered cobbles to his cottage, Ronnie to the chilly, echoing house to try to warm her frozen bones in a bath, then sit with the dogs in the armchair by the Aga, using the house phone to call Petra to find out if there was any word on Pip. She was on a crackly car Bluetooth.

'She's fine. I'm just driving to pick them up now.'

'When will you be back? I need to come and apologise about the stallion.'

'Oh, good, you can stay for a drink. Say sevenish. Charlie's dying to meet you.'

It wasn't what she'd intended, but Ronnie knew a degree of diplomacy was required. 'Thank you. I'll see you then.'

She pressed closer to the range, remembering this kitchen thundering with glugging bottles, clinking glasses and laughter in its Christmas heydays, all horse and hunt types, a vat of mulled wine stewing on the simmering plate, a scene she'd often re-created, the places and faces changing, the foundation deep set. It had patterned her life.

On a whim, she called an old friend, her Wiltshire landlord, catching him dressing to go out to a recital. 'When are you coming back?' he asked hopefully. 'We're all in mourning.' He chattered amiably about mutual acquaintances for a few minutes, the comforting shallow lap of safe harbour until: 'You heard from Blair?'

'No.' The pain was getting easier to endure, she told herself.

'They've finally found a live-in carer for Vee, whom she's willing to tolerate. Rugged young Australian chap, queer as you like. Look of Blair about him. He says she gets them muddled up, which works out quite superbly.' He laughed uproariously.

Ronnie smiled, glad to hear things were getting easier.

'I'll tell him you called.'

'I'd rather you didn't.'

'Fair dos. How's the Cotswolds whirl, darling? Knowing you, it's more of a non-stop game of Twister. I bet your feet haven't touched the ground.'

She tucked them tighter beneath her. 'You got it in one.'

Petra found her husband and Pip cosied up in the hospital café, eating their third round of chocolate brownies.

'I've told Pip she must come and stay with us!' he announced cheerfully.

Her smile froze. Somebody appeared to have swapped her husband for a man she didn't know.

Pip was given the box bedroom in the attic beside Petra's old study, all hastily tidied in her honour. It felt like a little suite, with its own small shower room, Sky TV and many hundreds of books to read. Feeling like an honorary teenager, she was in Heaven, settling for an evening of box-set catch-up.

Petra or lovely Charlie checked on her every hour, the girls made her a get-well-soon card with two horses hugging on the front – 'Mummy wouldn't let us draw mating' – and Wilf the spaniel bounded up to share her bed. Pip was particularly touched when age-defyingly glamorous granny Barbara Gunn came up to interview her for her blog, and posted a very flattering photograph of 'the bravest woman in the Bardswolds' on her @GunnPoint Twitter feed. 'I have almost ten thousand followers,' she told her, with a discreet eyebrow shrug. 'That's more than *Antiques Roadshow*'s Fiona Bruce and she has five accounts.'

Too polite to point out that the real-life Fiona Bruce wasn't on Twitter, Pip shared the picture on Facebook. It got almost fifty likes, one of them from Ronnie's daughter, Pax, as she was quick to point out when Ronnie came to visit her that evening, bringing a stack of unread *Horse & Hound*s that Pip had put out for recycling.

'I'm afraid I don't do any of that social-media business.'

Pip had expected her to be purring apologies with classic Percy élan, but Ronnie was gruff, bluff and couldn't wait to get away, backing towards the door barely a minute after coming through it. 'Well, if you need anything, just say.'

'I have actually written a short list.' She held up her phone. 'Shall I email it or would you like a hard copy? The printers are all networked here so it's no trouble.'

'Just tell me it, Pip.' Ronnie hovered reluctantly at the door.

'Could you check on my Home Comforts clients? Make sure they're eating? Drop off some edible treats? They're very fond of home-made nougat.'

'I only do soup,' Ronnie told her.

'Soup is good. I'll text you their names and addresses. Oh, and there's Kit Donne.'

'He doesn't need soup, surely. From what I can tell he's already on a liquid diet.'

'I just want him to know I'm all right. He was so kind, keeping me conscious until the ambulance arrived.'

Ronnie sucked her teeth. 'Anything else you want me to do? Feed your cats? Water your plants?'

'That's very kind, but there's no need. The neighbours and I take turns. They're in my debt by three family holidays and seven mini-breaks to none so if I need longer to recover they say it's fine.'

'But you're only staying the night here, right?'

'Charlie said to take as long as I need.' She settled back on her pillows. 'He's a lovely man, isn't he?'

'I think you're stuck with that one for at least a week.' Ronnie tracked Petra down in her big, trendy kitchen knocking back a stiff gin and tonic. The house was very glossy magazine, all tastefully decked in its Christmas accessories. No wonder Pip looked like a pig in clover. Taking a bump on the head and ending up in the Gunns' gorgeously furnished warm little attic room must feel like a luxury spa break. Ronnie far preferred Petra out of context, hiding from her friends behind stone walls.

'I bloody knew it.' Petra had closed her eyes in horror. 'I've no idea what possessed Charlie. I'm spoiling for a fight, but he's hiding in the annexe with his mother, pretending to show her all the Christmas presents he's bought me. Stay and have a drink.'

'Just water's fine. I can't stay long. I'm desperately sorry about what happened with the stallion. I take full responsibility. I don't want Lester involved in any fallout. He was working under my instruction.'

'What fallout? We're hardly going to force them to do the decent thing and get married. I think the Redhead rather enjoyed it.' Petra smiled over her shoulder, stretching for a glass from a cupboard. 'Gill's coming to check her over tomorrow, but she assures me that having sex comes quite naturally to horses. Far worse if he'd bored her about his work stress over supper before presenting her with a semi and suggesting they get it on to some porn.'

Ronnie bit back an emerging smile. 'Would you like me to try to persuade Pip to recuperate at the stud with me? It's cold and damp and there's no internet or phone signal. She never lasts in the house more than a couple of hours.'

'It's fine. Writers need mad women in their attics. I'll make Charlie take her home tomorrow.' She cleared her throat. 'Some men never come back, they say.'

'Mum! This came out of the printer in the playroom!' A mop-haired boy appeared with a piece of paper and grinned at Ronnie. 'I'm Ed. Are you the Bardswolds Bolter?'

The water dispenser in the fridge door started spouting across the floor as Petra turned round and shushed him.

Ronnie found her smile bedding in more, winking at Ed, who saluted her, took an apple from the fruit bowl and sloped off again.

'Bloody hell!' Petra was reading the printout. 'This is Pip's list of things she might not manage while she's recovering. All her clients are on here with details of their special requirements and favourite cakes. She's added links to *Bake Off* recipes. And listen to this: *The Old Almshouses is signed up to my Home from Home Comforts platinum package, and I've promised the full works next week. Janine Turner's team are booked to go in on Monday to clean, tidy and launder, plus there's fuel deliveries to supervise, provision of basic groceries, cooking for the freezer. Mr Donne will be visiting his children and then seeing friends for Christmas and it must be perfect for his return. The key is kept under the boot scraper.*'

'You'll have to drug her to get her out of here.'

'I'll just turn the WiFi off and unplug the Sky dish. Works for the kids if I want them to have fresh air.'

'Opposite problem growing up where mine did. Hard to hide all the horses.'

'That would have been my *dream* growing up. That and the cast of *Robin of Sherwood* as neighbours.'

Ronnie's gaze drank in all the evidence of family life: the abandoned games and tablets on the kitchen table, colourful fleeces hanging off chair backs, the different-sized shoes littered around the boot rack, a small outcrop of Emma Bridgewater by the sink hoping for the Dishwasher Fairy to wave her wand. Feet thundered overhead as two small girls in pyjamas ran in and out of each other's rooms.

Petra was topping up her own gin and tonic. 'Will you come out riding with the Saddle Bags between now and Christmas? We'd so love to have you along.'

She shook her head and laughed. 'I'm travelling too light to need a bag, Petra.'

'Bitch-walks, then?'

'Any time. After mucking out tomorrow. Bring the beard.' She patted Wilf.

In his attic room in the opposite gable to the Gunns' unexpected house guest, Fitz was stewing furiously. His father was predictably useless, leaving an emotional bomb ticking in London. At some point around lunchtime that day Charlie Gunn had deleted his account on the app, wiping out his son's surveillance. The final message from Lozzy, sent in the early hours, threatened all manner of vengeance. But Gunny had waved away the idea. Charlie, meanwhile, had stooped so low he was using a human shield, planting his mother's awful cake door-stepper stalker in the house.

He called Carly. She was waitressing at Le Mill, calling him back during her break.

'Can I come and buy you a drink after work?'

'Reasons not: I don't finish until midnight, you are under age, I'm married, you're a Liberal Democrat. Do what teenage boys do. Watch a few *Game of Thrones* episodes, eat, play with yourself, eat more, listen to depressing music, spend mindless hours on social media, pretend Tumblr is social media.'

'I've been doing that all day. I'm rethinking the bisexual thing.'

'Cool. Whatever makes you happy.'

'I think you do. My life is pointless without you.'

'Is this about your father?'

'There's a bloody smokescreen going on here. I'm sure Gunny's double-crossed me. She's covering for him.'

'But that's a good thing, isn't it? *You*'re covering for him.'

'I'm protecting my mother! It's different.'

'Oooo-kay. What do you want me to do about it?'

'Run away with me?'

'I'll have to check my diary and get back to you.'

'Thanks for cheering me up.'

'Pleasure. Now get back to your depressing music.'

55

Petra realised how fast that long, swinging country stride of Ronnie's could go when they walked together the following morning. She practically had to run to catch up, the snow crisp as sea salt underfoot, the sky uniform blue.

'How's the patient?' asked Ronnie.

'Very undemanding, but showing no sign of budging. She thinks she needs another day in bed. We're going to Stratford this afternoon to see the RSC Christmas play, so she's insisted she'll be doing us a favour being home to look after the dog and fight off burglars.'

'She'll stay till Christmas,' Ronnie predicted.

'She'd better not.'

'It's her way of hiding from all the poor old souls she's told she'll cook Christmas lunch for. Now she's gone off the idea and can't face breaking it to them.'

'Someone has to tell them.'

'I'll do it. She invited them to my house, after all. I haven't blackened my name nearly enough yet.' She cast across her wicked smile. 'Lady Windermere's fan can come back out on the soup run.'

'I told you, they'll all be relieved, I promise.'

'Until they try the soup. I'm only doing it because Pip's worked for nothing on the stud for God knows how long.'

'The strange thing is, she and Gunny have bonded like besties. I caught them both up there cackling over some dreadful old repeat on the Gold Channel this morning. They have the same taste – all old glamour soaps and reactionary sit-coms that would cause a social-reform march on the Beeb if they were made today.'

She was totally out of breath now, trying to keep up with Ronnie's relentless pace. They were already deep in Comptons countryside, far behind the stud, skirting along the few hedgerows left in the Sanson estate's great moonscapes of high-yield farmland, which all looked the same to Petra, covered with white snow. 'How come you know the way?'

'I rode these fields a thousand times as a girl. It doesn't matter that they're all kept shaved nowadays, like bald men's heads and women's pubic hair. You navigate by the horizon.' She pointed at the different woods and hills, spires and roofs visible. 'Same with cross-country riding. Don't look at the fence, line up two points on the horizon and ride for those.'

'Is it true you rode round Badminton?'

'Twice. I might have won it if I wasn't so rubbish at dressage, but we all said that in those days. We were also terribly naughty. I'll give you some good stories one day.'

'Why not now?'

They paused at the brow of the hill on the edge of the woods.

'Terrible time of year for getting nostalgic and maudlin, like Dickens's *Christmas Carol*.' She set off at speed along the track leading into Compton Bagot. 'Best not to think back.'

Petra panted after her. 'The Ghost of Christmas Past was the jolly one.' She finally caught up as Ronnie held open the kissing gate at the far end of the woods, leading to a path at the side of the Bagot allotments, the roofs of the Orchard Estate just visible over the far fence.

'That's what I'm worried about. Lester's my Bob Cratchit and Pip's Tiny Tim.' She clipped on her dogs' leads. As they walked back along Plum Run to Upper Bagot Farmhouse, Petra sensed Ronnie's mood had blackened. She's thinking about her children, she realised.

'Come in for a coffee.'

'I've got to get back to make soup.' The big smile came back up, humour and self-deprecation never far away. 'Sorry you caught me bitch-walking on a black-dog day.'

'I enjoyed it. Can we do it again?'

'I'd like that. Enjoy the theatre.'

As Petra watched her go, a taxi pulled up outside the farmhouse, the female driver winding down her window and calling, 'Passenger left a phone in my car yesterday. Forties, black coat, lots of bags. Been told he lives here?'

Petra reached out to take it. As she did, Fitz hurtled onto the gravel turning circle and grabbed it out of the driver's hand. 'I'll take that to Dad.'

'Wish my kid was that helpful.' The driver grinned, touching her phone screen in its dashboard holster. 'Which one's the Old Almshouses?'

'Opposite the church. Curly chimneys.'

'Oh, yeah, I remember. The man who went out with Orla Gomez.'

'Did he?' Petra was astonished. 'Can you wait there a minute?'

She dashed inside, reappearing with the red coat and a bottle of champagne. 'Can you give this to him and say a huge thank you from Petra for gallantry? I'd drop it off in person, but he probably needs to wear it if he's going out.'

'This is from Petra for— Hang on, what did she say? For gallivanting with Orla Gomez.'

'She said that?' Kit took the red coat and pulled it on over his suit jacket. It smelt of perfume and horse, a combination that made his nerve ends tighten uneasily.

'That's what she said. Bottle of champagne back there for you too.'

Kit was grateful that the driver had the radio switched off this time, talking in a Bluetooth headset on her phone as they drove towards the Micklecote road. He kept his eyes averted from Upper Bagot Farmhouse.

'That's right. Rang all flipping night. I thought I'd find out whose phone it was if I answered it, but this voice just shouted that my husband was cheating on me. I said, "I know that, love. I divorced him three years ago!"'

Kit watched the white-topped Cotswolds walls slide by as they made their way into Bagot. The banner outside the pub was now boasting a grand New Year opening for the fruit-ale and raw-food enterprise.

'Stratford-upon-Avon, then?' His driver had finished her call.

'Yes.'

'Seeing a show?'

'Christmas shopping, then a drink with friends.'

'Getting in the mood, eh?' She turned the radio on: Cliff was singing 'Mistletoe and Wine'.

He supposed he had to accept at some point that Christmas was actually happening.

'No harm done,' was Gill's verdict when she checked over the Redhead, still squealing flirtatiously at her devoted Shetland admirer through the stable divide. 'Looks like she'd go again, in fact.'

'What are the chances she's in foal?'

'Unlikely after just one covering – I'm impressed he got it up in that blizzard – but there's an outside chance. Do you want me to give her something to make sure it doesn't happen?'

'No.' Petra looked at her beautiful, hormonal chestnut, sympathising with her rampaging mother urge. 'Let's leave it to Fate.'

'I'll scan her in eighteen days just in case.'

There was an uncomfortable pause in which Petra was expected to offer coffee and didn't. She was still smarting from the thoughtless way that Gill had broken the news about Bay coming out of Pip's bungalow. She was also embarrassed to be harbouring the bungalow-seduction suspect in her attic, currently watching an old *Lovejoy* episode with a tray on her lap, eating beans on toast.

'Right, well, I'm off. See you out with the Bags. Monday, I think we said? Winter solstice.'

'See you then.'

Gill looked downcast and Petra felt mean-spirited, so she followed her round the drive to open the gates with a peace offering of news. 'Did you know Kit Donne had an affair with Orla Gomez?'

Gill's long face adopted its upside-down smile. 'Petra, everyone in the village has known about that for weeks.'

'They don't know he's been your Safe Married Crush for two years.'

'Longer.' The upside-down smile straightened. 'One hardly needs reminding of the cruel truth that men like Kit can have their pick of beautiful young women, whereas old trouts like us rarely ever get tickled.'

'Any-fin is possible.'

The mouth twitched, the bear-like eyes sparkled. 'See you Monday.'

Petra hurried upstairs to change for the theatre, then chivvy the children into coats and shoes. Finally, she went to check on Pip. 'How are you feeling? Are you sure you're going to be okay?'

'A bit in and out of focus, you know.' She leaned sideways, trying to see the television around Petra.

'Oh, God, shall I call a doctor?'

'I'm sure I'll be fine. You look nice.' Pip admired Petra's long wool dress, which clung to her curves and had beads the colour of cranberries sewn round the neckline. She had lots of lovely clothes. Pip was dying for the Gunns to go out so she could have a good snoop round the house, including Petra's wardrobe.

'You can call me if you need me – although obviously we'll have mobiles switched off for the show,' she was saying, plumping up the pillows behind Pip's head distractedly, smelling delicious. 'Charlie made Fitz give our phones back. He's going through this weird obsessive thing at the moment. Revision stress, I think.'

'You are so good with him,' Pip said sympathetically. She had yet to find out what syndrome the Gunn's strange son had, but sharing a house with him was a worry.

A few minutes later the mad teenager himself came into her room, making her scrabble back against her recently plumped pillows. He had his hoodie so low she couldn't see his eyes, just a beautiful Cupid's-bow mouth, whispering, 'Swear on your life you won't repeat to my mum what I'm about to say, because if you do your life won't be worth living.'

'I swear.' She crossed her fingers under the covers.

'If anybody called Lozzy turns up while we're out, will you tell them to fuck off for ever?'

'Yes,' she squeaked, trying not to think of *We Need to Talk About Kevin*.

★

Carly and Ash had spent the morning Christmas shopping with the kids in the big retail park near Broadbourne, returning home feeling considerably poorer, grumpier and less festive than they had been when they set out.

'I still think they're too young for pets,' she said.

'You like animals, Carl.'

'Not rodents.'

They now had three guinea pigs, a hutch and lots of small bales of bedding, hay and feed, the main Christmas presents the kids were getting this year. Ellis, briefly excited at first, was already more interested in the Smyths toyshop bags, full of cheap stocking fillers. Sienna and Jackson were asleep, the little creatures in the boxes beyond their comprehension.

'Someone's been splashing out!' Janine cruised past with Social Norm. He was so well wrapped up that he looked like he was in a body bag, sitting in his wheelchair with an oxygen-tank tube coming out of it. 'What have you got there, then?'

'Wilson, Brewster and Koko,' Carly muttered.

'Nice one. Let's hope that mad dog of Jed's doesn't eat them, eh, Granddad?' She laughed, the body bag chuckling and coughing uproariously.

'What dog's that?' Carly tried to keep her voice casual.

'One of Jed's dogs got out last week and killed little Jaden's rabbit and a couple of Tex's cats. Savage bastard it is. He's letting the Brummy boys have it. They don't care what gets killed as long as it's on camera. Jed says it's useless at coursing anyway.'

'Which dog is it?' she demanded. 'Not Tequila?' That's what they'd called Pricey.

'They all look the same to me. What's its name, Granddad?'

The phlegmy wheeze could have been saying anything.

'Taser, Granddad says.'

Carly breathed out. 'So he's still got Tequila?'

'Just leave it, Carl.' Ash carried the hutch on his shoulder into the back garden.

Granddad Norm was wheezing away at her. She couldn't understand any of it.

'Granddad really rates her,' Janine explained, 'but Jed's still not got her measure. Can't get her to stay focused on the job. They're taking her out again next week.'

'I'd like to come.'

Janine pulled a face. 'No offence, Carl, but now him and Ash have fallen out, it's not worth asking.' She patted her arm and wheeled Norm off.

Carly got her sleeping children out of the car, put the guinea-pig boxes on top of the buggy and wheeled them all into the garden.

Ash had left the hutch where he'd set it down, still in its plastic wrap. She could see the flicker of the television screen through the window. He was back on his games console, shooting his way out of a gang crime.

Carly knew better than to tackle him. It was a way of dissipating anger, of avoiding another fight that went round in circles about him skipping college, about his late nights, about money, about Pricey, about the army. She filled the hutch with sawdust and hay and set the terrified little creatures inside, her heart going out to them, thrust into a cold little house after the companionable warm routine in the pet shop. She knew how they felt.

She could hear Jed's dogs howling on the other side of the estate, Pricey among them, her traumatised rebel who had lost focus.

He was right. She liked animals. Even rodents. Even damaged humans.

She was going to talk to Jed.

Pip was in heaven. In the Gunns' absence, she'd taken a thorough tour of the house, looking in drawers and cupboards, acquainting herself with the day-to-day, the secret, the squalid and the odd. Families never ceased to amaze her.

She enjoyed a lengthy session of Call of Duty on the Wii console in the playroom, black plastic gun cases wrapped around the controllers in each hand, double-shooting as she jumped out from behind the sofas and SAS-rolled between dolls' house and space-hopper. Wilf the spaniel watched with interest.

She found an iDock, with a fully loaded little brick of Charlie and Petra's lifelong record collection uploaded onto it, put eighties

Christmas songs on, piped through speakers everywhere downstairs, and drifted along to Tom Jones and Cerys Matthews singing 'It's Cold Outside' – it was: she'd just let Wilf out and felt her eyebrows freeze over – letting the love sink in. She loved this house; she loved this family. She'd been wrong to transfer her allegiance to Ronnie. Petra's world was a perfectly self-contained M and S Christmas advert.

Both her phones were on the kitchen island, rattling against the granite as she got more Facebook likes – being a have-a-go hero was great – and now chimed with a message. Kit Donne: *Can you make up the spare bed when you go in next week? May have guests soon. Many thanks, KD.*

She texted Ronnie to pass this on, enjoying the power enormously, until the reply came: *Who are you?*

She hasn't even saved my number, Pip realised forlornly, sending a sharp message to Janine to make herself feel better: *Almshouse client v. demanding. Change all beds on Mon, air rooms, fluffiest towels.*

She fired up the family Mac that had been left on the kitchen table and started looking through its browsing history, loving the Gunns more and more as she travelled between Barbara's latest reviews – oh-so-harsh but oh-so-fair – Charlie and Petra's secret Christmas internet shopping for each other, Ed's Steam gaming account, Prudie's vlogger favourites and Bella's pony sites. Somebody had even googled a present for Wilf. And weird teen Fitz, trapped in his ever-decreasing spectrum of rationality, had searched one name repeatedly.

'You must be Petra,' a deep voice said behind Pip, shaking with a vibrato of emotion. 'You don't know me. I'm Lozzy.'

Where was the dog? was Pip's first panicked thought. As she turned to face the intruder, she slid the black Wii controller guns from the table in front of her. 'Fuck off for ever!' She aimed them.

Petra had taken the restricted viewing seat behind a pillar for the RSC show and now had a crick in her neck and a pulled muscle in her back because she'd decided it would be romantic to hold Charlie's hand as they watched the play, a sweet moment of connection negated by the hour and a half of discomfort that followed because her arm was at such an awkward angle.

Back home, windmilling her arm, like a spin bowler at the crease, she went upstairs, passing Fitz charging down them, smiling to himself.

Pip was in her attic room, looking wan in front of a back-to-back Christmas rerun of *Last of the Summer Wine*.

Petra put a cup of tea and a plate of biscuits beside her. 'How are you feeling now?'

'Soldiering on,' she said in a small voice.

'Everything been okay here?'

'All very boring.'

'You'll feel better soon.'

'I already do. Lots!'

'That's good. Charlie will run you home first thing tomorrow.'

'But there's two of you, Petra.' A hard look, leaving Petra uncertain if she was seeing double or doubting her sincerity.

She plumped her pillows, then stopped. 'Pip, what are these doing here?' She drew out two plastic guns.

'I get scared on my own.' Her voice shrank. 'At the bungalow I'm scared all the time.' She ate a biscuit, watching Compo rattling down a hill in an old pram.

Petra sighed, folding her arms in front of her chest so the guns crossed, like Lara Croft. 'Do you still want a big, scary tattooed man to look after you?'

'Do you know one?' She glanced up hopefully.

'If necessary, I'll find a blank one and get him tattooed especially.'

'You're so lovely, Petra. I said that to Bay after the carol-singing, when he was at the Bulrushes. "Petra's really nice," I said, "like really, *really* nice."'

'You two had a good chat, did you?'

'I didn't remember anything about him coming back at first.' Pip selected another biscuit, snorting with amusement as Nora Batty started hitting Compo with a broom. 'I think I must have blanked it out with the trauma.'

'And Sloe de Vie. Your "Frozen" was up there with Amy Winehouse in Belgrade.'

Without warning, the big pug eyes filled with tears. 'Don't hate me, Petra. Don't hate me for what he made me show him.'

Petra sat down on the bed, casting her guns aside. 'Christ, what did he do to you?'

'When we got back he made a horrible cup of coffee and I showed off all the detective work I've done online about people in the village. He loved that, especially the stuff about the Percys. While he was looking at it, I cleaned my teeth and got changed into my best nightie and told him he could have sex with me.' The lip wobbled.

'Right.'

'And he made me some more coffee and went home.'

Petra gave her arm a squeeze. 'Probably for the best.'

'I know. I was only doing it on the rebound, seeking meaningless skin on skin to make up for JD breaking my heart.'

'This is the man you thought was Ash Turner? The one with the, um, piercing.'

'I loved his piercing. All of it, really. It's huge. Wait a minute, I still have the pictures on my phone. Here you go. He's at full mast in this one.'

'Gosh, that *is* huge.' Petra stared at it. 'Really. Very. Big. Christ.'

Pip looked proud. 'You don't get many like that, especially not round here. I'll share it with you, if you like.' Her thumb patted the screen.

'Really, you don't have— Oh. You have. I suppose we could put up a Have You Seen This Willy poster on trees around the village?' Looking at JD's extraordinary appendage, she battled an upsurge of giggles.

There was a jingle of bracelets from the door, and Gunny said, 'Oh, do hold it there. That's splendid!' She had her iPad aloft, the red recording light glowing.

Petra jumped up. 'Barbara! Gosh. How long have you been there?'

'Just a ten-second soundbite. It's going to work perfectly for my Christmasculine vlog. Oh, *Last of the Summer Wine*! What a treat. Budge up.'

In the kitchen, Fitz helped himself to a snack – the fridge was always a treasure trove at this time of year, his arms barely able to hold the tall stack of treats he'd unearthed – and closed the door with a satisfied smile.

Lozzy was gone for good, he was convinced of it. Good old Pip, the mad cake-baker, had seen her off. The Gunns might not yet be able to evict their unwanted guest from their attic, but she was a gunslinging heroine when it came to scaring away ex-mistresses. And she'd reassured Fitz that her father's tall, deep-voiced lover was definitely female. Not that Pip knew Lozzy had been anything to do with Charlie. She'd assumed she was an older girlfriend of Fitz's, and he wasn't about to disillusion her. He'd take this one for the team. It was Christmas after all.

Meeting early the next day, Ronnie walked with Petra and the dogs down through the orchards opposite Upper Bagot Farmhouse, crossing over Lord's Brook and skirting behind the beautifully sculpted hedges belonging to medieval Compton Manor, its half-timbered grandeur quite separate from the Austens' farm that had long ago served it.

'It's been on the market for ages,' Petra told her. 'Belongs to a company director whose wife doesn't like it because it has no land.'

'A Brummy rock singer lived there in the seventies,' Ronnie remembered. 'Kept a hostess trolley full of cocaine. We thought he was impossibly glamorous. Complete pervert, as it turned out. Terrifyingly endowed – a friend and I took one look and ran for the hills. Never seen anything like it. Rumour has it he fathered several round here.'

'Could this be one of them?' Petra handed her phone across with a photo displayed.

'Good God. Quite possibly. Did you take that? Please tell me it's Charlie.'

She listened as Petra told of Pip and her Tinder conman. 'The tattoos were someone else's, but that seems genuine.'

'I think our rock star's reborn.'

Crossing into Austen land, they indulged in a delighted medley of seventies dance classics – Petra's superior memory for lyrics making Ronnie laugh in astonishment and complain, 'You're far too young to know these songs!' – then stood on a gate to scream. Crossing back over the brook into the church meadows, Petra kept her in raptures describing her *Black Beauty* fantasy life growing up in Yorkshire.

'My parents just didn't get it. They were modern groovers. That music played all the time at home. I was an Edwardian throwback. While they were tuning in and dropping out, I was making a bustle out of loo rolls strung together under an old curtain.'

'That's glorious.' Ronnie trudged along speedily, grateful to have found someone who was human Prozac.

'They're arriving tomorrow, so listen out for Jefferson Airplane blasting from a Prius. How did it go with Pip's oldies?'

'They were cock-a-hoop to be let off the hook for Christmas lunch. Yet they all obviously adore her. They grumbled like mad about the lack of baking and gossip. I told them Pip has run off with the vicar and Judi Dench had moved into number two, the Green. Should keep them going until Midnight Mass.'

They were at the gate by the church, Ronnie's arm already up in farewell.

'Can you smell something burning?' asked Petra.

Smoke was billowing along the lane. 'That, maybe?'

'Oh, hell, there's a lot of thatch down there.'

They reached for the gate at the same time, Ronnie sprinting ahead. The source was a small bonfire in the garden of the Old Alms-houses on which a red coat was burning merrily. Kit Donne was heaving something long and heavy, like a roll of carpet, into the boot of his car. Both women retreated before they were seen.

'Do you think he's murdered someone?' wheezed Petra quietly, hands on her knees, blowing hard. 'They always burn the blood-stained clothes, don't they?'

'I'll find out, shall I?' It was about time she made peace for Hermia's sake. A citizen's arrest for murder might complicate things, but she'd risk it.

'I'll keep you covered,' Petra offered nervously. 'Cagney and Lacey should split up for this, I sense.'

Ronnie grinned, then marched across the road. 'Kit!'

Clean-shaven and shivering in a thin corduroy jacket and his newsboy cap, he tucked his hands under his armpits, looking far from pleased to see her. 'Good morning.'

'Have you killed someone?'

She heard Petra let out a quiet groan across the road.

'Of course not,' he snapped. 'They're Tibetan rugs. I'm dropping them off to be cleaned on my way to London.'

'I heard you're getting the full service. In fact, I rather fear I've been left in charge of it.'

'I'm sorry?'

'Yes, extraordinary, isn't it? Thought it best to warn you. I won't snoop, but I know you're not my biggest fan.'

He looked at her in silence, jaw offset, clearly trying to work out if this was a wind-up. 'Wait there.' He let out a withering sigh and disappeared into the house.

Ronnie prodded the rugs and turned to the lane with her thumbs up. 'No stiffs.'

'Are you okay?' Petra called.

'Perfectly. You go.'

'Okay – see you tomorrow, I hope.' She disappeared behind the cherry trees.

Kit emerged just as Ronnie called, 'It's a date!', his brow creasing as he looked around and saw nobody.

He was carrying a shell-inlaid box. 'Your letters to my wife. You might as well have them back. I was going to burn them, but I couldn't face it.'

'Did you read them?'

'Yes.'

She waited.

He cleared his throat. 'Your writing style is very idiomatic.'

'I was hoping for an apology, not a critique.'

'Why should I apologise?'

'Because you accused me of letting her down. Now perhaps you understand why I thought she'd be better off without me.'

'I certainly agree with that sentiment.'

She turned away with frustration, then back. 'Can't we just call a truce?'

'What difference does it make if you and I get on?'

'Because she wanted us to.'

'It won't bring her back. Our memories of her don't even cross over.'

'You're right,' she said angrily, taking the box to the bonfire. She started to pull out the letters and drop them onto it. 'Let's forget all the things she told me about you. About how maddening, stubborn and self-destructive you are. And so, so bad at being alone. About how funny you are, how your brain is this divine fusion of maths and emotions that adds people up in an instant, but rejects anything that can't be explained logically. About how much I'd love you, ha-ha. About how much *she* loved you. Christ, she loved you. I have pages of it in the letters she wrote to me, her love for you. My friendship might be worth ashes to you, but I've carried her bloody-minded love around for twenty years and I'm not burning that.' She handed the box back. 'Merry Christmas.'

As she turned away, he started to speak, that lilting Cumbrian all too oddly familiar: 'After the accident, I was so grateful she was alive I didn't care what they said about managing expectations, about preparing for a much more limited life. She thought she'd get better. I thought she'd get better. But it's like she was always just around the corner, waiting to come back. She was in there. We kept trying to reach each other. And the longer that went on, the more frustrated and angry we grew. It became this slow-burning grief. I started to resent her, as though she was the accident itself. She hated my martyred patience, my *well*ness. I was no saint. On really bad days, I thought she'd be better off dead. Now she is, I don't know how to live without her.'

Ronnie turned back. His hands were tucked under his arms again, his newly shaven cheeks hollow, eyes tortured.

'Yours was this flawless childhood friendship that she held up, a perfect example of life before pain, unsullied by domesticity, children, sex, anger and trips to bloody neurologists who say your clever mind is for ever broken. All the time the village was closing in claustrophobically. I stood at that door God knows how many times fobbing people off because she didn't want them visiting. And you had escaped. The one person she held up as this fucking perfect paragon in this fucking idyll had escaped. Had got away.'

Without thinking, Ronnie stepped towards him, her hands reaching out to touch his arms, then his face, fierce with dignity.

'Sorry, Ronnie, it's me again!' called a voice behind the cherry trees. 'Your dogs followed me home, so I brought them back.'

With a brisk nod, Kit turned and walked inside.

56

It had not escaped the Saddle Bags' attention, particularly a quietly hurt Gill, that Petra had been seen on more than one dog walk with Ronnie Percy. They were all agog to know the gossip, but Petra was loyally tight-lipped as they headed out in bright, ski-resort sunlight to ride up to the windmill. She was also deeply embarrassed to have broken up the fireside conversation between Ronnie and Kit Donne, suspecting the acquaintance to be a lot less casual than she'd assumed: Ronnie hadn't been around to bitch walk that morning.

Increasingly short of breath as they kept up a fast trot, the Bags started talking about Christmas visitors, grumbling about their respective husbands' families.

'Barry's told his parents we'll have… lunch with them in Micklecote… on Christmas Day,' said Mo, between puffs. 'He knows Mum and Dad won't come because they only have their turkey after the yard's done, so I'm going round to cook it for them and Pam after.'

'We're flying to Poland tomorrow,' Bridge said. 'Aleš's family invited my mum too, but she's booked herself on a cruise. I don't blame her. All Aleš and his brothers talk about is cars, computers and mobile phones. There's usually at least one fight. And a *lot* of pickled beetroot.'

'Charlie's mother is with us for… almost a fortnight.' Petra laughed breathlessly, grateful to be able to vent her frustration. 'Which means I am on camera constantly… am redundant, as a failed wife and terrible mother, and in…' she checked her watch '… just over three hours' time my parents arrive, which signals the start of a political debate that will rage until the day after Boxing Day. And I *still* can't get rid of Pip.'

Gill shot her a you're-not-suffering-enough look. 'Thank God Paul's lot only venture across from New Zealand once a decade.' She wasn't remotely short of breath. 'Ma and Pa are dead, of course, but one keeps one's chin up. Both dying at Christmas is always a bit of a sore point.'

Petra blanched guiltily.

The tough, no-nonsense smile picked her up. 'Pip has an aunt on the Isle of Wight. My old nanny is in the same sheltered accommodation. Young Pip – or Pauline, as Auntie calls her – is flavour of the month after writing a lovely letter recently, and would be most welcome for the festive period. You can still get a passenger-ferry gift voucher, Nanny tells me.'

'Gill, have I told you I love you lately?' By way of thanks and rebonding, Petra somewhat guiltily shared Pip's Tinder conman selfie among the Bags when they pulled up for a breather at the windmill. 'We need to find this bastard.'

Mo deleted it immediately, Gill stared at it in disbelief, and Bridge made it her phone wallpaper. A shocked silence reigned.

'I'll ask Paul,' Gill said eventually, then looked surprised as the rest of the Bags protested. 'Why ever not?'

Ronnie arrived at the Old Almshouses armed with Pip's home cooking from the stud's freezers and supermarket bags of cupboard supplies.

Carly Turner was already waiting on the doorstep in a pink tabard, casting her a bemused look through the pretty dark eyebrows that contradicted her blonde hair. 'I was expecting the Home Comforts lady.'

'I'm undercover, recruiting you to come and visit my neglected foal.'

She snorted with laughter. 'Seriously, though?'

'Long story, could easily have been shortened by a quick "Bugger off" but I'm glad it hasn't. Pip's indisposed. And you're here, which is kismet. Shall we start with a cup of tea?' She dug around for the key under the boot scraper, trying not to feel too disconcerted walking into Hermia's half-life.

Carly was in no mood for introspection. 'You're kidding? I'm due waitressing in two hours. Get these rubber gloves on, lady.'

'You're the pro.' Ronnie watched her marching in and followed reluctantly. It smelt, not unpleasantly, of incense, Scotch and baking. And it was a bombsite.

A super-efficient blitzer, Carly tidied and recycled at warp speed. If Ronnie had been planning on staying on in the village, she'd have been tempted to offer her a job on the spot.

'This'll do,' Ronnie said, with relief, once the place looked reasonably clear, cramming the last of the food away, deliberately blinkered to her surroundings, eyes on the practical, not the personal. 'The oil tank's being filled later today, logs coming tomorrow. All done.'

'Are you kidding? It's not even clean yet. These are for you.' Carly handed her a big sachet of anti-bacterial wipes. 'They're Janine's specials. I nabbed a pack.'

'What does one do with them?'

'Find dirt. Wipe. And dance.' Propping her phone up on the peninsula, Carly set off to work to Jess Glynne's 'Hold My Hand'.

Ronnie followed suit, her eyes inevitably following her hands round the room as they ran the little throwaway cloths over surfaces and ornaments, picture frames and personal knick-knacks, piecing together a life that had all the enviable trappings of a chaotic, bright family, yet the secret it harboured showed up at every turn if you knew where to look: the widened doorways from the wheelchair years, the lowered surfaces, grab rails, aides-memoire, sensory stimuli, the rows of books on the shelves, their titles starting 'Neuro', the labels on things, and the many pictures of Hermia on stage to remind her of who she was, whom she had played.

Ronnie wiped a framed photograph of her as Medea, hauntingly beautiful.

'You're a slowcoach, you are.' Carly hurried past with a mop bucket.

'I knew her.' She held up the picture.

'Oh, yes?' At the kitchen sink, she was only half interested.

Ronnie set it back. She drew out a collection of Dorothy Parker's poetry from the shelf behind it, finding her own name in the front. *To H, Happy Birthday 2004. All love, R xx.*

She turned down the page on 'A Very Short Song' and put it back. 'While we're scrubbing along, Carly, tell me what a girl with healing hands is doing cracking them in a bucket of bleach.'

'I'm saving to train as a farrier,' Carly said, without hesitation. 'I'm going to do it.'

'I don't doubt you could, if you put your mind to it, but I very much doubt you should.'

Carly turned off the taps, running this round in her head. 'Come again?'

'You have a gift.' Ronnie's deep, rumbling laugh reminded her of a talent show judge announcing, 'You have four yeses.' 'Yours is one of those unique skills that needs no apprenticeship. You must work with horses, Carly. But heal them, don't shoe them.'

'You serious?' She put the mop bucket on the floor, water slopping.

'Of course I'm serious. You could take formal training as a holistic practitioner in Reiki or massage therapy, if you prefer. Or simply trust to Fate and start straight away. I have an old arthritic horse that would really benefit from those hands of yours.' She ran a disinfectant wipe along the work surface beside Carly. 'Word will soon get out.'

She made it all sound so possible. Carly was struggling not to whoop and dance around with her mop, like Belle with the Beast. But she knew embracing the dream would break the spell. 'I'll think about it.'

'You'll *do* it.' Ronnie's forthright way of putting things reminded Carly of the officers' wives in garrison. 'And that husband of yours will be the one who trains as a farrier, if he has any sense.'

'Flynn asked Ash to be his apprentice in the first place,' Carly admitted. She was quite certain Ash didn't want to be a personal trainer any more, his ennui and rebellion worsening because he was too proud to admit he'd chosen the wrong direction along Civvy Street. He and Flynn trusted and looked out for each other, the lance corporals of the old gang. They'd make a brilliant team, if only Ash could be persuaded to stop keeping everyone at a distance and to work with brothers in arms again.

'Your young chap was bred for the job. The Turner family has more instinctive horse sense than a Monty Roberts convention trapped in a round pen. Besides which, he's strong and immensely practical.'

'That's what Flynn said.'

'There you go. I'm rather fond of Flynn. He might look like a Bonnie Tyler in drag, but he balances a hoof perfectly. And he'll certainly need another pair of hands once the stud's back in full swing.'

'Ash says animals tie you down,' she said uncertainly. 'He doesn't like it that I'm so fond of dogs and horses.'

'The healing works both ways,' Ronnie said gently. 'They're very soothing and intuitive creatures. They know when somebody's been through a bad time.' A blue eye winked. 'You, Flynn and I have plenty of time to talk him round. He will be very, very good. And *you*, my healing naiad, won't have to mop floors much longer, trust me.'

When Ronnie said it, Carly believed it.

'I'm so grateful to you,' she said, deciding Ronnie was like the ultimate fairy godmother.

But she'd lost her attention. Ronnie was looking at a black-and-white photograph of a swashbuckling blonde in a ruff and cavalier hat, a sexy eighties New Romantic.

'*As You Like It*'s such a wonderful play.' She sighed. '*Love is merely a madness.*'

'Why's she dressed as a bloke?'

'Rosalind wants to turn the man she marries into someone as strong and upstanding as she is. I've been guilty of trying to do that. Maybe the secret is to wear doublet and hose.'

'Or seriously big granny pants.' Carly turned up the music on her phone.

'It comes as a shock to realise that having grandchildren means even my thongs are technically granny pants.'

As they worked their way round the house to a chart medley Ronnie didn't recognise but rather liked, in a home she didn't know but was surprised to find quirkily cosy, she pieced together enough clues to realise that, in the years before her death, Hermia had been loved, frustrated, depressed, safe, and utterly addicted to all manner of distractions from *Agatha Raisin* and *Charles Paris* mysteries to BBC Shakespeare and comedy box sets. But her ghost was long faded, her inner life hidden from view. While the photographs still radiated life, the house was now filled with a buzz of recent thought and chaos, fresh ring marks on the surfaces, fans of papers on the desk, recently published books spiralling in piles.

She also figured out that sleepy-eyed Carly was incredibly switched on, pissed-off and tired out. Her wounded soldier, whose pain was all in his mind, had gone through so many thresholds he was unaware of how much he was hurting her. Ronnie knew that scenario, however differently framed. It was within these very four walls.

'You should get away from this village,' she told her, as she polished an enamel box when they tackled the main bedroom together. 'A gift like yours can spread its wings.'

'Why run?' Carly wiped down the window frames. 'Trouble just runs with you.'

The little box fell open. It had a Silver Wedding crown in it: H on one side, V on the other. Ronnie spun it between her fingers. 'My father used to say that if you walk in a straight line long enough you'll always end up in the same spot.'

'Well, the world is round, I guess.'

'Try staying on a straight line circumnavigating it.'

Carly chuckled, forcing open the window, snow falling in dull thuds from the gutters above. 'I like your long words.'

'I prefer wise ones. You're a wise child.' She was right. Trouble always ran with you.

They both breathed in cool air gratefully.

Outside, a voice below called, 'Only me! Just seeing how you're doing. Need to sit down. Can you let me in?'

Carly growled under her breath, 'Don't let her too close to me.'

Pip was soon reclining in the chair by the circular window, hand to her brow, eyes checking critically round the room. 'I walked here. Petra said she was too busy to give me a lift, what with her parents and everything. They are *so* demanding.'

'It's only a few hundred yards,' Carly huffed.

Pip gave her a martyred look. She disliked Petra's parents intensely. Very blunt, Yorkshire and jovial, the elderly Shaws had seen straight through her hypochondria.

'Charlie would have driven me – he's super nice – but he's taken his mother and the kids to the cinema. *Such* a good dad. They invited me, but I'm still too frail and I've got to get home to pack. I know this is going to come as a shock, and I'm sorry to let you down, Ronnie, but I'm going away over Christmas.'

'Oh, that's quite all right,' Ronnie said quickly.

Pip appreciated her selflessness. 'The Gunns are treating me, and they're right, I deserve it. To be honest, it's a relief to get away from that place. It's very crowded.'

The overbearing Shaws were also very harsh on Barbara, roping her into cooking and clearing up to give 'exhausted' Petra a break: 'Let's give her and Charlie boy a bit of grown-up time together. I'll ring and bewk a restaurant,' Petra's dad had insisted that morning. Petra and Charlie had both looked appalled at the idea. Pip sensed a marriage excitingly close to implosion. She didn't want to stay away too long and risk missing anything.

'I'm back on Boxing Day,' she told Ronnie. 'I've broken it to my oldies.' She'd sent a mass text, which the ones with landlines would probably think was a PPI recorded message, but at least she'd tried. She was too weak for personal calls. 'Can you keep an eye on this place for me? I know you're having a quiet Christmas so you'll have the time.'

'It's hardly going to fall down in three days,' Carly pointed out.

Pip glared at her, looking pleadingly at Ronnie, whom she found it particularly thrilling to extract favours from. 'I've done so much for you and the stud and—'

'I'll check in on it.' Ronnie was turning a large silver coin in her fingers.

Pip smiled gratefully. 'You can't be too careful. I've been targeted for my kindness. All sorts of chancers in this village.'

'Don't you accuse my Ash of anything again!' Carly flared.

'How was I to know his tattoos weren't JD's?'

Ronnie cleared her throat. 'I gather one feature was genuine.'

Pip frowned. 'How do you know about it?'

'I may well know who his father was.' She gave a knowing smile.

Pip was agog. 'But who is the *son*?'

'One of six,' Carly butted in, picking her phone out of her pocket. 'I've got a list of names, and I think I know which one he is, but I've no proof.'

'Will this help?' Pip took out her own phone and summoned her favourite picture.

'Bloody hell.'

'I know! Isn't it just?' She looked at it fondly.

'Can you send me that?' Carly shared her number. 'Give me till you get back after Christmas. I'll make him squirm.'

Feeling she might have misjudged her, Pip stood up and headed unsteadily to the kitchen. 'I know where there's a tin of my best chocolate treats. I think we all deserve some Rocky Road, don't you?'

'Have you any plain sailing?' Ronnie sighed, sending a ghost of a wink to Carly.

Carly watched as Pip returned, forgetting to sway fraily, eager to ingratiate herself with her new crime-fighting team.

'Tell JD,' she sat down breathlessly, 'I'm prepared to forgive him if he still – has feelings.'

Carly caught Ronnie's eye, grateful for their grounding amusement. She forwarded Pip's picture text to Janine. *Look familiar?*

Carly had three hours off between lunch and her evening shift at Le Mill, enough time to pick up the kids from her mother-in-law, give them tea, bath Jackson, and catch up with Janine, who hurried straight round after her last cleaning client of the day, her spider eyes blinking fast.

'It's Jed,' she confirmed, sitting down and taking Jackson to bounce on her knee. 'I checked with his ex.'

'Hardly a master of disguise, lifting his cousin's Facebook photos and dropping the *e* from his name.'

'Jed's been dropping Es for years, hun. 'S how he got so fruit-loop. Even his dogs don't trust him. He's going out lamping later. Taking that lurcher you're so fond of.'

'Pricey.'

'Tequila.'

'Not for much longer.' She stood up and shrugged on her coat. 'Can you mind the kids? Take them back to Nan's if I'm longer than half an hour. My lift to Le Mill goes at six.' She looked at her watch. 'I thought Ash'd be back by now.'

'Seeing a man about a bike, I heard.' Janine gave her a big in-on-a-secret wink. 'You're a lucky girl, Carl, that's all I'm saying. What wife wants a dog for Christmas when they can have a Ducati?'

'A dog's for life, Janine. Like a marriage.' She stomped out.

In the garden, smashing his 'Splorer Stick against the shed, Ellis watched his mum striding purposefully into the estate.

Glancing into the house, where Aunt Janine was playing coochy-coo with his little brother, and his sister was gazing catatonically at *In the Night Garden*, he shouldered his stick, like a rifle, and marched after her.

Sticking to the shadows, as he'd seen his dad do in his sniper games, Ellis followed her to Apple Rise. At the far end there was a little row of terraces, a van parked outside with its tailgate open.

Ellis hung back behind a tree trunk as his mum marched up to the door and hammered on it. Dogs barked. Not Pricey, though. Ellis knew she was kept in a run further along the dead end, through double-padlocked gates in what had once been a stockyard.

Now Mum was shouting at Uncle Jed, pointing at those gates and at him and at her phone. He leaned against his door frame and laughed.

Ellis crept closer, teeth chattering. The snow had melted a bit today, rubbish for snowballing, and was now freezing hard and slippery. He struggled to stay upright, then held his breath as his trainers lit up. But she hadn't noticed.

'I could shop you for this!' his mum shouted.

'For sending a dick shot? Who wouldn't, Carl? You want a bit?'

'Get lost, Jed. You know what I want. Ash had no right telling you about that dog.'

'So you thought you'd blackmail me?'

'It's not blackmail. It's just saying I know what a low-down scum-bag you are. I'm appealing to your better nature.'

'Do that to your own husband, love. He's yours for better or worse, and he's a lot worse than me.'

'What are you saying?'

'We all know he's fencing.'

'Says who?'

Ellis had made it behind the van doors now, ducking under one and creeping closer to watch through the blackened glass window of the other.

'Whole estate knows he's up to no good. He's just like his dad was. You never met him, but that man was a hard bastard.'

Ellis's teeth were chattering. There were blankets and dog beds in the back of the van. He crawled inside, pulling two checked blankets around him, listening hard.

'I'll buy her off you. Fair and square.'

'She's not for sale. Granddad Norm says she's the best of the lot.'

'She doesn't like you, Jed. She doesn't want to hunt no more.'

'Give her time. Not many dogs resist instinct. And she's a fighter. I have to keep her on her own. She'd take a hind down.'

'Don't even think about it.'

'What are you going to do? Shop me to your friends the Austens?'

'If that's what it takes to stop you hurting Pricey.'

'Do that and your Ash is nicked. Shame, a war hero like him, but a lot lose it on Civvy Street, don't they? Won't be able to work as a nice personal trainer then, will he? Have to do security, bodyguarding maybe, protection. Dangerous work. Not home much.'

'I know my husband. He's no criminal.'

'Your little boy's growing up fast, isn't he? Chip off the old block. His dad got in a lot of scrapes at that age. Near misses, you know.'

'You threaten my child and I'll tie you up by that bloody piercing, Jed.'

'Now there's an offer.'

Ellis snuggled further into the van, feeling tired now. He didn't understand what they were talking about any more. Not dogs anyway. On they shouted. He was sure he could hear Pricey howling, picking up on her voice. He closed his eyes to listen. A moment later, he was asleep.

Petra and Charlie, who would secretly have preferred to stay at home so they could both drink, went to Le Mill, faced with picking through small portions and even smaller talk. Squeezed between a raucous table of twenty and another of sixteen, they smiled gamely and politely at each other over their menus and wine choice, but rapidly descended into long silences as the thrill of making a decision was shrugged into inevitable disappointment. Stony sober Petra found it hard to hold her tongue as Charlie drank his way down a bottle of Chablis within the first half-hour and couldn't stop his eyes checking out Carly, who was waitressing their table.

Embarrassed that someone she knew was witnessing their lacklustre attempt at marital bliss, Petra put on a big show when their plates were delivered and wine poured, sagging back into exhausted people-watching afterwards while Charlie talked about the Boxing Day shoot he was going on, highlight of his week ahead, Christmas paling into insignificance by comparison.

'Neville Ogilvy's going to be there. Now he is one big, swinging dick in the City, just bought a huge place over near Winchcombe. And Dave Goldstein – d'you remember him? Both crack shots. We had a day out last year on the Wyckford Estate. Huge mixed bag. Loads of partridge, a woodcock and three beaters I shot by accident.'

'Ha-ha.'

'Just checking you're listening. Now Dave's wife's a good shot too...'

She supposed it could have been worse. He could have been passionate about golf.

'Henry's offered to stand me a round of golf at his club,' he said, leaning across to scoop up two slices of the duck she was saving until last in her salad. 'See how I like it.'

A gale was forecast. Petra still had fifty-eight presents to wrap. She was missing the *Last Tango in Halifax* Christmas special.

'Everything all right for you?' Carly took their plates.

'Fabulous! Delicious!'

'I'll get you dessert menus.'

Charlie looked across at her cynically.

'We could just go home?' he suggested, already hard-eyed and horny from chasing down the Chablis with a very good Burgundy.

Sober and distinctly unstirred, Petra needed a bit more revving up. 'Where's your spirit of adventure? I expect pudding, Arabica coffee and a romantic walk to the Hare's Ladder.'

'Is that a pub?' he asked hopefully.

'It's a waterfall.'

'It's minus eight out there.'

'Two puddings, then.'

'Are you sure you should, darling?' His eyes nudged towards her thighs.

'Do you want sex later?'

He gave a Terry-Thomas growl.

'Then I want two puddings.'

Ellis hadn't woken when the dog was put into the van, despite having his face washed enthusiastically and a back wriggle against him. Deep in his unconscious, dreaming mind, she was familiar and protective. Nor did he wake as the engine started and the van rumbled out of the estate and onto the Broadbourne road, swinging onto the track by the millstream and following it as far as the little wooded parking spot dog-walkers used by day and doggers by night. It was only when the doors were pulled open and Pricey snarled that he started, eyes snapping open.

'Come on, you bitch.'

She bared her teeth viciously at the shadow in the door. Another shadow joined it, another car engine approached, dogs barking.

The rumble in her throat was low, deadly serious.

Ellis was frightened.

'Come *here*!' The shadow pointed something at the dog. There was a shrill beep and a little red light glowed near Ellis's face, where Pricey's neck was, a box on her collar. The next moment she'd dropped to the van floor with a yelp.

Ellis pulled the blanket over his head. A torch beam crossed the back, glowing through the rough woollen weave. Then Pricey had gone, the doors banging shut.

He waited for what seemed ages, the voices fading, the cold setting in.

Whimpering, he felt even more cold and scared. He couldn't open the van doors from the inside. There was a sliding glass panel behind where the driver sat, open just a fraction. His fingers were small enough to thread into it and tug until the glass panel slid aside enough for him to crawl through, taking his 'Splorer Stick with him.

Carly was helping Petra and Charlie into their coats when Babette, the maître d', beckoned her over urgently.

'Thank you again,' gushed Petra. On a two-pudding high, adorably Christmassy and sentimental, she'd left Carly a big tip and now hugged her farewell. 'You must bring your little one to ride our Shetland after Christmas.'

'Yeah, thanks gorgeous,' Charlie smouldered, making Carly back away quickly.

Babette handed her the phone, signalling that it was important.

At the other end of the line, Janine was talking so fast she didn't make any sense at first. Something about Ellis and Ash, all in a breathless rush: 'I didn't know he should have been home with the other two – I thought he was at a mate's or still at his nan's. Then Ash got home, and your phone's on voicemail so we couldn't check with you, then we had a beer and he was on the Xbox and we was chatting and, ohmygod, Carl, he must have been missing *hours*. When did you go? Half five? It's nearly ten! Oh, shit, poor little mite.'

'Ellis is missing?' She felt ice cold.

'Yes! Yes!'

'Where's Ash?'

'Out looking.'

'Has he got his phone?'

'Yes.'

'Call him and tell him to find Jed, yeah? FIND JED!'

'I told you he's out with the dog. A load of them was meeting up near Hare's Ladder, Carl. Don't you go there. He's with the boys from... Carl? *Carl?*'

She was already running out of the door.

Ellis knew he'd be safe while he had his 'Splorer Stick. It was magical, his mum said. He could hear voices up ahead, men with dogs. Ellis liked dogs.

It was really dark, but the moon was big and white above the trees, making the snow seem whiter, and if he focused hard he could just see the path. The ground was slippery, rock hard. His breath clouded in front of him. He needed the stick to feel his way.

The men were across to the left, a big dark dip in the ground between him and them. He prodded it, found a solid surface and stepped onto it.

He could see torches now, bright ones sweeping through the trees. They must be looking for him. His mum and dad were always telling him not to run off, and they'd be searching. He called: 'Here! I'm here!'

Something started cracking beneath his feet. They felt cold and wet. As he stepped around, trainers glowing, trying to find dry ground, he looked down and saw water bubbling up through broken ice.

'Ellis!' Carly ran along the path, stumbling and slipping, her breath coming out in great hoarse racks making shouting his name a pathetic wheezing breath. 'Ellis! Ellis!'

She passed the vans and off-roaders parked together, tucked tightly away in the clearing with tell-tale stealth.

'Ellis!'

The path blackened in the woods, making her fall more, her arms and legs lacerated with thorns, the ground a skating rink. 'Ellis!'

A small, distant cry: 'Mum. It's breaking, Mum.'

'Where are you? Ellis! Ellis!' She stood still, turned, listened, trying not to breathe, her heartbeat deafening in her ears.

'Mum!'

'Ellis! Where are you?'

She heard the ice cracking first, a splash, a scream. It might have been her own. She ran in the direction of the noise, legs tightly netted in undergrowth, trying to fight through brambles and brash as high as her waist. 'Ellis!'

Then she heard the dog, its panting breaths, solid body crashing through the woods to her left beyond the hollow. It was running her way. A man shouted, a small red light flashed. The dog yelped, dropped and rolled over as though shot. It scrambled up and ran on.

More shouting. The light flashed again. It barely broke stride this time, making a flying leap and disappearing into the hollow. A skittering of feet, more splashing, a cry. 'Help. Pricey!'

'Ellis!'

He was in water.

Carly waded through the brash, her shirt and skirt shredded now, kicking her way out to a steep bank at the far side. She pulled off her shoes and slid down it, hearing a motorbike screaming along the path beside her.

Her foot went straight through the ice. She pulled it out. Balanced on the bank, she peered into the gloom and saw movement in the centre of the black pond, the dog trying to swim through the ice towards her, a boy clinging to her back.

Not pausing to think, Carly dived in.

Christ, it was cold. Colder than cold. She could barely feel her arms to pull herself along. Her legs were flailing in frozen silt, ice shards trying to cut her throat. She'd made it about six feet into the pond and couldn't move, her body just shaking in horrible, paralysed inertia.

With great effort, she forced it on, focusing on Ellis, not caring if she lived or died as long as she saved him. All she had to do was save him. Her mind was freezing too, her vision so black. Keep going. Pricey was pulling him towards her, sinking right below the surface with the effort. She was a big dog, a strong dog now, but the water was freezing her senses too.

Carly reached out, almost able to touch him.

'Carly!' Ash's voice, somewhere higher up behind her.

'Here!' Why was no sound coming out? 'Here!'

The dog disappeared under the surface again, Ellis almost slipping in too. She plunged onwards.

'Carly!'

The dog burst up, copper eyes blinking, bright as coins in the moonlight. She let out a bark, deep and demanding. And again.

Ash came crashing through the brash towards the pond.

Carly felt a freezing cold little arm beneath her fingers, sobbed with relief as she gripped it, pulling Ellis to her, turning onto her back with him on her chest and kicking back towards the bank with the fragments of strength she had left. A great splash behind her and she was lifted out in one deft movement, still clinging so tightly to her son she worried she'd broken his arm.

On the bank, Ash ripped off his coat and wrapped it around them both, his hand first on her face and then Ellis's, checking they were conscious and breathing. Carly's teeth were chattering too much to speak, but she waved him away and crouched over their son too.

Ellis wasn't breathing.

'It's all right, little man. I've got your back.'

Ash was applying CPR before she could even start to think what to do, counting and compressing, then breathing into Ellis's mouth.

She took his little hand. It was still gripped tight round his 'Splorer Stick.

He gave a faint moan, the sweetest sound she'd ever heard. Then another and a splutter. Then he said, 'Pricey.'

Carly dropped her face to his small, cold hand, hot tears against it. The dog. She hadn't got out. As Ash knelt back, Carly gathered their son into a tight hug, feeling the tears start to shake through him.

'The dog,' she told Ash. 'She saved his life. She's still in there.'

He shook his head. 'She'll be gone, Carly.'

She swallowed blades. She remembered seeing it on television. People who had drowned in frozen water were brought round hours later. Surely the same was true for dogs.

'We've got to get her out.'

'No, Carl.'

'Yes.' She tried to pass Ellis to him and stand up, her legs refusing to work at first. 'I'm getting her out.'

'Stay there! I'll do it.' He settled Ellis back against her, pulling the coat tighter round them, looming over her as he pulled off his sweater. 'Take your wet shirt off and put this on. There's a phone in the coat. Call an ambulance.' He gazed across the pond at the field beyond the trees where the lampers had moved to the far corner, not bothering to come after the dog or follow the shouts. 'And call the police too. I don't believe I'm bloody doing this.'

Then, with a crack and a splash, he waded back in.

Fingers still steel hard, Carly dialled 999. So much for healing hands. She couldn't even feel them, struggling to hold the phone steady enough to her ear to hear. At last the message was conveyed, the location given as best she knew it. She clutched the phone to her mouth and Ellis to her chest, rocking and listening, rocking and listening. A splash here, a crash there, Ash cursing, then a whoosh as he went right under to search.

Ellis's teeth were chattering like hers now. 'Where's Pricey?'

'Dad's looking, love.'

'Want Pricey.' He took her hand and held it against his face, and she realised that her fingers were warm once more. Not just warm, they were hot.

There was another loud whoosh, a grunt and a curse, then wading and scrabbling, feet on the bank, the big black shadow of a man covered with pond weed clutching the big black shadow of a dog covered with it too.

'I expect you want me to give her bloody mouth-to-mouth as well, do you?'

'Too right we do.'

'Make her wake up, Dad.'

He laid her down beside Carly, who cupped her hands around Pricey's cold domed head.

'Here goes nothing.'

As Ash crouched down to start compressing her chest, the dog let out a great roar of a splutter, her big lungs pumping out, coughing and sneezing and heaving until she stood shakily up and crashed closer to Carly and Ellis.

'Guess she didn't want to be kissed.' Ash laughed.

'I do.' Carly reached up to his face. 'God, but I love you, Ash Turner.'

57

With two days to Christmas, the grocery deliveries were coming thick and fast to the village, vans parked in drives and on verges unloading plastic Tesco and Waitrose crates, posh hampers, cheap booze, and Amazon couriers wandering around with boxes, looking for houses with names, not numbers.

Among the dog-walkers on Plum Run, Christmas spirit was building fast, smiles widening, good will radiating. The thaw had set in. Although much of the landscape had started to reclaim its browns, golds and greens, the snowmen were still standing. Some joker had dressed up the Old Vicarage's gate eagles in dark glasses and Santa hats.

In the Orchard Estate, the illuminations were switched on twenty-four seven, old rivals staging stand-offs between icicles, nets, inflatables, ropes and projections. Carly and Ash's modest fibre-optic tree at number three Quince Drive was letting the side down a bit, but none of the Turners minded their understatement, given the heroism of the rescue that had just taken place. The family was reunited after a night of high drama, with one new member in situ, so thoroughly excited that she'd already broken the coffee table, the cat flap and the kitchen bin, and threatened to eat three guinea pigs. Ash was tolerating her for now, although his temper was blackened by the messages he'd stumbled upon on his wife's phone the night before, declarations of love – as well as Liberal Democratic allegiance and bisexuality – from someone called 'Gunn' and, more disturbing still, a dick shot of almost unnatural proportions bearing the family crest.

Like a Christmas e-card, mystery man JD's glorious appendage had now been shared via picture text among a great many ladies of the village, and he was gaining legendary status. Having left for the Isle of Wight, Pip was none the wiser that the man with whom she'd discussed tea-break KitKats had just been sent home on a charge of Trespass with Equipment Specifically Intended for Trapping and Killing Animals.

'She couldn't wait to race off first thing this morning – Gunny's already in decline,' Petra told Ronnie, as they walked to Eyngate through the ancient parkland that had once belonged to Ronnie's distant cousins. Petra was getting better at keeping up – walking with Ronnie burned more calories than working out at the gym, she'd decided – although the topic of conversation soon made her miserable.

'I'm going away myself in a couple of days.'

Petra's face fell when she learned that Ronnie was leaving for Germany straight after Christmas, her stay there open-ended.

'You can't go! I'll pine. You only just got here.'

'I was only ever stopping off here. I did try to tell you that.' Her chin lifted, the thick bell of blonde hair swinging. 'I'm taking the stallion back to the stud that bred him to stand there again. There's a Dutch dealer who wants to give me my job back. I can make ten times the money out there than I can here, and that's *my* legacy for my grandchildren. The stud is my father's and I'm going to leave it in very good hands. You wait. By the time you've written all your lovely trilogy, I expect it to be in the black.'

'So you are coming back?'

'Of course I will.' The blue eyes sparkled. 'Probably.'

'Is this to do with Blair?'

The sparkle hardened. 'Petra, I never stand still. Women in my position can't afford to.'

'Well, I think you should.'

'Thank you. I'll bear your opinion in mind.' The ravishing smile reappeared. 'Now tell me about your night out with Charlie. Did the spark reignite, or are you going to need Zip firelighters, rolled-up newspaper and extra-long matches with the flues let out?'

Petra had been too busy unravelling her own emotional knitting lately to remember that others had theirs sewn up in a brightly patterned sweater they wore like armour. Ronnie wasn't like her old London friends, who poured out their souls with a third Pinot Grigio, or the Saddle Bags, who spoke bitterly behind their whip hands, like Regency wives muttering behind fans. She was a veteran campaigner, emotionally scarred and rewardingly open. Accustomed to being admired, pursued and kept secret, hers was a code of conduct that most women would abhor, yet she struck Petra as deeply pragmatic as well as unerringly positive. If life dealt Ronnie a marked card, she always found an ace up her sleeve.

'It was fine,' she said, a smile creeping onto her face as her eyebrows shot up. 'More than fine.'

The Gunns, both contrite at their own misdemeanours, remained on their best behaviour both in and out of bed. Last night, after two very large nightcaps at home to get her in the mood, marital sex had turned increasingly giggly and silly until they were rolling around having a whale of a time.

'Good.' Ronnie hooked her arm through Petra's. 'No more Father Willy, then?'

'No more Father Willy. I kill him off at the end of the book. A jealous mistress poisons him with the old arsenic-Bible-pages, finger-licking trick.' She kept quiet about a possible haunting plotline she had up her sleeve for the second in the series.

They walked back into a lowering sun, waving at a group of riders out for a blast along Bay's new three-mile point.

'He rents it out for twenty quid a pop. The man is Croesus. They're hunting over it again on Boxing Day, coming up here after meeting in Chipping Hampton.'

'Do you mind that part of it is your old land?'

'That my father would have loved to field-master the run makes it easier to bear. Austens look after their land far better than we can afford to.'

'But press your ear to the ground on Percy land and you can hear hoofs, just like you can hear the sea in a shell. Don't get that on Austen land.'

'Oh, I love that.'

'Stay.'

She laughed. 'You sound like Lester.'

*

While the women made their way home, the stud was cast in its most golden of winter-afternoon glows, the water racing along its guttering as the last of the snow melted off its west-facing roofs. Lester fed the grey stallion a carrot through his bars – bribery was his new tactic – then headed into the adjoining yard to feed one to old Cruisoe, and went on to find his son. Spirit sauntered up, bright gold in the sunlight. 'All hopes are riding on you, little fellow. You and some bogtrotter she's got coming over here. Unless we can make her bloody well stay this time.' He went into his cottage and picked up the phone that tethered him to the wall, dialling out. 'Mrs Petty, it's Lester. I have something I must ask of you...'

In his attic room at Upper Bagot Farmhouse, Fitz was still studying the threatening message he'd received the night before from Carly's phone – he guessed the scary husband – and deciding regretfully that it was time to move on. He was never going to get long-distance Sophie off his back with a married woman. Deleting Carly's number, he messaged Dix Wish instead.

The last of the snow melted on Christmas Eve, leaving sludgy brown mud skirting the lanes, the few scarves, carrots and twigs on the Green, where snowmen had been, now buffeted by a bitter wind. Unfamiliar cars had been turning into drives throughout the Comptons all day, visiting family spilling out in festive jumpers, throwing open boots to reveal brightly wrapped gifts and weekend bags.

The boxes Kit carried into the Old Almshouses contained no presents, just more books, notes and files. There was always a distracting amount to do in London, but he saw no point in delaying his return with displacement activities. Ferdie was right: the first car alarm had seen him itching to be back in the peace of the Bardswolds. He was looking forward to spending Christmas close to Hermia and the project he hadn't finished in her lifetime.

He'd already shared seasonal gifts and meals with his children, their Christmas the movable feast typical of a theatrical family. They would share Christmas with their companies in the pocket between today's early-evening show and the Boxing Day matinee. He'd enjoyed the road trip visiting them, seeing the shows again, sharing his plans over late-night curries, assuring them that the relationship with Orla really was well and truly over, the brief press furore ridden out in glorious isolation. They were happy that he was going to be in Compton Magna for a while – they still thought of it as home in the way Kit had once thought of the Lakes as home until the generation that had raised him there was lost – and happier still that he had company on Christmas Day. Ferdie and Donald had insisted that Kit must share the celebration with them.

'If you won't come to us, dear boy, then we must follow you there with the Fortnum's five-bird roast and a case of Shiraz.' It was far from the first occasion that the Falstaffian theatrical agent had invited himself to the Bardswolds, this time with actor-husband Donald and their cockapoo Mopsa in tow.

'You two don't celebrate Christmas.'

'We celebrate seeing you.'

'Nothing whatsoever to do with the fact you're having your place in Stratford redecorated?'

'We'll forgive you for having a suspicious mind as long as you have a hospitable hearth.'

'The house isn't very habitable at the moment. There's an outside chance it might be clean.'

He'd heard nothing back from his message to Pip at Home from Home Comforts, which didn't come as a surprise so close to Christmas. He'd told Ferdie and Donald to bring hot-water bottles, thick clothes and a bag of kindling.

Her service was beyond impressive, though. The oil tank was full, a fresh load of logs lay beneath a tarpaulin by the store, and the house was spotless. He'd gone shopping en route, for some basic supplies – mostly cask-matured malt – but the cupboards were stocked with tins and packets, the freezer crammed with home-made meals and trays of ice.

Pip's alter ego Sabrina ffoulkes-Hamilton was right. She needed to be paid a lot more. He started unpacking his boxes, awaiting the riotous arrival of Ferdie and Donald. He stopped when he saw a silver crown on the work surface, picking it up to examine the letters crudely painted on each side: V and H.

Lester's eczema – last active when the hunting ban had been passed – had returned with a vengeance since he'd learned Ronnie was leaving, the skin behind his ears, elbows and knees crawling with itches. At Midnight Mass, he sat proud and upright in his favourite pew – which he usually had to himself but was typically crowded with drunken villagers, who treated the annual service like a Christmas singalong – but his body flamed beneath the tweed as though the anger was scratching its way out of him a pore at a time.

Ronnie had declined to come. He felt some prayers should be said for her safety with that big grey brute. Bribery was getting Lester nowhere. The stallion spent all day pacing, wall-biting and board-kicking, like a spoiled brat. He had no manners. Lester had shut the top door and retreated to Cruisoe's box to groom the old stallion, telling himself it was good that the horse was going. He was too messed up, too much trouble. Ronnie was right. Let him go back to his routine in the big German stallion factory. Cruisoe remained dignified, taking no notice of the grey beast shrieking in the next yard.

Lester could hear the wind getting up outside the church, howling through the yews and around the churchyard. The horses had all been upset by it.

As the congregation launched into a slurred Lord's Prayer, Lester fought a furious urge to scratch, his neck straining high above its crisp white collar.

Further along the pew, Petra was deliciously tight after a three-bottle family supper and much flirting with her husband, who for once played along – having sex last night had made her brazenly libidinous. Charlie looked very dashing in his long black Richard Gere coat and striped scarf wound as wide as a ruff, his bald head hidden beneath a watch cap that was surprisingly on trend for him, the sliding blue-grey eyes beneath knowing it. There was enough stubble dusting his chin to declare the holiday officially under way.

'Have we found out yet if the vicar's a woman or a man?' he whispered.

'It remains the biggest village mystery.' She closed her fingers through his, grateful that he was unambiguously male, and that tonight would almost certainly have been heading towards another seduction, had she not still to wrap the stocking fillers and slather the turkey in butter and bacon rashers. Christmas sex was always the wafer-thin mint that melted before you tasted it, an overindulgence taken amid excess.

The little village church was packed. There was a big mob of Turners on show, all very well oiled, ready to have a good sing-song. Janine Turner, who had terrifying Santa-hat nails complete with bobbles, was distributing beer and sausage rolls from a coolbox. Pretty Carly and her handsome tattooed husband weren't with them.

Petra was conscious of the entire Austen clan gathered on the opposite side of the aisle, close to the chancel, an affable army doing their duty in fur-trimmed herringbone in the VIP zone beneath the family plaque. In the furriest tweed of all, hat like a fluffy pouffe, Monique hadn't stopped tapping a long, skinny thumb on her smartphone. Craning round, Bay had tried to catch Petra's eye so often he might as well have got out a laser pointer, his flirtation springing up like the inflatable scarecrows that guarded his winter wheat, terrifying passing horses. She ignored him, empowered because her husband was alongside her, and because her crush was now in the afterlife. Father Willy's ghost might be haunting virgins' dreams – her new book's synopsis was mapped out in her mind ready for her to start work again in the new year – but she was firmly in control.

She reached for Charlie's hand again and squeezed it. It was cold and sweaty, she noticed, pulling it around her shoulder and snuggling closer, feeling the warm wooziness of the evening's wine still coursing through her.

The vicar was inviting them to take communion now and Petra watched the devout shuffle up to swallow the blood of Christ. She could have done with another drink, but that wasn't a reason to shrug off her agnostic doubts or her husband's warm arm. She could see Bay at the fore, a head above the others, and just for a moment a part of her liquefied at the memory of his kiss.

Glancing at Charlie, her fingers curling into his with playful familiarity, she drew guilty comfort from the thought that she'd kissed her husband this week with far more love and passion for having kissed Bay. He looked very pale, a muscle ticking in his jaw. 'Think I'll go up.'

'You never take communion.'

'Feeling quite close to God tonight. Good to keep the heavenly insurance premiums up.' The big Gunn smile flashed and he kissed her hand in a curiously chivalric gesture.

Petra watched worriedly as he loped along the aisle, peeling off his hat, bald head gleaming as he passed under the Advent candles. He was behaving very oddly.

Was lying to yourself in church a sin, she wondered.

In her heart, she knew full well why Charlie was behaving oddly. He was feeling guilty about something too. About someone. About his London life from Monday to Friday that she pretended had no content beyond work, drinks with the boys, sport, TV and sleep.

She jumped as a tall Grim Reaper shadow in a stockman's coat stopped beside her pew and swooped down on her.

'Only me.' It was Gill, plonking herself in Charlie's gap, pink-cheeked from a similarly wine-soaked evening. 'No smalls tonight?'

'I've got thermals on.'

'I meant the children.'

'They didn't want to come this year. The candlelit carols were enough. We left our parents trying to explain to Bella how Father Christmas can get his sack through the wood-burning stove.'

'You got rid of Pip, then?'

'Gunny's furious you tipped me the wink about the aunt in Cowes. She was going to adopt her, rename her Araminta and buy her a pony. She actually asked me if I was going to do Pip a stocking as well!'

Gill laughed. 'Santa will get blown off course in this.' She shuddered as the wind roared against the windows, the little church seeming to groan. 'No bad thing – I need him to be late. I've still got a mountain of stocking fillers to wrap and mine don't even believe in the man with the beard any more.' She stood up again. 'I'm going to ask God for help.'

Petra closed her eyes briefly, wishing she had more faith. Sod it, she wasn't letting Charlie get all the forgiveness. And she wanted a closer look at the hermaphrodite vicar. She stood up and stepped out of the pew.

Which was when, with a loud rumble, a slab of plaster as big as a dining table fell from the north transept ceiling and landed where she'd been sitting.

'They evacuated the whole bloody church!' Janine told Carly, as they crammed badly wrapped sweets and chocolate bars into the kids' gift sacks, her Santa-hat fingernails making it look like ten little elves were at hard work. None of the Turners were church-goers but, like many villagers, Janine made an exception for Easter Sunday, Harvest Festival and Midnight Mass – 'It's good PR' – and she'd seen drama as good as *Corrie* that evening.

'They reckon thieves must have nicked a load of lead off the roof just before it snowed, but nobody noticed because it's been covered in white all week. When it melted, the ceiling got soggy and fell in. Going to cost a mint to fix.'

Carly was shocked. She had been in there only last week with Sienna on her knee and Jackson in a buggy, watching Ellis line up with the rest of Compton Magna's reception class to sing 'Silent Night' in the school carol service. 'Did anyone get hurt?'

'It's a miracle they didn't. Petra Gunn had been sitting right under it – she'd only just stood up. Covered in dust she was afterwards.'

There was a chuckle of laughter from the other side of the room, followed by a bark, and the two women looked across at Ash, who had stopped watching his action movie to listen in, looking over his shoulder at them, wolf eyes bright for once. 'That's classic, that is. Serves her right for looking down on the rest of us from that big horse of hers.' Lying at his feet, Pricey cocked her big, square head as if opening the debate to the room.

Janine's eyes narrowed. 'Do you know who took that roof lead,

Ash? What is it you and Skulley are getting up to when you're out late at night?'

'Don't you *dare* accuse him!' gasped Carly.

'Ducatis are expensive, Carl. 'Sall I'm saying.'

Ash ignored them both, his entire focus on the television again. Janine gave Carly a 'Told you!' look.

Carly scowled down at the last of the presents as she crammed them irritably into the sacks. She wasn't about to spoil Christmas by kicking up a fuss about it, but she had no idea where Ash had got the money to buy it. Jed's accusation that her husband was fencing goods played through her mind, but she quashed it.

This time next year would be different, she reminded herself. Ash would be back at college, training to be a farrier. He just didn't know it yet.

She couldn't let it rest. 'What do you and Skulley get up to, Ash?'

'Stuff.'

She glared across the table at Janine, who was admiring her Christmas nails again.

'You know my little brother,' she said, smirking. 'He doesn't say a lot.'

'But what he says means a lot.' Carly stood up and walked across to Ash, bending over the sofa back to wrap her arms around his shoulders.

'Merry Christmas,' he said now, lifting his beer bottle, his eyes not leaving the screen, where a muscle-man with a machine-gun was wiping out everything in sight.

We'll fix you again, Carly promised silently, as Pricey propped her chin on Ash's knee and looked up at her with her kind, tawny eyes. Maybe not this year, but we'll sort that mess in your head out, Ash Turner. She dropped a long kiss into his hair.

58

The gales had dropped away completely by Christmas morning, adding to the sense of time standing still at the stud, with no wind in the sails to blow them all towards New Year. Still, cool and gossamer misty, the snow of a few days ago was a distant memory.

Ronnie took no pleasure from its tranquillity. Pax hadn't called. Now that she knew not even her most forgiving daughter would be coming to visit before she left for Germany, Ronnie wanted the next two days behind her. The day after Boxing Day her crossing was booked to Oostende. Today was just another twenty-four hours to tick off the wait. The worst mother in the world was about to tiptoe away carrying her shoes, as she had so often through life.

'Tell me I'm a not stupid, stubborn woman?' she asked her dogs, who cocked their heads, bat ears pricked.

Having wished one another a merry Christmas with brisk formality at seven a.m., she and Lester mucked out stables as though it was any other day, working as far apart as possible, listening to carols on Classic FM, and ignoring the announcer's constant references to opening presents and putting the turkey on. Yet there was a Scrooge-like companionability between them, which Ronnie found rather cheering.

In the spirit of a brief seasonal armistice, Ronnie followed the family tradition of inviting him to share a Christmas drink with her at midday. She'd found a very fine amontillado in a cupboard that she hoped would win him round. Her father would undoubtedly have been appalled that she hadn't gone through the hollow process of offering lunch too – an invitation that had been issued and declined every year in perpetuity – but Ronnie had seen no point: Lester had been too bad-tempered yesterday for her to flatter him with ritual. She was having soup, and Lester had his pie selection; he had a ferocious appetite for a septuagenarian built like a whippet.

But when he took his coat off, she looked at the neat leather patches sewn onto his increasingly threadbare tweeds, and saw the rim of angry red skin around his crisp white collar – 'Lester's rain scald', her father had called his eczema – and felt a rush of pity for this strange, insular, ageing man, who had once been such a hero. Was it possible that she had missed him more than she realised? There was an uncomfortable ache in her chest telling her so.

'Stay and eat with me.'

'No, thank you.' He looked quietly pleased, the custom honoured.

They raised a glass. 'To old friends.' It felt reassuringly secular.

Ronnie tried not to think of the many friends she had abandoned over the years, habitually repeating that first unwitting purge, the ability to walk out of one life and into another her blessing and curse.

Lester had downed his sherry in one. 'We'll toast your father.'

She was too dutiful a daughter to decline. Glasses refilled, they raised a toast to the Captain.

'And your mother.' He scratched the eczema on the back of his hand.

The glasses were charged and raised again.

Ronnie had never been a big drinker. By the time they'd toasted her grandfather, the stud's first foundation stallion and the Queen, she'd had enough to make the room spin. Even taking small sips, she could feel the fire spreading inside her. 'Let's leave it there, Lester.'

With a determined look, he picked up the bottle, filled both glasses and lifted his. 'To Johnny Ledwell.'

Ronnie knew he was trying to get a reaction out of her. Some memories should be shared rarely, she'd always found; she and Lester had very different ones of Johnny.

Lester was waiting, statue-still, small and stubborn. She suspected she could go and eat her soup, have an afternoon nap, listen to the Queen's Speech and come back to find him still here, toasting the man who had taken away her faith in love.

What was it she'd always said to gloss over her unhappy first marriage? 'He's the only husband I've ever had that I couldn't hand back to his wife!' Such a vaudeville line to wish away a tragedy.

She lifted her glass to the ghost in the room. 'To Johnny.' She drained it.

There was a long silence. Ronnie knew the fire was stealing through him too.

'He'd have been sixty this year,' he said quietly.

'I know.'

'Never liked Christmas, did he? Said it was the dull day off between Christmas Eve and Boxing Day meets.'

'He loved his hunting.'

'He did that.' The rheumy eyes were fixed on her face. 'More than anything.'

She met his gaze. 'Not quite.'

Lester's empty glass broke the deadlock, thrust up like a magnifying lens. One grey eye bulged in its convex. 'I never left him.'

'No.'

'Now you're up off again.'

'I…' She was feeling increasingly muddled, light-headed and angry. 'I was never going to stay, Lester.'

'Just like last time.'

'That was different.'

He had the bottle again, sherry spilling everywhere as he splashed more into the little crystal glasses.

'Young Ronnie Percy!' Lester barked, back in a schooling ring in the sixties now, relentless in his determination to make her ride better than the best. 'Let's drink to her, shall we? The girl who never gave up, no matter how many times she fell. The girl who looked after her friends. The girl who loved the stud, the horses, this house. She would never walk away from this place a second time. Drink to her!'

Knowing that taking on his fight would just bait it, Ronnie closed her eyes and drank. 'Now, I think you should go, Lester, before we toast the devil too. This is for you.' She picked up a small parcel and thrust it at him, eager to get it over with. 'Merry Christmas.'

It was a new recording of the Water Music by the London Philharmonic. Lester loved Handel with a passion bordering on obsession;

Jocelyn had once enjoyed a long-running joke of giving his stallion man a door handle every Christmas and watching Lester's poker face for reaction.

He muttered his thanks, and turned away, one tweed forearm brushing swiftly across his eyes. 'Yours is outside, Mrs Le— Ronnie. You'll see it later.' Stubbs the fox terrier gave Ronnie a withering look and followed his master out of the room.

In desperate need of food to mop up the sherry – a stack of Fray Bentos pies would have been ideal – Ronnie ate her soup, followed by the last of the biscuits Pip had left in the larder, now horribly stale, chased down with coffee. Two industrially strong black Javas later and she was feeling, if not entirely sober, awake at least.

Her phone was crammed with Christmas messages. When she'd deleted her contacts, she hadn't anticipated that they would all insist on staying in touch so vociferously. So few of them were signed with more than a row of Xs that she had no idea who they were from.

She had been determined to leave them all: her darling foxy admirers, old neighbours, her event riders and grooms, fellow owners. Over the sea and far away, drifting back into view occasionally if they forayed to the Continent: 'Ronnie's always such *fun*, isn't she?' She was good at fast friends. But they took longer to let go every time.

Was it possible that she was already missing them too?

She replied to everyone with an even longer row of kisses, irritated that Christmas was such a minefield of sentimentality. There was a message from Angus, signing himself off with her old nickname for him, 'Angst'. A five-month love affair that had led to a decade of mutual dependence. She sent him a row of kisses too, grateful that their drunken, angry Christmases were long gone, grateful also that he had stayed in touch all these years when she had tried so hard to keep rolling.

Nothing from Blair. The familiar stab of pain.

Had she barred his number? She tried to remember. She knew it by heart.

She had been so good. She mustn't crumble now.

She pressed the phone to her forehead.

It was Christmas. She'd had a drink. She must pull herself together.

Sitting at the kitchen table, she looked at her sleeping dogs by the

Aga, heard the clock creaking on the wall, felt the first involuntary jerk of her head growing sleepily heavy.

It was Christmas Day. It had been her choice to spend it alone.

She stood up, striding into the boot room for her coat. She had to ride.

Having arrived late the previous night and gregariously polished off six bottles of Malbec while talking into the early hours, Kit's house guests had slept through the whole of Christmas morning, which he rather liked.

Ferdie and Donald were big men – one as wide as the other was tall – so cat-napper Kit had put them in the master bedroom down-stairs and used one of the children's old rooms upstairs for his four hours of restless sleep. He'd walked at dawn, glancing up at lights glowing in bedrooms, imagining stockings being unwrapped; he'd visited Hermia's grave and spoken to her at length about their children and his Sassoon play, apologising for being tedious, knowing she would understand.

He'd intended to go to the morning church service – a piece of theatre he rarely sought out and enjoyed when he did – but there was a hand-written sign on the door saying that St Mary's church was closed due to unforeseen circumstances, so he'd returned home, vexed that the Comptons had lost both its pulpit and its public bar this year. If there was nowhere to sin and nowhere to repent, what was left?

He'd looked forward to sharing this notion with his guests, but they were still in bed. As the clock crept on towards lunchtime, Kit's relief at venturesome, ever-partying Ferdie and Donald not demanding authentic village revelry started to wane, but he was still enjoying the tranquillity enough not to demand company. He was simply grateful to have it close by. There'd been no sign of a breakfast raid or hung-over tea-making in his absence, let alone the five-bird roast. Instead, Ferdie's snores resonated through the door, Radio 3 still playing as it had all night.

Incredibly hungry, Kit investigated the freezer, indebted to Pip at Home from Home Comforts for stocking it with seasonal food.

There was every imaginable variety of canapé in there, along with multifarious themes on cooked goose, which might come in handy. When he went to put the oven on for the Danish pastries he'd found, he discovered the five-bird roast inside, already sizzling happily. A Post-it note had unpeeled itself and fallen on the floor.

Baste. Turn up at 1.00 and put potatoes in. Peel things, chop things, drink things. Do not disturb the head chefs. We may be attempting sex. If we are not with you in an hour, call it a vintage shag. If you don't see us by the time it gets dark, call an ambulance.

Laughing, he pinged the pastries into the microwave and enjoyed their stolid sweetness.

Pressing himself to the round window to get a phone signal, he wished his children a merry Christmas while drinking a large Scotch, feeling strangely content. It was, he realised, the first year he didn't feel angry with Hermia for dying. He'd never particularly enjoyed his own company – a running joke for an ambitious theatre director who wanted his own company very much – and yet he was the perfect sort of alone this Christmas, one shared with friends who had witnessed what he had gone through and understood that he needed to unfold very slowly from loneliness on a day like this.

He took his drink outside into the garden, completely neglected and overgrown in recent years, the huge old greenhouse that Hermia had loved to potter in now full of brown, frost-scorched weeds, its wood split and windows mouldering.

Setting his drink down, he started pulling up the weeds by the roots.

Out in the stableyard, dogs at her heels, Ronnie passed a large pot containing what at first she took to be a Christmas tree, a single tag shaped like a bauble attached to one of its branches, which she doubled back to read: *Time to put down roots. Merry Christmas. Lester.*

It wasn't a fir at all, but a young Cedar of Lebanon. A new family tree. Ronnie bit her lip hard, chest tight with emotion. She needed to ride off all this sherry-soaked sentimentality.

Crossing the yard, she felt light-headed again. She had to hang on to two saddle racks in the tack room and breathe deeply to recover.

Photographs of her younger self surrounded her, fast-riding Ronnie Percy, some of them muddy-faced after she'd picked herself up from a fall but refused to give up. What was it Lester had said again?

She shook her head. The words were gone, just his anger and disappointment in her remaining.

There was no sign of Lester.

'You two have to stay here,' she told her dogs, cupping Enid's grey muzzle in her hands. 'You're too much of a stopper… and you're too much of a goer.' She kissed Olive.

She tacked up Dickon, who was delighted at the prospect of an outing, his big blazed head almost legging her up into the saddle on its own.

'You're in charge,' she told him, as they clattered out along the driveway and turned right into a village currently muted by collective turkey-carving. He took immediate exception to a small hatchback with a roof box, almost dropping her in an undignified heap at her own gates. 'Okay, *I'm* in charge. Just let's not move too fast.'

The village was bathed in milky sunshine, its ironstone cottages the colour of the roast potatoes being pulled from the Agas inside them. However hard Ronnie tried to tell herself that she didn't belong here any more, that it had reinvented itself in her absence, she felt a deep, loyal sense of kinship.

Was it possible she had missed this place?

She stood in her stirrups as Dickon took a long, contented pee on the wide verge by the post-box. She envied him the freedom, her bladder already uncomfortably full from drinking so much coffee. She waved at a family in paper hats who were watching her through the window of one of the thatched cottages on the Green, mouths open.

Would they bring it up every year between crackers and seconds? she wondered – 'Do you remember the Christmas that woman stopped outside the window while her horse relieved itself?' It hardly mattered. She'd be long gone.

Only a handful of those now living in Compton Magna were familiar to her, mostly old farming families and a few elderly retainers.

There was a new breed in situ – career-couple families, often incomers from London, a clever and sociable bunch with self-confident children and badly behaved dogs. Moving into the area in their thirties, they juggled a work–life balance, their oldest friendships too far away to reach, new ones slotting into categories that seldom saw a whole picture – neighbours, school parents, fellow commuters, dog-walkers – while second cars and spare beds suddenly took on prodigious significance, drawing in distant friends and granting freedom to travel to them. Petra Gunn was one of the new breed.

She'd had such fun talking to Petra in their short but sweet acquaintance. Was it possible that she would miss such an instinctive friend, with her soulful eyes and wise wit?

Life went in circles, they said. Circle of life, circle of friends. Running in circles only to end up in the same place. That straight line right the way around the world that took you back home. Oh, bother. She was still drunk.

'All the world's a stage, and all the men and women merely players,' she said out loud. How many of her seven ages had she had? Hermia would know the whole speech.

Ronnie had always made friends easily, but none had held a candle to Hermia. That she had extinguished the friendship so unequivocally made its end all the harsher.

Since then all friendships had felt transient. Experience had taught her that it was easiest if you treated them like much-loved animal companions. While they were around they made the world feel better, but their lives would always be shorter than yours. Villages could be very lonely, paranoid places without friendship. Kith and kin were lifeblood in a quiet spot like Compton Magna. One had only to look at Lester.

Poor Lester didn't make friends easily, yet he'd once had the greatest of allies in Johnny, the friendship born in the hunting field where one had been huntsman and the other amateur whip over four seasons of the best runs the Fosse and Wolds had ever known. Lester had offered Johnny his undying loyalty and still lived by that promise.

Ronnie legged Dickon into a trot to leave the thought behind. Whizzing through the village now, she peered over hedges and garden walls, feeling far better, enjoying the snap of frost in the air and the pricked ears in front of her as Dickon bowled along on autopilot.

She'd been planning just to loop around the manor fields and the orchards – a route she and Hermia had regularly thundered along at full tilt, talking breathlessly all the while – but now that she was out, the cobwebs blowing off, Ronnie felt she could last all day. Far better out here than cooped up watching family viewing with no family.

'How fit are you feeling, Dick?'

He loped along, brown ears pricked like beetle claws, a horse for whom stamina came as naturally as speed to a greyhound.

'We'll take it steady,' she promised. 'Lots of middle-aged breathers.'

She was going to try out Bay Austen's three-mile point.

When Kit went back into the house, there was still no sign of Ferdie and Donald. Radio 3 had been turned up a few notches; Bach's Oratorio was playing.

Hermia, who had adored the couple, would have been delighted by the deliberate love-in. 'Leave them there and see how long they can last without food,' whispered her playful voice in his ear.

Wanting to be alone with her longer, Kit took the bird out to rest and turned the potatoes, knowing the cooking smells would flush Ferdie out eventually.

He listened to Van Morrison while he prepped veg, the familiar songs they'd fallen in love to. It hurt less than he'd feared. The second large whisky steeled his nerve enough to put on a much-scuffed, sacred family CD while he peeled carrots. His children played it at Christmas every year. Usually he couldn't stay in the room.

Hermia Austen's radio recording of *The Happy Prince* accompanied Kit's vegetable prep. And although he laid down his peeler to cry more than once and shout several times – the director who had overlaid his wife's beautiful voice with strings had been an idiot – it made him proud and humble to listen to her voice again. She wasn't talking to him, she was performing, which brought her to life in perfect abstraction, a Princess Leia hologram projected a safe distance away. The story was exquisitely sad, its pompous over-sentimentality largely lost on him because Hermia was in the room.

'My goodness, she was good!' Ferdie appeared in flamboyantly striped pyjamas, his eyes baggier than hammocks. 'Didn't you direct this?'

'Yes.' He nodded. 'It was recorded live at Chichester Festival.'

'Marvellous.' Short and broad-girthed, with a neat black d'Artagnan beard, a bald pate and hair curling over his ears ('I model myself as a fat Shakespeare,' he was fond of saying), Ferdie always looked as if he was two bottles of wine up even when he'd slept off his considerable capacity. 'How long until lunch? Donald's eaten all the chocolates we brought for my mother and is about to start on the pot-pourri.'

'It's almost there.'

'Excellent.' Ferdie tapped his large red nose. 'Better have a cuppa and get dressed.' Pouring Merlot into two mugs, he carried them back into the bedroom, pausing at the door to listen. 'Strings are too loud.' Whether he was talking about the Oratorio or *The Happy Prince* was unclear.

'Ten minutes to curtain!' Kit warned.

59

After half an hour in the saddle, meandering happily into Eyngate Park to ride up to the folly and pop some logs, Ronnie was still uncomfortably aware that she should have had a wee before she set out. After an hour, hurrying to find the start of the three-mile point, she was in age-old pelvic-floor-twitching territory. After two, having diverted so far around a flooded culvert near Manor Farm trout hatcheries that she'd practically ended up in Broadbourne, she was sitting as tight-buttocked as a hussar, wishing she had somebody with whom to share the joke. She shouldn't have stayed out so long, but the winter sun was so warm and the views so beautiful that she hadn't been able to drag herself away from old familiar fields and tracks, unable to bear the fact she was about to leave it all behind again.

Thank goodness Dickon was forgiving and still full of oomph, happy to bowl towards home along the verges.

But as she rode back past the church, pelvic floor threatening to burst, like its poor leadless roof, Ronnie knew home turf was too far, and she had to find a discreet bush.

Typically, the post-prandial villagers were now coming out in force, dogs being walked to burn off too many pigs in blankets, children pedalling new bicycles.

'Merry Christmas!' she greeted each one, as she thundered past, increasingly desperate, almost mowing down a middle-aged male couple, one as short, sallow and black-bearded as the other was tall, dark-skinned and white-bearded.

'Now that's a magnificent sight, madam!' boomed the short one, laughing as he leaped aside.

When she spotted the Old Almshouses, Ronnie almost wept with relief. She knew where the key was kept. This was an emergency. And Pip had even asked her to check the place while Kit was away for Christmas, so now she could.

She unhitched the gate faster than a Pony Clubber at a hunter trial and rode straight up to the door, abandoning Dickon there with his reins hastily knotted round his neck – she trusted him to wait a few minutes, he was a collie of dependability – and searched round the porch beneath the boot-scraper.

They weren't there.

'Bugger.' She pressed her forehead to the door, quickly girding her bursting loins to nip round the back and make do with a bush in the garden. With a click, the half-latched door swung open. The house smelt of sumptuous cooking and expensive aftershave. In her experience, burglars didn't splash out on Jo Malone and microwave an M&S chocolate fondant mid-raid.

'Hello?'

There was no sign of life. She was too desperate to question herself as she hurried inside.

Filled to the brim with five-bird roast, Kit had sought out the sofa and nodded off in a Scotch-and-Malbec-induced slumber while Ferdie and Donald washed up. Unaware that they'd gone out to walk the dog, he dreamed he'd gone back to visit Hermia's grave, far more elaborate in his sleep-scape, guarded by a gold-leafed stone angel, with sapphire eyes and a ruby mouth.

When he heard a voice say, 'Bugger', he half woke, uncertain if the figure hurrying through his house was part of his dream. A flash of blonde hair. Slight and light. Another husky curse as a knee caught a chair. The Ghost of Christmas Past.

'Hermia?'

But she was already gone. He closed his eyes again. He had to cut down his drinking. He'd quit through January to work on Sassoon.

He awoke very definitely when the cistern flushed. The house had old plumbing. It always sounded like a plane taking off.

He watched the figure steal back across the room.

'Hello.'

'Shit!' The blonde figure spun round. 'Hi! Happy Christmas!'

Kit sat up, rubbing his forehead in his palms. He should have guessed.

Ronnie was standing close to the door, the smile illuminated by the casement glass. Blue eyes as bright as buttons on a sailor suit, her face too intelligent and defiant to be so silly, so rude, so alive. It caught his heart in a mousetrap pinch.

'Just checking all A-OK. Pip asked. No idea you were in situ. Sorry. I'll go. Horse outside.'

'Wait, I—' He started to speak, but the words caught, like a bone in his throat.

She stood as asked, still beaming apologetically. 'God, this is awkward.'

Dry-mouthed, Kit reached for his glass, forgetting that Ferdie had got the fifty-year-old cask malt out before he'd nodded off. Flames scorched their way down his throat.

'*Chide me, dear stone,*' he stood up and walked towards her, '*that I may say indeed. Thou art Hermione.*'

The smile got very confused. If Kit had been directing an actress to play *The Winter's Tale* trial scene he'd have asked for just that – the way it dropped away and danced, her eyes darkening like opened camera shutters.

'*But yet...*' He tilted his head, noticing for the first time how high her cheekbones were, the old-fashioned dimples, the weathered skin.

'*Hermione was not so much wrinkled, nothing so aged as this seems,*' she finished, that deep, hypnotic purr of laughter in her voice. God, she was quick, far quicker than his wine-soaked reactions. He could see the thoughts condense, process, emote on her face.

Now the smile came back, bolder and more arrogant. 'Kit! What a great surprise.'

'Ronnie.' He pulled his chin back, tilting his head the other way. 'What a bad lie. Merry Christmas.'

'I really am enormously sorry, barging in like this.'

'Let's call that truce.' He held up his hands, backing away as though held at gunpoint, unable to face a barrage of overpolite Jeeves and Wooster apologies. 'You were quite right. We should try to be cordial, for Hermia's sake, if only for today.' He found himself adding, 'Stay and have a drink.' God, he must still be half cut.

He watched her face across the room, saw the mask slip then re-form, the smile as blinding as the low winter sun. 'A Christmas peace pipe?'

'An armistice.' He nodded, pouring her a slug of Ferdie's malt and moving across to hand it to her.

She took it, her nose tipping away from it. Her face was running its gamut of expressions again. It was fascinating in its fruit-machine emotion. Three jokers came up, a mask of badly judged good manners. 'Aren't we supposed to share cigarettes and play football? Swap photographs of sweethearts?'

'Take your bloody pick.' He waved his hand at the many shots of Hermia, mood instantly darkening, whisky meeting Malbec dyspepsia, like a firework thrown into an oil barrel.

But she just danced closer to the flame. 'I had no idea you'd be back! I heard you were away until New Year.'

'I changed my mind. I like it here.'

'We can all do that. I like it here too.'

They both registered a moment of surprise, more in their own sentiments than each other's.

'This house is very special,' she said.

'Noisy plumbing.'

'I never trust plumbing that doesn't sing like a church organ.'

From what little he knew of Ronnie, he might have guessed she was the sort to commandeer a loo if she needed one.

You will love her.

'Drink your Scotch.'

'I might need some water in it.'

'Ah, yes, the temperance disciple.'

'And the Bacchanalian.'

They looked at one another levelly and, for the first time since they'd met, shared a wide smile.

Kit Donne had eyes like a fox. Ronnie hadn't noticed their vulpine quality before. Wily, predatory, instinctive.

Conversationally, she was waving a loaded gun. She couldn't stop herself. Every time she tried, the trigger squeezed. 'How lovely to be spending Christmas here!' There she went again, fully loaded with vapidities.

The eyes drew hers again. Hermia had rescued a fox once, like Lester's cub, only hers had been released back into the wild where she remained convinced that it came back each year to watch them perform in the church meadows. Mr Fox, the theatre critic.

He plucked the glass from her grip and went to pour water into it. At last she could breathe properly. Scotch reminded her too vividly of Johnny. Heaven to kiss, hell to try to keep pace with drinking.

Ronnie watched Kit standing at the sink. He had reading glasses on a rope around his neck and a red-wine smile, like Joker from *Batman*, on his scowling lips. And fox eyes. Seeming to forget the drink was hers, he knocked it back himself.

He looked across at her as though he'd forgotten she was there and was astonished to see her all over again. He seemed miles away, years away maybe.

She tried for a hearty farewell, the rough shot turning a few more circles, firing out a hail of plastic-bullet smiles. 'Like I say, I really am very sorry. Terribly bad manners.' Hermia would be laughing like a drain now, once all too familiar with holding an extra set of reins when her friend got caught short out hacking. 'Too many sherries before lunch. Shoot me.'

Still unsmiling, he held up two fingers, like a gun, to the sky, narrowed his eyes and lowered them on target.

'Bang,' she said good-humouredly, taking the shot with an under-stated feigned death against the door frame. She and Hermia had once been very fond of staging melodramatic mock-deaths.

'Awful,' he critiqued.

Ronnie jumped back to life. The fox eyes stared.

'Shoot me again.'

He ran his hands through the oaky pelt of his hair with a rather cranky sigh and aimed again, a double-handed shot this time, looking one-eyed down the sights, the voice loquaciously dry: 'Bang.'

She gave it the full swoon, face contorted, clutching her chest, reeling, pirouetting, pinpointing her landing spot, and then death.

'Worse.'

'Well, you bloody do it!' She stood up.

'I'm not an actor.'

'Neither am I.'

'Could have fooled me. You're more theatrical than most green rooms I've been in recently. Have you ever thought of taking it up as a second career?'

'Not if I can't die.'

'Immortality looks great on the CV. That, horse riding and sword fighting.'

She smiled, realising it was getting dark outside. She'd abandoned long-suffering Dickon, who would be waiting patiently, like a mustang outside a saloon. An evening of couch-potato television and naff snacks beckoned. Lester may yet be persuaded to join her. 'I must go.'

'I think I was too hasty to judge you, Ronnie,' he said. 'I apologise.'

'Likewise. I hope perhaps we can make friends.'

'I'd like that.'

'How long are you staying?' she asked.

'On and off, indefinitely. You?'

'Two days, on and off.' She smiled apologetically, wishing it was longer.

The door opened behind her, amid much bass chatter and laughter, and Ronnie turned to find two bearded bystanders with a waggy-tailed cockapoo, the jovial little and large she'd met when out riding.

'Ferdie, Donald, this is Ronnie.' Kit introduced them all.

'My God, you look like—' Stout little Ferdie stopped himself. They were both terribly excited.

Donald said, in his deep, rumbling bass: 'You do know there's a horse in your greenhouse?'

'You've got to hand it to Ronnie Percy.' Barry Dawkins's round pink cheeks glowed like coals as he stood at Gill Walcote's elbow, watching a horse wearing a metal greenhouse frame, like medieval armour. 'She adds to the entertainment round here. Never a dull day.'

The drama of the horse trapped in the greenhouse on Christmas

Day had united the Compton Magna village faithful. All hands were somewhat drunkenly on deck, delighted to rally to the rescue.

Feeling peckish, Dickon had spotted the debris of recently pulled weeds close to the old glasshouse, had ambled up for a sniff and a munch, following the trail inside and getting stuck. Lifting his head in surprise, he'd hoisted the entire frame off its brick course. Potentially dangerous as it was, Dickon was an immensely patient, self-protective horse and had stayed put, waiting for rescue to come.

While the village rallied and Kit seethed once again – he could forgive most things, but not horses – Ferdie and Donald cracked open another bottle of Malbec and watched the proceedings.

'She does look extraordinarily like Hermia,' they observed, as Ronnie alternately thanked, helped, praised, apologised and – in unguarded moments – looked impossibly sad, gazing round at the villagers, the brightly moonlit lane and the church.

'Amazingly expressive face.'

'Do you think she and Hermia had the same father?' Ferdie, thoroughly excited by so many strapping young village men carrying plate glass across the garden, was in a reverie of imagined illicit rural affairs.

They watched Kit stalking inside, slamming the door.

'*My only love sprung from my only hate!*' Donald intoned.

'They're a bit long in the tooth to be star-cross'd.'

'You're right. And who wants to end up dead in a crypt with a family reunion going on?'

'*If it be love indeed, tell me how much.*' Ferdie gave his husband his best Egyptian-queen eyes.

'*There's beggary in the love that can be reckon'd.*' Never had Antony been darker, deeper or sexier.

'*I'll set a bourn how far to be belov'd.*'

'*Then must thou needs find out new Heaven, new Earth.*'

'Now that's more like it. He falls on his own sword and she's bitten by a snake. Thoroughly Cotswolds.'

They looked at each other hopefully, then watched as Ronnie knocked on the door in the porch.

*

Bracing herself for his most irascible demeanour, Ronnie sucked her teeth and rolled her lips as the door opened. In the glow of dim lighting, the fox eyes gleamed.

'I apologise again for my horse. I have arranged for a new greenhouse to be delivered tomorrow.'

'Tomorrow-tomorrow? As in Boxing Day?'

'Sorry – is that inconvenient? Someone called Skulley, who was helping out here, is going to deliver and erect it. Apparently, he has a ready supply. He'll fix the lead flashing on this porch while he's about it. He seems charming. Bit of a Yorick theme going on with the tattoos.'

'Right. Thank you. Well, *bon voyage*, if I don't see you before you go.'

'It might be slightly longer than two days, actually.'

'Right. Good.' The fox eyes gleamed more brightly.

'Merry Christmas.'

'And to you.'

Lester was sweeping the yard after putting in afternoon hay nets when Ronnie came up the drive leading Dickon. Putting down his brush, he hurried to her side, taking the reins from her. 'You all right, Mrs Le— Ronnie? You've been gone hours.'

'Thank you, I'm fine.' She stooped to greet her dogs, who raced forward. 'Lester, I've decided I'm staying on here after all. I'm not going to Germany.'

He couldn't immediately speak, but she could tell from the way his eyes creased that he was happy.

'Beck's staying too. You're right. The Horsemaker should be allowed to try to work with him.'

'If you say so.' He looked slightly less delighted.

'I say so. And what I say goes around here.'

60

Kit Donne took delivery of a new greenhouse the following morning, a pretty Victorian oak-framed one, far comelier than the bent, broken-glassed armour that had preceded it. Painted lichen green, it came complete with finials, opening roof vents and a sticker with a delivery address in Worcestershire that the skull-tattooed erector scratched off while Donald and Ferdie were plying him with tea and biscuits, asking eagerly about horticultural matters.

With the greenhouse came packets of rosemary and pansy seeds, and a note that Kit propped up on his kitchen windowsill. 'Don't let's throw any more stones. Your friend, Ronnie Percy.'

He couldn't wait for everyone to bugger off so he could crack on with Sassoon.

In Chipping Hampton market square, under another snow-heavy sky, the Fosse and Wolds Foxhounds were admired and patted by the crowds at the Boxing Day meet, stirrup cups passed around the hundred or more mounted followers. Today they were being field-mastered by dashing Bay Austen, his cool Dutch wife at his side for once, keeping very close tabs on him, wrongly imagining that Ronnie Percy might be joining them and trying to muscle in on both its handsome joint-master and a mastership of her own next season.

Being marked closely didn't stop Bay riding across when he spotted Petra on foot, laughing his head off. 'I thought you were anti, Mrs Gunn.'

'I'm silently protesting,' she insisted, having been press-ganged into bringing mother-in-law Gunny, who used it as an excuse to dash off to the sales, and Bella, who was sulking because Tilly and Grace were both riding. Charlie was shooting, her parents and the other three children taking Wilf up to the windmill, where she longed to be too.

'What did Santa fill your stockings with?' Bay growled, in an undertone.

'Varicose veins and swollen ankles.'

'Stop pretending to be anything other than gorgeous, Mrs G. You must bring Bella round to play before they all go back to school, mustn't she, Moni?' he called, as his wife charged up, like a polo player about to ride off for a ball. 'Bring Bella round to play with Tilly.'

'Absolutely.'

Petra backed gratefully away to say hello to Mo and Gill, who were both mounted, the latter looking distinctly jaded under her frayed-brimmed beagler: 'Three hours of charades, an entire Stilton and two bottles of port late last night are taking their toll,' the vet reported weakly. 'The only fresh air we got all day beyond checking horses was when Ronnie's horse walked off with a greenhouse on its head.'

'I'm sorry she's leaving.' Petra sighed.

'No, she ain't,' Mo reported eagerly, kicking the cob closer. 'Lester's telling everyone as'll listen that she's staying and has some fancy sort coming over from America or somewhere to make the stud a world-beater.'

Petra cheered up immensely, guiltily excited at the idea of the 'fancy sort'. She was in desperate need of a new SMC. Bay sent her another smouldering glance over his shoulder, lifting his big hunt whip to his hat brim. He looked far too rakish on a horse for safety. She couldn't wait to retreat to the Plotting Shed and start rattling his priestly chains.

Pip had arrived back in Compton Bagot at lunchtime, after catching the morning ferry, her palms permanently scarred from digging her fingernails into them as she listened to her aunt talk about the ones that had got away. She had changed into her pink horse gear: she was missing morning hay nets, Lester and baking. And even the horses a little bit. She raced to the stud to find Ronnie nowhere in sight. Instead Carly from the estate was rolling round the yards with the ubiquitous buggy and snotty children, plus the big tattooed squaddie and a terrifying-looking dog on a string.

'Does Mrs Ledwell know you're here?' she asked archly, as they went to hang over the fence and talk to Spirit. She couldn't look at Ash at all.

'Yeah, we saw her,' Carly said, putting a hat back on one of the snotties as the first few flakes of snow started to fall. 'She's gone to watch the hunt come up from Eyngate to draw something called Compton Thorns.'

'I'll go there too.' Pip had no desire to stick close to the tattooed one. She hoped the tack room was locked.

'Pip.' Carly called her back as she hurried away, making her heart stop a little. 'JD was Ash's cousin Jed. He's been sorted out.'

'Gosh, thanks.' Being 'sorted out' sounded terrifying and nothing like what she was doing with the stud attic. She hoped they'd left his best asset untouched. She could, she felt, bring herself to forgive him in time.

As she hurried down the drive and onto the lane, she stepped aside to let a red Shogun swung into the stud entrance, then spun round in shock, watching it thunder up the drive, Alice and her lanky farmer husband in the front, three enormous children in the back and wrapped presents sharing boot space with a collie.

Further along the lane, in the gateway to the Sixty Acres, the Fosse and Wolds car-followers had already gathered in force, off-roaders parked at the usual haphazard angles, binoculars trained on the horizon. Ronnie was standing with the round-faced chairman of the hunt supporters, Barry, both laughing uproariously.

'Hello, old Pip!' Ronnie's ever-amused voice was full of affection.

'Hello!' She bounced forwards. 'Did you miss me?'

'Too buggery fucking right I did!' boomed a joyful voice, from somewhere in the midst of the donkey jackets and waxed cotton. 'Bloody shaggingly good to see you again, Pip.' A blonde Boris

Johnson mop popped up. Roo Verney, in purple Puffa, pearls and Hermès scarf, was beaming over a burly Turner shoulder, camcorder in hand.

Pip smiled shyly back. Purely platonically speaking, it was overwhelmingly nice to be liked. And Roo did have tremendously sparkly eyes. She also listed Boyzone under her music choices on Facebook.

'Give her some space, chaps!' Ronnie lectured the foot-followers and terrier men.

'Yes, give her some space,' Pip ordered, earning a wink from Roo, who turned round as the huntsman's horn blasted in the distance.

They watched the field canter up from the direction of Eyngate, the pace leisurely, no line being pursued, just a big Christmas-card tableau of hounds, horses, red coats and black jackets in a beautiful Cotswolds valley. The snow was thickening: scent would be poor. Compton Thorns would almost certainly be the last covert drawn, so Bay would achieve his ambition to jump his way home from a day's hunting across his hedges, if he so wished.

Ronnie spotted Lester in the field, still best turned out by far and riding with terrific panache, even though his hips needed fixing and he couldn't see much beyond his cob's ears. She was glad she was staying to look after him. The Horsemaker was a lovely guy, but had no sense of the importance of Lester and the wisdom of Lester, the last of the great holy trinity of the stud.

'Hello, Mum,' said a low, sweet voice at her shoulder. 'Sorry I didn't call. We all thought we'd take you by surprise. Then you weren't there.'

Hands flying to her face in surprise, she turned to Pax, a head above her, deep red hair already flecked with snow, freckles creasing together in a smile.

'Merry Christmas and all that.' The beautiful hare's eyes blinked warily. 'We brought lunch. We know you only do soup.'

'We?'

'Alice and her lot are up there. Tread carefully. I think Lester threatened violence. I brought my two men, four and forty, and the doughty in-laws, sorry.' She pulled a face. 'Tim's in the Cape, as you know, but he chose the wine and is going to call. It'll be a proper Percy Massty.' She looked across the valley as the horn sounded.

At the head of the field, standing in his stirrups, Bay charged along on a huge, rangy chestnut. 'Nice-looking type.'

'Not your sort.' Ronnie threaded her arm through her daughter's, patting Barry's shoulder farewell. 'No staying power. Got to sit tight and kick on in this life.'

As they made their way back up the drive, her phone rang, an unlisted number.

'That might be Tim.' Pax unthreaded her arm while Ronnie answered it, going to talk to Dickon and Horace, the point-to-pointer who had been turned out in one of the front paddocks, old-timers who were listening to the hunt pass with wise, delighted eyes, high heads and pricked ears.

'Hello!'

The voice was the deepest, gravelliest she knew, as Australian as the Great Barrier Reef. 'Ronnie, I have to see you before you go.'

She stopped, gazing up the drive to the beautiful house and yard her father had entrusted to her care. 'There's no hurry. Really, there's no hurry at all.'